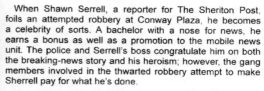

By James G. Davies
On sale now

When Shawn Serrell, a reporter for The Sheriton Post, foils an attempted robbery at Conway Plaza, he becomes a celebrity of sorts. A bachelor with a nose for news, he earns a bonus as well as a promotion to the mobile news unit. The police and Serrell's boss congratulate him on both the breaking-news story and his heroism; however, the gang members involved in the thwarted robbery attempt to make Sherrell pay for what he's done.

His new found fame generates more publicity than he needs. Sherrell receives a mysterious phone call asking him to investigate wrongdoing as the Alma Welborn Institute, a private and government-funded institution catering to disabled veterans. This assignment intrigues Sherrell who has become know as a news-action magnet. But the price he must pay to cover the story may be too high.

First, Sherell's apartment is struck by an arsonist, and he loses the paper evidence related to the hospital case. Then, his contact goes missing. Sherrell, who feels as if he's being continually followed, doesn't know who he should fear.

When Worlds Collide
By James G. Davies
On sale now

What have we here!

We have two people - individuals with a sense of humor all of their own, who have been under the same roof together for over forty years. Not only have they been sharing the same interests, house food children and now grandchildren, but also their 'wit' and understanding required to make such a bonding last this long.

We have a man {George} and a woman {Rose}, two names which hold many fond memories for us. But in reality they could be anyone or anybody you will come across in your life - they may coincidentally even be you!

They are also two individuals, personalities, who suddenly find each other thrown together now that hubby is retiring. Only now do they realize that the one thing they had not really prepared themselves' for when George's time came - was the actual amount and meaning behind the words' 'more time' together.

The worlds they had lived in while he was at work and she taking care of the family and home are now about to collide.

And now - much to your good fortune, they are about to share some of those rare golden moments and situations often springing forth out of that time with not only you - but anyone willing to have their funny bone not bruised but instead tickled.

If you should somehow see in our couple a little bit of yourselves, or someone you know, then it's only because they in all probability also exist.

Sit down, put up your feet, and get ready to pick your side, or maybe even add your own, in a match of wills that are sure to strike close to home on hopefully more than one occasion.

iUniverse books by James G Davies

    Lateral Gains

    When Worlds Collide

Later this year - watch my web site for;

    Creative Art Through Welding

    Short stories

Shifts

James G. Davies Sr.

iUniverse, Inc.
Bloomington

Shifts

Copyright © 2011 by James G. Davies Sr.

All rights reserved. No part of this book may be used or reproduced by any means, graphic, electronic, or mechanical, including photocopying, recording, taping or by any information storage retrieval system without the written permission of the publisher except in the case of brief quotations embodied in critical articles and reviews.

This is a work of fiction. All of the characters, names, incidents, organizations, and dialogue in this novel are either the products of the author's imagination or are used fictitiously.

iUniverse books may be ordered through booksellers or by contacting:

iUniverse
1663 Liberty Drive
Bloomington, IN 47403
www.iuniverse.com
1-800-Authors (1-800-288-4677)

Because of the dynamic nature of the Internet, any web addresses or links contained in this book may have changed since publication and may no longer be valid. The views expressed in this work are solely those of the author and do not necessarily reflect the views of the publisher, and the publisher hereby disclaims any responsibility for them.

Any people depicted in stock imagery provided by Thinkstock are models, and such images are being used for illustrative purposes only.

Certain stock imagery © Thinkstock.

ISBN: 978-1-4502-9847-6 (sc)
ISBN: 978-1-4502-9849-0 (dj)
ISBN: 978-1-4502-9848-3 (ebk)

Printed in the United States of America

iUniverse rev. date: 5/20/2011

Hello there.

Looking for a good time? No, this is not leading you into entrapment. Well I guess it is, in a sort of way now that I think about it. But only because I want you to read the book. In fact I'll tell you right now, right up front, that if you're looking for a fantasy filled story containing nothing but explicit sex scenes, rata ma tat shoot-um up's, ear singing foul language, you should stop right now and take a deep breath, because this definitely isn't it.

Come. Take a brief walk down mammary lane, where it was sometimes fashionable for the little head to do the thinking for the big head. A time when a woman was smart enough to let her husband think he actually ruled the roost. And it was an era when most people truly had enough common sense, the smarts, to really care and get involved with one another.

This is simply a fantasized fable from a time involving a group of everyday shift workers in industry, possibly your parents of even grandparents. In their youths they would in all likelihood seem to be or maybe even have been a part of a group of workers busy filling their time and lives with whatever it was that made them laugh. And like at times, mostly in the center of such a group, there were generally one or two individuals who always seemed to lead the way. Below is just such a story, sometimes so close to reality that you might envision it fits like a tailor made suit onto someone you already know. In fact, even though it's impossible to write a story that doesn't sometimes offend or step on someone's toes, it is only a story meant to entertain with the intent of shooing away some of the present days ensuing stresses. So sit down with a treat of whatever it takes to chase the blues away, and enjoy what I sometimes felt my past was actually like. And if I've pleased you, I know I was entertained just writing about it, great. If not, then try one of my other books. We're both bound to get lucky sooner or later.

I realize that some of the words or language used in the story may by today's standards be considered as offensive. But in the era this book represents, these are the terms often used. So sit back, curl up, or into whatever position of relaxation you prefer, as there never was or ever has been any animosity intended.

This fantasy is dedicated to all in the present workforce, about a time for most, the seventies, when it was deemed more important to care for each other than just oneself. It was an era when the prejudicial words of today were mostly thrown around as neither stick nor stone.

So come spend a little time from the present to visit the past, a decade where fun and good times were on most peoples minds, generally involving family and most friends.

Allow yourself the pleasure to be as one with your parents, and maybe even your grandparents. But whatever you may feel, see, or experience, just remember that it is highly unlikely most of it will ever pass this way again.

Hint. For a true feeling of reality, think of your favorite stars chosen to play each part of this story as it unfolds in your mind eye. Play it out up there on the big screen, as an entertaining comedy!

All rights reserved, and 'No!' It's not a story about the plight of the Indians. This book is intended 'strictly', I repeat 'strictly', as a work of fiction. Characters and situations although often as not sometimes questioned as coincidental, I'm sure it's bound to happen occasionally with any author, are strictly a product of my debatably unusual imagination. Any similarities to actual real people or events are entirely absolutely and purely unintentional, obviously as well as coincidental, animosity never being the reason for its creation.

No part of this book may be reproduced in any form or by any means without the prior written consent of the author James Gordon Davies.

When someone 'wise' once said something along the lines of 'laugh and the world laughs with you , but cry , and you'll cry alone.' they obviously had just hit the 'nail on the head', their 'finger nail' that is! And why is that? Well, because for some strange reason it seems to be imbedded into most of us that the antics usually associated in the aftermath of such an incident, almost also instantly attacks our funny-bone. And even though we just as quickly offer genuine words of condolence, we also find ourselves instantly fighting back, unsuccessfully at times I might add, the effort to laugh outright straight into the misfortunate individuals very often pain ridden face.

Prologue

Shit!, Shit!, Shit! And then one more time, 'She-e-e-it!'

Aren't you shocked?

Well, maybe you're just a little bit disgusted, no doubt by the messy detailed images this 'crappy' word might have just brought to your mind. And especially, if it's a long term disturbing recalled picture nobody really wants or needs to flashback onto.

But then, why should you be? I'm the one typing this out, and I usually draw from familiar images somewhere out of my past, when logic dictated that we use reclaimable cloth diapers. Now for those of you not old enough to remember those glory days, you'll never be able to understand that one such disgusting item could come in so many variable shades of brown green or yellow.

So, back to more reality. It's a 'given' fact of our lives that without the ability to get rid of 'it', 'it' meaning you know what, 'poo' we'd in all likely-hood 'die', and in a very unpleasantly way mind you! And then even further, let's not forget to mention the disgusting assault on some of our other senses it also brings with 'it'. But without the ability to pass 'it', we'd all either rot from the inside out, our breath undoubtedly giving an advance warning, or maybe, possibly sprout the nicest botanical home for flowers any horticulturist would be proud to be seen 'pruning'.

Then again 'verbally', possibly by to-days moral standards not exactly considered to be that 'flashing bolt of literary lightning', or maybe again even remotely, a strong 'interest grabber'. But then only some further invested time will lead us to that truth.

In 'fact', nor is it the best of topics to start a good story or decent conversation with, unless you happen to have just accidentally stepped in 'it', or be up to the 'old' literary proverbial neck in the stuff. But for whatever the excuse, regardless of the fact that 'it' is a word that even those with the most limited amount of 'intelligence' can almost always immediately understand, I use it as an excuse to get the majority of 'crap' out of the way. It is also, [no pun intended earlier, at least not just yet] usually expected in tales like the following, as well as to hook, line, and, 'stinker' your attention. The 'stinker' over 'sinker' pun 'was' intentional. So get yourself a clothespin, put it on the end of your nose, set your common sense on idle, and then let's carry on.

To an educated person the exclamation would have simply been an expression for excessively consumed food. To another less fortunate, it could implicate their present emotional frustration over something presently going wrong in their life. And possibly, lastly especially for a few individuals you might know, the self-imagining word in all probability is the best thing that could be said about their overall general piss poor attitude on life.

But, before we venture any further, let's get our own priorities and values in this all too often crazy world, reasonably straight. For instance - if you feel that something unfortunate such as a funeral is only supposed to be emotionally depressing, last minute weeping in dark clothing with the usually surroundings of miserable rainy weather, then you'd better give up reading right now. Why? Because, the following more real than fantasy 'slice of life' is definitely not for you, or anyone else lacking even the slightest hint of a ticklish 'funny bone'!

Now another 'why', you might already be asking yourself, should you do that? Well, the simplest and most often as not honest answer to such a negative attitude, is that you most likely may not be able to accept or understand the more often illogical existence of the very individual the following story is centered around, one 'George Allen Stone'. Here is a man whose three basic beliefs to survival in this all too often cock-eyed crazy world are; "Any day above ground, even if you are a 'minor', is a good one!" "No-body, but 'no-body' remembers you when you are nice!" And finally "When things seem to be at their worst, even though it is another 'given' that they often can and do deteriorate even more, if you don't find some reason to laugh, you'll cry!"

And now, for those of you even remotely confused, let alone still here, read on to find out the reasons for the final 'why!'

Normally being stuck with a handle like 'George', especially at a time when the rhyme 'Georgie porgy puddnin pie, kissed the girls and made them cry!' was popular, would have in itself been bad enough. But, when your humorously sadistic 'old man' also saddles you with the middle title 'Allen' to go with the surname 'Stone', you are in for a very large amount of razzing. Why? Well, because the kids you grew up around, kids an awful lot just like me or yourself, figured out real fast that the first initial from each name spells 'gas', something strangely comical and appealing to all ages. And from there, you really learn fast that there are purposely two different ends to every animal, as well as to which divided location you want to be associated with. Then, after understanding that we all live in two very distinctive worlds, one a sometimes roller coaster wild ride roaming fantasy inside our heads, the other also occasionally shockingly real one that we all struggle to survive in, should help you understand why our boy sometimes just naturally prefers to spend more time in the one 'he' foolishly believes he has the most control over.

So, with this kind of attitude in life, our boy George just couldn't help but be the benefactor to more than his fair share of really 'Wow!' 'Hot-dam!'. Or even really 'Yahoo!', 'Hot diggetty daggetty dog days!'

Okay, since you've apparently read this far, something that tells me you're either very persistent or curiously confused, so let's take another big 'potentially messy' step into his world. Let's get most of the 'crap' out of the way and just start in with the exact type of situation I tried to warn you about, right from the very start.

'Oh', and by the way, just in case some might think we're off track from where we started, the verbal expression of 'Shit!' around our boy Stone, is that the substance, other than the obvious, is really only considered by him as a referral indication of one's very 'limited' vocabulary. 'Or', for any individual with an even shallower uneducated grasp of the English language, it is something needed for expressing their present frustrated emotions or in a situation over one of vulgar profanity.

James G. Davies Sr.

But most importantly of all, without animosity or regret in your heart, laugh at every opportunity that presents itself during your lifetime. Why? Because unfortunately, more than enough reasons to cry will also present themselves along the way.

Chapter # 1

Why 'Time fries.'
Or
The 'Friday flue.'

Apparently someone is presently in a position, and not on just the 'horizontal' plain, to prove what is said about the 'almighty buck', 'you 'can-not' take it with you!' At least it would seem so - since none of what the 'dearly departed' had hoarded during his limited time here on earth is presently visible. And since there is also no 'Wells Fargo' or 'Brinks' truck anywhere to be seen in the immediate vicinity, it would appear that it's safe to say, that, 'when you go, you 'really, really' 'go'! Plus, you 'definitely' no matter what anyone else might try to tell you, 'you do not', well, other than what you are wearing and farewell trinkets, 'take anything else materialistic acquired by said 'loot' with you!

Now the 'who' or 'why' of the recently deceased is not really overly important at this time, well, at least not just yet. But, even though soft religious music is being pumped in from somewhere, a minister presently delivering one of his best often rehearsed eulogies to apparent friends of the literary 'poor sole' in the closed casket, there all traditional similarities - abruptly grind to a stop.

There is also the suggestive appearance of it being a hot sticky mid-July afternoon. As well, the atmosphere from the open aired service is noticeably affecting the strange antics of the large gathering. Instead of beads of sweaty tears or sorrow showing on the group's faces, soft smiles and light joyous conversation is floating among the just short of boisterous crowd, with the minister busily reminiscing about memories that were not any part of even his. Joining the festivities is an aroma of fresh summer flowers blooming close-by, blending in with the pleasing overhead clear blue sky. Also present are the sounds of passing chirping birds, as the chattering mob continues to act just as if they were really at some sort of joyous outdoor festivity, instead of the intended heart rendering farewell tagged onto the end of ones eventual departure.

In life the recently deceased had been recognized as an individual who was often considered as an all-around 'pain in the prostrate' to most of the men he controlled, with that definition being by far one of his good points. Justifiably nicknamed the 'Evil Dwarf' by the gathering, by factory workers he had intimidated or invoked anger from, the man's presence would obviously be far from missed. The fact that in life most found their departed foreman anything but likeable or friendly, it was something which apparently no longer really mattered. And it was only our singular smiling George Stone, his reputedly 'most' antagonistic worker, who truly and fully appreciated the exact extent of just what was really going on right now.

Constantly during the 'service' this well-groomed devilishly grinning individual 'I already warned you that our soon to be main man 'George' was a strange human who evidently found humor even in the all inevitable departure called 'death', had allowed his attention to float continually back and forth. Up down and across that is, through the sea of seemingly happy and also very familiar work related faces before him.

Suddenly now, as the minister's voice grew louder, our boy Georges' concentration finally belonged to this man of the cloth, and to him alone, as his eyes hypnotically followed the 'man of Gods'' every over-exaggerated gesture.

Strangely his body suddenly felt pleasantly warm, and yet still contently hypnotized. In the background he could see a half dozen sardonic grinning 'pawl bearers' suddenly surround the bright acrylic red coffin, no doubt after a short wordless order from the minister. On more than one occasion, he could recall, it had been remarked that the foeman had been enough of a male's 'doniker' to warrant having to carry his own casket to the graveyard when the time came. But then again - as six men dressed in black tuxedos with matching stove pipe hats aligned the 'oblong box', it was just possible that a further remark about how most people would 'gladly' go to their bosses' funeral - strictly to make sure the wasn't just playing a trick on them. Hell, that would be too obvious, but then again , it just might very well be the main reason responsible for such a large presently rambunctious turn out.

Finally, as he continued to watch, each man then reached up and pulled the shining tubular stiff black hats down tightly against their now pushed out protruding ears. But when they quickly picked up the eye dazzling 'bloody nose red' container, a gun magically materialized held high over the clergyman's head, George couldn't help but start to laugh uncontrollably ahead of what he strangely knew could only be about to happen next.

Instead of a loud thundering 'bang' emitting from the weapon clenched in the minister's raised outstretched hand, a short ear-piercing 'ring' irritably echoed inside of his head. It was also, apparently for this gathering, a normal phenomenon, which in turn instantly seemed to prod the rest of the smiling funeral party into letting out a loud roaring cheer.

Then, from the gathering, came a pair of identical and beautiful obviously built for breeding scantily clad young women, edging themselves closer to George's knee-crossed seated form. He in turn, even stranger for those who knew him and his attraction for 'top heavy' overly endowed young ladies, seemed entranced, as his eyes joyously engulfed the now uplifted casket being comically whisked away by the six work-related pawl bearers. And as they moved jerkily, just as if they were on a thirty-three and a third rotations record presently being played at an advanced seventy-eight speed, the sound of joyous pulsating applause once again filled the gay atmosphere around them.

Even passing pigeons seemed to be a party to what was happening because one, an obvious critic, now flew low over the bobbing coffin and made a noticeable deposit as if to signify it also had know of the deceased man's memorable virtues.

Suddenly, just as when things going all too well always seemed to do, something happened that was about to bring an abrupt end to our boy's joyous festivities. When the second ear-piercing ring from the minister's weapon reached his ears, it somehow caused the comical dream like world around him to instantly freeze, only then to start melting, like raindrops running down a car's windshield. In one foolish last second of desperation, as if his brain had already sensed what was happening, he tried to wrap each of his arms around the two voluptuous cud-able creatures now smiling on each side of him, their hands resting on his neck and shoulders. But when his arms passed right through the intoxicating creature's bodies, the often contagious smile that had been at home on his face, regrettably likewise started to drain away to join them.

Some as yet still unknown wave of invisible pain now caused his head to suddenly feel as if it were the 'clapper' inside a gigantic unseen church bell. Then, while the fading images reverberated and echoed down the corridors of his interrupted dream world, his body slowly acknowledged its beckoning back to the harshness of reality, a reality with its painful existence now once more calling out to him.

It was in this passing 'twinkling of an eye', as had happened on over countless other such similar nights, that the often humorous protective fantasy world of our George Allen Stone regrettably once again 'died' the unavoidably inevitable death.

Our boys' material world, although very often closely associated with that of his fantasy domain, was sometimes exactly as he dreamed himself and others to be. It was something he brought with him from his childhood, something that had made older women wanting to scold and pinch his little cheek each time his devilish nature had acted up. The only thing different between then and now, even though he was still inclined to act up, was that now that some older woman he knew, and even some of those who didn't really know him - now just wanted to occasionally 'slap' that very same cheek.

His quick biting wit and overall friendly attitude had more than once brought people forward, in search and appreciation of his well-intended acid tongued comments. It was this personality, something we more sense and feel towards one another rather than see or hear, that helped make him always smile in even the touchiest of situations.

All of these things, only led to the fact that he was about to wake up in his own bed. This, in itself, was a 'real' rarity, considering places such as the backyard, bathtub, pool deck, front lawn, and unlimited other similar strange places that had served as his mattress on past occasions. But the originally anticipated location would 'not' prove to be the 'first and only' highlight of his soon to be pain-ridden day.

A deep-rooted habitual instinct caused one of the arms on his now tortured horizontally resting form to sneak out and 'kill' the reverberating monster that had summoned him back to the existence he had once more almost successfully drowned in alcohol, only scant hours earlier.

Using that same instinct to push his groggy body fully erect from the bed beneath him, because he'd never been a 'five-minutes-more' type of sleeper, George's hands automatically shot out to carefully and gently encase a pulsating head that suddenly felt as if it were about ready to go off like a giant roman candle. Letting gravity make his body fall backwards into a sitting position on the edge of the bed, a small moan escaping his lips, only managed to slightly relieve the throbbing time bomb straining to explode inside of his aching 'pumpkin'.

Slowly now, more through instinct than necessity, he forced his eyes to scan the room's fuzzy familiar surroundings in search of a usually non-sympathetic wife, a consistently on the go individual he presently and secretly hoped would now be in the kitchen putting a silencer on his 'snap-crackle-pop' breakfast. Instantly he found that even 'they, his 'stained portholes' to the world each time they were forced to try and focus on the razor sharp outline of any object in the bedroom encasing his tormented form, ached in protest to their every movement. Holding them closed, his pulsating head agonizingly matching and counting off the tormenting passing seconds, he talked to himself briefly "You damn idiot!" before once more foolishly feeling ready to challenge the enemy again.

Cautiously using only one eye at a time this time, but just as 'slowly' as earlier, he let the windows to his conscious world hesitantly flutter open until they both could eventually lock onto the object most nearest him. As the reality that it belonged to the alarm clock, sank into his aching thoughts, he instantly remembered that it had been this obviously devil created instrument that had brought him out of sleeps peaceful sanctuary, only without mercy to toss him into his present tormented condition. And the biggest thing he 'really' hated about repeatedly being treated with no respect, was that he always seemed to land on his 'head', or why else would it always give him the most trouble when arriving back onto the first step of his next new journey

Mature intelligence told him that the act he was about to perform couldn't possibly ease any of the terrible pulsating pain he was still presently experiencing, but he did it anyway. In one fluid nonstop motion he scooped up the mechanical device now silently performing a function it was also created for, and tossed it sidearm out through one of the bedroom's two opened windows, directly across from him. And as he watched the alarm clock sail majestically out of view, something he had also done countless times before, he at least felt psychologically satisfied when his ears registered on the loud unseen 'plop' it made when landing in the backyards similarly located swimming pool.

Something previously undetected, now in the room's doorway, moved at the side of his present line of tormented vision. Forcing his head to pivot in its direction, even though he already knew what the intrusion could only be, he wasn't at all surprised when the outline of his reputed 'better half' came into full view. And when her soft seemingly unconcerned voice said, "Morning hun. One of these days I guess we're just gonna have to find out if someone makes a cheap waterproof alarm clock that's available to the public." he didn't even attempt to acknowledge the sarcastically weak remark.

Wordlessly watching her as she then made her way towards their bed he was still sitting on, another ritual they were often a part of because he wasn't yet sure if he was capable of speech, he made no effort to move. And his evaluation of her present attire, her bandanna wrapped head said that she was either about to totally dust down the house as soon as he was off to work, or they were going to too have Aunt Jemima pancakes for breakfast, he kept to himself right up to and after as she spoke once again.

"Breakfast is almost ready, and Fred's still comatose in his car out in the driveway."

Concentrating fully on simply standing erect now, with as little discomfort as possible, he finally managed to mumble "Good morning yourself." through lips that felt as if they and the tongue they were concealing had been used as a 'doormat'. Smiling a little sadistically, the object of his affection almost unintentionally, set her-self up for a fall. "Did ya have a bad time last night, hon? You kept waking up and touching me."

George, again more through instinct than necessity, didn't even hesitate, let alone consider the agony he would have to pay physically and psychologically for the reply, shot back brokenly, "Oh, I was probably, just checking to see which 'nightmare', I was presently visiting just now."

He next cautiously used one hand on the nightstand close-by so as to help steady his already anticipated tormented shaky movements. Then, for reasons probably known only to his warped sense of humor, the very reasons why he had not kept the waterbed they had purchased a year earlier, flashed through his memory.

On more than one occasion he and the wife had heard of so many therapeutic benefits of a waterbed from friends and relatives, not to mention its rumored sexual attributes that they had decided to purchase one. But right from night 'one', the rippling creature had proven to be an unwise investment. For him it had been a long time since he had experienced an intoxicated induced floating bedroom, and the first night had quickly brought that queasy sensation back fresh into his memory. The second night had started off a little more hopeful, after, a sometimes more comical than clumsy contortionist bout with 'laying a little pipe', meaning attempting sex, but it soon only preceded more bobbing hours of lost sleep. And when on the third night the wife had developed a bad case of body shaking 'hiccups', something he still swears gave him his first experience with a nauseating bout of 'seasickness', they had both decided that the rippling monster would have to find a new home.

Even, though all of these memories had flashed through George's tormented head in less than a second, he knew he didn't have to glance at the 'love of his life's' face to know that the whimsical grin that had been seated on it as she had entered the room, was no doubt still there. He was also smart enough to realize that any attempt to 'lying the-afford mentioned 'pipe', although he constantly was commenting that it was one of those things you couldn't 'save up' or 'put in the bank', would not only have been totally one sided. He also knew that any strenuous activity could be a lot more painful than the threat of 'death itself',, although he thought, its painless sanctuary 'did' sound appealing, especially just now. Also, since Judy was far from being an exhibitionist, it was highly unlikely that sex had entered either of their heads last night, considering his present condition. Besides - similar past experiences told him the 'chub' he was sporting just now was only full of kidney strained booze, 'not' anticipation.

Twenty years of living together as husband and wife had given both of them more than enough time to know and adapt to each others personal oddities or traits. And when George finally managed to perform the maneuvers he had missed on the first try, grabbing the night stand securely, he made no attempt to look in Judy's busy direction, when finally asking if she had sent one of the kids out to the car to wake Fred up.

"Ya, Ian's going to do it as soon as he gets dressed." there was a noticeable brief split second's silence at the end of her reply. It was almost as if she were waiting for George to respond to it, but he in turn only used the pause to finally glance in her direction. The gesture, as their eyes met, told her that it was safe enough to quickly add what else was on her mind.

"I sure hope you don't expect me to show any sympathy for a couple of guys foolish enough to sit up half the night making 'love' to the stuffing's in a 40 oz. 'glass turkey'."

"I --- I may expect," it was easily evident by George's shaky appearance and words that he was still having enough trouble 'breathing', never mind 'talking', "a lot of things in this world, lady --- but 'sympathy' from you --- isn't one of them."

Smiling mostly inside, while moving to the opposite side of the bed, George's present aim couldn't hit the floor, even if he fell on it, Judy added, "If you were a real drinker I'd offer you a quick start, a shot of booze, to get your day restarted. But we don't want to let you off that easy, 'do we'? Not only that, I'd swear it sounded as if you were dragging an elephant up the stairs behind you when you finally came to bed last night. What was the matter, your feet beat the rest of your body to sleep?"

As she deliberately and loudly snapped the bed sheets free of most of their wrinkles, there could be no doubt from her antics that she was sadistically enjoying George's still noticeably painful hangover, as he stiffened briefly in reaction to the loud 'crack' they made. It alone prompted him, while totally failing to recall just how in the 'Hell' he had actually gotten into bed, to let her finish with whatever else she might have to say before we would seek his no doubt expected revenge. He even vaguely, as he knew he had tried before, remembered trying to find someway to somehow stick himself to the ceiling. And as crazy as it sounded, he kept telling himself that if he ever did manage to wake up there someday - he promised himself that he would never drink again! Why, because he had often heard that some people repeatedly 'fall off the wagon', but no ones ever 'fallen off the ceiling'.

"I also thought I heard you splashing around in water briefly last night, when you failed to float on 'tipsy' toes into the house. The rug in the dinning room is still a little damp in a few places. What happened - you and the sponge trying to sneak up on that proverbial 'glass of water' for your booze?"

"Very funny!" he finally lamented, 'tipsy toes.' One of his hands gently caressing the side of his pulsating head, as the other maintained its vise-like grip on the nightstand - now acting as a third leg. "I was only teaching the new goldfish a lesson for 'barking' at us when we came in last night."

"Oh no!" Judy moaned. "You didn't put 'jell-o' in the tank again, just to slow them down to the speed your world was moving at, did you?"

"No I did not!" He didn't have to force a smile, as the memory of what she had just brought up, flashed through his tormented brain. "I was only trying to teach them a 'lesson', not to hate me."

"Well you can't blame the poor little devils for that. They probably heard while you were still in the pet shop what happened to the previous tenants, and figured that you or the other guy with you was going to swallow them alive too."

"Well it wasn't Ken Anderson! It was only Fred. And the closest to swallowing any fish or water he's come to since Nancy left him, is doing a little swimming in the booze." George answered defensively.

"He's a little to far from 'shore' to be calling it just 'swimming' don't you think?" Judy chuckled, still keeping the mood light and lively.

"Well don't you worry," George continued to snap. "He won't drown as long as I'm around to keep an eye on him."

"And just who, may I ask," Judy shot back, a hint of her own form of sarcasm again dripping from every word now, "is keeping an eye on the 'lifeguard'?"

"Don't you worry about someone keeping watch over me," he tried to brush the smile from his face now, "I can swim or float with the best of them. It's when they start using' my head for 'rugby' that I can't take." At this time, mostly for his benefit, both of his hands came up to carefully cradle his 'heart pulsating' head, his brain silently repeating one more time the alcoholics pledge of 'Never Again'!

"Well to me it just shows you that there is a 'God'. and he's no doubt a little perturbed at the way you and your Thursday night snooker league define a regular booze-up as a rollicking successful night of excitement."

"We call it - exercise!" George butted in.

"Exercise!" Judy almost chocked on the words, a loud snap of the last bed sheet both emphasizing her regard for George's words, as well as making him again cringe noticeably in reaction to the sudden pain the 'crack' once more brought with it. "The only 'exercise' your body was getting was when you 'bent your elbow' or 'shuffled your feet' off to the 'John' in order to take back some room for the next round of bladder expander!"

As she started to move on to her next chore, she let her privileged nagging trail her. "The closest thing to muscle toning you 'sponges' ever got after that most likely happened on your way home. I hear you were all doing fine one night, until someone passing by accidentally stepped on your finger tips!"

As much as it hurt to laugh, George couldn't help nut snicker slightly as an image of himself and all of his regular drinking partners crawling on their hands and knees like a 'herd of turtles' instantly popped into his head. It was a brief pleasure that his hangover instantly rewarded him for even as he spoke, "Well at least we all seem to get home safely. Besides, it may not be five hours in the gym, but at least it does involve a lot of movement. Before our night's out the only excuse for any real caloric depletion Fred was getting, was from regular sex, something I can honestly say he hasn't seen 'hide' nor 'hair' of since his separation."

George instantly paid dearly for the rude pun he had just made. But, as was his code, it didn't keep him form painfully adding, "Why, if we were still teenagers, I'd say Fred has a record holding case of 'blue-balls, especially after having become so accustomed to regular trips to the 'playing field'."

Pausing long enough to deliver a combination half frown and soft smile to go with a low 'Ntish.', to emphasize her contempt for his remark, the real head of the house just smiled. It was something else customary when playing this type of little verbal game with each other. Judy simply and honestly answered, 'Ya, you're right. You all seem to at least make it home in one piece.' And even though it was on the tip of her tongue to add the extra words of 'Or should I have said 'to the right peace!', she instead carried on with, 'I guess we women should be thankful for at least that much."

"Ya know what, you're right!" George quickly shot back, anticipating that it was now his turn to get in a few more verbal digs. "At least we're not all out chasin skirts, like some of the other 'boob snoopers' from work always do."

"Other, 'boob snoopers!" Judy almost gagged. "Other?"

Now human enough to instantly realize his 'slip of the tongue' George expertly took the foot that had just been in his 'mouth', and started to tap it on the floor in front of him, in such a manner to indicate that it was still snoozing. "Sorry! Not all the little guy's are up yet."

Still busy with the bed Judy gave out a short "Huh." in response to the brief diversion, before continuing with, "Oh don't go patting yourself on the back to much, or you might dislocate your shoulder. All females aren't so stupid as not to realize that their husbands look at other women. And personally,' she winked in his tormented direction, "I don't care who or what gives you the incentive, just as long as you remember to come home to get that 'itch' scratched.'

Pretending to ignore the little 'innuendo' George frowned at Judy while using one of his hands to cover the very area she was referring to, but not for the same reasons. In fact the closest thing he had to resembling sex, and not on his mind, could easily be drained away with a visit to the bathroom, something which was increasingly becoming very necessary with each passing minute. But fortunately with that passing of time came not only very slight relief - but also growing courage.

"Speaking of eating, I hope you de-boned whatever it is we're havin this morning. Right about now, I feel like I could gag on air! Oh, did you say you sent anybody out to hunt up Fred for breakfast?"

Giving him another "Ntish.", Judy wanted to tell him to give his head a shake - but she knew he could never live through the agony the movement would bring with it. Instead she half frowned, "Yes - I already told you - I warned Ian to be kind when he goes to wake Fred up. As a devilish image of just what her son was capable of - her frown was replaced with a silly grin, as she continued with "And speaking of Ian - he says you paid a little visit to his bedroom again last night. Would I be correct in assuming that you don't remember that little incident either?"

As his brain fought in vain to recall what his wife had just said, George let his still aching form temporarily re-find the edge of the freshly made bed. Stalling for as long as he dared, he was finally forced to admit "No, not really." And even before words he knew would be coming in his direction next had a chance to even start, he tried to relieve some of the torment still evident in his head by gently rubbing at it once more.

"Your son says that when he woke up you were sitting on the edge of the bed in front of him. He also said that you had a mirror in one hand and a flashlight in the other. And that after shinning the flashlight into his face, you then held the mirror up in front of your own face, while looking at first him and then yourself - a couple of times. Finally you mumbled something about 'it was okay for him to stay for another year', before getting up and falling out of the room."

Scratching his head more through necessity than desire to make it look as if he was still trying to recall the incident, George had no trouble forcing a smile onto his face while answering, "It sure sounds like something I'd do. I guess it's lucky for him he's got my family's nose and forehead."

Picking up George's discarded clothes at arms length from beside the hamper, a pinched nose and distorted face testifying to their desirability, Judy lost no time in doing justice to his last words. "That's not all he's got from your side of the family. Sometimes I swear he's got most of their brains too, especially when it comes to makin' historical blunders. Lucky for him he's got a lot of my family's traits too. As for the rest from your side of the line of evolution, time should work in his favor. If not, I've heard they're makin' great advancements with plastic surgery or even backup shock treatments nowadays."

"That's a nice way to talk about our son!" George frowned, while forcing himself erect once more. "As for the rest of your attitude - I didn't think you'd stoop so low as to pick on me while I'm so mortally wounded." He knew it was now or never to head for the bathroom, or he and Fred were definitely going to be eligible for being classified as legally late for work.

Watching his comical struggle, Judy answered his appeal for sympathy with, "You were never that wounded, especially after all of the rehearsing you've done! And as for Fred, I don't know why the 'Hell' that poor man doesn't just go sleep it off on the couch in the rec-room! Heaven only knows what he's got to go home to."

"Exactly!" George butted in. "He has to have someone's ear to bounce his troubles off of. Best friends are 'supposed' to be around for things just like that!"

Letting his eyes search out his bathrobe as he had been speaking, his face found it at almost exactly the same time when Judy tossed it in his direction. And as the next words out of his mouth, "The way his luck's been going lately, he'll probably get struck by lightning next time he's takin' a shower!" were almost totally muffled as the robe had landed over his head and shoulder.

"Speakin' of a 'shower'!" Judy pinched her nose, the rest of her wrinkled up face expressing how he presently smelled, as her hands did their part and rested one on each hip to indicate an unspoken command.

"I know! - I know!" George grimaced, as his right hand fought with the bathrobes first sleeve. "I'm goin', I'm goin!" he added, before bravely taking the first step in the afford mentioned rooms direction.

"It's not just 'you', I was hinting about." Judy then added. "After one of your nights out with the boys you're not the only one who smells like something any 'decent' bloodhound would try to bury."

"Oh - Fred." George half, grinned.

"Yes 'Fred'!" Judy smiled openly now herself. "Did you leave the windows down on the car?" she added with a hint of sarcasm.

"Yes, I left all the windows open", George bluffed, his eyes squinting as his brain fought once again for any memory of doing exactly that, and then saying to itself, 'I think I did.'

Reading him better than he could himself, Judy chuckled, "You are going to 'Hell', and you know that don't you?"

Pretending not to know what she was hinting at, even though it was on the tip of his tongue to respond 'Anybody 'special' on your side of the family you want me to say 'Hi!' to when I get there?', George kept on moving, while continuing to defend his earlier answer. "Even if I hadn't - Fred wouldn't have suffocated. That only happens if you leave the car's motor running and there's an exhaust leak."

"That's not exactly, the kind of 'suffocation' I was thinkin' about - or 'gas leak' I was referring to." Judy chuckled.

"Oh?" George feigned blankly, pausing. "And just what sort of asphyxiation are you referring to?"

"You know exactly what kind of contaminating suffocation I'm referring to." Judy's words sounded more hummed than spoken, as her hand continued to pinch her 'nose' as she spoke. "You guys are probably so hung over that your senses don't start workin' again for another two days. When I use the car after you and your buddies have been riding in it, not to mention 'Fred' sleeping there, I have to drive around in the contamination for about three hours, all windows at full mast, until it's been decently fumigated of all your left behind party odors."

Already knowing that it would be wrong to say, "Oh come on, it's not that bad!" he said it anyway.

Judy in turn, lost no time in zinging him even further. "You're right! It's even worse! More than once I've been tempted to drive it, windows all the way down, through a car wash. And if that didn't work I was going to put our garbage in the back seat and drive it around town until it stopped 'smelling better'."

A sudden both foolish and definitely 'death wish' wanted him to say, "I've tasted your cooking, and as garbage it's an improvement!" but even 'his' warped sense of humor wasn't that rude, not to mention his will for survival wisely prevented it. Such a remark was not only a little harsh right now, but such a slamming deserved to be saved for a better occasion or audience. So instead he wisely just mumbled, "Fred's sleepin' in his own car. Don't you remember I sometimes get him to drop his car off in our driveway so we can ride together, just in case one of us is to drunk to drive."

But the expected remark as his face had temporarily flinched didn't go undetected, and Judy pretended to lean her head closer to his once more departing figure while asking, "What was that?"

"Oh nothing, nothing." he smiled, while carefully guiding a few more steps towards the rooms' slowly approaching doorway. "Just thinking out-loud."

"Well don't get too involved with whatever it is that's presently taking short trip across your brain, or you just might forget where it is you're eventually going."

"It's just that I had a little idea about the barbecue running around inside my head." George continued, while rubbing at the back of his neck.

"Well you better get the thought out while you can." Judy smiled. "Otherwise it's liable to die of loneliness in there." she then chuckled.

While answering, "Boy, you're on a roll today!" he fought back the temptation to extend both of his arms straight out in front of him, as if their extension would somehow shorten the distance still separating him form the shower he so desperately needed. "Why don't you pick on Fred? I'm sure he'll prove to be an even easier prey for your witticisms."

Instantly, even before she spoke, the humor that had been a constant in Judy's voice and movements, were now noticeable going to be missing. After over twenty years together they had each become capable or reading sincere sentimental changes in each other even before they were expressed, such as now.

"After every night you two stay out late drinking lately, you tell him to go sleep in the basement. And after every time he says 'No. he's going home.', we always find him sleeping it off sawing logs in either our car or his own."

Stopping in his tracks, and not just because he still wasn't fit for the rest of the world, George felt the change in his wife's tone even before he heard it. From past similarities he knew that just his presence would give more moral support than he was still verbally having trouble expressing.

And the too often taken for granted warm sensation he still got from his wife's presence, was there as he let her continue.

"I don't know why you don't just take Fred's car keys off him when you get back here. You're supposed to be his 'friend', aren't you? One of these times he's going to kill himself or somebody else, if he ever manages to get the 'Hell' out of the 'damn' driveway."

George knew that when his wife used the words 'Hell' and 'damn' twice within a minute, it was definitely time too speak up. She wasn't far away from shifting to a depressing mood he personally wanted to avoid, and he intended to steer her present feelings back to how they had been only long moments ago.

"Ya know what?" he said, while carefully turning his body to totally face the only real woman he could finally admit to himself that he had ever really known and loved in this world, his body still painfully protesting his every sluggish move. "Sometimes I think a little of me has rubbed off on you and you've learned something from all my intelligent remarks or actions. Then - sometimes you remind me of your brother 'Slow pitch.' Right about now, you're acting about as sharp as "bathtub 'Fred' out there."

He had to work at forcing his shaky right hand to point towards the same window the alarm clock had left by earlier. But when Judy's eyes failed to glance in the windows direction, he kept on speaking anyways.

"I've been switching Fred's car keys for weeks with a dummy set I had made up for whenever we're going to end up here - and he never catches on either! I also have a deal with the boys that whoever wakes him up after switching his own keys back from where I hide them under the cellar stairs, gets a couple of extra bucks in their allowance after pay day."

Like almost always his special mixture of sarcasm and humor was doing exactly what it was intended, as other parts of the world fought for existence around them. A soft breeze of refreshing midsummer morning wind trying to rejuvenate the bedroom's contaminated air wasn't the only thing floating in through the room's two half opened windows. Recognizable faint opening and closing sounds associated with the house's aluminum spring door leading into the driveway also floated in.

Soft footsteps realizing that retrieving the customarily Friday morning discarded alarm clock was also apart of the task he was about to perform, faltered from their present course just long enough to use the backyard pool's skimming net to snare the submerged timepiece form it's chlorinated watery grave.

Ian, the youngest of George and Judy's three sons, and like most others in their early mischievous teen years, 'over-emphasized' every move and gesture as he tiptoed quietly up to the vehicle containing the still dormant form of his dad's best friend. What he had been asked to do was not unfamiliar to him, but it never ceased to amaze his maturing humor at the variety of strange positions and facial expressions he generally found Mr. Owens presently involved in.

The aroma of stale beer and old cigarette smoke was about the only unpleasant sensation Ian experienced during these missions. But his youth still served as a protector and buffer to the type of bad habits generally accepted by the adult world as being normal.

Seven o'clock in the morning provided more than enough daylight to fully illuminate the car's interior, as Ian playfully and cautiously peeked in through its open left window. And his adolescence couldn't completely kill the silly youthful giggle presently being born in his throat.

Quickly clasping one hand over his mouth in an effort to muffle the uncontrollable gesture, his whole body dropping to the ground to rest on one bent knee, he forced himself to take deep breaths of fresh morning air, until he felt he was capable of continuing with his mission. Inside his head he likened the adventure to some earlier childhood imaginative fantasy, possibly where he was on a perilously dangerous 'dragon killing' expedition.

It would be only a few scant more years before Ian would fully understand the depressing reasons behind the present condition of the still sleeping man's sad situation. But until that time, strictly because of the youthful ignorance still protecting him from life's maturing realities, he could be content with the comical visual aspects of Fred's twisted dormant snoring form.

Reaching in through the car's partially opened window, a devilish grin and restrained half-snicker blending in with his actions, the reward for exchanging the vehicle's keys was his first accomplished act. Then placing his right hand gently onto the awkwardly positioned leg bent up in an angle no doubt intended to provide more horizontal sleeping room, Ian slowly started to shake the knee of the man often referred to as 'Uncle Fred' - while softly calling out his name, "Mister. - - - - Mister Owens." It was an already accepted routine that he knew also would have to be repeated quite a few more times with growing force, before he would eventually obtain successful results. It was likewise an act that blended in verbally with what his father was presently still talking about, less than sixty vertical feet away.

"As far as really sleeping it off in the rec-room goes, I guess in a sadistic sense we should be glad Fred doesn't 'imitate the dead' down there."

George was glad when he detected a small smile creeping into the corner of his wife's lips, and it only served to encourage him with what he had already intended to say anyway.

"If he smells anything near as bad as I think I do right now," a small nod instantly coming in his direction to confirm his statement, "then the rec. room no doubt could start smelling as if we've taken to raising a herd of wild 'beer guzzling' goats down there."

This time a short laugh came with the broadening smile on Judy's face, and it not only told him that he had succeeded in accomplishing what he had wanted to, but also to say what else was still in his thoughts.

"Besides, when we come here after the league, sometimes I drive his car." lowering both his head and voice, "At least I think I do .... most of the time." Securing the housecoat's belt loosely draped around his waist even tighter, he pushed off wobbly for the bathroom once again.

Instinctively he knew Judy's smiling face would still be enjoying his tormented little one act play once more, and when her voice dripped with phony sentiment as it asked, "Don't you ever get tired of having to relearn how to walk every Friday morning?" he quickly replied, "No more than what you have to go through whenever you get behind the steering wheel of our car." Then he forced himself to try and look less nearer 'death's door' than he actually felt.

The sound of her warm chuckle floating over his shoulder as he concentrated on the room's doorway, now seconds instead of miles away, magically enlightened his self-inflicted agony, as it generally did.

Then also as was part of their 'morning after the night before ritual', Judy genuinely now asked him if he was going to be okay. "You going to make it today - hon?"

Halting in his movements, he pivoted his body back in her direction just enough again to make sure their eyes were once more smiling into each others' before speaking. "If time really does 'heal' all things as people say, then I should be fine, in about 'five years', 'Kid'."

Kid was a nickname that had somehow become a part of their lives , as well as their feelings for each other during the years.

A small giggle escaped Judy's lips as she watched his more comical than agonizing movements start up once more. She then quickly offered, "I put some fresh appropriate clothes in the bathroom for you." as he finally reached the doorway. "And try not to take five minutes this time if you find out you're puttin' you socks on from the wrong end again. We haven't got that much time to waste. Oh, and if you get stuck thinkin' there's only one sock there, check your feet before you call me. I still remember when you once put them both on the 'same foot', and then went crazy looking for another sock for your still bare one. And no, I don't want you, like you've done in the past, to have one white and one black sock on after you're dressed. I didn't believe you then and I won't believe you 'now' - when you tell me it's just your way of showing that you don't believe in discrimination.

With an outstretched hand he pretended that he was briefly inspecting the door frame, instead of actually using it as a brace while responding, "I think this room's about due for a new coat of paint."

Not until now did Judy realize that her hubby's 'war wounds', a term she had developed for him since he had started spending more drinking time with Fred since his separation, were no doubt giving him a little more agony than he wished to let on about.

"You've been saying that about once a week for the last month and a half hon.' And instead of verbally objecting about his growing habit, she instead just silently loved him a little more for trying to help a very dear friend during a rough period in his life.

"But then you said exactly the same thing for about two years before we painted the room last time."

As she spoke, while putting the finishing touches on their pillows, George remained stationary in the doorway, looking back at her maneuvers - while waiting for the last of the remarks he knew were yet to come.

"So - I guess it means we're good for another year before it gets done this time."

It didn't take George any real effort to smile as he watched his wife expertly and effortlessly float around the room, straightening or touching just about everything in her path. She, like a lot of others, had been made the butt end of a lot of his jokes during their years together, and it had taken him a lot of that time before he was publicly able to admit that he really loved her. It was a fault he now maturely was able to accept and reason that had probably come from an almost fatherless childhood. But thank God in his wisdom had only let their separation last a short time.

There had been true strong affection between himself and his brothers and sisters, there still was, but outwardly displays of genuine physical emotion had not been one of his parent's stronger points. And it was this he believed that had cost him and his wife a few touchy beginning years of their marriage, for his emotional insecurities to be washed away.

Working among such a large number of people he had seen a lot of marriages go 'bad' and break up during the past couple of years. A few of them being very close friends, such as Fred's. And when others who had also noticed, questioned 'why' his of all peoples lately hadn't gone the same route, he never once denied the fact it might have , if not for his strong willed wife's commitment to marriage.

It was this realization that caused him to smile softly in Judy's direction, just a little bit longer than he normally did. And she, almost always with and occasionally ahead like now briefly of his special kind of 'wit' knew it was time to feed him the fuel to help bring him back home to where it belonged between them.

"Oh - and by the way. Don't forget it's my dad's birthday today - and we've got to phone and wish him a 'happy birthday' when you get home from work tonight."

"Not again already!" he frowned. 'You know how much I like talkin with you dad."

"Stop whining." she continued to grin. "You never hear me squawk when it's time to congratulate your parents on anything during the year."

"Why would you. Every time we have an argument, they're on your side."

"Can you blame them. I heard through the family grape vine that you were such a little bugger when you were little that between the truant officer and the school principal they had to book an appointment if they wanted to spend some time with you. And it wasn't their idea for you to move so far away that it takes special occasions to warrant a family reunion. A smart man would know that when everyone in the audience always votes against him," Judy continued to smile, "then chances are he's never right."

"Ha!' George threw back at her. "I might not always be right - but I'm never wrong!"

No sooner were the words out his mouth, as Judy broke into laughter, then it dawned on him the potential consequences of the ammunition he had just offered her. And just as quickly as he realized that there was no way to take them back - he tried to reinforce them in his favor. "I married you didn't' I?"

Dropping back to less than a smile, Judy straight faced him, "Make up your mind. One minute you're telling me my dad took advantage of you, and in the next one you're taking credit for the smartest thing you ever did in your life."

"I know, I know." He answered, the pain he was presently experiencing coming not from within the words themselves - but rather in just the fact that any kind of movement or verbal expression was enough to make the pounding in his head increase in volume. "It's just the way your dad seems to smile all the time when we're having a conversation. Whenever it looks like I might get the best of him on anything, he always glances in your direction briefly, and then back at me with a big silly grin on his face. I always feel like he's giving me a little 'dig', like he somehow outsmarted me into taking you off his hands."

"Oh you're just being 'picky'." she smiled once more.

"Am I?" he quickly retaliated. "And you don't think those two little words of 'Thank you!' in brackets he always manages to slip into the remarks someplace when thanking us for the cards we send to cover all of the seasons special occasions, aren't his way of getting a little personal 'jab' in?"

"Stop being so 'paranoid'." Judy smiled. "Besides, even if he doesn't say or show it, I know for a fact that he's actually quite fond of you."

Inside of his thoughts, he reasoned, 'He should be! After all I took you off his hands didn't' I!' but instead settled for, "Well, regardless, it still bugs my ass!" George frowned.

Reaching out just far and quick enough to give his posterior a quick rub, while saying, "And what a nice little 'ass' it is!" She then quickly pulled her had back just in time to keep it from being swatted at by his automatic reflexes.

"Slow down lady! One of the kids might be close by, and we don't want to scare em to early in life. Besides, man's supposed to be the hunter, at least that's what they're teaching in school I hear."

"Well now you know why they don't program the boys in homeck. They don't want them finding out the truth." she laughed once more.

'They're learning more than everything they'll ever need to know in later life around here!" George snapped.

"Okay." Judy smiled, as hubby once more massaged his temples "If you say so. But if you don't get back on track, you're never going to get out of here."

Wisely, he started to move towards the bathroom once more, ignoring the discomfort his movements brought with them.

Finally, after telling himself that this was presently the longest trip to the 'john' he could recall, as well as 'Come on 'powder puff' keep movin.' he actually was feeling a fragment more alive than when he had first reached the doorway. Bravely he let go of its security while saying, "I'm going to try for a shower and shave. If you really cared - you'd light a candle - or at least say a small 'prayer' for me."

Willing his feet back into motion, he restarted for the bathroom while words of "A good or bad prayer?" followed him. Pausing long enough to reply, "You always were sadistic. But you better put my life insurance policy on the mantle over the fireplace. It should be kept close-by, you know, just in case."

He didn't want to give her the chance for a last wise crack, and made a sudden quicker movement to cover the last remaining feet in the room, but she did in a low voice anyways. "I already did."

Now, strictly for her benefit, he quickly covered the mile still separating him from the new sanctuary he was after, the bathroom's now visibly partially opened door. The fact that words of wisdom from one of his retired older friends suggesting that when he gets to be his age all trips will be calculated by the distance from fire hydrant to firehydrant although somehow fitting in right here, didn't help any. And it was only for his own benefit, after telling the information to get lost, that he mumbled to himself, "I guess we should be glad she isn't in one of her 'vacuum' till the color's all gone out of the carpet's binges. If the noise didn't kill us, the vibrations would be more than enough to make us wish we were in its sanctuary."

At one time during the last few years, one of the boys, and George was pretty sure which one, had made up a sign warning of the washroom's possible contamination ration after being used by none other than dad himself on a Friday morning. One time he had overheard his oldest boy say, 'You can always tell when dad's been in the washroom after Thursday nights 'booze up' - the cat runs in circles and cries at the front door to let you know it wants out!' It was a brief memory that made him chuckle when remembering how 'human' their pet actually acted at times. He even on occasion prided himself as being able to see - or at least think he could understand things from the poor creature's point of view. And if it was true, then he could understand why the feline had hid from him for almost a whole week after he had accidentally stepped on its tail when trying to sneak up the stairs one night. Its ensuing loud 'Me-e-o-o-w!' had not only wrenched his heart form its protected ribcage and up into his throat, something he swears he had to swallow at least five times just to get it back to where it belonged, but also cost him the three stairs of advancement he had won, only to end up sitting ass down back at the foot of the stairwell and gripping at his chest. And even though he had used some pretty risqué words to define the heart pounding situation - he was pretty sure 'Snowball' was also presently using its 'ear singing' vocabulary to express its dissatisfaction at their unintended one-sided encounter that night.

At one time, especially after almost tripping over her as she had slept on the same set of stairs, he even wondered if the fact that she was the second female in the house, been in on a conspiracy to do him in. Especially since in that incident, he was fresh out of bed and not yet totally awake while using one hand to give himself a good 'everybody up' scratching, had left him with a groin injury he treated delicately for months - he thought he had torn his left testicle off while trying to maintain his footing.

But where most people looking for sympathy would have tried to take their agony out on the world, especially if people had laughed at how the injury had happened, he wisely blamed it on something that could be work related, saying he had accidentally walked into a blind corner or blunt edge on a piece of equipment he and Fred had been working on. And as always, with his good buddies confirmation, he had worked it out into a very humorous 'one man play' whenever re-enacting the 'rain dance' that such a male injury would have insisted upon.

Pushing the door open, he allowed his vision to pan the cubicles area real quickly. Fresh clothing was stacked neatly on the vanity just inside the door, as he had been pre-told. Forcing himself to cover the last few steps still separating him from the bathroom's prelude to salvation, he bravely locked the door behind him, a precautionary act he told himself was mainly for the safety and benefit of the other dwellers in the house - not his.

At first, as all of his present clothing quickly disappeared onto another strategically placed clothesbasket, he had every intention of stepping right into the shower. But as strange noises rumbled around deep inside his body, he instantly knew what his new first priority was. Even in his present state of still hindered reasoning he was smart enough to realize that his exterior body wasn't going to get any 'dirtier' than it presently felt, but the bathroom floor sure might. And the only reward he got for the quick decision, as he strained momentarily for an act that usually came easy while mumbling inside of his thoughts 'I gotta start leaving those triple cheese pizzas alone.', was the magnified sensation of his blood painfully pulsating through his once again throbbing temples, after no doubt having first tripled in size.

He then in turn, only now strictly and selfishly for the benefit of the sorrowful looking sight presently looking back out of the mirror now in front of him, allowed his face to go through a short comical pantomime routine, showing the passing of agonizing self induced pain in its various stages.

Shifts

From then on, and more than once as he continued through a ritual that would hopefully prepare him for the day's existence, he thought of his best friend Fred, and the similar biological agony he must surely be suffering also. But instead of showing any real outward sympathy for the man, just as he silently wished someone would do for him, he once more instantly regretted the painful short laughter that escaped from his lips. He then did something he often did for his own amusement - he mentally visualized some of the humorous and 'fuzzy' antics that he could remember, Fred, and the rest of the gang, had been involved in last night.

Personally he felt his shave was more an act of courage than necessity, after the shower, even with its brief high pitched scream and freezing cold shock, had accomplished only part of what he had prayed it would do. Unlike the dirt, odor and last remnants of sleep that had gone down the drain with the water from its needle-like spray, the pair of large symphonic kettle drums that had been playing continually inside his head earlier, now felt more like rhythmic bongos beating in time to the pulse of his pumping heart. Even though the ordeal felt longer to perform then he knew it did, only about ten minutes had passed before he felt close to human enough to leave the room's rejuvenated life-giving protection.

Stepping back out into the hall, the broad grin that was now on George's perfumed face was mainly from the 'tee shirt' he was now wearing. Over the years in the plant where he worked, comical or fact-related undershirts had become a running gag with most of the crew, himself being one of the worst offenders. And even though he hadn't chosen the clothing he was presently wearing, Judy herself knew of the men's child-like antics at work, and liked to occasionally get her own 'two cents worth' in, such as his present tee-shirt reading 'T.G.I.F.'

Normally he would have chosen his favorite 'Friday flu victim' but the one she had chosen was just as symbolic. On the front the lettering read 'Approach with caution.' with the evenly spaced letters boldly displayed in white on a black background on the back.

The letters 'T.G.I.F' throughout most of the working class were instantly recognizable as standing for 'Thank goodness it's Friday'. But George in his sadistic wisdom had strategically added the letter 'F', which those associated with him understood to read, 'Thank 'fuckin' goodness it's Friday!' which definitely fit in with the way he was still feeling.

Leaning against one of the small hallway walls, 'Morning pop.', was the son he believed responsible for the presence and construction of the small sign now hanging on the door's outer surface. Darryll, their second eldest boy, was obviously enjoying his father's recognizable hung over condition.

If necessary, especially after being occupied by someone in his condition, there was another washroom in the house available to use. But George knew, 'Good morning son.' that his offspring was no doubt there for a special reason.

"Is it 'safe' enough to go in there and take a shower dad?"

The question had more or less been exactly along the lines George was expecting. It also caused the grin already on his face to broaden even more - before starting to walk away while giving his answer, "I don't know son. I guess it really depends on how long you can hold your breath. - But if I were you, I wouldn't chance it, but that's only because I already know what it's like in there."

After watching his father disappear down the stairwell leading to the main floor, Darryll then pinched his nose with one hand while using the other to reach blindly into the bathroom's interior to return on the rooms exhaust fan. He then gave the unit a long cloudy spray from a blossom scented deodorizer he had been concealing. Still grinning, he then closed the door and flipped a small pointer on the cardboard sign he had fabricated, with it ending up resting on one of the three categories it was made up to display. Grinning openly he then once more read the wording he already knew by heart.

'Warning! Room presently undergoing life saving fumigation. Advisable to allow five minutes for decontamination. Then and only then, enter at own risk, if you dare!'

Giggling a lot like his younger brother Ian had done moments earlier Darryll then set out to join the rest of the strange family he sometimes questioned as to why he had been born into it.

Friday mornings, what with hangovers and company, were getting to be an expected experience for most of the family members. And when George finally made his awaited entrance, his arrival was greeted with cynical gestures more of humor than emotion.

But life's regularity was still presenting itself as a small challenge in the back corridors of his low throbbing head. His oldest son, George junior, nicknamed 'Wubbles' by him, was there at the kitchen table with Ian. And as he headed for the opportunity to sit down again, Fred was sitting with his head resting over crossed arms at the breakfast table as, Darryll appeared from the same doorway into the room - only seconds behind him.

Gently lowering his freshly attired frame into its customary location for breakfast, after a brief stop at the sink for a glass of cold water, a fresh round of 'Good mornings' exchanged among them. George then let his nose take in a long pull of the pleasant aroma of hot coffee and cereal floating everywhere in the air. Almost instantly, as his reawakening senses feasted on the pleasant odors, he was 'more' than glad that they were encouraging his growing will for survival. And even the background music Judy liked to play constantly on the radio on the kitchen counter, a commercial from the hometowns radio station 'WWWP.' playing an old favorite 'Elvis', 'Teddy Bear' tune, couldn't weaken his presently improving mood.

Similar recent experiences had taught George that his very rough looking friend, presently looking like he had been mauled by a bear far more vicious than the one Elvis was presently singing about, was not quite as awake or human as he himself was now only starting to feel. So before speaking he reached across the small table and gently rested one hand on Fred's folded elbows. "Why don't you nip downstairs and risk a quick shower buddy. Maybe you'll get 'lucky' - and go down the drain."

The laugher that was being deliberately suppressed now flowed freely from Judy and the kids, as Fred's ragged looking body slowly crept into motion. Then, just as quickly as it had filled the kitchen's interior, the mood disappeared when his tired and definitely abused unshaven face gradually lifted itself in his hosts' direction.

The well meant bubbling humor the Stone family was presently experiencing, as they each stared into a face that looked as if it had just been dragged over ten miles of rough road, no way on Earth held any intentional animosity in it. And when a pair of red-veined bloodshot eyes blinked repeatedly, while his tongue dragged itself sideways between two dry lips before saying, "I hope we had one Hell of a good time last night George. I'd sure as Hell hate to feel this bad for nothing!" the temporarily suppressed laughter was immediately set free again.

No verbal request was needed or given for the two cups of steaming black coffee that appeared in front of both men. And as Fred's trembling hands eagerly wrapped themselves around the one obviously intended for him, he shakily added the words, "I think I know where your cat did its business last night." while once more licking his lips before taking a few quick sips of the hot life-giving brew.

The two bowls of cereal that were also about to touch the table in front of the men, the boys previous nickname 'serial killer' now justifiably depleted thanks to more variety, froze in midair at the mention of the family feline pet. A look of menacing displeasure also came over Judy's face, as she suddenly said, "Speakin' of Snowball, I don't know what you two 'shit disturbers' did to her last night but I can't get her to come up out of the basement. You better not have been," her eyes glaring directly into George's now, "stretching her or half-picking her up by the tail and walking her across the floor again, Mister Stone. I'm warning you!"

"I don't pull the cat's tail!" George quickly answered, a perturbed look on his face trying to overshadow his lying answer. "I just hold onto it, the cat does all the pulling! Besides, you're still mad at me because at Christmas when you saw 'tinsel' from the tree hanging out of Snowball's rear end, and I offered to pull it out because she looked like a wind up pull toy, you thought I had fed it to her in her food on purpose."

As he had been speaking, an image of their jet-black feline flashed into George's mind. The poor creature, and for apparently good reasons, was constantly trying to avoid him, and his renowned playful rough handling. Not to mention the times he had put Rice Crispi's' into its Kitty litter box, just to watch its hysterical tap dancing reaction to the 'snap, crackle, pop' as soon as the cereal was wet upon. Besides, how tough could the spoiled animals life be? Other than having to keep track of his movements late at night and in the dark, it's biggest worry would seem to be as to when or where or its next treat was coming from.

"Don't evade the issue." the outstretched cereal in Judy's hands retreating a little, as if indicating it just might be removed is she soon didn't get a proper response.

"Are you sure it was us? Maybe one of the boys 'drop-kicked' her off the front porch when they put her outside, you know, to get rid of her 'excess' cat food last night. Instead of trying to crucify me, I should be praised, since I probably only let her back into the house when we got home."

The absurd remark instantly proved to be an answer that obviously only someone like he could believe. It also brought with it a loud and almost in unison reply of "Dad!" from all three of the boys.

"You're the one who's always pulling Snowball's tail with one hand while holding onto her neck with the other, and then telling us it's just to help her to grow longer," Ian said. "And you're the only one she avoids 'constantly', so don't try and put any blame onto any one of us for her present behavior."

"Well maybe she was 'carpet surfing' again. I really don't mind her laying on her back tits up under the furniture. But when she reaches up, sinks her claws into their under parts only to push herself along the carpet as fast as she can go, then that I mind. Besides, nobody seems to worry about what happens when I get home late, and through an act of respect so as to not wake anybody up, I leave the lights off. An act I might add that almost brought on a heart attack the first time when seeing bits of sparks emitting out of the darkness, making me think my time was up and I should be expecting my past life to start flashing in front of my eyes." Pausing long enough to enjoy the sparse laughter, he quickly followed up with, "Sometimes lately I swear she's going to build up enough static electricity to explode!"

"Maybe she remembers how you've built up static by shuffling your socks across the carpet a couple of times, and then touching her on her moist nose." Darryll laughed.

"Ya, Dad. Maybe she's just priming herself to get even with you, if and when the opportunity presents itself." Ian giggled.

As the bowls of cereal that had been held back momentarily now continued their journey once again, George junior, while reaching for more sugar, accidentally bumped his mother's arm. Even though he automatically said, "Excuse me mom," George instinctively remarked, "Stop reaching for everything. Haven't you got a tongue in you head?" Junior, as often as possible 'a chip off the old block' lost no time in answering with a reply that George himself would have been proud to come up with.

"Sure I have, dad. But my arms are a lot longer."

It was on the tip of George's own tongue to quickly add," As long as the girls you hang around with know that too." but instead he held it back, mainly because he knew he wouldn't be able to stand the pain across the back of his head he would be receiving from Judy for saying it.

Laughter preceded the cereal's eventual contact with the kitchen table. And Fred's head, even though he had hypnotically watched their approach and landing, jerked instinctively at the sound of the bowl's magnified crashing contact with the flat hard surface.

"Even the kids can read you two bad actors like an open book when it comes to trying to pass on the blame." Judy half snarled, while heading for the refrigerator.

"If you're still worried about the cat," George acknowledged a little sarcastically, "Just don't feed her for a while. I'm sure she'll come out of hiding quick enough when her stomach starts taking control of her decisions." He then bent fore-ward slightly to sip at his coffee, while snapping off a quick wink, once detecting his buddies blinking bloodshot eyes across from him.

Fred, for foggy reasons still know only to him-self, noticeably had to force himself to blink back in a manner that made George wonder if he really 'did' know something more positive about the cat than he should. But before he had a chance to pursue his friends tormented condition, 'Wubbles' excited voice cut in with, "They're 'guilty' alright mom, I just saw them winking at each other!"

Glaring in his namesake's direction, a two hundred and thirty pound boy he just loved to bounce 'fat' jokes off of, someone more than once he had jokingly said about 'You should have been born in the wild. All you ever do is look for food!' George sneered menacingly with each word that next fell from his lips.

"Keep it up 'son', and you and the other members of your 'Hubba Bubba Club' can find someplace else to go nibble on furniture over the weekends.

'Little George', another pun and gross understatement his brothers loved to use on him, was smiling while saying, "Ha, ha, dad!" in a manner giving no doubt that he was unimpressed by his father's familiar smart remark. But the rest of his rebuttal was stopped 'cold in its tracks' - by the real boss of the house.

"Knock it off you two! It's getting late, and I've noticed that neither one of you can walk, talk, and chew gum at the same time lately." Judy's eyes had encompassed all of the tables' occupants while speaking. but strangely only one of them somehow felt signaled out over the words. And as much as it must have hurt to do so, Fred comically shoveled several spoonful's of cereal into his dry mouth, before forcing a big silly grin onto his aching face. and while staring into her face, "See, I'm eating, I'm eating!" The words spilled out of his mouth almost as fast as the food he was having trouble stuffing in did.

Deliberately forcing herself not to smile at the silly gesture, everyone else not being as graceful, Judy simply remarked, "As for you - don't get to close to a 'mirror'. I don't think either of you could take that much bad luck."

Waiting until he was pretty sure that the kids were preoccupied with their own breakfast, after encouraging it along with a few quick verbal barbs in their direction, George leaned a little bit closer to both his bowl of rejuvenating energy and Fred. And even though it was done in the hopes that no one else would bother to pay attention to what he wanted to whisper, it was an act about to turn on him.

It was another maneuver that instantly rewarded him with something he could only assume an old English castle's inactive moat might smell like, which thankfully each of the kids sitting closer to Fred had obviously pretended not to notice either. So rather than embarrass his best friend by telling him that he possibly had the breath of a 'dead lion' George let the grin that was always hiding close-by inside, show itself by asking, "Just what the Hell 'did' we do to 'Snowball' last night?"

"I'm not sure." Fred answered, while carefully inspecting the inquisitive ears trying to unnoticeably eavesdrop on their conversation, but more so as to make sure the only real person he was intimidated by was busy elsewhere. "But I seem to remember a bit of you holding the poor creature up in front of your face, and then going 'gobble gobble' at it a few times, like an excited turkey.

As the full significance of Fred's answer suddenly flashed into George's still slightly groggy mind, he couldn't suppress the chuckle that always seemed to come with it whenever recalling how he always re-acted about evaluating the need for pets. And when their cat's last visit to the veterinarian had cost them over seventy-five dollars, it had encouraged him to come up with a new saying, "The 'next' pet that comes into this house better go 'gobble gobble' or taste good with 'gravy' if anything ever happens to it!"

As pain rewarded George for the chuckle, Fred's voice made it obvious that similar pain was no stranger to him either, let alone about to take an undetectable back seat, when he asked, "What in the name of 'Sam Hill' was it supposed to mean?"

George, while using both hands to rub at his temples, offered only a quick whispered response, "Not here! I'll explain it all to you later."

The kids hadn't totally contained themselves when hearing broken parts of their father's familiar phrase. They each, in their own way, fought in vain to hold back their varying degrees of humor. Then, as they each got up from the table to leave in order to get ready for school, a short phrase of "Don't forget to brush your teeth." followed each of them out of the kitchen.

Glancing in Judy's direction, George was just in time to catch her performing another customary ritual with the very alarm clock he had thrown out the bedroom window earlier. She had found that the best and quickest way to dry out the instrument's mechanical interior was by placing it in the microwave oven for just under a minute. He then nudged Fred's elbow and gestured in her direction while saying out the side of his mouth, "Time's fryin. We better get movin!"

Even though it was painful, the more than once used pun once more got the only recognition it deserved, as an elongated 'E-e-e-w.' escaped from Fred's lips. He then gave George a now not so depressing smile, before quickly downing what was left of a breakfast he prayed he could hold onto.

A follow-up quick glance at the wall clock over their heads told them that they were almost ten minutes behind their regular schedule. In a since, they were getting nowhere fast. Their Friday morning routine after a night out barhopping usually always ran ten minutes late, and it was not yet seven-thirty. The large steel plant they both worked for was less than a fifteen-minute drive from where they were now standing. As any kind of overly speedy movements were still one of the things they weren't ready for just yet, they each grudgingly accepted the fact that now was indeed definitely the right time to get their 'far from fat asses' unglued off the kitchen chairs, and into motion.

Pausing briefly, as if suddenly remembering something that had slipped his mind, George inquisitively frowned in Judy's direction while asking, "Hon, who used the upstairs shower last yesterday?"

'Why, your son who just discovered he's in love." Judy hesitantly replied, her face already reading everything inquisitive in advance of his question, and then quickly added, "Why?"

"Oh, just curious." he smiled, while standing erect. Then, as if on cue to an un-given request, the boys filtered back into the kitchen. It was more than perfect timing, as they were just in time to once again briefly scrutinize the humorous antics of their father, and his very regular lately weekend guest. Darryll and Ian, also on an apparent schedule, were now noticeably more interested in what their day yet consisted of. Without a hint of hesitation George retrieved the glass of water he had brought with him to the kitchen table, and then threw it straight into Darryll's unsuspecting face. And as his startled son, a surprised 'Yelp!' instinctively escaping from his lips, everyone including Judy looked just as shocked as he was, froze in his steps. George, while placing the now empty glass down onto the table, remarked, "Now you know what it's like to get hit smack right in the 'gate' with 'cold water' when you're least expecting it. Now next time you have a shower, you'll remember to put the dial back onto 'tub' before you leave it! And when 'I' decide that if I ever need a 'cold shower', that will be strictly between me and your mother!"

Laughter lost no time in returning to everyone's face, as well as Darryll's, even though the boys totally failed to understand the reasoning behind why in the world their dad would 'deliberately' want to take a cold shower. And as they each started out through the screen door Ian had used earlier. Judy, always quick to react to anything George might surprise her with, quickly threw a towel she had somehow magically managed to come up with in her dripping wet sons direction. Then, while giving George and Fred her full attention - she let her face more than her words express what she had in mind for them. "You two can run, but you can't hide. You'll both pay for this later, that I 'promise' you!"

James G. Davies Sr.

Only George chuckled at the threat he considered to be hollow, as Fred's tormented face said the contrary, while trying to put himself behind his best friends form and hers. It was a reaction that only served to make Judy snicker, and she couldn't help but add, "Oh forget it. I'm sure the 'big guy upstairs' will eventually get even enough for all of us."

Little did she realize that as fragile as he was feeling, Fred was absorbing her every word. And just the mention of the 'almighty' getting even, made him think to himself, 'If God had wanted to punish us because of whatever happened to Snowball, all he had to do was make us a witness to her trying to cough up one of her legendary furballs. I'm sure just the sight of that happening would have me matching her fur lined hack with a gut wrenching shoulder shaking similar gut wrentching hack, only mine possibly bringing up my intestines. And if it excellerated the pounding now at home in me even one iota, it would be the last bit of energy needed to take the remainder of my already exploding head, like puff wheat exploding out of a cannon, right down to my shoulder blades."

Each of the boys lately always seemed to be involved in some sort of physical school sport. George himself however, whenever any reference was made of the young being overly active, often just said he instead was entering into his 'slowdown years'. It was something Judy just as often laughed about, while stating that his drinking habits sure hadn't changed any. But when all was said and laughed at, George always liked to encourage the boys into any type of physical activities whenever possible.

George junior, carrying a wrap-around motorcycle helmet under one arm, was himself presently deeply involved with school football. But only he out of the three youths, no doubt because of his maturing, offered any assistance towards his father's noticeable aggravated movements.

"If you want, dad, I could drive you and the rest of your car pool to work, and even pick you all up afterwards. Football practice isn't for another hour yet, so I still have lots of time before I really have to leave for school."

The smile that came with the answer, "We're experiencing pain, son, not lack of co-ordination or memory as to how to get to the plant." was an honest one, as far as father and son were concerned.

As he returned senior's gesture, junior answered, "Okay. But don't say I didn't offer." before starting to squeeze into his motorcycles helmet.

The comical looking maneuver, no matter how many times he had watched it happen, instantly struck George's semi-conscious funny bone. It also made him instantly remark, "Every time you put that thing on your head, your face reminds me of the first time I ever saw you - on the day you were born."

"Very funny, Pop'. But everyone knows fathers weren't allowed into the delivery room nineteen years ago."

"Well, if they had been," George chuckled, "no doubt there'd be a lot less kids walkin around today, let me tell ya."

"I like your other putdown better Dad," junior half smiled, indicating it was just another repeat of something he had already heard before, "Ya know, the one about, if it wasn't for the dark, a lot of ugly kids wouldn't get born!"

Somewhere along the way as they had all started traveling out into the driveway, Judy joined them. And it was only the sound of her soft chuckle that gave her presence away, before she said, "I need thirty dollars, hon."

"Another thirty bucks!" George cringed, even though one hand was already starting for his wallet. "Yesterday it was twenty, and the day before that it was forty. What the 'Hell' do you do with all my money?"

"Oh, nothing." Judy smiled, while accepting the three tens George had fished out of his vault. "You haven't given me enough to buy what it is that I want yet! And by the way, it isn't 'your' money, it's 'our' money."

George was a firm believer that everyone in the world was subject to emotional-related ups and downs in their everyday existence. He was also more than glad that his family had greater opportunities for these 'highs and lows', which in their true content seemed to keep short bursts of laughter and humor always close at hand.

Today was definitely in line for one of those very 'up' periods, regardless of his and Fred's touchy hung-over condition. It also, so far gave no indication of changing or faltering any, as they continued to struggle towards the car. Fortunately for George and Fred they were also both firm believers, due to recently repeated past performances, in the saying that 'Time really does heal all', which now alone possibly seemed to give them each courage and momentum to carry on in their movements.

Instinct in turn also did its share in helping guide their movements out of the house. But getting into the family wagon was apparently going to be another adventure in itself. For Fred just the effort of forcing his body to bend over slightly, as he almost crawled into the vehicle's rear seat, caused the pneumatic hammer that had been idling inside his head to pick up momentum. And as a low painful sounding moan of '"Oh!" escaped from his lips, he allowed gravity to suck his tormented form fore-ward, to land across the rest of the vehicles rear leather seat.

It was for just such a comical display that each of the kids had hung around. But only their faces gave any hint of the humor they were presently experiencing, as they wisely remained quiet beside the car.

For George and Judy, apparent bad examples, Fred's movements were everything they appeared to be. And as they both chuckled in their poor friends' humorous 'ass held high' comical looking position, only George paid for that pleasure.

Next came a brief hug followed up with an exchange of kissing pecks on each other's cheeks, an act their youngest son still obviously found embarrassing as the sound of "Sheeash!" escaped his lips, before George himself was ready to attack the car. Two prepared lunches magically appeared in Judy's hands, as she watched her hubby gently lower himself onto the drivers' seat. She then handed the bags to him in through the car's open window, once it was apparent he was as comfortably settled as his present condition would allow.

"You might have to buy something from the canteen for dessert. I thought I had piece of chocolate cake safely hidden in the back of the fridge but your son probably got to it first."

"If it was white with a dark icing, I flushed that thing down the toilet yesterday." George grinned.

"You mean, you ate it!" Judy frowned.

"Isn't that what I just said!" he continued to smile.

Leaning closer to the car so that only George should hear her if she whispered, Judy warmly said into his ear, "You two don't have to go to work just because it's 'Friday' you know. I'm sure the plant won't close down over you two taking a 'day off'."

This was not only another routine they had gone through in the past many times before, but also a falsehood for this particular Friday.

"We 'know' that dear." George beamed back just as softly. "But we're close enough to our pensions that we don't want 'them' knowing the plant 'can' actually run without us."

He didn't bother to offer her the information that they still had to pick up some more fellow workers yet, because he liked his reply to her remarks better, not to mention he expected to sell and collect money for the company yearly stag today also. Besides, something very special, something he and Fred had both helped plan and were a very important part of, was to take place on this almost too normal lately particular Friday.

It was not only something they were both looking forward to, but also a little happening that most other workers also involved needed and appreciated occasionally, in order to add some spice to their otherwise sometimes 'hum drum' everyday routine jobs or lives. It was for reasons such as it, just like the predicament they were suffering for right now, that helped make George answer Judy the way he did.

"And another thing, the last time we used the 'ole car trouble' routine, someone at work squealed and told the boss that it just meant that we were probably just still 'too drunk' to drive it."

"Well," she shrugged her shoulders, "at least they weren't 'totally' lying to them." Reaching fore-ward long enough to feel his pale forehead, a bigger than ever smile still on her face, Judy quickly added, "I guess it's going to be safe enough to put your insurance policy away again for awhile." in a loud enough voice that the kids could surely hear now.

Quickly, as all of the kids started laughing and drew in closer to their parents' present location, George played the change in scenery for everything it was worth. Letting his face add features to the pain already there, he deliberately fumbled with the key in the vehicles steering column. With a different audience the little whimsical demonstration would have instantly been rewarded with a verbal comment of 'Do you think a little 'hair' around that thing might help?' But such 'digging' sarcasm's were strictly for the mature, or was that the demented? Whatever, as the key found its mate and the motor eventually started, all giving him time to prepare for his retaliation.

"I really appreciate your sympathy 'dear.' But right now I feel as if I was born on 'Labor Day', and I'm presently wearing my 'birthstone', a bloody 'grinding mill-stone' around my neck. So if you glance inside my 'last will and testament' you'll be surprised to see just who I've 'really' left all my possessions to!"

Letting his eyes relay part of his next words, "But I'm sure there must be others who feel worse than I do though." they ventured briefly in Fred's still reclining strange direction. "But seriously 'kid', don't go worrying your-self about me." With one foot on the brake he used his right hand to engage the vehicle's automatic transmission. "I'll try to call you from work later, that is if I can still remember how to use a phone."

Turning both eyes and full attention toward the rear window, George released the pressure on the brakes just enough to let the car noticeably start to roll backward. Judy in turn immediately backed away straightening her leaning body, the words of wisdom trailing her 'Remember! You don't 'have' to be the first one to 'every' red light!', while still keeping her eyes focused on George's form. And when his vision darted back to hers long enough to relay the final farewell she knew was always yet to come after an attempt at having the last logical word it came in the form of the tip of his tongue flickering once and long in her direction, her left hand instinctively waved as her face pleasantly mouthed one last 'Good-bye.' towards his.

Almost instantly, and unfortunately, as had also happened on other similar hung over occasions, George's temporary diversion of attention brought brief humor once more into his already troubled world. Without even slowing down, the green rubber trash can he'd hit now being deformed and wedged under the rear fender of the wagon, he completed the vehicle's swerved trip until it was totally out of the driveway and into the center of the street.

This wasn't the first time George had unintentionally backed over his very own garbage, or taken it for a drag. At least he was pretty sure it wasn't, even with one of the neighborhood kids being close enough to catch him at it. Now, it wasn't the tormented voice coming from the vehicle's rear seat that caught and held his attention, "Please George! no Kamikaze runs today!" but rather the excited words from the youth, as his own family watched while laughing out loud.

"Hey! Hey, mister! There's something sticking out from under the back of your car!"

Without hesitation, while glancing into the excited youth's shocked face, just as if nothing unusual were happening, George put the vehicle into forward gear while letting his farewell reply trail his 'devil may care' departure. "Unless it's got arms and legs, or wearing running shoes son, don't worry about it!"

The deformed trash can, once set free from its compressed entrapment, rocketed almost straight up out of the mouth of the metal monster that had snatched it from its resting spot. Its 'fifteen seconds of fame', as it vomited out its most recent lunch, were once more ignored as everyone's attention remained glued to their swaying departure. And the strange sight of the upward bound container reminded him that it had been almost ten years since mankind had last managed to not only have a man walk but as well also ride on the moons surface. And yet here he and Fred were still having trouble not only just walking and talking, but occasionally driving to work.

Unknowingly behind him and fading in the distance his namesake was shouting, "Hey, Dad! You better get that noise checked! I think there's a 'car' in there someplace!" before asking his mother if maybe he shouldn't follow them a little ways, just for safety's sake. But the only sounds George was presently aware of, as Judy answered "No, you better not. Given the chance I think he just might back over you too!" was the occasional moan still coming from the vehicles' rear compartment.

As strange as their world already was, he couldn't help but start to smile at the sound of his 'buds' torment. But it was more the site of Fred's rear end protruding up into the air then the sound of his 'hangover' that helped him carry on with what had just jumped into his mind. With one hand steering the car, he used the other to reach back over the seat and push his best friends posterior down out of sight, while saying, "Sorry buddy. But I'll probably have to contend with enough of the usual 'assholes' on the road along the way, without yours adding to the scenery every time I look in the rear view window.

If there was only 'one thing' George Stone could ever be 'really' sure of in his crazy little world that day, no matter how many times he had jokingly said such a thing to others around him, 'Thanks for leaving!', it was not about to happen to him now. And as his castle and clan finally disappeared from view, it was the fact that he knew none of his family was ever really glad to see the 'back' of his departing head. Trick him from the front, maybe, but never from the back. He had learned real quick that if Judy knew he was planning a long active night out with the boys, he could be down right positive that he would be getting 'beans and toast' for supper that day.

But then again, as was most usual, he had left them laughingly 'begging' for 'more' and 'more', and then even an 'encore'!

Chapter 2

The 'Survival kit'.
Or
Time for a 'Table break'.

'Shit!'

'Oops, sorry! Let's save some for later.'

Other than finding ourselves unavoidably and occasionally stepping in that unsavory topic, I believe it's safe to say for those with a weak stomach that we've by now more than well disposed of 'most' of it in the prologue.

Fred's present physical position, strangely his rump seemed to be on some invisible string which kept pulling it right back up each time George tried to press it down, didn't overly allow for much 'deep thinking' conversation at this time. His posterior was still noticeably by far the highest elevated part of 'intelligence' in his body, so George used his suffering friend's silence, after making an invisible footnote to catch up on his shop diary at work, too mentally 'relive' an incident he'd more than once considered experiencing with the neighborhood youth left dumfounded at the end of his driveway.

On several occasions he'd found reason to believe that the same boy, as well as another similarly aged youth from further on down the street, had been responsible after 'garbage pick-up' for kicking the emptied plastic garbage pails out into the center of the road. It no doubt was a childhood prank geared to make any passing motorists comically 'swerve' erratically to avoid them. George in retaliation had been 'sadistically' tempted to lay a trap for the boys, by leaving them tied 'stark naked' to the containers, in the center of the same road. But he knew Judy, if ever getting wind of it, would never have allowed any such form of justice, especially since she had found out about the time he had briefly locked a pair of similar pranksters inside a hot steamy sauna at a close-by community center.

The fact that the youths had just 'urinated' on the hot rocks with the intention of quickly vacating the cubicle, to wait for some unsuspecting poor buggers reaction to the stink that would have built up in the small chamber. After five hot minutes subjected to the smell and taste of their own liquid waste the boys had ended up just short of throwing up, hadn't mattered to Judy. But for George, it was basically what life was all about, justice. He was a dedicated believer that everyone in this world, regardless of their age or gender, is accountable for such actions, no matter how trivial. And in a sense, especially if there really is a 'God', he liked to believe that he was just occasionally helping the 'almighty' along with his very busy and no doubt 'staggering' workload.

Within minutes George was braking the car for the first of two stops he would be making that morning. Two men doing their best to imitate standing at the curb, both outwardly looking like a 'bag of shit with shoes on', were the other half that often made up the foursome to their car pool.

Anyone knowing George would know that the big smile presently on his face was only there because he had deliberately braked hard, just to watch his friends 'cringing' reactions. And it was only the vehicles abrupt stop that could cause Fred to shift his tormented form into another comical looking position, one that would allow for one of the new men to join him.

The older of the two co-workers, one with six years seniority over George's twenty two in the plant, was a heavy chain smoker - something which appropriately earned him the name of 'Rusty' due to the slight brown discoloration on some of his fingers. Their other new passenger was Bob 'Pop Bottles' Logan, who wore glasses with lenses reputedly thick enough that you could see the craters on the moon , on a cloud filled night. He was also not only the youngest of their group, he was also the very reason for each of them being presently in varying degrees of 'hung over' conditions. Fortunately enough for all of them though, they, as well as the rest of the 'Snooker League' had helped celebrate the final arrival after three girls, of Bob's first son. today was their last shift in for the week.

No real conversation was needed to express how most of them were feeling that day as Rusty and Pop Bottles gradually and carefully became a part of the car's structure. But then again, if only for the sake of being practical, one of them grunted "Mornin guy's. I sure hope this isn't going to be one of those days where I'll feel safer riding in the trunk!"

Inwardly regretting that he had purchased what was considered as the Oldsmobile 'Visit Cruiser' station wagons bottom line, he briefly scolded himself with the thought that cruise control would sure have come in handy right about now, especially if it would also have come with the ability to drive itself to any programed destination. But the radio was something he did have control over. And as much as his personal since of humor wanted to briefly crank up the volume, he fought off the temptation with another realization that the drum roll presently under way inside of his own pumpkin would only serve to aggravate those still now pulsating inside of his head.

George instead answered the remark with a simple extension of the soft grin already on his face, a smile that read, 'Don't worry, I'm not an elephant and you're not a peanut!' And Fred, as the two new arrivals sarcastically fanned at the contaminated air of the car's interior, simply mumbled a barely recognizable 'Harrumph.'

Bob Logan, quickly rolling down the vehicles window beside him while still fanning at the abused air, commented. "By the aroma and looks of Fred I take it you 'gruesome two-some' were gluttons enough to party a little more after leaving us last night."

"Just enough to regret it!" George continued to smile, while letting one hand pretend to massage an enlarged aching head.

"I was Seriously thinking about taking the day off," Rusty added. "But after one look at you Freddy, I guess I just ain't that bad off. You both look like 'a bag of shit', 'with a hole in it'!"

Fred found it hard to make himself look less hung over than he actually felt, while mumbling out an answer of, "Thanks for the 'ole vote of confidence, buddy.' But you still don't exactly smell like no 'bouquet of roses' yourself.

"I don't think any of us is in any condition for any 'beauty contest', or 'fifty yard dash'," George chuckled. "But then the celebration of the arrival of your first boy 'Pop Bottles' is more than enough excuse to keep any good party going for as long as consciousness allows. And all of this must have been pre ordained , or why else would your son be born at the exact time we're in the middle of our 3 weeks of days and 1 of afternoons changeover shifts?"

"Well, you could have invited us!" Jack offered, while lighting up one of the 'tension tubes' he was so famous for. "Oh!" he then quickly added, while lovingly looking first at the smoking cigarette now in his hand, then at George, "Is it 'okay' if I smoke in the car?"

Rustys' paced actions and remarks had both been deliberate because he just loved to hear George's 'well know' and 'famous phrase', only one of many that he had already heard proverbially a 'thousand times' before. And when George Replied, "Only if you're on fire!" he honestly replied through habitual instinct, than choice of words. But when he quickly followed up with, "I vaguely remember asking you two guys back to the house for an 'after hours' 'nightcap'." His brain was working a little harder than usual, as it fought to remember if the thoughts presently occupying it were real or just imaginary. "But I think one of you said something about there being a curfew you just had to keep, or being in before all of the doors and windows were locked. Something like that."

"It's more like all the locks on the doors being 'changed' if he wasn't in before a certain time." Fred said painfully.

"Well look who's alive!" Rusty grinned, while taking a long pull at the cigarette in his hand. He then blew a long stream of its smoke in Fred's direction, while adding, "For a while there I was afraid I was going to have to notify 'National Geographic' and report you as possibly being on the 'endangered species' list."

"Hardy har-har-har." Fred moaned, while using his hands to encourage the smoke on out through the opened window. "Some times I don't know what smells worse, those 'thousand for a dollar' 'coffin nails' or your 'breath'."

Quickly pinching his nose, Pop Bottles only a fraction of a second behind copying the gesture, Rusty reminisced, "And just look who's calling the 'kettle black'."

Butting in, while steering the car along a route so 'familiar' it in all probability could have traveled it on its own, George quickly added, "Why don't we save our animosity for someone special, like say our 'foreman'!"

None of them really cared about what they were presently bantering about, let alone remember all of what had happened last night. Presently was a little game they continuously played back and forth, not knowing what each other was really talking about as true or something just off the top of their 'groggy' heads. But just like always, it provided the kind of laughter, a type of humor that seemed to relieve some of their agony, a comedy they were enjoying right now. In fact, as another part of their male bonding during the past, as well as their wives, they had been described as more devious collaborators, than friends.

"Getting back to the kids, George," Rusty turned his head away just long enough to exhale the depleted smoke in his lungs out through his own opened window, "are yours still eatin you out of house and home?"

"I guess you might say that. Instead of puttin any money into a retirement savings plan like most rational people are doing, all mine goes either into the fridge, or the kids. Anytime I finally do get a little extra cash ahead, the little 'carnivores' quickly eat it up to."

George had no intention of letting the 'chimney' beside him get away without offering information on his own family's present situation. He even managed to sneak off an undetected wink through the vehicle's rear view mirror and into Fred's smiling face, while asking, "Speakin of kids, how about your son? Has he managed to find any work yet?"

"Are you kiddin? right now he's trying to make up his mind between two very highly sought after top jobs. For the first and the one he says is his favorite, he's been practicing to take over for 'Lil Abner', as official 'mattress tester', if and when the job becomes available. And as a backup, if that one doesn't work out totally to his fancy, he hopes to blend his first choice in with his second 'weather forecaster'. He goes to bed when the sun's rising and gets up when it sets. right now I think he's running on 'Arctic time'."

"Mine are all like their mother!" George laughed. "They could fall asleep on a 'clothesline wire', in the middle of a 'windstorm'."

"Ya, I know what you mean." Rusty chuckled. "When Eric dozes off I'd swear he's just short of knocking on 'death's door', or at least gone into a 'deep coma'!"

Pop Bottles, for some strange reason, maybe he felt neglected, provided the next avenue for George's quickly recuperating rebuttal. "I don't know what you guys are complaining about. I've had to live with four females so long, that I don't feel comfortable unless I'm sitting down to take a 'leak'."

"Well, look at the bright side." George smiled, but this time he was winking in Rusty's direction, "With a son now, you not only don't have to start buying 'man hole covers' by the carton like you were afraid of, you also now have someone else to share the blame with if you ever do start leaving the toilet seat up again during the night."

Even though they each continued to pay dearly in pain for the pleasure of laughter the conversation was providing, only Fred smelled as if he had actually lived through the drinking 'shenanigans' that had left them with their present afflictions. When Bob, one of his hands carefully caressing at the throbbing temples of his head brought on by their now almost constant laughter, gave out with the old "Thank goodness it's Friday." phrase, Fred quickly repeated the well know routine while adding the unmistakably meaning letter 'f' while pointing at George's tee shirt.

Laughter, like the smoke from Rusty's cigarette, overflowed out through the cars opened windows. It also had no trouble remaining with them through the rest of their almost completed journey, as the company's parking lot finally came into view.

As a short clear whistle close-by informed those familiar with its purpose that it was now exactly a quarter of eight, Pop Bottles made the well intended mistake of offering George a piece of breath freshener.

"How about a little gum buddy, to help your breath along?"

Quickly blowing into the palm of his hand and then holding it up close enough to his nose to sniff, George smiled, "No thanks, 'buddy'! It doesn't need any help. It's strong enough to 'walk' all by itself."

Pinching his own nose once more, Bob threw a lot of sarcasm behind his words, "That's not as funny as you think. 'I' for one believe ya."

A silent negative shake of the head, almost lost in a cloud of more exhaled smoke, was offered even as Bob shifted the position of the still out-held gum in Rusty's direction. And when the generous gesture was moved on to Fred, he also silently begged away from the minted chewable breath freshener.

Shrugging shoulders while saying, "Suit your-selves. Personally I don't want a bad case of 'garbage mouth' if we happen to run into 'Louie' 'too' early." He then, a big grin on his face, popped two pieces of the scented gum into his own mouth.

The brief reference to one of the plant's 'by far' prettiest and most available young woman caused a variety of immature 'male chauvinist' groans and 'devilish' grins to find their way onto each man's face, as they each mentally recalled the woman's overly endowed buxom figure. And as George happily recalled how he had often remarked that Louie's large chest made most other top-heavy woman look as if they were all wearing a 'training bra', the spearmint gum that was wisely being reoffered, was instantly scooped up and utilized by each of them.

Risking another brief glance into the rear view mirror, George couldn't help but grin at his closet friend's still obviously suffering condition. "Hang on a little bit longer buddy." he said. "Your salvation is only minutes away now."

"I can wait." Fred answered. "Last time I took the 'cold shower' cure, I think I chewed off three gallons of hard water while my teeth were chattering."

Traffic had grown heavier with their approach to the large steel complex, soon about to be blessed with their presence. As George instinctively started to brake the car for the entrance to the parking lot now only feet away, he turned Fred's remark expertly into an advantage for his next comeback.

"I'm afraid you're still not thinking straight 'ole friend. Right idea, wrong hangover. It's cold water for the little head's problems and hot water for the one supposedly carrying your brains around, remember?"

James G. Davies Sr.

The childish giggles the remark had brought, as George pulled into the already almost full parking lot, was cut short as Rusty's excited gravel voice half shouted "Look! There's a parking spot in the front row!"

The sudden surge of excitement instantly brought noticeable results as the vehicles rear tires kicked up loose gravel, when George's foot stomped down on the accelerator. It was a tactic that surely would have resembled the response of cavalry horses when General George Custer had shouted "Charge!" at the battle of the 'Little Big Horn'. And as the car surged fore-ward, someone else close-by and as yet still undetected at the opposite end of the lot, immediately performed the same maneuver when spotting the very same rare prime piece of vacant real-estate.

Almost simultaneously, from opposite ends of the front row of parked cars, both speeding vehicles entered the unpaved aisle. Instantly, once spotting each other, both drivers pushed the accelerator beneath his foot even closer to the cars floor mats. The gray clouds of disturbed dust behind each now racing metal dinosaur, widened with the passing gravel spitting from the rear of both speeding cars.

Fate fortunately must have been on George's side, or maybe it was one of his passengers, because he easily beat the other vehicle to the open prime spot. And as he coasted into the vacancy he and each of his cohorts couldn't help but childishly and sarcastically smile into the irritated face of a co-worker most often ignored by other men in the plant.

The frown belonged to a middle aged man justifiably nicknamed 'Motor-mouth', who after having more than once come away a loser during any verbal confrontation with George, simply forced a just as phony smile onto his face as he coasted past George's car.

Laughter filled the vehicle once more as they all briefly reverted to their childhood days and took turns punching each other on the shoulders, while remarking how they had put one over on 'ol Motor-mouth.'

"I'm not sure," Bob offered, "But I think he was wearin his favorite baseball cap again. Ya know, the one that reads 'Room for rent.'

"The only way that guy's ever going to get ahead of me on anything, George answered as he and the others rolled up the car's windows before vacating it, "is to be 'born' there!"

"Well he got a new fully loaded Cadillac before you did." Rusty chuckled.

"He had to work almost three years of overtime to get his!" George snapped at Rusty. It only took me a bloody day to get mine! And unfortunately it was only because its owner, some idiot in a hurry, was backing out of his driveway at the time without looking first, smart ass! And that's not funny."

As always George's funny bone, even though it had not been that way at the time, was once more being tickled, and he let it show.

"I'll go along with what you said earlier." Rusty added, while closing and locking his side of the car. "He's so over impressed with himself that you have to almost promise to sacrifice one of your kids on the alter, before he'll even do anything for you."

"Ya!" Pop Bottles had also on occasion been involved in the past in a few verbal un pleasantries with the very one who was the subject of their recent victory. And he was more than eager to follow in with how he appropriately felt about 'ole nasty disposition. "The only people I know of who would be glad to see 'him' are 'all' blind!"

"Don't forget his 'better points'." Bob carried on. "He's also the kind of guy who if he can't put you down, he'll at least try to kick you while you're in that position."

"Especially if he can't find anyone else to annoy or talk to." Rusty led the way as they walked past the security guard and into the plant. "he'll find a mirror and bore his own ears off."

Mainly because of the condition he was still in, Fred chose to remain silent, while letting his closest friend George express their feelings for both of them.

"Bet I know of at least six guys who work with him who've gone to the 'first aid' to have their ear drums deliberately 'punctured', just so they don't have to listen to his 'jabbering'."

A new voice from behind, "Hey guys, wait up!" cut into their laughter. Altering their attention in its direction, they found another member of their regular group doing a mixed half walking and poor jogging effect coming towards them.

The paging plea belonged to someone else who had been in on their celebration Thursday night, a Terry Purcell, alias 'Eagle Beak'. Each co-worker's nickname, although chosen with that individual's traits or obvious physical attributes in mind, was never intended to be used for malicious purposes. And since nicknames, the 'funnier' sounding the better, were often far easier to remember than a person's real name, the men very rarely chose to use each other's birth-given handle.

So 'consequently' most workers found conditions in the plant less strained to work under, especially if an individual could periodically come up with a joke-like comical situation or 'slamming' which was related in any way to their own identifying nicknames deliveries. And it was partially due to such a repetitive assault on chosen people, no doubt due to years of practice and studying people's personal habits or mannerisms, which sort of made George a small 'plant-wide' legend.

Even before their friend and coworker had caught up with them, George had a put-down ready for him. "Ya better slow down Terry. With your nose you could hyperventilate if you started vacuuming up to much 'oxygen' so rapidly."

In less time than it had taken for their friend to join them, "Oh, very funny George! and I hear you were a beautiful baby. What happened, did your parents drop you a lot? Besides, you know I'm not into jogging. I hear it's a 'dying' fad!" the group soon found themselves back into the same labored pace that they had been moving at when interrupted. George in turn and with an over exaggerated hurt look on his face, as the group chuckled at Eagle Beak's quick comeback, then laughed as hard and sincere as they did. He also, and not because he was at a loss for words, made no further attempt to jokingly insult the friend now walking with them. And why would he do that? Why, because he was a firm believer that you had to be capable of 'taking' a ribbing, if you were willing to 'give' one.

Glancing at his wristwatch instead, he chose another avenue of conversation. "Time's dragging guys. It's ten to eight. I guess the 'Friday flu' is making us all 'run' a little behind schedule."

Without intending to George had made a bit of a joke by using the word 'Run', and only Terry picked up on it. "Never mind trying to get in another pun in at my jogging by using the word 'run' in your remark. Just tell me what the 'Hell' you were all laughing at before I caught up with you."

"Nothing really important," Rusty replied. "Just justifiably raking mister 'Motor Mouth' over the coals one more time."

"Why? Someone accidentally get some 'dirt' on his precious car again? His isn't the only car to end up with red fallout dust from the company's venting stacks."

"Maybe we'll pick on him for that later." Pop Bottles smiled. "But we just happened to beat him out of a piece of 'prime' parking 'real estate' in the front row."

"Ya," Rusty cut in, "And he in turn rewarded us with one of his best alligator smiles."

"Gee, that's too bad. If there really is a God I would have been just a little bit earlier, and had a chance to see it happen. But, you'd think anybody who has a car as 'spotless' as his would want to keep it as far away from our 'dirty wrecks' as possible."

"I don't know." Rusty said, while shaking his head. "The way the bloody thing never seems to deteriorate, I think he must have bought ten identical cars, all the same 'damn' make model and color."

"I wouldn't doubt it." George added. "But personally the way he always keeps the darn thing so clean and spotless, I think he just takes it into the house with him at night whenever he's not drivin it."

One of the huge company's many change rooms, the one 'they' were after, was now only short steps away. The big stone complex really had a dual purpose, in that a smaller portion of it at the opposite end also housed a percentage of the female workers change rooms also. Some of the men even jokingly enjoyed telling friends and relatives that they shared 'co-ed' washrooms and accommodations at work.

Rusty, still leading the group, reached forward to open one of the two doors leading into the change-house, but was surprisingly pushed aside by someone from behind.

"What the .....!"

"Sorry Jack!" George explained, as his eyes and attention fluttered briefly in the direction of the reason he had shoved Rusty so hastily aside. "That 'shit-hawk' just missed you with something that would have drilled you into the sidewalk, if it had been allowed to make contact!"

Rusty's vision glanced first upward at the group of seagulls noisily circling overhead, then down to the grotesque stain on the ground where he would have been standing if George hadn't pushed him aside. With Fred and Pop Bottles chuckling in the background. He then smiled simply in George's direction, while saying, "Why does it seem like I'm on always on everybody's 'shit-list'?" before completing the task he had first started.

The new atmosphere that instantly greeted their senses was not only by far 'familiar', but also filled with all sorts of mixed contamination. Other workers, in a variety of attire and stages of undress, were busy getting ready to perform whatever duty their period of shift necessitated. The air itself, as their presence was acknowledged by friends and coworkers, was filled with a strange mixture of cologne and old body odor fighting to hold on to their identities. But it was a losing battle for both as the building's ventilation system softly hummed them away, giving way to a wall of far off music blending in with human conversation now waiting their turns to go home.

The complex also consisted of two levels joined by stairways. and as the men split up in order to reach their own personal metallic cubicles, only George and Fred's were situated close together, they parted with the usual promise that they would see each other at the shop lunch tables.

Fred's forced walk increased noticeably as he pulled ahead, and George couldn't keep the humor he was sensing to himself. "You can almost taste that shower, can't ya?"

Mumbling as he went, Fred answered, "Shower! What shower? My bladder's so full, every stride I take feels as if I'm stepping in a 'puddle'! And if that isn't bad enough, the sound of the water rushing out and then back in, splashing in both directions, in itself is enough to make me want to piss my pants!"

If there was an answer to his remark, as Fred disappeared around a corner, George first kept 'Another forty years and I'm sure it will be quite acceptable Buddy.' then missed the opportunity when a new voice said, "Mornin George." to him. It also caused a falter in his direction of travel after his vision found the owner of the familiar sounding friendly remark. He didn't have to force a smile onto his face to match the one presently beaming straight at him, while answering, "Mor-r-r-rning Sid."

Both men were now only feet apart, and it wasn't until they were standing almost side by side, after the man had added the remark, "Come on over here, and bring you ears with you." that any real conversation broke out.

Shifts

Reaching out to shake the hand offered in his direction, George boomed back an answer that anyone else knowing of his reputation would have called him a 'softy' for. "What do you say, you 'old fart'!" his face flushing slightly from the fondness he felt for the one across from him.

"Nothing more than I have to 'buddy'. Nothing more than I have to." Sid continued to smile.

"Smart move." George beamed. "Ya know what they say about better being 'thought' of as an 'idiot', then opening your 'mouth' and removing all doubt."

"Ya. And I almost missed you too 'smart ass'!" Sid quickly half laughingly retaliated.

George then, still jokingly raised one hand to shield his eyes from the flashy Hawaiian style shirt his old co-worker was wearing. "Wow! Did that thing come with batteries and a 'dimmer switch', or is your memory on its way out thinking it's summer and you're at the beach?"

Sid Parker was a past partner and drinking buddy from 'way back' - when George had first started in the factory, and the jab at his present memory status hit closer to home than he would like to remember, especially since joining the 'sixty and over' club. In fact he was now at the stage where the two main memory concerns in his life were, was the name he answered to really his? And secondly, by far the most important, a seemingly never-ending and constantly ongoing dilemma, was his 'barn door' his 'cage gate' his 'zipper' his 'fly' open! Not to mention the stallion kept in that barn was actually at times looking more and more forward to spending more time in the pasture than chasing young colts around. That whenever planning on going very far from home you always try to plan the length of the trip on the distance between 'fire hydrant' to 'fire hydrant'. But then again, why 'pee' in his young friends' cereal. Why dissolution him with the possibility that this was only the tip of the 'ice-burg' for things changing, and also taking some of your scant remaining sanity with it. And last but not least, he was starting to think about what someone older than him had said to him, 'Don't worry about entering 'old age', it likely won't last very long.'

And when George grinned, "Are the 'dognuts' in the canteen fresh this morning?", Sid answered by opening his mouth and letting out a big long burp right into his face. The response, as those passing close enough to hear the escaping gas' release smiled, was retaliated even further along as George pretended to sniff the air in front of him, before answering, "Naw. Those were definitely more than 'day olds'."

But, back to present-day reality. He was about the oldest and closest person inside of the plant, other than Fred, that George had become emotionally attached to. It was all from a time before they had been split up and put onto different work crews. Consequently, by being on shifts that very rarely overlapped, they had as could be expected drifted apart. But anyone presently passing would never have guessed it, as they noticeably enjoyed each other's verbal company.

"Just burning off some old cloths buddy. When you get to be my age you'll realize that you're not as fashion conscious as you used to be, and this place is good enough for anything you wouldn't normally wear." he then answered. And as he did one of his hands rubbed at his stomach while his face squinched up to indicate that he might be experiencing heartburn. It was a common reaction that he shared with many other night shift-workers, suggesting that the late hours were anything but kind to his digestive system. And as his face now imitated how he was feeling, he offered, "This working nights, is strictly for 'pimps' and 'whores'!"

"Oh!" George instantly grinned, the statement just begging for his kind of response, "So, how many girls you got working for you now?"

Instead of a justifiable harsh rebuttal, which would have been totally out of character anyways, Sid faked a short jab at George's mid rib-section while saying, "Still haven't changed, eh?" And as George instinctively flinched away from the undelivered blow, his face a mixture of anticipated pain and humor, Sid instead easily reached out and messed up his hair, while adding, "Haven't you heard we're all on the endangered 'species' list? They're just not making any more of us. You slam the wrong guy some day, and you're likely to be added to the 'extinct' side of the list. Or should I have said that you'll be given the opportunity to jump your present place in the 'cue' line."

"Well, we all need something to live for." George grinned. "Some people need a cigarette. Some need a drink. Fred Owens needs a good 'rattle'. You need to 'retire'! And as for me, 'I' just need to be recognized!"

"Like I already said," Sid laughed, "you pick on the wrong person and you just may end up being 'recognized' alright. You'll be getting recognized at the 'city morgue'."

"Not much fear of that happening around here," George smiled, while glancing at his wristwatch. "If brains were rocket fuel, most of the people I work with wouldn't have enough liquid to launch a 'ping pong' ball."

"Ya, I know what you mean, jellybean. Some of the youngsters I work with now think they've really got it rough. I can still remember having to 'hand balm' the same type of jobs when they were still 'shitting green'!"

"Been there, done that." George grinned. "I know a lot of guys who couldn't find the ground, even with the help of a compass and a map."

"I wasn't exactly referring to the 'working class', ole buddy. I hear your new boss hast a 'hit list', and your name's on it, 'five times'!" Sid chuckled, apparently having similar memories of his own.

"Probably." George said. "But in his case seniority breeds 'senility'. He's so slow on the uptake I wouldn't doubt it if he put 'turtle wax' on his shoes. And to give you an idea, let's just say that if we were standing in the middle of a boat with a hole in it, and he has the right sized plug in his hand, we'd all be dead from drowning before he ever figured out where the 'cork' goes."

"You mean, he's got the 'IQ' of a potato."

While repositioning his body so that he was as least aiming in the right direction for his eventual departure, George smiled. "Not to mention that he's also the type of guy you could throw a stag for, hold it in a phone booth, and still having enough room left over to make at least two long distance calls."

Sid, as expected, couldn't help but let a chuckle slip out of the smile on his face. But before he had a chance to do his part and keep up his end of the meeting, George's now noticeably excited voice, suddenly no doubt thinking of something else worth adding started to offer more to the mood he had already started. "Say! Didn't I hear that that you just got your 'thirty years' of service ring?"

"If that's what you want to call that thing in the little cardboard box they gave me was for! Sid frowned, a hint of sarcasm dripping from every word. "After checking the box again, I spent the next five minutes wondering where in the 'shit' the 'cracker jacks' went!"

As George kept up his end of the agreement by laughing out loud, Sid checked his own watch, before continuing. "Speakin of stags and the company's finest - how's the ticket sales going for this year's purging of the elderly. Is there anything in the wind I should be leery of?"

"Well," George smiled, "as for the stag other than having everyone wear 'name tags' for identification this year, I'd say that the best thing you can do is keep both your eyes and ears open, and your prostrate covered. In other words, it's probably going to be the same as every other year"

"Name tags ya say." Sid frowned.

"Ya. Name tags." George frowned a little, knowing that his friend was up to something. "What's wrong with name tags?"

"Oh nothing I guess." Sid continued to frown. "It's just that I think they're a waste of time."

"How's that?" George quickly asked, now willing to bet his own pension that his buddy was setting him up.

"Well," Sid smiled. "I know many years ago when we tried to use them a lot of the men, which doesn't surprise me I might add, not only found them slightly confusing, but sometimes outright embarrassing. Right then and there I made up my mind I wasn't going to let something as simple as wearing a bloody name tag get me mocked at in front of a lot of people, so I memorized mine, and threw it away."

Giving the joke the recognition it deserved, a big grinning chuckle, George quickly got back on track.

"I hear the company's profits are so bad just now, that instead of a '25 years service watch', they're giving out a toll free number that you can call night or day, just to 'hear' the correct time! But other than that,' George continued to grin, "it's going about the same as last years. Some guy's will give ya their wife and kids if you asked them. Then it's either the ones who pay you with a ten dollar that looks as if it's been riding around in the bottom of their shoe for about a year. Or their idols, the guys who reluctantly go into the vault and pull out a bill where the picture of the Queen's 'squinting' when they pull her out of her tomb, all because she ain't seen daylight in about the same amount of time."

"Ya, I know what ya mean!" Sid chuckled. "And let's not forget the type who can squeeze a dollar bill so hard before they let go of it that there's ink stains left on their fingers when it finally does make it back to freedom."

After another quick glance at his wristwatch, as he again chuckled at his friend's remark, George couldn't help but start to move when the device told him how short he was on time. "Wish I could stop and talk longer, ole buddy, but I'm way behind schedule. I gotta fly!"

"Of course ya do!" Sid suddenly cried out, as George's body disappeared into the same area Fred's' had earlier. "Buttons went out with the 'horse and buggy!" And then he added silently for his own benefit, 'Just wait until your time comes buddy. You'll be surprised how many times you question yourself if 'it's' up or down! And it's not going to be very easy every time you have to explain to your doniker when you take it out to drain your bladder that the reason your hand is shaking, is just due to old age setting in, and not 'happy hour'. Plus the pressure you have now that will let you blow the color out of porcelain, is long gone while sometimes remaining just barely strong enough to keep your shoes dry. And that there was still a lot of truth in that old saying of, 'Remember. One thousand 'Atta boy's' can all be wiped out by just one 'Oh shit!' especially around this place.'

Rounding the last corner separating him from his locker, the rest of the facility still a small 'bee hive' of varying activity, George's eyes and ears instantly locked onto Fred's cursing frustrated form wrestling with some hidden object totally concealed within his two cupped yanking hands. Instantly George knew what both the object and problem were, so he quickly moved forward in order to correct his friends irritated predicament.

Using both hands, George firmly grabbed Fred from behind at the shoulders, and in one smooth motion, jerked him free of the combination lock still firm in his grasp, only to move him over one more set of twin lockers. The act, totally noticed by two other men changing close-by, brought both laughter and brief embarrassment. The laughter belonged to the small audience, and the embarrassment was Fred's when he realized that he had been trying to open the wrong combination lock, again.

Leaning close to Fred's ear, George whispered, "This is about as bad as the time you came back from one of your vacations. I found you scratching your head, while staring at this lock. and when I asked you what your problem was, you told me you couldn't remember the 'fourth' set of numbers for your combinations lock."

When one of the two onlookers commented, "I take it you two were out over workin your bladders again last night." George snidely and calmly replied. "It's a hard rough job at times, but someone has to do that kind of work when it's called for." while concentrating on opening his own set of lockers.

In less than a minute Fred was nude, his thin frail body looking and smelling every bit as hung over as he still felt. Gathering up his soap and towel, he quickly became a part of the still lingering few who were working the twelve to eight shift, after telling George he would see him at the usual lunch tables.

George, after grinning an acknowledgment to his friend's remark, finished with the short note he had been scribbling into his diary, while also hurrying into his worn work clothes. He then just short of ran to the big canteen located half way between the change house and lunch area he and his coworkers waited at in order to receive their daily job instructions.

Bursting through the front doors leading into the always busy lunch bar, other passing familiar workers nodding in brief recognition, George almost knocked down a piece of 'bad news' that apparently was on its way out of the canteen.

It was Carla Daniels, a recognized middle-aged man-hater with enough reputation to be known and avoided whenever possible. She was with three other almost just as notorious women, each one's mind 'pregnant with trouble' whenever confronting any of the plant's males.

Behind Carla's back, most men considered it to be by far her best side, the males often joked that she was tough and mean enough to take any three of them two out of three falls in an arm wrestling match - with both hands tied behind her back! Some of the guys even swore they had once seen her wearing a tee shirt with the wording 'Beware of dog' on it. And if the woman's features were to be rated on a scale of from 1 to 10, as was customarily part of an old craze, then Carla's anatomy warranted a double digit evaluation, only starting from zero and working down.

Built in reflexes more than instinct had made George sidestep the almost wall of rough looking human flesh. The suicide he had briefly considered when first waking up would have been gladly delivered, it would appear, judging by the present look in each woman's eyes. and even as they each opened their mouths to protest the near collision, George cut them off with his own kind of defense.

"Sorry ladies. But I just haven't got time to stop and 'trade' insults with you right now."

Without any form of hesitation, he instantly moved away from their noticeably frustrated protesting forms, and left them with the grinning words of, "I am afraid I'm almost late, and I've only enough time to pick up two 'survival kits'. Maybe we can find some time to 'spar' later."

Disappearing behind a row of soft drink machines, a few of the so-called ladies 'cat calls' registering on his ears, George silently let out a small "Whew!" while wiping at his brow, and whispering to himself. "That was a close call. No man really wins an argument when having a dispute with a woman, especially the ones that ruled in this place."

"Do you believe that!" No doubt the emotional delivery of Carla's words were due to her rising blood pressure. "I don't care if he is in the top ten standings of the plant's 'short order club'. I still think he's rude and crude."

"Well, 'Long Dong Silver' or not," one of the other women quickly added, which was not only totally out of character but also frowned upon, "he can put his shoes under my bed anytime."

"If it wasn't for the fact that 'any man' could kick his shoes off under your bed, dearie, "Carla said sarcastically, "I'd think you were pickin sides."

"Well, he is one of the few men that we know of for sure that isn't 'peepin' in on our side of the change house." Kit Fryer's pride had been slightly irritated by Carla's remark about her preference for men, and she felt justified in letting a bit of her true beliefs about George Stone's character express itself. "We've never caught him with an eyebrow full of 'graphite', or a ring around one of his eyes under ultraviolet light."

"Humph." Carla grumbled, her vision briefly trailing George's long gone figure. "That only means he washes his face and hands before and after work, as far as I'm concerned."

"Ya!" two other women of the group, Judy Smith and Mary Jackson, added in Carla's defense.

"You're startin to sound like those softies who started the "short order club'. Just because they think his boys would make an ideal husband for their daughters, or just because daddy's financially secure and has a reputation for being a decent human being in their eyes, doesn't mean he wouldn't cheat on his wife or sneak a peak at any of us in the nude if he thought he could get away with it." Judy Smith added sarcastically.

"Well, if he is sneakin a free look, "Kit answered, now noticeably perturbed with her friends, "I don't think he's overly wastin to much time on any of us."

"And just why not?" Carla half-snapped.

"Because I've seen what a few of us look like in the shower." Kit started to grin, "And if it wasn't for rape, I doubt if some of us 'body-beautiful' would ever get the chance at bearing children."

Though she was both childless and unmarried, Carla knew that Kit's put down was aimed directly at her. And even though she hated to admit it out loud, she finally realized that Kit was putting them all on, especially when it came to taking sides with the male part of the work force. So instead of pursuing a lost cause, she did her best to have the last word at getting even, and still keep the group together.

"I can live with the reality that I'm not on every man's secret dream list as the woman he'd most like to be marooned on a desert island with, just as long as I'm not on that same dream list of any woman's."

As Kit laughed at Carla's remark, Mary made a disgusted look with her face, and Judy did almost the same while stating, "Hell no! I'd definitely rather 'fight' than switch any day!"

Once more two-faced 'lady luck' seemed to be temporarily showing her friendly face in George's direction. There was apparently only one man in the usually long line waiting to be served at the facility's main counter, and even he was in the process of receiving his requested order.

Stepping silently in behind the individual, George could now detect that it was not only someone who wasn't supposed to be there, but also a co-worker and Thursday night team member. George patiently and still undetected, watched as the friend appeared to have trouble totaling some loose change that was now in the palm of his hand.

The young female counter worker that was still waiting to be paid made a mistake when she tried to be customarily friendly by leaning closer to the counter, while asking, "Have you got enough?"

Not until now was George's presence given away, when his automatic verbal reflexes quickly answered before his friend could speak.

"You're asking the wrong person, young lady. I think his 'wife', is by far better qualified than he is to reply to that type of personal question."

The young waitress, already knowing and having dealt with George's strange sense of humor in the past, gave a mixture of half-smile and embarrassed blush when realizing what the words really referred to. And when she sheepishly said, "You're terrible, Mister Stone."

"Every chance I get!" he grinned back. "Nobody', and you can trust me on this one, 'nobody', remembers you when you're 'nice', or is that for 'being nice'?"

The butt end of his joke, a friend nicknamed 'Scratch' because of his habit and record for absentees from work, looked far rougher than the smile in his voice. "Mornin George."

"Morning Scratch. You told us last night you were going to play 'hooky' today, and maybe lay a little 'pipe'. What happened?"

Pivoting his head back in the young blushing waitress' direction long enough to pay her the money she was still waiting for, George himself now holding up two fingers in the girl's direction and silently mouthing plant-wide familiar words of, 'Two survival kits, please.' Scratch steeped away from the counter while offering an answer to George's question.

"I wanted to take the day off, but I don't know who'll 'scream' my ears off the most if I take any more time off work, the boss, or my wife."

The grin growing on George's face, was always, more sickly humorous than serious - as he said, "A stranger might ask who you are more afraid of. But the fact that you're here should answer that question. Besides,

I always thought that in your case, the wife and your boss were one in the same."

"And yours isn't?" Scratch half-laughed.

"Not as far as the kids are concerned." George bragged.

"That's too bad." Scratch scoffed, a little dryly. "Just imagine how shocked they're going to be when they get married and find out that a man ruling the house is only a fallacy."

"Speak for yourself, chicken shit!" George retaliated.

"I wish I could." Scratch continued, just as disappointed. "But then I guess letting the 'little woman' think they're the boss is worth it, just to get a little peace at home."

"Oh!" George quickly laughed back mockingly. "And is that 'p-i-e-c-e' like in 'laying pipe'. Or is that 'p-e-a-c-e' like in 'quite!', we're talking about?"

Hesitating slightly, as if really having to contemplate an answer, Scratch was about to answer, "Both, I guess." when the waitress spoke first, in Georges direction. "That'll be $1.30 please."

Using one hand to drop the exact amount of change into the girl's hand, George used the other to scoop up the bag containing his regular order of coffee and doughnuts.

"Thank you." he beamed into the young woman's face before starting for the same door he had entered through. Scratch's shorter steps had to hurry to match George's time-saving elongated strides, and once they were both back outside they continued with roughly the same issue George had been concerned with all morning.

"See you at the motel tonight?"

"I'll try to be there. It just depends on how I have to use that word 'peace' when I get home tonight."

"Getting a little behind on our 'ass kissin' are we." George beamed.

Both of them had a smile on their lips as they went their separate ways. And once alone again, George, after allowing his watch one more quick glance, half-ran the distance still separating him from his next destination. It was a journey that he covered in just over a minute, and not because it had been peppered with short bursts of "Hello's and Good-morning's.

The lunch tables, they were used exactly for that purpose by any of the men not being sent out of the shop to work in ant of the plant's mills that day, contained everyone expected to be there for that shift. Everyone, that was, except tormented friend Fred. But he was only a few seconds behind George's arrival. And as he went through he same "Mornin!" ritual, George placed their 'survival kits' onto the table in front of the vacant bench seats they always occupied.

Peter Farkas, the 'Evil Dwarf', was still in the main office, along with the knowledge of each of what each of the men would be working on that day. Even though he very rarely ever arrived at the lunch table before five minutes after the starting horn had blown, he had the type of disposition that left people wanting to see more of the 'back' of his departing form - than its arrival.

George, his own tormented memories of last night now gladly more vague in his mind and stomach, smiled into his best friend's eyes when saying. "Thank goodness I can only guess as to how you're feeling now buddy. But at least you look, or should I say 'smell', one Hell of a lot more human than you did earlier."

In the process of trying to wash down the last bit of a doughnut now occupying his mouth, as his best friend had been speaking, Fred first returned George's smile before answering, "Remember the weekend we got into some homemade red wine and hot chili? That combination had each of us busy at both ends!"

"Do I!" George laughed. "My ass was so sore after washing down that chili with home made red wine, by the end of the night I was dabbing at it - instead of wiping it."

"Well, I wish I felt that good now!" Fred moaned. "Actually, I could use about an hour undisturbed in the 'library', and not because the ole plumbing is plugged up."

"I should hope not!" George grinned. "Normally one thing I don't need after a good 'booze up', unless I've had some of that extra cheese pizza, is dynamite to keep the bodies plumbing pipes blown clear."

Dropping one hand below the lunch table just enough to carefully rub his queasy stomach in reaction to the prospect of what he knew was not only inevitable but also close-by, Fred fought off a little lost gas while saying, "Well, when that time comes, try to make sure I'm not in any of the 'traps' close-by."

"Never mind me." George smiled. "But you still look like you couldn't survive a good flushing, not to mention I don't know who I'd feel sorrier for, you, or anyone else who might be unfortunate enough to be in the 'John' at the same time you're in there."

"If you were a real friend, you'd offer to do it for me when the time comes." Fred beamed.

Instantly recalling his own time in the washroom at home, George made an immediate sour face in reaction to the terrible odor that accompanied the memory, and he let it flow over into his voice. "No way, ole buddy. Besides, if you'll remember, the true description of a real 'friend', is someone who goes to town, gets two 'blow jobs', then comes back and gives you 'one'! And since I'm religiously dedicated by far from ever being that friendly with anyone, I'm afraid you're just going to have to suffer through this thing by yourself, when the time comes to 'go- o - o' that is."

The brief instant laughter the remark had brought was lost in the same type presently already underway by the co-workers at the other end of the table. It also caused both George's and Fred's attention to abandon what they had been joking about, only to turn in the loud laughter's direction. And in that same split second of transition, they not only knew what was presently responsible for the attack on everyone's 'funny bone', but also by whom.

It was all thanks to Pop Bottles, and as should be expected, it was still over the arrival of his new son. The men were without mercy while taking turns running through all the more common expected puns of sons being preferred over daughters.

Some of the men were even verbally pushing each other for positions as to who could be the first at 'needling' Pop Bottles. And just like always, once started, there was no shortage on puns or slamming's to draw from, such as him now being a common victim of 'son stroke'. Or there was the remark that since he was a graduate of prenatal classes with his wife, he was no doubt more or less expected to be able to 'breast feed' also.

"Don't let them razz you, Bob." George said. "They're all wishing they were in the same boat as you, only knowing what they all know now. I bet you that most of them would think real long and hard about doing it all over again, right guys?"

The variety of instant negative responses, "Hell no!" "I'd rather run away first!" "Not me, I'd rather adopt!" "I blame it all on 'my' father." "Mom tried to warn me!" although worded and delivered separately, were all comically expressed, and meant to mean the same thing from each of the workers answering George. When one of them even went so far, while frowning into his open lunch pail, as to say, "Boy! if I was ever single again and knew what I think I know now, I'd never give 'it' away again!"

Everybody there already knew that the 'it' that had been referred to was the word 'sex'. but it was only George, as a few of the men answered, "Here!" "I'll say!" "You better believe it!" that responded in a manner to do humorous justice to the man's referral to sex, as well as slamming him. "Ya, but sooner or later, Willey, you'd have to start sending your hand flowers!"

Maybe it was just the fact that it was Friday that made the men's happy attitude so contagious. But George was always appreciative of the sound of genuine laughter, and he even went so far at times as to seemingly set himself up for some possible verbal abuse.

"Don't feel so bad Bill. I've even said something similar to my wife on past occasions when we've had a little 'tiff'. I've said to her, 'If I ever get out of the marriage alive!' and she always cuts me off with the remark 'Don't worry, you won't! And I'll give you a little bit of extra free advice to go with that type of verbal bantering. It must work, especially since we're still together."

As intended, George made sure that he had shot himself down just as quickly as he had set himself up. It was the type of situation that proved to be once more contagious in the other workers minds, as they all ended up laughing even harder than before, especially when someone else added, "Just wait until your boy gets old enough to get the 'shit' out of his diaper. Ours used to paint the crib, walls, themselves, and everything else quite regularly. At first it's funny, but after the first half dozen times the novelty wears off. The only way the wife could keep her sanity was by calling the little stinkers her potential 'Vincent Van Gooogh's'."

"That's nothing." someone else quickly added. "Wait until they start 'eatin it'. If that don't help you with your diet, nothing will!"

"You guy's are all still 'amateurs'." one of the much older men with children the same age as George's cut in. "Just wait until they get to be teenagers. When they're little they walk around with their 'mouths' wide open. Then when they become 'teenagers' they walk around with their 'hands' stretched open!"

"Amen!" another of the group in the same boat half frowned.

"Speakin of other kinds of 'slow death'," another worker offered, his staring eyes just naturally drawing everyone else's in Fred's direction, "Is 'suicide' still illegal in this state?"

Then, unfortunately for the individual foolish enough to say it, one of the men at the table made the mistake of being the last to comment on Fred's still easily noticeable haggard hung over condition.

"Gee Fred, if I looked as rough as you do, I'd go home and smash every mirror in the house."

"From where I'm standing," George quickly shot back, "you better do it anyways."

The comment had belonged to Eagle Beak, or 'Gonzo as some of the men liked to joke, Terry Purcel. And George had no intention of letting him or anyone else, even other close friends today, putdown or dump on Fred. "Fred'll be sober sooner or later and you'll still look like you should be sitting on a perch someplace, eating crackers."

"Very funny, Mister ol Acid Tongue Don Rickles." Terry answered, only half-laughing now. It was easily obvious for everyone to see that he wasn't overly impressed with George's remark, at least not near as much as the rest of the men at the table now seemed to be.

"Just because Fred's your best friend doesn't mean he can't verbally stickup for himself. Or is it just that you're still feeling a little 'bottle fatigued' yourself?"

"Ya better watch it. Terry." someone at the table quickly butted in, "It's when animals are wounded that they're the most dangerous."

The warning was totally unnecessary, especially with the sound of the King singing somewhere in the background. No-one, weather, mood, or situation, with most of the men in the plant, was allowed to put a damper on any day when Elvis was performing in the building.

George, content to let his own intended remark wait a little bit longer, used the previous remark to the best of its ability, by simply laughing menacingly in Terry's direction.

No doubt sadistically looking for blood, all of the men's eyes shifted in Fred's direction, and he surprised even himself when he slammed Eagle Beak with a putdown that instantly struck everyone's funny bone, even Terry's. "Anyone who automatically has to alter the direction they're facing every time the wind blows past their face, shouldn't be pickin on anybody else."

"Very good, Fred," he acknowledged to the slamming. "Not bad, not bad at all."

There was a small round of applause from the men as Fred pretended to take a bow, while Terry, his eyes squinting and words dripping with sarcasm to indicate he was ready for a verbal sparing, kept right on speaking.

"And if I were the vindictive type who needed revenge for such a personal snide remark, I'd bring up the rumor about you being seen 'brown bagging' it a couple of snorts in the change house last week."

"How right you are Gonzo!" It wasn't only George who could anticipate that things weren't going as comically intended, but he was the one to quickly cut in and prevent things from getting any further out of hand. "Fortunately for all of us we can laugh at ourselves over such personal afflictions when necessary. Especially if we're going to take a chance on puttin' someone else down, then we're going to have to be prepared to be slammed back if the need arises, right?"

As happened sometimes, the mood of the men faltered slightly while realizing that poor 'ol Terry was getting a little too emotionally involved. But then again, Terry, realizing that he had to save face, let the mood deteriorate only temporarily before setting it back onto happier grounds himself.

"You're absolutely right again as usual 'ol wise and wonderful know-it-all. But at least Fred didn't come out with one of your old put down lines about how my big nose makes me look as if I'm the first to arrive for a 'fruit loops' convention."

The laughter that once more filled the air was just as quickly interrupted again, when one of the men detected the approach of their foreman "Peter Farkas, alias "the Evil Dwarf!"

"Uh-oh! here comes 'ol pain in the prostrate' now."

"Shit!" Fred said. "Is it that time already? he's more than enough to make me wish 'I'd' taken the day off."

James G. Davies Sr.

"You too?" Pop Bottles frowned. "Personally, sometimes I'd rather lay on the railway tracks for half an hour, than getting here five minutes early for his shift."

"Me too." Gonzo added. "I tried to do an impression of him once. But I had to quit. It kept 'hurtin' my face."

Laughing, George deliberately and verbally over pronounced, "Puuuuuleeease!" in Gonzo's direction. "We're supposed to be settin' up the 'boss', not ourselves!"

"Ha, ha." Eagle Beak said snidely, as George continued.

"From my own personal experience I doubt if the 'Dwarf' could even open an envelope, without the proper combination."

"For years," Fred added, as the other men snickered now that their enemy was only about twenty feet away, "I thought he was physically deformed. It never dawned on me that the 'lump' deformity on his rear end was really only a pocket book he was carrying in his back pocket."

And when someone else added 'Pay attention boys'. He not only looks as if he's already taken his first 'nasty' pill of the day, it also looks like it's just about ready to kick in." the familiar phrase not expected, it also received a round of disgruntled 'Harrumphs'.

Not until now, as the overly large yet short foreman stopped at the end of the tables, his usual expressionless face in place and company clipboard in hand, did most of the men realize that there was another human being in behind him. And this was only possible because the man was actually smaller in frame, than the 'ol paper pushing Evil Dwarf himself.

Peter Farkas, the sound of his name almost summing up his disposition, knew and accepted the fact that he had very few true friends - with not one of them presently being present at the table. It was a fact that he justified this situation to himself by believing that all of the men working under his authority were just jealous of his present authoritative position. He, just as the workers seemed to do with him, tolerated the quite noticeable icy change in atmosphere often brought on by just his presence. And he in turn tried not to be around them any longer than necessary. More often than not he was not only successful with this outlook on life, but was also appreciated by the men for having enough limited mentality to know that his enduring presence was never overly welcomed by them, going doubly for George.

All of the men knew that George and the Dwarf were often like fire and water when they got together, George playing the part of the water and easily smothering out the boss's heated surges of hostility. He also had added anther nickname of 'Athlete's Foot' onto the foreman, much to the other workers pleasure, meaning that they often just had to put up with his presence until he finally went away. And today, as he irritatingly dropped the clipboard containing the days' worksheets down onto the tables' surface, it was easy to surmise that he was going to be no more of a thrill to have around, than any other day.

Pop Bottles started to get up from his place at the table, but was temporarily halted in his movements when the boss remarked, "Sit down! Sit down. There's no need to stand up just because I'm here."

Even as slow on the 'up keep' as some of the men often thought of him, Pop Bottles was just as quick as the other workers when realizing that their bumbling leader had either misinterpreted his gesture, or was trying to fit in by whimsically pulling his leg. It was an opportunity, even though his co-workers failed to hide their own reactions to the remark; he played for all it was worth, by adding straight-faced, "Why? Can't I put my lunch pail in the fridge?"

Only the stranger who had arrived at the table with the dwarf managed to control his tickled funny-bone, if indeed he did had one, as a noticeable touch of embarrassment crept onto the bosses face. But it was only George who had enough nerve to chuckle openly enough to draw everyone else's attention in his direction , while adding, "The guys and I were having a little argument, and I was wondering if you could answer a question for us?"

The blush that was already present, possibly because he already suspected that his antagonist just might be up to something irritating or even stupid, stayed while answering. "That's what I'm supposed to be here for, or as I've often heard you guys infer under your breath, that's why I get that extra nickel an hour."

"Good!" George grinned. "Good. Could you possible tell us who played the character 'Fred Murtz', on the old 'I Love Lucy' shows?"

Letting his eyes and head emotionally express the only answer he intended to give, one rolling upward awhile the other twisted back and forth in a negative gesture, he turned his attention to the others at the table.

"Good morning gentlemen. I trust the rest of you, along with 'William Frowly'," he glared directly at George so that there could be no misunderstanding as to whom he was referring, "are here to work, and not to just entertain each other."

What little acknowledgement he got for the remark was only through courtesy, as everyone's eyes inquisitively floated towards the short grinning oriental man now in full view beside him. So in order to reward them with as much recognition as they were giving him, he continued with, "Before I give anyone their jobs for today, I'd like to take this time to introduce you all to the newest addition to out team. He's originally from Chicago, and since today will be his first day in the plant I, I'm going to put him with a pair of you for the remainder of the shift. I know all of you will each gladly show him 'the ropes', when it's time for him to be with you."

Each of the men took turns in nodding a reply of recognition to the almost humorous grinning face now passing over theirs. And if there really was anything to the belief of first impressions giving a true indication of that individuals personality or traits, then the little fellow gave every indication of being prime material for a whole series of new and old oriental short 'slamming's'.

Starting with the men closest to him, for some unknown or appreciated reason Fred and George seemed to be the always the last or at the opposite end of the tables, the 'Evil Dwarf' started to read off from the clipboard in his hand, jobs and locations requiring their expertise. And as the number of co-workers started to instantly dwindle, two at a time for each mentioned maintenance location, George leaned closer to Fred's ear while whispering, "I hate to say it, but it looks like 'Ol Athlete's Foot' is saving 'short-ass' for us."

'Oh, by the way, did I forget to mention that the men often have more than one nickname for 'slamming' of humorously picking on each other?"

Letting his eyes roll skyward, the accepted human trait often used to emphasize ones present irritation, Fred offered what he knew his buddy would already be thinking. "Great! just what we need today. An 'ass-dragging' 'burp as you go' 'babysitting' job!"

Shifts

"Take it easy." As usual George's sense of anticipating humor was not only ahead, but also working overtime. "Let's not be in to big of a hurry to condemn the poor little fellow, at least not until 'after' we've had the trial."

"Is it just me, or does he look kind of 'wimpish'? Fred added, while letting the features on his face change just enough to look remotely related to the new mans. "I'll tell you one thing, I hear people of his culture are known to be greatly musically gifted. But if he ever comes in here carrying a violin case, I'm not hanging around to see if he's one of them."

As the last two men who had been sitting closest to Fred and George left for their jobs, the foreman repositioned himself so that he was now standing within feet of his last and by far from favorite two workers. The new man, the smile on his face for some still unknown reason somehow ever broader than when he had arrived, changed the location where he had been standing also. In fact, George thought to himself, 'he gets any closer, and he'll be on the other side of the Dwarf'!'

Scanning the surrounding area, first no doubt to make sure that they were not only alone at last but also out of potential earshot from anyone who might be passing, Farkas introduced the new man once more. Using his head as a kind of pointer, he tilted it when saying, "Bob Wong, this is Fred Owens and George Stone.

Fred and George immediately offered an outstretched hand of friendship at the sound of their born given 'monikers'. Farkas apparently feeling now was as good a time as any, let a small hint about how he really felt about the two of them show itself, which only served to justify any of his given nicknames.

"I would like you to spend the shift with these two gentlemen. They, as well as a few others of limited mentalities, seem to feel that they are not only the best tradesmen around here, but also the main reason the 'plant' is presently operating in the 'financial gain' column."

"Ah, ah," George quickly interrupted. "maybe not the best, but definitely in the 'top ten'. And might I also add, that as of yet we've never had the opportunity to meet the other eight gentlemen currently referred to as existing in that special category."

"Humph." was the only response Farkas gave in reaction to George's whimsical remark? But there could be no doubt from the very noticeable contemptuous displeasure now on his face, when he continued, that there was anything but distaste for George or Fred, both often becoming as one when spoken about.

"Once you realize the statement 'Once you've worked with the best, you can forget the rest.' doesn't apply here. It'll be easier for you to pick up and understand the right way of doing things around here, especially once you're with any of the other groups."

Now for the first time since he had arrived, there was a big smile - often the kind associated to that of a 'crocodiles', on his face. And since the new man Bob's grin never seemed to fade totally from his face, it would appeared that at least two of the four people there had appreciated the attempted personal vindictive 'put-down'.

But George was often never one to let anyone have a last say on just about anything, like the one he had just sat through, especially such as a derogatory remark against him or any of his friends. So he effortlessly added his own personalized kind of turntable 'slamming' come-back.

"One of the biggest differences between you and 'I' 'Sir', is that some people live for the company, myself not being like 'you' or them."

Both instantly and easily, it could be seen that his remark was about to leave another scar. But before Farkas could even start to open his mouth to spar back, George 'slammed' him just a little bit harder.

"In fact, you ought to be glad I'm not 'your' boss. I'd be up your ass so far at times that I'd be able to tell if your teeth were your own, or 'store bought'."

"Ya." Fred beamed, while making sure that the new man would have no difficulty in understanding that he was speaking directly for his benefit, "And if you eventually can't understand or do anything properly around here, the company'll make you a 'foreman'."

This time there were only three people smiling, ol Athletes Foot not being one of them. Instead his face had returned to its old placid self, as he coldly said, "If we're not careful boys, Mister Wong here might get the wrong idea on how we work and respect each other around here."

"Well, if he does," George smiled, looking directly into Bobs eyes, "it sure as Hell won't be from anything we've said."

Fortunately for Farkas, his face flustering, an older of the company's employees from another department, happened to be walking by. And as he called out, "Good morning everyone!" his friendly gesture was just as happily acknowledged verbally by George and Fred in almost perfect unison, Bob only silently nodding his head.

"Morning 'Did-Ya'! How's it going?"

Slowing in his steps long enough to answer, "Oh, you know how it is on a Friday fellas. I'm just as pleased as a pickled bowl of punch to be here."

Their brief guest was by now almost totally past them. And as soon as the sound of his husky voice, at the end of his comment, faded into the areas awakening activities, George's own words chased after him. "Ya, but fortunately that 'idiotic' feeling generally goes away at quittin' time!"

With the words, "Catch ya later." trailing 'Did-Ya's' smiling form waving good-bye before disappearing into the structures surroundings, George lost no time in picking up where he had left off, before the Dwarf had a chance to recoup his losses.

"Now then, where were we? Oh ya! Just because the company likes to think they've destroyed everybody's individuality or judgment as a person so they can control and manipulate the employees, doesn't mean it's true. Besides, you're the one who said we should teach 'ol Laughing Larry' here the ropes. And since you've indicated that you obviously want him to start at the bottom and work his way up, reference to present posteriors not intended, I figure I'd better specify just as to 'whom' is considered to be at the bottom around here, and 'who' isn't."

The intended reaction the remark was expected to achieve, a flush to the bosses' cheeks was instant, which also caused his voice to falter slightly as he spoke. "I know, that you, and the other men resent me, but I guess all leaders and famous people have had to deal with such feelings of animosity."

Bob, still smiling naively, may not have be smart enough to understand exactly what he was being privileged to, but so far he was intelligent enough to keep his mouth shut, while just grinning quietly.

Continuing to stoke the fire he had lit under the bosses' posterior, George almost gleefully added, "Oh, you're famous alright." and Fred, matching almost gesture for gesture the new mans innocent bystander approach, also copied his silence. "Your name's already plastered over every shit-house booths walls from one side of the plant to the other,"

"Very funny." Farkas frowned, only a hint of sarcasm now in his voice. But it was there, and it was still just enough to express it-self as he added, "At least I'm smart enough that I don't have to crawl around in the dirt to earn my wages."

"From what I hear, you do your crawling in a different type of work area. And much smarter men then you'll ever rub shoulders with, have already passed up chances at a position like yours, not just because the prospect of checking out the gum collection under some higher-ups desk didn't appeal to them. On the other hand you might consider yourself overly intelligent. But as for myself, personally I believe that you wouldn't know 'dog shit' if you stepped in it. And one more thing, if you don't back off with these 'tainted' verbal confrontations, you're going to give yourself a coronary. For that, I applaud you."

Pausing as if to take a deep breath, but in reality more to give the Dwarf a chance to get in his kicks, George also gave an undetected wink in the direction the other two men still wise enough to remain as silent spectators. And when he could once more see a hint of a red blush on his bosses' face, it told him that he had won another verbal confrontation. So rather then continue to berate the man into a possible anxiety attack, he chose the prevailing silence as an excuse to possibly get the remainder of the day underway.

Turning his attention in Fred's direction, he winked once more. "I take it there's no change in the menu, and we're on the same job we've been on all week. And if that's the case, we better get going or we're never going to get anything worthwhile accomplished today."

Reaching forward as they stood erect, while picking up the same blueprint and work-order sheet they had been using all week long, Fred apparently felt that it was his turn to prove he was more than just part of the scenery.

"Hey! There's nothing on this paper."

"Flip it over, you idiot." George smiled.

"Oh!" Fred smiled, while doing exactly that. "Some moron must have accidentally put all of the information on the wrong side!"

Only now, as they started to move, did George quickly correct himself for not mentioning their newest teammate's name.

"I'm sorry buddy, ah, Bob. I didn't mean to forget you. You better come with us." Briefly glancing back into the foreman's still flustered looking direction, he then added, "I think you'll be a lot safer where we're going."

If the little oriental had deciphered anything at all out of what had transpired in front of him, than he failed to let it show through onto his still silly looking little grin. And as George and Fred started to walk away a little faster, he quickly readjusted his expected little stride to match theirs, without once looking back in the direction of the sour face now fading in the distance.

At first it looked as they were about to ignore the new mans slightly trailing presence, but that instantly changed just as soon as they were out of sight of the heated lone figure still seated at the lunch table behind them. Opening a gap between himself and Fred, he waited until the created cavity was filled.

"Sorry about that." George smiled at the newest addition to their group. "But every once in a while we seem to feel the need to justify our positions around here.", his head tilting back to where they had just left. "Don't let what happened back there throw you. I'm sure he must take everything we say or do with a 'grain of salt', I know we do, or he's eventually going to snap. "

And as a loud laugh suddenly interrupted from Fred and his own lips, obviously from some as yet little unknown joke between them he, carried on with. "No - o, we're not crazy, although I'm sure some of the other men will argue that point once you get to know them. But in case you couldn't fathom what was going on, it's just that old 'shit-head' and I almost always never see eye to eye on most things around here, and not just because I'm taller."

Now for the first time since he had been in their presence, did the silly little 'Charlie Chan' like grin fade away, and his accent free voice gave no indication of being wimpish when he spoke. "Aren't you afraid of getting fired?"

"What!" George laughed. "For what happened back there? Never! Someone probably pissed in his cereal this morning and he's got his customary 'skin off his ass' on his forehead again today. Our boy's one of those guy who tries to rule through intimidation. No doubt he can't do it at home, so he likes to try it in here on us. I've got to much plant seniority and savvy to be threatened by the likes of him. At times like this, I just consider him to be a 'waste' of human skin."

"He can still give you the dirtiest or hardest jobs available around here, can't he?"

There were sudden sighs of maturity and wisdom showing through in Bob's otherwise timid looking features. But Fred and George were still on so much of an emotional high, they both failed to detect it.

"Naw. That was just about an average get-together for us." George smiled.

"What he knows about anything important around here," Fred grinned, "you could print on the balls of a very small animal!"

"We've worked on just about everything there is to repair in this place." George cut in. "We not only know how long it takes to get the job done, but also the easiest and cleanest way there is to do them. Farkas only 'thinks' he's in charge."

Now looking directly at the newest to be member of their team, his face suggesting that he still had something on his mind, George stopped with whatever was presently in his thoughts to comment, "Say, what ever happened to that 'happy-go-lucky' stupid grin you were constantly flashing at us earlier?"

"Oh, you mean this one?" Bob answered, the expression mentioned suddenly reappearing. And as Fred offered with a half chuckle, "Ya, that's the one!" it once more disappeared.

"Oh, that's just a little wall I put up until I get to know what kind of people I'm round. I was always taught that 'When you see great men, think of becoming them,' And as strange as it may or may not seem, when people first see me or anyone of my heritage, they almost always expect that we should be acting like those stereo typed in the movies. Believe it or not, it actually does come in handy occasionally. Especially when I throw things like, 'Great men always understand what is right.' Or 'To go too far, is as bad as not to go far enough.' in their direction.

"Turning his head just far enough to notice that a grinning George was also apparently enjoying himself, he added, "Well it sure as Hell looks like it didn't take you long to evaluate us. Does what you just said mean we pass, or should we start worrying?"

"Well," the silly gestures that had shown earlier, returned, housed by just as foolish looking "Confucius" mannerisms. "Wise man once say, do not underestimate oneself. Leave it to others. Or. Before put foot down, be sure to have leg to stand on."

"Well I'll be." Fred grinned. "We've got 'Charlie Chan' working with us today."

"That's not 'Chan', you imbecile. George laughed, while reaching out and punching his buddy in the shoulder, "He's quoting "Confucius'. And as Fred reacted with a loud 'Ouch!' George looked back at Bob while asking, "Am I right?"

The answer he got, "'When three are walking together, they are sure to have a teacher among them.' And it is just as wise to remember that, "Speaking without thinking, is like shooting without aiming." which actually made him sound as if he had just answered his own question.

"That does it! 'Confucius' it is." George chuckled.

Suddenly, just as quickly as they had appeared, the new man's fable impersonation vanished. And his voice and body mannerisms were just as intelligently mature as when he had spoken earlier.

"Seriously, some individuals you can read like an opened book. I've been around enough people to almost instantly categorize them. And even though it is an old Chinese proverb, it is true. 'The time to make a friend, is before you need one!'

"Whoa! wait a minute!" George interrupted, while stopping in his tracks. "We've got people around here who have enough trouble just thinking in a straight line. You start talkin' in riddles or quote logic in a manner they're not used to hearing, and they'll be afraid to open their mouths whenever you're around." Then, just as if someone had just slammed the door of realization in his face, the suspicion that had been in his voice returned. "And just how in the hell come you sound just like the two of us now?"

"Just because 'one' looks like 'ones' ancestors, does not mean 'one' has to sound or think exactly as they did." Bob grinned back. "Or, maybe it has to do with the fact that I was born and raised 'third' generation in this country."

The answer not only made sense, it was more than acceptable as was evident by George and Fred's once again grinning. But even that was altered briefly as they started moving, when Fred asked, "Categorize? Earlier you said categorize. What do you mean by categorize?"

"Well firstly, there's the people in the world you know who you are responsible for 'totally', and they in turn, for you. Secondly there are people you know because you need to 'know', just to exist, such as mister Farkas back there. And lastly, there's the people you get to know because you want to know them. They're a kind of gift you give yourself. They generally are the ones you want as close friends."

"Oh!" George injected, his face now a mixture of grin over confusion. "I don't know exactly why, but it all seems to make sense. But it still doesn't tell us as to what kind of people you think we're going to be."

Once again the more silly now than foolish grin that had started the conversation reappeared on Bob's face briefly, before he acknowledged "I think it's safe to say that you two are 'as one', 'a pair', 'a duo'. 'To live and walk in the company of greatness, is the finest of things possible.' I look only forward, to working with you. And the reason for that, would be that I have often found it best to be oneself, no matter how painful or detrimental it may be. It is something, from what I have seen so far, and also believe, that you two have already succeeded at."

George looked seriously first at Fred, and than at their apparent new close friend, his brain as always busy in thought. And when he finally said "And that I would predict dear friend, every pun intended, is a very wise and noble prophecy." It was an evaluation which only served to have them all soon lost in laughter. Laughing not because of what he had said, but rather due to his best over exaggerated oriental imitation manner in which he had purposely delivered it.

Chapter # 3

'Why for a why.'
Or
'Truth for a truth.'

Their destination was still long minutes away when Fred once more made a noticeably sour face, one of his hands coming up to gingerly massage at his still queasy stomach. George noticed his closest friend's ongoing agony, and instantly read the symptoms for what they could only be. Trying to sound at least a little bit sympathetic, even though he really was, a streak of sadistic humor in him helped make a smile appear on his face, as he said, "Abused body chemistry nagging at you again buddy?"

"Ya." Fred acknowledged, in a sour tone genuinely belonging to the rest of his answer. "And It's about to make its presence shown, very very soon I'm afraid."

'Well, why don't you take off and dispose of some of that torment." George continued to smile. "We'll meet you at the job site later."

Starting to move away, even before all of the wise suggestion offered had finished, Fred let one of his hands come up and cradle his tender stomach again, while adding, "Very intelligent offer, 'o wise one'. But then answer me this, how come lately a trip home always seems much shorter than it took for the original journey to get you wherever it is you went?"

"No doubt," George chuckled, "because lately we've probably been to 'shitfaced' to remember half of the return journey."

"Oh." Fred frowned. "Now it makes sense." He then, George and Bobs' smiling eyes watching his departing form, disappeared around another of the ever endless supply of corners, fortunately not far away from one of the company's many 'libraries'.

Chuckling on their way, George had no intention of wasting the next private moments he and the new man were about to have together.

"While we've got time Bob, I think I better fill you in on a few little things it takes to survive around here. But before I tell what they are, there's one question that's been nagging at me since we've been introduced. If you don't mind, I'd like to get it out of the way before anyone else brings it up."

"Go for it." Bob smiled, two rows of even very pearly whites enhancing his reply.

"Well," George continued to smile, a hint of seriousness now in his voice, "before I recommend what it takes, the thing that's on my mind kind of goes hand and hand with you and your people, their heritage and all that stuff."

Bob, his face instantly loosing its smile let the tone of his own voice match George's, while cutting him short. "I'll have you know I come highly 'recommended'! My last boss was always telling everyone he met that anyone who gets me to work for them, was 'damn' lucky!"

"That, I can believe." George chuckled. "But that's not what I'm talking about. It's, well, it's just that, you're not one of those screaming all arms and legs flailing 'Kung Fu' fanatics are you?"

Bob knew that he had been jokingly mocking himself earlier. But he was still more than just a little bit leery about George's capability to sound convincingly serious while being sarcastically funny at the same time. So he let this hopefully new friend continue, while changing his facial expression just enough to indicate that he didn't have the foggiest idea as to what in the 'Hell' George was talking about.

"I was just wondering, well," possibly without even realizing it, George started to put a little 'body English', slightly jerky and chop chop movements with his arms and hands, as he spoke. "I was wondering that if, how can I put it delicately, well, if you were one of those guys who go around making sounds like they're filling their laundry. You know, while kicking boards, breaking, bricks, or punching holes in perfectly good water-melons"

Hoping that just his leg was being pulled, it had to be he told himself, Bob half-chuckled and smiled while answering the silly sounding question with what he hoped was the right answer. "I'm afraid you've been watching too many imported oriental movies my friend. I know there are those out there who think that everyone of our heritage all look alike. But then we think the same about your race. And as for Bruce Lee, I know I shouldn't be assuming that he is what we are talking about, well, I have seen most of his movies, with 'Enter The Dragon' being my favorite. But I am not Mister Lee or even Jackie Chan, although I have nothing but the highest of resect and admiration for those with such devotion to the martial arts. It's obvious that it is not something to be acquired on just a weekend or two. And as for the years of devotion and training, well, let's just say as for myself, I'd be happy if I could just handle the wife."

Without deliberately trying to, his own sense of warped humor created mental images to match George's remarks. And as the images appeared inside of his head, he deliberately did his best to awkwardly attempt to demonstrate movements required too achieve what had been suggested. "Besides, from what I understand, anyone really serious about martial arts is usually mature enough to refrain from having to use their acquired capabilities to defend themselves, let alone use them to show off."

"Okay, okay!' George offered, his expressions only changing slightly. Anyone like Bob not really knowing him had yet to learn no one would still think him serious with his present remarks. "I was just trying to find out if you were capable of protecting yourself if some of the guys jokingly get on your back. You know, ethnic jokes and all that crap."

It's not exactly like the United Nations around here, but occasionally some of the workers feel it's time to do a run on ones heritage background. Case in being, if you'd joined us a month ago you would have heard the comment on how electrical copper wire was really invented. Rumor had it that it was born when two Scots men were each holding onto one side of a copper penny one of them had found. And as they each tried to pull it out of the others grip, well, I'm sure you can envision the penny being stretched and stretched and stretched. And I'm pretty sure once most of the workers get just a visual glimpse of you, I think it's pretty safe to predict that your turns comin."

A brief semi-sarcastic sigh slowly escaped from Bob's lips, which in his way erased any doubt that he was anything but pleased with George's remarks. He then took his turn in using over emphasized body gestures to enhance his answer. "Sticks and stones may break some peoples bones, but I'm not the type who runs into the 'john' to throw up when it does happen. Or should I have said that if someone does somehow manage to come up with some embarrassing insulting innuendoes that I've never heard before, I'm not going to run home and throw myself on top of a sharp knife."

The involuntary images the words conjured inside George's warped mind also brought almost contagious laughter with them. It also almost made it impossible for him to act serious about anything he was about to hear from there on. And he continued to chuckle while offering, "Wonderfully put Bob, or is it Bobby, or even Robert?"

"Whatever suits you or the other men is going to be fine with me." Bob smiled.

"Okay, Bob it is. And remember, it never hurts to have an answer ready for even the simplest insult, especially if they think they can intimidate you. For example, if they hit you with the ol line 'I know where you live!' my favorite comeback used to be 'That's great! Can I have your phone number?' And when they ask me why in the Hell they should give me their phone number, I hit them with, 'Well I drink so much, sometimes I can't remember where I live. If I had your number I could call you up and you could tell me where to go! And personal experience I've found that it's hard to stay mad at someone if they just made you laugh, especially after they add, 'I for one would sure as Hell welcome the opportunity to tell you where to go!"

As Bob was busy doing exactly that, laughing, George carried on. "But that now brings us to our next point in question. Do you have a nickname?"

Whatever co-workers they passed George acknowledged with a simple nod. He had decided that they were not quite ready for an introduction to each other, especially since Bob sure as hell wasn't verbally attuned for them just yet.

"A nickname?" the question must have sounded more than strange to Bob, because it brought a grin along for the ride, as he repeated it. "What do you mean, ' nick name'?"

"You know," George smiled back. "something sounding unusual or comical. A 'moniker' someone might have labeled you with during your childhood, or even on your last job. Think about it, something that's destined to be associated wish you during the rest of your life. Something pleasing, or even irritating, depending on how you might feel about it."

Just from the sudden look of confusion now on his face, his brain possibly lost in thought searching for anything to offer, George could see that Bob was definitely going to need some assistance, even before he confirmed it. "No, not really."

"Shit!" George quickly said, noticeably disappointed. "It looks like I better think up a harmless moniker real fast, before the men label you with something like 'Yellow Jaundice' or 'Chicken Ball Bob' or something else not quit so friendly, something you wouldn't want to hear in front of the wife or kids."

As they had been walking Bob had periodically been letting his eyes and curious attention stray away long enough to scan their surroundings, the occasional individual standing around doing seemingly nothing, all no doubt in an effort to familiarize him-self with his new 'home' away from 'home'. But the note of urgency in George's voice told him that he better keep both on the concerned gentleman now trying to educate him. "Is it really that important?

Instinctively checking where Bob's attention had been straying to George then changed the direction of their conversation without even missing a smile. "Don't mind those guys. Aside from being brainy enough to end every conversation with 'And will there be fries with that order?' they're on what we commonly call 'pigeon patrol'."

When Bob's face said "Huh?" even before he could, George carried on. "You know, for people who have got nothing better to do than stand around all shift 'day-dreaming' up at the ceiling."

Bob's face, while glancing back at one of the men in question, was apparently still slightly ahead of his brain, as the same "Oh." of recognition came out of his mouth. And George, still grinning and obviously pleased with himself, lost no time in carrying on with what he was originally taking about.

"But let's get back to what I was trying to warn you about, nicknames."

"Come on." Bob smiled a little sheepishly. "It can't really be all that bad."

"Around here it is. Almost all of the people you'll come into contact with will have a whimsical label somehow associated with either their personality trait or job qualification, 'or' the very obvious I should add, their physical appearance. We've got a fellow nicknamed 'Mumbles'. This guy is very hard to understand, because half the time he sounds as if he has a mouth full of marbles. A 'Stan Stumbles'. This guy can trip over air, straight or wavy. A 'Thumper'. This boy loves to argue and then get physical. Then there's 'Picky Joe', and no it's not an 'innuendo' to his nose. He's just one of those guy's who likes to pick everything presently going on in the world apart. 'Scratch'. He'll take a day off work at the drop of a hat. 'Harpo' This guy whistles more than he talks. A nail biter, 'Starvin' Marvin'. And a 'Dee Jay'. This guy loves to play a musical game at the lunch table occasionally where we will draw out of a coffee can a piece of paper containing an old song title from a particular year, lets say, Rod Stewarts 1971 'Maggie May'. You in turn will have to come up with a comical punch line or quip using the song title amusing enough to tickle the funny bone in most of the other men also eating there. If you get more thumbs up then down, you're 'home free', at least until the next time. If you don't, you get to put a quarter into the coffee clubs can. In this case where you have been hit with 'Maggie May' the rather obvious respond would have been, 'Maggie may what? Meaning of course, Maggie may do what? Or better yet, there's 'Up on the roof.' by The Drifters. For criminals it's merely a potential escape rout. For some it brings to mind an almost private place to grow flowers or even raise pigeons. For young lovers it could represent a secret meeting place when wishing for privacy or to just look up at the stars in a cloudless sky at night. And then there's the perverts, who just go up there when there's nothing good on the television that night, and look into adjoining windows with the hopes of being entertained."

"Wow!" Bob half laughed. All that out of one little song title.

"But there's more." George chuckled. "Around here there's always more. In this case its simply as with any good contract, there's always an escape clause. With us, it's a simple case of just being able to sing a couple of lines out of the song if you can't think of anything comical to put the title to. And since most of the workers in here are tone deaf, or to put it in much simpler words, they couldn't carry a tune in a bucket if their life depended on it, unless you've got a voice that can shatter glass, most of the audience generally ends up cracking up in laughter. And that's generally more then enough to let you off the hook."

"I think, I like that idea." Bob smiled.

"Good. A coward would have simply said 'Pass the can!'. Then at the end of the year any profit in the can would go to the Salvation Army to help those less fortunate with a Christmas dinner." George grinned back, before continuing.

"I like that even better." Bob continued to smile.

"So do we." George smiled back. "And for the summer we've even got a 'pop' fund going where you can buy a can of cold pop out of the fridge, with all of the profits going into an account used to aid anyone having a tragedy where a bit of financial aid will help lighten the burden. It's a kind of insurance policy where everyone is willing to pay into with hopes they never have to benefit from it.

"This just keeps getting better." Bob smiled softly.

"Well, most of us do what we can." George offered, before getting back on track. "And then there's even a man we nicknamed 'Rabbit'. But I don't mean like in 'Bugs Bunny'! All of which you'll understand if you ever get to see the amount of woman this guy dates. Then there's a 'Motor mouth'. This one's even been suggested to as having to have his mouth shot in order to get it to stop moving when he dies. But then I've been called that one myself occasionally. And then there are the tags that can cover more than one individual. 'On Golden Pond' or 'Old farts' relates to older people. 'Ticker tape' or 'Jones' for those who play the stock market. 'Craps' or 'Antae' and not because of a bowel movement or family relation. It's just do to their gambling habits. 'Buffalo Butt' or 'Baby Hughie' for those noticeably over weight."

Even though Bob was floating back and forth between grinning and chuckling, while thinking 'What could be left?' George kept right on enjoying himself.

"And that's only the tip of the workforce. Believe me as comical or cruel as they may sometimes sound, the nicknames are often used over their real given name tag. It's come to be kind of a tradition around the plant, goodwill and all that stuff. Some even consider it to be a sort of 'badge of honor' or recognition. Why, there's even one guy in the plant with the nickname of 'Windbreaker', which let me warn you has nothing to do with the brand of coat you would wear on a chilly evening! And, if you should ever encounter this guy on your own, just be sure to wet the tip of one of your fingers before holding it up to check which way the wind is blowing. Obviously this would be with the intent of standing on the proper side of him, especially if someone else should happen to walk by shouting 'There she blows! after the standard 'Speak ol toothless one!"

Chuckling slightly, even though George had made it all sound serious, Bob had to force his own voice to sound as just as concerned.

"Well, what can I do about it? I don't think it would be proper if I picked out my own nickname. Or should I have said, 'I would be grieved if other men did not know me.' But alas, 'I will also be grieved not to know other men.' He quickly added while slipping back into character."

Now it was George's face that had a chance to express one that was in deep thought before answering.

"Let me think about it for a little while. Sometimes the best nicknames often arrive on the spur of the moment, spontaneously by a reaction to something. We've got people in here that if their picture ever showed in a newspaper with their real names underneath, you'd possibly be confused, unless their nickname was listed there also."

Pausing long enough to scratch at the back of his head, a common gesture often associated with those searching their mind, or in some cases also often referred to that the individual actually had something, George let a small frown show itself, before continuing. It was also a gesture, but never in his case, that some individuals like to comment, 'He's one of those guy's who can't walk, talk or chew gum at the same time.' while slipping in an extra dig like, 'Not to mention he also has the morals of an alley cat!' "I like to think of myself as being petty fair at picking out names, let me think about it. I've generally got a few extra ones floating around inside my head, but let me play with them, and I'll try to have something for you by the time we're on the job."

"Well, okay." Bob offered, while trying to keep his features a rigid mask of seriousness like earlier. "But remember to try to be kind, if you can't be gentle. And if it's your name you want to see in a newspaper, just walk across a street full of traffic, while reading one."

"I might be a little premature," George grinned, a humorous gleam in his eyes, "but I think you just might fit in around here, real quick, not to mention easy."

"Quick and easy?" Bob smiled. "That not only sounds like the description of a soft hearted prostitute in a hurry, you also make it sound as if most of the people are here to 'play' instead of 'work'."

George appreciated that their new friend might seemingly be as quick-witted as he liked to think of himself, and he wasn't above showing it.

"Not bad Bob. Not bad. In a sense you're right. But personally I always like to think of my job as being a hobby. If I really took it serious and had to do it for a living, I'd quit and go on the 'system'.

"Oh, you mean 'cash for life!" Bob quickly smiled, which instantly had George just short of laughing. It was also the kind of infectious response that he couldn't help but imitate.

"That's another good speedy 'comeback'. George continued to chuckle. I can see that I just might finally have some real competition around here, -- ah -- 'slingshot?"

"Slingshot -- sling -- shot!" Squinting, no doubt rolling the name repeatedly over and tasting it in his thoughts, Bob finally shrugged his shoulders while saying. "I guess 'Slingshot' sounds as good a handle as any to me. 'Hell', it's got to be better than the more obvious you already mentioned. 'Charlie Chan' 'Confucius' 'Mister Motto' or any of those not so friendly you also brought up earlier. Hell, right off the bat I haven't even touched upon the two most obvious slamming's that I'm pretty sure most of the other workers are going to come up with as soon as they meet you."

"And they are." Bob said more then asked.

"Well, with your last name being 'Wong' the first and most obvious attempt at humor at your expense your going to get is that someone's sure to comment that every night when you go home, you obviously go home to the 'wong' house."

Even to an audience of only one, George waited for a response. And as soon as Bob chuckled, he carried right on with, "The big one in your case is going to be along the lines of whenever you get into a discussion with anyone in the plant and you think you are winning a disagreement. The one you're verbally sparing with is probably going to hit you with 'You're 'wong' I say! You're 'wong', 'wong', 'wong'!" And that one's going to spread like 'wildfire', right after the first time it's used. From then on, need to use it or not, the jokers are going to throw it up in your face every time they think they can get a laugh with it."

As soon as Bob replied, "Been there, heard that!" George, apparently a new idea exploding inside of his thoughts, lost no time with blurting out, "Luckily you're not into farming, or you just might have gotten stuck with something like "Shop Suey!"

"That," Bob quickly frowned, "I can do without. So why don't we just stick with your original, 'Slingshot' for now, or at least until you can come up with anything else you might feel appropriate."

"Great!" George smiled. "ol 'Slingshot' it is. Now let's get on with some of the more important popular 'slang' terminology you're going to come up against around here. And when you do remember, don't be afraid to add to any of it. Everybody does, and everyone loves it. Okay?"

"I'll do the best I can." Bob smiled.

"Good. And I'm sure you can." George acknowledged. And as he continued with a chuckle, the impish attitude that had occasionally popped up along the way, was back. "Remember, 'Wise man' once said 'Better a slip with the foot, then the tongue'."

Bob, realizing that his earlier doubts about feeling comfortable or fitting in were both needless, while enjoying the bonding and humor coming in his direction. And then as if in almost perfect timing to confirm most of what they were talking about, Bob caught a glimpse of a worker passing in the distance, apparently talking to himself while making strange hand movements in the air around him. The view in itself was not only have seemed unusual, but the fact that there appeared to be no other human activity for the words and actions to be directed at, only made whatever was presently going on even more confusing.

But it wasn't about to be a mystery for long, as George had also noticed the man, as well as the look of confusion on Bob's face. And he put it all at ease by offering, "Oh that's just 'Signals'. He's once of those guys reputed as going to be late for his own funeral., as well as the reason they only put one door on a shithouse stall. Any more and he'd get confused as to which one he entered and which one he should be using to exit. It's even been joked that he could get lost on a 'one way' street. So now, as long as nobody beaks into his line of concentration, and like someone riding a bicycle, he uses his arms to point in the direction he is heading or next going to be moving in."

Once more giving Bob a chance to briefly absorb and enjoy what he was hearing, after he had chuckled, 'You mean like if an elevator ever went anywhere else but up or down, he'd probably get lost?' George then started right back into where he had left off.

"You'll find that most of the wise remarks should be almost self explanatory in how and when they are used. Take the word 'Groceries' for a start. Around here they refer to the food you are about to eat. Got it?"

Bob, while nodding his head silently in an affirmative manner, gave out with a smile that was definitely a close cousin to the one he had noticed for some reason that George found so humorous to look at. And as usual, it also made him react appropriately.

"Okay. Now sometimes two slang phrases can mean exactly the same thing also, such as 'pounding your ear' or 'pressing the bed-sheets'. Both means that someone's sleeping or napping."

"We called it 'catching some 'z-e-e-e-e-e-'s'." Bob smiled.

"Great!" George chuckled. "Like I said, if you have a slang saying for anything or any of the one's I give you, throw them back at me. It never hurts to add to one's verbal repertoire, especially if you can get a smile or chuckle out of them'

"Sure thing." Bob continued to grin. "If we're going to 'zing' or accidentally take a 'pot shot' at one-another, we just might as well know what it is that 'other one' is talking about."

"Believe me," George chuckled, "If I 'zing' you, you'll have no trouble understanding that you've just been 'slammed, and it won't be by accident."

"Remember." Bob grinned, "One does not have to be very smart, to outsmart oneself."

Realizing that a challenge had just been thrown up, George did his best to imitate Bobs' oriental imitation when spewing words of wisdom. "A man is never licked, until he quits."

"Ah." Bob replied, also quickly falling into his Confucius disguise. "You mean, 'It is better to fall down, then to lie down'."

Purposely taking a deep breath, it also gave him time to search for something to continue with, George crossed his arms and bent forward slightly before saying, "Wise man never test depth of water with both feet."

"And one should always remember their truest friends." Bob continued to grin, already accepting the fact that he was fighting an enemy with far less verbal ammunition then he had. "But not until they have remembered their enemies." he quickly added.

Also realizing that he was less qualified then first believing, George started looking for a way out of the challenge he had been feeding. "Well, how about, 'Life is a test that often has more questions then answers."

"Or," Bob quickly added. "If your life is one that is to be scrutinized, make sure it is a life that you are proud to be living."

"That's it!" George replied, throwing his hands up and reverting to the one wisest man he knew and imitated best, himself. "I should have known better than to let you pick both the type of battle and choice of weapon. For now , we'll just concentrate on the simpler things, the plant and those who make it run."

"The lack of information about each others background falling away with every smile and word spoken, Bob told himself he just might be in his kind of 'heaven'. "Sounds fair to me! But just remember, every time you talk - your mind is on display."

Twisting his head from side to side as if in disgust, even though he was also smiling George stopped solid in his tracks once more while saying, "Why do I feel that I've just been slammed again!"

"Sorry." Bob half-laughed. "I guess you're just too easy to talk to."

"Well there's sure as Hell's nothing wrong with that!" George smiled, his feet once more in motion. "Just remember that being ones-self is always best, no matter how painful. Or, wise man once say 'He who mind own business, stay in business.' And I meant every word of it."

As an instant look of surprise registered on Bob's face George let out a small laugh while adding, "I read quotable quotes too." And as Bob then joined him in laughter, he added, "But let's 'worry' about that when we come to them. Let's go to some of the ones you're more apt to hear around the job or lunch table."

And as Bob smiled out a singular 'Shoot!' George shot back, "Don't tempt me!" before carrying on.

"Now, if someone asks you what you're 'barkin' about, they generally want to know what you're talking about. 'What's on the menu?' means what job are you on for that day. "Bottle' or 'Friday flue' generally refers to a hangover."

"You mean like you and your buddy Fred." Bob cut in.

The realization that this new man had already picked up on the closeness between him and Fred brought a hint of an emotional glow to George answer. "Ya. Like poor Fred and me, as well as a half dozen other guys around here today. Only I didn't think I still showed the symptoms that much. What gave me away - my breath? The wife's always saying that after a night out with the boys I've got the 'breath of a lion'.

"You don't." Bob chuckled. "It's just that I heard Mister Farkas talkin about how close you and Fred were. I just reasoned out that you're the type who sticks by a friend when he's in trouble."

For one split second George could swear that his head was now registering a warm buzz, much like the kind it used to tell him that he was drinking too much. But he already knew what it was really from, and he passed it along with a smile towards the little man walking beside him. It was also a sensation that made him want to get to know the short oriental one Hell of a lot more.

"If you don't stop interrupting me, I'm never going to get you ready for the other workers."

"Soul solly." Bob chuckled. He then added, "Hit me again!" before pretending to zipper his mouth shut.

George, already anticipating that the remark 'Hit me!' didn't really mean just that, but rather 'go ahead' and start the slang expressions again. So instead of answering 'Only if you insist,' while faking a punch to Bobs mid section, he simply smiled, "Okay, let's continue."

"Now then. 'When the 'Big bird' shits!'. it generally means that it's payday around this place."

Even though he loved such a reaction, George totally ignored Bob's instant and honest attempt as suppressing a chuckle.

"A 'gravy' or 'hummy' job, a real rarity around here, is used to depict an easy 'fabricating' or 'repair job' you will be working on for that shift. 'Tiny time capsules' or 'firin up the 'gas chamber' are 'pork and beans' 'Brown baggin it' means drinking on the job. 'Close your 'gate' is shut your mouth. A slap in the 'pumpkin' or 'thump upside your noggin' refers to a punch in the head."

"Speakin of jobs," Bob cut in, "one of the places I used to work at actually had two very high paying jobs that nobody ever applied for."

Already anticipating that they might be being set up for something, especially since he knew that he would have used the same opportunity to make some smart aleck comment, George kept a serious face, as Bob continued. "One was, while wearing boxing gloves, you had to separate fly shit from the canteens pepper shakers. And the other was to go around and pull out all of the old staples, for re-use, from across the company's posting boards."

Even though both suggestions had been heard before, George did give it a brief chuckle, before an excitedly new voice picked up from where the ball had seemly been dropped.

"And let's not forget a couple of my favorites" Fred cut in." his surprised reappearance just as comical as his hop skip and a jump attempt to match his awkward footsteps to their marching pattern.

"He's got to be referring to food." George frowned. "He's always thinking with his stomach."

Ignoring the 'dig' Fred quickly carried on with, "So it's about 'food'. Everybody knows ya gotta eat, or ya can't shit! And if you don't 'shit', then you're goanna 'die'!" For the words used he looked directly at his grinning 'bud', who instantly recognized the hidden phrase for what it really meant, 'Eat shit and die!' before continuing. "As I was about to say, before someone so rudely butt in, I just wanted to let you know about the different kinds of sandwiches you might come across at the lunch table. Firstly there's the 'air' sandwich, a simple joining of two pieces of bread with no meat or butter in between. Then there's the 'temptation'. That's where you get two pieces of bread, butter, pickles, ketchup or mustard, but no meat. From there we move onto the 'grueler'. With it you have everything in the sandwich. Bread, butter, pickles, and sliced cheese, only with the cheese still wrapped in the cellophane it came in. And then last but not least, there's the 'last word'. That's where your favorite sandwich has all the lip smacking ingredients that make you drool just thinking about it. But the thing that turns you off about it is where it's topped off with something gut-wrenching you can't stand, such as ketchup or mustard, horse radish, or whatever."

"Now you know why he spends so much time in the 'crapper'. George grinned.

"They don't sound so bad, especially when you've bitten down and found a sock in your sandwich!" Bob laughed.

"A persons sock!" Fred chocked."

"Yes, a sock!" Bob grinned. "A folded, with the heel cut out of it, smothered with your favorite mayonnaise lettuce and tomato 'sock'!"

"I take it you were having a disagreement at the time, and this was her delicate way of telling you that you're a 'heel', if I hear you right. - And as for it being cut 'out', I think that has something to do with that when it 'comes', to relieving the old eye ball pressure, that privilege just might be 'cut off' also." George smiled. "When Judy wants to make a point, she just turns one of the arms on my work shirt, or pant legs inside out. That way, especially with my pants, she knows my routine by heart by now, I usually end up falling over while hopping around and trying to get my left leg into its proper socket."

"Lucky you weren't having Chinese food, sweat and sour 'sliced and diced' chicken balls." Fred smiled at Bob, while dropping his hands down to cover his crotch area. "You can just image what the implications behind that servin' could lead to!"

"Sounds like the voices of experience!" Bob answered with a broad smile on his face, indicating that he was enjoying everything he was hearing, almost as much as George and Fred were having fun in saying it. And when Fred suddenly commented that he must have missed something and had to find another 'john', real fast, George tilted his head in his buddy's jogging departing direction, while offering, "Sometimes, if the jobs to big to handle, you just have to make more than one trip to deliver the load. Oh, and while we're on the subject. I 'm not trying to 'but' into your private business, with the word 'butt' being spelled with a double 'tee'. 'But' 'again' when it comes to your constitutional I recommend you try to arrange to take care of all of your 'sit-down' business at home. There's been rumors of 'crabs' spotted in here so big that you could put a 'dog leash on them!"

Alone again, except for the buildings other normal personnel, George didn't even take the time to take a deep breath, even though his new companion was now occupied chuckling, before picking up where they had left off.

"When someone says they're going to 'evaporate'," he smiled, "they want to disappear for an early shower or something. A 'mop chop' is a haircut. 'Eggs' or 'nut's' shouldn't be that hard, especially if someone was to kick you there, it means your 'testicles'. A 'chicken shit' is a coward. 'Piss flies' are those little 'hang-gliders' you'll some times find around the urinals and garbage pails at the lunch tables."

George made no effort to follow any pattern that would relate one slang definition to another, but rather chose to let whatever came to his mind first fly from his lips. And without even realizing it, he even started to use one hand to count off finger by finger each saying as he went.

"'Breckie' is your breakfast. Your spoon is generally labeled as a 'shovel'. The 'white rain' means its snowing. 'Fast food' involving hamburgers, are 'racehorses'. 'Manhole covers' are tampons. 'Shit hawks' are seagulls and 'nose bleeders' are high heeled shoes."

The original chuckle that Bob failed to suppress as they were walking had not only managed to slip out occasionally, it had also brought a host of others to join it during a few of George's humorous sounding definitions. It also, and not because George was starting to get tired of the sound of his own sweet voice, think of an idea to get Bob involved. It would give him time to let his own mind race ahead in order to remember more shop slang.

"Why don't we make this a little bit more interesting?" he suddenly said to Bob.

"How's that?" Bob answered, a hint of skeptical surprise in his voice.

"Well, say I give you either the phrase or the definition, and you try to think of what the answer would be to either one. That way you're not only more involved, you just might come up with a few newer or funnier forms of slang terminology."

It was on the tip of Bob's tongue to ask, 'We've been walking so long, have we crossed the boarder yet?' but instead he wisely just replied, "Sounds good to me. I already had an idea on the answers for some of the ones you've already covered. This'll give me a chance to see how close I really was."

"I'll start you off with an easy one." George smiled in acknowledgement. "What's passin wind?"

"I don't now about here," Bob smiled. "'but' , and it's the 'appropriate' word to use if you think about it for a second, but where I come from it's either a 'fart', a 'gas leak', bad breath a 'room divider' or you're considered to be just blowing someone a kiss."

"Right!" George smiled. "And if you're wanted on the 'blower'?"

"You're being paged for the telephone." Bob instantly replied.

"And the gentleman wins another cigar!" George laughed. "Now I'll make them a little bit harder. What does it mean to 'slam' or 'goon' someone?"

Only pretending to frown, since he believed that he had already been a witness to their usage, he finally answered, "I don't know exactly, but I'll bet it's safe to say that it refers to literally putting someone verbally down, or even just in their proper place."
"Close." George smiled. "Real close. They both mean to wisecrack, irritate, or potentially bother someone. Now if you wanted to go to the washroom for a leak, what would you say?

"Well-l-l, we called it the 'crapper' or 'keibo'." Bob laughed. "And instead of a leak we would say 'We're going for a whiz'."

"Very close again." George continued to smile. "There's all kinds of slang terminology that can fit in here. For the washroom we could call it anything from a 'john' to our personal favorite 'the library'. When contract time comes around you'll even find the occasional 'Vote here!' sign on their doors. But when it's time for a leak, it could be referred to as 'relieving bladder pressure, or again a favorite 'drainin' the main vain!' Now then, what's a 'brown noser'?"

Staying away from his first thought of 'someone into kinky sex.' Bob grinned, "That sounds like another easy one. That's someone who suck-holes around the boss, only we used to call them 'dickey lickers'. Now let me ask you one, what do you call homosexuals around here?"

The humor that was so much at home on George's face instantly faded noticeably enough that Bob had no trouble realizing that he had for as some as yet unknown reason had either stepped in the proverbial 'shit', pardon me 'poo pot', or probably hit on a touchy spot.

"I've heard some people around here," George answered straight faced, his voice just as bland "refer to them as 'queers', 'faggots' or 'ass-bandits'. As for myself, and not because I believe in any part of their life style, prefer not to pick on anybody I consider to be mentally disturbed."

"Oh." Bob said, both shocked and noticeably confused. "Sorry." Had he stepped into 'taboo' territory he asked himself.

"I'm the one who should be sorry." George quickly said, the smile that had vacated his face now back. "I didn't mean to put a damper on our conversation. But that was just a prime example of what I want you to understand about this place, as well as the kind of people your going to be working with eventually. You're going to have to learn to be either yourself, or a little bit of everyone you come into contact with. Try to pick out only their good points, it'll make it a lot easier for you to survive.

"I see." Bob replied, the humor he had been enjoying earlier still noticeably missing. "Well, what about the other guys? Is there any 'one' person in particular I should be careful with?

"No!" George snapped, a little more seriously again. "'Be watchful of 'all of them'!"

George's strong emphasis on the words 'All of them!' left Bob feeling totally confused. And he wondered if he had somehow misjudged the man he was being so open and friendly with."

"You mean 'everybody's' not to be trusted?"

"Exactly!" George blurted out. "Not even me!" And then he couldn't keep the bigger than ever smile he had been deliberately holding back off of his face any longer. "If I told you which workers around here to be leery of, I would just be prejudiced against certain individuals I'm overly fussy about in the plant. But if I warned you to be cautious about everyone, even 'me', and then you still got slammed by one of these people, then you've got nobody to blame but yourself, if and when the times comes. Remember, being your-self is always best, no matter how painful."

Bob's already inherited thin eyes once more narrowed even more, as he again deliberately imitated features and actions long since associated with fictitious oriental wise men, while saying, "It sounds 'wise one', it is 'you' who should be 'philosopher'."

"Ya, well, it's still not quite that easy." George sarcastically chuckled, his receptive audience apparently back. And since he couldn't miss Bob's theatrics, he let it inspire him, as such reactions often did in the past.

"You're going to find that most people are like turkeys. One panics around here, and a bunch more want to jump in the barrel 'head-first' with him. And if you think I'm kidding, first chance you get when taking a shower here, just yell 'fire!' you'll be surprised many people will run out from under the water. It makes me kind of glad I don't own shares in this company."

"We had a few of those guys in my old job too." Bob chuckled.

"I guess it's kind of a universal disease." George grinned. "If I thought any of my kids were ever going to turn out like them - I'd rush home and do up a complete sanity check on their mother's side of the family tree."

"How about the kind of people who world screw a snake if they could find it's shoulders." Bob added, the bonding between them once more growing with each passing second. "Have you got any of them around here?"

"Fortunately only a few." George answered, disappointment in his voice. "But thank God we already know who most of them are."

"And just how am 'I' going to know who these people are? Or do I have to let them have sex with me first to find out?"

"Let's hope not." George laughed. "If your instinct for survival doesn't kick in I'll have to think of some way to warn you, without as I said getting personally involved."

"Instinct?" Bob faltered.'

"Ya, instinct:" George continued to chuckle. "You know that thing that sometimes warns you about your fly being open when you're standing in the middle of a crowd."

"Hell, if that's the case, I'm in big trouble! Bob said seriously. "It's always taken a cool draft or someone to say something along the lines of 'Your barn door's open.' before I've realized my zipper's at 'half mast'."

George, while laughing, chuckled out, "Well, if your instinct doesn't warn you, maybe I'll just start hummin something along the lines of the tune 'Having your baby.' whenever we're around anybody who likes to verbally rape or abuse anybody they can."

"You've got people really that bad around here?"

"And then some." George said. "You're going to come across individuals in here who are going to try to use you, or abuse you. Some will test you to see if you carry tales. And a few will try to get you to pick sides in everything from opinions to arguments."

"You'll not only have to make up your mind as to which of the people you'll work with are going to be your friends, if you want them to be that is, but also if you are going to one of the workforce. Or, if you'd rather, just another piece of machinery that makes this 'circus' run. To survive sanely in a place like this, you not only have to be able to do your job. but also occasionally become a bit of a psychologist. There's an awful lot of children in here walking around in grown ups bodies, and they are not all foremen! Remember, good friends are generally made through many acts of kindness, but can be lost with just one of stupid foolishness."

"Wow!" Bob's face back to using the heritage expressions he'd donned earlier. "I see, you can be real serious when you want."

"Well," George smiled, "you did ask. Now get the silly theatrics off your puss. I'm a firm believer that if you tell someone the truth, then you can forget it. But if you tell a lie, you not only have to remember exactly what the lie was, but also everyone you told it to."

'You're doing it again." Bob smiled, but with less of what was requested. "You're being philosophical. Next you'll be telling me that 'if you can't be big', than don't 'be little'. And here I used to think 'Ann Landers' was a woman."

George opened his mouth with every intention of making another comment. But as soon as he realized that it would sound exactly like Bob had just suggested, it never had a chance to be born. And as soon as he started to laugh instead, it became contagious, as he started to twist his head in a negative manner while saying, "Ya, you're right. And if we don't start talking about something else, I'll probably have you so scared of me, you'll be looking forward to being with anyone else."

As if on cue, their destination came into view. And after saying "We're here." George told Bob that he would get him a spare set of keys made up for Fred's and his tool storage lockers. That way, he told him, if the need arose he would at least have access to some decent equipment until his trial period was up.

"Remember." he quickly added. "You are not a 'bee', and this is not a 'beehive'. If you don't produce, they're not going to sting you to death and throw you out of the hive. And the most 'important' thing to remember about what I've talked to you about told so far, is that 'everything is to be taken with a 'grain of salt'. I'm sure one of your families 'words of wisdom' prophesies would have covered what that means. Even if it should look as if we are picking on someone, it's always to be considered as just in jest. And yes, even when discussing mister Farkas! Harsh words or feelings are never overly intentional."

Feeling like he'd just spent a half an hour on the 'psychiatrists couch', Bob's smile was definitely genuine when answering, "Thanks." And as he continued to match George step for step, as they walked around to inspect the huge piece of equipment they were there to repair, he asked if there was anything else, political or otherwise, that he should know about.

"If you mean 'union' wise," George answered, a hint of disgust in his voice. "About the only sure thing you can rely on them for, is to take their dues out of your pay every month. But if it is company policies you're referring to," there was no noticeable change in tone or words, as he spoke. "then just remember to keep your eyes and ears open, and your mouth shut, especially for as long as you're on probation. A lot of people in here, yours truly being one of the biggest offenders I've heard, have been known to have hanged themselves, their own tongues having been used as the rope to make it possible"

Suddenly, and definitely looking as if his second little detour had actually left him rejuvenated this time, Fred's smiling form whistled its way up to where they had stopped. And when George sarcastically intoned, 'Speak of the Devil.' a phrase Fred had heard a hundred times before, he quickly lost no time in retaliating with an answer George loved to use himself.

"He couldn't make it, so he sent me!" And when only the strange new man smiled in reward, he quickly added, "What's the problem?"

"The Problem, "George over pronounced every word, "is 'that' it's Friday! There's Louie's prank staged for around two o'clock. We've got a new man on our hands. The 'ol' 'pain in the prostrate' the 'Evil Dwarf' is sure as Hell to show up around here a couple of times just to impress both himself and Bob here. We've still two coffee breaks, one lunch period, clean up and shower time on our hands. And that's all without allowin for even picking up our tools to do some work yet. Plus, that's not counting some much needed time for trips to the 'library' yet. You're not the only one born with an affliction to get rid of excess food, you know. Personally I don't think we've enough 'Friday' left in this shift to handle even half of it. Now do you know what the problem is?"

Fred looked, first from the smiling little oriental he still didn't know anything about, to George before letting his totally relaxed emotions answer, "No, not really. The work as usual will just have to wait. No problem."

"Wise man once say, 'It is better to wear out, then to rust out'." Bob added in character.

The spontaneous laughter that broke out in unison told Bob that he was going to have very little trouble if any adjusting to new workmates, nor they to him. And as George unlocked the pair of tool cupboards they were now standing in front of, he rattled off most of their contents, no matter how familiar or common they were to men of their classification.

Time, as is often said when one is busy, flew by. They just had the tools out and set up to go, when it was time for the first of their coffee breaks.

"I know you're going to hate to hear this fellows, but it, is, 'break time'.

"Gee, that's too bad." Fred grinned. "And just when I was finally getting the urge to really 'dig in'."

"Well, fortunately for the company that it is break-time." A smiling George quickly shot back. "It's because of guys like you that they have to put a 'fifty, fifty' warranty on all work performed around here."

Bob's face, indicating that his brain already knew he shouldn't be gullible enough to ask just what the Hell George was talking about, made the inquiry any ways.

"What's a 'fifty, fifty' warranty? Or, shouldn't I be asking?"

"It's to late now." Fred frowned. "You've opened the door." And as he added, "He's just trying to be sarcastic. It stands for 'fifty feet' or fifty seconds', whatever comes first when one's expecting something to fail or breakdown.

Bob may have led the laughter that followed, but it was a chuckling George that led the way to the closest canteen, as well as what was too be talked about along the way.

"And another thing you might as well know now Bob. If you finish to quickly any job they give around here, they'll sure as Hell make sure that they give you more than enough to keep you busy during your next shift."

"And that's the truth-th-th-th-th." Fred cut in, using his best imitation of Lily Tomlin's 'Ernestine' from 'Rowan and Martin's' 'Laugh In'. But as quickly as he had taken control of the conversation, he just as quickly dropped the humor, while continuing. "Especially our sweet lovable ol foreman. No matter how quick or long it takes to finish a job - he automatically thinks you've finished early enough to stand around and 'screw' the company for a few non productive work hours any-ways."

"Which only goes to justify my philosophy." George grinned. "I'd rather do 'dick all' and get 'shit' for it, then work my 'ass off' and still get dumped on."

The surroundings as they walked and talked, a new route unfamiliar to Bob, only seemed to be of secondary importance to the rest of the structures' activity, but as earlier he let his curiosity swivel his head back and forth as they went.

"We wouldn't mind the attitude problem around here if the Dwarf was at least a little bit worth idolizing. But as a status symbol he stinks. He's got one of the worst track records for absenteeism in the plant." George said. "Why, the only guy I know who gets more time of then him is 'Santa Claus". And another thing, when he asks you something, don't let him pick your brains. Even if it is, 'Slim Pickens'.

"Whoew" Fred shot back, with a wounded smile on his face, and Bob chuckling. "Who you 'pickin' on? Me or the boss?"

"Take your 'pickins'. George grinned. "I'm sure there's enough insinuated insults to go around for everyone."

The canteen they were after was the same one George had used earlier. And as they gradually covered the distance separating them, they purposely found other things less irritating to talk about by showing their new friend the wide variety of comical 'safety' signs mounted on the walls. But the biggest rounds of laughter that came their way, was when they encountered wall mounted 'Herman' jokes that had been purposely altered to identify with places and personnel Fred and George knew worked in the plant.

Since coffee break periods were universal throughout the plant, they were far from being the only ones on their way to the canteen. And as it grew nearer, so did the number of people briefly acknowledging Fred and George's passing presence. But it was the appearance of one of the company's stranger type employees, even by George's standard that suddenly caught their attention. Faltering slightly, George altered only his course, while saying, "Wait here." he then continued towards what had to be the strangest looking sight Bob could ever recall having crossed paths with.

The worker, if he was aware of their presence, didn't acknowledge it even the slightest. He even continued to sit perfectly motionless as George walked up to where he was at. And as George reached out and yanked free the paper that was scotch taped to the center of his forehead, the seemingly hypnotized individual didn't twitch even the tiniest bit.

George, his attention now on the magazine page now within his grip, flipped it over to see what was on the side facing inward, before mumbling, "Hmm, not bad Billy boy, not bad. Real breeding stock this time I'd say." as his eyes took in the glossy picture of the overly top heavy nude young female printed on the surface of the paper. Then, in just as easy a motion as he had used to lift the picture - he replaced it back onto the almost identical spot, before adding "Enjoy your break Willy. We'll talk to you later." He then headed back to where he had left smiling Fred, and a dumbfounded looking Bob. And before he could even ask 'What in the h - e - double upside down seven's was that all about?' George smiled out the answer.

"Not everyone lives on solids alone you know. Ol 'tit-man' Wilhelm back there once told me he was never weaned as a youngster. And every time he sees a real healthy looking 'heifer', he not only gets a 'boner' and a craving for a big glass of milk, but he's also good for the whole day."

Needless to say the air hung with laughter, and when they finally entered the busy complex, it didn't take long to realize that he was walking into someone's potential 'gold-mine'. He was also just about to comment on the amount of human activity, by asking who was keeping an eye on the rest of the plant, when his eyes fell onto something that briefly made him question his vision, or was he really seeing double?

Even though they were still moving George detected Bob's brief gesture of confusion, and offered the answer to what had caused the perplexed reaction.

"You're not seeing double my friend, that's only the Langly twins. You might say that God in his wisdom decided not to put too much lack of intelligence all in one body, so he split it up."

"Ya." Fred chuckled. "And you'll probably have the chance to see some woman around here who could use the same kind of blessing. Only are 'the-e-ey' ugly!"

Because of the sudden large selection of company personnel now around them Bob's vision once more eagerly started eating up everything within their range. Even as they all laughed at something new they had found briefly to pick on, George's right hand dug deep into his pant pocket in search of money while saying, "Since it's your first day with us we'll buy. I'll get the coffees and Fred'll get the dognuts - or would you rather have a hot chocolate?"

"Hell no!" Bob's answered, his face matching the excitement in his voice. "All that stuff's good for is giving your 'crap' color." If it's okay with you, I'd just as soon have a caffeine, free pop."

"Say, does that caffeine, free shit really work? Fred asked. "I've heard it helps you sleep better."

"All I know is that it works for me." Bob smiled. "I used to wake up in the middle of every night, just to drain my bladder'. Now I sleep right through the night, just like a baby."

"Gee, that sounds great." Fred continued.

"Not really." Bob frowned. "I still have a 'whiz', only now I sleep right through it."

Trying to hold back the laughter the remark had invoked in each of them would have been futile, especially when George had added, "Now there's an image I don't need in my head. You in a big diaper.", even if it was enjoyed by only them. And the small beehive of activity going on around them, was just as eagerly involved in its own existence, as Bob split off to head for a close-by pop machine.

Once there, someone else had beat him to the unit containing the brand he preferred. As well as being occupied rocking the metallic monolith back and forth on its legs, Bob was just in time to hear him mumble "Puttin money in these damn things is like gambling in Vegas."

It was very obvious that the person still emotionally shaking the mechanical thief had not really been speaking to anybody in particular. But it didn't stop Bob from adding something from him brand of humor to the frustrated comment. "Personally I think the odds in Vegas are one a Hell of a lot more in your favor."

The small chuckling smile he received in return for his comment was the only thing Bob got out of that area. Not being a gambler by nature, he quickly walked over to another monolith dispenser and settled for an alternative brand of soda.

Returning to where he had left Fred and George, he was just in time to join them as they were picking up the refreshments they had ordered. George, obviously still the one in charge of their small trio, said, "We better have our break on the job site. That way if 'you know who' shows up, it'll give him one less thing to gripe about."

Heading for the door, they were almost out of the building when the same group of women George had almost collided with earlier, only now larger by three familiar members, came into the canteen. Instantly, as if their eyes were magnetized poles searching out each other, their vision locked onto one another's as the distance between them quickly started to dwindle.

Bob's glare was proof that beauty was universal to all ethnic races, and it was more through animalistic instinct that he stared at a beautiful blonde-headed creature almost centralized by the marching group. George's attention was instinctively preparing itself for a possible defense, as he looked into a small sea of bobbing faces only briefly friendly towards his. Fred, still a slight emotional coward since separating from his wife, forced his eyes to glance towards George, as if hoping to be able to drain off some of his closest friend's seemingly endless courage.

The women in turn, Carla Daniels man hater leading the pack, altered their course just enough so as there could be no doubt that their paths would collide, especially if no-one failed to give any ground.

Most of the charm present, although no one appeared overly aggressive as of yet, was mainly on the faces of the men. And just when it seemed as if their worlds were indeed about to mix, both ranks split just enough to allow them to pass between each other. George offered a 'Morning, ladies." as Fred and Bob smiled on in bewilderment. The only decipherable reply they received in return for their friendly gesture, was a mixed barrage of short mumbled obscenities, masqueraded as light womanly giggles.

Once out of the canteen only Bob bothered to look back, George remarking, "That's another thing we're going to have to fill you in on, later." The remark only served to snap his attention back in George's direction, as he continued, "I don't know how you and the wife get along, but around here we call married ladies in that gathering 'dragons', with the nastier of the group naturally labeled as 'Dragon Ladies'."

Fred, as always eager to get in on the fun, no doubt because they were out of ear shot, offered, "In case you didn't notice back there - some of that double ugly I was telling you about had made its way to a few other members of that group."

Chuckling slightly while looking from George to Fred and then back again, Bob said, "I realize some of them were a good argument for bachelor-hood, but whose gorgeous daughter was that blond 'goddess' in the middle of the group?

"Oh that was Louie Zupanic" Fred eagerly answered. "Poor girl lost her husband over two years ago in a car accident, and since then most of the older man haters in the plant have taken her under their protective wings. "With her 'Playboy' bunny body" using both hands to outline an invisible shape in the air in front of them, Fred groaned slightly, while continuing with, "even some of the married men have hit on her for a date, if you know what I mean, jellybean."

In reaction to Fred's suggestiveness, and in keeping with the innuendo, a low almost crude 'wolf whistle' escaped from Bob's lips.

And then his voice was dripping with regret when he spoke. "If I wasn't so addicted to 'Chinese food' even I'd be tempted."

"And you wouldn't be the only one." George cut in. "Fortunately being 'over the hill' doesn't mean we can't occasionally stop, look, and enjoy the scenery. With Louie, and she's really one of the nicest members of the female gender you'll ever get to meet around here, as well as 'don't go there' if you're thinking of making any crude references about her looks, she has the habit of wearing jeans so bloody tight I swear you can almost read the dates on the loose change in her pockets."

While pretending to look back in hopes of visually confirming the remark, the women were long out of view, Bob instantly and justly also gave it the 'rib tickling' it deserved, by starting to comment, "I thought you just said," which George quickly cut off with, "Never mind what I said. This is one of those cases where you 'do what I say', not 'what I do'." And even though bob looked like he was about to object, George cut him off with what else was also now on his mind.

"While we're enjoying ourselves with the subject of Louie, I guess now's as good a time as any to fill you in on what's planned for later this afternoon." And as they walked back towards the job site, he did exactly that, periodically peppering the information with the occasional bit of lewd suggestive gestures.

Fred, always at the ready to assist and help out, took just as much pleasure in adding his 'tidbits' of information, his hands cutting a shapely figure through the air as George had done. He told a grinning Bob of how some of the other men in the plant liked to infer that Louie's noticeably large breast endowments were often referred to as 'Donald Ducks' mostly unseen members of the family 'Hewie' and 'Dewie'. He also couldn't contain his definitely contagious emotions while informing him that he was about to become a part of something that would within the plants vast community, live long while probably going down in the facilities memorable history.

Chapter # 4

'Louie's prank.'
Or
The 'Axe man cometh.'

As predicted earlier by George, the 'Dwarf' was indeed waiting at the job site when they got back. The sour looking expression on his face, as usual, gave every indication that he was no doubt in the mood to open his mouth to exchange feet. But George had no intention of allowing him that privilege, at least not until he had earned it.

"We were just showing Bob where one of our canteen is located, especially for when it's his turn to buy. We don't mind giving him a 'free ride', carrying him until he gets to know the routine, but we'll be dammed if we'll feed him for free along the way to."

"And it took 'both' of you to do that? Farkas said, his head pointing in Fred's direction.

As to be suspected it was immediately clear that Farkas was looking for fault in their action, no matter how trivial. But George still did his genuine best from letting their meeting deteriorate to that level just yet. And fortunately at times, such as now, he had no trouble in conjuring up a false smile when answering, "You know how it is sometimes. We wanted to show him a little bit of the plant along the way, and two pair of eyes can sometimes pick out things that one person might overlook. Since it is his first day on company land, we figured we better show him his way around. Ya know. Just in case of an emergency and he had to get out of here real fast."

"Ya. And next we're going to show him the locations of a few washrooms." Fred quickly added. Bob just as quick to fall into the verbal debate around him - assumed his silly looking idiotically grinning disguise, as Fred added, "Just in case of another kind of an emergency."

His added remark brought a smile to only their features. Ol Athlete's Foot apparently still preferred to remain frigid to their reception, as his face fought hard to maintain its dignity, when he said, "If you guys insist on consistently trying to drown your livers, why don't ya just take the following days off work. That way you'll feel better, and I'm willing to bet the company will be just as happy about it to."

The little slamming on most other occasions would have been all that was needed to invoke a justifiable verbal rebuttal from George. Instead, mainly because of Bob's presence, he handled it as gently as possible.

"We can't. Our wives don't want us hanging around the house when their 'soaps' are on TV." His nature wanted to add the rest of what was in his mind, "Besides, we're a Hell of a lot more afraid of 'them' then we are of you or this place." but he successfully fought off the urge.

The Dwarf, obviously still suicidal, kept right on feeding George remarks that even anyone with a registered 'I.Q.' lower than that required to become a foreman could have answered.

"If you guys are not going to get this job finished today I just might change my mind about leaving Bob here with you."

As soon as the word "Uh." popped out of Fred's mouth, George knew that his friend was about to-do exactly what he himself had so painfully been trying to avoid.

"Well if you do change your mind, please call us and let us know what you 'got' for it."

"Is that supposed to be an attempt at humor at 'my' expense?" Farkas snapped.

"Not if you have to ask." Fred grinned in his frustrated opponent's direction. It was a 'slamming' proving that his years exposed to George's verbal sparing was not all in vane.

George, even though he could easily stop the present sparing of wits, let it continue just a little bit longer as a favor to his friend, especially since he considered the foreman to be only half-equipped for the battle. And when the boss shot back with, "You've been hanging around with George Stone so long that you're startin' to sound exactly like him, 'ridiculous!'" to which George couldn't help but chuckle. "Why thank you! Now, are you going to let us finish our coffee break? or are you going to keep us tied up gabbin' so long that there's no way we're going to get this job done today?" he said.

The Dwarf may have been under matched when it came to a verbal confrontation with George, but he wasn't so stupid that he didn't recognize a rare chance to make a safe retreat when it presented itself, like now. Turning to leave, he simply replied, "I'll be back later." before parting.

George was usually the first to reply with a sarcastic witticism. "Thanks for leaving!" being one of his favorite for someone departing, but it was Fred who verbally gored the Dwarf just a little bit more before he was totally out of hearing range.

"Right! And if we've got ten minutes spare time at the end of our shift, we'll 'paint' the shop!"

Bob wisely waited until the boss had finally disappeared from view before expressing what had been in his thoughts when the foreman had essentially warned that he would be back later. "In our shop when someone used to tell us they'd see us later, we would always say similar, 'Thanks' for the warning!"

"We used to say that too," George said, before taking a large swig of his coffee. "But we've always prided ourselves in constantly trying to improve or create new slamming material, especially where 'ol shit-for-brains is concerned. Personally, I find that when he starts talkin' to you it's just like having long strands of stringy gum you've just stepped on, irritatingly stuck to the bottom of your shoe. And even though you end up trying to scrape it off, or whatever else you might try, you just can't completely get rid him."

"Ya, and he's just being kind about what some of us really feel about the boss," Fred added. "As for myself, I always felt he was so stupid that he thought a 'watchdog' was an animal that cold tell you what time of the day it was, but only if you asked him."

Reading the sometimes look of confusion occasionally passing over Bob's face whenever the foreman was verbally abused, he knew that now was as good a time as any to let him know the reason and whole truth about why George justifiably had reasons to pick on or dislike the Dwarf.

"Just so you don't get to thinking that we're a little bit twofaced when saying to always be nice, and then pick on the 'Dwarf' every chance we get, I guess it's about time you got to know the reasons why."

George, smiling, "Go ahead! you row for awhile, and I'll try not to let my feet drag in the water. Besides, you're apt to be a Hell of a lot kinder with the details when telling him the story."

"Don't bet on it!" Fred chuckled, before turning his head back in Bob's direction. "But I 'am' the only other man in the plant who knows the whole reasons as to why they're always at each others throats."

Noticing Bob leaning a little bit closer as he had been speaking, Fred couldn't help but continue to grin as his apparent desire to hear gossip, just like every other man he knew in the shop.

"Well, as strange as it might sound, I guess you might say that the start of their dislike for one another, 'dislike' being the gentlest word I can think of to use at this time, was born even before knowing each other existed. Before Farkas arrived in the plant we used to have a shop leader with just a warped sense of humor, and almost just as off center as most of us. He not only could give a joke, but could also take one with the best of em. And it was just the kind of 'good nature attitude' that often set him up for involvement in a variety of jokes or pranks, mostly spontaneous."

'Try to keep it down to a thousand words or less will ya." George chuckled. "Just give him the abbreviated edition."

"Don't, rush me!" Fred snarled. "Or I just might forget who's supposed to be the 'villain' in this story."

"Well you better hurry up and spit it out," George smiled back. "Remember, just the facts 'Jack', just the facts."

"Well if you'll stop butting in 'buddy', " Fred shot back, 'I'll get err done!"

Not giving George a chance to retaliate, even though it looked like he wasn't going to, Fred turned his attention back onto a wisely silent smiling Bob.

"Now then, as I was 'saying'. Before our previous boss retired, he and 'shit disturber' here were involved with a classic. We were all involved with a repair job where we needed some measurements before ordering any new replacement parts, and you can guess who among us in their infinite wisdom forgot to bring their measuring tape with them."

As Bob's vision faulted long enough to glance in George's grinning direction, Fred kept right on with his story.

"Well, after shifting the blame onto someone else by saying that they must have borrowed and forgotten to return it, he quickly rectified the problem by asking to borrow a tape from one of the other men standing close-by. As fate would have it the foreman just happened to be on his hands and knees in order to get a better lower view of the worn segment. And old' 'smart-ass' here, never one to pass up an opportunity to utilize anyone else's disadvantage, reached out to take the requested measuring tape now being offered from the man across from him."

A quick glance at George by both of them only found that he was apparently more interested with cleaning his fingernails, then basking in the glory of one of his pranks. But it didn't stop Fred from using a little of his own body English to emphasize the words and action he was presently mentioning.

"In one fluid motion he instead of taking the tape - grabbed the unsuspecting man by the wrist and pulled him forward. Surprise being on his side, he easily caught the worker off balance. The poor bugger ended up arms and legs flaying spread eagled across the back of our just as unprepared foreman. From there on, and I'm sure by the smile on your face that you're having no trouble envisioning the image inside your mind that this would have created, everyone, and I 'do' mean everyone, especially after someone had shouted 'I hope you're wearing a 'rubber'!' was to worn out from the ensuing laughter to get ay decent work done that day."

"But you said that was your old boss." Bob chuckled, but in a questionable like manner.

"Bare with me." Fred continued to smile.

"That incident was to be only a part of the groundwork given to Farkas during his introduction when being informed about the best and worst of each worker he would have working under him when he took over. George having a bit more colorful reputation preceding him was just naturally on the Dwarfs mind when something happened that seemed to have just too much of a similar end result to have been just accidental, especially since it took place within the first week of meeting us."

"George and I were running a little bit late, as was customary for a Friday morning, when we were scheduled to meet Farkas on site. We were to help with refurbishing a large cast-iron ram, with a thin protruding extension located unfortunately at just the right height to be both dangerous and humiliating to any average unsuspecting male."

Still using body English, the palm of his right hand facing downward and at manhood level, Fred let his face express the pain and sickening feeling anyone who had received a bump to his testicles would have experienced, which every male member of the human race could in all probability relate to. Bob, his own face almost identically imitating through his own past contacts the sickening sensation that went with them, even managed to let out a small moan to emphasize that he knew all to well exactly what Fred was trying to describe.

"Well, to put it as human as I can, Farkas was bent over this segment in order to get a better view of the cracked area in question. George, always a leader instead of a follower, was the first one around the screens set up to protect the surrounding area and personal from any welding to be performed. With Farkas bent down out of sight, and with us thinking that we had actually beat him there, George unintentionally walked right into you know whose rear end. The free 'goose' he must have got was never mentioned, possibly because it was lost in the loud scream that had followed when the protruding segment had jammed him right in the middle of afore mentioned delicate location, his 'nuts'. And just as unfortunately, as we all seem to for some strange reason have the urge to laugh after witnessing any such incident, we couldn't totally control ourselves while watching poor old huffing and puffin Farkas hobbling around on tipsy toes, while holding onto the family jewels."

"Needless to say, he qualified for some justifiable recuperation time off. And before the accident investigation committee had a chance to investigate the incident it, especially after the 'Dwarf' swearing it was no accident and looked as if we were going to get some time off too. Not even George's repeated apologies to Farkas, while swearing that it really really was an accident could make him see that it was just that, a freak' accident. It apparently was a no win scenario, especially after it came out later that a few of the other workers also didn't believe it either, something that only seemed to encourage them to be at each others throats from then on. Let's face it, I'm sure all of us can only say that we're sorry so many times, before getting tired of hearing it even for ourselves."

"Well I would say that was a little shallow for a good leader to act." Bob smiled. "He should be able to overlook such an incident, no doubt even be forgiving to promote an atmosphere of goodwill among the workforce."

"Oh he was 'forgiving' alright." Fred continued. "He was 'for giving' everyone a hard time, probably right after every time he had to urinate!"

"Especially after someone was stupid enough to bring in a couple of old 'jock straps' and leave them laying around with a pair of oranges stuffed inside for Farkas to see." George offered. "It had about the same results as waving a flag, or in his case a pair of red blood stained shorts, in front of a bulls face. Personally, I think he should have just looked at it as taking one in the testicles for the team, I know on occasion I have!"

"But the 'piece de resistance'," Fred cut back in, "was when someone told him about an incident in the change room where someone, someone who had been approached about being considered as foreman material, had ended up with their shorts being repeatedly yanked down around their ankles, at the most 'embarrassing' of times."

"Oh, now I see." Bob grinned. "Everything seems to be aligned towards our mister Stone here picking on the foremen, whenever he can."

"Not all of the time." Fred frowned. "In the last situation he is only reputed to be the culprit. In this incident a worker was in the process of getting dressed to go home. Another man who changed beside him, as well as looking ten month pregnant, was bending over drying his legs when he lost his balance. In that brief instant, something born to manipulate all of us, genuine instinctive reflex's kicked in and he just naturally grabbed as the closest object nearest to him in order to keep from falling down. Unfortunately the closet thing to him just happened to be the bare legs and 'jockey shorts' of his next-door buddy. And again, as fate would intervene, someone else on his way from the showers just happened to be walking by the end of the change isle just in time to see one man on his hands and knees, facing the exposed genital area of another. Needless to say a pregnant rumor was instantly born, which fortunately only someone here with our friend's talents has the ability to stop in its tracks."

Chuckling, no doubt due to the insinuating images that must have popped into his head, Bob inquisitively asked, "Why's that?"

"For just two very good reasons." Bob answered. "Firstly because the unwritten rule among most of the workers has always been that no-one will deliberately say or do anything which can inflict long term harm to another fellow worker. Which is just as well in this case, because one of the men involved is the timid type who will break out with a nosebleed if you so much as sneeze loudly in his direction. And lastly, because almost no-one who still has control over their bowels has enough intestinal fortitude to really tangle 'assholes' with one of the plants reputed 'leading' 'assholes', the 'Axman'!"

The wink he gave George at the inference to his reputation, was just as quickly returned with a short protruding tongue from his best friend, as he continued.

"Unfortunately though there are still a few who haven't learned that lesson which is probably why there was a short run in the 'rumor mill' that George was possibly one of the men."

"Didn't you ever dispute or verify it" Bob asked, while glancing at George.

"Naw. Why give any of those idiots even the breath it takes to mention it. I've had a Hell of a lot worse things thought about me, and I'm still here. I only let the truth bother me."

"Well, I guess it's true." Bob chuckled. "Some problems in this world are consistent no matter where you go. In our old shop we used to joke about one particularly arrogant foreman having a flock of geese on his farm, each named after one of the men working under his authority. Rumor has it that each and every time one of these men gave him a rough day at work, he'd go home and kick shit out of the goose or goat labeled with that guy's name.

"Sounds like one Hell of a great idea to me," George laughed.

"Gee, and here I thought we had the only 'Poop Head' in this town workin' over us." Fred added.

"I say this more as fact than an unneeded shot at revenge" George said. "But the Dwarf's definitely got what you might call a 'laxative' outlook on life. If everything doesn't 'look' shitty to him, anything he eats or touches soon is."

Pausing long enough to add his laughter to Fred and Bob's, George then quickly added. "But enough pickin' on such an easy target, not to mention the fact that it's startin' to throw me off my break. Let's pick on something else for awhile."

"Well at least he didn't throw the 'Overtime Kings' at us this time." Fred chuckled.

"Overtime Kings?" Bob more asked then said.

"Ya." George offered. "Whenever he thinks he can drop a 'guilt' trip onto or shoulders, he throws a couple of what he likes to refer to as 'dedicated to the company' names at us. You must have had them where you worked last. You know those guys who worked every bit of overtime they could get their greedy little pay cheques on."

Instantly zeroing in on what their next topic was apparently going to be about, Bob let out a soft 'Oh.' before offering a small piece of his history on the subject. "We use to refer to them as the people who would play 'Hide and seek, for a thousand a week.'

"You got it." Fred beamed, before George could offer, "With our 'Kings' came such rumors that they spent so much time in here that they had the mail forwarded to this place."

"As well as their home phone having the exact same numbers as the company's" Fred laughed.

Chuckling himself, Bob threw in, "We use to like to say that they spent so much time in the plant that it was highly likely that all of their kids were adopted."

"Oh, that opens to many doors." George quickly added, a look of mischief on his face before adding, "Especially if any of their kids looked even a little bit like any of the foreman they worked under."

"Under!" Fred exploded. And then looking directly at Bob he added, "You realize that he's insinuating that it was their wives that worked under the foreman."

"I now. I know." Bob acknowledged with raised eye brows. "I'm not so slow that I didn't get the drift. And I thought we were bad when we used to ask them if they got Christmas cards from the income tax department thanking them and saying, 'Thanks! And please keep all that green stuff comin' in.'

"Our boys are a lot cruder then that." George smiled. "A few years back someone with a bad since of humor managed to paste together a combination of photos and magazine pictures that made it look as if the 'Kings' actually had their tents and campers set up in the company's parking lot. And as true as it hinted at, it only lasted a few hours once the word got around that one of the men was using all of his extra cash to set up his aging parents in a good rest home."

"And the moral of that story," Bob smiled softly, "is to make sure you do your homework first."

Pretty soon doughnuts and coffee weren't the only things being eaten away. Time and information about the women's part of the workforce, as well as Louie's upcoming prank, were also being consumed as George and Fred took turns doing what women were supposed to do best, "gossip". In the hour and a half it took lunchtime to work its way around, they had managed to pinpoint, often humorously while working, people and incidents that were more than memorable during some of their years in the plant. And they toped it all off with the statement, "You're going to come across those who believe that to know them is to love them, those who think the sun shines out of their wazoo, and those who are easily hypnotized by just the referral or sound of their own voice.

Unavoidably and almost instinctively, as they headed for the lunch area, free flowing friendly conversation became a natural part of their time together. It was as if all of the other things around them were of secondary importance, but not intentionally. And the fact that Bob was originally from both a different culture and living location, only served to give Fred and George fuel to humorously prepare him for gags or ribbings that often went with such topics.

They also informed him that there was a lot of 'local' truth to the old philosophy 'out of sight, out of mind.' when describing some of the other workers, a good example being the worker they had just passed.

"See that guy back there." George smiled, his eyes pointing the way.

"Sure!' Bob smiled. "I saw him, why?"

"Doesn't he remind you of somebody, even a little bit?" Fred asked.

Staring momentarily at the individual, someone apparently more interested in the pigeons' overhead, he smiled "Why yes, now that you mention it. He does looks a little bit like the 'King'."

"And that's why a lot of the other workers refer to him as an 'Elvis' stand-in." George offered.

"He's an Elvis Presley stand-in?" Bob said- bewilderment in his voice and on his face. "Why's that, does he also sound just like him, and can he sing?"

"Neither." Fred chuckled. "He just looks a little like the King. As for his being a 'stand-in', that's just a little dig the men have put in. It refers to his working status ability. Chances are that if we come back this way later on in the day, there's about a ninety nine percent chance he'll still be 'standin in' the same spot."

Curiosity still being what it was, even as they all laughed, Bob naturally inquired as to how the words applied to the men in this plant were any different than the ones he had just left behind. George gladly then told him that most of the men liked to consider themselves 'as one of a kind' and classify themselves as being literally 'out of this world', when describing there own personalities, while he in turn just liked to classify them as mostly being 'out of their minds!'

"We used to say," Bob added with a hint of laughter to his words, his eyes narrowed and hands clasped in front of him again, "Every mans work - is portrait of ones self."

"Well then that other fellow we just nodded 'Good morning' at as we passed him fits your words of wisdom to a tee. Around here he's called 'Windbreaker!'

Glancing back just long enough to easily see that the man's dark high cheekbones and jet black hair hinted of heritage, Bob asked, 'I can't see where anyone would deliberately name him after a light winter jacket, so it must have have something to do with his tribes ceremonial background."

"Neither!" George smiled. "It was born out of his preference of eating hot spicy foods, and their often 'silent but deadly' assaulting side effects."

It only took about two seconds, as Fred quickly used one of his hands to pinch his nostrils while the other fanned at the air in front of him, before Bob let out a face wrenching 'O-o-h!' of recognition.

And George, while making the same gesture in Fred's direction, briefly smiled at his buddy, "Remember what they say about people who live in glass houses shouldn't be throwing rocks." before turning his attention back on to their newest friend, and adding, "Exactly! His ability to 'break wind', sometimes seemingly on demand, has the capability of splitting a room in half much quicker than any thrown tomahawk!"

When they finally found themselves back at the lunch tables, they weren't the first or last to arrive. some of the men were well into their groceries, inhaling a sandwich or de-boning a piece of fruit, while busy talking all about one of the more morbid subjects they often liked to make fun of - 'death'.

George's philosophy on the subject, most of the workers already knew his feelings about life and death because of past conversations on the morbid topic, was that when you're born they pull you out of a small hole - and when you die they drop you back into a bigger one. And the rest of his attitude on the subject was - that nobody in this world really 'owns' anything. They only got to 'use' whatever it was that they had spent most of their lives acquiring, while their time here on earth. And with their passing from where-ever it is they may have been that they originally came from, everything they thought to selfishly call 'theirs' will likely pass to someone else with the same foolish belief.

Along the way to the tables, after having tried to talk Bob into joining in on their little poker game get-together scheduled for later that night, with a possible 'maybe.' being the answer, it had been mutually decided that he would permanently sit beside them at their reserved seating arrangements. And when they finally got to sit down, their lunches retrieved from a company refrigerator supplied to the eating area, George made sure his voice was loud enough for every-one there to hear.

"Anybody have any objections if our new man Bob here joins the 'coffee club'?

The response he got was not only immediate but expected - when they let their attention focus in his direction. All that is except one genuine 'half wit' had offered 'Bob-Who?' for the rest the replies were a series of smiling 'No - o - s.'

George then proceeded to explain to Bob what the coffee club consisted of by telling him that each man paid five dollars a week into the club, and was then entitled to drink as much coffee as his greedy little bladder permitted. Those greedy enough to want to make sure they get theirs and everyone else's moneys worth often develop a caffeine induced rush side effect."

"And it also makes them capable of being able to stay awake long enough to watch all of the 'late shows' even if they didn't want to!" Fred added.

An immediate big grin from Bob was all that was really needed to confirm that he would gladly join, even after his eyes had temporarily looked at one of the other man's obviously oversized coffee mug. Fred caught the brief stare and quickly responded to it once more, with, "That's not a coffee cup! It's really a small bowl, with a handle on one end."

George quickly followed in with his own interpretation, "Personally it always reminds me too much of the potty I sat on as a kid."

"I heard that!" the one being zinged half-laughed. "You don't hear me barkin' about your bottomless cup, do you? I just like to save trips."

"Which he always spends on just trips to the washroom, and more I might add." one of the other workers chuckled.

"Ignore them," George smiled at Bob, "Believe it or not, the one with the bottomless bladder actually used to be talented at one time. In fact, he was one of the best 'arm fart' players this place ever produced."

"Pretending to ignore the slamming, the other man took a short sip from the big mug now in his hand before saying out of the side of his mouth, "Chuck you Farley".

"And I love you, too, 'Fart Face'." George smiled back,

Fighting a battle he knew he couldn't win, the now smiling coffee drinker shifted his attention in Bob and Fred's direction temporarily, before adding. "When you guys are ready to leave again, remind me to be the first one to thank ya's".

"With your memory, I'm sure we'll have to remind you." George shot back.

Wetting the tip of one finger with his mouth, his eyes now back on the coffee in front of him George's opponent then pretended to mark off an invisible number one in the air above him, while adding, "That's one I owe you."

Bob obviously enjoying what he was watching, whispered in George's ear, "Does that mean he thinks he's won the battle?"

While saluting, his heels clicking together, George smiled and answered, "Around here, we all win, or we don't play. Teddy boy over there is one of those rare few you believe would die for you if he had to. So if he likes to think he's one up on me, I'll do my best to confirm it,"

In between pretending to stick his finger down his throat, Fred said, "Boy! What a load of sentiment. The only time you let anyone off with the last word, is when you know you're going to dump on them again later!"

"Could be." George winked in Bob's direction. "Could - be."

As was becoming a custom with them now, they all laughed at the remarks, and it lasted right up until they all had a hot cup of the debatably rejuvenating liquid in front of them. They then, with George naturally leading the way, got into the conversation already underway - while eating their lunch also.

By this time, the men were into funerals and their fears of being buried alive, when Rusty said "When I die, I'm not taking the chance of being buried alive. I'm going up the chimney. I'm being cremated."

George used it as his chance to get into the conversation, and quickly commented, "You just keep suckin' away on those 'cancer sticks' the way you do, and you just might get that chance a Hell of a lot sooner than you think. As a matter of fact, you keep smokin' at all the way you are right now, I'm pretty sure you'll eventually get all of yourself into that astray in front of you. Then where would your family be?"

"Very funny, smartass, "Jack Ellis shot back sarcastically. "And I'll thank you to leave my family out of your sarcasm."

The men more than loved opportunities to watch one another getting slammed. In fact, they practically thrived on it, especially if they were in no immediate danger of getting picked on also. So it was not unusual when the smart ones just sat wordlessly smiling and watching the entertainment unfolding in front of them, as had happened when George had first arrived.

"Well, just because you don't smoke," Rusty continued, no real animosity in his still sarcastic sounding voice, "you didn't think any of us should either."

"On the contrary," George chuckled. "Go ahead and smoke. That way if you do get terminally ill and croak, you'll not only make way for a new worker, but chances are that just maybe he or she won't have your same bad habit."

"It's easy enough for you to condemn smoking," Rusty answered. " you've never had the habit."

"Look" George replied, a note of noticeable seriousness in his voice now. "I'll make a deal with ya. If you'll quit smoking for the rest of the year, I'll take you, with all of your family, out for a free meal at a restaurant of you choice. But if you start 'puffin' away again before the time's up, and remember that being a non-smoker I can detect old fumes a mile away, you'll take me and my family out for a meal under the same conditions."

"Are you kiddin?" Jack more choked then laughed.

"Seriously." George imitating his gestures by pretending to 'hack', coughed out his replied. "And just to give a little bit of more incentive to stop, if you do decide to take the offer, I'll even bring a family snapshot of everyone involved standing around the fridge."

"That's why I asked if you were kidding." Rusty continued to choke and laugh. "I've seen the size of you family, especially your growing boys. And that wouldn't be the refrigerator they would be standing around, it would be the family vault! Why, if I lost out on your idea of a bet, I'd have to mortgage the house just to pay off the restaurants' cheque."

"And with no money left over for a tip," the same as earlier co worker jumped in once more, "the waiter will probably be out in the parking lot, waiting to thump ya."

"And that's where the incentive part really comes in." George beamed. "You break down, you have to spread for our meal, consequently leaving you with enough of a monetary shortage that you will not be able to afford those 'cancer sticks' for at least the next two years. Either way, I win."

"No - o - o - o - o thank you. I'll pass." Jack laughed. "Besides, if I quit, it'll be just one less thing you have to bitch about around here."

"Well, in that case, "George said, still noticeably serious, "I don't think you should stink up the lunch area while someone who doesn't smoke is still eating their lunch, even if the odor of smoke isn't anywhere near as bad as the smell of your breath.

Unfortunately, even though most of what was being said was transpiring in 'jest', smokers for some reason known only to them, always seemed to feel that they are being discriminated against as soon as they are asked to temporarily refrain from smoking. And since most of the men at the tables were addicted 'lung burners', it was inevitable that some of them would feel the need to defend their polluting habit.

The first of them, a John Weller, tried to defend Rusty's earlier remark by saying in his defense. "Well if any of us do pass on due to our nicotine addiction, I guess the bright side of the situation will be that we wouldn't be around to listen or be subjected to your line of sarcasm any loner."

Feeling justified in offering his 'two pack a day' opinion, Slammin Sam jumped in with 'I used to look up to you."

"You're so short you have to look up to everybody." George quickly retaliated, his face still aglow.

As Fred jumped into the melee with, "Get that into ya!" in John's direction, someone else whining, "Why is it always the non-smokers who seem to know what's best for us, not to mention constantly giving us their unwanted advice on why we should quit."

Then someone else in the group, another apparent smoker, chuckled out, "He-e-e-re! Get that into ya!" which was another recognized symbol through out the plant, as a verbal putdown. But none of what had been said deterred George from getting in his own barbs, as the other men were laughing.

"Well, if you're anything like your Aunt Martha, we'll never get rid of you."

"And just what do you mean by that?" Weller asked, a justifiable hint of sarcasm on his face and in his voice.

George, obviously already pleased with that he was about to answer, couldn't help but have a big grin on his face, the features also being instantly contagious. "You may have the company fooled, but I know for a fact you were off work for her funeral at least three times in the last ten years. And if they had to bury her on three separate occasions just to get her underground, I don't doubt you're going to take a Hell of a lot longer - unless they smack you with a shovel just to make sure you're not faking it. Hell, now that I think of it, I'll even bet she died of embarrassment, rather than tell anyone she was related to you."

As could and should be expected most of the men who could relate to the words spoken actually seemed to lean closer, maybe in order to offer verbal support, but it was an act of encouragement George didn't need to keep the comradely alive.

"Don't you laugh. 'pickle puss'." George shot at the buddy almost straight across from him. "Everyone knows the only reason you can afford a new car and lots of other toys now is really due to the death of a very close and rich uncle, who was obviously very fond of you. Or should I say, 'What happened, they finally drain the harbor and find 'your ship' resting on the bottom, ya know the one full of money your were always saying was coming in some day'?"

As those not under fire at this time continued to laugh and chuckle on the sidelines, George continued back on the co-worker he had first started picking on. "But, anyway, you know what they say about absence making the heart grow fonder, I guess those of us left behind when you do 'burp out' will just have to look forward to bragging about how crazy we were about you."

Strangely enough, once on a roll, George swore on occasion he could sense his adrenaline starting to build. It was also something which just as strangely seemed to be contagious to those around him, and just as obvious when occasionally throwing themselves on their own sharp tongues.

"And in your case Danny," George pivoted his head and attention away from Rusty long enough to briefly 'slam' directly his next victim. "if they should happen to accidentally bury 'you' alive, you've got enough calories stored up to be able to hibernate for about a year. In which case I'm sure you'll just probably eat your way up out of the ground."

"I'm not 'fat'." Danny grinned, a little forced hint of being indignant dripping from his words, something none of the men really believed. "I just happen to hold more water than the average person."

"We'll I'll be damned." George continued to grin. "I always thought you were full of 'something'. But plain old 'water' would have been my last choice if I had to hazard a guess as to what it was. In fact, if what your saying is true, I've seen waterbeds that hold less fluid then you."

"Hell, if that's true," someone else offered. "instead of paying someone with a water truck to fill my pool, I'll just get you to come over and jump in."

"Ya," someone else laughed. "you do look more like your mother beat you with a 'drumstick' than an 'ugly stick'."

"Not to mention" another of the group jump in. "someone as big as you shouldn't be eating 'apples' in public."

"Well I'm trying to watch my figure." Danny continued to pretend to pout in defense.

"Next time you go to the fridge, just pretend it's locked!" someone in the outer circle of the gathering offered.

"Well if you don't get off that diet you're on, "George butt back in. "pretty soon you won't have to tilt your head in any direction to be able to see the outline of your body. And if you want to know when that time has come, just watch to see how many people there are sitting in your shadow on a hot sunny day at the beach."

Bob wanted to offer his own comment, his philosophy "If you're shittin twice a day, you're eating to much." to the barrage of 'slamming's' presently underway, but realized he possibly wasn't quit ready to be recognized or accepted into the gathering. So instead he just quietly sat and made sure to smile or laugh only when the rest of the incited mob did.

The relentless cannibalistic verbal attack, as often happened when their male bonding and humor was flowing, carried on when new fuel was thrown on the fire. "What's your gross weight Danny?" And when the joker beside him cut off any rebuttal with 'Who - o, cares!' But you were right when you said he was 'gross'!"

The follow up of "You'd care if he ever stepped on your foot, safety shoes or not!" were lost in the ensuing laughter.

"He eats any more, and I swear he's going to blow a rib!"

"Don't say that!" an escalating voice was heard. "I have to work with him occasionally. I can't afford any time off work."

This time it was Fred who gave out with the elongated "He-e-e-ere!" and when Terry Purcell opened his mouth to speak, "Well, I," George lost no time in throwing him into the barrel. "Don't worry 'Eagle Beak'. If someone ever accidentally buried you alive, with your nose you'd be dead through asphyxiation long before they ever got your carcass out of the funeral parlor."

As generally happened once the ribbings had become contagiously impregnated in everyone's mind, almost someone always eventually grew enough of a thick skin to almost grow a backbone to pick on George - but only because they foolishly believed in the old saying 'There's safety in numbers.' "What about you? I know for a fact you're not exactly on everyone's 'Christmas list'. Aren't you afraid they'll ever band together and you'll end up being buried alive?"

"The broad grin already at home on George's face grew noticeably wider now, and the men habitually knew they were in for something either hilarious or ridiculous. George, as usual, then did his best to live up to their expectations.

"When I go, I'm having a telephone buried in with me. That way if I wake up unexpectedly, I can call all of you bums, long distance I might add. And you can bet your ass it'll be collect. That is, if the line isn't dead also. But remember if you should return my call, just because I don't answer right away, doesn't mean I'm not home."

While the men were laughing, Terry asked, "And what do we do if the line's busy?"

"Well," George paused while shrugging his shoulders, as if seriously pondering the question, "Unless it's a matter of 'life or death'," which made the men laugh even harder. "you're just going to have to wait, and then try me again later. Don't forget, I could be on a party line."

"Well, if you do get buried alive, " Rusty added, "be sure to call "ol Farkas first. Hearing' from you, especially after thinking' you're safely 'planted' should be more than enough to make him croak and join ya. Shit! Now that I think of it, talk about a 'going away present'! Getting ride of you two at almost the same time, why, you'd be immortalized! The men would probably be burning a candle in your honor for years to come!"

As Rusty had been talking his voice had also been escalating with each word spoken. and it got to be so emotionally noticeable, that one of the men said, "Whoa! Slow down. Buddy or not, you hyperventilate, and I'm 'not' giving you mouth to mouth when you pass out, regardless of what you had to eat last!"

"And what makes you think that 'mouth to mouth' isn't what he's been after all along?" George grinned.

'Slingshot Bob' still stayed smart enough to just sit there, quietly smiling and laughing at the appropriate times. Fred also, also apparently feeling a little left out, waited until he was sure he had good reply for his friend's earlier remark, before jumping in.

"Well I think you getting stuck with a 'party line's' justifiable, especially the way 'you' like to party."

Everyone there, even Bob, got the significance of the intended pun well before Fred could let one of his hands cradle his still faintly hung over head. He continued speaking, "But maybe you should get one of those answering machines, you know, just in case you're out,"

"Out!" George's voice was not only loud now, but also excitedly fluctuating in tone with an over-emphasized expression on his face.

"Who the 'Hell' do you think I am, Dracula? The only 'out!' I'll be, is like in 'out cold!"

"Like you were last night!" someone on an apparent 'suicide' mission jumped in.

"Oh! And you were a 'beacon' of sobriety." George shot back. "At least I didn't have to keep asking for directions to the 'men's' room."

"Instead of the word 'out'!" another smiling partygoer offered in his friends' defense, "I think Randy should have said something along the lines of 'stiff', 'inebriated', 'ridged', or even 'shit faced'."

Enjoying the moment just as much as everyone else, as a few of the men let out a small gasp over the word 'shit faced' George offered only a big grin in rebuttal to reference to their weekly ritual. And it was here, as soon as it became apparent that he had no intention of verbally fighting back, that Rusty felt it was safe enough to pick up where he had left off.

"Well I guess every day will be like a Thursday for you then." he sarcastically laughed. You've drank yourself 'rigid' almost every Thursday since 'I've' known you".

"Very funny, brown finger's," George chuckled, "I just might take up Fred's suggestion and buy that answering machine, just to program it to phone wise guys like you in the middle of the night, so I can 'slam' ya!"

Bob's appropriately timed laughter, at least he had thought so, hadn't gone unnoticed by some of the other men at the table, he had even foolishly thought himself still immune to the friendly verbal 'back biting' just as long as he kept his mouth shut. It proved to be a gross misjudgment, just like George had tried to warn him about earlier, as soon as he decided to have a cigarette after his meal.

Reaching for an ashtray not presently being used on the table in front of him, three of the men in the group were presently already smoking, he instantly froze in his movements when a stern voice asked him just what the 'shit' he thought he was doing.

Immediately after his eyes had briefly sought out George's in the hope of obtaining a hint as to what was going on, his vision then settled onto that of the man who had made the surprising remark. And even though George's face had yielded only a slight hint of surprised humor in his search, which was natural considering it was the first time he had lit a cigarette in front of him, his own face and voice was one of genuine confusion when he almost timidly answered.

"Uh, why, I thought I'd have a cigarette."

Rusty's voice was still very stern as he continued, "You don't have to look to George for clearance when one of us is talking to you, or is he in charge of all of your decisions already? If that's the case, I guess we'll just have to nickname you as one of the 'Three Stooges'."

Still noticeably bewildered, Bob weakly only managed to get a singular confused word of "But" out of his mouth before Rusty continued his attack.

"There'll be no 'butts', until after you've had your smoke. 'But!', Before you earn that privilege, all I want to tell you is that if you're going to get along in here with us, the least you should do is to have the decency to ask if we 'minded' if you smoke?"

Still a little confused over if his leg was being pulled, even though it was plain to see that a few of the other workers were having trouble holding a serious expression on their faces, Bob slowly started to retract his hand away from the ashtray while offering, "Sorry. I didn't know I needed permission."

"Well you do!" Rusty then said his little act still in play. And as if to add more special effects to the tiny drama, he slowly and deliberately took his time while pausing long enough to light up one of his own coffin nails, while slowly over emphasizing every movement. "And if you had bothered to ask, we would have given you the same answer we give to all newcomers to the shop. Do you know what it is?"

Still justifiably hesitant, Bob's eyes once more quickly darted in his newest friends direction, only to surprisingly find himself looking at the back of George" head. He then timidly asked, "What?"

Playing the moment for everything he could get out of his audience, Rusty took a long pull on the cigarette in his hand. And not until had the total interest of everyone there as he blew two small rings and then a long stream of exhaled smoke into the air over his head, did he finally answer.

"Well, if you'd taken the time to ask if we 'minded if you smoke'," while pretending to reach up and grab at the two dissipating smoke rings still hanging close by, " we'd have said 'Only if you're on fire!"

The words were loud and almost spit in Bob's direction. But as soon as they were out everyone at the table especially George and Fred, broke out into a loud roaring laughter. And as soon as Bob's face indicated that he had finally realized that he was the victim of one of the many pranks his new friends had warned him about earlier, the laughing grew even stronger with as his vibrating body blended in with theirs.

In a way it had been a small joint invitation initiation into the group. and now that it was over, Bob not only leaned closer to the conversation he had previously only been a spectator to, but now also felt justifiably inclined to join in.

As was also common whenever the topic they had been talking about had become interrupted, the men just naturally floated away from it long enough to give the reason for their interruption a quick verbal going over. And since Bob and his desire to smoke had been the two reasons for the group's detour, George kept the topics in motion.

Glancing in Bob's direction, as Bob finally got around to lighting up the cigarette still in his grasp, George said, "If you knew how obscene that thing looks hanging out of your mouth, you'd quit smoking."

"How's that?" Bob said cautiously, now smart enough to checks the faces of the other men there for any clue as to what he might be being set up for.

But before George could answer, and only because they had used the same verbal insulting set up on other smokers' Fred quickly but in with the words, "You're thinkin'" about guys who smoke cigars, George, not cigarettes."

The other men at the table had also been a part of George and Fred's verbal attack on smoking, and they started to cough even before Bob could realize what he had insinuatingly been insulted about.

But just as soon as Bob did get the drift of the insult, he deliberately fought back with a sarcastic grin. "If the smoke bothers you, let me know." I'll move my cigarette, closer!" while recalling the advice given to him earlier about the three most important things to the men in the plant 'girls', 'gas', and 'gags'.

"Right idea, wrong direction." George grinned. " And even in the right direction, you couldn't move your cigarette away far enough to suit me."

As a gesture, even though had been smiling as he had spoke, George used both of his hands to fan away the sudden barrage of deliberate irritation now floating in his direction, courtesy of most of the other smokers at the table. One of the men, possibly accidentally on purpose but definitely well timed, gave out with a series of coughing wheezes that prompted George to add, "Boy, that stuff you're on must be doin' wonders for your body. If you can keep from spittin' out a piece of lung, ya just might be lucky enough to pull all your hemorrhoids back up inside."

As other men at the table, including Bob, made faces of disgust while saying," E-e-e-e-e-w", the man with the cough paused long enough to quickly say, "if you haven't tried it, don't knock it."

"No-o-o-o-o thank you!" George answered, using both his voice and his head to elaborate his true feeling about smoking, " I don't have to try something that could kill me, like washing exterior windows on the hundredth floor of the empire state building, just to know that I won't like it."

"Well if you fell, "Rusty grinned, "it'll be the first time in your life that you ever got anyplace real fast."

"Not much chance of that happening." someone quipped. "With our luck the wind would probably blow him onto one of the ledges."

"Which goes to show you that even 'God' doesn't want him!" another brave co-worker quickly added.

The remarks, like always, not only gave some of the men who would never have dared offer their opinion, kept on coming - as another of the men followed up with another round of "He-e-e-e-r! get that inta ya!"

George, like the rest of the men, even his closest friend - laughed. But he also made sure to pan them all while saying, "You bums aren't going to get rid of me that easily, even if the only people who'll be sorry to see me go are the ones holding the insured mortgage on my house."

"He's right." Fred spoke up, not just because he was so close to his best friend. "When you die, it doesn't matter if you have a million, or owe a million. And since you can't take any of it with you when you pass on, I figure there's no sense in havin anyone looking forward to or even glad to see you pushing up daises. Besides, we all know there's only one individual around here we'd all like to refer to as the 'dearly departed'."

Fred's last words had been dripping with humorous sarcasm. and as soon as one of the gathering whispered what was already on most of the other men's minds 'The Evil Dwarf!' another of them laughed, "Hell, when he does his best to 'make the heart grow fonder', I'm sittin in the cheering section at the farewell party."

"Don't hold your breath waitin for it to happen." Terry Purcell said. "It's a proven fact only the good die young, and ol Farkas is no doubt going to retire in better health then all of us put together."

"Say, that's an idea." Fred smiled. "When he retires maybe we should have a 'twenty one gun salute' for him."

"They only do that for funerals as a show of honor." Rusty said in disgust.

"Ya I know." Fred grinned devilishly. "Maybe someone will do us the honor of getting sloppy with their aim."

There could be no doubt by the way everyone instantly broke up laughing that the ides had tickled their funny bones. But George, his mind always ahead of the crowd, especially after enjoying the 'cheering section' chuckled, "It may sound like a great idea, but with most of you guys and your cross-eyed capabilities you're more apt to end up shooting each other, ya know, like in a 'Newfie firing squad'."

Unfortunately, at least people having a great time will always tell you, their brief break together was 'gone', confirmed by a brief horn blast close-by. But before any of them had a chance to get up from their tables, the very loved one still fresh in everyone's thoughts made his soon to be presence felt, which caused Rusty to whisper. "Oh, oh. Speak of the 'Devil'. It must be that time of the week again."

The remark, once checking to see what Rusty was looking at, made everyone there grin, everyone that is except Bob. He in turn, looking in George's direction for assistance once again, prompted a whisper response from one of the men beside him. "Just pay attention. If you're smart enough to still be able to identify yourself from a photo, you're smart enough to be able to figure out what we're talkin about."

Stopping at his customary location at the end of one of the tables, his crocodile smile was acknowledged half-heartedly by most of the men. The rest, especially George, just pretended to ignore his presence by turning their heads and attention away towards some imaginary destination. But the 'Dwarf', or rather this time the 'Devil' wasn't about to be ignored by the very people he had come to talk to, and he had to repeat his first remark before everyone finally gave him their attention.

"I'm sorry, are you talking to me? Or are you just talking?" George said?"

Naturally the remark, as the rest of the men wisely sat silently by in anticipation of the verbal abuse the foreman and 'Slammin Sam' usually threw at each other, brought an instant flush to the face of the one the remark it had been directed at. And the foreman turned his attention towards the other workers just long enough to tell them that it was time to get back on the job site, before venting his present feelings fully on George's direction.

"Are these constant verbal battles between us really necessary?"

With all indications of humor gone from his face and voice, George answered. "They must be. You keep coming back for more."

Those of the lingering workers still within hearing range chuckled just loud enough for Farkas' ears to pick up, which he wisely and purposely ignored. Instead he foolishly fed George more ammunition to make insults with.

"I know you and some of the men are just praying for the day I retire, but don't hold your breath. It won't be happening any time soon."

Even though George easily had a rebuttal ready, it was Fred who instantly shot back with a real 'zinger', a slamming well worth the pats on the back he would get later on. "Prayin! That's an understatement if I ever heard one. Why I know for a fact that 'Mister Acid Tongue' here has a two foot tall candle right now stashed in his change locker, and every morning when he comes into work he lights it up for about thirty seconds, just in case someone 'upstairs' is listening. Now I admit I can't hear whatever little prayer he's chanting under his breath, but apparently he's not whispering the right words."

Justifiably now, as George and Bob fought to suppress their emotional reaction, it was Fred who now became the subject of the dwarfs intimidating look, when retaliating.

"I can now see it was a big mistake to put Mister Wong with you two characters."

"Oh no!" Bob quickly blurted out, surprising everyone still there - as well as himself. "So far today I have learned far more than I had dared anticipate for a first shift."

At first Farkas was genuinely confused at Bob's remark. But as soon as the words, "If you know what I mean?" were quickly added to the end of his remark. Farkas believed from its delivery that his new employee was possibly trying to tell him more than what he was actually saying. In fact the words were so double edged that it made him do some quick back paddling.

"Ya, ya I guess my first decision was the right one. You better try and bear it out with these, these, two men a little bit longer."

The last remark, even though undoubtedly sounding as if it had sarcasm written all over it, could also be taken in a matter of different ways, all of which only seemed to make Fred and George, along with the rest of the backup choir, grin even more then they already were.

"But that's not what I'm here for." Farkas continued. "I have to go out of the plant on business for the rest of the day, and I have to know if the job you men are 'dogging', I mean 'working' on is a 'carry over'."

"It'll be done before four, at least our segment will be." George smiled. And Fred added, Ya, I guess the afternoon shift will have to find something else to lie about on their 'time sheets' tonight. Oh, I forgot. Only foremen are supposed to be able talk about the workers that way, I'm sorry."

Only Farkas straight faced the delivered obviously intended insult, to which he let his departing words fall in Bob's direction.

"Unfortunately I may be forced to leave you with these two comedians all next week, but I won't know that for sure until Monday. I wish I could leave you with better news, so instead I'll just wish you a pleasant weekend."

Indignantly turning in the direction he had arrived from, ol athlete's foot Farkas then walked away, without even attempting to offer George or Fred the same courtesy. But both ignored snickering men simply reacted to his appreciated departure in a way that was almost ritual.

"Company business 'my ass'." George chuckled. "Anyone who still believes that line should be lying on a coach someplace looking up at the ceiling and paying someone to listen to them lie."

"Doesn't he ever say anything about you or any of the other men always thinking of him as being so unlikable, may-be even an asshole? Bob smiled.

"Of course he does." George grinned. especially when he's not here. But then, we have no real big secrets between us."

"It's probably more like time for a haircut I'd say." Fred followed up with. And Bob immediately added something more to the remark, something he had noticed about his boss when first meeting him.

"When you hair's as rare as his, you don't just pay a barber to cut it, you also pay him a finders fee to locate it first, then pretend to be busy cutting what there is of it."

The remark not only made both men smile, but George to also add. "Well it's about time you got involved "Slingshot'"

"Slingshot. Slingshot! Fred said, noticeably totally confused, even as he and a few of the men who had rejoined them still chuckled about the 'slamming' they had shared in. And the look on his face prompted George to explain how he had come up with the 'handle' of a nickname, for Bob.

As soon as George swung one of his legs over the tables bench seat, both a gesture that it was time to get moving, as well as to stand up, the rest of the remaining men quickly imitated his moves. Once they were all erect and heading back in their job site's direction, George continued with "Don't anyone forget we've got "Louie's little prank scheduled for right after the two o'clock break."

James G. Davies Sr.

Even though Bob didn't ask what was planned for two o'clock, George could read the need to know on his face, and happily offered an answer. "Louie!' You remember the young woman back at the canteen don't you? Ya know, the one with the glass hour figure, lookin like it had recently been turned, and now most of the sand was still in the upper half!" Having mentioned one of those 'key; words that strangely always seemed to trigger something else they it is related to, George instantly went off topic long enough to say, "Speakin' of 'sand', one of the workers I forgot to mention to you is nicknamed 'Sand Trap', which in this case has nothing to do with golf. We'll probably be crossing paths with him sooner or later and now is just as good a time as any to warn how he got his moniker. His real handle is Billy Sands and he likes to play tricks of the other men, without them knowing it, by tape recording induced conversations about other workers in the plant, thus the word "trap', and then playing them back when the individual happens to be visiting, or whatever."

As a smile instantly appeared on Bob's face, George didn't wait for the verbal reply he didn't really expect, before continuing with what he had originally wandered away from. "Well, the company sponsors a 'first aid' course to any employee interested, and right now Louie is about half through her enrollment. Today is one of her classroom days and we know the exact time and route she will be taking in order to get there."

When Bob, still silently smiling, nodded his head in recognition to what he was listening to, George continued. "I wasn't kidding when I told 'Laughing Larry' back there that we'd have our job finished today, so if all of us hustle for the next hour, I'm sure we can have it wrapped up and out of the way in time for Louie."

Consuming the distance still between them and their destination, joking and laughter their constant companions, Bob apparently now feeling comfortable enough to speak his thoughts, suddenly asked something that had been on his mind since their last meeting with Farkas.

"I hope you don't think I'm nosey, but just out of curiosity - how do you always manage to have such a quick comeback. In the short time I've been here with you, you always seem to get the better of the boss each and every time you lock horns."

"Oh that's easy." George grinned. "Most of the time I just pretend I'm him, when confronting me."

Even though it was Bob who said "Huh?" Fred noticeably also found the statement bewildering.

"Sure." George continued. "It's really easy if you think about it. Sometimes when I know 'Old Dumbrowski' is due to show up, I just think to myself, what kind of stupid or insulting remarks is he going to come up with time. Fred'll verify that our 'lost' leader is so quick on any decision making, that he has to sit in his office a half hour just thinking it through before he finally comes out and makes an attempt at it."

To give credence to the insult, a grinning Fred nodded his head affirmatively when Bob glance briefly in his direction.

"As for myself, I immediately have no trouble coming back with an answer of my own. And then I ask myself how would I reply to such an intimidating remark if I was Farkas."

"Such as?" Bob quickly asked, a big smile beating George's answer.

"Such as -" George beamed. "And these are to be putdowns that I've not only used before, but also sarcastic slammers that ol Farkas would never have the ingenuity to come up with."

"Go ahead." Fred butted in. "I've been around you long enough to know all of your best material by heart."

"Well," the grin on his face growing even more devilish, "More then once I've been tempted to say to him , 'Go ahead, admit it. You wish you were me, don't you?' And ol Farkas would reply something like, 'Ya, you're right. That way I could do the human race a favor, and commit suicide!"

Instantly Bob reacted, his body gestures saying that he had just been stabbed through the heart with some sort of very sharp instrument, "O - o - oh! That is a nasty one." The homage, as appreciated as much as it was, only served as fodder to keep the master at work.

"But that's not as bad as if I'd said, 'Go ahead, smile, make my day.' and he'd come back with 'Why? You got terminal cancer?'"

"Wow!" Bob grimaced. "Talk about being cruel. Last time I heard anybody spurting anything that rough - Don Rickles, 'Mister personality' was making a living out of it."

"Where do you think he got the nickname "Acid Tongue' from. Fred laughed. Or 'Slammin Sam.'"

"But, any-ways," George carried on with, while doing his overly modest best to emphasize that his inflated ego was overflowing into his swelled head. "I do not 'slam' people solely with the deliberate intention of hurting them emotionally. If I think someone can't handle it to be joked with, then I do not pick or even participate in such bantering. And that goes for 'Ol Farkas too, even if he does deserve it most of the time."

"Well, how come you guys seem to have more than one nickname for him?" Bob asked.

"Because" Fred offered, "he's the kind of character where one descriptive nickname can't possibly describe all of his inadequacies. While, as you'll probably hear more than once around here, it's true that most people are often a lot like hairs on a toilet seat, they occasionally get 'pissed off'. Ol 'Fart Face' has a knack for going out of his way to encourage such treatment."

The chuckles the remark had brought, as well as being enjoyed by all, also prompted George to pick up where he had left off.

"It's been said that many a true word is often spoken in jest, and this is one of those times. But if I really thought that the boss couldn't live with our little verbal sparing sessions, then I'd somehow find a way to put up with him. I know it looks so far as if we're overly picking on him, but he's generally the one, as you just heard, who encourages it all."

George's face and tone had turned to one of complete seriousness by now, while Fred's was one of disgust. but Bob didn't get a chance to express his own feelings about what he had just heard, as Fred let his own reaction to what his friend had just said spill out.

"Care about hurting 'shit-heads' feelings! In a pigs ass you care! You might fool Bob, but that's only because he doesn't you as well as I do. And I know from personal exposure, there's nothing more you enjoy than 'slamming' 'the Dwarf' every chance you get."

"I know." George beamed back, his chameleon expression once more changing to one of total happiness again, which as always affected his tone and body language. "I just thought I'd give Bob a lesson on the facts that everyone's fair game around here, even him and you 'ol fish-breath'."

Shifts

Once more there was harmony in the air around them. There was still over an hour before Louie's prank was scheduled to take place, but it was destined to pass as quickly and easily as most of their time together had faded into the past, and it did just that.

Some of the men in the plant, as well as the foremen, carried 'walkie talkies' for the purpose of safely being able to communicate with each other whenever ready to test or operate any piece of dangerous equipment not visible by sight. It was these static plagued squawky instruments that were to be used to keep contact between themselves, when Louie was ready to fall prey to their little scheme.

Logic suggested that the more people who knew about the stunt to be played the greater the chances there were of it leaking out, going wrong before hand. So originally the amount of workers involved in the prank was to have been very limited. But as time would soon tell, someone must have written about the stunt on half of the plants 'library' stall walls. And as the minutes approaching two o'clock mounted, so did the number of curious onlookers, which George reluctantly handled.

Carefully lifting the 'walkie talkie' to his lips, as Louie's lone figure finally came into view, the first of two posted lookouts softly gave the coded message that had been agreed upon. 'Ten to eleven, eleven to twelve, twelve to thirteen.' until it was feared that she might detect him in his hiding spot. Most of the men had graded Louie's intoxicating body and features as by far above the perfect 'ten' stereotyped in the movie off the same name. And since her beauty logically grew with each approaching step taken, it was decided that escalating numbers were logically the only appropriate way to signify her approach.

Instantly, as the pre-warning was eagerly accepted about a hundred feet away, adolescent like men quickly headed for their already prearranged locations, like flies being temporarily brushed away on a hot sticky day.

The brief sharp 'crack' caused by George from the tightly rolled up newspaper when he slapped the selected victim's forehead - was totally lost in the sounds of shuffling feet hurrying to hide. In just a matter of seconds only the lucky chosen men needed for the prank were left huddling around the form of Cory Allen, as he dropped his body horizontally onto the cool cement floor beneath him. Cory, rightly nicknamed 'bashful', didn't know if the nervousness his thin twenty-four year old body was experiencing was from anticipation, or the very nature of where his nickname had been born form. Regardless of what it was, he had originally wanted to avoid the labeled 'lucky draw' used to decide who would play the part he was in, but now he was glad that it was him who had won. Wordlessly inside of his head he asked his pounding racing heart to please behave itself. In fact, the men had on more than one occasion remarked that he was too timid to even take 'the Pepsi challenge.'

Each man in the group had been looking forward to what was hopefully about to happen for so long that each of them was almost qualified to be eligible for an Oscar nomination, proving it by acting out their parts. The second lookout's voice was now heard to fade out and the excitement that was in their voices, as Louie's shapely feminine form finally came around the last corner separating her from the gathering, was totally genuine, with only the words spoken being false.

Whispered words of, 'She's here!' prompted "bashful' to slowly and quietly drain his breath, his eyes then snapped closed, leaving only his ears to tell him what was going on in the visible world he had just shut out. But he had no trouble in distinguishing each man's excited voice presently taking joy in her every movement.

"Hey Louie! Quick! Over here! Cory Allen's been hurt!"

Instantly, as her eyes visually confirmed the dormant horizontal form of 'Bashful' on the floor, Louie broke into a half-run, quickly covering the small distance still separating her from the gathering. Her new sudden direction of concern involved her thoughts just enough that she totally failed to see the sudden pleasure that was registering on some of the men's faces, when their eyes ate up the pleasant sight of her tightly clad well endowed body bouncing with each step taken.

The small gathering divided itself even more to allow her perfumed form into their group. And as she knelt beside 'bashful's seemingly dormant body, one of the workers offered information that was already in her thoughts, an instant evaluation of the situation.

"He must have walked into something. Look at the size of that red mark on his forehead!"

Doing exactly that, she was about to put the middle three fingers of her right hand against Cory's neck so as to check his pulse, when someone else excitedly added, "I don't think he's breathing!"

Instantly remembering the three critical 'Bs' of her First Aid course 'breathing', 'bleeding', 'bones', along with the order of their importance, she quickly discarded the gesture. Instead she lowered her head close to Cory's partially opened mouth. Failing to detect any sign of air entering or exiting, she immediately started with a life saving procedure she had already practiced in her first aid training class, with the ever hopeful intention that she would never have o use it.

Using her half-opened mouth to completely cover 'bashful's, her right hand pinching the nostrils of his nose closed, she carefully blew air softly into his lungs, while watching for his chest to rise. The small gathering of hypnotized men, one of them whispering. 'The lucky bastard!', while another answered, 'I think I'm in love.', to which someone else added 'I'm in shock!' and then a nasty 'Not me. I'd rather be in Louie!' while rearranging their positions in order to get a better view of what was going on. Bashful Cory in turn did his best to accept the warm breath flowing from Louie's pleasant perfumed body into his. And after she had applied her life saving technique only a few times, the inevitable happened, something every normal healthy red-blooded young boy or man constantly lived in fear of uncontrollably happening whenever he was in the company of a pretty girl or beautiful woman.

It was one of the men now in the elbow to elbow crowded huddle, someone obviously not totally as interested in Louie's beautiful kneeling form and life giving techniques as he should have been - that noticed 'Bashful's' growing predicament. And he let the humor of what was uncontrollably going on with Cory, flow over into his choice of words when he spoke. "I think you're lo-o-o-sing him!"

Instantly, her face a mask of concerned confusion, Louie looked up into the direction the remark had come from. The rest of the men there also imitated her gesture, and when all eyes were on the one who had made it, their vision then followed his as he looked down towards what it was that had brought the first and now continuing urgent sounding words to his lips.

"Either 'rigarmortis' is startin' to set in, or he's 'definitely' got a 'pickle in his pocket'!"

The results, as the true realization of the crude remark slowly started to sink in, were instantaneous by both Louie and the rest of the gathering. As an immediate blush filled her face, after a small surprised

'Oh!' had escaped from her lips, all of the standing men instantaneously broke out into loud uncontrollable laughter, the odd 'wolf whistle' splitting the air. And as the workers who had been hiding close-by filtered out from their hiding places to quickly join first the crowd and then the laughing, the total reality of what was really going on finally sank through Louie's embarrassed and confused thoughts.

Lowering her vision back onto the face she had been pressing her lips against only brief moments earlier, bashful Cory's facial skin now also fully engulfed in a deep crimson red blush, Louie's right hand seemed to act on its own as it shot out and slapped his already embarrassed face. The laughter that was busy filling the air, if possible, grew in volume and magnitude as the gathering once more watched her enticing every movement. And as she exploded erect, while stumbling through the words, "I, I'll remember your part, in this, this childish prank, 'Mister, Mister Allen'!" the group once more parted just enough to allow for the anger fuelled departure they knew would be coming next.

In almost the same instant, after having fought and won the urge to kick at the tongue-tied horizontal form still in front of her, Louie's hot anger filled eyes scanned the sea of laughing faces around her - Cory's embarrassed body started to jump erect. But his awkward unbalanced like actions were just a little bit behind those of the female that had just fanned the flames of his growing embarrassment, which naturally by now in a sense had vacated the building. And as her angry body stomped away in a huff, his pleading words of 'Wait! Please! Let me explain!' were lost in the excited antics and laughter of his wound, up coworkers now lost in hysterics.

Someone in the crowd mumbled, "What a dynamite broad!" another added, "Ya! And you can't even see the parts I'd date her for!" while another spurted out "Now there's a 'stroke' worth dying for!" All of which were only a few of many lewd comments somehow just naturally expected from such a prank, only confirming the rather obvious fact that not all of the 'kids' were in school that day.

Before Cory could make any attempt to even follow Louie's hurrying departing figure, the group closed in even tighter and continued to congratulate him on his performance.

The men were not only joyously loud, but also very physical, as embracing arms and hands came out to grab and poke well-intended intentions into his side. Helplessly entrapped, he was left to accept the praise being bestowed upon him, with one last look at Louie's departing form, before it eventually disappeared around along a walkway it had originally been destined for.

There had also been another pair of concerned eyes watching Louie's angry retreat, an individual who had strangely chosen to remain in the background, and George knew it would be best to get away as soon as possible. Chuckling, but for more reasons then was now before him, he and the others had just earned not exactly an honorable place in plant history, but what had just taken place would always be worth a mention.

Suddenly, while both of his arms were being pumped as a showing of appreciation and congratulations, a closer and louder voice than all of the rest must have realized that Cory's strangely distracted attention was keeping him from enjoying the moment. Snapping out the words, "Hey man!" brought Cory's distracted attention back to the groups. "What in the Hell's wrong with you? Smile! Whether you appreciate it or not, you're famous! People are going to brag about you and this day for years to come!"

Someone else, another 'bud' and co-worker also obviously overcome with the joy of what he had just watched, offered, "Gee, if my wife were only built like Louie. Dam it, I'd be at home right now trying to save my marriage!"

Then another worker, one with a more limited vocabulary, rudely yelled. "Not me! I'd be to busy walkin around with a constant 'Chubb' on!"

"You mean you don't now!" the man beside him quickly harpooned him with, and then quickly added, 'O-o-ops sorry. That's your nose!"

"You would too." now the co-worker on the other side of the adlibbing jumped. "Especially, if the best sex you ever had was when your wife sneezed in your face 'at just the right moment', if you know what I mean, 'jellybean'."

The smile the remarks brought to 'Bashful's' face was more forced than genuine, and he knew that the deep personal secret between him and Louie would be in danger of discovery unless he started to act as happy as the rest of the still excited men. Now that Louie was out of site and no longer subjects to any more of their crude smart remarks, or silly antics, he gradually found it easier and easier to pretend that he was really having as good a time as they were. After all, the true intention of the prank had been to give everyone involved something to look forward to occasionally, not to mention some incentive to come to work, while hopefully breaking up the sometimes monotony of the to often routine jobs. And just like always in the past, when other pranks had been pulled on even some of the men now enjoying themselves, any hard feelings encountered would hopefully be soon forgotten, by the time someone else became the next target in a hopefully victimless joke.

Another voice that had chosen to remain in the background finally made its presence known once its owner had also zeroed in on the large welt now on the side of 'bashful's cheek. And even as the man started to talk, George used it as an opportunity to whisper in Bob and Fred's direction that he would meet them in the change-house.

"You better hope those marks fade before anyone who doesn't know what happened here sees them."

The sudden silence from those close enough to hear the remark, as Cory himself replied, 'How's that?' caused the others still talking and laughing to become silent also, obviously curious enough to wonder what was going on now.

"Well." the fellow worker continued to grin while letting his eyes pass suggestively over everyone else's now grinning back into his, no doubt letting the anticipation of the rest of his answer to build. "The last time I was wearing a noticeable red blemish like you're sporting on my face, and to this day I still swear it was from an ingrown infected hair, someone here at work spread the rumor about how I got it. It happened just before you started working here Cory. Someone, and I know I'll find out who someday, said that I told them I was impatiently helping my wife off with her underpants in bed one night when the elastic banding in them broke, letting them snap out and whack me full tilt in the face."

Even though it was one of the most commonly used comments, it still instantly, as some of the older men there remembered the occasion, possibly even the culprit responsible for the rumor, caused contagious giggling to once more took control of the gathering. The man telling the story, as George had told Bob earlier, had just demonstrated that not only was no intended animosity when anyone is 'slammed', such as he had just done to himself. But he had also demonstrated that each and everyone at one time or another, was expected to do their time in the proverbial 'barrel'.

Just when it looked as if the prank had played itself out, another fresh voice, after having glanced at his wristwatch, was solely responsible for the gatherings instant disbursement. as the words 'Clean up!' exploded out of his mouth and over the dwindling entertainment, the men evaporated in a variety of directions. one of the unwritten 'golden rules' recognized universally throughout the plant, was that you didn't waste the companies time, especially when it came to one of the periods allowed for dinners, coffee breaks, or everybody's favorite 'shit, shower, shampoo and shave' time. And it was usually these all too short and rare break periods dividing the employees work days, that most of the workers used to punctuate their long hours in the company during each shift. It was also the type of 'fodder' George most times looked forward to keeping track of when making his daily entries before heading home. He also kept telling himself, other than having information to refresh his memory with if ever having to call out the big guns to defend himself on anything out of his control, 'Heaven forbid', it would also hopefully give him one Hell of a laugh during his retirement years. After all, like he kept telling his kids, what you see on television or commercials were only a small portion of what was related to as the real world. And as hard as it would be for a stranger to believe any of the pranks or situations he and his motley crew of coworkers got themselves into, it 'was' the 'real' world!

Chapter # 5

'That's what friends are for.'
Or
'Locker room rituals.'
Or
'Joe the janitor.'

Being older, and supposedly wiser, George not only knew his way thoroughly around the plant, but also all of the time saving shortcuts. A few of the ruder and cruder men would have in fact simply said that he knew the inside of the plant as well as he knew the inside of his nose. But it was actually his age acquired knowledge that had let him manage to get ahead of Louie during her angered trip to what could only be the change-house now, especially considering her condition when departing.

Stepping out from between two vertical columns used to support and divide the building he was leaving from the one he was entering, he found himself only a few short feet in front of Louie's hurrying form. There could be no doubt from the way she reacted to his sudden appearance that he'd genuinely startled her, but only temporarily. She kept moving fore-ward, only now with her head tilted slightly downward and away from him, there had been still noticeable anger on her face

Shifts

as well as in her movements. But George had detected something else there, something that she was now apparently trying to hide.

There were noticeable trails of moisture on Louie's cheeks. George, easily recognizing it as residue from the tears they were, as he deliberately tried to block her avenue of travel even as he spoke.

"Hold up a minute Louie! Please! There's something we just have to talk about!"

Louie, her eyes still tilted towards the ground in front of her, easily dodged George's obstructing figure, and he had to do a silly kind of sidestepping 'Shuffle off to Buffalo' before he could manage to get his body once more in between her and her line of retreat. She was just about to out-maneuver him once more, when his pleading voice, "Come on Louie! if you'll calm down for just a minute, I'm sure I can justify every 'stupid' 'childish' thing that happened back there!" This made her stop temporarily. She then raised her eyes, apparently not caring anymore if he saw the paths of moisture still on her face. She then let the anger still within her flow through her voice and eyes when forcefully spitting out the words that were meant to represent all of the rage still in her thoughts.

"I, doubt, it!"

Starting to move once again, her right hand in the air and sweeping sideways as if brushing aside some invisible pest, Louie's voice was now noticeably emotionally disappointed as well as angry, as she continued speaking.

"I always thought you were different! Different then, then some of those depraved animals back there. I guess I was wrong!"

George made no effort to block her movements this time. Instead he let one of his hands retrieve a small bulky white envelope he'd hidden earlier inside of his work shirt, while offering, "If what you just said is true, then at least don't loose your total respect for me for at least one more minute, please. If you won't listen to me, will you at least read this? I'm sure you'll agree there's no possible way I could have had enough time between what happened back there and now to write down what's on the piece of paper inside this envelope."

By this time Louie had managed to put about ten feet between herself and where George was now standing, his feet straddling the ground, the bulky envelope held high in his right hand and over his head. When she finally looked back in his direction, not just curiosity making her want to do so, the caring smile on George's face was more than one hundred and ten percent genuine. And as he waited for even a small part of some signal indicating that she was willing to take a gamble on what he had just said, he made sure that he didn't even accidentally lean forward towards her one fraction of an inch. He wanted her to understand that only she would decide if the distance still between them would be breached.

Letting her eyes go from first the letter to George's smiling yet pleading face, and then back to the envelope again, Louie's curiosity couldn't help but eventually give George the signal he was waiting for. Quickly closing the distance separating them, he stopped a few feet short of her while leaning forward just far enough to offer her the envelope still in his grip he offered her what else he hoped she was willing to listen to.

"Go ahead. Look inside, please! Hopefully you'll realize that everything that's happened, even if I can't begin to imagine how bad it has upset you, is not really really as bad as it all seems."

Hesitantly at first, a look of mixed curiosity and contempt on a face that had been totally angry only minutes earlier now gone, Louie reached out and snapped the thick letter out of George's fingers. He in turn, as she tore open one end of the envelope and extracted two smaller thick envelops with a singular piece of folded paper, stepped back away a foot in order to act as a gesture of his sincerity. He then allowed the surrounding area a quick inspection to make sure they were still alone.

Louie's eyes, at first imitating his to make sure that this was not just another trick, then let her vision concentrate on the strange collection of items now within her grip. As curiosity took full control, she slowly unfolded the singular piece of white paper, still not sure that it might yet ignite within her grip. After giving George one last glance to make sure that his location had not changed, she let her eyes glance down the crowded page and relay the information written on into her brain. It took less than a minute to realize that George, as well as Corey, although involved in the terrible prank, had not really or intentionally been making fun of her. It also took her about the same amount of time to understand that George also apparently knew about the secret between

Cory and her, a secret she believed that absolutely nobody within the plant could possibly know anything about. When her eyes next found George's, he was still, almost boyishly, or better yet 'the cat who had swallowed the canary', smiling in her direction.

The red-hot anger and frustration that had occupied her heart totally earlier, now no longer had a home, as curiosity itself took deeper roots. And when she finally spoke, her voice was soft and caring, as a woman's was meant to be.

"But, how, how did you find out about us?"

"It really wasn't that hard." George answered. "Surprisingly, as some of us people get older, we don't just get uglier, sometimes we somehow even get a little bit smarter too."

His smile and present attitude was now noticeably contagious - which only served to keep him talking. "Let's just say, it was a wishful sort of lucky guess, not to mention those little biological signals between you two that any old romantic like me would have picked up on. And no, I'm not Ann landers in drag."

An unintended surprised 'Oh!' escaped from Louie's lips. But George was quick to assure her that what he had just said, was not common knowledge throughout the plant.

"Don't go getting worried just yet. As far as I can detect, nobody else knows about you two, yet, that is."

"You mean," the torn envelope and all of its contents were still in Louie's hands, and she glanced at only the letter briefly, as she continued speaking in a surprised voice. "You, you mean you haven't told anyone?"

"Hell no!" George smiled. "Why would I?" And he kept grinning while adding, "If you two wish to keep your friendship or feelings for each other a secret, it's none of my business, or anybody else's around here for that matter as far as I'm concerned. I may be one of those people you left back there, but I'm only an occasional jerk. I know how immature or cruel some individuals can be sometimes, but believe it or not it's the occasional such stunt that also makes this place bearable at times.

Louie's face might be showing slight confusion, but she still understood enough to nod affirmatively at the right time, as he spoke.

"And that's why I figured I better let you know that Cory isn't worth giving up over one little immature prank."

With a hint of doubt still about her, Louie asked, "But why didn't he warn me about what was going to happen"

"He couldn't." George continued to grin, while his eyes briefly dropped to each envelope still in her hands. "He didn't know he was to be the lucky 'Billy-goat' until about an hour before we had staged it to happen."

"But in the letter," Louie started to shake the page held tightly in her right hand in a frustrated manner, "you said it was fixed so that Cory would be the winner of some kind of raffle used to decide who the 'bill-goat' as you called him, would be. Just how did you arrange that?"

"That's where those other two little packets you're holding come in. Would you be able to recognize Cory's hand written signature if you saw it?"

Louie, her face once more showing confusion, looked curiously at the two small still unopened envelopes, before answering, "Why, yes. Yes, I would."

"Good." George said with an actual hint of relief in his voice. "Then you better examine what's inside the envelope with the 'X' on it first."

Lowering her eyes once again to both of the sealed envelopes, she then used the hand holding the letter she had just read to first stuff it and the larger torn package into one of her skin tight jean pockets. She then used the same hand to put the unmarked white envelope under her left armpit. Letting her bewildered vision once more briefly glance in George's direction, she tore the end off the 'X' marked package and shook out its contents. Inside had been approximately twenty pieces of equally sized folded pieces of paper. And when she started to open each paper one at a time, confusion still in her movements, she discovered that each small paper contained the handwritten signature of men she knew of within the plant, including George's.

"Those are the original ballots for the raffle." George said. "Now look at the signatures on the ballots used in the raffle. They're in the other sealed envelope."

Stepping forward just enough to reach out and take the first of the two small packets and its contents, George once more stepped backwards to the location he had just vacated, as Louie now turned her attention to the remaining envelope. Quickly and eagerly tearing it open, she extracted its similar contents, and proceeded to examine the folded papers in the same way. The only difference she found this time was that each ballot contained the handwritten signature of Cory Allen, to which George asked her if they were or were not his signatures.

"Why, yes, they are. But if he wrote all these, then he must have known he was going to win the raffle, and he could have warned me!"

A slight hint of hot anger had let itself slip back into her voice, but George soon extinguished it.

"Yes, you're right. He should have warned you, 'if', if he'd signed all those ballots that is."

Extracting a pen from his shirt pocket, Louie's eyes hypnotized by his action, George then wrote something onto the outside of the envelope within his grip. He then reached forward and handed it to the once again baffled Louie. Then, as she took the envelope, he offered her the full and true story behind how Cory had actually won the draw.

"As you can see, I signed all those ballots. Normally my writing's so bad, I've said it before and I'll say it again, if you could get my signature onto a prescription, you could take it anywhere in town and no questions asked, get whatever drug it is you're on!"

Realizing that the smile the remark would have normally received was never going to materialize, he quickly picked up from where he had left off with the original point he was trying to make.

"And once I had everyone's signature, it was a simple case of practicing Cory's handwriting until I could copy it good enough to fool everyone who might be close enough to read it once the ballet was drawn. You'd be surprised how many 'children' were upset because they didn't win."

There was still a little bit of cynical humor in his last sentence, but it also soon left as he kept speaking.

"The original ballots I sealed in the first envelope and kept strictly for you to see. If the word got out on what I've done, my name would be 'mud' around here for the next couple of years. Why, my forging was actually good enough to fool 'ol bashful' himself, when he looked at the ballot. Thank 'God' he didn't win the draw used to earn the privilege to pick the person to be chosen for our prank. Fortunately someone else got to pull that ballot out of the can for that one. Can you imagine the 'hoopla' if it looked like he'd actually picked his own name twice!

"You mean, he didn't know that he had won dishonestly?" Louie asked.

"Believe me," George answered with a hushed tone to his words, his eyes comically pretending to search the area around them - as one elongated finger had come and touched his lips to emphasize the need for secrecy. "I learned long ago, if you tell the 'truth', you can forget what it was you had said. But tell a 'lie' - and you not only have to remember the exact details of what it was that you said - but also whoever you have told it to , let alone anyone else who might have overheard it, and 'forever'."

Reaching out once again, Louie's face reading that she was occupied digesting everything that had happened between them so far, George quickly added in a still almost hushed voice, "Nobody knows, that is, except you and me. And once I've safely destroyed all of this evidence, paper trail, nobody will ever be able to prove any suggestion otherwise about anything then what they actually saw. And unless you or I 'talk in our sleep', we should be safe."

Some doubt still apparently in her mind, Louie more said than asked, "Well, then Cory still played his part in the prank believing that he had just accidentally been lucky enough to win that stupid bloody raffle?"

George, let his head twist back and forth from side to side as a suggestion of saying 'No, no, no and again no!' as well as saying it.

"Now don't go getting all wound up again over nothing. He had to make the 'best' out of what was happening, and play the part to the limit. He might be one of us, but doing what he had to do - took one 'Hell' of a lot of guts, especially in front of some of those animals back there. Besides, if not him, who would you like to be giving mouth to mouth to back there ---- me?"

Louie didn't answer his last actually humorous remark right away, even though it also hadn't actually been a question either. Instead she just stood silently letting her eyes travel back and forth between George's forced smiling face and the opened letter she had just retrieved form her pocket. Her face said that she was debating something still unknown to him, and he did his best to grin more and more whatever the doubt was out of her, each time she looked in his direction.

Only 'now', did she realize that this person, an individual other woman in the plant were always telling her to avoid, was more than just another man she had noticed always smiling at her as she had passed. He was actually a friend, a friend of the closest kind. A friend she now believed to be trusted. And if he could be trusted here and now, then he can be trusted in the future."

For what seemed much longer than it actually was, only the sounds of the factory's inner life filled his ears, but not his thoughts. Then suddenly, which even startled George slightly, Louie reached out and stuffed the remainder of everything she had originally been holding into his already overcrowded grasp. She then also, which once more caught him totally off guard continued to lean even closer just enough to give him a soft gentle pleasantly scented kiss on his cheek. Turning and almost running away, with George frozen dumbfound to the floor beneath him, she then disappeared into the buildings inner structure. And only when she was totally out of sight, did George let out one long elongated 'Whe-e-e-e-e-w'! while turning to head for his own shower room, after saying to himself, 'Normally I would say that this is one of those things you take with you to the grave, but I just gotta write this one down as definitely one of Lawrence Welks 'Wonerful! Wonerful!'. Nobody will ever believe me if this ever comes out in the future, well, maybe Fred.'

He was glad he didn't have to go into more detail on the various forms of stress within the human body, let alone the multitude of ways it had for relieving that tension. He considered Louie young enough to still be a stranger to some of the older workers sometimes 'rude' and 'crude' methods for expressing themselves. For most of men something as simple as the referral to making a 'pit stop' would surfice for the disposal of body waste, whereas the remaining few might say they were going to 'drain the main vein' or 'chop off a log'. And whereas a woman could sit down and have herself a good cry if things going wrong got under her skin, men either had to get aggressively physical or find some other method to let off steam, something like what had just happened. Sex, or excessive 'eyeball pressure' as the men liked to refer to it, was often the maker or breaker of real people, again where such comradely often helped purge many forms of such tension. And yet strangest of all, no matter what the age or gender, the many methods of evacuation for the bodies built up of body pressure 'gas' was always a whole new ever ongoing field in itself.

A quick glance at his wristwatch told him that there was no sense in trying to catch Bob or Fred back at the job-site, because at this time of the day most of the workforce was either on their way to their change-house, or already there. He was so relieved that 'Louie's prank' was over with that is normally active 'sixth sense' would have picked up on the female figures still hiding in the distance. And not only had he missed their presence when he had been so involved with Louie, he had also failed to detect the singular 'click' when she had kissed him on the cheek, but then again nobody's hearing in the plant was that good.

Along the way the only person of any immediate importance to our George was another close friend and 'bud' 'Joe the janitor' Benzik. Joe was exactly what his nickname implied and because of his harmless looking short balding early sixty-ish Italian features, he also was often the target of some of the worker's devilish pranks. But Joe, his deep hearty laugh and well know good nature, could play as good a prank as he could take. That, as well as the fact that he was a devoted bachelor, made him a prime candidate for every extra curricular activity going on in and outside of the plant. And it was also the reason he was one of the men invited to a little drinking and poker party scheduled for later that night, which he asked him about. "How about tonight Joe? You going to make it down to the motel?"

"Ya." Joe grinned, showing his uneven and brown aged teeth. "I goanna be there." Joe was a thirty-five year man in the plant, and although ready for retirement, he had never quite managed to totally master full control of the English Language. "How abouta the entertainment? Doesa Fred asuspect anything?"

"I'm sure he doesn't yet, but time'll tell."

George half laughed. Either way, you don't want to miss out on tonight. He also doesn't know it yet, but I'm going to talk him into having supper with us tonight, that way I can be sure he'll be there. I know for a fact he hasn't had a good 'rattle' since his separation, so no doubt he's just about ready to explode."

An immediate loud laugh was the reward George got for his remark, and as he returned the gesture, he started to walk away while saying, "Same time, same place Joe. Remember, if you're not there you're square."

Once more temporarily alone with his thoughts, he had deliberately not told Joe about the outcome of 'Louie's prank', strictly because he didn't have the time to hang around and do it justice. Another quick glance at his watch then made him widen his stride. And when he finally passed through the change-house's front door, his hands already busy undoing the buttons on his work shirt, George's body told him it was more than ready for a hot rejuvenating shower.

Entering the men's locker room, the women's were at the opposite end of the huge complex and no doubt often suffered the same affliction as their male coworkers did. It was like walking into a combination of the worlds united nations building and the city's 'funny farm', with coming, going, and time all being irrelevant. For some their lockers were like a small extended room from their homes, as the two cubicles interiors were decorated with everything from family photos to lights and radios that automatically came on once their doors were opened. Others loved nothing more than to be able to take care of their personal hygiene and biological inconveniences on company paid time and material. With some, it was just a small entertainment center, where they used everything at their disposal to humorously involve or irritate others, strictly in order to entertain only themselves.

For George it, it was an accumulation of all, and a new experience each and every day, especially if he got an opportunity to do a little slamming along the way also. He not only loved the blind conversations with people changing aisles away, but also the visual comedies as people sometimes did things to each other they would have whacked their children for. And of course there were always a few who still suffered from a childhood affliction. They had an allergy to water, something always more noticeable during the summer months, which also seemed to keep them from taking their dirty work clothes home weekly.

Smiles and short nods usually distinguished those ending their shifts from those about to start them, and George did mainly both as he covered the last bit of distance between himself and his lockers. In fact, he was in so much of a hurry that he didn't even stop when he passed a familiar recognized 'health nut' presently doing push-ups in the vacant aisle by his locker. Instead, he just mentally plied himself with short quips that he would have offered if time had allowed - such as, 'Strong back, weak mind'. He's as strong as a bull, and just as smart'. 'What's the matter - your girlfriend leave you?'

The few men in George's isle working the same shift as him were no doubt already in the showers. All that greeted him as he passed their opened lockers was one set of fold out mirrors, a religious statue, one set of family photos, no not the 'Adams family', and a small tape recorder presently belting out an obviously preferred 'olden golden' pop from out of the sixties era.

Habit, more than reasoning, opened the combination lock sealing his two cubicles. As instinct then tore as his dirty work, clothes, making sure to stuff all of the papers from the prank into the bottom of his workbag, his thoughts then registered mental images to the present conversation underway close-by. Someone, George knew almost everyone's name in the lockers around him, and those he didn't he knew well enough to put a face to any voice he was hearing, was saying, "Did you see the size of his nose? No wonder him and the wives don't have any kids. She probably can't get serious about sex while screwing that close to a wind-tunnel."

"Not to mention he probably has to have an extra meal a day just to keep it alive!" the second voice in the insult added.

The 'slamming' just naturally made George chuckle slightly to himself, especially when another mental image of who he thought they might be talking about jumped into his head. But it was only a brief interruption before zeroing in on the next conversation, it was actually bragging, he was also eavesdropping on would. This time George not only knew the face and voice he was hearing, but also the man's name and personality. 'Beautiful Brad Nagie', a definite ladies man and always ready to boast about it, was on every male workers 'hit' list. If in fact the braggart knew George would be listening in on his latest exploit, past contact and experiences would in all probability would have cautioned him to keep his big 'trap-door' shut, instead of putting himself in the position of having it sprung open beneath him, like now.

"As a matter of fact, my parents were always telling me about how fast I was to learn anything. They often said that I was walking on my own by the time I was only six months old."

"I can believe that!" George called out, without letting even a fraction of a second pass, his ever-racing brain as always leading his mouth. "By the looks of you now, you were probably so ugly as a baby - nobody would carry you!"

Instantly a barrage of scattered 'He-e-e-e-eres' filled the air around where the remarks had taken place. And as George stepped out of his last piece of clothing, saying to himself, "I just love it when you can use a good slamming more than once!" he acknowledged the other unseen admirers' remarks with a simple happy, " I thank you, thank you - one and all."

Grabbing his soap, towel, face cloth and shampoo, a smile still on his face as he slipped into his flip, flops, he then broke out into an almost half-run as he headed for the shower room. He was still looking forward to the stimulating warm spray on his body, but now a newer and definitely more important matter was making its need known in his body, thanks to all the coffee breaks and excitement, he desperately needed a brief pit stop in a 'library booth'.

In his impatience, the workers often added graffiti on the outside of the shithouse trap doors that ran from 'reserved', 'vote here', 'room for rent', 'shitting room only', 'personal confessions heard hear' right on through to the inevitable 'out of odor' George forgot to check for occupancy, as he pushed on the first partially opened stall door he came to. And when he heard first a dull thud - followed by an even duller, 'Uh!' he quickly moved on after apologetically saying, "O-o-ops - sorry!"

People, as well as conversations, were now all around him as he found success on the next door he tried. And as he rushed through a routine normally punctuated with either a twenty-minute short rest, or book of some sort, George mentally told himself that he would just have to make it up next time.

The people, like their conversations, were often music to his sense of humor. Walking into the drying area to hang up his towel, the bald and the abused everywhere now, his ears instantly picked up the loud assorted duck calls the men used. Someone was shouting, 'Answer those damn things, will ya!' as they tried to get a little bit more of the company out through their noses. Someone else in the background was doing a terrible job at singing, 'Rock-a-bye-your-baby,' and it made George wonder if sung in its appropriate location, if just maybe it couldn't be one of the unknown possibilities for crib fatalities.

Soap, flannel, and shampoo in hand, his eyes having already picked out the wet semi lathered bodies of Fred and Bob, he half-ran under the vacant shower heads towards them, while dodging a half dozen other soaked surprised bodies that only a mother could love.

One startled form yelled 'Hey, what do ya think this is, a car wash?' which also warned Bob and Fred of his approach. Naturally, as George already expected, they just happened to be still talking about the stunt that had pulled on Louie.

George, his aim as bad as ever, tried to hang his wash cloth over the vacant showerhead he'd ended up under, while offering, "Sure sounds like 'I' wasn't missed."

Gravity, as the small cloth slipped free of its intended resting place, did its job and sucked the now wet flannel towards the even wetter floor, where it made a loud wet 'plop' when landing. Without even hesitating, George quickly bent down and retrieved the cloth, before being instantly rewarded verbally by one of the familiar friendly co-workers he'd rushed past only brief seconds ago.

"Gee, isn't amazing how some guys will do anything to get a closer look at another guy's 'family jewels'. If you wanted to know who's been circumcised, why didn't you just ask?"

Smiling as the other men in the stall started to rib him about the very insinuating put-down, George started to lather his soap into the flannel - but not without having verbal restitution also.

"I hate to be the one to break the bad news to you Bill - but when the doctor circumcised you, I think he threw the wrong piece of skin away. Another half inch shorter and you'd have been just another peasant, with a scar on your ass."

The laughter already in progress grew even louder briefly, to which George after offering his latest victim one of his best over emphasized grins, turned his attention back to his still chuckling friends.

"Don't believe everything you hear around here." he smiled at Bob.

"I'll say." Fred chuckled. "especially not after what you did to John Maylin."

"And what was that?" Bob asked, already smart enough to realize that he was expected to ask, while rinsing down his body.

But George, as Bob's inquisitive eyes looked into his, made no effort to answer the question, mainly because he didn't like to and also believed that bragging about ones conquests wasn't the proper thing to do. Besides, he also knew that if enough time lapsed, Fred would do his bragging for him, which was exactly what happened.

"We used to have a guy in here who would always run up and hang his 'doniker' in your face whenever you bent down to retrieve any dropped shampoo, soap, or for whatever reason. But George soon got him out of that habit."

"How's that?" Bob asked again, only this time with his eyes remaining on the one telling the story.

"Well, when he tried to pull the stunt on George once to often," Fred started to laugh as he continued, "Our buddy here was more than ready for him. When George bent down to retrieve his shampoo on that memorable day, he was actually only setting John Maylin up. And when John fell into his trap - George quickly reached out and quickly stuck a spring-loaded clothespin he'd hidden inside of his facecloth onto the bottom of ol Maylins hanging 'sack'. Well, if you could have been there, I'm sure you'd understand why when I say 'We never had any problems with John after that' you'd know why.

Bob, no doubt because in his mind's eye he could envision someone half hopping and screaming through the shower room - while trying to get the cloths-peg off of his 'bag', made a grimacing face, before breaking out into the same laughter his new friends were presently enjoying. In fact, the humor was so contagious that the other men there unintentionally eavesdropping also broke up, which for some strange reason also caused one of them reward them with a big long what sounded like a 'bu-u-u-rp', or at least they all would soon wish that it really had only been a burp.

Now 'natural gas', in their present location the men just liked to think of it as someone being 'squeaky-clean' especially if bubbles were present, was always an occasion for rude or humorous rebuttal. Fred, apparently the 'in house' specialist of the day, lost no time in starting off acknowledging the sound with one of the more common remarks it almost always seemed to deserve. "Speak - on mighty toothless one!"

His accentuated verbal offering, like almost anything else whimsical to the men, only served as an encouragement for others to follow, which someone else quickly did. "I think my ears just popped." Then, another co-worker obviously not to be outdone offered his attempt at comedy, "Say --- that sounds like a pretty bad cough you've got there. I think you better get it looked into." And then the final indignity, "That 'almost' smells as bad as your breath!"

The laughter, once started, as always became contagious, especially after the original perpetrator pretended to cough, before repeating his earlier performance. And as always to be expected, George never to fail to get his 'two cents worth' in, added, "That's 'probably' the first intelligent thing he's said all day!" - in his friends direction. "Now then, where was I before we were so rudely interrupted?" he smiled. "A-a-ah." As his train of thought instantly got back on track. "I can see, I wasn't missed after leaving you two bums earlier."

"Hell no!" Fred grinned, while continuing to scrub at his body. Louie, yes! But 'you', never!" It was almost twenty after three before everybody finally split. Everyone must have thought poor ol 'bashful' was an old fashioned water-pump or something. The way they kept priming his arm I wouldn't even be surprised if he eventually loaded his laundry."

One of the obviously eavesdropping men still in the shower, while snickering, decided to add his feelings to their conversation, "Boy - that Louie's got 'knockers' bigger than my wife's ass." To which George lost no time in adding, "I've seen your wife's 'ass', and you're wrong, they're a 'Hell' of a lot smaller!"

Bob, still new to most of the other men in the shower room, wisely once more just stayed in the background during their conversation. But his presence wasn't forgotten, as George more than once winked in his direction whenever he himself was involved in any of the never ending verbal contest going on.

As if waiting in the wings, fresh fodder entered the showers, an electrician whose chronic body hair made him look as if he was standing in a 'five o'clock shadow, to which one of the others there remarked.

"That reminds me, I've been told I have to shave before I can come home tonight."

"Why's that?" someone else foolishly asked, and was instantly rewarded with, "Because the wife's developed a bad rash, and is starting to walk funny."

Silly giggling was once more contagious as soon as they each had figured out the suggestive rudeness behind the words just spoken. But for some strange reason it also made Fred lean slightly forward to look at Bob's face, while saying, "Boy, I guess your people don't grow very good beards, do they."

Obviously already anticipating what Fred was hinting at, Bob continued to shampoo his jet-black hair, while answering what really hadn't been a question. "Well - what can I say. Everybody knows that things always grow better if fertilized. And we all know what the best fertilizer is made of don't we?"

"You could be almost right." George laughed. "There are some real' 'shit-heads' walkin around the plant with a full growth that keeps them in constant disguise. Personally, all this time I had just thought that it was because they owed a lot of money, and were in hiding."

Fortunately for all, non-physically enhanced verbal 'slamming's' didn't require the use of any of their extremities, at least none of them at this time were into knee slapping' when hearing a good joke. Hell, due to past similar conversations, those listening were more interested in not getting caught by the ol 'snuff of soap' incident. That was the type of situation where one got so involved in the humor that they accidentally inhaled some of the soap being applied to their face, and generally ended up blowing burning soap bubbles out of their nose, which only gagged those never having seen a big 'booger' before.

When Fred and Bob were finished and on their way out to the drying area, George's words followed them.

"What about tonight Bob? Have you given any real thought to what I mentioned earlier, can you make it?"

"Ya." Bob grinned. while reaching for his towel. "After what I've seen so far today, I think I better be there, for one reason or another."

"Good boy." George smiled, his head now bent forward and covered in shampoo, making him comically looking like he was really talking to the wet floor. "Give Fred your address and he'll tell you what time we'll pick you up at. The most it should cost you is a bottle of whatever you like to drink, but we'll talk about that when we're on our way there, fair enough?"

"Okay." Bob answered with his towel now busy in hand and imitating Fred's actions. George then quickly followed up with, "Get his phone number also buddy, and I'll meet you outside when I'm done."

George was alone now, but only as alone as a man could be in a building busy with a shift change going on. As the other men had filtered out they had left with a small grin on their faces. And by the time he picked his towel up from its resting-place, while saying to one of the men now drying beside him, "You must be from the east coast, the way you like hot water. I'd swear you're part lobster!" He then haphazardly used it to wipe at his body, in an effort to save time, as he almost ran back to his lockers.

His isle now, as he was afraid, was partially obstructed by a human wall of semi dressed bodies. For some strange reason, these men always seemed to prefer the second set of showers directly across from the ones George had just used. And as he excused his way past each of them, friendly conversation once more seemed to be everywhere.

The first half-dressed man that he had squeezed past, a friend and crane-operator who liked to jokingly say that he had control over a hundred men working under him, was in the nude sitting down and for some strange reason busy examining the skin between his toes. George, without even having slowed down, simply said, "What are you doing Lenny, learning to count up to twenty one?"

The next fellow was an individual with soft 'sixties' music playing out of his locker, a rather appropriate 'Working On the chain Gang' by Sam Cooke presently filling the air. He had been busy trying to get his pants on, when George couldn't help but accidentally 'bullshit!' bump into him. The result, as well as looking hilarious, brought another comical remark , when the individual ended up with both of his legs crammed into the same pant leg of his pants. All of which prompted out of George, "Well, at least now you know how a pair of Siamese twins must feel like, when they're only half dressed."

The third, and second to last obstruction that had been blocking his hurried movements, was a man who liked to periodically brag about his wife's knitting abilities. And as luck would have it, he was presently trying to unsuccessfully squeeze his head into something gaudy enough to direct traffic in. Even to the untrained eye it was quite obvious that the neck of the homemade sweater was overly small, and as George had passed he had said, "Maybe you should just get your wife to knit you a head that'll fit through the sweaters neck opening."

When his goal had been in sight, really only feet away, he had been forced to brush past and definitely the strangest of the group. The co-worker and very good friend had the reputation of always having his hair perfectly and rigidly groomed, with never a piece out of place. In fact it was often jokingly said that if he ever went outside on a windy day, it would in all probability snap off before even starting to bend.

Over their years together short put downs and comments from George had come to be expected, which was why most of the men he passed had just ignored his verbal barbs, all that is except for an occasional sarcastic grin.

Content that damp dry was good enough, George was starting with his clothing when the last man he had just almost brushed bums with asked his opinion about something. Because of his fine crop of hair he was know to be constantly and always looking for newer and seemingly better ways for taking care of it. And after having just rubbed in one of the most recent found tonics into his scalp, he asked him how he liked the smell of his hair. George, without even hesitating as he slipped into his underwear, replied with a straight face, "For your benefit I'll assume that we're talking about that creation on the upper part of your body. And if so, well, it's okay if you're into that kind of stuff, but personally I think you should just shave under you arms."

Rebuttal had always proven useless when dealing with George in the past, but his now indignant looking friend tried anyway.

"Well, at least I haven't got a lot of gray hair like you."

George, letting his vision wander just enough to make sure that everyone else in the isle were listening to what was going on, then looked directly into the eye's of the 'slamming' he had just taken, while saying, " Just mark my gray hairs down to constantly living in fear."

"Fear! I know I shouldn't ask this, but, " the man already staring to shake his head in contempt for the rest part of George's explanation, but did it anyway. "fear from what?

"Fear," George himself was now already starting to grin even before he had finished with the rest of his explanation. "anybody here's kids just might grow up to be anything like you."

As well as bringing a round of laughing 'He-e-e-ers' out of the group, it also made the guy fully dressed at the end of the aisle; his name was Lenny Lammont, comment. "I don't know how he manages to keep his wig in perfect place all the time, and yes even in the shower, George, mine's always all over the place.

"Ya, we can 'see' that!" One of the other men in the isle grinned back. And just by the way he verbally emphasized the four words - the other men instantly understood that Lenny would probably have been better off keeping his mouth shut and opinion to himself. "It's in your comb, it's in the shower room, it's on your shirts caller, it's etcetera, etcetera, etcetera."

As snickering became rampant in the tiny area once more, the one originally responsible for the 'hairy' topic being bantered about, used both of his hands to comb and pat his into place, while feeding more fuel to the fire that just wasn't ready to go out yet. "Who's your barber Lenny? I want to make sure as Hell I don't accidentally ever go to him."

"Very funny Nick. And just what's with the ol 'Mirror mirror on the wall' routine? What the 'shit' you getting all dolled up for this time? It looks like you've got enough 'Brylcream' on your hair to lubricate a very large army truck."

Running the palms of his hands along the sides of his perfectly placed jet black hair, a smile of appreciation over the comment and recognition now on his face, Nick grinned, "I've got a chance for some real 'kinky sex' tonight. But then, I doubt it if any of you 'pickle pusses' ever get a chance for a thrill like that."

Smiling contently at the reflection grinning back at him, obviously very pleased with his remark, he then ran a finger over his freshly brushed teeth, no doubt checking to make sure they were also measuring up to his expectations. But George being George was not about to let anyone so vain think they'd had the last comment, 'right or not' particularly about anyone there, so he quickly shot back a huge ego bruising 'put down'. "I'm not admitting to you being right or wrong buddy, but in your case I'm pretty sure the other guy doesn't want you lookin or smellin bad either."

Someone in the next aisle over could be heard to snicker, which made Nick ask sarcastically respond. "I wonder what the Hell he thinks is so funny?"

George, now into his socks and pants, didn't even look up from what he was doing, let alone miss a beat, while adding. "Oh, he probably just walked in front of a mirror or something."

By that time almost everyone there, everyone except George, was dressed and ready for the 'time clock'. And as each of them noisily slammed their lockers closed, the only guy still not heard form in their gathering finally added his voice to George's last 'barb' at Nick.

"Well, if what you said about lover boy here is true," he smiled, "I guess that kind of makes Nicky a vegetarian."

"How's that?" one of the other men quickly smiled, no doubt just doing his part in the game, realizing that what was to come could only be a real 'pip'.

"Well, what else would you call a person who only eats fruits"

"Oh ya?" Even though Nick's voice sounded as if he was really irritated by the 'gang up' he as well as they only smiled when adding, "Well at least I don't have teeth that would make a beaver envious, or a tree nervous. And as for you 'dumpy'," he was looking directly into the man standing fully dressed beside him, "you're probably the only guy I ever knew who as a kid went around singing, 'I wish I was an 'Oscar Meyer wiener' - and made it!"

Not waiting or giving any chance for a rebuttal, while stuffing his dirty laundry into a duffel bag, Nick then turned his head and full attention in George's smiling direction, while remarking, "Is that your breath or mine I can smell?" George, knowing and accepting for now that it was his time in the barrel, answered. "Well it sure isn't mine!" And Nick quickly followed up with, "I didn't think so. Yours doesn't usually smell so good." before turning and heading out of the aisle with the other two laughing men.

George, still chuckling after wishing them all a good weekend, was now once again all alone in the aisle as he put the finishing touches to his own wardrobe, a splash of after-shave, 'whore oil' the single men used to call it, topping everything off.

A quick glance at his wristwatch told him it was now two minutes to quitting time, which caused him to hurry even faster if possible. Slamming his locker closed, its sound like a delayed echo that had been repeating itself throughout the crowd area, George scooped up the bag containing everything dirty and jogged for the building's exit.

Fred was waiting just outside the complexes' front doors, and as he said, 'Slowpoke!' he quickly matched his steps to meet George's long hurrying stride. Rushing hadn't paid off, as they were just in time to be at the tail end of the line when punching out. And when they got to the parked car, Rusty and Pop Bottles were already there, their laundry and lunch pails hanging at their sides.

Stopping at the vehicle's trunk long enough for each of them to deposit his well-used and scented laundry, George then unlocked the passengers side of the car before walking around and doing the same for his side of the vehicle. They, as always, used the same seating arrangements they had used earlier that morning. As should be expected the conversation before each man's stop, and a promise to meet again later that night, was solely about the stunt they had played on voluptuous Louie. And when George and Fred were finally alone in the car, they turned the topic to other things.

"Got anything planned for supper tonight?" George had taken his eyes off the road just long enough to softly smiles in his best friend's direction, as he had asked the question. Fred, in turn, returned the warm gesture while answering.

"Naw, nothing special. I'll probably just hit the 'Colonel' on the way home, and then do up my laundry before we go out tonight."

His latest home, as George already know, was a small depressing one-bedroom bachelor flat that had all the suggestive traits of making a freshly separated man seriously contemplate suicide. It was also, while having the privacy and sex appeal of a 'padded cell', a place of Fred's choosing, after George had unsuccessfully tried to get him to move in with them for a while. His reason, running from seeing that Fred got good meals and clean laundry, on through to him having constant good companionship in order to keep the mind from working against itself when he was alone, were all well intended with strictly Fred's well being in mind. But each and every good intention was just as quickly also rejected. Fred had inwardly wanted to accept his best friend's offer, but pride had kept it from happening.

This time, instead of glancing in Fred's direction, George let his voice show his pleasure when he next spoke, obviously ignoring every rejection from Fred's lips. "Good! I already warned the boss before we left this morning that you'd be staying for supper tonight."

"But, but," Fred started to object, his voice noticeably emotional, but George easily cut him off.

"If you can't stay for supper I'm afraid you'll have to talk to the head of the house, not me. Besides, it was more her idea than mine anyway."

"Gee!" Fred said, his voice still displaying how he felt. "I already spend more time at your house than my apartment. My poor landlady keeps thinking I've skipped out on her, and now I'm going to take some more food out of you kid's mouth.'

George pretended to laugh lightly at Fred's last remark, and he tried to lighten the mood between him and his best friend evermore.

"Well, if you're going to look at it that way, then just think of it as taking food out of only the oldest boy's mouth. A little bit of less calories won't hurt him any, and you'd be doing me and his mother a big favor by helpin knock a few pounds off him. Besides, that's what true friends are all about."

By the look that instantly came to Fred's face, it was obvious that he had a response to George's last words. But George as always was far ahead of his friend's reasoning, and he easily cut him off with the words, "And never mind what I said earlier about what a 'real' friend really is. 'That' definition does 'not' apply here!"

The expression on Fred's face faltered only slightly, as his brain recalled what George was talking about. But as soon as he had remembered what the words were referring to, he started to chuckle. George, in turn, his house now in view, instantly joined in and kept their present mood constant, right up until he pulled into the driveway.

Climbing out of the wagon George spotted his second oldest boy Darryll presently busy with his newest and apparently most favorite now, pastime. It used to be lifting weights and body building, 'pumping iron' the younger generation liked to call it, but now it was apparently holding hands or talking with the next door neighbors oldest daughter

Pat. And as soon as the his son realized that he was watching them, the boy let go of the beautiful young girls hand, while acting like the kid who'd just been caught with his hand in the proverbial 'cookie jar'. The young girl, looking more and more like a younger version of a young developing Louie Zupanic, acted just as bashful as his son whenever he was around. And it made him on more than occasion remark to the boy that if they had built girls more like her when he was young and single , he'd at least still be single!

As both of the youngsters youthful faces almost identically and in unison said, "Hi dad! Hi mister Owen!" both George and Fred couldn't help but openly smile at their noticeably blushing young faces.

"Hello kids!" they answered. But only George recalled that the girl's earlier nickname of 'Fatty Patty' was no longer descriptive, let alone suitable. And again, it was really only George who noticed that the pretty young girl was not that far away from becoming a beautiful young woman.

"Are your brothers home yet?" George called out, as they walked around to the rear of the vehicle.

"Ya." Darryll replied. "I think they're both hiding in the house, someplace."

Retrieving both his and Fred's work bags from the vehicle's trunk area, Fred both tried and failed to object, as George easily cut him off again by saying that he was doing it for the benefit of the car's atmosphere, not him.

"It's bad enough the boys smell up the car when they borrow it on the weekends. I don't need the raunchy aroma from your laundry hangin around in there, and giving me flashbacks at to where we work. I get enough of that place up my nose while I'm there. Besides, with any luck you'll be in no condition after tonight or tomorrow night to do laundry the next day. And this way at least you won't have to worry about having clean work clothes for work on Monday.

As they headed into the house Fred already knew and accepted that he could in no way win any of the verbal battles ever laid on him - especially in their present surroundings. So, he just silently, while nodding, fell in line behind his truly best friends moving form.

Even before the screen door had a chance to slam and 'kiss the ass' of the last one through the doorway, 'Fred', Judy's pleasant smiling face was welcoming them home.

"I'm glad to see that you two managed to make it through another workday, as well as all the way home on your own."

Reaching forward to trade them two ice cold bottles of the 'related dog' that had bit them, for their work-clothes, she continued smiling while adding, "How about the rest of the 'sponges', everybody make it to work today?"

"We had one close call. One of the group must have got ahold of a bad piece of chicken or something. He said he spent part of the night sleeping on the white telephone, and by the time he was done he figured the only thing he hadn't passed were his tonsils. Other than that, I'd say they were 'all there'." George grinned back. "But then again that would only be 'half true', if you know what I mean, 'jellybean'?"

"I know what you mean, 'jellybean'! And if you're going to continue using the wagon for horizontally transporting those to inebriated to remain vertical under their own power, try to remember to occasionally leave the tailgate window down a crack for ventilation during those trips home. But most importantly, just because it might look a bit like one, try not to turn it into a Hurst."

"Hey!" George smiled. "We both agreed on buying a station wagon. I told you that feeding the kids just every second day wasn't going to keep them from getting any bigger, remember?"

Judy chuckled, while turning to head for the laundry-room. "Supper won't be ready for another twenty minutes - and I'm pretty sure which half of the group you two belong in, so why don't you two take your beers to the basement until I call you."

George, while tilting his head in the rec-rooms direction to tell Fred that it was where they were now heading, added, "I'd say her suggestion sounded more like a combination 'slam' 'command' ol buddy.' So they did exactly that.

Chapter # 6

'Boys night out.'
Or
'She sickness.'

Six o'clock supper was well on its way around the bend and into the plumbing by the time George and Fred stopped off long enough to pick up Bob. Climbing into the vehicles rear seat, after returning their smiling 'Hello's'!, Bob's nose twitched both unnoticed and unintentional when picking up the last remnants of Fred's not that long hours ago 'crash' site. Allowing his form to sink into the cars soft seats, he let the grin that had been present when first watching the vehicles approach, return as Fred started to fill him on what he might expect later.

George, although occasionally still subject periodically to certain displays of bigotry, prided himself that he was successfully avoiding its ugly head from appearing around their new close friend. It was, he mentally told himself, just another of his capabilities rising over some of his fellow workers' limitations, such as the ability to walk, talk, and chew gum at the same time, when necessary. And as the distance between them and the motel they were headed for disappeared under the vehicles wheels he periodically jumped in and out of the verbal comments such as the one his best friend was presently making.

"I hope you brought lots of loose change for the card games." Fred said a little cynically. "Rules are, we don't borrow or lone money amongst ourselves during these outings. Nobody wants to be gambling against their own loot."

Briefly altering his facial features, instantly telling George and Fred they were once again about to be the beneficiaries to another of his many ancestral proverbs, Bob answered "Money not true way to keep score. And wise man never loan money to friend, have found it ruin their memory."

George, snickering in Bob's direction, slammed him with "Hell, as long as he doesn't play poker anywhere near as bad as you do 'buddy', I don't think he'll need much change, or luck. You're the only guy I know of who can constantly guess wrong two times out of three on a two headed coin toss."

"Oh ya!" Fred shot back, deliberately trying to look as if he had been verbally wounded, "And I suppose you're mister Las Vegas material?"

"I don't have to be." George smiled, "As long as I don't play five card stud with a six card draw - and a buy at the end, like you do."

"Oh ya!" Fred shot back again; "Well at least I didn't throw my body on the 'crap table' and yell, 'I bet it all!' just because I was down a few bucks."

"That's not even close to what happened when I was in Vegas." George grinned back. "If you remember, I had just said that one of my brothers had perfected a proven system for gambling in the big sand trap, and it had taken all of his money to prove it didn't work. For me, I told you that my usual run of bad luck had the guy in front of me at the airport win a new car when he had opened the door marked "pull". Me, all I got, was my foot stepped on when I yanked on it."

"Then why do you bother going? Fred winked back, keeping the opportunity for his best friends humor open.

"Because the time before when I was at the same airport and I'd put three quarters in one of their storage bins, not only its door, but all of the other storage compartment doors flew open at the same time. Boy, you talk about a 'rush'!"

"I give up!" Fred feigned in hopelessness, his hands waving in the air above his head. "Let's play cards, but not your way!" he quickly added.

Neither of them had bothered to ask Bob if he knew how to play poker. But judging by the way he chuckled after George's last remark, it could be assumed that he must have at least been associated with the basics, especially since there was no such game that George had mentioned earlier.

"Would I be correct in assuming that if I'm lucky enough to win any big money tonight," Bob chuckled, "chances are that I'm not likely to be asked back for a return match?"

"He walks away with a bundle of anybody's loot tonight," Fred grinned in Georges' direction, "with emphases being on the word 'walked', 'chances' of him even getting a ride home tonight are slim to none. Right Buddy?"

"It could happen." George half laughed. "After all - he's been lucky enough to meet us hasn't he?"

"Should I consider that as 'good' or 'bad' luck?" Bob added, a definite attempt at a humorous slamming imbedded in the words.

"Definitely bad." George sneered. "And that's the only reason we would ever think of asking you back for any of our get togethers'."

"Oh, and what's the next treat to be?" Bob asked. "Darts, snooker, tiddlywinks?"

"More likely the latter than the former." Fred laughed.

"He's right." George butted in. "Wait-ill you've had a chance to be around this bunch a few times and you'll not only be glad - but you'll understand that you don't want to be around these characters for a variety of reasons when comes to other avenues of entertainment."

Smiling first at Fred and then at George, Bob asked with a hint of skepticism in his voice. "Should I be taking those as words of wisdom or just some friendly advice?"

"Let me put it this way." George carried on, with a half chuckle. "There isn't enough money in the world to get me out into the woods on a hunting trip with any of the men you're about to be with tonight, especially where booze is involved. I just can't imagine any of them loose with a loaded weapon in their hands. Besides, when it comes time to be 'mounted', I'll take my wife, over anyone's fireplace.

As Fred smiled, "Right about now, I'd be happy to get mounted anywhere." Bob grinned, "Since most things are generally "stuffed' before they're mounted, what say we stuff a mixture of booze and entertainment under our belts."

And when it comes to darts, well, you might just as well as give them a bow and arrow! In their cases they both would require lots of running for cover."

Failing to totally suppress the chuckle borne of the mental images Georges words had instantly brought to his thoughts, Bob asked, "Well what about snooker? I fail to see what damage could come out of that game."

"You don't know the limitations of or boys." George smiled. "Other than occasionally swearing that they some times felt as if they were living behind the 'eight ball', when it comes to playin with a cue or rackin up their balls, well, considering that there's no potential for a Willy Miscony hiding in the bunch, I'll let your imagination take you there on that one."

"And the only good thing that can be said about 'bowling'," Fred quickly offered, "is that with any luck, you'll wake up with 'one pin' still standing in the morning."

You haven't mentioned the 'gentleman's game'." Bob smiled. "Golf. What about golf, or does it require to much physical activity?"

"That's only the half of it." George offered.

"Oh that game where it never rains." Fred quickly added.

"Exactly." George just as effortlessly cut back in. "Who in their right mind would go out in the middle of a thundering rain storm, metal spikes in their shoes sunk into the wet ground. And then repeatedly waving a metal rod over their heads, which is like saying 'I'm over here! I'm over hear!' Why, I can almost hear Gods answer of, 'Just a second, and I'll be right with you! 'Za-a-a-a-ap'!"

Giving his passengers the benefit of a few seconds to enjoy his interpretation of the game of golf, George kept right on grinning while adding. "So you can see where when it comes to any great amount of any safe physical activity, sit down cards and good repetitive arm bending for a booze up just naturally go hand in hand for most of us."

It was the type of deliberate mood setting comment that not only had Bob laughing repeatedly, especially when George had allowed Fred to slam him back with a verbal. "Well at least I'm not such a compulsive gambler that I keep trying to bump the ante," but also the kind of friendly jesting that stuck with them during the entire drive to the motel.

Dusk was already making its impending arrival known as they pulled into the motel unit's parking lot. Two other cars George instantly recognized were already parked in front of the end unit they had often reserved in the past for such similar get-togethers. Wasting no time in pulling in alongside the vehicles, he quickly got out of his own car just in time to see and hear the noisy arrival of another two co-workers also involved in the plans for the evening, the 'Langley twins'.

Instant smiles appeared on Fred and Bob's faces also as they pretended to jump out of the path of the approaching car's swerving erratic behavior, just as it gave out with a series of short loud bangs, no doubt due to a long overdue tune up. As it squealed to a lurching stop only inches from where they stood, its radio loudly at work screamed out a modern song that protested the plight of the garbage men. It was also now easy to see that the two now laughing men it contained had obviously gained a slight head start on the night's routine drinking.

The driver's tongue, as he yelled out, "He-e-e-y! Are we la-late or early for the pu-party?" tripped noticeably over a few of the words. But before anyone could answer, the sudden sound and appearance of a door opening with a hurrying man only half-dressed carrying his pants and shoes, froze everyone's attention in the strange happening's direction. And not until the confused and frightened looking man had nervously fumbled his way into his car, a woman's voice from within the unit shouting, "Don't be afraid, honey! Come back inside!" did the reality of what was happening finally sink into their heads.

Laughing almost uncontrollably, as the terrified man's vehicle noisily burned rubber all the way out of the parking lot, a just as nervous and semi-dressed woman appearing in the unit he had just vacated opened doorway. George, his imagination conjuring up images to fit what was unfolding before him, proved he wasn't stronger than the contagious humor under way around him. Over-reacting like everyone else, he used one of his hands to slap at the top of his car's roof to noisily amplify his almost sidesplitting present laughter. And it wasn't until the woman, glaring at their presence - mumbling some unheard obscenity under her breath had disappeared back into the motel unit's privacy, that the humor finally started to look for a new reason for living.

Leaning forward finally, small trails of moisture running down his cheeks, George had to force himself to concentrate on what he wanted to say, into the face of the second man in the car who was holding a bottle of beer on his lap.

"I see you guys have been into the "brown pop" on the way here."

"Sure, why not?" the driver, Bob Langly, smiled. "Me, me and my brother figured we we'd c-elebrate a little in advance be-before taking everybody's money off them in the poker game."

The insinuating remark not only made all of them laugh, Bob Logan and Jack Ellis had walked over to stand beside the car too, but it also gave George a chance to once more verbally slam the two brothers, mainly because they honestly believed the foolish comment just made.

"Ya know, two half wits don't make a whole wit. And the sunny day you or your brother, 'ol Laughing Larry', end up with any of my money, I'll personally drive you two to the bank and roll out the red carpet when you're ready to deposit it."

The humor that had deteriorated just slightly enough to hear rebuttal quickly came back in full strength when the car's tires once more squealed, while Bob called out. "We-e-ll, keep tomorrow mornin' around eleven o'clock - free."

The car then lunged forward after a parking spot all of its own. Turning their attention back towards the vehicles they had arrived in, while still chuckling, each man then stepped forward and lifted a cardboard box out of their trunks, once they had been opened. Each person participating in any of the little get-togethers had always been responsible for their own personal kind of 'poison' and mix. Fred, carrying the three twenty-six ouncers of 'Superman in a bottle', he and George had picked up a rye for Bob as a sort of token welcoming gift to the group, let Bob struggle with the two cases of tinned mix that would not only help make their consumption of alcohol slide down just a little bit slower, but also help slow down the pickling effect their livers were about to undergo.

George, in turn, carefully carried the box containing his video machine, which he always volunteered to make available as long as someone else would supply the 'blue' movies.

By the time he got to the doorway of the motel unit with the movie unit, Fred had the room's door opened and ready for his arrival. Leading the way inside, Bob almost bashfully in tow, it was not only easy to see that they were almost the last people to arrive, but also that their anticipated presence was immediately appreciated, as the men already there started to cheer their appearance. And when on of the men stepped forward and slapped stickers on Fred and George's shirt, only Bob acted genuinely confused. Confused, that is, until Fred offered, "Oh, these thing are just part of the atmosphere." he beamed - one finger jabbing at George's nametag. It's a little game we play, just to see who ends up wearin' whose tag the next day."

Still smiling, Bob feigned looking at where his would have been if he had been offered a tag, to which Fred quickly said, "Don't worry, we should have some spares around here someplace. First chance I get, I'll see if I can find one for you."

"Tell him the only embarrassing part." George piped in.

Faltering only slightly, as if lost for an answer, Fred grinned. "Oh - you mean how the women put our names and addressed on the inside of our clothing, just so that whoever should find us when we're to 'plastered' to know who we are or where we're going, will know where to ship our bodies home to."

Fred and Bob's laughing was lost in the activity as two men rushed forward to get the room's television set ready for George's video unit. And when the Langly twins walked noisily into the room only seconds later, their presence was briefly acknowledged by only a few of the men, and barely at that. "It's about time you 'bums' got here!"

Concentrating only on the installation of his machine, George's ears failed to pick up on the conversation two men were having about his phobias on having most of the latest video equipment on the electronics market. He didn't hear the words, "I'm surprised he hasn't run out and bought a parabolic dish yet.' And he totally missed the reply, which he had expressed himself already many times before, 'He would have, but he's heard rumors about satellite signals eventually being scrambled and he's afraid of being stuck with a five thousand dollar 'bird bath'.'

Finishing with the last connection between his video unit and the TV set, a drink with his name on it, "Here you go, George", appeared at his side. His ears told him who his new found friend was even before he could look in the voice's direction. But when he did, he found himself staring into the smiling face of a man who was presently off work on compensation due to hand injury, incurred on the job.

Returning the smile, while accepting the healthy shot of rye, George allowed his vision to briefly alter its direction just long enough to get a quick glimpse of a cast half encasing the man's other hand, while saying, "Thanks Ralph. How's the mitt?"

Raising the hand now free of the drink it had been carrying up in front of both of their faces, Ralph opened and closed it repeatedly while answering, "Okay, I guess., Not as good as the 'wife' mind you, - close - but definitely not as good."

To show his appreciation of the pun, George raised the drink now in his grasp and silently saluted at the still flexing fingers in front of him, chuckling and smiling, while adding, "Here's to the wives. Can't live with em, can't live without em!"

With a big grin still on his face, as one of the men mumbled, 'I sure wouldn't mind givin it a try at least one time!', but so as to give an honest answer to the genuinely concerned question, Ralph raised the cast-enhanced hand this time and said, "Oh, did you mean this one? Well, the doctor says it won't be around long enough to crack nuts open with at Christmas, but it'll take another few months before it'll be ready for a workout back at the 'ol sweatshop."

As the memory of how his coworker had receive the injury, the hand had been badly cut and mangled while testing a broken gear housing, George's face instinctively started to allow the recalled gruesome scene to wipe the smile from his face. But before the mood could deteriorate any further, Ralph glanced quickly across the room at Fred, who was still busy fixing drinks. He then leaned closer to George, a rather futile gesture considering the amount of noise and commotion presently under way by the other men there, and whispered, "Does Freddy suspect what's up yet?"

"Are you kiddin?" George said a little sarcastically. "Ol 'sharp-as-a-bathtub' Fred suspect what's up? Why, sometimes I have my doubts that he could even fall 'down', without first asking directions."

"Other than that," Ralph laughed, "How's he holding up? The 'Dragon Lady' stills in his stomach?'

"Well, personally," George said dryly, "right about now I think he's feelin lower than 'snake-shit' in a wagon rut."

"Oh." Ralph said a little dejectedly. And then as an almost second thought, he raised his injured hand up to eye level once more before saying, "Well, ya know there's no real excuse for a man ever having to do without - except for some of us that is."

George had no trouble deciphering Ralph's insinuation - which was quite evident by his following remark. "I realize 'beatin ain't cheatin', and the closest he's come to gettin 'raped' lately - is when he takes himself in-hand to take a 'leak'. But Fred's the kind of guy who's too bashful to even date himself. No - I'd say 'ol high blood pressure Fred' is more than ripe for the companionship of someone of the opposite gender. Oh, and as for dragons, let's leave the wives at home where they belong. As for our surprise, she's supposed to be a potentially pleasant memory, not, a constantly continuing existing nightmare."

"Well, I guess later will sure show if there's any truth to that reasoning,' Ralph laughed. "But if he don't score tonight, you better find some other means of him getting rid of the 'ol excessive eyeball pressure real quick, before he gets a chance to explode. And remember, while we're waitin, none of us is getting' any younger."

"I'll say," George chuckled." And if any of our wives ever find out what we're doing, you or I won't be around long enough to get any 'older' either."

"Well, maybe the movies will be just the thing needed to make the 'trick' work later,' Ralph said."

"Just remember," George grinned. "when it comes right down to sex it's the 'magician', not the 'wand' that really makes the 'trick' work."

Glancing back in Fred's direction, he and Bob were now in the process of loading their hands up with the drinks they had just poured. Ralph, now with a slight hint of sarcasm in his voice, quickly offered, "Well, if there is any truth to the recent rumors I've heard about him 'brown bagging' it lately, we better do something real quick. Ya know - just to make sure he doesn't get too 'pissed' to know which end of the so called 'trick' he's in control of."

"Don't worry." George smiled, while glancing briefly in Fred's direction. "I plan on keeping an eye on him."

"Well we don't want him doing 'throw rug' imitations on the floor." Ralph said, using the same attitude. "Tonight's supposed to be an opportunity for him to 'shine' up his image, not tarnish it."

"He'll be a 'beacon of light' guiding ships on a foggy night." George smiled. "Just you wait and see. I'm sure he'll surprise everyone."

"I sure hope so. But more for his sake then ours." Ralph added.

Just short of being on 'cue', with Bob in close tow, Fred started to glide in their direction , his hands overflowing with drinks. It was a comical looking balancing act that was rewarded with a passing remark of, "Ya know when someone yell's 'drink's for everyone', they generally don't expect you to try and carry all of them, all at one time."

Ralph and George, watching every move, used a little body English to help guide them in for a safe approach, big smiles and outstretched open hands offering assistance for their eventual arrival.

After dancing around a few of the other men, Rusty and Eagle Beak lightening the load of refills they had asked for, Fred with Bob still in close tow finally stopped in front of his best friend and Ralph. Only now noticing that George already had a drink close-by, he wordlessly offered one of the few drinks he had left in Ralph's direction - while saying, "How's it going Ralphy! How's the ol 'hammer' hanging?"

Both George and Ralph couldn't help but keep grinning, not so much for what Fred had just said, but rather for what they had been talking about. And the next order of business to introduce their newest friend Bob to Ralph was totally forgotten as Fred's curiosity made him ask, "Why do I get the feelin I'm missing out on something? Just what are you two sneaky bastards up to?"

It was on the tip of George's tongue to say, 'Oh, about five foot eleven each.' as he reached and lifted one of the extra drinks from his friends hands any-ways, but instead just laughed a little bit harder, as Ralph was doing. And when he did speak, he said, "I thought I told you before to never ask a question leading to an obvious answer. You know there's time's I can't help myself."

Letting the good feelings on his face turn into an obviously over reacting frown, Fred sneered, "Ya know, we're all looking fore-ward to the day when you get yours 'wisenheimer'. Now are we going to play cards and get into some serious drinking, or just stand around 'pickin' on each other?"

"What's wrong with doing a little of both?" George laughed. And as the others there chuckled lightly, he quickly added, "But what say we introduce Ralph and Bob to each other first."

A small card game had already been in progress when they had entered the room, and by now the Langly twins, Bill and Bob, were both noisily and monetarily involved in it. Allowing his laughter to subside completely, but also making sure to smile appropriately after doing exactly as he had suggested, George nodded in the poker game's direction before saying, "Why don't we take Bob around and check out the action? If we find anyone we don't trust we can always get another game started."

"Sounds like the perfect plan to me." Fred beamed - while using one of his elbows to nudge Bob in the side.

Ralph started to excuse himself by saying, "I don't know about you 'girls', but I gotta drain something." But before he could move, he suddenly became aware of George's drink empty hand pinching his pant-leg - in a manner that only he could detect. Instantly realizing that George obviously wasn't finished with him yet, he pretended that he still had something on his mind that he wanted to ask George about.

George in turn saying that there was something he needed to talk to Ralph about concerning the upcoming shop stag, told Fred and Bob to get started, and he would catch up with them in a few minutes.

Watching both men walk away, waiting until he was sure they were both completely lost in the room's noisy atmosphere, Ralph unnecessarily once more leaned closer to George before whispering, "Poor bugger. He's kinduv old to be getting 'blue balls'. Why it's probably been so long since he's been with a woman I'll bet he almost forgets what they smell like."

George's reply, like always, was quick and double-edged when he wrinkled up his nose while saying, "That's bad?"

The laughter it brought was just as instantaneous as George's remark had been, and he offered a silent salute with his glass in Fred's departed direction, while adding the rest of what was also in his thoughts.

"Here's hoping all of that changes real soon."

Matching the toast with his own drink, Ralph didn't laugh this time as the full meaning he knew to be behind the 'innuendo', but instead sincerely added. "That - my good friend, I will drink to!"

The sudden interruption of a new voice from behind them, 'What's up, the Queen comin?' broke into their present train of thought. It was Jack Ellis, a drink in one hand and a big piece of 'burning rope' in the other, busy making love to his two favorite vices. And as someone close to him chuckled 'No. You can whip out to your car and put your dress back on if you want!'. The thick gray smoke from the cigar slowly floated up into their faces, it eventually caused George, not the only one to chuckle at the put down, to squint and fan at the air in front of him, while commenting through a rattling cough, "That thing reminds me of a 'coach-fire' Jack. why don't you give everybody a break and take that thing outside before someone calls the 'fire department'."

The remark, although said in a half jest, and already obviously expected, caused Rusty to hold the 'smoldering small log' behind his back - while retaliating, "Let's not get all emotionally 'choked up' George. I just wanted to give you the movies you had asked for. Gee!"

As George and Ralph both pretended to be poking holes in the building cloud from the cigar, Rusty brought it out from behind his back and stuck it into one side of his mouth. He then let the now free hand continue on its way and retrieve two small black plastic cases that had been tucked under the armpit of the hand still holding his drink, while grinning out. "If these 'baby blues' don't start the 'ol coals down below a-glowin' we're to late. Fred's either 'dead', or 'switchin'."

"That, 'cinder-breath'," George said sarcastically, "is not one bit funny. It might be acceptable in your family, but I personally wouldn't want my brother, let alone best friend, to marry one of those people."

"You mean it's legal now!" Rusty instantly and jokingly added, while over acting his best at being totally surprised.

If laughter is indeed the 'best medicine', then each man with their present form of sick humor were each overdue for a thick 'cream filled pie' in the 'kisser'. It took almost five full minutes, as they took turns running through all the present day puns on homosexuality ranging from, 'his and his' towels. Are they 'entitled to wear white at their weddings - as well as who leads on the dance-floor?' And right on to 'What will their children think of them?' before they accepted the fact that it was time to let the subject have a rest. And when Ralph used the break in the laughter as an excuse to take care of prior business before getting a new drink - Rusty said that it about time he got financially involved in one of the two poker games now in progress.

George, after glancing at his wristwatch and wondering just what kind of jokes the people they had been poking fun at would use to describe them, he called after Ralph to bring him back a refill too. And then just as quickly added on 'Grab some of those chips pretzels and nuts to pass around to will ya.' before leaving him with to also make sure he washed his hands first.

An unhappy sounding eavesdropper in the gathering shouted out, 'I hope you didn't buy any of those chocolate covered nuts like last time. Somehow I got some of that melted brown crap on my lap and it looked like I had forgot to wipe myself before pulling up my pants after a visit to the crapper.'

The comment, as some might have warranted as 'keeping to ones self' was instantly acknowledged with a barrage of mixed 'Yuks and E-ewes. George, after adding his own insult of 'I thought you said you had your hemorrhoids fixed. Oops, sorry, wrong color.' quickly returned his attention back towards the video machine, a much larger barrage of filled with a mixture of chips pretzels and nuts being thrown in his direction.

Inserting into the video machine the first of the two provided 'porno tapes' he was still holding, George started spot checking its contents at random. The sometimes graphic material, the plot also no 'Oscar' winner, was as Jack had promised, tongue dragging on the floor potential, as was evident by the short outbursts of whistles and wolf calls coming from the men viewing the short scenes.

The screening took almost another whole five minutes, and in that time not only the drink he requested had been consumed, but also the last men they were expecting finally showed up. Twelve regulars had made a definite commitment towards the little party, and surprisingly, the whole rowdy bunch had shown up, with Bob making it an uneven 'baker's dozen'.

But the time hadn't been wasted by everyone just waiting for the movies. Some had distracted each other just enough to slip in the odd pantomime, such as one of them falling noisily backwards out of his chair. And once he was sure that he had most of his buddies attention he put both of his hands around his throat as if choking before letting first one leg and then the other shake like the tail on a rattlesnake, only to suddenly fall motionless. It was a performance that was instantly rewarded with a bland remark of, 'That'll teach ya to drink out of someone else's glass.'

Past experiences had seasoned most of the men enough that they realized a trip to the 'bar' for a refill was something to be avoided as long as possible. Anyone foolish or drunk enough to forget the reasons 'why' generally found themselves not only getting their own 'poison', but generally half a dozen more requested by the men, 'sponges', too preoccupied in the card games. Jamie Weir, the last worker through the door, was busy suffering such a fate, as George and Ralph walked up to the motel unit's tiny kitchenette, now substituting as their refreshment center. He then made another mistake when, after saying 'Hello.' asked George how in the 'Hell' he managed to get out once again by himself on a Friday night. And when he instantly got 'zinged', "The same way you did Woody, by lying to my wife about where I was really going." he knew his presence for the remainder of the night had been officially recognized.

The man, George had given his nickname of 'Woody' because he had a hollow wooden leg, and whenever George was looking for revenge on him would always threaten to throw a 'woodpecker' on him, 'Woody Wood Pecker' cartoons also being popular at the time, chuckled slightly before continuing.

"Ya know 'Acid Tongue', If you ever said something nice - or ever failed to pick on any of us, I think we'd all really feel offended."

"Offended!" George said. "If I didn't like you, I wouldn't even spend the air required to talk to half of you 'Einstein's!"

"Like us!" Ralph quickly added, just as sarcastically emphasized as George's words. "Hell, what with your brown eyes and laxative outlook on life, we just naturally assumed that you're full of that messy brown body waste any-ways."

Once again George knew that it was time to let one of his buddies have their brief 'shot at fame' 'time in the spotlight' over him, especially since he knew that he could 'pick them off like 'fish in a rain-barrel' any time he wanted. And he was more than happy to move onto the next issue at hand, when one of them made the mistake of adding, "Come on now. Don't tell us a man with your limited vocabulary and 'IQ' is going to let the truth finally have the last say!"

Altering his attention, and not because he was lost for words, but just long enough to refill his empty plastic cup, as well as two others, Ralph and Woody hung on his every silent movement. George, 'milking' the little 'one man play' for every thing it was worth, looked directly into their eyes to mentally access if they were primed enough yet. And from his estimation it was plain to see that each opponent's facial expression was indicating that they indeed were just begging for more abuse. So, being the close friend that he was, he gave it to them.

"Only my scruples and personal commitment not to pick on dumb animals is keeping me from doing justice to your weak verbal attack on my integrity. Instead," while picking up the three shots of 'high test' he had prepared, "I'd rather leave you both guessing at what I'm mentally saying about you two. That suspense in itself should mentally antagonize you both into total frustration." He then turned and left their laughing figures behind him, while happily whistling in his best friends' direction.

The last time he had looked as his wristwatch it had been just short of nine-thirty. The party, as well as growing in volume, had noticeably grown a little wilder in language and antics, apparently in accordance with their present growing good mood. Dropping two spare extra drinks he had brought with him off in front of the men he had arrived with, lower building internal pressure told him that it was time to lower his waterline, before even attempting to occupy the empty seat they had saved just for him.

Placing his own drink onto the table while winking in Fred and Bob's direction, 'guard that with your lives.' He noticed that by the amount in front of each of them it looked as if 'lady luck' was sitting someplace else in the room. He was just about to leave, when one of the men in the same poker game asked him he was going back to the bar. And if so, would he mind bringing him back a couple of anything wrapped in brown pieces of glass.

"Sorry Terry. I just gotta have a 'whiz'."

"Great!" 'Eagle Beak' grinned. "Have one for me while you're at it, will ya."

"I'm only goin to drain the 'main vein', not perform surgery to relieve pressure off of your brain."

The hand of poker presently in progress at the table was held up just long enough for each man to express their appreciation to the verbal 'slamming'. But it was only Bob who continued to watch his new found friend's form until it disappeared into the unit's small imitation of a decent washroom.

On his way back from the 'john' he happened to cross only paths at this time when "Beautiful Brad, who was up for his own refill - grabbed George by the elbow and asked him what was on most of the other men's already drooling minds.

"How much longer before we get into the movies, George? Some of the guys are startin to have trouble keeping a straight face whenever they look at Fred"

Before George had a chance to answer, Joe the janitor joined them, just in time to hear the end of Brad's question. And as he added his own words of, "Ya, howa much longer George?" George glanced down at his wristwatch once more, before stealing a quick look in his best friends direction while answering. "It's almost a quarter past ten now. Say about another half-hour. Everything's rented for the whole night and our surprise isn't due for almost another fifteen minutes yet. And I said the exact time was very important when setting this thing up."

Satisfied with the answer, Joe and Brad started to walk away, but halted just long enough to hear the rest of the words coming out of George's mouth. "Tell them 'shit-heads' who are having trouble containing themselves that this is strictly a peaceful mission, and I shouldn't have to explain the full meaning behind the spelling of the word 'peace-full' to any of them, I hope."

A big grin was all that was needed to signify that both of them emphatically and fully understood the emphasized word "peaceful".

After pausing long enough to gaze around the smoky room, George then made his way back towards the seat still awaiting the pleasure of his big 'butt', ass, against it, while adding over his shoulder, "Now go tell em 'I' said so."

Regardless of the real reason each of the men were together that night, they had all agreed a long time ago that poker and drinking could only make for a bad feelings, no matter what the stakes were. So in an effort to try and minimize the risk of anyone's feeling or financial status from being overly abused, they always kept the limited three bumps betting in the games at strictly the nickel, dime level. In that manner it could truly be said that each other's entertainment was their only real reason for justifying their get-togethers. And even though Lady Luck had never really been a constant stranger to George, he liked to tell himself on the nights that he did loose that he was only putting minor deposits into the bank, to be withdrawn at some future game.

Pausing at the first poker table long enough to return some of the all-knowing winks and nods for what was yet to come, George couldn't help but laugh out loud when his ears picked up some of the conversation presently underway.

"Hurry up and deal, will ya!, I have to be to work by Monday!"

"Come on, come on, let's go! I'm used to losing my money a lot faster than this!"

"Okay, okay!" the dealer 'Pop-Bottles' finally said, "Red's wild, and you have to win it twice."

Still chuckling to himself as he finally lowered his body into his seat, Fred smiled into George's face while asking, "What's up, buddy? What's so funny?"

"Oh nothin' in general," George continued to grin. "It's just that after being around some of the people here I have to ask myself, where else could I go for entertainment this cheap."

Just as Fred answered "Ya. I know what ya mean." Bob nodding his head in agreement also, a bowl of passing potato chips paused under George's nose, just long enough for him to scoop out a small handful. The bowl then continued on its way and stopped next in front of Beautiful Brad, who instantly refused them with the words "No-o-o-o thank you. I don't do salt!" And when someone quipped at the cloud of smoke sitting beside him, 'Are you cheating?' everyone else in almost unison yelled out another standard reply of, "Of course! Aren't you?"

Brad then, always eager for a chance to show off his muscular physique flexed his arms and chest as if he was hoisting some invisible set of barbells, while saying, "You guys should watch yourselves. A body like this doesn't just come in a bottle, you know." Without even a split-second passing, one of the other men at the table held up his half-consumed bottle of beer and said, "Gee, that's funny. Mine did!"

The always as is contagious laughter that broke out was magnified even more by the loud sound of George clapping his hands in approval. As should also be expected, the remarks overflowed into the next table, only to build in volume even more until someone felt they had done their share to keep things going, going that is until someone else could find the next direction to take them in.

Reaching way down deep inside, much like we did when we were kids at the 'matinee' Rusty set free a 'burp' so loud that it actually seemed to startle a few of the men close to him. And when someone quickly retaliated with the remark, "That one's gotta have 'food' on it! Give me another second, and I'll bet I can tell you what you had for supper!" the puns were off again.

"If you could only put that kind of 'gas' in your car, I'm sure you could drive to Florida and back - on less then half a tank."

"Well, it sounded more to me as if he was just about ready to give 'birth', on that 'puppy'."

"Birth nothin!" Kim Langly added. "I felt the vibrations from here - and it felt more like there could have been a bit a 'lung' on the end of that gasser."

"Well, all I can say," Ken chuckled, "is I sure feel a lot better since it left home base ! Or would you rather I use the old standard, 'better up and out, then down and out.' remark?"

"I'll say, fart-face." George laughed. "Normally your breath's bad enough. We don't need to hear from just another 'bunghole' to challenge any part of it."

"Why don't you save your 'crap' for the next time you're near the 'crapper'!" Rusty snapped in George's direction, a big smile on his face. "Come to think of it, with your rumored shitty outlook on life, you probably don't get too far away from one, do ya?"

"Only when I've been drinking!" George grinned back "But if I forget, my tiny bladder never fails to remind me."

"Speakin of drinkin." Fred interrupted loudly, while holding his glass high in the air. "Will the next guy going to the bar for a refill get me one. Oh 'Hell', make it two!"

Almost instantly the air around Fred was cluttered with bits of thrown potato chip and peanut wrappers, as well as verbal abuse, such as, "When did your personal servant die!" and while trying to smack away some of the flying debris coming in his direction, he threw back at them.

"Gee, if I'd known you guys were so touchy about your drinking problems, I never would have sat with you's."

As earlier, it took someone complaining about their luck that night, the next dealer now, to get every-ones minds back onto the game.

"Now I 'know', it's time to quit. I'm dealing and I still can't win!"

Brad, obviously in an effort to irritate the dealer even more, said, "I got a flush." while dragging the pot of small change towards him. And the dealer, over exaggerating everything, tossed his loosing hand onto the pile of other discarded cards, while countering, "I know what you got! I dealt, didn't I?"

"Don't mind him." George smiled. "He's got a head like a doorknob."

"How's that?" Fred asked, just knowing that his 'bud' would no doubt have some other little 'innuendo' to add the jabbing remark.

"Easy." George started to laugh. "Any girl in town can turn it."

"Eat you heart out!" Brad shot back, looking directly into George's grinning face. "You're just feeling jealous because I'm always getting opportunities at more ass than a toilet seat."

It was on the tip of George's tongue to say, 'Could be, but at least we're still only using women.' So instead he just went with the more obvious, and along the same lines. "I don't doubt it." he continued to grin, Fred and Bobs heads smart enough to silently just turn back and forth to face who-ever was talking at the time. "But if you want everyone else to know that you're just another 'ass bandit' that's your business."

After a few of the men had offered the 'ol slamming salute' of 'He-e-e-re! Get 'that' into ya!' in Brad's direction, Brad picked up the cards in order to deal, while sneering, "Ante up, children. The night's not getting any younger, and the mortgage is due."

Occasionally, as he glanced at the 'hole card' in his poker hand, George also let his eyes stray just enough to check the watch on his wrist, to confirm that everything was right on schedule. He had also, in between taking a few personal 'slams' as well as giving the same amount out, caught the occasional silly antic and inquisitive gesture from some of the other men close-by. They in turn had silently mouthed words suggesting that they all wanted to get involved with the double bill movie features of the evening, a few even using their arms to assist and magnify the importance of hurrying.

Finally, the time for the next move in the men's hopefully beneficial evening finally arrived. And as Fred, apparently still fully ignorant of his fellow coworkers real reasons for getting together that night, did his best to get inebriated as conveniently as possible, George watched his already mellow mood loosen up even more. In the short time they had been there, Bob doing his best to keep up with him, Fred had managed, not counting the half dozen and one spiked drinks dropped off by friends, to kill off almost a half of the soldier he had brought. If nothing else, he was obviously and quite noticeably on his way towards a hangover to rival the one he had only recently dumped - either that or he was ready for what they had planned for him.

For a beginner the amount of alcohol presently being consumed would have had them by now ready for 'la la' land. But for a pro, most of the men present easily falling into that category, a 'twenty sixer' or 'forty ouncer' was considered as just 'All in a days play'.

Saying, "If you'll excuse me gentlemen, but right now my bladder feels as if it's being pressed between a rock and a hard place. Then I'll get the movies ready." George pushed himself away from the small table, and his ten-dollar bank deposit. The brief trip to the washroom gave him a chance to use another of his favorite one liner comebacks, "In my case, I'd have to watch out for whiplash!" after someone had thrown at him one of the oldest washroom puns know. "Remember George, if you shake it more than once, you're playin with it."

As he re-entered the area of the room housing the t. v. and video machine, he couldn't help but smile when seeing that most of the men had re-positioned their chairs in front of the television set, fresh drinks in both hands. 'Perverts' row, the isle of seats closest to the viewing screen, was overflowing with its loud and lewd regulars.

A few of the men, the Langly brothers and a 'woozy' looking Fred, were busy at the bar, apparently having a debate about nothing, while preparing extra drinks. They like everyone else, only obviously slower, were intent on not having to get up for another drink once the movies and bodies in motion have started.

Then, as the room's interior started to escalate in volume as each man did his best to crudely outshine one another, pun after pun peppered their antics, all in the hopes that their remarks would add to the groups already happy mood. It was also evident that if there is one thing all normal red-blooded healthy young men have in common with each other, it was their attitude towards abnormally endowed young nude women.

A few verbal appropriate shouts soon had the last three standing men in a strategic seating arrangement that was known by all but one, Fred, hurrying to be seated.

Even if he hadn't bothered to make an extra supply of drinks for himself, Bob and George, a means to have him sitting in the back row and closest to the unit's only exit would have somehow been found. And even as the room's interior slipped into brief and almost total darkness, George's voice was easily recognizable above the rest as he said, "Now let's not have a repeat performance of our last get, together guys. There's to be no rude or physically intimate contact while the movies are in progressing. No drooling or wetting, and positively no thumb sucking. However, giggling, constructive suggestions and maybe even a little hand holding will be permitted, but only while the lights are out."

Almost as soon as the T.V. screen burst into illumination, its entirety filled with images at work performing physical activities that everyone in the room at one time or another no doubt would have volunteered to do for free, as the players' names and story title floated across the screen. A low barrage of childish actions that not only seemed accepted but encouraged simultaneously came from most of the men's lips. Maturity or not, suggestive grammar was crude from the very start.

The plot, like the actors, was embarrassingly acceptable only because physical attributes and performances dominated everything else in the film. And none of the men, starting with remarks like, "Wow! When I was eighteen, most girls were built like a carpenter's dream, flat as a board and no one wasted to 'nail' em." had any trouble finding answers to comments such as, "Gee, I would have sworn that it was physically impossible to do that."

"When you get to be our age," Rusty added, "it will be."

"Well, at least I can see what I'm doing right. And what the wife's doing wrong." came another follow-up.

"You mean like snoring in your face, before you're finished," somebody quickly offered. "Yes sir!" someone else said. "It kind of makes you wanna run right home and smack the little woman, doesn't it?"

Like always the passing of time was fast, smooth, and enjoyable as suggestive antics were quickly followed up with comical remarks. And when one of them in the front row foolishly tried to do shadow images with their hands in front of the TV. screen, it took George's loud voice to break up the comical mayhem it had induced. But when a soft knock registered on the outside of the unit's door almost every eye in the place, even Bob's, instinctively went to either it or to Fred. It was only George's normal quick thinking that kept the men's suddenly strange actions from being detected by his friend.

"Grab that, will ya buddy!" he said, while looking directly at Fred. "It's probably just the food we ordered."

An effort was made to turn the darkened room's lighting on, as grunts and moans continued to emit from the television. Fred, his eyes darting repeatedly back to the entangled group of human images in the center of the TV screen, half-blindly fumbled his way to the door. It was not until he had opened it and grabbed a quick glance of a young uniformed figure almost completely hidden behind the pile of containers in its arms did he realize that he'd forgotten to pick up the money usually allotted for such extras that was left in a plastic cup at the bar.

Gesturing in the youth's direction while saying, "Come on in for a minute, I have to get the money," he quickly closed the door behind both of them while trying to keep most of his now partially drug-induced attention on what was happening in the movie. And as he quickly retrieved the cash from the bar, he still totally failed to pick up on the sudden drop to almost silence and change in the men's antics.

Giving his attention briefly to the small capped head just barely visible over the pile of boxes whose aroma could now he attested as hot chicken, Fred asked how much the order had come to, before quickly counting out an even fifty dollars from the bills in his hand. In an awkward gesture, that kept him from getting a full clear view of the person who he had just let in, he managed to exchange the money for the food, while saying, "Thanks'. And keep the change."

Taking it for granted that the delivery boy could let himself out Fred turned his back on the youth, and staggering slightly, started back for the bar. He had still failed to detect, except for the occasional sounding giggle, that the barrage of crude comical comments on the movie's antics had vanished almost completely. Then, as a few of the men got out of their seats to follow Fred and the chicken, the person responsible for its delivery quickly went through an astonishing metamorphosis.

Skin-tight coveralls that had been stretched to their limit were almost ripped off to reveal a form that could definitely no longer be foolishly mistaken for that of a male's. And when one of the men standing erect in an effort to camouflage the shapely young woman's moves let out a low anomalistic sounding moan when viewing her overly abundant chest, someone close instantly punched him in the arm while whispering. "Knock it off, Pop Bottles, or Fred's goanna hear ya!"

Within seconds the innocent looking individual who had delivered their late night snack, had transformed herself into a voluptuous tantalizing long-haired creature in a jumpsuit so tight you could almost read through it the embossed writing on the manufacturer's label.

In a routine that was so quick and effortless that she had probably performed it a hundred times before, no doubt under similar circumstances, she expertly applied lipstick and perfume to a figure that had the hearts of the men surrounding her beating more rapidly within their already excited chests.

Ralph had gotten up and followed Fred to the bar as soon as he had realized what was happening, and he tried to keep his separated coworker busy temporarily.

"If you want to start unpackin the food Fred, I'll start passin it out.

"Huh? Oh, hi Ralph." the statement, possibly because of his present condition more than the limited illumination in the room from the still playing movie, caught Fred temporarily off guard. But it was only until he realized who was talking. "Ya, sure thing."

Behind them the men's comments, like the film, were still in motion. And when the 'surprise package' seated her-self in the suggested last row near Fred's chair, Jack Ellis positioned himself between her and the vacant seat - while using his cigar to provide a heavy smoke screen.

Occasionally, as everyone waited for Fred to finish what he was doing and return to his seat, some of the men's curiosity got the best of them and they tried to nonchalantly steal a quick glimpse at the lady of the evening who was now seated among them. One of them even commented, after a pleasant smile had come back in return to his, 'Boy! she's enough to make any man wish he hadn't been weaned!" The girl couldn't help but overhear the remark, as someone punched Terry in the arm while saying, "I don't know what you're complaining about.

you're wife 's so big she always looks like she's just about to give milk." and she had to clap her hands over her freshly painted mouth to keep from giggling out loud.

Kim and Ken, noticeably drooling, seated themselves so as to not only block out any view their young guest might get of the television screen, but also as an aid to help hide the women's deliberate slouching figure when someone whispered. "Here he comes!" The rude remark of, "Well, if not now, then definitely later!" was lost in the room's atmosphere as a few extra large puffs of cigar smoke succeeded in altering Fred's course of travel, as well as getting a n often used and just as expected comment of, "That thing smells almost as bad as your breath!"

But the maneuver succeeded in him making his way to his seat by a route that would not have him passing in front of the girl.

Only now as the men occupied themselves between the food their expensive guest and the images still active on the television screen was there any purposely-true silence, since they had all entered the motel unit. As the food in front of them quickly disappeared, because of what they knew was still to come, most of it being washed down with alcohol, each of the men then slowly one by one started to mysteriously vanish from the room. In only minutes, all but six of them including Bobs' grinning face after George had given him directions with his eyes and head had left the room or building in a variety of exits.

Strategic viewing from the bungalow's two small bedrooms, on occasions a few of the men had gotten too drunk to drive home and after refusing rides, had ended up sleeping it off in one of the rooms. It was this location that had been decided upon as a temporary viewing port for most of the men.

As 'Joe the Janitor' and 'Pop Bottles' crawled clumsily into one of the bedrooms, their liquor-induced moves hindered even more by helping hands from their just as inebriated friends, 'Beautiful Brad' tried to keep all of them as quiet as possible.

A few of the men were already outside, with George and Bob being two of them. And as they took turns trying to catch a glimpse of what was happening inside the building, George headed for the rear of his car. Retrieving a special camera for night shooting that he had borrowed, he always told people he needed a camera with a 'Ph.D.'-

'push, here, dummy', he carefully lowered the vehicles' tailgate until it snapped locked again.

Without intending to, his face was busy betraying his present emotions, as it smiled devilishly at the thoughts now in his mind. But it wasn't until he was headed back for the room windows his cohorts were using that he realized that something felt unusually wrong.

Slowing in his steps, he let his eyes do a slow and inquisitive scan of the area around him, until they found what he believed his instincts had sensed. At the far end of the motels' parking lot was a car he instantly recognized, a vehicle that hadn't been there when they had arrived earlier. It was a site that made his body involuntarily react with a quick chill running along his spine. It also was enough to make his next movements slow and deliberate, until he had moved himself where he was positive he couldn't be seen from the other cars' line of view. If necessary, as some of the men liked to say, he would 'bet his left nut' that the vehicle, although at first glance looking vacant, was one, if not the very one, just like the one Fred use to own. The magic words of 'use to own' now only meant that thanks to a shrewd lawyer it was in his wife's possession, along with almost everything but 'his nuts', even though Fred occasionally swore he had a sensation that they were being squeezed periodically. And ironically at those times he has just put it down to the sensation of his friends building eyeball pressure due to lack of 'nookie', something they were there to hopefully correct.

A mixture of curiosity and loyalty told him that he had to look even closer, so that he could make a positive identification. But his common sense also told him that he head to be cautious enough not to be detected doing it. Suddenly remembering that the camera was still within his grip, he stuck it and his head just far enough around the units' end wall to allow for a close-up view of the still apparently vacant vehicle. Focusing the infrared lens on the camera until he had magnified the cars front windshield crystal clear directly into the center of it, his timing and ingenuity seemed to pay off almost instantly.

A black silhouetted head belonging to someone who had obviously ducked from view when he had shown up, slowly popped up from inside the car, no doubt as to view the parking lot for any lack of human activity? Then in a movement his ears failed to register on, he watched the human form slowly let itself out form its hiding place. The chill that had run down its spine earlier instantly repeated itself as he realized that he was indeed actually watching Fred's wife Nancy. And there was no doubt in his mind, by the instrument that she was carrying, a cheap polaroid, that she had somehow found out about their little get-together, - possibly even what was about to happen to her husband.

Inside the bungalow, the food still being consumed by Fred did nothing to slow down the effects the large amount of spiked alcohol he had consumed was presently having on his body. He had detected the gradual decrease in the presence of his friends, but he had learned long ago that their strange antics were sometimes to be expected, as well as ignored. And not until the rest of the gathering got up all at once and started to leave the room did he realize that something was going on. Apparently something he as of yet knew nothing about, but also wasn't invited to.

It was in this same instant, as someone passing the television set shut it and the video machine off, allowing the room to fall back into almost total darkness - that he even thought to question what was happening. But with the darkness also came something he thought his groggy senses had briefly detected earlier, a slight hint of strange sweet perfume, probably from one of the men trying a new aftershave or deodorant. But as quickly as the strange odor had appeared, it had been just as quickly suppressed by the smell of mixed fried chicken and cigar smoke. and as his nose beat his sense of smell as it pulled in a much stronger sweet scent of perfume this time, to late did he realize that he was not alone in the room.

As the 'lady of the evening' made her move, her thin soft arms wrapping themselves around his neck, he instantly realized two things - both just enough to sober him slightly. The first, something that any mature male could recognize no matter how drunk he got, was that the other individual in the room was definitely and wonderfully a tantalizing scented female. And secondly, for strangely some much more important reason at the moment, she was apparently after one Hell of a lot more than just his unfinished chicken!

Instinctively at first, his drugged reasoning had him foolishly and unsuccessfully trying to deter the pleasant smelling silhouette attacking him. But fortunately for him, the woman presently stripping him of his clothing was an apparent professional at her task. Time usually meant money to her --- the less time she spent with one customer generally gave her more time to accommodate another one sooner --- but not tonight. Tonight her specialty and eager attacking company was to be available only to the male figure finally ceasing to detest her physically aggressive movements. And in what was really only a minute, they were both soon eagerly assisting each other to undress - with only one obvious mission in mind now.

A devilish plan with sadistic overtones had formulated itself inside of George's mind, as he had watched Fred's wife trying to sneak up on the bungalow he was still hiding behind. As he had awaited her cautious inevitable arrival, he'd had enough time to 'shoo away' any of the men who might have been detected by her 'Everybody get around the back, and stay there quietly until call you!' as well as put his plan into motion.

Now, as an unsuspecting Nancy leaned closer to the unit's front window, no doubt in a hopeful attempt to grab a view of its interior, two pairs of human eyes carefully watched her every move.

For a brief instant it looked as if she was temporarily shocked by whatever her eyes had managed to detect. But then, as her composure quickly returned, she lifted the camera within her grip and aimed it in through the window. From a silent signal not even intended for her, George and a cohort rushed towards her still occupied figure from opposite sides of the unit. In quick movements already discussed, they both easily managed to secure her surprised body and maneuver it, as a strong hand was held securely over her mouth, in through the routed unit's front door.

Holding the door securely shut with both hands, hushed laughter filling his ears, George could detect a few quick silent tugs on the handle he was locked onto. And as soon as the jerking pulls had failed to release the obstacle from his grip, his ears then heard a short burst of whispered obscenities that he honestly believed Fred's wife really didn't know the true meaning of. But when even they eventually disappeared, only to be replaced with sounds and muffled voices he now couldn't fully make out, his curiosity soon found him joining his coworker's smiling figure as it stared in through the same front window Nancy had been using only brief seconds earlier.

Shock logically would have been the first reaction from a normal person after getting a look as the sight presently underway inside the room in front of them. But George's instant behavior was no different than not just the man's beside him, but also all of the other men still hiding inside of the unit's bedrooms, men he had temporarily forgotten about. And as he laughed out loud at the comical looking antics of the three almost totally naked human figures rolling around on the floor of the bungalow, he once more suddenly remembered his own camera.

Turning to Eagle Beak beside him he whispered, "Quick! Get around to the back and get the rest of the guys quietly out through the bedroom windows. Then bring them and the rest of the other kids all back here and I'll explain what I've got in mind."

After a quick reply of 'Gotcha!' he watched Terry Purcell disappear around the same side of the building he had attacked from. By the time the group of adolescent-giggling men finally joined him in front of the window, a finger up to his lips to imply that they 'Keep quiet!', he had already taken five intimately suggestive photos of the 'love triangle' presently underway inside.

Before starting with what he reasoned would be the best for his friend Fred, he gave the still immature acting group a sharp long drawn out 'Sh-sh-sh-u-sh!'

Apparently someone had been smart enough to grab a few of the bottles of liquor as they had vacated the room. And while 'dying soldiers' were passed among the group, some of them tried their damnedest to get a clearer first hand view of what was still happening inside. It was at bit of a mayhem that had George deliberately leading them all away from the unit as he spoke.

"This thing could turn out better than we had planned fellas."

"How's that?" Jack Ellis asked, in his slightly inebriated state.

"Easy." George smiled. "I'll still take the pictures we had planned as a souvenir for Fred, only now they'll be of a more beneficial purpose."

"In what way?" Sid Parker said, even though the question was already on most of the other men's faces.

The Langly brothers had turned in their tracks with the intention of returning to the front window, but were stopped even before they could get started back in its direction.

"Don't try it you guys, or you could spoil this whole thing. If I can get enough intimidating pictures of what's going on back there, Fred's wife won't dare take him to court for support-money, or anything!"

If someone passing had caught sight of the large gathering of men and their silly antics, they in all probability would have just kept right on going, for their own safety sake of course. And when one of them whined "Just what in the Hell are we supposed to do for the rest of the night?" George told them.

"Either do what you had planned on doing if these new circumstances hadn't come up. Or go home early and put the half buzz you're all presently feeling to bed. Who knows, you might get lucky and catch the wife with someone she's not supposed to be with. And if he says that he's just over to borrow a cup of sugar, you can tell him to take his sweet tooth someplace else."

Most of the men instantly got the drift of the pun intended and their laughter was contagious among those who didn't. Ken Langly, after taking a swig from the bottle now within his grip, asked George, "And what about you? Why should you get stuck with the depressing job of having to force yourself to take pictures of what's going on back there? Aren't you the guy who's always telling everyone that you don't believe in torture?"

As to be expected the men once again started to laugh, especially those who remembered having heard George say exactly that when passing up a chance to peek into the women's side of the change-house at work. And he even had to laugh himself while trying to justify the reason as to why he should be the one to stay behind, alone to do the dirty work.

"Believe me fellas, I realize it's a disgusting humiliating job that no decent man should be asked to perform, but Fred is my closest friend. So who but I should be willing to make the sacrifice this kind of disturbing long term mental imaging this nasty job demands?"

As one of the almost empty bottles passed near him, George reached out and grabbed it long enough to take a short gut warming gargle of its contents before continuing,

"Now seriously, if you bums all go to the bar on the next block down, I'll hang around here long enough to get a couple of good shots, and then I'll join you there."

No-one in the group really protested his suggestion, but it took a little bit more verbal abuse to get them into gear and on their way towards the bar.

"And I want a couple of you characters to keep an eye on Bob here until I can get there. We don't want to loose him before we've had a chance to show him what good hangovers are really made of."

Their voices and laughter still echoing in the distance, George took one last picture of their comical antics, before walking cautiously back to the window, but only after he was positive all of the men had been safely out of sight.

Peeking in through the same opening in the curtains everyone else had been straining to see through, he was genuinely surprised when he saw that someone had turned the TV. and movie back on. He even felt slightly embarrassed for being a 'Peeping Tom' when his vision took in the tangled images of his best friend and the two women busily occupied in positions that only a chiropractor was supposed to know about.

Quickly snapping off a dozen shots of highly provocative scenes, he then moved completely away from the window with the intention of letting his not so mysteriously now energetic friend have the rest of his enjoyable looking workout in privacy, while telling himself that apparently it was true, 'Sex is the most fun you can have without laughing!'

Criss crossing back and forth about the parking lot, the alcohol inside of him keeping him warm as he discarded the empty liquor bottles, he used up the rest of the exposures left on the film by taking photos of anything he thought that might associate each picture with the present time and place of what was happening. And not until he had locked his camera, and the Polaroid taken from Nancy earlier, safely under a seat in the wagon did he think to even glance at his wristwatch.

It was just after midnight, a time when some nights out on the town were just starting for the afternoon shift workers. For no particular reason, he decided to wait around a few minutes longer, since being alone with himself never ever bored him, before deciding to head out to join his cohorts in the nearby 'den of iniquity'.

Walking down to where the motel's parking lot met and then became the main street it was situated on, he seated himself on a section of ornamental brickwork before letting his thoughts run wild with the multitude of nightlife sounds presently filling his ears.

Allowing his eyes to trail after some of the late night traffic passing before him, he more than once found himself staring in the direction of the bar now within view. With the sight of it he found himself also chuckling at the wild crazy antics that his imagination told him that some of his 'buds' were probably involved in right now. In fact, he became so engrossed with his own little fantasy that he almost failed to detect the approach of someone from in the parking lots location behind him.

Turning his head abruptly in the figure's direction, the grin that was on his face faded just long enough to turn itself into a questionable smile. Just why the beautiful looking young 'woman of the evening' they had hired for the night was fully dressed, and leaving was still a mystery to him. But he had every intention of finding out, just as soon as she was a little bit closer. He had always disliked hearing the words 'prostitute' or 'hooker' used to described women forced to use their attributes to make enough money to live on, but it was just another one of those cases where people with limited vocabularies often used words to depict someone they felt warranted such abuse.

"Hello!" He'd not had a chance to get a very close look at her when they were inside the motel. But now that he could see her up close fully dressed in her regular working cloths, it was easy to assess her to be about twenty-five years old, even though she could pass for someone in their late teens, especially if his guessing was any good. It was also plain to see that she was definitely overly qualified as a centerfold for any of the popular 'girlie magazines presently on the shelves. And if anybody ever had a truer reason for having the saying 'bang for your buck' tied in reference to them, it definitely was her, especially in her profession.

In a way he was glad to see that the smile coming back to meet his was overly pleasant to look at.

"Nothing wrong inside I hope?" he asked.

"Wrong!" placing her hands on her hips, her purse hanging looped from one arm, the young woman stood with her feet spread apart so as to give emphasis to her soft voice as she spoke. 'I might be short on a lot of things in this world 'fella', but intelligence isn't one of them!"

There was a definite noticeable humor in her gestures and words, but George made no effort to butt in just yet, as she continued.

"I've got nothing against 'group therapy', but when it comes to being almost ignored and made into a bystander, I can take a hint and know when to leave!"

"You! - Ignored!" George meant every bit of emphasis he had put on the two words, and he used one of his hands to pat the area beside him so as to indicate that she should join him, as he had said it.

"Yes! Ignored! Do I know you well enough to lie to you yet?" Not losing any of the pleasant grin on her face - she kept right on rattling off what was on her mind. "And don't think you're going to talk me out of any of my commission. No-one said anything to me about a third party becoming involved. Being 'kinky' isn't exactly my specialty - but when I find myself being strictly a spectator on the sidelines with no hope of participating anymore, well, then it's time to head back to work."

George found almost all of what she had said puzzling, and his face showed it as he said, "No-one's asking you for a rebate young lady. But, and I'm not trying to be rude, but what did you mean about not participating anymore? Are they both pooped out already?"

Sitting so close to her perfumed body, George could see how any young man ready to offer his services for populating the world could become addicted to her shapely youthful body. And when she started to speak again, her prior over-emphasizing and acting ability seemed even more exaggerated this time.

"Ya gotta be kiddin! I've been with guys who've been separated from their wives before, and believe me, whoever said you can't save it up sure hasn't had to go without sex for very long!"

George couldn't help but laugh openly at her remarks about sex, which only seemed to encourage her to continue.

"I know a couple of woman right now who'd just love a chance to rent your dynamo friend back there for the evening. Men aren't the only ones, using expressions I've often heard from them, who get 'excessive eyeball pressure' or need their 'itch' scratched you know. Besides, those two in there are probably still so busy enjoying each other's company that I doubt if they even realize I'm gone yet!"

Allowing his vision to briefly follow hers in the motel's direction as she had been speaking, George soon found himself once more staring at the young woman's shapely figure. It was a male reflex that also had him thinking about just how much she compared in not to far off in age or appearance to the girls his oldest sons were starting to bring around the house. She in turn, upon detecting his pleasant smile and stare, pretended to readjust her skintight outfit. While using one hand each on her oversized breast to lift and readjust they way they were presently resting, she returned the glow it had brought to his face by commenting. "Ya know, I am paid up for the whole night. And by rights I am yours to do with as you please until morning, if you know what I mean?"

George's wicked mind, as the words 'jellybean' briefly ran across his thoughts, had absolutely no trouble at all in instantly deciphering the absolute whole wild idea of what the tantalizing sexy young creature was hinting at. And even before she added, "If you want, I'm sure you could get another room, and we could put it and the remaining time to good use." he knew that his face was very 'very' definitely going to develop a quite noticeable visual blush.

What he didn't realize though was that the last syllables out of his mouth would not only be words that he had never dreamt himself capable of saying seriously, but also so honestly believing that they had come right form his heart. They were also the type of a 'mushy thing', that if any of his coworkers ever found out about any of it coming from his mouth, he would never be able to live it down.

"In all probability, if such an offer or opportunity had presented itself fifteen years ago, I honestly just might have foolishly considered it. Ah, on second thought, I most likely would have 'jumped' on the opportunity, if you get my drift!"

The broad smile that was already on the woman's face instantly changed into an almost childish-like giggle, at her own interpretation of his last words. Her mouth then in turn settled into a big wide grin showing two rows of well-manicured ivories, even as he kept speaking.

"But that was fifteen years ago. Unfortunately, especially for our present situation, maturity isn't the only thing that comes with time. Self- esteem and worth also seem to mean a lot more at my age, I guess. So, not because anyone else might find out about what you and I might be able to achieve, but rather because I myself would always know and have to live with it, I'm afraid I'm going to have to turn down your tantalizingly tempting offer."

By this time, the rest of the world and its reality still existing all around them was totally lost, as they stared into each other's eyes and minds. Yet, even though they both lived in worlds seemingly alien to each other's, their emotional feelings briefly touched as only those of the human species at times could. For long seconds, they each relished in the sensation that there was no longer any right or wrong, good or bad, but instead just perfect harmony that knew nothing about age or morality.

Then, in a gesture, which broke the mood of seriousness, they each had unintentionally settled into, George lifted one arm and used it to cover his eyes while forcing his voice to over emphasize into the next bit of terrible acting. "Now go! Go before either of us weakens any more! Let us always remember this moment of each other with only honor and kindness in our hearts."

The sudden faint sounds of scraping beside him told George that the 'lady of the evening' was lowering her body from the ledge they were sitting on. And when he felt her soft scented form briefly press close to his while whispering "Thank you." into his ear, he was genuinely surprised but made no effort to look just yet in her direction, as his ears now detected her spiked foot steps starting to fade in the distance.

Finally, risking one eye, he lifted his arm just enough to be able to watch her departing figure, as it ambled down to the curbs edge of the sidewalk, before sticking out a thumb raised hand in the 'universally' known hitchhiking manner.

Feeling safe enough to allow his arm to fall into his lap, a long slow 'sigh' of relief escaping his lips, he was amazed at how fast she got a reaction to her gesture. If he had to guess, he would estimate that only about ten seconds had passed since her arrival at the curb's edge, and the braking vehicle presently pulling up in front of her tantalizing form. So when she turned back in his direction just long enough to blow him an invisible kiss, he quickly smiled and pretended to reach up and catch it, before yanking it down and pressing it hard against his genuinely pounding heart.

The maneuver, as over-exaggerated as most humorous things he was a part of were, cost George his balance on the small wall. Legs stiff and spread wide apart while falling awkwardly over backwards, his hands instinctively grabbing at only vacant air as he went, he landed out of sight on his back in the small decorative garden just behind it. Bobbing straight up erect like a 'Jack-in-the-box', he was just in time to see the woman's giggling body disappear into to the car's interior. Laughing now himself, he watched the vehicle until it became a part of the night's glittering silhouettes, before finally lifting a hand to his forehead in order to wipe away some invisible beading of sweat, while a loud and winded "Phe-e-e-w!" escaped from his lips. And if he had even one tenth of the ability for premonition as he often believed Judy had, the fact that he had not seen the last of this beautiful creature and that their paths were destined to pass once more under similar circumstances would have more scared than bothered him.

While brushing any loose soil or debris from his cloths he might have picked up, he looked down at his watch, the last of the chuckle still in his throat leaving with the dirt. Glancing back in the motel unit's direction, apparently still containing Fred and Nancy, he said to himself, "Na, no sense in disturbing a good thing." He even then thought to himself 'maybe I should have packed an overnight bag for him. But then just as quickly as he had asked himself the question, he sick sense of humor brushed it aside once more with another 'Na.', 'He's already got an overnight 'bag' And I'm pretty sure it's' safe to say - it's 'more' than 'packed', it's probably ready to explode!'

Then, a soft whistle on his smiling lips, he headed in the bar's direction, with only himself for company. And since as always, since his ego would never let him tire of himself, he let his minds eye relish in the departing images still fresh within his thoughts. The only big thing out of the ordinary, other than the beauty and pleasantness of the 'eye candy' they had hired to entertain Fred, had been the surprise arrival of his wife. And where he had originally only anticipated maybe just a small paragraph or two entry into his 'book of memories' since real men don't have diaries, Nancy's present physical involvement was going to require 'far' more than just a 'foot' note. This, although possibly overflowing into a new book, to date this would be four that he had filled, was working out far better than he had even dared to imagine.

And as he allowed his wicked imagination to continue, it brought him a slight tickle as it tripped over the sex related innuendos of 'pok - er' and 'a, foot' when he forced himself to try and concentrate on just how he could as delicately as possible put the definitely raunchy facts down on paper, without hurting anyone down the road.

    He knew it was too late to get into any really serious drinking, especially without Fred there to pick on or keep him company. So he consoled himself with the thought that maybe Bob, an apparent diamond still in the rough, could fill in the temporary vacancy. If that idea failed, there was always the reality that the men always appreciated his company, more than he needed theirs. And to prove that he had earned that respect he still had one more trick up his sleeve to not only prove it, but also help protect his friends from themselves. Extracting a small round ring of scotch tape he had brought along for just this time, he set off to place a small piece over the lock leading into each mans car. That way if they were to inebriated to get into their vehicles, they were definitely too drunk to drive.

Chapter # 7

The 'Meat' Market.
Or
'Foot in mouth disease'

Inside the bar, 'The Meat Market', a rather appropriate play on words because of the amount of male and female flesh advertised there. The men were only just now seating themselves at a freshly vacated table. A few of them, beautiful Brad and the Langly twins being the worst offenders were already prime candidates for a trip to their chiropractor in order to get an re-adjustment for whiplash. The place was well populated with noticeably healthy woman displaying tight jeans and chests that gave the appearance that the tops of their bent knees were being pushed up and out through the unbuttoned area of the shirts or tops they were almost wearing. In fact it would have been hard to find even one woman within their view who fit the phrase 'she was built for comfort, not for speed'. It was also a scene that prompted Rusty to ask, "What do you call a guy who's lucky in love?" to which Pop Bottles quickly shouted, "A bachelor!"

On the other hand, some of the men wore the appearance on their faces that looked like someone had been feeding them knuckle sandwiches, with them in turn being noticeably sloppy eaters. And as if to give credence to the summation two men within hearing range were in an apparent disagreement over apparently nothing. But that was not uncommon when an overabundance of alcohol was so readily available. So when one of the inebriated started to pick on the antagonist, they wisely tried to ignore the remarks, until seats were available. But it wasn't going to be that easy, as words floated into their desire to become unnoticed, let alone involved.

"See that wall over there! Run over and try banging your head off of it a couple of times!

"Why in the world would I want to do something as stupid as that!" the second fellow complained, a small grin giving away their true feeling towards each other.

His antagonist apparently finding the time to take a drink out the raised glass in his hand, lost no time in following up with, "As much as words referring to "you' and 'stupid' being appropriately together in the same sentence, well, you can believe me when I say we'll definitely be getting back to them later. But first lets talk about 'your head' making contact with the wall. Maybe, just, maybe, you'll shake loose some of that 'shit' you've been using for 'brains'. And if I can, in your case, put in a 'proper pun' to good use, you'll really be taking a 'load off your mind'.

Still grinning, his drinking mate swallowed the remainder of the contents of his glass before retaliating, "Look! Sis said to keep an eye on you - and that's exactly what I'm doing, although I fail to see what good bouncing my head off the wall is going to do me,

"You! Who in the hell said you banging your head against the wall was going to do 'you' any good! It's me.! It's 'me', who's going to feel better!" the first man laughed.

The place did have a reputation for wild women and very physical brawls. And that was with just the women, which was not totally virgin information as far as George and the rest of the men were concerned. All this, plus the mixture of present day and old time rock and roll, was always a good excuse to see the shapely ladies shake their booty.

Pivoting his leering head in Eagle Beaks direction to whisper, "Hey Terry, get a load of that one over there in the spray on jeans and concealed football helmets." Brad said. "How would you like a chance to take that one home?"

Easily picking out the young woman in question, the man beside her sporting a face suggesting that he had possibly and repeatedly had to defend her on more than one occasion, Terry swallowed hard at the stunning view. Putting his hands up to his eyes, suggesting that he was looking at the creature in question through a pair of binoculars, he then swallowed hard once more before answering. "I'd love to!- But I honestly don't think my wife would let me keep her!"

As those of the group close enough to overhear the remarks laughed, beautiful Brad turned his attention towards Pop Bottles, one of the few men in the group apparently not interested. "Hey Bob! - what about you? How would you like a chance at something like that?"

Letting his line of vision float over to match the others, Pop Bottles shook his head in a negative manner, while answering, "No thanks. I got one at home right now I can't afford. What in the Hell do I want with another one!"

As all of them started to go through varying degrees of purposely choking laughter, Bill Langley vulgarly offered, "Shit!, Go ahead and ask me. Normally I don't believe in torture, but for one like that I'll do three days on the 'torture rack' or even locked in the fruit cellar, anytime!"

"Don't ask him!" one of the men quickly added. "Or he'll go into 'How many Clydesdales' it would take to drag her off his face."

And when Jamie Weir asked, "What's that strange smell?' after one of them had snuck out a deliberately detectable silent but deadly room divider, Sid Parker answered sarcastically, "Probably just your breath blowin' back in your face."

"Smells more like where the 'beer and the cantaloupe play' to me." Ralph quickly added.

"Well, you're right about it smellin'," someone else added, two fingers comically shoved up his nostrils, "Smells more like germ warfare to me!"

"Well, whatever it is," Bob Langly said, two fingers of one hand quickly pinching his nose as his other hand fanned the air around him. "I think someone ought to seriously consider leavin' that 'ol pee in a bottle' alone until they can find a cure for why it affects certain people this way."

"Beer helps keep me lean." someone quickly threw in, to which another of them just as quickly added, "Ya, so I've noticed at work. It helps keep you leaning against the walls, leaning against door frames, leaning against your ego, etcetera, etcetera, etcetera!"

It was more humor than booze that had kept the pleasant tune and smile on George's lips as he had covered the distance between the motel and the bar. And although it was not the type of establishment that a rational man would take his wife or healthy sons to, its reputation for brawls were justifiable as far as he was concerned, it was a convenience and not a preference that had brought him and the boys there that night. But the fact that the place also had entertainment in the way of loud live bands with occasionally 'strippers', not the paint or wallpaper kind, was not to be rationalized as a deterrent either.

Holding the door open for an obviously lucky young fellow and his date to exit through, George acknowledged the 'Thank you.' that had come in his direction with a pleasant 'You're welcome.' before rewarding himself with a quick glimpse of the shapely young woman's wiggling departing posterior.

Shaking his head while mumbling to himself, "Poor bugger. Hope he doesn't hurt himself," George felt good while walking inside the bar. And the humor that was already in his mind had no chance to subside as his vision took in the sight of an overly inebriated individual loudly saying, "Hello! Hello! Hell-o-o-o-o!" into the phone within his grasp, just before tapping it on the wall in front of him, no doubt possibly hoping to shake some words apparently caught inside loose .

Pausing in his steps long enough to snatch the receiver out of the drunk's hand, a half laugh and smile on his lips, George simply turned it end for end before sticking it back into the slowly reacting confused man's still outstretched hand. And as the realization that he had been arguing with the wrong end of the phone slowly sank into the drunk's head, by sayin, "Idiot! This is an outgoing call, not incoming!" George couldn't help but chuckle out loud before continuing on his way.

If there had been a contest on, it would have been a close call as his eyes and ears fell on where his rambunctious friends were hiding. They were at a table near the rear of the crowded bar, and a few of them were already busy calling out his name, while waving him in their direction.

Letting a big smile on his face acknowledge their actions, George instantly made his way in their direction, carefully making sure to step around or grin at any obstacle he assessed might be looking for a chance to impress itself. The closer he got to the table, the easier it was to detect more and more of the people and activity presently going on at it. But as soon as he was able to see that a couple of women were also seated at the table, its surface already littered with a variety of bladder filler, a silent 'Uh-oh.' went off inside his head. Normally he would have been more then happy to view lovely women in his surroundings, but not right now, especially since one of them was what some of the lesser sophisticated men would normally considered to be as a real 'barker'.

It wasn't the first time during their nights out together that previous unknown women had ended up at their tables, no doubt looking for a free drink - but past experiences had always proved that they were strictly for wishful dreaming fantasies, for looking at - not touching.

Dropping his body into an awaiting seat, Bob wearing one of his ridiculous over-exaggerated oriental grins again, had managed to save for him, George was just in time to hear Beautiful Brad whisper in the younger looking of the two women's direction, "Baby, where have you been all my life?" And even though the answer instantly springing into George's head wasn't new or original, he used it anyway.

"By the looks of 'her' Don Juan, I'd be willing to guess, she probably wasn't born for the first half of it."

Ignoring George's words, Brad continued to hustle the younger woman with, "If you can guess what I've got in my hands," his two hands now cupped together so as to conceal anything he might be holding there, "I'll let you give me a great big wet kiss."

The young lady, no doubt playing along with his little act, answered, almost genuinely confused, "Uh, an elephant?" And Brad, playing the 'ham' right to the end, pretended to peer with one eye into the concealed area within his hands before answering, "What color?"

As was hoped the two bar room regulars giggled, with the younger one then forgetting that it was supposed to be her kissing Brad, and not vice versa.

Pretending to blush, Brad then added, "Gee, am I ever glad I cheated, and told you the answer earlier."

As the woman continued to laugh, George added. "I don't know what's funny?" to nobody in particular, "Earlier he had to look twice himself, just to make sure 'he'd' have the right answer."

As customary most of the men broke into a variety of laughter and chuckles over the slamming, Eagle Beak letting out a low "H-e-e-e-re in Brads direction

"Ask them if they believe in the 'hereafter'." one of the men then offered, to which one of the woman instantly answered, "We're not going to talk about death are we?"

"No, not really." Brad chuckled. "When he said 'hereafter', he meant, if you're not 'here after' what we're 'here after', then you're going to be 'here after' we're gone!"

One of the woman, the noticeably older of the two and one referred to during his approach, for some reason seemed to have taken a dislike to George, and it was just enough to be noticeably indignant, when remarking "What's the matter mister? - Don't ya like girls?"

"Can't live with 'em, can't live without 'em." George smiled. But I sure as Hell hope I never have to find anything better."

He wasn't the only one at the table who could sense when the atmosphere had the potential to deteriorate. So Sid Parker quickly said in the woman's direction. "Don't mind him, ladies. He's like an old baseball game that's confused with sex. So far tonight all he's been doing is striking out or walking his balls. He hasn't even gotten to 'first base' with anyone - let alone 'score' yet."

"That's me, girls." George grinned. "I must be getting old - because the best thing I've gotten out of any ball game lately is the excuse to drink cold beer. And the only thing I end with are 'beer nuts'. - Ya know, the kind that always has you standing in the 'John' 'bat' in hand, and wonderin why you're there."

The rest of the men, although mostly preoccupied with their own brand of entertainment, didn't miss the fact that George's little repitwaw seemed to be falling mostly on unsympathetic deaf ears. And as soon as it was evident that neither of the two women were about to smile, let alone laugh, they tried to cover up any building hard feelings that might be still be fighting for recognition, by laughing out-loud. But the older second girl, definitely the one who was a prime candidate for 'needy' and not 'greedy' sex, apparently felt that she had to come to her friends' defense. "listen, wise guy! we'll have you know you can't treat us like some 'nickel and dime' prostitutes."

George, not only seeing that someone else was now wearing the proverbial 'skin off their ass on their forehead' today, not to mention letting his alcohol lubricated mouth lead his mind, didn't even pause before replying. "Oh, does that mean that you ladies 'don't come cheap'?"

As a few of the men, mainly Brad, grinned at the full understanding of George's pun, the rest simply did what they had come there to do, laugh it up and have a good time. Unfortunately the woman weren't so inclined. And as one of them almost spit out an over emphasized 'We-e-ell!', someone quickly added "Well, at least now we know where the water came from that's trying to wash away our happy mood." they instantly got up from the table and stomped away with a big shoulder shrugging 'huff'.

As quickly as the women had started to disappear, Brad was right behind them.

"Wait a minute girls, wait up! He just thinks he's Edgar Bergan - but I can speak for myself." and as he disappeared into the crowd behind the women, Ralph offered, "The way that boy's been scoring lately, I think it's safe to say there's not much fear of him ever gettin cancer of the prostrate."

"If that's all he gets from those two 'bimbos" Bill Langley quipped, I'd say he got off easy, and I don't mean 'got off'!"

"Don't knock his sex life." Bob grinned at his brother. He's the only guy I ever met who found out the hard way - that Vaseline turns green under a 'black light'."

Just then a waitress, yet another noticeably 'well-built' girl wearing a provocative 'V'- neck sweater, arrived at the table in order to clear away some of the empties, as well as take any new orders. And as she was bending over the table directly across from George, he couldn't help himself for starting to say, "Ma-a-am." quickly realizing that he had almost said 'mammary', he just as quickly shook the word out of his head, and continued with, "Miss, if you only knew how much that bothers me, you wouldn't do it." when his eyes couldn't help but take in a full view of her exposed hanging cleavage.

The girl, a blank look on her face as to what she had just heard, opened her mouth to say something, but was cut off when 'Joe the janitor' let out with a long reverberating belch that seemed to have no end to it. It was instantly obvious that he was well into the term 'drunk as a skunk', and as he grinned a little embarrassed, Eagle Beak remarked, "Oh my God! I think he just wrote the first line of a new melody!"

The waitress, apparently immune to such behavior, cut into the conversation long enough to take their order, which a few of the men tried to make as humorously difficult as possible. And as she walked away, expertly balancing the tray in her hand, the same men, Jamie Weir and Pop Bottles let their vision and voices follow her.

'She must jump off the dresser to get into those jeans." Jamie said.

"Hell, I'd jump off a bridge into a creek with no water in it, just to get a chance to jump into her jeans!" someone else snickered rudely.

"That's not for me." came out of the group. "If I ever got the chance to meet her I'd pull the ol 'hooker' routine. You know, where I get to brag that I don't come cheap!"

"After someone had shouted out 'Get some new material!', Pop Bottles quickly added, "For me, I'd just love to be there when it happens, so I can count how many bounces it takes her boobs to stop vibrating after her feet hit the floor. And her buns aren't bad either."

"I'll say." Jamie moaned. "If you can't get an air tight seal on them then there's something wrong with the shape of your face."

"She must have had a 'boob job'." Eagle Beak added to their remarks. "Nobody's built like that on purpose."

"Ya." Ken Langly joined in. "With most of the money being spent on one side I'd say."

"Well gentlemen, you're looking at positive proof to the old saying 'there's nothing wrong with money well spent.' Rusty smiled.

"Especially, in her case!" George had tried not to add his 'two cents' to the conversation. but it was a well-known fact among the rest of the men that he was a 'lung man' from way back. And when he lewdly added "If that's true, I'd sure like to volunteer to be the one to run my tongue over them in search of any 'dead spots'!" the crude remarks, especially considering the comments that had started it all was more expected then encouraged.

The topic, like always once started, encouraged more of the same. And as the band walked back up onto the stage after one of their breaks, the sounds they made drew some of the men's attention in their direction just long enough for Kim Langly's eyes to fall on another vision of beauty. Straining his neck to get a better view, he than said to no one in particular, "Will ya look at the 'knockers' on that one! What do they do, breed them in the basement here?"

"How'd ya like to jump on her bones? Sid added, as all of their eyes fell onto the unquestionably obvious girl Kim had remarked about.

Standing up to over-emphasize the stare he was taking, George pretended to frown a little before answering, "No thanks. I've already had one 'rattle' after work, and I doubt if any of us here has enough lead in his pencil right now to keep that one happy."

"Speak for yourself," Sid sarcastically added, someone else in the background saying, "Piss up a rope."

Reaching to clutch at his chest, noisily wheezing, Rusty did his best to give the acting profession a bad reputation. "Knock it off you guys. You know my old 'ticker' won't take such remarks, especially after what we're used to working with."

Bob, still grinning and content to evaluate his new group of friends, raised his glass in a silent toast each time he heard something that tickled his funny bone, a gesture that was not only copied but followed up with a series of 'He-e-re, he-ere's!' from some in the group.

Since most, pardon me, all, of the 'boys' were there playing in the hopes that some big-chested woman might just accidentally expose her mammary glands in front of them, their conversations continued with the topic of sex. And since women naturally went with that preoccupation for all of them, they each took turns expressing their different opinions on the art of how best to pick up a woman.

Sweet talk or appearance came first, most of them agreed. But technique and delivery had no trouble in going from sweet talking baloney, down to the 'ol pair of rolled up socks' stuffed down the front of ones pants. And when Bob, now apparently feeling 'booze enhanced, accepted enough to speak, asked if that type of thing really worked, someone joked, "Someone better write the instructions down for this boy. Or he's liable to use a pair of month old 'stinkers', and drive everybody away with the odor."

Again the harmless laughter among them came easy, even as they searched for new material to pick on. Bob was so glad that he had so far been accepted into the group that when a seemingly pregnant woman walked past their table, one of the few ladies in the place that God in his wisdom had created the dark for; he used her as a chance to strengthen the bond even more.

Tilting his head closer to George, but speaking loud enough for everyone else at the table to hear, he said, "It must have been another case of 'rape'"

"Rape!" Ralph chuckled, more sarcastically then excitedly. "Who still in control of their faculties would want to 'rape' that?"

"I meant 'she' must have raped someone." Bob laughed.

Suddenly, once more proving that they were still only little boys at heart, one of the men made no effort this time to hide the built up residue of 'natural gas' his body no longer had any need for. And as they all broke up, while fanning at the air around them, Jamie Weir started to sing "Blow me a kiss from across the room. Tell me I'm nice when I'm not." as someone else added, "Is that really a bad cough you got there, or were you just trying to clear your throat?"

"Well, just remember what they say," the offender offered, making sure he had everyone's attention. "To 'air' is human."

"And to forgive 'divine'" Rusty quickly added. "Only in your case - it would read 'stupid' instead of 'divine!'"

"But 'wise' man would say," Bob added in his 'Confucius' smile, "Man who vacate present premise, show superior 'sense' and wisdom."

Fortunately for those close to the offender, who was now busy rubbing at a kneecap that had been kicked in recognition to his 'ghastly' deed, the bars already contaminated atmosphere helped dilute the alcoholic induced odor. Eagle beak, even though everyone knew he didn't really mean it, apologized by blaming the 'foul act' on the beer now passing through his kidneys.

"You guys are getting off easy." he smiled. "If I did this at home - the cat won't come near me for days, and I always get terrible pains in my right arm."

"More than just your arm should ache." Kim said. "Especially when you smell like something had crawled up your 'bung hole' and died there. But it's your 'left arm' that's supposed to ache when having a heart attack. So how in the 'Hell' can excessive internal combustion make your 'right' arm ache?

'That's easy." Terry laughed. "Especially if that's where your wife keeps punching you whenever you 'break wind'."

"My worst time is when I've been drinkin this 'brown pop' too." Pop Bottles offered, while reaching forward and picking up to drain the 'culprit' in question in front of him.

"Ya." Rusty added. "But the worst thing I hate about beer is that after about seven bottles I can't seem to get my bladder totally empty - once I prick the bubble and start trying to drain it."

"Sounds like a universal problem that could make you a millionaire, if you ever found a solution to get around it." Sid said, while downing the remainder of his drink.

Chuckling even as he spoke, "Ralph offered his own answer to the problem. "Maybe someone should invent a real cheap beer that you just dump directly into a urinal, thereby eliminating the middle man, not to mention the amount of time saved not standing in front of the worlds biggest 'bill board'."

"Sounds great to me." Kim grinned. "I'm tired of splashing water back onto my pants, every time I put the 'snake' back in its cage."

"If your 'asp' wasn't so short, the 'dead beer' wouldn't have so far to jump, and you wouldn't have to come up with a new excuse every-time you 'go-o-o' to the 'John'. George laughed.

Before Bill had a chance to verbally retaliate, his brother pushed his chair back from the table, while offering, "Is it just 'me', or does everybody else suddenly get the urge go for a 'whiz' when hearing someone talking about it."

"Sounds like an 'old mans' disease." one of the men answered.

"You keep offering answers like that," Kim smiled. "and you won't have to worry about getting 'old' enough to find out if it's true or not!"

As the words, "Who cares!" followed the threat; the journey that had been started was continued. "I'm gonna have to let you guys work this out. If I don't get close to a urinal real soon, you guys are probably gonna be real embarrassed to be seen with me."

"We already are." Sid lost no time in adding. And as Bob Langly walked away from the table - Rusty got another of his 'putdowns' in. "It's amazing the amount of booze that guy can put away - and not end up making splashing noises when he walks."

"He may be my brother," Bill offered, "but lately he's been drinkin so much I think his livers startin to shrink. Notice how he pulls to one side when he walks."

"Speakin of splashing noises," George said, his head searching back and forth around the very active crowed bar. "Where the Hell's Brad got to? Sometimes I'd swear he sees more 'ass' then a toilet seat."

"I'll say one thing for him." Sid added, admiration dripping from every word. "That boy's got balls. How much longer he'll have them is anybody's guess. But for now, I gotta admit, he's got balls!"

"The part about how much longer he'll have the 'family jewels' sounds good to me." Tom grinned, his face indicating that no doubt inside his head he was probably mentally envisioning Brad's possible castration. "But if I were in his shoes, I'd be sleeping with some kind of protection across the main artery in my throat."

"Say." one of the men laughed. "Isn't the 'main vein' the reason we're worried about him?"

"Ya." Sid replied. "I love my nookie' too. It's just that I'm not ready to 'die' for it yet!"

"Well if he ever has to go to jail over his sex life, I'm sure he can always plead 'Not guilty!' by reason of insanity." George smiled.

"How's that?" Bob bit.

"Easy." George continued to grin, everyone's eyes and ears on him - waiting for the rest of what they new had to come. "From what we all know about Brad and his lewd sex life, I think it's rather obvious he's just 'crazy' about it."

"Never mind Brad." Rusty laughed. "How was 'lucky' Fred doin when you left him?"

Using a side to sweeping side hip gyrating motion as body language to emphasize his answer, he instead asked, "Is that a sarcastic or envious 'lucky' you want to know about?" George laughed just as hard as the others of the men who broke into instant jeers and wolf whistles did, some of them imitating George's insinuating vulgar gestures did.

"What the Hell's this supposed to be?" a familiar voice called out. "A twist contest or a handicapped convention?"

It was Brad and he had somehow managed to snare another healthy-looking woman. Looking straight at George, so there could be no doubt, as to whom his words were intended for, "Is it safe to sit here?"

Brad started to pull a spare chair in beside his still vacant seat. A few of the men, while gladly answering, "Sit down! Sit down!" repositioned their own chairs in order to make room at the table.

George, in his usual humor, quickly objected, "Hold it! They didn't mean here!" Kim and Pop Bottles in turn just as quickly booed him before returning their attention back onto the woman still half wrapped around Brad's elbow. "Ignore him lady, he thinks he's someone important." and the topic of how 'lucky' Fred was making out, and you can believe me he was, was once more briefly forgotten about.

A few of them, Rusty and Ralph even, gentlemanly half-raised themselves out of their seats, as Brad helped her into the chair beside his. And when she pulled a cigarette out of her purse while saying, "Does anybody mind if I smoke?" two lighters instantly materialized in front of her face, as Brad stared at George's grinning face while saying, "Don't you dare answer that!"

Winking in Bob's direction, George pretended to be a little hurt, when saying, "I don't know why you guys don't like me. I like you!"

Rusty, the flame in his outstretched lighter now kissing the end of the woman's cigarette, turned his face to look at George. "Personally, if I liked 'guys', which 'I' 'don't'! Or even had them liking me, which I sure hope 'they' don't! I know 'I' wouldn't be bragging about it in public - especially in front of strangers."

As George already anticipated, most of the men instantly gave him the standard slamming of 'He-e-e-re!' and when Bob, a big smile on his face, also took part in the ritual, George beamed back at them. "Thanks for the recognition fellas. But just remember, I'm not the only guy who keeps droppin his soap in the showers at work all the time."

There could be no doubt, especially since she had a big smile on her beautiful young face, that their guest was just as use to all of the attention she presently receiving as she was loving all of it. And when the returning waitress immediately dropped off the draft beer in front of where she was now sitting, no one complained.

Placing the rest of the order in front of each man who had requested it, plus a half dozen extra silently nodded for drafts, she didn't have to ask for the amount of money mentioned when first arriving at the table. It and more, even before she had a chance to drop the last beer, found its way to her tray thanks to George's smiling generosity. And while still stooping, she was smart enough to wink in some of the other men's direction as well.

Watching her ever movement until she disappeared into the crowd, no doubt to deliver the remainder of the alcohol still on her tray, George explained the reasons for his grinning behavior. "Don't mind me," he said. "Everybody here knows I'm a 'sucker' for big boobs." It was a pun that even their newest smiling guest also acknowledged, as the rest of the men gave him of mixture of jeers and 'Bo-o-o-os', a rebuttal that once more made their table unlike any other in the place.

Acting almost near as drunk as he really was, Bill Langly, fortunate enough to be seated beside their pretty guest, asked her what time it was. She in turn, at first not knowing if he really needed to know the time or was just making conversation, answered 'Friday.' before giving him the real information.

"I must be going crazy!" he exasperated. "All day long I've been asking people everywhere the same question, and every-time I get a different answer!"

About the only benefit of their seating arrangement was that the sea of human bodies separating them from the band area was that the loud music lost most of its heart-pounding pulse by the time it filtered back to them. But when a few notes from the ballad presently being played did manage to find its' way there, it prompted Eagle Beak's courage to show itself. Letting his movements lead his voice, he started to stand half-erect before asking, "Would you like to dance?"

Since there was only one woman at the table, there was no real need to guess as to whom the question was directed at. But before she could reply, the smile on her face already answering for her, George cut in with, "I'm sure she would - just not with you."

Raising from her seat, and failing to suppress the humor she was now sharing with the rest of the table, it was hard to tell if her acceptance was out of sympathy or genuine desire as she accepted Terry's request. Standing up himself Brad grinned, "Don't forget where you got her buddy!" before using their absence as a chance to make room for more beer.

As expected, the rest of the men left at the table were more interested in how Eagle Beak was making out on the dance floor, and took turns straining their necks to watch more of the woman's than his booze enhanced gyrations on the crowded dance floor, someone saying, "Boy! I wonder if she'd like to sell some of that energy?"

"Down boy! Down!" Sid chuckled. "Even if she did, I doubt if you could afford the service charge, let alone feed the meter."

"Well, all I can say," Woodie offered, "is she'll always have a place to 'sit' as long as I have my face."

"You mean 'place'." Rusty quickly added.

"No-o-o." Sid chuckled. "He means his 'face'."

Rising a little wobbly from his seat, time and amount of liquor consumed obviously guiding his movements, Joe the janitor had every intention of trying to sneak away as unnoticed as possible. But as always, nobody got to do 'anything', without being noticed by someone in the gathering. So Bob said, "What's the matter Joe - the 'cement truck' here?" Joe rewarded the oft-used familiar remark with an over grinning "Do-o-onna you worry. I leta you know when she's a ready wit your newa shoes." before finally saying that he had things to do early in the morning. And when George asked him if he needed a ride Joe answered that the big yellow taxi that passed by outside the bar went right by his house also, so there was no sense in anyone missing out on any fun just for his benefit.

Watching him blend in with the crowd until they were sure he was safely out of the building, the men's interest soon changed when they picked up Eagle Beak and Brad's date returning. And it wasn't until they were actually back at the table that it became evident that they had brought company with them. Two similarly dressed, and roughly old enough to be half of the men's at the table young daughters, had followed them back to the table.

The broad grin that was on Terry's face, as he introduced them, "Boy's, this is two of Julie's friends, Bunny and Roxanne." grew even larger when one of the ladies eagerly occupied his offered vacant chair. The other woman, as another chair was squeezed into their gathering, giggled likewise when sitting down, as George said, "Bunny! Is that bunny like in rabbit?"

Julie, already in her own seat, led the laughs as she told her two friends, "Careful, girls. He's the one I warned you about. He's the kind of guy who'll ask you to dance, and when you say 'No, thank you.', he'll try to get even with you by answering, 'Does this mean that I have to give your girlfriend her dollar back?"

"No-no-no!" Pop Bottles laughed. "If you said 'no' - he would have slammed you with, I wasn't talking to you, I was askin the girl beside you!"

"Or he would have offered," Rusty more coughed than said, "Well - then what the 'Hell' did you come here for! Right, George?"

George, even though he hadn't thought the remarks had warranted it, had laughed right along with everyone else. But now that they were being foolish enough to ask for his attention, even though he already had every intention of putting them all down as soon as possible, he gladly gave them what they were asking for, and more.

"As for the lovely ladies here, and you prime candidates for Alzheimer disease, I would have simply given them the old standard, 'Don't thank me, thank God I asked you.' if one of them had said 'No thanks' to my offer to dance."

Arriving back at the table just as everyone was laughing at George's remark, Brad lost no time in joining right in, especially once he had detected the two new young faces at the table. Leaning closer to Julie, he quickly whispered in her ear, "Who are your friends?"

Julie deliberately and still in a happy mood thanks to a combination of the most recent remarks, the free booze she was sipping at, and in all likelihood that she had heard all of the familiar sounding such sweet-talk before, indignantly snapped back in his direction, "They are not whores!"

Brad, his face instantly turning a deep shade of red, tried to defend his whispered question.

"No! No! I said 'Who'! Who are you friends?" And it wasn't until he realized that he was the only one at the table presently not enjoying his embarrassment that he finally realized he was being made fun of. As slow as he sometimes was, Brad mentally said to himself, 'Thank goodness one of them wasn't named 'Denise'. I probably would have been accused of saying that's where she spent most of her time.'

The young girl that was beside Eagle Beak, possibly because she and her two friends had played similar games with each other before, turned her head in his direction and answered a question he hadn't even asked.

"You mean if I don't agree to go to bed with you, you're really going to commit suicide?"

Eagle Beak, just as totally caught off guard, didn't have a chance to answer the accusation, as George quickly offered, "That, young lady, has been his usual procedure on past occasions."

Bunny, not to be outdone by her friends, looked at Pop Bottles while saying, "How about you? Are you afraid of sex?"

"Afraid of it!" Brad exploded before Terry had a chance to answer. "Hell! Woman never ever fall asleep 'on' him during sex. He just jiggles them unconscious."

"Other than being the most fun you can have without laughing," Bill slurred, "it's definitely not to be considered a spectator sport!"

"I take it that's a positive reply then." Bunny smiled into Pop Bottles face, while giggling just enough to make her chest rise and fall noticeably for the benefit of those paying attention.

"Lady!" Ralph beamed. "I wouldn't get to close to that boy just now. It's been awhile since he's been with a woman. You keep doin what you're doin - and he's gonna hyperventilate right in front of ya."

"Hy - hyper - per, - is that bad?" Bunny said, noticeably confused, as everyone but Pop Bottles laughed.

"Well, let's put it this way." Rusty answered. "If you three gorgeous creatures had just gotten out of a nice hot sauna, Bob here could probably drink all the water out of it in one downing."

Even as he had been speaking, Rusty was pushing his chair away from the table. Ralph and Woodie, already knowing what he was up to imitated the maneuver. It was a known fact that they usually rode together during their little special nights out, and when Sid asked, "Leaving so soon?" Jamie Weir answered. "Have to. We're not as young as some of you bums. And we've still got tomorrow night to live through don't forget."

"Oh, the barbecue at George's place." Sid said, no doubt remembering another potential booze up. "I did forget." standing erect, a little noticeably wobbly, he pretended to tip an invisible hat in the women's directions, while saying, "If you'll excuse us ladies, we all have prior commitments. But first, a phone call."

"He means they're married." someone chuckled."

Starting for the same door they had come in through, the old standby 'Thanks for leaving!' trailing them, they, like Joe the janitor, were usually escorted out of the building after Sid had paused long enough to use the phone.

"He has to phone home." Eagle Beak grinned, in answer to the confusion on the woman's faces.

"Boy, has his wife got him trained." Bob smiled, a slight chuckle in his voice while watching Sid's comical detour towards the phone's area. "What does she do, 'kick the boyfriend out of the house before he gets home?"

"Nah" Eagle Beak grinned. It just gives her enough time to check and make sure the kid's bikes are out of the driveway, as well as their new cats in the house. He's already run over two."

"Bikes?" Bob asked.

"No, cats!" everyone else answered in almost perfect unison.

"Boy, the odds are getting better all the time." Brad winked in the girls' directions.

"Ya, and as soon as you leave they'll be even better!" George smiled.

Totally ignoring the remark at first, Brad rested his hand on Julie's arm while saying, "Let's dance." He then turned his head just enough to be looking solely at George, while adding, "It's probably not as crowded up there, as well as a lot quieter."

Bill and Bob, once more proving they were brothers, almost simultaneously asked Bunny for the same pleasure. And when she accepted, while shrugging as to which identical looking brother she should dance with, they both in unison positioned themselves on opposite arms, before wobbly leading her giggling form to the dance floor.

Roxanne, her head slowly pivoting around the whole of the table, pleasantly smiled, "Well, what are the rest of you, cowards?"

"Sorry." George quickly answered. "Hell, I even step on my own toes when I dance."

"Not to mention," Pop Bottles smiled, "he couldn't get rhythm if his pants were on fire."

"No-o-o look at me." Bobby lost no time in offering in his best over accented oriental dialect, when her eyes settled onto him, "I have 'chicken fleet'!"

"What ever the Hell that means!" Jamie Weir offered. "And since the rest can't be trusted, I guess it better be me."

It was easy to understand why George and the rest of the men were well into being legally declared intoxicated. Between them that night they'd consumed enough alcohol to permanently preserve anybody's kidney. But the woman's good behavior was either similarly induced, or they were all looking for an Oscar nomination. Before any of them could get too far away from the table, George reminded the men to leave a little of that stuff 'dreams are built on' - money. And even before the requested green stuff had a chance to hit the tables' surface, George and Bob made sure that they threw in their share also.

With just the three of them left at the table now, Pop Bottles turned his head in Georges' and Bob's grinning direction, before saying, "Thanks for the vote of confidence guys."

"Don't mention it." George smiled. "Someone had to watch out for you young studs."

"You ain't 'that' old!" Pop Bottles laughed.

"That's what I used to think too," George answered. "Until I whistled at a pretty young thing the other day. She turned around and asked me what my dog I was whistling for looked like. I guess when it comes to the ladies - we all can't be like Brad."

Rising out of his seat just long enough to get a brief peek at the dance floor. Bob's and George's instinctively following his gaze, Pop Bottles' leaned a little closer to them, before leading off what was on his mind with a smile.

"I'll let you guy's in on a little secret. Ol Brad's confidence isn't doing as great as everyone thinks it is."

"How's that?" George grinned back.

"Rumor has it that after picking up a real eye teaser last weekend, he was about to get rid of some excessive eyeball pressure when his egotistical world got a tear in it a mile long.

"That, I'd like to see." George smiled devilishly now, Bob still just grinning.

"Seriously!" Pop Bottles continued. "Apparently he was lying half naked on the bed with the girl supposedly locked onto the 'horn' of his saddle when while trying to get her sweater off over her head without being thrown, she lost her balance and toppled over backwards off the bed. After that she was laughing so hard Brad couldn't keep up his end of the arrangement, if you know what I mean."

"We know what you mean, 'jellybean'." George laughed. "I guess it just goes to show yea that occasionally there is such a thing as justice. Next time we're in the change house and he starts braggin about 'poundin himself short', I'll just nonchalantly remind him about this little incident."

"Hell, don't tell him I told you. Bottles spurted out, while checking the dance floor again.

"Don't worry, I won't." George smiled. "The first thing to remember about hearing secrets is to never tell who told you, or you just may not ever get to hear any more."

Poking his finger lightly into George's side, Bob whispered in his ear, "Careful. Everyone's coming back." And as George and Pop Bottles automatically looked towards the dance floor once more, Bob quickly added, "Remember - diplomacy is thinking twice, before saying nothing."

The waitress, as the group of dancing fools dropped their sweaty tired frames back into their chairs, reappeared at the table at almost the exact same time. Pop Bottles, even though they didn't really need it yet, used only his eyes and index finger of his right hand to order the same next round. And not until she was gone again did he remark about something he had detected on Eagle Beak.

"If your wife asks about that stain on your shirt collar Terry, just tell her it's a little bit of shoe polish, the Evil Dwarf's. I'm sure she'd accept and believe that."

Everyone's eyes had automatically turned to search out the stain in question, Eagle Beak trying to pull the collar far enough in front of him so as to be able to detect how bad the mark was. But even before he could find it for himself, as the men laughed, Roxanne was already busy wiping it away with a 'spit wet' hanky she had retrieved from her purse.

Building internal pressure reminding him that it was almost time for another trip to the library, George asked Bob if he was about full yet.

"No thanks." Bob grinned. "I drained the 'ballast-tank' just before you got here."

Excusing himself, a few of the men as always just naturally thanking him for leaving, George smiled mostly to himself as he set out for the 'little boy's room'. And just before his hearing was totally engulfed by the bar's present sounds of survival, his ears picked up on Eagle Beak's trailing words of, "Go for me while you're at it will yea, I'm kind of busy."

Passing the bar he was at first genuinely surprised when he saw what was obviously a drunk laying spread-eagled backwards on the floor, the bartender leaning over the bar saying, "Why don't ya sit up here Mike?" The drunk, either honestly or as a joke, with a glass in one hand, slurred back, "No thanks. I'd rather stand."

George wasn't the only one amused by the little skit, as others watching instantly broke into laughter also. But when he next saw another noticeably inebriated patron who had one of his shirt sleeves nailed to the bar's surface, he couldn't help but think to himself, 'Boy - business doesn't look that bad!' and the humor stayed noticeably with him, even as he walked into the smoke filled washroom.

Even before he had entered, he recognized the contaminated air for what it was. The tiny room reeked of the stuff the younger generation was always saying should be legalized. The thick atmosphere, even though George was old enough to be considered as part of the older generation, was something he had often found humor in - even if he didn't always agree with it.

Walking up to a vacant urinal labeled, 'We aim to please. You aim 'too', please.' his ears as always eagerly eating up things he couldn't see. Purposely, he eavesdropped on any of the conversations or remarks presently going on around him. And his first chuckle came from the individual on his right who was presently looking downward and seemingly talking to his penis, "Look! Make up your mind! It was your idea to come in here! Do you have to go or don't you?" and as he chuckled to himself, his ears kept right on working.

"I must be getting old." he heard someone say. "It seems the only time I ever take my pecker out of my pants lately is to use it to pee out of."

"I know what ya mean." came probably from the man he had been speaking to. "Ya know you're getting old when you look down - and your thumb looks bigger than your doniker does."

"I don't know what you guys got to complain about." another voice and apparently someone else involved in eavesdropping on the ongoing remarks, offered. "When I was your ages it never took more time to drain it than it did to fill it."

But it was the comment from the end stall that grossed them all out. "There's a sign on the door in here that say's all turds over two pounds are to be lowered by rope. Anybody out there got a rope?"

Taking care of his own business, George couldn't help but notice that the man on the other side of him was just short of falling over in a stupor. Feeling that conversation might help bring him around, he used the friendliest voice he owned, while using one of the old standard lines of, "I hear this is where all the big pricks hang out!" and then moved right into "The water sure feels cold today!"

Apparently startled by the sound of George's voice, the inebriated individual, while zipping up, smiled while answering, "Yep. And it's deep too." before heading for the door. Chuckling slightly he then turned his head in the opposite direction something usually frowned at in a sober world, to smile into another set of whosey looking features, before commenting about the condition of the urinal in front of him. "Someone pretty ugly must have stood here. They've not only cracked this porcelain trough, but the wall behind it also."

"Well don't look at me!" the other man quickly shot back, his balance disturbed just enough to let his already hampered reactions fail to keep his body from doing a slow melt sideways down the very wall George had just referred to. And as he thought to himself, "Boy, water spots on the front of your pants is bad enough, but how do you explain the whole side of your body being wet." others in the room totally ignored the poor mans new position.

Under normal circumstances George would have been one of the first to run to the now snoring mans' aid, but in his present condition everything seemed strangely acceptable. Grinning to himself, his senses fast approaching the condition he and Fred had been in the night before, he continued to let his attention float around the room.

Close-by, a few men were passing around the reason for the room's strong odor, and when it was offered in his direction, George smiled his reply. "No thanks. I never learned how."

"Go ahead man! It's good shit!" one of the men said.

"Thanks anyway." George smiled. "But my hands are full right now."

"Don't you wish!" the same man laughed.

"Don't we 'all' wish!" George laughed back. "Besides, when it's time for some good 'shit', I'll take it in there."

He had used his head to point in the direction of the room's cubicles as he had spoken, with the men puffing on the 'joint' letting their blurred vision trail his. It was a gesture that instantly made them all react slightly surprised when they happened to see someone's head, a feat that could only be accomplished if the man were standing on the 'stall's' toilet seat, peering out in their direction.

The patron who had offered George a puff on the cigarette earlier indignantly asked in the cubicle's direction, "And just what in the name of 'Hell' do you think you're doing?"

George, his business finished after shaking his long time companion goodbye, a small wet spot on the front of his pants, laughed while offering, "From where I'm standing, I think it's rather obvious that he's either afraid of water, or he's bragging."

Starting for the door after drying his hands, one of the men he had joked with called out in another departing patron's direction, "Around here we wash our hands after taking a 'whiz'."

George, without even breaking his stride or glancing back, called over his shoulder, "Where I come from our 'dicks' are long enough that we don't have to worry about getting 'pee' all over our hands."

Retracing his route, he happened to pass the table where the two girls he had scared away earlier were now sitting. Spotting them at about the same time they noticed him, the grin already on his face broadened even more after hearing what they had to say to him.

"We'd ask you to sit down, but with our luck you'd probably think we meant with us."

Instead of a verbal rebuttal he just offered them a part of his smile, while mentally telling himself, "If I had sat down, they'd need therapy treatments by the time I was ready to leave again. I guess they're a prime example of what people mean when they say that 'Some people are like pubic hairs on a toilet seat, sometimes they get pissed off'.

But the return trip wasn't going to be 'all' negative, as he passed an area where someone had noticeably thrown back to the material world, some of what they had routinely come there to acquire. And as he commented to himself while looking down at the mess of regurgitated food and booze, 'And 'that' is one of the main reasons why I try not to frequent these places anymore than I have to.' A joker somewhere close-by called out, 'Some-body here order a hot meal!"

Arriving back at the table, he was just in time to hear Brad introduce a now familiar face to the table. It was the female singer from the band. And in his seat was another new face, only this one belonged to a body that anyone with a kind streak in them would simply have remarked as having more than a hint of abused high mileage on it. Passing Eagle Beak he dipped just long enough to whisper in his ear, while gently smacking him at the base of his skull, 'That's for dribbling on my pants when you finished when it was your turn to go. Next time, shake it dry, sloppy!'

Stopping beside his chair, George couldn't help but notice that the singers' eyes were still on him. And if he'd had an ego, which most of those who knew him if asked would have commented that he most definitely did, then he would have overly exaggerated the pleasant smile now already on his face.

Using one of his friendlier true lines, he returned her attention by saying, "If you're not a superstar some day, then there's something wrong with the business you're in."

"Why thank you." the singer smiled provocatively. "Maybe I should get rid of my manager and let 'you' handle me."

"Careful what you say around this guy." Brad jumped in, his own voice dripping with over exaggerated innuendoes. "I'm sure he'd love to 'handle' you alright, but his wife would probably kill him if she ever found out he was even thinking about it."

"Oh.' the singer answered with a noticeable hint of frowning on her face and sadness in her voice. "You mean you already belong to someone?" she then pouted, while looking directly at George.

"For at least the next thousand years!" someone laughed.

"We all do." George grinned back, a slight hint of egoism to his words and face. "At least that's what the company we work for likes to think." and it took a quick, "Hey! No shop referrals during 'off duty' down time, remember?" to remind everyone of the golden agreement not to waste their time together away from work by talking about anything shop related. The term 'Off duty!' meant just that. At the present they were off company property, off company time, and for those who really knew them, off to one of their better attempts at all being 'shit faced' once again, before making it home.

Glancing around for a vacant chair, George's gesture didn't go undetected. The woman still planted squarely in the one he had first occupied, smiled up into his face, "What's the matter sonny? Did you loose your seat?"

Not intending to be rude, George returned her forced smile while answering, "Not really. I know 'exactly' where it is. It's presently hiding under someone.'

"Oh, you mean me?" the still grinning woman answered exaggeratedly, her posterior more grinding then twisting itself slightly into the chair beneath her as she spoke. "Well why don't I just give it back to you, and then sit on your lap."

"I'll second that!" Eagle Beak laughed. "And then you can both talk about the first thing that 'comes' up!"

"If you ever tried to 'imitate', not to mention 'second' that motion someone quickly threw in, "I'm willing to give odds that nothings ever going to 'come' up, and not just where Ol George's concerned!"

As the slamming originally intended for George instead found a new home to flaunt itself, he quickly scanned the area once more, while offering a reply to the remark originally intended for him. "Thanks for the offer, but I'm sure I can find another placed to put my butt."

Keeping with the act of being hurt by his replies, while thrusting out her already overly endowed protruding chest, the woman then offered, "What's the matter honey? Don't you like what you see?"

Normally there weren't many things in the world that could visually rattle Georges' composure, his warped since of humor screaming 'Mo-o-o-o'! But since he couldn't help but be in a position to be looking directly down into the open top of the woman's bare cleavage, a slight blush leapt to his face once more as he answered first only to himself, 'Lady, if I could drink all of the booze in this place, it wouldn't be enough to give me the courage to hustle you!' And then out loud, "Hell, of course I do! I'm married, not queer!"

Lady luck must have been paying attention to George's predicament, as a chair within arms reach suddenly showed itself. Its' present owner at a table next to them, his unsteady body more then once repositioning itself for balance as he went, stood up. Apparently calling it a night while scrapping up some loose change from the tables surface in front of him, a low mumbled burp attesting that he had been there longer then they had, he gave George just a silent affirmative nod in reply to the words, "Is this seat available?" And even before the area was totally vacated, George was busy squeezing it and himself in alongside Bob's, well away form the barracuda still occupying his.

No sooner had he planted his body firmly onto the chair, everyone enjoying his quirky intimidated predicament, before Bob was whispering into his ear, "You better watch yourself my friend. Speculation has it she's a 'hooker', no doubt trolling for business."

"Well if she is, on both counts, then she's sure got the right 'bait'! Her skirt gets any shorter when she sits down, I'll bet anyone willing to check will be able to see her mustache. But when it comes to 'trolling' for business - I'm not fishing today." he whispered back, a quick glance in her direction conjuring up an image of her having a mattress strapped to her back. And the only way he could get rid of the humorous picture inside of his head was by shaking it slightly, while telling his 'rude' and 'crude' imagination still wanting to shout out 'Mo-o-o.!' to stop working overtime. "But if I was," he continued, "the only 'catch of the day' I'd be interested in, is at home right now guarding the boat, and probably sawing wood as we speak."

From his new seats location he couldn't help but detect that the singer was also still showing a grinning interest in his direction, probably from his noticeably present uncomfortable predicament. Returning her compliment, he was genuinely a little sorry to hear that she would be leaving, when she started to stand up while saying, "I've got to get back to work gentlemen." a wink in his direction not going unnoticed. "Thanks for the entertainment and drink."

Gentlemanly politeness, 'Now that's talent! - Good looks good manners and good grammar to boot.' he told himself, which made him as well as a few others at the table raise themselves half erect, while watching her shapely form maneuver itself back to the stage area. And he then had to fight real hard to keep himself from asking the woman still planted squarely in his old seat, if she didn't have to do the same.

But his attention was briefly distracted by not so much the comment of "Boy! You talk about the grass always looking greener on the other side of the fence!' but rather the answer from the man sitting beside him of, "I don't care how much 'grass' you smoke, your wife's never going to look any better!' that broke him up. And another comment close-by of, "Why would you invite Ronnie to come here with us, he's practically deaf!" which was answered with, "Deaf yes, blind no. Just look at his face. Apparently he's no worse off than us when watching the shapely young women on the dance floor bouncing up and down in rhythm to whatever it is that they can hear."

But the conversations at the adjoining table were starting to head in the same downhill spiral he had experienced in the washroom, when one of the men comment to another.

"Say, isn't that girl over there the same one you were dating last year, what happened?"

To which his buddy replied, "Ya - that's Linda. It just didn't work out between us."

And his friend, while straining his neck to get a better look at her, quickly asked, "Why not?"

And when the first guy answered, "Remember when we were kids and used to go the Saturday matinees to watch the westerns, and everybody's hero was 'Red Rider' with his sidekick 'Little Beaver'?"

"Sure." the one who had started it all smiled.

"Well, I'm not a 'kid' anymore. When I got a chance to meet her parents, I realized that as she got older she was going to start looking more and more like 'Little Beavers' mother 'Big Beaver!" George knew he had overheard enough.

Pop Bottles, no doubt trying to be friendly, picked a package of the junk-food resting in front of him and offered it around the table, saying, "beer-nuts anyone?"

George normally would have been all over the perfect setup for one of his humorous reply's, but instead left it alone in order for the obvious reason of keeping him-self away from the center of attention. But as comical as the question sounded, another of the men quickly said what was no doubt possibly on half of the male gatherings' minds. "Not now! I just drained them."

Eagle Beak, while stretching the neck of his shirt away from his body, said, "Definitely! Dump some in here will ya!"

Brad, not wanting to miss out in anything that could have the girls' eyes facing in his direction, deliberately over-exaggerated by leaning his body across the table, while saying, "Sure! I'll take a chance on those denture wreckers."

But before any of the nuts now moving in his direction could reach his opened hand, a small squeal escaped from his lips, as he jumped erect. The hand that he had been using to hold onto the tables edge for balance had somehow picked up a small sliver. And as he visually inspected his newly acquired affliction, all eyes at the table stared in his direction, but not for the reason he had wished them to.

"Damn it!" he said, the injury now under his close inspection. "I've picked up some wood. Anybody here got a pair of tweezers, or something sterile?"

As each of the woman instinctively reached for their purses, most of the men's vision trailing their moves, George quickly took a full gulp of his drink. Pretending to gargle with the liquid before swallowing it, he then stood up while answering, "I'll get it ladies!"

In one quick movement he leaned across the table, and grabbed unsuspecting Brad's outstretched finger, only to sink his teeth into the inflicted area. And as Brad, reasoning finally sinking into his thoughts, instantly yanked his hand out of George's mouth, while excitedly yelling out a surprised, "Hey!" everyone else there broke out into loud laughter, while George pretended to spit out the rewards of his effort.

It was just another of the many comical spontaneous situations that once started - just had to be carried to its conclusion, as Brad realizing that he was being 'played with', out-loud next pretended to inspect and count one by one each finger on the assaulted hand.

It was safe to say that a few of them, as most laughed almost uncontrollably, were on the very edge of an acquired condition where they wouldn't in a probability be able to remember the next day much of what was presently happening. And to add proof of truth to its possibility, Bill Langly wasn't acting when his head suddenly made a dull 'thud' when contacting the table's surface in front of him. In fact the interruption seemed to be such a perfect continuation of what was going on that his brother reached out and lifted it, by way of his hair, back off the table, while saying, "Ya gotta hand it to him, he sure knows when to quit."

If Bills first meeting with the hard surface hadn't bothered him, Bob only a drink or two away from joining him, then in all likely-hood the second one wouldn't do much more damage, when his head was set free to quickly imitate the same noise it had delivered earlier.

"Isn't he supposed to be in on overtime tomorrow?" Sid asked, after lowering his head far enough to rest on the table, which would allow him to be able to look directly at the closed slits covering Bill's eyes.

"Maybe we should phone in and say he can't make it tomorrow, ah, I mean this morning." Brad smiled, while giving Julie a soft shoulder embracing hug,

"I'll do it." George quickly added.

"Oh no you won't!" Bob instantly shot back. "I still remember when you phoned in for me once. I'm lucky I've still got my job!"

New enough to the groups' rituals to in most men's eyes to be a kind of 'virgin' to their antics, Bob let a big grin accompany the words, "Why? What happened?"

Also without even knowing what had happened, a big grin seated itself on Brad's face also when likewise asking. "Okay - I'll bite. What happened?"

The answer, "Well - it was about a year ago." not only started with a glare in George's direction, but also with an exaggerated deliverance that had the rest of the gathering spell bound. "In fact it was on an occasion a lot similar to tonight. I'd had more than my share to drink, and like my brother, I wasn't going to be in any condition for work in the morning. When I let George phone in for me, I heard him say 'Hello!

Is Bob Langly there?' and when he got the obvious answer of 'No.' he quickly shouted into the phone, 'Well he damn well 'ain't' going to be either!' I swear I almost broke my wrist trying to snatch the phone out of his hand when he slammed it back onto the receiver."

The words, aided by a dressed up face stretching deliverance, would in themselves have been enough to crack everyone up. But when they all glanced in George's direction as if to confirm the story, they broke up even more when seeing him with an Angelic poise of clasping hands raised as if in prayer in front of him, his eyes lifted towards the heavens. And as new to the group as Bob was, even he knew that George and anything resembling 'sainthood' just didn't seem to go together. It was a view that those who really knew him - apparently felt deserved a materialistic reward, as it suddenly started to rain bits and pieces of the junk food that had been strewn about the table.

Detecting, while deflecting away some of the incoming barrage, that the one still occupying his seat was smiling at him each time his gaze happened to pass over hers, George deliberately forced himself to keep himself busy someplace else. Turning in his newest friends' direction, he asked, "Do you know why your nose is designed with the venting ports aiming down?"

Those close enough to overhear what had just been said, once again stopped what they were doing in order to concentrate on their new friends reply, especially since most of them had already heard the question before. But Bob wasn't as totally naïve as some of them felt he was and when he instantly noticed their sudden curiosity in his direction, he smiled slyly through 'Charlie Chan' eyes at George - while saying, "Wise man not say, 'I bite', but instead ask 'Why'?"

"Because," George grinned, "if it was on upside down, every time you sneezed, you'd blow your hat off."

"But, I don't wear a hat." Bob quickly shot back.

"Well - maybe some day you'll be wearing a 'rug' same thing. Every year around here we're known for the amount of rain we get, so, you'll eventually have to buy one. Otherwise every time you go out into the rain and take a deep breath, you'll eventually fill up and drown." George continued to grin.

As Bob's imagination envisioned inside of his head the potential comedy behind what had just been suggested, he broke up just as hard as everyone else did. It also let him know that reality was another thing that had to be paid attention to occasionally. And as his kidneys reminded him that the beer he was presently draining from the glass held to his lips would soon need to vacated some room to make way for its new arrival, he told himself that now was as good a time as any. Using the empty glass to salute in everyone's direction, he stood up to excuse himself from the table, his features exaggerating what he was no doubt about to say.

"Confucius once say, 'Man sometimes like boat on ocean, drifting to one side when moving. To acquire stability, uneven load must be removed."

"Did he really say that?" one of the women naively asked.

"Search me." Bob smiled, now out of disguise and totally back in his own true character. "Personally I never met the man. But when someone who's been eatin and drinkin as much as we have says it's time to dump some liquid balance, believe me, it's time to dump!"

Heading towards the washroom, a deliberate slight hint of being effected by the ratio of booze he had consumed showing in his movements, he was no sooner out of sight of the table then the woman George had been trying constantly to avoid quickly occupied his vacated seat. She then, leaning provocatively in his direction, a few eyes from those curious as to what she was up to watching her every move, she half-whispered for only his ears, "Ya wanna neck?"

The obvious answer, especially since he knew exactly as to what she was referring to, should have been, 'No thank you. I keep all that activity for the wife after she's seen my pay stub after some overtime.' But instead he went for the reply that everyone who knew him would expect. "No thank you, I already have one. And I'm not quite ready to stick it that far out just yet."

Undaunted, and still with a hint of a giggle leading her, the pursuer persisted with the more direct suggestive words, "Ya mean, you wouldn't like to, you know, 'take' me someplace!" her chest once more protruding.

Being the pursued instead of the hunter continued to keep George on guard and slightly off balance. And his answer, "Sorry. but I can't leave my buddies. If you want, I'll call you a cab. I'm sure he'll gladly 'take you' wherever you want to go." was strictly one of self-defense.

Finally accepting that she was either batting 'zip' or wasting her time and potential on an 'idiot', both noticeably irritating her, she verbally shot him harshly with, "Say. Are you deliberately trying to ignore me?"

George, fighting both her remarks and the booze he was more than feeling, let his eyes foolishly sneak another peek in her overly pleasingly scented direction, swallowed hard again before answering. "I'm trying to lady. Believe me, I'm trying. But you're not helping my concentration any."

Those still watching George, especially since there were very few things in the world that they knew of that could stump or disturb him, enjoyed watching him squirm while trying to back-paddle away from the 'barracuda' beside him. And the woman, apparently still not willing to admit defeat, continued her attack, but from a more direct direction.

Letting one of her hands find its way to rest on his arm, its unprepared for contact making him again noticeably flinch, she then softened her voice once more while continuing with, "Well, if not 'me', name one thing in here that you do like."

Stalling for time by pretending to glance around what he could see of the room, George indicated that he needed the arm her touch was starting to burn up - in order to take a drink from the glass in front of him. And when it was finally free, he used it too only take a sip from his drink -before answering, "The juke box."

"The juke box!" the woman answered, noticeable frustration in her voice as she looked directly into his face, "That damn things been broken for the last three days. The only bloody thing it's good for is to rest your drink on while you're on the dance-floor."

Faking another smile, as much as her choice of words just 'begged' for any one of a dozen possible and all rude innuendoes, George just grinned, "I was just looking for a 'safe' answer to your question lady, not an 'honest' one."

"Well, maybe you'd like to just dance with me then." the woman said provocatively.

"Sorry." George back-paddled again, even his rarely seen 'good behavior' finally starting to wear a little thin, "But right now I'm having trouble concentrating on just breathing, never mind anything as energetic as dancing. Besides, I've kind of grown attached to my 'jewels', if you know what I mean. As someone said earlier, my wife ever finds out I've been even considering any 'hanky panky' and she'll have them in a jar on the mantel over the fireplace real quick."

Looking for any excuse to get away from her and not the table, he quickly downed the remainder of his drink. But before he could even push his chair away from the table to justify the excuse he had just made about needing to use the 'john' again, a big almost glow in the dark fancily dressed negro bent down between his exit and the hustling woman. His sudden intrusion, while smiling, "Everything going okay here baby?" and the broad grin, as obviously 'crocodile as it was, did allow two rows of seemingly overly exaggerated white teeth pass over the gathering.

Only a blind man would have failed to see that the man was apparently the woman's, to quote a kinder definition, 'guardian'. Everything about him, his cloths, attitude, excessive amount of gold enhancing the one big gold platted tooth in the front of his mouth, seemed to brand him as the type of person always stereotyped in movies for his profession. And as the woman in question, answered, "Apparently the natives around here aren't restless enough yet."

George let the combination liquor and thinning impatience in him foolishly loosen his tongue to the extent where he more than just 'shot himself in the foot'. In fact what he was about to say, was considerably enough to warrant shooting everyone there in his group in 'both feet'!

"If I was a fashion designer, I'd 'highly' recommend that anyone with your complexion 'really' shouldn't wear that loud of a shade of yellow."

Almost instantly all of the men at the table stopped in their mid-conversations and antics, because unfortunately they already could anticipate what to expect next. The 'pimp', the 'guardian', or whatever slangish nickname the profession happened to be going under at the time, seemingly lost all traces of being in anyway courteous. Now, even for then, it was generally acceptable to call a 'spade' a 'spade', a non intended racial slur or bit of animosity intended which would have only meant anything only in the hearts of those with bigotry there also. And why, because the shit was now about to hit the fan.

Giving every indication that he was in control of the situation, , the ladies apparent guardian said sternly, "And just 'why', might I ask, is that?"

If you were to ask most professional performers how they managed to constantly repeat their routines time after time in almost perfect unison, they would tell you that once they start their monologue it fortunately often just flows out of their mouths, without even having to think about it. Unfortunately for George, especially in his present condition and like now, he often was subject to the same type of answering, speaking, without first thinking.

"Because it might make you look like a banana with bad spots."

A few of the men and all of the women fortunately, while a few noticeably cringed, had enough sense to try to laugh the failed joke turned insult away. It was something the offended not only picked up on, but also seemed to be enough to change his attitude if possible even more. Leaning his body in a little bit closer to George, while glaring into his eyes, he almost growled, "Is that supposed to be an insult?"

Not seeming to know or even care, George's cavalier like attitude remained unchanged, as he answered with a smile that indicated they were somehow age-old friends, which they definitely were not, just joking around with each other, "Not if you have to ask."

For one brief second it actually looked as if the man was at a lost for words, which was probably why he came up with a 'comeback' most would have considered as being out of 'left field'.

"Well at least I still got all my hair!" he snapped.

"My partial baldness is the result of a childhood affliction." George smiled. "When I was little I was so good that the grown ups kept repeatedly patting me on the top of my head - while saying, 'Good boy!, You're a good little boy!' which as you can see eventually trampled the roots of my hair to death."

Now there was no mistaking that the building emotion from the man only inches away from him was anything but sarcasm, as he continued with the verbal attack. "Boy! You must really think you're something special."

Still sober enough to know that the hole he had started to 'scoop out' with his tongue was getting deeper and deeper, George started to slide his chair away from the table while smiling, "Well, I know I'm not the best, but I'll just have to do until the other guy gets born." And even though he knew he was in the middle of something 'very' important, his bladder and short ability for holding fluid once more told him it had priority 'one'.

The negro, as everyone else remained a spectator, made the mistake of not giving George the room he needed. Consequently, and definitely not on purpose, George accidentally dragged one of the legs of the chair across an alligator shoe definitely not his. And even as its owner yelled, "Hey!" in surprise, George tried to apologize.

"Oops, sorry!" And while instinctively looking down, he instantly added. "Whoa! How in the 'Hell' did those babies get so far from the swamp?"

Almost instantly the already diminishing happy mood that had tried to remain at their table, dropped another two octaves, as everyone there waited to see what was going to happen next.

Using the mishap as 'fuel' the 'pimp' pretended to care more about his fancy shoes than he really did. Dragging a finger across the mark left by George's chair - he barked, "What are you , blind!"

Sometimes it's funny how fast the human brain can talk to itself, like now as it thought, 'The saying is, 'What are you blind in one eye, and can't see out of the other?' or 'I can't be blind, I hit your shoe, didn't I?' but instead he apologized once more.

"Look. I really am sorry."

"I'll show you 'sorry'! the now center of attention shouted angrily. "Do you want to step outside?"

Glancing up and down the table, it was now evident by the small crowd that had gathered the agitator was definitely no longer alone. In a last ditch effort to get the dangerous mood back into a happier groove, George smiled, "Unless 'that's' where they've moved the washrooms, I don't really see any reason to."

Surprisingly stepping away, anger in every word as his hands hung clenched at his side, the next words were hot and filled with anger from the negro. "Do you know 'karate'!"

To plead ignorance of any acknowledgement to the world of 'karate', especially since action movies were presently raking in mega dollars at theater box offices, would have been useless, especially since almost everyone in the group was a big fan of the 'king' of the 'Kung Fu' movies

Bruce Lee. But as was his nature, George threw gasoline on the already growing fire between them, with the words, "Could be." he smiled. "What does he look like?"

Once more all of George's male friends felt that now would be an appropriate time to chuckle. But it was a noticeable wave of nervous laughter that soon became obvious when it moved only among their gathering. And, as some of the men stole an occasional glance at the group growing around them, when one of them who had materialized put his hand inside of his shirt, Pop Bottles timidly chuckled, "When you pull that hand back out, the only thing on the end of it better be four fingers and a thumb."

"Is that a threat, 'four eyes?" the man snarled in his direction.

"Hell no." Pop Bottles smiled, noticeably a little nervously. "Just a prediction, I hope."

If there was any doubt in anybody's mind about the intentions of the bar's regulars and George's group, it was quickly washed away when the woman basically responsible for the potentially explosive situation, said with displeasure in George's direction "Can you read my lips?" and when she then silently mouthed an easily identifiable obscenity in his direction he lost no time in giving the rude gesture the only answer his warped sense of humor would allow.

"Normally we could. But not while you're sitting down, lady."

"That does it!" the negro growled. "It's time to take this thing outside."

Brad, trying to laugh the hostilities way, half-heartedly joked, "Ya better watch it. George turns into a real 'windmill' when he's fighting."

Eagle Beak, realizing that Brad was up to, instantly followed up with a few more short hopefully humorous puns. "Ya, he'll be all over you like a 'ham on rye', once he gets going. And if that doesn't work, he's been known to hit someone with so many 'left's they've actually been said to beg for a 'right'!"

"And most of that shirt he's wearing," someone else threw in, "isn't all air. There's actually some muscle in there too, someplace, I think."

"My religion doesn't permit me to fight." Ken laughed.

"Well, lucky us." one of the standing men answered, "Mine does."

"If any of you bums believe in 'God'," one of the seated men half-whispered. "now might be a good time to get in touch and use up any favors you might have comin to ya."

No one still seated had to take a look at the surrounding unsmiling faces to realize that their weak attempt to humor the situation away was failing miserably.

So George, even though he wanted to say, 'You mess with us and I'll punch all of the color out of ya.' simply returned the constantly unfriendly stare with a smiling, "Personally my favorite is, 'You mess with us and I'll hit you so hard, you'll have to jog for three days just to get back here'. But I can see it wouldn't be appreciated just now."

So far the audience George had always played to in the past had always been of a friendlier nature, but it definitely now looked as if all of that was about to change.

When not one person standing even gave any hint of a smile at his remark, George grinned himself, hoping that it might be contagious, as he said, "Loosen up fellas. We're only joking. All we came in here for was a few drinks and live it up a little. There's been no harm done. Look, I apologize if anybody's feelings have been stepped on. Oops, I mean, I mean feelings have been hurt, uh, that doesn't work either does it? Oh what the Hell! Whatever! We're looking for fun, not trouble!"

Sneering "Hurt!" indignantly, "We'll show you what real pain is, or are all of you cowards to?"

The last words caused a small ripple if building emotion to pass noticeably over the men still seated. Trying to avoid a fight was one thing, but being called cowards was another. It was only George who managed to let his unchanged face completely conceal the emotional anger building inside of him. And when the antagonist continued to let his voice drip with sarcasm when saying, "You guys can't just come in here anytime you want and abuse our women." George finally accepted the fact that there was nothing he could say or do that would halt what was fast approaching.

Mentally he had to agree that except for young Louie and relatively few other women, most of the females he had seen up to now in the bar were far better looking than anything he was used to seeing within the plant. But regardless, if it was true or not, he couldn't just stand there and take the man's continuous verbal abuse, no matter how much he had unintentionally begged for it.

"You're right." he finally said, while glancing around the gathering. deliberately stepping away from the woman beside him, he added, "Besides- it looks like God already beat us to it."

"Still have to make a joke about our women, don't you?" the negro shot back - his face once more only inches from George's.

"You're right again my friend." George said straight-faced. "They're nothing to joke about, are they."

Two men with biceps that looked as if they had been using cars for weights when working out, possibly the bar's bouncers, joined the group just as a firm voice from behind the bar's area shouted, "You guys get outside if you're going to get physical!"

Someone from about the same area and invisible to Georges' vision, not that he was willing to take his eyes off the ones still so close to his, excitedly added, "There's going to be a 'butt dancing' contest!"

In one last futile effort to save a bout of unnecessary trouble from ruining their otherwise successful night, George once more offered to settle their disagreement with a 'Why don't we 'drink' this over?'

It was a useless gesture that only invoked the angry 'pimp' to pick up a half-filled glass of beer from the table and toss it in George's direction, while saying, "Here! If the drinks are on you, why don't I get you the first one?"

George managed to easily dodge most of the liquid contents from the glass, which more then most of his coworkers seated around him couldn't do. Some of the beer even managed to splash across the exposed neck of Bill Langly, who was still resting face down on the tables' surface. It was an unintended act that comically made him bolt up direct in his chair, while slurring, 'Sorry fellas, I didn't realize it was my turn to buy again so soon." before letting his head slowly hug the tables top once more.

Using one hand to wipe away what little bit of beer that had managed to find its way to his face, George then used the other to give a silent signal of restraint in his coworkers direction, because he just knew some of them would be wanting to get up angrily from their seats. And when his ears picked up on the only words seemingly being offered in their defense from the bands singer, 'Why doesn't everybody just back off and have a drink. Then I can get back to what I'm being paid for, giving you an excuse to get rid of some of that excess energy your so eager to work out, by dancing!"

The gesture, even though well intended, was totally ignored. So George picked right up from where he had left off.

"No need to get excited, fellas." he said. "They say beer's good for the hair, so just consider it that you've had a little shampoo treatment, courtesy of our friend here."

"Jesus!" the almost totally frustrated negro spit out, his feet now braced with tensed arms and clutching fists. "What in the Hell does it take to get you guys into motion? We ain't your friends! And if you'll step outside, we'll prove it!"

Letting his shoulders shrug as a sign of hopelessness at the situation he had not only gotten them into, but also out of, George made sure to keep his eyes locked onto those still glaring into his, when he picked up his glass to drain the rest of his as yet unborn hangover, before saying, "You're right. I guess you're too much of a jerk to be any friend of ours. Show us your best side, and we'll follow you outside."

As the rest of the workers, fortunately still sober enough to realize that they should keep a cautious eye on the group of men surrounding them, except a snoozing Bill who was still assuming his last position, George managed an undetected, "Where's Bob?" Even the answer, "He's probably still in the 'crapper', saying goodbye to that chicken he was stuffin into his face earlier." Moving for the doorway, George whispered, "Good. No sense in getting him all bruised up the first time he's out with us."

Their exit from the bar must have been a fairly common occurrence, especially since only a few of the patrons who had originally gathered around their table, bothered to follow in behind their exit. On their way outside it had been hard for George or the boys to pair off fairly, due mainly to the amount of men apparently still on the 'pimps' side. And it was only the fact, George thought to himself, that the patrons who had chosen to remain behind possibly hadn't wanted to lose any precious drinking time, over that the fact that he and his buddies were definitely more inebriated then the bars regulars - that might still work in their favor. But as luck would have it, George somehow did manage to end opposite the negro, the bars probable leading instigator, who now seemed to feel compelled to put on a little intimidating display.

Planting his feet firmly on the ground, in a manner that looked as if they actually were gripping it, he then went into his spiel. "Remember inside I asked you if you knew karate? Well I'm a third degree 'black belt."

George, whispering to him-self just low enough that no one else would be able to hear, commented, "You would be! It's obvious 'brown' would just never be good enough for you." and even though common sense told him that he would probably stand a chance if he had brought along his 'Pete Rose' or 'Mickey Mantle' sluggers with him, his warped mind instead wanted to say out-loud, 'Get your hand off my zipper!' But then 'Superman in a bottle' and every other form of 'backbone builder' often had a tendency to do that.

"And this is what I'm going to do to you." the negro growled, using his voice to add to the already building intimidation. He then started through a series of obviously well trained expertly staged smooth flowing kicks and punches that would have easily disabled or killed the invisible opponent he was attacking. And as the sound of his voice and whip snapping movements chopped at the night air around them, George couldn't help but detect a couple of his friends swallowing hard, while looking as nervous as he was now feeling. He even had time to silently scold himself, by saying that his wagging tongue was finally about to get him severely thumped.

The thought that he might be able to get a lucky to kick in just above the man's prostrate even foolishly passed through his thoughts. But he was still sober and smart enough to realize that his wishful thinking - was just that. And when the normal sounds of the night were finally allowed to solely fill the air once more, he didn't really have to force himself to remain face to face with the one who in all likely hood was about to kick him and his ass into the middle of next week.

Suddenly, before the first expected blow even hinted at being delivered, a new voice floated through the air. It was a surprising interruption that instantly had every one in the gathering looking inquisitively in its direction.

"No, no, no! You were doing it all wrong!"

The words belonged to Bob, who was now walking briskly in their direction. "You did it all much too slowly. Me and my friends here have been training on how to take out some of the unnecessary wasted moves, so as to make the "kata' not only shorter, but much more effective.

By this time, Bob was only a foot away from passing George, where he smiled and delivered an undetected wink in his direction, while continuing to speak.

"Here, let me show you what I mean."

In a series of similar movements, after a scream that would of made the absolutely dead sit up and take notice, which also had over half of the men there blinking in disbelief, Bob went through the almost exact same maneuvers the negro had, but in a far snappier and expertly delivered manner. And when he was finished chopping, punching, and kicking holes in the midnight air, he jumped up what would later be estimated at least twenty feet into the air and landed directly in front of the antagonist's face, which instinctively made the man back up a few feet, before adding, "Now you come at me, and I'll show you what you're doing wrong."

The mans face, like almost everyone else's, was justifiably frozen in disbelief at what he had just witnessed, which Bob deliberately kept that way be quickly adding, "Come on! I promise I'll try not to hit you."

In what was really only a matter of seconds, a low murmur of awed surprise passed among both the bar crowd and his new found friends. It was a reaction that only served to fuel the reasoning racing through the startled mans mind. And when he finally spoke again, involuntarily taking another step backwards, his manner and aggressive voice had done an almost totally about face from his earlier attitude.

"Naw, naw. That's, okay, man. I think I know what I'm doing wrong."

In a brief display of wise false courage, George and a few of the other men from the shop had enough sense to rearrange their feet just enough to match Bob's, indicating that they possibly might know a little bit about karate. It was a maneuver that instantly had the bar room crowd cautiously giving them a little more respected room then earlier allowed, as Bob once more took a few quick jabs at an invisible foe.

It was also George's quick thinking next that managed to break up the little deadlock that was settling in among them. Stepping fore-ward, a move that made the pimp almost comically trip while making another backwards retreat, George smiled softly while sticking out his hand in a hand shacking manner, before saying, "What the Hell, I still apologize. Sometimes my tongue has a tendency to let it-self speak, before I even think. This is a bar, not an arena. Like I said inside, we came here to drink, not fight." he smiled. "We can always do that with the wives when we get home. Let's get back onside and stop wasting what little guzzling time we have left. It's got to be almost time for 'last call for alcohol' anyways.

In a hesitant move that soon became contagious among the rest of the men, Bob in the background cracking his knuckles, the negro slowly accepted George's fortunately work induced muscular hand, while saying, 'Ya, what the Hell. You're right, man. The first round's on me."

Starting for back inside the bar, some of its regular inhabitants now joking with a few of the men they were only minutes earlier willing to rearrange their facial features, George managed to sneak a whispered, "Remind me have a little one on one talk with you later." in Bob's ear. In return Bob just grinned devilishly after saying, "You take care of the leader, and the rest will fall into line real quick." while expertly delivering a friendly lightning like jab into Georges' unsuspecting ribs. It was an attack that not only happened far too fast for George to see, but was also a blow that he or any of the other workers had not even the slightest bit of knowledge on how to prevent. And when Bob continued with, in disguise of his now regularly popping up ancient proverbs of wisdom, 'Remember, man who willing to kick sleeping dog awake, must be ready to feed him also. But most importantly, when it comes to the Martial Arts, always remember 'He who speaks, does not know. Yet he who knows, does not speak'!"

George smiling back in apparent recognition, told only himself that he was pretty sure he would eventually figure out what the Hell it meant.

Pop Bottles, realizing that he was no longer in danger of having the proverbial 'shit' kicked out of him, instead listened to his bladder saying that it was considering otherwise. Stepping towards a dark shadowy section of the buildings exterior, his intent to get rid of some excess beer in order to appease his complaining kidneys, he was just starting to shift some of his watered ballast when something came out of the dark that almost did what the bar crew had ceased to do, 'Scare' the shit out of him.

"Do, you, mind!"

Instinctively freezing in 'mid-stream', the next reflex staining his pants with water as he tried to tuck his now traumatized penis back into his pants, his eyes were just in time to catch the start of a silhouette, as two human forms started to melt out of the shadow. And as the disturbed couple protested, she rearranging her blouse as he brushed at the big wet stain on his pant leg, "Haven't you ever heard of washrooms?" he in retaliation quickly shot back, "Apparently no more than you've heard of motel rooms." It proved to be a 'no win' scenario that soon had them each laughing, while going their own ways.

Pretending not to be surprised or hurt, even though his ribs were presently telling him otherwise, George countered Bob's earlier comment with what he himself was best at - words.

"Personally, I'd rather just kick your ass up between your shoulder blades, which by the way wouldn't be very far for it to have to go, but I think I'll just let you buy me another drink instead, for now."

He had no intention of telling Bob that until he showed up, he thought for sure that most of them were going for a swim on the parking lots asphalt. Instead, he just made a low grunted verbal comment to a question he had asked when they had first met.

"Don't know "judo' or 'karate' eh! Just want to be able to defend myself against the wife uh. Kiss my 'ass' you don't any martial arts!"

"I wasn't lying." Bob grinned. "How do you think I met my wife. She has a higher ranking then I do, and has been kicking my butt ever since I met her."

"Well ya must of pinned her butt at one time." George started to laugh, but then quickly added, "Or was it visa versa, and she had to marry you?"

"That, you will never know, Mister Stone." And then he gave away another well deserved lightning jab into Georges ribcage.

Not until now, almost everybody's attention occupied someplace else, did he allow himself the benefit of turning his face briefly away from Bob's grinning face, just long enough to let out a low moan in reaction to the pain his ribs were once more protesting.

The gesture didn't go undetected, and Bob said in sincerity, "Sorry friend. It's just that I wanted to be accepted for myself, not what I can do." But then, no doubt because he was truly fitting in, his sense of humor kicked in as he added, "Hell! Didn't you ever take any form of self-defense?"

"Sure." George answered in grimiest. "But only enough to keep the wife and kids in line. And I don't think they give out diplomas or plaque for screaming."

Once back into their seats, the women that had been beside George now gone and sitting in a huddle at the far side of the bar, George wisely made sure to instantly repay the round of drinks that had appeared at their table as promised. He then, with most of the men silently agreeing, suggested that it was wisely time to call it a night and head back to the motel for their vehicles.

With every intention of leaving a good impression of their visit, George started to hum in tune to the melody presently being played by the band, 'Go Your Own Way' by Fleetwood Mac, a rather appropriate message considering, he thought. The rest of the workers at the table, after a wink from him, quickly either matched him or started to sing the words to the popular tune. And when a woman at a table close-by instantly broke out into tears, George in sympathy said he was sorry if they had accidentally brought up any old unpleasant memories for her.

"Oh, that's not it." the woman answered. "It's just that I used to a professional singer at one time, and it always hurts when I hear a song being so terribly mutilated."

With a laugh on his face, George was just about to be the first out of his seat when Bill's restless head once more made noticeable contact with the table in front of him.

"Quick!" Eagle Beak said. "If he's going to be sick - you're supposed to put his head between his legs."

"If he could put his head between his legs," Bob slurred, "he'd still be single."

It was on the tip of George's mind to say, 'Well, if he can't get his head between his legs, maybe we should try the gams on one of the ladies at the table.' But considering what they had just been through, plus he didn't know any of the women there well enough for them yet to fully understand his brand of suggestive crude humor, let alone sound outright rude, it would also leave an obvious avenue open for someone else there to remark, 'Well, if Bill doesn't want to stick his head between any of the women's legs, can I?'

Still laughing, George did manage to get out of his chair this time, while saying, "You grab your brother's 'right' arm and I'll take what's 'left'."

But before he could walk around the table, Bob right behind him, the words 'Don't you ever give up?' floated in from someplace in the rear of the gathering. Pop Bottles also quickly stepped in and took over the job George had volunteered for, while offering, "I better do it. You're so tall his left foot will never reach the ground, then he'll really look like one of the 'walking wounded'."

As everyone else at the table started to rise also, except the visiting women that is, Brad cupped both of his hands together into the shape of a small ball like earlier. Leaning down in Julie's direction he half whispered for her ear alone, "If you can guess what I've got trapped in my hands, I'll let you take me home for the night."

Even though Brad's offer had been exactly what she had originally planned when first sitting at the table, Julie had no intention of making it look like she was over eager, or the one who was 'hustling' him. So instead of blurting out the obvious answer, she pressed an index finger into one cheek and rolled her eyes as if trying to think of the proper reply, before saying, "Well I know last time it was an 'elephant', but the answer can't be that easy. So, this time I'm going to take a stab at, a handful of 'dead air'?"

Since she had made no effort to conceal any part of her answer Bob and George, who were more than close enough to pick up on every word, and seemed to be on the same wavelength when similarly saying, 'You mean like in his head!' and as Brad only retaliated by grinning devilishly before wrapping one of his arms around her waist, they then gave him an acknowledged slamming of 'He-e-e-r-r-e!' as he then answered in her ear once more, "No-o-o-o. But like last time, it's close enough."

The smile it deserved, it got, as he helped her out of her seat. Bunny and Roxanne, as soon as it became apparent that they were not going to be invited along, smiled a 'Till we meet again.', before picking up their drinks and heading for another table.

Making for the exit, Ken and Pop Bottles looking like dancing Kazaks with Bill dangling in the middle, Jamie excused himself from the group with the words, "I think I'll phone home, and see if I still live there."

Not until they were outside and well out of earshot from the bars patrons did a few of the men make sounds and over-exaggerated gestures suggesting that they were thankful that Bob had shown up just in time to save them from a potential bad shellacking. And when one of the men walked by George, he whispered in his ear, "Next time try not to open your mouth and let out everything that crosses your mind!"

"That's okay." Bob grinned, as a few of them patted him on the back. "Don't mention it" And then, as was becoming habit, quickly added, "Remember. Pride often get man into trouble. Temper keep him there."

"If you had to do one of your color related comments," one of the other men closely offered, "couldn't you just give him the one about where you had a bicycle the same color as his cloths when you were little, and nobody ever stole it!"

"Normally I'm a very forgiving guy." Pop Bottles half-laughed. "But in this case the only thing that needed to be done was 'for giving' that 'pimp' a good thump up the side of his head." Bob smiled. "Mainly because he was willing to misuse a gift originally intended to protect the weak and oppressed. Unfortunately there is no sure way to ensure that the 'martial arts' are always only acquired by those with only honorable intentions."

"Whoa. Talk about real 'words of wisdom'." one of them added.

"Oh, listen to mister 'O.P.P.' him-self." One of the men laughed. And as Bob inquisitively mouthed the strange letters he had just heard, his brain apparently searching for their meaning, the same man gladly gave him the answer to their full significance.

"O.P.P. stands for 'One Punch Pete'. That's what we call someone we figure is good for one good punch, before they end 'tits up' and 'out cold' suckin in air on the floor."

"Well, let's not forget who helped get us into that predicament in the first place." Brad offered, while glaring in George's direction. And as soon as a few of the other men started say, "Ya-a-a-!" when they figured out what was suggested, George quickly gave them a smile similar to one Bob loved to use, while saying, "Think nothing of it fellas. Think nothing of it. You know me, I'm always glad to help out." And as someone, obviously intoxicated with booze and the realization that he was no longer in danger of getting his lights punched out, said, "What's that funny odor this time." he was rewarded with both a punch in the arm and an answer of, "That, you idiot, is fresh air."

Still carrying Bill more than helping him walk, they were almost at the end of the bar's parking lot when George spotted something he felt they might be able to use. Saying, "Hold it a minute guys," he quickly retrieved an old wheelbarrow from a junk pile that looked like it was more than 'ripe' to be picked up by the garbage department. And as soon as he it positioned in front of Bill's limp form, while saying, 'Someone here order a taxi?' Pop Bottles and Bob, while laughing into each other's face, gladly lowered Bills rubbery body into the barrow's dark dinted cavity.

Stepping away from the wheelbarrow's handles, George smiled at Bob while saying, "He's your brother, you drive." But before he could fill the vacancy created, "Sling Shot' Bob, quickly stepped into the cavity while suggesting, "Why not let a professional do it."

Turning around so that his back was facing the wheelbarrow and its very groggy contents, Bob bending at the knees lowered his body until his hands could grasp the two wooden handles. Standing erect, the well aged container now balancing on its almost deflated rubber wheel, he let his upper front teeth show through another of his comical oriental expressions, before offering, "Bobby's Rickshaw Service ready. Destination prease."

"Just follow us." Eagle Beak offered leading the laughter. And as they started for the motel's parking lot once more, Bob started to jog in almost pin-steps, while grinning, "Vely good."

Their often over exaggerated silly humorous antics were not only enjoyed by just them, Julie being one of their best customers, it apparently and definitely tickled the funny bones of other people of the night they passed. But before they could cross the last main road still separating them form their next destination, the sudden appearance of a police cruiser, its lights flashing, stopped them all in their wavering tracks.

As one of the two officers in the car climbed out of his side of the vehicle, it was easy to see by just the slow way he walked and placed his hat onto his head, that he was having trouble totally containing the apparent humor their antics had brought him and his partner. But even before the man had a chance to demonstrate his position of authority, Bob still supporting the wheelbarrow and its seemingly sleeping occupant, widened his smile even more while asking, "So solly! - Was I spleeding?"

As the police officer still in the car put one hand up over his face in an effort to conceal and muffle the humor he was experiencing, his partner tried to say as sternly as he could, "May I see your drivers license, please?"

Releasing his grip on the wheelbarrow's handles so that it would deliberately make a rough landing as it fell to the ground, Bill's inebriated form was now far beyond pain or reaction. Bob, as the office noticed Bill's condition, stayed with the pretext of searching in vain for his wallet. The rest of the men, some having to turn their heads away in effort to hide and choke off the laughter the antics before them was causing, wisely stayed out of the little charade, while also doing their best to look as sober as possible. Finally handing what he had been after from his evasive wallet to the officer, the guardian of the city deliberately took his time inspecting first Bob and then the piece of paper he had been offered. The officer, after having smiled in familiar Julies direction, tapped at his hat while letting 'Mam.' trail it.

Clearly looking for any excuse, or maybe even at a loss for words, the once more stern faced officer finally looked directly into Bob's face while forcefully saying, "Just as I thought! You're not licensed to operate any commercial or recreational vehicles other than your car. And I know," his head now turning back and forth over the faces trapped by his authority so as to strengthen his words, "you're all smart enough to realize that most of you are possibly to drunk to drive right now. I also trust that those of you still dry enough inside to drive safely, will do the smart thing and make sure that your buddies will all make it home safely with no more regular or even 'bladder' stops along the way."

Before handing Bob his wallet back, the men silently nodding like scolded little boys to confirm that they clearly understood what had been suggested, the officer added, "That 'is' right after you have put the wheelbarrow back from where you got it from, got it?" And as the heads that had been bobbing up and down earlier once more repeated the gesture, he climbed back into the cruiser. But before they could drive away, Eagle Beak dropped to his knees in front of a sewer grate at the sidewalks edge. Using both hands he then leaned forward and grabbed a-hold of two of the bars in the grate, while yelling into them, "Hey! How many times do I gotta tell ya, I'm innocent! Lemme outa here!"

Not to be left out, Pop Bottles got down on his hands and knees also. Starting to crawl towards the motels lot, Sid helped him with his little charade by saying, "He'll be okay officers, just as long as nobody steps on his hands."

Julie, while giving Brad's arm the occasional gentle squeeze, smiled back at the grins being offered to her, while saying, "It's hard to believe most of these guys are somebody's father, isn't it?"

"Get out of the way before he runs ya down!" Bob shouted, as they watched him then crawl over and join Eagle Beak.

And when he was greeted with a slurred, "Are you afraid of heights?" while looking into every-bodies kneecaps, Terry over exaggerated a loud 'hic' before answering, "Yesh."

"Well then don't look down! Pop Bottles added, while continuing to fake fear.

The still laughing police officers, apparently having seen enough, left them with the words, "Don't forget the wheelbarrow!"

Not until the cruiser had disappeared into the distance did all of the men start to laugh almost uncontrollably, while carrying on with their antics - but also doing exactly what they had been told.

Arriving like a 'brass band' where the cars were parked, an ear tilted temporarily in the direction of the motel room where they had left Fred, George realized that the room was still occupied and did his best to make sure no one else bothered to satisfy their curiosity also.

Brad, after using one of his 'Your face of mine.' crude remarks on the woman still happily clinging to his arm, added 'Rather than break up the set, why don't I drop off the twins."

"Well I guess I better see that Pop Bottles and Eagle Beak get home safely." Jamie said. "We can't have them showin up for work on Monday sportin scrapped knuckles and knees."

"Guess what?" George smiled at Bob, after reminding everyone about the barbecue planned for Saturday night. "You're all mine." and then as an after thought, as they headed for his car, he quickly added, "You wanna stop off at my place for a nightcap?"

"Naw." Bob smiled back. "I better not."

"Why?" George asked. "The wife and kids aren't that ugly?"

"Maybe not." Bob grinned. "But mine can get real bitchy if I get home to late. And 'No!' before you ask. She doesn't have a higher ranking belt than I do, at least not now."

"Ah." George laughed, while almost crawling in behind the steering wheel of his car. "If that's the case, I'm glad to see I'm not the only one who's afraid of his wife.

Looking at the motel while joining George in the front seat, Bob asked, "What about Fred? Who's going to give him a ride home?"

'Don't worry about him." George grinned. "After the ride he's getting right now, he'll be in no condition to 'walk', let alone drive anywhere."

Immediately the wagons interior was filled with contagious laughter, which only encouraged them to verbally keep building the strong bond they had now acquired for each other. And it wasn't until George had backed out of his parking spot and put the transmission into forward that another little potential heart attack presented itself.

In the same instant it took the vehicle to start moving ahead, his and Bob's attention still naturally on each other's after having watched the rest of the group drive slowly away, a body unexpectedly materialized smack dead center on the cars hood.

Instinctively jumping on the wagon's brakes, a dull 'thud' reached their shocked senses, even as the eyes from the man that had just landed only inches away from the windshield, looked back into theirs. George and Bob, their eyes now glancing into each others, froze in disbelief as the rubbery form then did a 'slow melt' first off and then down the front of the vehicles hood. And in that one brief instant, as inside Georges' mind instantly recalling Judy's words 'Don't turn the wagon into a Hurst.' All of the hours spent acquiring the soft fuzzy mostly pleasant sensation they had been chasing all night, instantly disappeared. Instead of being scared straight, they had all just been scared sober.

Bursting into excited movement after their reasoning had accepted the information their vision had just fed it, both of them in panicky movements scrabble back out of the car, leaving its doors wide open. Running to the front of the wagon, their pessimistic startled brains already envisioning the worst, both of them froze once more when picking up on the motionless form laying spread eagled on its back basking in the cars headlights. And the hearts that were already in their throats almost died there when the male form didn't move after George had grown enough courage to bend down to shake the protruding foot closest to him, while nervously saying, "Hey! Hey mister! You okay?"

Bob, no doubt hoping to sound convincing enough to make George, and probably himself, believe what he was saying, leaned forward and softly said over the still dormant form, "Hey buddy. You can get up now. You're scaring the 'shit' out of us." Looking briefly at George, his pale face almost matching his, he then nervously smiled at him. "He's only faking. Give him a second, and he'll get up."

Taking his eyes off of Bob, this time trying to shake some sign of life back into the man's motionless body, George slowly and just as disturbed added, "He-e-e-e'-s not getting up!"

Suddenly, as fear induced courage made them move in closer to the man's upper features, the night air was rudely interrupted in their face, as a loud elongated beer scented 'burp' erupted in their direction. And as a mixture of surprise, noise, and odor made them jump backwards, reality slowly returned in unison, with George being the first to break out into laughter, just in time to hear the horizontal form give out with a series of short inhaled and exhaled snorts.

Bob was only a split second behind George's laughter, while saying, "Well, I'll be - ?"

This time, when George vigorously shook the man, he got a response.

"Huh-huh?" the man slurred, apparently the recipient of an enjoyed evening, reality having interrupted into his bout of unconsciousness. "Ish the bush here already?"

Smiling a mixture of relief and sadistic humor, George answered, "It is now buddy." while trying to lift the drunk's 'dead weight' erect. Bob, eagerly jumping in to help with the opposite sagging side, couldn't hide the humor building inside of him, as he and George struggled the man's rubbery body into the vehicles rear seat, finally asked, "How the 'Hell' you ever going to explain the stale beer odor this guy's going to leave behind?"

"Once you get to know us a little better," George smiled, "you'll know that I don't have to. Fred's been using the same location as a home away from home for sometime now, but we can talk about that next time. And, speakin of next time, which isn't going to happen until we get to know a lot more about you, I guess I haven't really thanked you for getting us out of that 'very' tight spot back there. If it hadn't been for you, I'm willing to bet most of us instead of singing 'I'm Kungfu Fighting', if it had come to any real physical fighting, would have been 'Kungfu Pooing", in our pants!"

"Don't mention it." Bob grinned. "That is until I need a favor."

"Any time buddy, anytime." George smiled. "Even when you don't ask, we'll be watching your back."

After swearing them both to secrecy about absolutely 'everything' that had happened and might yet still happen during whatever might yet remain of the night, George then picked up from where he had left off, before they had been so 'rudely' interrupted. And from then on, after the addition to their team had uttered his address before passing out once more, a steady stream of 'z-e-e-e-'s" poring from of his inebriated sleeping form behind them, everything else was lost to the laughter that also seemed to be their ever constant companion lately.

Chapter 8

'Saturday struggle'
Or
'Meet the family'
Or
'To 'air' is human'

It was just a little after 'ten bells' before George felt justified in making his presence known for the day, or the world ready for him, as some would say if asked. Barely sitting on the edge of the bed, his throbbing head cradled in supporting hands, it could be said that the phrase 'hung over' truly had a duel meaning at this time. And even though only a devoted 'imbiber', a true leader of the often 'inebriated', like him-self could possibly relate to the fullest context behind the words, he as always successfully managed to keep his temple-thumping hangover from inhibiting his humorous outlook on life. As for why he was stark naked, he was pretty sure the wife had something to do with that as yet unsolved mystery. At least he sure hoped so, considering that after some nights of beer and chili when the body had felt the need to release a little bit of unprotested pressure, his shorts had often paid for the unwise decision.

    The phone proved to be only a temporary enemy when he checked on Fred's whereabouts at the motel. But having found out that he had missed his best friend by only minutes, he made a mental note to ring his apartment later. Turning his tattered attention back onto the world pulsating around him, he concentrated on getting it and a little of the day behind him, wisely realizing that only 'their' passing would eventually make his existence more bearable.

Most Saturday noon hours around the Stone house usually passed with half the clan being excused to perform functions sometimes only attainable by weekends. This Saturday proved to be no exception, with Ian at some school chum's house working on a class project, and Darryll probably shopping at the neighborhood mall, with the newest love in his protected young life, Pat Faylen.

Sitting alone at the kitchen table, George tried to shut the outside world out of his throbbing head by gently cupping his hands in a supporting manner over his ears. Leaning forward, his elbows resting on the kitchen table, he mentally told himself to concentrate on what he had to do yet today. It was a gesture so slightly successful that he totally failed to detect number one son's entrance. And not until George junior's deep voice half-laughingly rang out, "Morning dad. Still living through a bit of left over residue from last night?" did he realize that unfortunately he was no longer alone.

"Shouldn't you be out blockin a doorway someplace?' he retaliated, without even lifting his head from its supported cradle.

"Funny, Pop. Very funny. Can I help it if I was born with a strong affliction for food?"

"The price of meat keeps goin up the way it is son," George answered, still not bothering to lift his head. "and one of these days you're going to wake up hanging by your ankles from the ceiling."

Mimicking in his best sarcasm junior did one of his best usual tributes to Jackie Gleason, "Hardy, har, har, har." while walking to the fridge. "You can bounce all your best material off me you want, but I'm not going to let you get under my skin today 'Pop'!"

"I'll go along with that son," George added, only now raising his head. "I find it hard to believe that anybody could get under your skin. It looks to me at times as if there isn't even enough room for 'you' under there."

Not until now, as junior retrieved a glass from out of the cupboard over top of the refrigerator, while mumbling inside his thoughts, did

George's eyes finally take in the loud black and red checkered shirt his namesake was wearing. And even though his first instincts, especially in his present state, told him to quickly re-cradle his face back into the black void it had just vacated - he deliberately overreacted by instead throwing his hands up in front of his eyes while saying, "Holy mackerel! With that shirt on, shouldn't you be out laying across a table someplace, with someone eating spaghetti off your chest!"

"Boy! We're on a roll today, Aren't we? And don't say dinner roll!" junior remarked, while finally getting around to pouring himself a glass of milk.

"Forget the food and get me my sunglasses!" George continued to over-react, but only now by into squinting. "Does that thing also come with side blinkers and a battery?"

"Say!" junior smiled "Maybe there is a 'God! - And maybe this is just one of his many ways he has for making people like you and your buddies from work pay for their little' walks' on the wild-side."

"Oh, there's a 'God' alright." George grinned back. "And I'm pretty sure that if you shaved my head bald, and tilted it at just the right angle to the light, I'm pretty sure you'll find his 'thumb print' dead center!"

"And 'you' don't deserve it?" junior laughed.

While his son joined him at the table he kept the innuendoes going as he rubbed his eyes, plus in a shaky voice, he added, "Let me tell you from my long years of experience "Bubba', I just know it's going to be a 'lo-o-ong' day. Do us both a favor, just concentrate on your 'moo-juice'."

"Ya mean you're to wounded to lower yourself to pickin on the rest of my buddies next, like you usually do?" junior smiled.

It was instantly obvious, as he sat up more erect in his chair, "Oh! You mean the 'Hubba Bubba Club!"

Just the mention of his sons gang of friends, or 'herd' as George had on more than one occasion called them, had for some warped reason rejuvenated his blemished condition. And even though he may not have sensed it himself, it was instantly evident, as he continued to eagerly fuel the beneficial change.

"I don't know why you guys call yourselves a gang. Heavens knows that when you all get together it's more like a large crowd, or even a group.

Hesitating only long enough to let out a small moan while rubbing at his temples, a newer slamming already in his thoughts, he couldn't help but ignore the pain and chase it away with a chuckle, before adding, "Or when 'food's' involved, it's more like 'cattle-rustlers' in the middle of a stampede."

Killing the rest of the milk in his glass, young George rewarded his fathers' putdowns with only a weak smile, before offering, "Let's not forget the one about anything as big as any one of us should have signals and a license plate on it. Or, the one about anything our size shouldn't be seen eating apples in public."

"My!" George grinned, in an over-emphasized gesture that was compensated by a short sharp pain through his temples. "Aren't we touchy today! I know it's 'hard to be great when you're over-weight. But it's not my fault you always look as if you're seven months pregnant. Stop sneakin down here in the middle of the night to 'rape' the fridge. Then you wouldn't look like you're ready to pick out 'baby' names. You also wouldn't have to hear the toilet bowl let out a big groan every-time you squat' on it."

"Not bad pop." junior said, forcefully un-amused. "I've got to admit, I've never heard you use those two 'knee- slappers' before."

"Son, sometimes they just seem to fall out of the sky." he smiled, before filling his cheeks with as much air as pain would allow.

Happy to add fuel to their often 'on again' 'off again' continuous personal joke, junior ran two fingers around the inside edge of the empty glass still in his hand, and then licked them, before saying, "I can take your warped humor dad. But you've got to realize some of my friends don't come from a home as open to comical bantering as ours is. And when you asked Eddie last week if he'd eaten any good kids lately, or Stan if he'd ever thought of renting himself out as a spare piece of furniture, I could almost feel their desire to die of embarrassment."

Letting the trapped wind out of his cheeks in a laugh George chuckled, "You know my motto son. 'Nobody remembers you when you're nice'."

"If that's the case Pop - then there's no fear of you ever fading into obscurity."

"Good!" George laughed. "And I'm sure that whatever it is that you or your friends die of, it won't be from starvation."

· As a mental image of his son's chunky friends made a brief and painful passing through his head, he as always paid in pain once more as he also recalled how he used to tell people his oldest son was actually a twin, with both boys occupying the same body.

"I hate to break up our little get together," juniors eyes searching the surrounding areas within his view, "especially since you obviously get s-o-o-o much enjoyment out of them, but I've got something else to do." And when even his hearing failed to track her whereabouts down he added, "You got any idea where mom is?"

"Last time I saw her," George grinned, "she was giving all of you and your brothers' rooms an enema."

Shaking his head sideways, while rolling his eyes noticeably in retaliation to his dads answer, he couldn't also help but smile - while offering, "Oh, now we're going to switch over and do 'house' jokes are we?

"Not yet I'm not. I'm still not done with you or your 'weigh-scale breaker' friends yet." he continued to grin. I realize this place sometimes looks like 'boy's town', but I expect you and the 'Hubba Bubba Club' to behave yourselves if you have them over during our barbecue tonight."

"Meaning?" junior frowned.

"Meaning -," George started to answer, while briefly puffing his cheeks up full of air once more, "I hope that most of the food tonight won't somehow die a terrible death, or even suddenly or mysteriously evaporate."

Getting up from the table, his own face and movement still clearly showing that he was playing out his part in their little charade, junior 'waddled' over to the kitchen sink, to get rid of his empty glass, before saying, "Don't worry dad. If they do decide drop by I'll have them stop off at the 'Salvation Army' and pick up some old furniture, ya know, just so they have something to nibble on first."

"Good-boy son. At least if I see any of them 'double cheekin' it, I won't have to do a quick head count of the other kid's here, ya know, just to see if anybody's missing."

Answering, "I'll burp em all and check their breath just to make sure they're reasonably full before they get here." junior headed for the sanctuary of the same way he had entered the kitchen. But before he could make it to total safety, George quickly gaffed him with, "And tell them that if they're going to use the pool -- please -- no cannon balls! Ian just filled it and I don't 'ol cranky Falen next door complaining again that we're responsible for flooding his basement. The only good thing about it was that once I got his insurance adjuster to stop laughing, we both got to share a few 'dumb neighbor' jokes over a beer."

"I'll warn em." junior smiled, just before disappearing into the hallway. He had wanted to say, 'act your age dad, not your shoe size.' in response, but he also realized that such a pun was strictly amateurish and on a level his younger brother Ian was more apt to appreciate. So instead he just contently added a hum while continuing to smile in the knowledge that eventually someday soon, he would have the last word and laugh on good 'ol dad.

Alone with his thoughts again, once more company he never felt bored with, he was just about to let his head resume its earlier position when a new arrival into the room provided him with more fuel for need to exist.

Dropping the basket full of dirty clothing she had just collected from the boy's room's down onto the kitchen table, the loud 'plop' its contact making causing George to flinch in pain. Judy, loving the reaction it had caused, laughingly asked him if he was going to spend the rest of the day pressing his prostrate against the seat of the same kitchen chair.

Massaging his temples once more, while answering, "Only if you let me." George instinctively went back into his hung over routine. Not only was it unnecessary, it was also in search of something that wasn't there, sympathy.

Instead Judy smiled, "Didn't I hear George's voice?"

"Ya." he more mumbled than grinned. "He just went outside, probably to check the garbage pails to check and see if we were foolishly throwing anything still good enough to eat away."

Ignoring the remark both verbally and visually at first, Judy instead occupied her outward attention by checking the pockets on the dirty clothing in front of her, before attacking in another direction.

"How'd your little get-together go last night? None of the boys or I could find Fred anywhere this morning. Where'd you lose him?"

James G. Davies Sr.

The question instantly brought images of last night's little 'comedy of errors', including the spicy pictures he had taken of Fred and Nancy re-affirming their marriage vows. And even though the rough house like playing that had gone on was often more comical then crude, he only thought briefly about mentioning any part of it. Instead he just answered, "Oh, about the same as always. After a little shit-disturbing shoptalk over some poker playing, all encouraged by a lotta booze, everybody ended up a little more than shit-faced before we finally called it a night. As for Fred, he got a ride with someone else and is probably at home still 'pressin the bed sheets'. Besides, don't you remember we've all got 'If found, please return to.' labels on our clothing, or did you switch the address on mine again?"

Giving him one of her best 'Wouldn't you like to know?' smiles, Judy just wiggled her eyebrows before starting to hum to herself, while picking up where she left off.

George, once realizing that he was actually watching instead of hearing his answer, also returned to where he was before being disturbed. Falling right back into his sympathy seeking routine by rubbing at his temples, he even threw in a little moan to help emphasize the remnants of the hangover he could still relate to.

Each of them, when necessary and now, could read each other's thoughts almost as clear as yesterdays newspaper. So Judy, still making sure to sound as if she didn't really care one way or the other, fished for more direct information. "Well? What about tonight? If he's coming to the barbecue, I'd kinda' like to know how many seats to tell the boys to set up in the backyard."

George didn't even have to think about second guessing if Judy was baiting him to find out whither Fred was bringing a guest, but rather if she could invite one of her old recently available school friends. And if there was anything he was in agreement with in this world, it was that you could never have enough wet bikini-clad women jiggling around at any pool party.

So he enjoyed the moment for what it was worth, by pretending that he hadn't heard all of her question. "Sorry hon. My head's still pounding so loud, it's drowning out almost everything else. What was that you said?"

"You heard me 'hammy'." Judy smiled. "Save the theatrics for an audience who doesn't know you anywhere near as well as I do."

While responding, "Well if you're going to be like 'that'," he gave his temples one last rub, before leaning back in his chair far enough to let the ceiling become part of the rest of his answer. "As far as I know, he'll probably be here, 'alone'. But I'll make a phone call later to check, if you want?"

"No, no. That's alright." Judy said in one of her best couldn't really care less gestures, while picking up the clothes hamper once more. She then set out to finish her earlier journey, while just as non- shelantly adding, "I'll thaw out one more steak, just in case we do have an extra mouth to feed." And as she headed out of the room, he quickly called out after her, "Well don't worry about it going to waste. I'm sure the Hubba Bubba Club will make sure it never sees the inside of a garbage pail!" before one more assuming the pain-releasing position he had already been twice disturbed away from.

But, as was a constant in his world, its beneficial sanctuary was not to be totally reached just yet, as the slamming of a screen door disturbed him once more. Risking only one eye in the irritations direction, he was at first pleased when no one appeared in the kitchen, and then curiosity as to just who or where the individual responsible for the interruption had disappeared too. Letting his ears take over for his eyes, it only took seconds to pick up the squeaky floor in the room almost directly over his head. And with the sound came the realization that his number two son Darryll, must be in his bedroom. Forcing himself erect, he had something he wanted to talk to the boy about in privacy, he set out for his son's room. Looking floor ward as he started to move, the words 'Alright you guys, pay attention. Left right!' 'Left right!' being softly spoken, he could hear a slight giggle trailing him, as he headed for upstairs.

Darryll, his attention deeply occupied, was staring at something through the half opened window in front of him, also failed to pick up on his fathers' entrance into the bedroom.

Walking up behind the boy, movements slow and quiet attributed to his hangover George let his line of vision trail that of his son's, until they focused onto the shapely sunbathing bikini clad figure of the neighbors young daughter Pat. Also within view was the image of her father busy occupied on hands and knees, with his reputed second worldly love, digging in his garden. And it was this view that prompted George, something witch noticeably startled his son to the extent that if he had still been ten years younger he would have definitely wet his pants, to shout out, "He-e-ey Jimmy! You still looking for that 'two bits' you lost last year?"

Even as the attention of both Pat and the one in questioned being summoned swung upwards in George's direction, Darryll dodged for the safety of cover out of their view. George in turn just smiled broadly while over waving, with only the young girl's gestures retuning as friendly as his.

But 'lady luck', strangely always never far away where George was concerned, once again briefly turned her usually humorous face towards a kind of befitting justice when his over exaggerated waving hand accidentally knocked out the thin piece of wood holding the lower half of the opened window up. And when gravity started to pull the now unsupported section of the window down, instinct made George instantly reach out to catch its falling form, a reaction that rewarded him with the tips of his fingers on both hands ending up almost pinched between the windows sill and the window itself.

Fortunately for him the piece of tapered wood, which was just slightly thinner than his fingertips, ended up between the descending window and its normal resting place. So instead of ending up with squashed 'nose pickers, he experienced only minor pain and discomfort. But until his brain had a chance to register totally on this fact, protective instinct made him do a comical looking little dance, while blowing on the end of his fingertips.

Now, reality finally setting in as his vision passed briefly out through the now closed window, for him it was only Jim Faylen's laughing features that came back in his direction. But it was Darryll's concerned voice, young Pat's face locked into one of grimacing pain, "You okay dad!" that finally convinced him to realize that he wasn't really as hurt as he had first expected.

Using first one hand and then the other to gently examine the other's fingertips, George himself couldn't help but grin when he realized just how humorous he must have looked from his neighbors' viewpoint.

'Hell!', he thought to himself, 'If I'd seen what just happened from Faylens' location, I'd be just short of pissin my pants with laughter.'

"Ya, ya, I'm okay son." he finally answered. "But I think I just made ol 'fart face' Faylen's day. In fact, I wouldn't even be surprised if he wet his pants! But that's okay." He paused long enough to smile and wave in his still chuckling neighbor's direction. "Last week when he was up working on his roof, I got him down three times by phoning him, before he realized that someone was pulling his leg. And even though he knew that if it wasn't for the fact that Faylens boss occasionally 'didn't' 'wear the pants in the family' he would have spotted a 'For Sale' sign on their front lawn long ago, he still enjoyed their little sporadic pranks on each other, such as now.

Watching until Faylen had disappeared into the house, Pat returning to her sun worshipping, George continued to look out of the window while saying, "Don't you 'see' 'enough' of her when you're together, and I do mean 'see enough'?'

Quickly putting his head along side of his father's Darryll let his eyes pick up from where they had been interrupted from earlier, as George kept talking.

'When I was your age son, all of the girls were built like a carpenters dream, flat as a board, and never been nailed.

Darryll, while grinning from cheek to cheek, opened his mouth to say something, but George cut him off by continuing with the very reason he had wanted to speak to the middle of his three sons. "Oh don't get me wrong son. I can still remember when on more than just one occasion the vibrations of a moving bus had me end up riding it at least five stops past where I had really wanted to get off, no pun intended. Or where I had ended up on a warm day sitting all alone in a male female classroom until after everyone else was long gone."

Pausing long enough to look into his son's eyes, hoping that the boy was mature enough by now to get the meaning behind his witticisms, he was really happy to detect behind the youthful grin a glimmer of his own now long gone youthfulness. And then he quickly added, "If you know what I mean?"

In a surprise reaction, as his son quickly added, 'Jellybean!' the standard finish to one of his favorite sayings - he instantly knew that he was indeed on the right track, even as the boy added. "Ya - a - a - I know dad."

"Well don't let your imagination run too rampant just yet my boy." George smiled back. "And don't ever let me hear you refer to mister Faylen as 'fart face'. Just because he's such a 'neat freak' that he was caught cutting the grass of the houses all round his, just so his would look great, don't judge him to harshly. That's not only the result of private information between us, but also something you're not quit old enough to understand just yet. And don't ever let me hear you make fun of Mrs. Faleyns cackling laugh, even if it does leave you looking for an egg after she has gotten up to leave."

As Darryll, still smiling, just nodded his head enough to say that he indeed did understand his fathers' remarks, George picked up where he had left off. "Hell, I never 'Really' kissed a girl until I met your mother. Will you be able to say that to your son about his mother, when the time comes?"

"Probably." Darryll more laughed than smiled now. "But obviously not with such a straight face as you just did."

"Funny son, very funny. But just keep it in mind that when it finally comes down to 'sex', you'll in all likely-hood find that a 'runny nose' and a 'hard-on' usually go hand in hand with each other. And if and when that times 'comes', no pun intended, honestly, just remember that girls can't get pregnant on spit."

Blushing slightly, Darryll acknowledged, "Gee, dad. I'm not that naive. I have seen a sexually explicit movie before, you know, even if I can't picture you and mom ever doing things like that."

They do have a name for movies like that. They're called pornographic. But then, when it comes to raunchy encounters like that between your mother and me, either can I." George half laughed, a small blush being only felt by him. "But then, don't knock it." he continued. "If it wasn't for some of the antics you might have come across during your so called explicit movies, you or your brothers just might not have made it here!"

"Well don't tell Ian that!" Darryll pretended to be shocked. "He still thinks the stork had something to do with him being born!"

"Well let's not burst the bubble to his protected world just yet." George grinned. "I don't even know if I'm really the one qualified to be giving you any sound advice on sex or on marriage, at least not on the way I perceive them to be. Hell, I'm still happily married to your mother, or least she tells me I am."

"Is this," Darryll answered, his face a mixture of humorous frustrated inquisitiveness, "supposed to be one of those little father-to-son talks we're expected to have occasionally, dad?"

"Well." George paused, obviously glad that what he had wanted to talk about was now out in the open, "Ya, yes I guess it is son."

"Gee, I sure hope you're not going to tell me that the bulge on the end of my doniker is there just so my hand doesn't slip off and I end up punchin' myself in the forehead. All the guys in gym class have already told me that one." Darryll smiled timidly.

"No-o-o- ." George laughed back. "I kind of expected that the laws of physics and natural instinct had already taught you that lesson, especially since there are no sharp corners on it."

He just loved it whenever any of the boys displayed a sense of humor just as strange or warped as his, even if their mother didn't.

"But I'll tell you what stuck in my head from one of my fathers talks to me when I was around your age. I can still remember him telling me that the older I got, I would gradually start to notice that there was no such thing as an ugly woman. Well let me warn you son, I guess I'm just not old enough yet. And why would I say that, well, because there's still some real 'barkers' out there yet. And I don't say that to be mean, or as your mother often says when she's losing an argument 'You need glasses!'

Fortunately his brand of humor had also made it possible for any of his sons to speak openly on just about any topic under the sun. And it was for this reason that Darryll came right out and asked him what it was that he was beating all around the bush about.

"Well, What's on your mind dad? If you're having trouble sayin it, or if it's on the tip of your tongue, just open your mouth and I'll read it."

Oh, it's sex-oriented all-right son. But it's nothing like having enough brains to take all of the necessary precautions. You're a Stone, and inherited common sense about such matters should go without saying."

"Then spit it out!" Darryll said, while shaking his head a little in frustration. "The suspense is not only killing me, but if you don't hurry up and say what's in your mind, I'll either be told old to appreciate it, or may-by even participate in whatever it is that you're trying to get at."

"Participation is exactly what I'm getting' at son. Your mother and I've heard that the kids nowadays have a new version of the old 'post office' game, called 'postage stamp.'"

"Postage stamp?" Darryll squinted.

"Yes 'postage stamp'." George smiled. "Now I assume that you would be the 'stamp' with not-so-plain anymore, Pat Faylen next door being the envelope."

The blush that leapt to Darryll's face couldn't go undetected, but George pretended not to notice, as he kept speaking. "Now your mother and I think the world of young Pat, but we don't want either of you through a natural instinctive act of biological human behavior to end up with a say, 'little unregistered package', on the rest of your lives, if you know what I'm getting at."

Silently nodding his head, an even bigger blush now on his face as he fidgeted in his seat, Darryll answered, "Ya, I know. Especially if that 'little bundle' has a 'junior' after its name."

"Exactly!" George half-laughed. "Now we're not saying that you're having sex, but I want you to remember that your mother still does your laundry. We're both not so old that we can't remember what those strong first cravings for physical contact were like. We'd just like you both to practice a little patience and self-restraint for a little while longer. Believe it or not there will be lots of time for such urges as you get older, and believe me, wiser."

Inside of his head the saying he often used about sex, being 'it's one of those things in life that you can't save up and put in the bank, so get it while you can!' was meant for married couples. And for one brief second he tried to recall if he had ever used in front of his kids at one of the many back yard barbecues. But just as suddenly as the thought came he let it go by telling himself that it didn't really matter just now, especially since his sons maturing world was just starting to bloom.

"Probably more sooner than later son you're going to start getting chances at more ass than a toilet seat. And by that what I'm trying to say is that either of you don't have to 'jump' on every opportunity that 'arises'."

Darryll through years of similar exposure had no trouble imitating the humor on his father's face, let alone understanding the double meanings behind his play on words. And as he wisely, while silently praying that Pat would for some reason disappear into her house, made sure his own line of vision was returned undistracted likewise from his father.

"Now contrary to what you boys might sometimes think, your mother and I still have a lot of fun together. And by that I mean I hope you and your brothers aren't under the illusion that we're not just hanging around here keeping this house going for just you're benefit. Sex is not something to be used or abused carelessly, as well as a weapon for punishment. But then - that's starting to get a little bit deeper than I had wanted to 'bark' about just now. Both your mother and I just want you to know that if there is anything at any time you want to talk or know about, than you're to openly approach either of us, preferably her, and just ask."

"We've already gone through this kind of conversation with your older brother, and I guess in a few more years I'll have to repeat it for Ian. And with my luck, especially the way young people's moral standards are constantly advancing, he'll in all probability be filling 'me' in on what's going on in the neighborhood."

Grasping onto the mention of Ian's name with the hope of using it to get away from the subject they were now seemingly 'beating to death', especially as far as he and the present love of his life Pat were concerned, Darryll commented that he thought baby-brother just might quite possibly already be starting to notice girls.

"How's that?" George asked, a glimpse of confusion once more in his words. "Has he started to notice that they're starting to look a little different lately?"

"It's more then that Dad." Darryll replied sarcastically, his face working overtime on camouflaging the humor that should be there. "He's told me that they sort of smell different."

"Oh, that's okay." George beamed back, in a recognizable manner, apparently ready for another of his 'rude and crude' suggestive comments. "Just as long as he doesn't say they taste different. And by the same 'token', I'm still not drinking out of any glass he's had his lips wrapped around, until I 'do' see him with a girl."

Turning the conversation even more, Darryll allowed himself the pleasure of one quick undetected glance in Pat's direction. And it was all in the hopes that his silent prayers for her to go into the house had been answered. "I know this isn't exactly along the same lines of what we've been talking about dad. But how is it I never hear you swear around the house, not even in any of your jokes. I've been to a lot of my friends homes where some of their parents use language that could cause the wallpaper to peel off and roll up to hide in embarrassment."

George opened his grinning mouth to answer, but the sudden interruption of a previously undetected new voice cut him off. "It's probably because his father told him he was never to use words he wasn't exactly sure about the full true context of their meanings."

Not waiting for any retaliation against her mates little put-down, or 'slamming' as some of their friends liked to call them, Judy kept right on moving towards their own bedroom, a basket of clean clothing held in front of her. But George wasn't about to let her escape that easily. deliberately raising his voice loud enough so that in all probability not only 'ol man Faylen but everyone else in a three block radius could hear him, he called out after her.

"The reason I don't 'swear', son, and everyone who knows us will testify to the truth behind this statement, is that with your mother I've had more than enough justifiable reasons on various occasions to do exactly that. But I've never felt you had to 'shock' or 'impress' someone through verbal vulgarity. Not to mention that I've also always considered profanity as just an illiterate's way of verbally expressing to the world that he or 'she' has a very limited vocabulary."

Darryll, wisely staring along with his father in the direction his mother had now disappeared in, let the following seconds of silence after what his dad had loudly proclaimed to everyone within hearing distance, pass just that way, unchallenged. He was old enough to know from repeated past performances that no one ever interfered between or sided with mom or dad whenever they were taking verbal 'pot shots' at each other, at least not without crawling away in wounded humiliation.

After hearing no immediate challenge in response to his retaliation, George grinned a shallow winners smile in Judy's last seen direction, before in his original soft voice continuing. "Well I guess I told 'her' who wasn't illiterate." Returning his full attention back onto Darryll, he paused just enough to indicate that in his mind he was trying to recall exactly where he had left off. 'Now,' he finally said. 'if you had asked me about the secret of my success , I would have told you that whenever you've gone someplace to purchase or pick up something, and you have forgotten what in the Hell it was you went there for, pickup or bring back anything, no matter how trivial it might look."

"Huh?" Darryll said, noticeably terribly confused.

"Think about it son." George continued to grin. "The secret to that mystery is to never let anyone know how 'stupid' you might really be."

Slowly at first, like the rising sun passing over everything within its path, immature reasoning gradually fathoming out the logic behind what he had just heard, Darrylls' face said that he was actually getting the buried wisdom within his dads' words. And as George read and accepted the expression on his sons' face, he continued with the contagious expression that been with them since the beginning of their 'father to son' conversation. "Now then," he smiled. "if there's no other immediate questions, I suggest you put that stupid damn stick back up in your window, so you can get back to whatever it is that you were doing, while I do the same."

Not bothering to wait or hear if his son did have any questions or remarks he wished to talk about, George glanced briefly out through the window in young Pats' basking direction. Then, after letting out a low long and slow 'wolf whistle' in her direction, he grinned sadistically in his sons' now blushing direction while adding, "You lucky little bastard!"

Quickly turning, George headed for the rooms' exit, a very low and barely detectable elongated 'moan' trailing his departure. And not even the brief touch of something furry brushing against his leg as it entered the room, a most common maneuver whenever the cat wanted to make its presence known, could interrupt his busy mind.

Suddenly remembering that he had forgotten to ask his son if he would be bringing Pat to the barbecue, he faltered in his steps only briefly. Glancing back just long enough to see that his boy was once more occupied looking out through the window, no doubt at the rather obvious, and that "Snowball' had joined him, he chuckled silently as only he would at the thought that passed threw his mind at such a scene. 'How ironic getting older is. I look now, and all I see is a 'pussycat'. He looks, and all he sees is a 'pussy'.'

Turning away once more, he then answered his own earlier question, 'Judy's in all likelihood probably already checked. She has a knack for envisioning everything down to the last detail when planning out anything involving large gatherings.' And besides, his youngest sons' room and the second half of the reason he had come upstairs, was only feet away.

Ian's 'sanctuary', as the boy loved to call it, was just a little bit more extravagantly decorated than any other early thirteen year-old boys'. But then again, any kid with enough ego and imagination to draw and write his own comic books, as well as humorous television skits, probably wouldn't' be able to sleep in a room decorated in just any plain old fashion. As well as full sized postures of modern racing cars he had also hung a variety of sectional views illustrating modern weapons and designs of buildings envisioning what the future had in mind for the upcoming generations. The stereo system, along with a variety of computerized video games that had been purchased as presents for him, had been added to and altered just enough for him to be the envy of his friends. All were children who were growing by leaps and bounds, which George had often said in response to the noises always emitting from the room when Ian was entertaining there.

But it was none of these things that had brought George there at this time. He had come to check on something not normally present in his or any other normal young boys' life. But somehow at this time and present surroundings they seemed quiet acceptable in his sons environment. But worse than all that - they were now in full view.

Stopping only feet short of the small aquarium he had allowed his son to borrow from a friend in order to study for a biology project, he leaned forward just far enough so that he could see directly into the tank. Mumbling to himself "Beauty must be in the eye of the beholder. Those are the two ugliest fish I've ever seen. With those teeth, if they ever had to kiss, they'd probably circumcise each others noses."

Scanning the desk the tank was resting on, George was both a little sad and then glad when he failed to find anything to feed the 'gruesome twosome'. But then it was only his morbid curiosity, no doubt after having seen in movies where animals were striped to the bone within seconds after encountering such creatures, that had made him want to watch as the two piranha would churn up the water in the tank whenever they ate.

Satisfied that he had genuinely tried to accomplish what he was there for, George turned to leave the room, when his vision passed over something that somehow just looked naturally out of place, especially in Ian's room. His son, if nothing else, was at most times known to be just too much of a perfectionist, a 'neat freak'. And the uneven row of odd sized jars with a variety of brightly colored lids barely visible on a shelf at his eye level instantly jumped out and struck George as something demanding investigating.

Altering his direction of departure, without even a hint of hesitation, he walked over to the shelf and picked up the first glass container in order to satisfy his curiosity. At first glance the jar, much like the ones he used to hold a variety of odds and ends in, looked just like any other empty washed out glass container that might have originally held anything from jam to cheese whiz. But a closer inspection finally revealed a small white label stuck to the bottom of the container, with some sort of printing on it.

Turning the jar until the hand written wording was level with his inquisitive line of vision, George silently mouthed the strange lettering. 'Lenny Baker, June, backyard barbecue'. As to what the short obviously abbreviated wording meant remained a mystery, as he once more visually peered through the glass with the hopes that there might be something so small enough inside that it might be at first almost undetectable. And when another, only more thorough, inspection failed to detect anything inside - he turned his attention towards the next two similarly labeled jars bottoms.

Still just as confused as when he had first started, he continued to mumble to himself. "Billy Waters, May, Apollo movie house" from the container he was holding in his right hand. From the jar in his left he then read, "Peter Peter pumpkin eater, September, Wentworth Plaza Mall"

By this time the enigma in front of him was starting to become just a little bit irritating. So when another quick inspection of the jars still ended with the same results, he finally accepted that he was going to have to look directly inside of one of them.

After replacing the jar in his left hand back to where he had picked it up, he concentrated solely on the one still within his grasp. Using a firm grip to twist off the tightly sealed lid he then held the container up closer to his face in order to get a better view of its empty interior. At first all he got for a reward for his actions was the exact same results that he had achieved from looking in through the sides of the transparent container. But when necessity made him take in the next breath of oxygen so important to a human's survival, something totally alien came in with it. A grossly strange foul odor so offensively terrible that it made him instantly jerk the jar to arms length away from his face, while surmising that the containers original contents must have died a disgusting death. It also made his face also react by twisting itself into a mask of total disgust, while exclaiming out loud, "Wo-ow! What in the Hell was that!"

Once reasoning and logic returned with the next breaths of fresh air needed to clear his offended senses, he quickly replaced the lid back onto the jar, only to twist it on as tightly as his strength would allow. Without intending or realizing it, his face continued to cringe and wrinkle his aggravated forehead while contemplating what to do next.

Making his way to the rooms' half-opened window, its view almost identical to Darrylls', he quickly gulped down a large lungs-full of fresher summer scented air. He also reasoned that if he had come across anything so offensively bad at work he would have been tempted to run and dial the emergency 2111 hot line.

Finally accepting what he had to do next, he reluctantly went back and picked up the first jar he had pulled from the shelf. Slowly and cautiously, at arms' length now, he carefully removed its lid. This time, accepting that his eyes couldn't help, he let his nose lead the way while he slowly brought the jar inch by inch closer, to his flared nostrils Cautiously pulling in short spurts of air as it approached. And as soon as they started to detect a new and similar gut-churning aroma apparently set free from its restricted boundary, he instantly lost no time in quickly putting its lid securely back into place. Instinct for some reason, or was it because had seen the cat do the same thing whenever it had a nose full of something it didn't like, made him think he could 'spit' the stench out through his nostrils, assisted by a few quick neck twisting shakes of his head.

Not even his above-average insatiable curiosity, as he took the rest of the labeled jars from the shelf and placed them beside the ones he had already handled, could bring George to venture another scented examination of one of the mysterious glass containers. Instead he just gathered them all up into his arms to take down to the kitchen, for a future possible explanation he told himself.

This was to prove to be a wise decision that was rewarded almost instantly when young Ian walked into the room just as George was putting the jars down onto the kitchen tables' surface.

"Come here young man!" he said in his sons' direction. Ian in turn, only now getting a visual look at what his father was up to, froze briefly in his movements when his brain recognized the familiar looking containers.

But even before George had a chance to ask what the question at the front of his mind, namely 'What in the Hell was with these jars?' Ian excitedly beat him to the punch. "What are you doing with my biology project dad?"

Ian's very noticeably disturbed nervous response to the sight of the wicked containers only served to further fuel the ever-growing enigma that had been festering inside of George, which clearly showed itself in his voice and choice of words.

"Judging by your reaction young man, it would be kind of silly to say I found them any place else but 'in' your bedroom. Now perhaps you'd be so kind as to tell me, 'by all that's sacred', just what in the Hell they are!"

"You didn't open any of them did you dad?" the excitement that had been in Ian's young voice a moment earlier, was still inquisitively there as he picked one of the jars up, no doubt to examine it for himself.

"Well of 'course' I did!" George answered, noticeably indignant. "Why else would I be asking you what in the Hell they are? I've never smelled anything so repugnant in all my life! The leftover smell from whatever was originally in there could still 'gag a maggot'!"

Picking one of the jars back up again as he had been speaking, George's curiosity had him once more trying to figure out its mystery - by turning and rolling it end over end, while continuing. "It's rather obvious that the insides of the jars are clean, but what did you have in them originally that would leave such a putrid disgusting odor now?"

Placing the container he was still holding in his hands back onto the kitchen tables surface, Ian then slowly took a small step backwards. Still visibly excited, his answer was broken, and seemingly deliberately worded. "They - they're - a part - a sort of 'specimen' collection, - a long term project you might say. It's for a future - kind of science project. Something I've been working on - for the last couple of years. I know I'll be following some of the science courses Darryll is taking now, and I want to be ready for them when I get there."

"What'd ya mean 'science project'? You said biology earlier. And why so bloody long? What's it for, Nasa?"

George's face was saying just as loudly as his voice that he was still confused by his son's response. And as soon as he started to say, "Any fool can see that they're empty!" He quickly realized that he had opened a door that just begged for a comeback that could be summed up by his 'better half' in just one word, 'Obviously!' And fortunately for him she just happened to be someplace out of earshot, thank-goodness. Then, as if to convince himself for one last time, he held the glass jar still in his hand up towards the illumination from kitchens light so as to let its brightness pass through the containers transparency.

Silently taking another backwards' step, not only undetected but also bigger than the first one, Ian's voice now held a hint of gigglish humor that somehow naturally came with boys of his age - when he answered. "They all contain different mixtures of anatomical vapors that I've collected at different times and places with the help of my friends.

Lowering first his eyes and then the jar as a reality normally never a stranger to him gradually hinted at what he thought his boy was talking about, George slowly repeated the two most important words in what Ian had just said, 'Anatomical vapors?' into his sons' broadly grinning face.

And when Ian more giggled than laughed, "That's right dad! Anatomical! Like in human!"

In a genuine gesture of disbelief, as his mind instantly ran through everything he had done since opening the two jars, George only managed to get an elongated first letter of the word reality was now shocking his brain with, "F-f-f-" out of his mouth, before Ian cut him off.

"Right again pop. Human, gas!"

Instantly wrinkling up his nose in zestful disgust, George tossed the jar he was holding, as if it had suddenly began burning into his hand, back onto the kitchen table. Then, as Ian's youthful laughter filled every square foot of the room, George nauseatingly said through screwed up facial features, "If you'll excuse me, I have to go gargle through my nose!"

With one hand pinching the aforesaid protruding appendage, George overplaying his part started to stager out of the room, his trailing gasping voice warning that they would 'indeed' be talking about this later.

It was almost three o'clock before George finally managed to trace Fred's whereabouts. A beckoning ring, to which he had answered to an unfamiliar sounding female voice, "Sorry mam. You've got the wrong number." had not only brought him and Alexander Graham Bell's invention together, but also reminded him that he should be looking for his buddy.

Dialing Fred's home number it was hard to tell over the phone if the noticeable excitement in his best friends voice was from happiness or embarrassment of some sort, especially when all Fred would say before hanging up was, 'I'm kind of busy right now George! I'll explain it all later when I see you tonight.'

Dropping the phone's receive back into its cradle, George tried to interpret the meaning of his friends words, by comparing them mentally with past experiences together. But instead of coming up with anything his still slightly buzzing mind would consider as sensible, he just managed to confuse himself even more, especially when remembering how since after Fred's separation from his wife he was having trouble even thinking in a straight line.

If fact, lately it might justifiably be said that poor Fred's head wasn't even fit to use as an ugly hat rack. The incident on Friday in the change house where he had to move the hung over poor man over one combination lock, had been only one in a continuing series of minor comical incidents lately. Two shifts earlier on the job site he had found him struggling while trying to screw a big grease-fitting together. And after examining it, he'd jokingly called his buddy an 'Idiot', while telling him that the pipe had a left handed thread on it. Then Fred in turn, his brain apparently 'absent without leave', or not having its 'elevator travelling to the top floor' as others liked to say, had blankly replied 'Oh.' before placing the fitting into his left hand, only to continue trying to screw it on wrong again.

But that was then, and this was now. The only solid piece of concrete information he had managed to decipher out of their brief conversation was that Fred was planning on showing up at the barbecue later that night. If he was bringing someone or going to arriving all alone was still a mystery. It was also a little really immaterial mystery that was chased out of his head by the sound of Judy's far off voice paging him.

"I'm in the basement!" he shouted back in her direction. And she in turn, their echoing voices passing in the house's stairwells, quickly called back, "Well I'm upstairs in Ian's bedroom. I'll meet you in the kitchen!"

Softly grumbling to an invisible companion, past history had taught him it was unwise to keep her waiting, George took the cellar stairs two at a time. But the complaining he had been doing to himself was nothing compared to the suggestive remarks he made in his wife's direction, when he entered the kitchen and found her already seated sipping from an almost empty coffee cup. From the scissors and cut up papers in front of her it was obvious that she was presently involved with one of her present hobbies, coupon cutting. It was also instantly obvious that she had once more successfully conned him into doing all of the physical work required to bring them together.

Judy in turn simply rewarded his suggestion on where she should 'stick her head' next time she needed to call him for anything, with a sly grin, while commenting, "You needed the exercise more than I did. I've been on my feet all morning, and my 'dogs' need a rest. We've still got tonight to go through yet, remember."

Grinning menacingly while making his way to where the coffee cups were kept, he said, "That, 'lady', is one I owe you for." while grabbing a cup labeled, 'Lazy, is not a gift. It has to be learned.' And as Judy silently saluted him for his remark, he scooped up the coffee pot from the stove in passing and carried it to where her laughing form was seated. Refilling her cup first, while starting to say, 'Speaking of exercise, I forgot to tell you I had the company's yearly medical at work on Thursday." Replacing the pot back onto the stove, after filling his cup, George then seated himself across from Judy's still chuckling form , and got ready to verbally spar with her once more.

Waiting until he was totally seated, Judy knew that in order to coach something out of her hubby, she always had to let him have his little joke first. "Oh? And just what did their doctor say this time?" she grinned.

Even though the humor that had been on his face earlier had evaporated, no doubt to give a taste of potential seriousness to his statement, the silliness he was no doubt really experiencing inside did trickle through into his voice. "Well, at first I thought we were about to get engaged."

Up till now Judy had been having no trouble in keeping a sincere straight face. But she knew that when the time came she would break down and laugh - she always did. "Oh? How's that?"

"Well," George hung his head in an almost ashamed like manner, no doubt for her, in an effort to give more emphases to the rest of his remark. "at first, she said she wanted to check me for a hernia."

Chancing an upward quick glance in Judy's coffee sipping direction, George could see that like always she was keeping up her end of their little two person plays. "But when I dropped my pants in front of her rubber gloved hands, well, she coughed before I could.

The small hint of a grin that had crept to the corners of Judy's mouth in response to George's picturesque words were fortunately for her hidden by the cup still held to her lips. And it gave her enough time to regain most of her composure while fighting the urge to say, 'Are you sure it wasn't just a small chuckle in disguise she was having?' instead of her actual reply. "And what else? There has to be more."

"Well -" George continued just as seriously. "then she had me a little worried when she started humming 'Having my baby'. I even briefly thought for sure that I would be getting flowers delivered here before I could get home."

"Go on!" Judy said, rolling her eyes in disbelief. "If you can 'bare' to tell it, I can sure as hell 'bear' to hear it." while over emphasizing the desired meaning out of the word 'bare' each time she used it.

"And then there was the nurse who kept coming into the room to ask what time it was, only neither the doctor or I was wearing a watch at the time'" George continued. "I swear I was feeling so light headed by then that I thought I was going to faint. Besides, I probably would have, if I hadn't have been so afraid of waking up with 'money in my mouth'.

Leaning forward so as to let both eyes stare straight into her hubby's, both elbows resting on the table, Judy smiled directly into his, while saying, "It sounds more to me like you've been sniffing highly intoxicating fumes off something at work!"

"Honest Injin!" George grinned, while placing the palm of his right hand over his heart, the other elevated palm outward, indicating that he was ready to swear an 'oath' if necessary. 'But the real shocker came when she asked me if I had any holidays left this year. That's when I thought for sure she was going to suggest that we elope together."

"Oh brother!" Judy moaned. "If you can hold it a minute, I'll go get a broom and shovel out of the garage. This stuff you're 'pushin' should 'really' make the rose's grow!"

"It's not that funny." George quickly said just a little bit indignantly now. "When she next suggested that I should use them all up real quick, well, she really what you might say 'put a pin in my balloon'."

Just envisioning her hubby with a giant pin sticking out the top of his head, which just seemed to go with his fairy tale, started the laughter she knew would be showing up sooner or later. "She probably had to do that in order just to get your inflated ego unstuck from her office ceiling. Now what did she really say?"

"Other than being in great shape, you mean?" George smiled.

"Other than being in great shape for a man of 'seventy', what did she say?" Judy continued to laugh.

"Oh --- nothing serious." he answered, noticeably less humorously this time. "She asked if I was having a love affair with anything greasy or salty in the way of food. And when I reluctantly answered 'Yes' she simply replied, 'Not any more you're not!' She said my blood pressure and weight were in a race to see who could get the highest. So she recommended that I break off our engagement and leave the junk food alone for a couple of months. I told her it's not the food that bloating me, but rather that I'm the type of guy who's pretty sure that it's the 'air' that is fattening."

"And that's why you were so long getting home?" Judy continued to smile.

Once on a roll, as he liked to call it, George barely paused long enough to take a breath before answering. "That wasn't my fault!' he offered, his face still void of humor. "I just happened to be passing an apparent customer from the Optimists down the hall, or should I say attempting to pass, when I had a damn good reason for taking so long. She was holding what looked like what was a prescription up to within six inches of her face, no doubt trying to read what was there. Well, you know me, always the first to offer a friendly word of advice or little ray of hope to anyone who might need one. And when I asked her if I could help her with the prescription, she answered 'No, I'll be fine just as soon as I find my glasses.' From there, after watching her get into her car, no eyeglasses still in sight, I wasn't leaving that building until she was long gone zig zaging out of the parking lot!"

Without saying a word this time, except "Ha!' inside her thoughts, Judy picked up a pen that had been lying on the table in front of her. She then used it to scratch out something that had been written on a piece of paper also resting there.

Inquisitively, since he had never learned to read anything written upside down, after commenting, 'Why is it that everything that tastes so great is supposedly so 'bad' for you. And everything that is so great for you often tastes like 'shit!' George asked. And then added, "What's that? What did you just scratch out?"

Only now allowing herself a slight grin, she answered, "I'm just making it easier for you to break off your 'love affair'. I'm starting you on a diet. I've got way too many years invested for you to be skipping out of here because of high blood pressure. I know that more than once you've been accused of using your 'mouth' to dig your own grave, but that was just through verbal abuse of others you've come into contact with. This is the first time I've ever heard of you using it to dig your own grave through food. So starting tonight - - no more 'zit filler' for you."

"O-o-o-h," George moaned comically, his cheeks puffed out as if they were full of food. "Don't' you remember that thirty day diet you tried me on once, and all you lost was thirty days."

If he was hoping for anything more than the small grin his remark had invoked, the passing seconds quickly confirmed that he wasn't going to get it. "Why can't I start tomorrow. Everybody's going to be stuffin their faces all night long, and how's it going to look for one of their host's to be standing sucking on a celery stick with tears running down his cheeks? They'll probably think we've been fighting again, and you finally won one!"

"Don't I wish!" Judy half-laughed. "Besides, the day I clobber you it'll probably be over you gapping 'bug eyed' at another woman, not food."

Pressing the fingertips of both hands against his chest, he left them there as he gasped out the words, "Women! Is it my fault that God in all his wisdom made me a 'lesbian' instead of a 'homosexual'. Can I help it if I was never 'weaned', and have a strong affliction for ladies that look like they're just about to give 'milk'!"

"Very funny. Very funny." Judy offered, while pretending to be a little sarcastically upset, as she always did when they joked about his and every other males' parchment for large mammary glands. "Keep on bragging and you'll be on a lower calorie diet than you think - 'sex-wise' that is."

"Sex!" George snapped. "Lately I've been feeling as if that's just a number between five and seven. And if you cut me off the junk food, I'll probably end up hungry enough to eat a 'horse', saddle and all."

"I don't care if you get hungry enough to eat the 'asshole' out of a skunk, don't let me catch you filling your face with garbage." Judy smiled. "Is that clear!"

Resorting back to being emotionally hurt, just like one of the kids, George slowly answered, "Well, okay. but I'm 'not', I repeat 'not', givin up lookin at women!"

"That is alright." Judy continued to smile. "Just as long as that's all you do, is look. And as the saying goes, 'I don't care where you get your appetite, just as long as you come home when its time to eat'."

Picking the paper up from the table, she waved it in George's face while saying, "Now do you think I can trust you to go shopping at the 'plaza'? Or do I have to send one of the boys with you just to make sure you're back in plenty of time before everyone arrives for the barbecue?"

Snatching the list out of her hand, George kept right on pouting, as he headed for the car. "That won't be necessary. I think I can find my way there and back without an escort. Besides, at home it's alright if the kids call me Dad or Pop, but in public I insist they call me Mister Stone, and they don't like that."

"I should be so lucky!" Judy chuckled to herself.

"Gee I hate goin to the shopping malls on the weekends." George mumbled, ignoring her remark, but deliberately loud enough for her to hear. "I don't mind people retiring , I just hate it when they want to spend most of their time in front of me in the aisles when I'm shopping."

Pausing briefly at the room's doorway, he made sure to get in the last whimsical words, even if it was obvious that Judy was too busy laughing to fight back. "Believe it or not, I'm going to miss you all the while I'm gone. Not a hell of a lot, mind you, but I will miss your charming wit." Turning to leave again, he let the words, "For all of about four seconds, that is." trail him. And then to finalize his departure, while checking to make sure that he was still being watched, he made one last gesture to tickle her funny-bone. Stuffing the list she had given him into his mouth, he pretended to noticeably chew on.

Suddenly remembering the phone's earlier ringing, Judy called out after him, "Who phoned earlier?"

George, pausing momentarily to spit the shopping list back into his hand, leaned his head back into the kitchen while answering, "Oh, just some female clown who thought that our place was the weather bureau. She wanted to know if the 'coast' was clear."

Judy, with a gentle chuckle still in her throat as she heard the screen door at the side of the house finally acknowledge George's departure, got up from the table solely with the intent of putting their dirty coffee cups into the dishwasher. But the sudden interruption of the phone hanging on the wall now close to where she was standing instantly obliterated the idea from her head.

Placing the cups back onto the tabletop's surface, she reached for the vibrating instrument that was now well into its second ring. Scooping the mouthpiece from its resting place, a short customary 'Hello.' was all that was needed to excite the person on the opposite end into verbal action.

"Hi Judy! Are you alone?"

The strong clear voice belonged to Betty Faylen their next door neighbor. She may have been big and menacing enough to wear the pants in her own marriage, but she was also smart enough o know that George was nothing like her wishy washy husband, Jim.

Maybe that was why the two men, as close they lived together and constantly bumped into one-another, mostly had very little in common with each other. And, it was also why it was safer for Betty to call in advance when wishing to visit.

"Half the time he's 'here', I'm alone." Judy chuckled into the phone, the sound of the family car now pulling out of the driveway filtering into the house.

A secondary customary "Hello." for recognition wasn't generally needed whenever they wanted to get together. And the short phrase, 'Are you alone?' had become an accepted signal they each used to signify a visit was in order. So Judy only needed to add the extra words of, 'The coffee's on.' in order to say that it was indeed okay to rush over.

They, like almost everyone else, had plans for the barbecue. So with a little luck, they would have at least a half-hour all alone together in order to get in a little verbal relaxation and planning. It would be a period of time together that would let them bring each other up to date on any future probable childish little tricks either husband had tucked up his sleeve to be used in a never ending line of retribution against each other. And as Judy hung up her end of the telephone line, she half- laughed as she remembered what George had to say about their visits together. He often liked to refer to the two of them as being like 'Siamese twins', joined at the lip.

Dropping only her hubby's coffee cup into the sink, Judy pulled a clean one from the cupboard in preparation for Betty's arrival. Picking up the coffeepot from the stove, she was just about to fill the two cups she was now holding in one hand when the sound of the front doorbell cut into her thought filled mission.

"I don't believe this." she said to herself, while dropping the hot pot back down onto its previous resting-place, the cups finding a spot on the counter beside her. "Someone must be out-there watchin' to see whenever it looks like I've five free minutes alone to myself!"

Walking to the front door and opening it, silently cursing under her breath at whoever was now seemingly trying to set a new 'Guinness' world record for pushing the chimes button non stop, she was just about to express her opinion over the irritation still filling her ears - when her eyes took in a sight that even her broadmindedness wasn't prepared for. Standing smack dead center of her small front porch, one hand still vigorously giving the chimes a workout as the other clasped a hand of a young brown curly haired boy wearing what at first looked to be at a mild summers tan, was a negro woman looking just as irritated as Judy was now feeling.

While saying, 'Yes?' Judy let her eyes and facial expression say that the woman could and should take her finger off the buzzer. It was more in the way the single word of introduction was delivered, that seemed to be all that was needed to prompt the woman to do so, only noticeably apparent that she was a little reluctant to do just that. And as soon as she spoke, 'Is this the home of Mister George Allen Stone?' the tone on her voice told Judy that whatever their following conversation was to be about, it would be anything but friendly.

Never to be over reactive about anything she didn't know the full story behind, Judy slipped into one of her best acts of wimpish naiveté while answering, "I'm afraid my husband isn't home at this time. Is there something I may help you with?"

In a voice just as noticeably indignant as she had started with, the woman answered, "You may not want to, when I tell you why I'm here. But believe me, you're going to."

Under normal circumstances, and courtesy, Judy would have invited the woman and child into the house to talk, but not this time. As soon as the woman realized that whatever was about to transpire between them, it would be happening exactly where she was now standing. And even though the silly blank look on Judy's face seemed to turn to one of being even dumber, the woman leaned slightly forward in an effort to pull the porches screen door tight up against her form. She then, in explicit and harsh wording, unfolded a story that would have had any soap opera addict drooling.

Whoever the woman was, as she accurately described George's appearance, age, origin of work, and bowling buddies, she was apparently very well informed. And just when she finally dropped the 'big bomb' she had come there to deliver, Judy's ears picked up on Betty's arrival through the side door. But it was to be only a temporary interruption as the still talking woman's hot breathed speech behind her turned head, snapped it back in her direction when her genuinely shocked ears picked up on the words, 'And 'this' is your husbands son!'

With so many years of George's wild and unpredictable reputed exploits behind them, 'all' of which she knew about due to be their unwritten rule never to keep anything hidden that might prove be an embarrassment, Judy never for one split second believed that what the strange woman had just suggested could be anything but a fabrication of someone's corrupted imagination. This, plus he had told her that because of the most recent prank pulled on Louie Zupanick, he had good reason to believe that something might be in the wind thanks to some of the woman at work he had labeled 'man-haters'.

And with such a history, she had no trouble continuing to fake being naiveté while answering, "Oh, oh how can it be!" as the woman quickly and accurately described George's two day bowling tournament out of town four years earlier, while briefly flashing the child's supposedly birth certificate in her face.

Judy in turn continued with her involvement by acting genuinely concerned when saying, "Wait a minute! Wait a minute. It sounds to horrible to be true, but I think I know how we can prove if all of this is true or not. You two wait right here for a minute, and I'll be right back."

Backing into the house, while half frowning, "Now don't go away!" she closed the door just enough to show that it was still open. Judy then used the tip of a finger on her lips to indicate total silence in Betty's confused looking direction, as she brushed past her and disappeared briefly into the halls' closet. Almost just as instantly she was rewarded with what she knew to be kept there. Returning to the front door she yanked it open as fast and far as she could, surprising both the woman and child still waiting on the porch. And just as quickly she snapped off two Polaroid pictures from the camera she had dug out of the closet.

The first instamatic snap shot caught the woman's features in one of stunned bewilderment, with the young boy looking as confused as his years would permit. The second and now third flash from the camera, as the boy scooted in behind his mother's legs for protection, caught the woman with first her arms starting to swing up to block her face. And lastly, only half making it, as words never meant for childish ears escaped from her cursing lips. And before she had a chance to retaliate any further, Judy quickly put the woman in her place by telling her what she could do about what had just happened, if she wished to pursue the matter.

"I think you and your son, if indeed he is your boy, better take your wild accusation someplace else to look for a free meal ticket. Have you ever heard of the word 'vasectomy'? Well, my husband, and there's no racial pun intended, has been 'shooting blanks' for over the last five years. Now, as I already said, if you wish to pursue this supposedly recorded second 'miracle of conception on earth', just have your lawyer contact this address, and we'll really see who's bluffing who. I on the other hand will look into the potential of your accusation on this end."

At the beginning of Judy's rant the woman's face had started with confused anger, only to just as quickly change to surprised shock at what she was hearing. But by the time Judy was finished making her challenge, the woman's face was back to one of total anger, or more so, if it was possible.

In a movement that almost certainly yanked the young boy's arm out of its socket, or stretched it at least half a foot longer than it was supposed to be, the woman spun around and loudly stamped her feet the whole time it took her to leave the front porch. And as quickly as she disappeared into the cab that only now Judy realized was parked in their driveway, Judy, after snapping off another picture of the vehicles plate numbers, made sure to smile and wave pleasantly in the woman's direction. It was something that just came naturally, especially when she noticed the woman sneaking a quick peek back in her direction just before the vehicle passed out of view, again something that just begged for one last parting photo.

Almost choking on the laughter that came to her as she visualized the last looks on the negro woman's face, Judy closed the door. Not even waiting to be asked by Betty as to what in the 'Hell' had just happened, Judy smiled while sneaking a peek at the photos she had just taken. Offering, "Somewhere, someone, real soon, is going to be either very angry, or very very disappointed." Judy fanned the air around them with photos in order to help with their developing ability.

"What do you mean?" Betty said exasperated. "Just what the 'shit' was that all about?"

"I think," Judy smiled, while leading the way back to the kitchen, "George has irritated someone 'far worse' than even he thinks he's capable of."

"Huh?" Betty remarked, while following Judy around like a little lost puppy, eagerly waiting for the rest of the story seemingly getting juicier and juicier by the moment.

"Well," Judy grinned, reclaiming the same chair she had used earlier, as Betty did likewise from her previous visits, "from what little bits of what George tells me about what often goes on at work, I think the group of woman he says he's always bumpin heads with are after his 'ass'."

"The women?" Betty said inquisitively with the hopes of encouraging more of a bone to be thrown in her direction, her hands clasping the still steaming cup of coffee in front of her.

"Ya, the so called 'ladies'." Judy chuckled. "The more I think of it - who else but a woman, or better yet a group of women, could be vindictive enough to think up a prank this devious. And besides, George getting 'fixed' was not something we advertised back at that time. So I doubt if anyone at work ever knew about it, except his best friend Fred maybe. And Fred's never been one to talk about family matters.

No sooner were the words out of her mouth, when as if their mention gave birth to some idea from in back of her brain, when she snapped her fingers and quickly added, "Hold on, wait a minute! I think I just might have a way to check on that idea."

Excusing herself, the sound from her footsteps letting Betty know where she was going, Judy half ran down into the basement and back, holding onto three small booklets as she reseated herself at the kitchen table. Betty, wise enough to just sip from the cup now held to her lips, gave her friend a few seconds to catch her breath, and waited patiently while watching Judy's fingers leaf though the pages in front of her. And except for the occasional 'No, no, that's not it.', while skipping from one similar looking book to the other, it wasn't until the last cover was closed that Judy finally spoke to her closest friend again.

"I thought I might find something linked or suggesting to whatever that woman was trying to pull, but there's nothing that jumps right off any of the pages and says 'And here's why I think I deserve to be retaliated against.'."

Not being able to figure exactly what Judy was insinuating, her face saying the same thing, Betty asked, "What are you talking about? What are those little books?"

"Oh, these are just little notebooks George uses to keep track of things that go on in his life." Judy smiled, while sipping from her own cup.

"You mean, George, he keeps 'diaries'?" Betty added, total disbelief now leading her every word.

"Well," Judy continued to grin, "he likes to call them his little 'insurance money' records. But now that you mention it, in a sense, ya, I guess they are diaries."

"What do you mean 'insurance money?'" Betty asked, still just as confused as when she had started.

"Well, he always joked that if he got Alzheimer's and I ever thought of putting him into an old age home, he'd just go into them and start recalling memories from out of our past, just to prove that he still has control over his mind which doesn't really matter as long as I have control over his stomach!"

"And he leaves them around for you to see?" Betty more said than asked, the smile on her face only a hint of that on Judy's.

"Why not?" Judy answered. "We have no secrets from each other. I know that he takes one to work occasionally to make notes about how things are going in there, as well as here. Besides, I'm sure we'll both get a big kick out of them someday, especially when there's nothing good on TV."

"Why is it that as crazy as it sounds, it kind of makes sense for around this place." Betty chuckled. "But earlier you said you had him fixed, what do mean, 'fixed'?"

"Ya, you know." Judy chuckled, one hand raised and using an invisible pair of scissors to snip away at the air in between them. "Neutered, castrated, made into a soprano for the boys' choir. Don't you remember when I swore you to secrecy about him having a vasectomy?"

Even as Judy's words brought the faded memory of what she had just said forward in Betty's mind, especially since they had never talked or joked about it since, her face finally reacted to its arrival, followed by the words, 'Oh, ya!' escaping from her lips. You're right. I 'had' forgotten all about that." the grimace of pain the image had brought with it growing on her puckered up face.

"How else did you think I'd kept this place from lookin like the 'old woman who lived in a shoe's' house." Judy laughed. "Or did you think, like some of our kids do, that at our age we don't do anything related to animalistic argument settler 'sex' any more?"

"Gee, I should hope so." Betty winked in reply. "I'd sure hate to think you keep him around for only his money or looks."

"He's startin' to get a little low on both of those drawing cards. But then our 'bait' isn't what it used to be either. I can remember when the joke was that if you treated a man like a floor tile, and laid him right, you could walk all over him the rest of his life. But that was then, and this is now."

As Betty slipped in an 'Amen.' Judy kept right on with, "But so as long as he does all his 'fishin' at home, I'll put up with the rest of his oddities. In fact, I've got to admit that it's his little oddities that make life around here so interesting some times, especially when they prove to be better than what's on the television, days or weekends"

"Television again!" Betty half grumbled. ""Who has time to sit in front of the 'idiot box' when there's so much to do around the house?"

"Oh?" Judy smiled. "What's hubby got you working on now?

"Remember how I was telling you about our bathroom looking so old that if it ever laid down to take a nap, it would never wake up? Well, Jim says that he'll do the major work. But if I want him to replace all the old wall and floor tiles, he doesn't have the patience to fill in every one of those little valleys and crevices, so I'll have to learn how to 'grout'."

"You're pronouncing the word wrong." Judy started to laugh. "All I had to learn was how to 'grunt'! And now I can get 'anything' I want."

At first Betty's face was lost to confusion. But as soon as the realization eventually started to sink in as to what her friend was suggesting, both were soon lost in equally wicked twisted laughter.

"It's a lot easier for someone who after giving birth to three kids and still has an hour glass figure to get what they want." she then added. "It might look like I've still got an hour glass figure to, but the big difference between you and I is that in my case most of the sand is now in the lower half of the glass."

"There's nothing wrong with having more sand in one location over the other. Judy smiled. "How else would you be able to make sandcastles? And everyone knows boys, young or old, just love to play in the sand, beach or no beach, and I don't mean, 'son of a beach'!"

Giving the terrible pun only a half giggle and smile, Bettys' tone was one of noticeable envy when she finally picked up her end of the conversation once more. "Still, any stranger lookin' at you would never guess you gave birth to three pachyderms!"

"Pachyderms?" Judy said, a look of total confusion on her face, even though she could figure out that Betty was referring to her sons.

"Ya, pachyderms. Elephants! You know, those creatures with trunks hanging down their front." Betty smiled. "You have three pachyderms plus George, and I barely have one, regardless of what Jim thinks."

Judy wanted to add that if it was 'pricks' she was referring to, a raunchy term usually left for places like bars and the workforce, then she really had five in her house. And that was only because George had told her that some of the people he came into contact with at work had often called him a 'prick', so in reality he could be marked down as two. But instead she just smiled, "Don't let it get you down lady. With what your daughter Patty's got, when she grows up she can get all the 'pachyderms' she wants. Think about it."

"Oh! You mean like us!" Betty chuckled, her seemingly dropping spirits once more raised. "Stupid me! I'd forgotten all about that!"

"Being married will do that to you." Judy laughed. and being around my hubby hasn't exactly been all rib ticklers and belly laughs. But when it comes to being a 'pachyderm', well, let's just say, he may not be the leader 'bull' of the main herd, but he sure does a fine job for just being who he is."

"Speaking of the 'bearer' of oddities', oh, or should I have said 'the dud shootin' stud'!" Betty continued to chuckle.

Judy, still giggling herself, offered, "I guess I'm lucky his name isn't 'Hank', or you probably would have called him 'Blank Hank'.

"Or even 'Scary Harry' with his strange sense of humor." Betty smiled. "But getting back to the devil, where is your 'macho machine'?"

"I told him to make sure he puts on his good running shoes, and then sent out to pick up some last minute stomach stuffers for the barbecue." she answered, before draining the rest of the contents in her cup. "At his last checkup the doctor told him that if he takes good care of his feet - then his 'feet' will take good care of him."

"Well what if he's only got six inches?" Betty blushed, knowing quite well that Judy's sense of humor would not only enjoy the comment, but in all likelihood attack it.

"Are we talking length or width?" Judy giggled back.

"Either would be nice!" Betty burst out laughing. "But now that I think of it, aren't we getting away off topic? Isn't the 'barbecue' what we're originally supposed to be talking about?"

"The 'Barbie' can wait a few more minutes." Judy smiled. "When it comes to having 'six inches' I'm not so naïve that to most men they would like it to mean 'six inches from the floor'.

Glancing at the table and its contents, Betty chuckled, "If you'd had George 'clipped' earlier, say by about three kids, you wouldn't need to be 'clipping' coupons right now."

"The operation wasn't available that far back" Judy frowned. "Besides, we didn't get married to sit around in a vacant house. And when it comes to my 'hubby', you're never off topic. Especially if you can leave him with a 'Zinger.'"

"Such as?" Betty smiled.

"Well, when he gave me one of his ol' sympathy seekers, 'Well at least 'I'll' miss me when I'm gone!' I hit him with the truth, right between the eyes. "You'll have to miss you. I sure as Hell don't think anyone else will!"

"And he wasn't upset?" Betty chuckled.

Keeping the same tone in her voice, Judy went right into, "He knew that wasn't the time to try and get even. Especially after what he had pulled earlier when he had asked me at the last minute to fix a small tear near the zipper in his pants. He was in such a hurry that he said he didn't have time to take them off, so I just gave the rip a couple of quick stitches. But unfortunately when I was biting off the excess thread our oldest came into the room just in time to catch me doing it. Smartass without missing a beat smiled, "It's okay son. I was just going out for awhile and your mother was just kissing me goodbye."

Giving Betty a few minutes to get her breath back, before she could enjoy the last comment, which was obvious as she once more eventually broke up with laughter, Judy next let out a big sigh after her emotions took over for the new information now fresh within her thoughts. "But ya know, when it comes right down to the bottom line, you just gotta love um."

"And how the Hell do you figure that!" Betty added, no sign of humor back within sight, even though she knew it was someplace close by.

"Well," a hint of mellow now in her words, Judy answered, "at the end of the day, when all is said and done, shit disturber or not, when he rolls over during sleep and puts his arm around me and tops it off with a gentle squeeze, let me tell you, the rest of the world doesn't matters. And any woman that hasn't learned that over the years of being together, I feel sorry for."

The words, even though it was hard to forget the earlier comment, were enough to end up giving way to a soft smile. And it was all because it was also now easy to see that her thoughts were apparently busy somewhere else. Betty had let her eyes drift homeward just enough to give Judy an inkling of where and why they were gone.

"Ya. I know what you mean. The big lummox may be short on words, unless he's got a bug up his ass, but when we're all alone and the mood is just right, well, let me tell you, even your George can't upset him. And believe me I know, your hubby just loves any excuse to 'shit disturb', especially if he thinks he has a chance to get under my Jim's skin."

"You mean like the time he dropped hints about having all of our lawn ripped out and then asphalt put in. And how he was going to have it then sprayed grass green, the occasionally yellow dandelion painted in for reality effect!"

"I don't know if it was the green asphalt or the thought of yellow dandelions that almost drove my hubby through the roof. You know how he hates the sight of weeds anywhere on our property! And those dummy estimates for the job your hubby deliberately left on the ground to blow onto our property didn't help any!"

It may have been what they had just been through as they raised and touched refilled teacups together in a salute - or maybe even the memories of past barbecues together that made them feel anything but old. But whatever it was, as always seems to happen with women who have bonded, they were almost instantly back to chuckling out loud, busy with the pleasure of enjoying each others company.

Chapter 9

'Fish food'
Or
'Is nothing sacred?'

Chris Hutchinson and his wife Vicki were the first to arrive for the six o'clock barbecue, or 'barf on cue' as some had reason to call it, depending on how much junk and juice they could cram down their throats. But then, being close neighbors, just how long could it take to walk across a road and one house down, especially if the misses was back packing most of what you were bringing that evening. But it was their tee shirts reading 'I'm with stupid! and, 'No reward! But, if found, do please return shirts occupant to 56 Maple Ave.', that made their arrival even more pleasant.

Fortunately the local weatherman was on a roll lately, and the clear evening he had forecast was right on schedule. George, as well as Judy, already had a partial glass of their favorite preference in their hands, as they walked hand-in-hand down the still warm driveway to greet their first guests. It was in Chris' mind to remark about how romantic the two of them looked holding hands, but better judgment told him that in all likelihood George would only reply something like, 'It's the only way I can keep track of her hand, not to mention keeping it out of my pocket.'

As Vicki struggled with the twenty-four pack of their preferred 'brown pop', Eagle Beak Purcell and his family pulled into the driveway, using both brakes and horn to make Chris jump sideways in a startled reaction to their noisy abrupt arrival. And when the Faylen's dog appeared at almost the same instant, a few of the women there remembering the large German Shepherd's past preference for certain private female parts, they all instantly took precautions to protect the aforementioned areas, from the aforementioned wet nosed pest.

George, already chuckling, ran for the garden hose, the dog easily avoiding the attempts by Judy and a few of the men to block it from its favorite pastime of sticking its inquisitive big nose into the first exposed female 'crotch' it could find. Not even loud shouts of 'Shoo! Shoo!' or 'Get-away!' accompanied by lots of waving arms and stamping feet could deter the animal from its apparent hobby. But as soon as George shouted, "Get back everyone!" the shepherd's memory must have also realized that what normally went with the familiar sounding loud command was more than enough reason to head for the safety of its home. And as the jet spray of water from the hose in George's hand hit the dog smack in the face, the animal's apparent allergy to water sent it yelping all the way back into its own yard.

"Why does that animal always do that?" one of the women half-shouted indignantly, as she used one hand to brush at the wrinkles incurred in her dress.

George, always never one to let an opportunity at potential humor get away, lost no time in answering, "Probably because its owner's wife won't let him do it!"

"Well he should be locked up!" another of the women added, brushing at her own attire.

'The husband, or the dog?" George smiled, while fending off a 'rib jab' that Judy was trying to deliver to his side.

But George's suggestively comical slamming wasn't to be the only attempt at humor the neighbors dog was going to bring forth, as one of the men smiled into his wife's face, "I'm not surprised he was after you dear. You were probably 'his' 'bitch' in a previous life." And as he was rewarded with the expected punch in the arm, another of the women smiled at her husband, "Well, if it's reincarnation you believe in - I'm sure he would have watered down your leg, ol' Fire Hydrant Dan."

One of the woman, still apparently bothered by the animals rude infatuation, and noticeably perturbed, snapped out, "Why don't you people just keep a big stick handy for his visits." And her husband, just like most of the men there, was glad for the opportunity to zing her. "What good would a bloody stick do? Anybody who knows dogs can tell it's not a retriever."

The atmosphere of burning charcoal was already noticeable in the air, for now enhanced with the sound of midd sixties 'I'm a believer' by 'The Monkies' memory music playing softly in the background. As two more men and their wives arrived an occasional wink and 'Where's Fred?' went totally unnoticed by all of the women except Judy. And as she deliberately started to walk past George on the first of many such trips into the house, she whispered, 'What, are you 'clowns' up to now?'

"Oh, nothing really much." George grinned innocently back, after taking in one long pull, finishing the remaining liquid in his glass. "Everybody's just naturally a little concerned about Fred, and his present state of welfare."

"Oh I'll bet they are!" Judy harrumphed, while making sure nobody else was close enough to become a part of the conversation. "But just in case anyone else is really interested, Lucy Carlson promised me she'd be here. And I hope that the fact that she's briefly receiving 'welfare' assistance from the city just now was just a coincidental 'pun' on your behalf."

George's usage of the word 'welfare' when referring to Fred's present well being had indeed been coincidental, something he often like to think of as 'God' having a sense of humor'. But it had been strictly as he had worded it, an accidental 'close call' on his behalf. But now that his wife had reminded him about Lucy, 'luscious loose Lucy, or even 'meal ticket Lucy' as some of the men liked to call her, and her rumored financial assistance courtesy of the city, he suddenly saw the connected comical aspects of the word. And as always, and not just because of the booze in his hand, he couldn't help but break out into a short snicker. Judy in reply, while giving him a short quick pinch in his midsection, replied, "Just as I thought! You're off to a good start!" She then turned and stomped off into the house, leaving him to his warped sense of humor, something which meant a lot of silly giggling, mainly to him-self.

Wisely having waited until Judy had disappeared, before following her, George was in the middle of pouring life back into his empty glass when his ears picked up the loud arrival of another husband and wife team. Ken and Kim Anderson were regular 'gathering' members whose affliction for humor was usually just a little wilder then everyone else's. And as for their marriage, well, there was 'lots' of love, with the general opinion being that where they loved each other, they probably loved 'themselves' just a little bit more.

Smiling, 'Long time no here!' in Kens approaching direction, he let the right time get itself ready for what was on Ken's mind to present itself.

Ken was everything a man physically healthy usually daydreamed about, with limited 'tact' and 'intelligence' unfortunately paying for it. He was said to have, on more than one occasion, phoned ahead wherever he was going and asked for him-self, just to see if he was there. Kim was a good match. Only her ego surpassed her beauty and charm, which she teasingly flaunted repeatedly in any interested males' direction. In other words, although not really having the morals of wild alley cats, they were made for no others.

They were firm believers that everyone is recognized and remembered for their outstanding deeds. Ken's favorite absurd stunt was stealing and then swallowing live tropical fish from people's fish tanks, which indeed in anger did keep his memory alive in his fortunately tolerant friend's minds. And many a time whenever another individual was in the front row of anyone's interest, he or she would always try to replace them with one of their own attention grabbing silly deeds.

In a fluid motion that was a natural part of their reason for getting together, George turned in their direction, with only one task in mind.

"I recognize the 'pounds of patties' along with the 'miles of marshmallows' Ken, but what the Hell's in the jug?"

"Oh, that's 'bean soup'." Ken smiled, while holding it up for George's curiosity to examine.

"Never mind what it's 'been'!" George continued, a little indignantly. "What's it 'now'!"

"Don't start already!" Kim quickly chuckled in her husbands' defense. At first George's voice had not been any louder than any one of the others verbally acknowledging Kim and Ken's arrival. But now that it looked as if Ken was going to become suppressed under his wife's wing, George quickly cast out a new line in his direction, by asking if he's happened to pass Fred anywhere in his travels.

"Not that I know of." Ken answered with a look of curious confusion leaping to his face. "But I did hear a little about what happened last night. Is it true?" he leered.

"Depends on what you think ya heard, my boy." George devilishly smiled back, in his best W.C. Fields imitation.

He then gave an eavesdropping Kim a 'We-wish-to-be-alone.' glare, which she instantly recognized by saying she would put what they had brought in with the others food, before he continued. "I was the last to leave and I only 'think' I know what happened!"

"Do tell!" Ken begged.

Letting his eyes this time noticeably flutter to imitate Groucho Marx, his drink free hand twiddling an invisible cigar grouch was also know to sport occasionally, George leaned a little bit closer in Ken's direction. Almost whispering, he offered "But something has happened that I don't really want any of the others to know about just yet."

Letting his vision copy George's antics, Ken closed the gap between them just slightly - before whispering, "If I say the 'magic word', will you tell me what's up?"

Now that he had swallowed the bait he had been tantalized with, George easily and expertly reeled Ken just a little bit closer, before gaffing him into the boat."

Leaning even closer, anymore and he would have legally been behind him, George lowered his voice another octave while offering, "I talked to Fred on the phone briefly this afternoon. Well, from what he wouldn't tell me, I think he had a Hell of a lot better time last night then we can begin to imagine. In more ways than one it might be said that the body slams we try to give each other in jest, he no doubt got plenty of - only his were all delivered physically!"

Ken's instant recognition of "Wow!" was a definite mixture of sadistic suggestive gloating, while adding, "To bad he didn't take as good care of himself as I do. He'd probably have to fall asleep in the saddle when it comes time to catch some 'shuteye'."

"I sure hope he got 'some' 'ze-e-e-e-s' in, as well as his 'itch' scratched. Heaven knows he was overdue for both. It was getting to the stage where I expected to catch him doing pushups over a 'Playboy' centerfold."

George had to let his eyes once more glance around them as he had been speaking, before feeling it was safe to continue. But to make sure that it was, while nodding his head in its direction, he said, "Let's go upstairs where we can have a bit more privacy. I need to get a few extra chairs out of my son's bedroom anyways."

Detouring long enough to pick up another refill, he then signaled in Judy's passing direction that they were off to get the fold-up metal chairs stored in the back of Ian's closet. And once they were well out of earshot of the rest of the gathering, all apparently more interested in each other over them, he continued to feed Ken just enough tantalizing tidbits to keep greedily interested.

"After all you guys had left last night I decided to give old Freddie one last visual check. Ya know, just to make sure he wasn't being physically taken advantage of."

Ken was more than evil enough to guess at what George was suggesting, and his snickering soon became contagious enough for George to start imitating as they walked, with his own rendition was his ears were being subjected to.

The chairs were exactly where George had said they would be. Reaching blindly into a small pocket area behind Ian's closet, his body all but about a third protruding out of the area, George was beginning to think he was going to have to verbally encourage Ken to take the first two chairs from his extended grip. But when he finally felt their weight being lifted from the ends of his outstretched arms, he then returned his attention back towards the three remaining seats while continuing to talk.

"I'll be amazed if Fred isn't at least two inches shorted after the poundin he must have taken last night."

"Hell, I'd be disappointed if didn't at least 'limp' a little." Ken quickly quipped, while George emerged from the closet."

"Probably both!" George laughed. "Especially if the workout involved any part of that top heavy gorgeous little thing we hired for him. One good look at her, and if you saw Fred standing beside her and a two by four, you'd think you were looking at a couple of 'studs'."

As George readjusted the grip he had on the chairs within his grip, Ken chuckled, "Ya. It sounds rough enough to make you almost want to try a brief trial separation, just to see if the guys would do the same favor for you." And then, as if pondering what he was about to say, added, "How about you? What would you do if you and Judy ever split up? Wouldn't you miss her?"

Without even allowing a second to pass before he had an answer on his lips, no doubt to the amount of comical situations he had often fantasized about over just such a situation, he blurted out, "Only for as long as it took me to get to the closet open Liquor Store. After that, it's 'party time'!"

Ken I turn, his humor also working overtime, quickly added, "Take me with you!"

The instant laughter that followed Ken's remark was almost in unison, as they started for the rooms' doorway. But before either of them could pass through it, George was leading the way verbally also, he stopped abruptly in his tracks while saying, "Shit! I almost forgot again."

"Huh?' Ken instantly replied, almost bumping into the back of George's form. "Forgot!, Forgot what?"

Resting the chairs he had been carrying against the doorway, George kept speaking as he sidestepped Ken's bewildered form, and walked totally back into the room.

"Oh, my son Ian's babysitting some bloody fish for one of his schoolmates. I was supposed to feed them earlier but forgot the food."

"Fish!" Ken said, his voice dripping with suggestive mischief. "You've got 'fish' in this house that I don't know about!"

Quickly placing his chairs along side the ones George had been carrying, his tongue almost hanging out, he lost no time following in his hosts footsteps.

"You don't want 'nothin' to do with 'these' babies." George offered, while stopping in front of the tank he had visited earlier. He then, with one eye checking to make sure that Ken was as curious as he wanted him to be, bent over and tapped on the outer glass as if summoning its occupants to come forward to show themselves. "These little darlings are the type that can bite back, that is if you're foolish enough to try any hanky panky with them."

"Huh?" Ken inquisitively remarked. "What do ya mean?" while instinctively leaning closer to the murky watered fish-tank.

"You ever heard of 'piranhas'?" George answered, while grinning wickedly in his direction. "Ya know, the ones that can strip an animal to the bone in a matter of seconds."

Almost as if on cue, both of the gruesome looking carnivores appeared at the very spot where George had tapped the tank. And just as if they had somehow been trained to do so, were baring their teeth in a sardonic grin in Ken's direction. It was almost if they somehow knew of his favorite trick, and would just love to return the favor. Ken in turn, as George, while letting his teeth imitate the fishes, said, "How would you like to try swallowing those babies?" Backing up slightly, his face already started to show his distaste for the gruesome looking little creatures. And when George next dropped a piece of hamburger just like the blood red meat already cooking on the barbecue in the back yard, Ken backed up even further while saying, "No-o-o-o thank you! I've never even liked the looks of those things, let alone the thought of what they do with those razor sharp teeth of theirs."

Dropping the rest of the hamburger into the tank in one big plop, George continued to grin menacingly as soon as the water was churned into a frenzy, as the fish viciously attacked the raw meat even before it had a chance to reach the bottom of the tank. "Greedy little buggers, aren't they?" he then said, while enjoying the look of painful disgust now on Ken's face."

"Ugh!' Ken shrugged. "I'll take a 'dog' for a pet any day!"

Under normal circumstances George would have been all over the remark like a 'ham on rye'. But now was not the time to spit out the obvious reply of, 'I can see that, I've met your wife.' Instead he stuck with, "goldfish are my favorite." he laughed. "I don't have to worry about following them around to clean up their mess, And when it comes time for exercise, I just smack the top of their tank with a flyswatter."

"Dogs are still the best." Ken said. "They're friendly, obedient, and masculine to be seen with."

"Hell!" George continued to laugh. "At least if the goldfish don't do as they're told, ya just flush em to a new home."

"Ya, but can goldfish protect your home against burglars?"

"If I wanted something for home protection, "George smiled, "I'd get an elephant. Just the size of them is enough to intimidate anyone. And if it's tracking you're after, just put bits of peanut butter all around the outside of your house. Any crook steps in that stuff and your elephant will gladly track him down for you."

"Don't you think that's doing things the hard way?" Ken said, humor starting to fade from his words.

"Not really." George grinned. "You're forgetting that an elephant never forgets. He gets a view or the scent of the burglar, and he'll be able to give the police a perfect description of who to look for, not to mention that they'll work for 'peanuts'."

Turning and heading for the doorway with chairs once more in hand, Ken said, "Let's forget I begged for that remark. Besides, if I watch those damn fish any longer, I'm going to loose my appetite."

George allowed himself the pleasure of one last silent chuckle, before joining Ken at the doorway. Picking up the same chairs, as he retrieved his, he then allowed the tank one last final thought, "I'll see you guys at snack time." before once more setting out for the backyard. He then smiled at Ken, "You're right. But I'd still hate to see what they could do to a human being."

By the time they emerged back out of the house the activity and loud crowd had noticeably grown by the additions of three more friends and their families, with Fred and a surprise guest being among them. Once spotting his buddy and his wife Nancy, who for some unknown reason was grinning from ear to ear into Judy's smiling face, George quickly disposed of the chairs he was struggling with by saying, "Set these things up around the picnic table, will ya Ken. I have to check on something."

Without even waiting for any acknowledgement to his request, George headed straight in his best friends' direction. But before he could cover the distance separating them, he saw Fred's vision pass over his advancing form, which instantly made him whisper something into his wife's ear, before heading out to meet him.

The big smile that was filling most of Fred's face was easily matched by George's, even before he said to him, "Hi buddy! I'll bet you didn't expect to see Nancy here tonight."

"No." George lied. "I sure as Hell didn't." He had a brief impulse to tell his bud about the roll of undeveloped film still in his trunk of the car, as well as what he had seen through the motel window, but quickly decided against both - mainly through respect. His sense of humor even had a passing thought about putting a dig in about the chesty prostitute, but it was just that, a passing fancy. Instead he reached forward just enough to indicated he was going to shake Fred's hand, but instead quickly punched his left shoulder, while saying, "let's get a fresh shot of courage while you fill me in on how this all happened."

"Well - from what Nancy told me," Fred started, while making sure to punch George back just as soon as the opportunity presented itself as they walked. "I understand that although you weren't directly responsible for her showing up at the motel on Friday night, you did do your little part in getting us back together."

"More than glad to help." George interjected. "If you remember, I always said that a good 'rattle' will settle many an argument."

"Well, 'whoever' or 'whatever' the original reason, when we did end up in each other's embrace she so glad, I thought for a while there she was going to suck my tongue right out of my head!"

"It was wonderful, wasn't it?" George laughed. "Since I've been approaching forty, Judy has been constantly complaining that I'm oversexed. But I tell her that I'm just trying to keep her involved with her half of me from getting 'cancer of the prostrate'."

"Well, for a while there I'll admit I was afraid the hole in the end of my 'dink' was going to grow shut, and I'd end up havin to pee out through my nose, or some other orifice." Fred smiled.

"Well, as long as you don't end up having to sit down for a 'whiz'. Now that 'would' be embarrassing." George quickly added, as they refilled their glasses once more.

Glancing around, Fred remarked, "I don't see our new buddy Bob. I take it he couldn't make it?"

"I tried to talk him into it." George grinned, his face only a hint of what was racing through his thoughts. "But it's best not to overexpose him to 'too much' 'to fast', especially after last night."

"Oh!, Fred said, while trying to red George's face and thoughts. "Am I to take it something happened after you left me?"

"Boy, did it!" George chuckled, as an abbreviated version of the avoided barroom brawl flashed through his head. "But this isn't the time or place to go into every juicy thing that transpired. Unless somebody's lubricated tongue later on tonight 'spills the beans', I'll phone and fill you in tomorrow, maybe even sneak away for a coffee."

"Good enough for everyone there to take the 'ol pledge of silence'?" Fred smiled, especially since he already had a rough idea of what his buddies when inebriated were capable of.

"One hundred percent, and more so." George grinned devilishly. "Now let's mingle, before we're missed."

"Well I've got some new information for you to." Fred smiled. "We can swop it all then."

Passing two wives apparently busily engrossed debating a topic, George's hearing telling him it was something trivial enough that it would only be important to them, they for some strange reason thought their opinions might be able to help solve whatever it was that they were presently dissecting. And when one of them smiled in his direction while saying, 'Jean and I are stuck on something and were wondering if you could help us decide which one of us is right. Do you know anything about 'family trees'?'

Without even hesitating, while grabbing Fred by one arm to encourage him to move faster, George used one of his best pleasant smiles to say, "Whoa ladies. Do we 'really' look that suicidal this early in the evening?" while in the back of his mind he really thought, 'Don't get me started! I'm willing to bet that if they ever rattled either of your ancestors trees, one of you most likely would have a few of the deceased fall out, no doubt hanging off the end of a rope. And as for you Jean, you'd probably find that most of them were at 'home' just sitting in it.'

Rejoining the party, they were just in time to see a little incident that would convince even an 'atheist', that occasionally some kind of superior intelligence intervenes into man foolish antics.

Ken was standing behind the barbecue verbally busy entertaining himself and anyone else that would listen. Chris, a straight rye drinker, was flipping steaks on the grill, and obviously paying more attention to Ken's remarks than the cooking beef in front of him. Without looking, or even realizing it, he accidentally picked up the cup of water used to sprinkle on the meat to keep it from burning. It was resting right alongside where he had placed his drink. Almost as fluidly as he had swallowed the first big gulp of clear liquid, his full attention still smiling in Ken's direction, the hand holding the cup to his lips jerked the container away from his mouth. And just as the water still in his throat burst outward in a loud wide spray, once his taste buds told him what the terrible tasting fluid was passing their way, the airborne water let gravity do its job.

Instantly the laughter that had been solely Ken's as he was talking, only joined and much louder now, remained his as he was engulfed in the wet spray emitting from Chris's lips. And as he, obviously loving every bit of it, held one hand out palm up to match his sky searching eyes as if testing for rain, a towel was thrown in his direction by his biggest admirer, Kim.

During the next few hours, in between washing down everything from steaks to hotdogs and hamburgers, the group took turns taking pot shots as each other. And Fred, each time he thought his joke would be lost in the noise of the party, whispered little bits of information about how glad he was that he and Nancy were going to try and work their problem out.

George, taking turns with Judy, eagerly accepted Nancy back into their activities, just as if she had merely been away on a long vacation. Fred, picking up on the slight truths and faults being altered by his best friends, just as happily forgot the bad parts. And George also, while making sure to show lots of attention to most of the others by means of his expected slamming's and comical insults, genuinely did everything within his power to make Nancy feel at ease with the noticeable discomfort she was experiencing after such a long absenteeism. He even deliberately held back on obvious and easy remarks that would normally been subjected to humorous 'putdowns'. In fact after a while it became so obvious that he was being 'unusually kind' rather then his expected 'sarcastic self' that someone mentioned his silence, by way of an occasional 'dig' into his ego. His wish to take it easy on the on and off hand holding Fred and Nancy was something that he realized was a minor mistake. But then again he told himself, it was an even bigger mistake by those 'lipping' off the "Axe-man', and he had every intention of 'crucifying' those responsible later, one by one.

It wasn't until about almost nine thirty that the older part of the gathering noticeably started competing against the antics of some of the children. Only theirs, was attributed to going from carnivorous meat eaters to potential alcoholics. The sun had called it a day hours earlier and Ian had switched on the multicolored flood lighting around the pool, needed to compensate for the fading daylight. By all standards, even though the water had been commandeered by the kids, the day was still young by the grown-ups standards. And if nothing else, it was the time of the evening when the party animals were starting to drop hints about their presence.

Again nothing remained sacred, as they took on everything from the unswayable 'religion' to 'ratters' at work. Each and every little opportunity for humor was jumped on, no matter how trivial. And when Pop Bottles opened his mouth in respond to a loud long hiss caused by his wife opening a fresh bottle of 'brown' pop, his face twisted up as if in anticipation of something foul yet to come. Kim, way ahead of his intentions, cut him and his no doubt incoming rude remark short by saying, "Don't even think it mister! Take your foul 'bud' remarks someplace else."

"Ya!" another of the woman quickly added. "Besides, it can't smell any worse than your breath."

"You know what?" someone offered. "If this was the 'old west', I wouldn't doubt that most of us by now would have been shot, or at least hung."

And when one of the men quickly responded with, "Hell, I'm just grateful to be 'hung'." his overhearing wife added, "Sorry hon. Although, I could gladly help you out with being 'shot', I'm afraid not even the almighty can do much about the part where you're presently 'hung'."

"Believe it or not" one of the women offered into the conversation, "there could be worse things in your life. You have no idea what it's like to be married to a man that has to have every type of hand or power tool on the market. Why when he dies, I'll bet he probably has a tool in his hand." And when another of them quickly came back with a catty remark of 'Sounds like every-mans fantasy to me!' it was evident that their 'claws' were coming out and ready for anything.

Shifts

"Well just as long as it's his 'own' tool that's in his hand." another of the women added to the cascading laughter.

"Well look at the bright side." one of the eavesdropping men threw in. "At least when he expires, so does his warranty."

"Well if I ever find out that he was loaning his 'tool' out," one of the so called ladies, added, a hint of menace in her tone, 'after what I would have done to him and his 'tool', and believe me when I say there was never much 'power' in it, he'll be glad he's already 'dead and buried'!"

"Wow!" someone threw in. "What are we drinkin tonight? With that attitude I'll bet poor Sam's looking forward to his exit."

'Let's not paint them all with the same brush." Marie added, in obviously her hubby's defense.

"If I ever thought Bill was even considering looking at another woman, Susan barked, "the brush I'll use will be dripping with 'tar', with the bag of sharp pointed feathers not to far away!"

Those of the men close enough to overhear the women's bantering, silently smiled at each other and headed for where Rusty and the other men were sitting, but not before raising their drinks in a smiling but silent salute to each other. And Sid, always the acclaimed 'lover' and not a 'fighter' whispered. "Never upset the enemy any more then you have to. Last time I lost a battle I didn't even know I was in, I ended up shittin through the 'eye of a needle' for three days! I didn't mind that, a little body flush is supposed to be good for you, but I couldn't for the life of me recall what I had done. And when I tried to question her about it, 'boom', I was right back to 'dabbin' over 'wipen for another three days. I say, let em think they're in charge, even though they are."

A few of the men, shaking their heads at their co workers defeatists attitude, raised the drinks in their hands and pretended to 'toast' his 'pearls of wisdom', before moving on.

"So your dog's a pointer!" Rusty said, completely unaware of the conversation at the other end of the picnic table. "What's so special about that Nick."

"Nothing to a 'normal' hunter, I guess. Pop Bottles grinned. "Except I trained my little buddy to only point out 'well endowed' young women."

"What'd you use to train him," Eagle Beak quickly asked. "a picture of Louie from work?"

"Don't I wish" Bottles answered, after visually checking to make sure his boss was still busy gabbing with the other woman on the far side of the yard. "If my wife was built like Louie, I'd be at home right now trying to save my marriage."

"If your old lady was built like 'Louie Zupanic', I'd be at your house right now trying to 'wreck' your marriage."

"I don't know what with." someone with booze-breath cracked.

"I know enough to remember that you bums are using material already done before." another voice deliberately slurred slightly.

"Well I think you should get yourself another dog with shorter legs." George smiled. "The way you've been draggin your ass around at work lately I think the one you got now is walking you to death."

"I don't take him out that often." Pop Bottles sneered at George.

"Well, where do you drain him?" one of his earlier antagonists asked.

"Or do you just put him out with the garbage when he gets full, and then buy a new one?" Rusty laughed.

"Very funny, guys." Bottles snapped. "I just let him out at night to take care of his business."

"Oh! And just what 'business' is he in?" George chuckled, after taking another gulp from his drink.

Arriving back from the washroom just in time to catch everyone occupied with laughter, Ken asked, "What's so funny what'd I miss", while lowering himself into the lawn chair officially his.

"Never mind what we're laughing at." Rusty answered. "Where the hell you been? Or did someone move the 'john' further south?"

"It's that damn junk food!" Ken smiled. "For a while there, I thought I was about to give birth."

"Ya." Pop Bottles added. "It's not the way that 'crap' gets into the house, it's the door it leaves through, that sometimes gets to me."

"You're lucky." Chris said. "At least the lights work. Last time I was here and went for a 'whiz', the light bulb was burnt out. And when I started to fumble around in the dark I got so excited I almost got an erection so hard I couldn't 'pee'."

"You're not going to tell us your 'donicker' doesn't know the caressing grip of your hand by now, are ya?" George scoffed. "Besides, if you can't find your 'dick' in the dark by this time of your life, either your memories going, or its so small you need a light to coax it out of its cave."

Boy, if you can't even find it when it's hanging in front of you, what does your wife do if she's interested in a little 'nookie'?" Ken asked.

"Oh, that's easy." Pop Bottles chuckled. "She already knows what his 'breath' smells like, even in the dark. So she just searches a little lower."

"Hell!" Chris laughed along with the others. "When it's time for getting rid of a little 'eyeball' pressure, I join the 'search party' and help her look for the little guy!"

As one of the woman sitting there, one of those who had chosen to be close to their husbands instead of the other woman, mumbled, 'Poor woman.' another one said, 'I'll bet he wasn't to far off when he called it 'little guy'."

And when another of the woman who had kept rambling on and on about how she wished her husband cared enough to do his part in keeping the adventure alive in their marriage, he in turn remained seemingly content to sit idly by wordlessly nourishing his beverage. It took a very noticeable break in her chatter before anyone really paid any attention to what she was 'beating her gums' about. And when he finally did speak up, it was only to add fuel to the party's present already merry attitude. "Oh, I'm sorry Dear. Is it my turn to talk? You were doing such a wonderful job all by yourself telling both sides of the story, I didn't want to stick my 'butt' in and confuse the facts."

Draining the glass in his hand, the booze once more encouraging abuse, Ken said in his best sounding serious voice, "I wish it was that easy." And once all eyes were on him, he added, "Do you know how hard it is to get serious about sex when there's a piece of jewelry hanging in your face? If it's not bouncing or scraping off the end of your nose, it's doing 'teabag' dips in your ear!"

"Don't knock 'teabags'." George added. And when everyone looked a little confused as to what in the Hell he was talking about this time, he quickly continued with, "It's a well known fact that to make coffee they have to crush your 'beans', whereas for good 'tea' they simply have to gently squeeze your 'bag'.

As everyone laughed, even those not getting the real meaning behind his witticism, Ken let out an elongated 'E-e-e-e-ew!' while pinching the end of his nose long enough to steal everyone's attention, before saying, "I 'knew' I shouldn't have asked."

"Do you ever think before you speak, let alone take your foot out of your mouth?" Rusty added.

"Only long enough to give the one I'm sparring with enough time to prove how much of a bigger 'ass' they are then me." George chuckled.

Dumping a bag of briquettes onto the barbecue, more for effect than necessity, George winked in Fred's direction. Fred in turn, after scooping up two dogs from an almost empty platter while saying, "Funny how before our last contract raise I used to be able to afford steak!" returned George's gesture before heading out to check on Nancy. And Rusty, while cramming more brown pop into the cooler half full of still mostly frozen ice-cubes, smiled in Fred's direction, before saying to George, "The wife say's you're coming to our house for supper one night next week. What're you trying to do, get even?"

"That is funny." George smiled. "Mine didn't warn me."

"O-o-ops, sorry." Rusty laughed. "Maybe the invite was meant for just Judy and the boys."

"I doubt it." George grinned back. "But either way, I'll warn you right now that startin tomorrow morning, I'm starvin myself, just to get ready."

Glancing in Judy's and Nancy's direction just in time to see her pointing at him, George gave her a small smiling wave, before scooping up two big handfuls of potato chips from close-by, only to awkwardly stuff as many into his mouth as purposely sloppily as possible.

"See!" Judy said to Betty. "I told you he was worse then the kids. It's not bad enough that he gets religious at these get-togethers and practically cremates his food before he eats it. Now he has to start scooping out his grave usin both hands and his mouth."

"Jim isn't any better. "Betty answered, while chuckling at George's antics. "Watching him guard the couch after supper every night, I find it hard to believe he fathered two hyperactive kids."

"Sometimes I think the only real reason George snores at night, is to get some exercise"

"Jim talks in his sleep." Betty offered. "Does George?"

"Na-a-a" Judy answered. "He's a lot more annoying then that. he just giggles a lot."

"Ya can't win." Betty frowned, while glancing in her spouse's direction. "In the winter time, he thinks he's part 'bear', and wants to hibernate most of it away. Then in the summer he says it's too hot to move around, and still wants to spend most of his free time in a horizontal position, and I don't mean sex-wise!"

"George is lazy, but not quite that bad." Judy smiled. "His cure for a hot day is to put a Hawaiian shirt and shorts, make himself up an ice cold drink, take it and the newspaper into every-mans favorite room in the house, sit on the edge of the tub, with one foot resting in the toilet bowl. Then, in between sips from his drink, while reading the paper, he flushes the toilet occasionally just to keep the water in the bowl cold. And to confirm that he really is 'lazy', if the 'urge' to 'purge' does strike, he's already in the right room."

As ridiculous as the truth sometimes sounded, none of the women presently laughing had any trouble not believing what Judy had just said. And just like the men, some as big tipsters as their spouses, they used similar remarks to take humorous 'pot shots' at their hubby's.

"Terry is worse than the kids' sometimes," his wife added to the conversation. "I used to wonder what people meant when they said Joey sure seems to have his father's brains. But now I know. The way he's been forgetting things lately, I knew someone had to have them."

"Not to mention that the older they get the more they complain about the slightest little thing. When my Harry's asleep and has even a little bump or bruise, he moans and groans about it all night long."

"I can remember," one of the ladies chuckled, "When moanin' and groanin' all night long really meant something, especially if I was giving him a reason to."

"Don't be crude." another of them smiled. "The kids could be listening. - Or are you just looking for an excuse to brag again?"

Kim opened her mouth and tried to tell the women how great Ken was, but Judy shot her down really quickly by saying, "Don't give us that old bit again about how important he is because he has almost a hundred people working under him. Everybody here already knows it's only because he's a 'crane driver'."

"Well at least my husband's not on a 'hit list'." Kim retaliated, not as hurt as she was making out to be, especially since she was getting a chance to put a 'dig' into Judy's George.

"Are you sure?" Judy smiled, with half of the women there looking genuinely confused over what was going on in front of them. And when Vicki asked her to fill the rest of them in on what Kim meant, Judy did, but in a way that had them all roaring with laughter.

And when Randy, puffing and panting, dropped off the purse his wife had sent him to the car to retrieve where she had forgotten it, his brief remark about the short inconvenience only added to the woman's gaiety.

"Now I know why all you woman have one mammary gland bigger than the other. It's for ballast, so you don't drift to one side when you're carrying these damn small suitcases around."

He had also 'noticed' during his trip to their vehicle that the wife of one of his buds', only recent members to their gatherings, was sporting an infected pimple on the bridge of her nose. Knowing that the man was as much an imbiber of even than far fetch topics of humor they chose to pick on, related woman folk were mostly considered as a 'no', 'no', unless absolutely worthwhile. But when he had 'noticed' the pimple, and then quickly looked away, the husband had 'noticed' that he had 'noticed'. And when he 'noticed' that his wife hadn't 'noticed' that she had been 'noticed', he took 'notice' to slip away and catch up with Randy, who pretended not to 'notice' that his co-worker was now matching him step for step.

"How's it going Randy?" the worker smiled once 'noticing' that his presence had been 'noticed'.

"Oh, hi Pete. Sorry I didn't 'notice' you there." he lied. "How's it hanging?"

"Oh, at about the same angle and in the same location, in case you hadn't noticed." he chuckled.

"Why the Hell would I 'notice' that?" Randy frowned, now feeling that a little retaliation was required. "I did 'notice' though that you look a little bit bigger than last time we met, you gaining weight?"

"You 'noticed' I'm getting bigger just by looking at my pants. I didn't think anybody could 'notice' that!"

"Stop referring to I 'noticed' your pants!" Randy just short of shouted, their conversation going 'unnoticed' to the other activity going on around them. And in case you haven't 'noticed' - you've worn out your welcome." he smiled. "Now get back before the wife 'notices' you're missing, and has to put a 'notice' in the newspaper asking if anyone has 'noticed' where you're hiding."

"I 'noticed' that you're a little bit irritated today." Pete smiled back. "Did the wife give you 'notice' to move?" he quickly added, while turning and then jogging back in his wife's direction. And Randy, not so much to save face - but rather just glad to get on with his mission, shouted back in his friends direction. "In case you hadn't 'noticed' no-one even 'noticed' you were gone! And now either will I." with the rest of, "Even if I did 'notice' that bump on your misses nose usually went well with a broom and pointed black hat!" added at a barely audible level.

Bringing his hands back around from where he had been hiding them, a big smile still on his face, Randy calculated inside of his head the number of times he had managed to use the word 'notice' into the skit he and Pete had been able to keep going. And as he silently counted off the numbers, unfolding a finger to match each one, he was also thinking, 'I sure hope nobody 'notices' what the Hell I'm doing.'

On the other side of the yard, a few of the woman, as everyone there generally did, had floated back to join their mates by now. George was still doing his best to encourage those sitting around the red smoldering ashes in the barbecue to get into whatever they considered as 'doing' their 'thing' was.

A lot of old tunes had been passing in the background, with a related wisecrack always not far away from the title. 'Born to be wild' had help temporarily stir some of the men up. 'Heard it through the grape vine.' was joked about as being dedicated to gossip from work. 'Suspicious mind.' They said was dedicated to the Dwarf. And when 'Let's spend the night together.' was played it encouraged a few of the husbands and wives to actually and openly show some emotional feelings by dancing with each other.

Woody was now inebriated enough to have taken his hollow artificial leg off and placed it in front of him to use as a combination ashtray and holder for his drink. Eagle Beak was up to his old tricks of going around with a pair of scissors snipping off the ends of peoples' lit cigarettes, or stealing every lighter he could get his hands on. And Ken, in between mimicking everyone else's personality traits, was trying to set a new record for having some people there who sometimes felt lonely, wishing they could be again, especially when he was around.

The night was also progressing just enough, as more and more people dragged their seats into a growing circle near the barbecue, to settle into their routines of letting their hair down, bald or not. And since there was no given rhyme or reason as to which order the nit picking should start or be pursued in, a comment not to bring their stinky cigarette with them was briefly shot down with, 'Just hold your breath!' until a rebuttal of 'I always hold my breath when you're around!' set the rules, to which there were none.

But if an opportunity didn't presented itself, it was often a race as to who was going to use the pause to their advantage. Such as when Rusty was simply going to use a close-by towel to wipe off his damp lawn chair after one of the pools occupants had briefly sat on it, Pop Bottles wife Helen, yelling at him that it was 'her' towel he was about to use, he went ahead and dried the seat any-ways', while replying, "It still is!" before tossing it to her.

Right now it was fat people and dieting that was on the tip of everyone's tongue. Especially after someone when being asked how he now felt after having lost 10 pounds, had answered, "I don't feel any different , and you sure as hell don't look any better!"

George was still successfully limiting himself to trying to behave, but it was a no-win scenario that he soon realized and accepted sooner or later would lead him full tilt back to his old acid tongue self. And when Rustys' wife commented, 'I lost ten pounds in four days while dieting once.' he successfully held back a reply of, 'Oh no you didn't! If you could turn around real quick, I'd show you where it's hiding!'

But when someone else's wife reluctantly added, while patting her own hips, 'I know what you mean. I haven't been able to look down and see my toes without bending over, for the past ten months.'

George, again, beat everyone else to the punch, with what was probably on most of the men's minds. "I don't know what the Hell you've got to complain about, lady. We've got a guy at work called 'Corky', because he doesn't need a plug when in the tub, and rumor has it he hasn't seen his dick 'face to face' in at least ten years."

As expected, the remark instantly got the appropriate response. But before finding someone else there to continue with, he slammed himself a little first by bloating out his own tummy and saying, "But then in case you haven't noticed, there are some of us here who aren't to far behind 'ol Corky'. A couple more pounds and you'll be able to place me face down on the floor, belly down, and then spin me. And whoever I end up pointing at after I've stopped wobbling, gets a free low calorie lunch."

"Now that you mention it," Ken added, along with everyone else's laughter, "I've noticed that George junior 'is' starting to resemble his father".

"Ya-a-a-a!" George frowned. "Whoever he was!" and then stuck his tongue out in Judy's smiling direction.

Pointing at George's protruding tongue, Chris remarked, "Well, at least now we know why Judy's stuck it out with you for so long."

Most of the women there instantly puckered their faces into an elongated, 'E-e-e-ew', as the men roared with laughter. And Kim, who was sitting closer to Chris than his wife was, punched him in the arm just hard enough to make him spill a little of his drink, while saying, "And what are you - a vegetarian?"

Chris in turn, in between dipping the glass free fingers into the spilled liquid and then sticking them into his mouth in order to suck off the recovered alcohol, indignantly answered. "What? The 'dragon' been complaining about our sex life again?"

From the men who knew how to, a stretched out soft 'H-e-e-er' was delivered in Vicki's confused direction. But George had no intention of letting off the overly plump men there also go 'virgin free'.

"Well, you've got to at least admit some of us here," he bloated his stomach out over his swimsuit again, "were built for comfort, not for speed. right Rusty?"

"Right on, oh 'son-of-the-Goodyear blimp'." Rusty smiled, before stuffing the rest of an uneaten hot dog he'd been nibbling on totally into his mouth. And as everyone laughed at the humorous attack he and George had taken at themselves, he continued to speak - even though his cheeks looked as if they were just about ready to explode.

"Go ahead, laugh. I'm not the only guy here who gets requests to rent out as a billboard when I'm wearing a white tee shirt."

"Take it easy Jack," Chris smiled. "We all know there's no truth to the rumor that you've made special arrangements when you die to be buried in a 'stand up piano'."

"Hold it, h-o-o-old it! Fred butted in. "That's impossible! we already know he's not only not musically inclined, but the musicians union would never allow one of their instruments to be so morally abused."

As everyone laughed, Rusty said, "Go ahead and live it up you guys! At least I don't have people standing in line wanting to be my partner during a 'spot dance', just so they can cover more floor space and better their chances of wining a prize."

While he had been speaking, a few of the men there had unintentionally glanced at their wives, a once detected gesture that had them being rewarded with a nasty look or physical thumping. And it only encouraged Rusty to quickly add the words, "And whenever I get a tummy ache, I really don't ache all over, as I'm sure some unnamed individuals here must!"

"Well, it's not our fault your wife's such a bloody good cook." Fred said.

"A good cook!" Rusty over-exaggerated, grinning in his wife's direction. "Hell, I've seen flies commit suicide by flying into an open flame, rather than land on 'her' meatloaf!"

"Don't believe everything he tells you." Betty shot back in her defense. "He just likes to think he can enforce his manhood. But every time he tries to put his 'foot' down, I step on it!"

"That's the only way I could trap her cooking when we first got married." Rusty chuckled, his foot shooting out to catch some invisible fleeting foe.

"Well, whatever." Betty shrugged. "But remember it's still his foot that's on the bottom. And when he gets that shovel he calls a 'spoon' in motion, well, more than once I've seen him almost scrape the color right off the plate."

"And if you believe 'that", Rusty exclaimed, "then you better start wearin' a hat whenever you go out, cause the sun's been baking your brains."

"Oh ya !" Betty smiled, someone obviously on her side adding, 'Go get him lady.' Then, 'Take off your shoes and socks and show everyone here there's really no bruises on the instep of 'either' of your big feet."

"I wouldn't waste their time." Rusty answered, a little reluctantly. "Most of the guys already know I've got a 'bruise' on my right foot. Some of them have got one also. For all you ladies who don't know what the 'Hell" I'm talking about, it's from a game we play called 'Captain Crunch'." He then, as often did when feeling that he was losing control of the situation between him and the 'boss', took out his false teeth and offered them in her direction, while saying, "Here, you always seem to know what to say better than I do. maybe this'll help you."

Betty, while wrinkling up her face and shuddering out an elongated 'No-o-o-o thank you!" as everyone else imitated her show of disgust, eagerly got the subject back onto the track it had deviated from.

"Well, next time you want to use your foot on something," she laughed, "try exercising it by going for a walk around the block and not to kick the fridge door shut because your hands are full."

"I've seen him in the canteen at work." Ken butted in. "And I'd rather eat shit off a stick than 'down' some of the garbage he's getting ready to consume."

"Gee, there really must be some truth to that saying 'you are what you eat'." one of the wives quipped. "But then your 'preference' for recycled food is your business. Personally I'd keep that kind of information to myself."

"And how about the time at work he was braggin' how Betty bought his sandwich meat spread by the pound, to which the "Axe-man here shot him down with 'Maybe that's why after lunch your breath always used to smell like 'dog-food'."

"Or the time he was boasting about his waist being in the thirty inch range again, and then got wounded with, 'Unless you're talking about your 'pecker', inches from the floor doesn't count!"

As most laughed just short of choking on the last part of the insult, others jumping in with the occasional 'Here, here!' while Rusty asked sympathetically, "What the 'shit' you all pickin' on me for! I'm not the only easy material sitting here! Is it my fault my mother always used to say to me, 'eat'! You don't' want to go to Hell hungry do you?"

"Well it's nice to know you've already got your place of 'retirement' picked out!

James G. Davies Sr.

"Don't knock 'his' eating habits." George added. "Every time I see you lately, you're eating watermelon. It's only an old wives tale that it will put the curls back in your hair."

The short slamming's everyone there was eventually getting, periodically impregnated with more and more booze, helped keep the mood and entertainment flowing smoothly, especially since everyone knew that animosity was never a part of their delivery. And the kids, occasionally glancing in the direction of the molders of their future, just shook their heads while keeping mostly to themselves and making remarks like, "And they call us the 'wasted' generation."

So far Randy Butler had been wise enough to keep a low profile during the party. He was also smart enough to realize that sooner or later he would have to take his turn as the center of attention, so he decided to make it on his time and terms. It was no secret that he was an avid jogger who prided himself in taking care of his body. Leaning forward in his chair, he made an attempt to dispel any such related barbs that might be gradually working their way towards him. Holding his drink airborne in a toasting manner, he said, "I know some of you think I'm the kind of guy who could eat a herd of elephants and never gain a pound. Well I'll tell you here and now that I ran and suffered through a lot of 10 kilometer marathons to stay this thin, and now I'm going to enjoy it, even if it kills any of you bums watching me do it."

"Don't listen to him!" his wife Tracy quickly added, before anyone else had a chance to retaliate. "He might look as 'fit as a fiddle', but after a little bit of a workout, if you ladies know what I mean," she winked, "He huffs and puffs enough afterwards to blow out the torch on the Statue of Liberty."

As most of them laughed, someone adding, 'Now who's bragging?' a few slipping in 'He-e-e-e-e-re!' George asked, "And just 'exactly' what kind of physical activity are we complaining about here?"

Giving his wife a 'Gee-e-e - thanks for the support honey.' look, Randy made sure she knew exactly 'whom' he was speaking about, before saying, "I'd say it's fortunate for some woman that looks aren't everything, because she can't cook either."

"Gee, I always heard that the mind was the first thing to go." Judy smiled in George's direction. "I can still remember the time he spent an hour looking for a second sock, before he realized that they were both on the same foot!"

"Don't stop there." George retaliated, in between the laughter and finishing the drink in his hand. "Don't forget to tell everyone about how much control you have over our marriage."

Smiling, before blowing him a kiss, which he accepted with such force that it half blew him out of his chair, Judy chuckled, "You do it hon. Every-one here already knows you plan on doing just that anyway."

"I was only going to mention what you always say to me before heading off for my nights out with the boys." George smiled pleasantly.

"Ya mean, 'Don't hurry back'!" Judy laughed.

"Not exactly in that manner." George grinned - speaking to the whole gathering instead of just her now. "When the other men's wives used to ask them when they were coming back, you used to ask me 'if' I was coming back."

"That's only because I was concerned about you. Never knowing exactly what you and your cohorts were up to, and I've seen bruises on you in some pretty strange places, I just naturally worry about you."

"About 'me', or my paycheck?" he replied.

"Well, 'both' now that you mention it, because you sure as Hell don't earn enough to bury you so deep you can't come back and haunt everyone."

"Just don't forget what I said about when the time comes, I want a phone put in there with me." George grinned devilishly. "And just because I don't answer when you call, doesn't mean I'm not there."

"Well what if the 'line's' dead?" someone quipped.

"Then it'll be in good company." George shot back.

"Do me a favor, take the doctor's advice and leave the junk food alone for a while." Judy smiled. "I don't expect you to work yourself into an Arnold Schwartznagger, but at least have the decency to stick around until all the bills are paid off."

Most of the women quickly added, "Right on!" "Ditto!" "You can say that again!" each glaring in their husbands directions, as Betty said to her spouse, "Did ya hear that? You ain't leaving me here all alone to face everyone you owe money to."

"Don't you say anything." Rusty comically snapped in his wife's direction, her mouth noticeably starting to open, a 'barb' of her own no doubt ready to be delivered. "I feel quite comfortable with myself, and I don't mean whenever I'm 'in' the fridge, metaphorically speaking."

Someone, as others chuckled, offered, "For someone as big as you, it wouldn't be called a 'fridge'. it would be called a 'freezer'!"

And then George, after politely waiting his turn again, remarked, "I don't know what all the complaining is about. Most men would normally be 'proud' to say that their wife is twice the woman she was - then when he married her."

"Speaking of being 'oversized'," Judy piped in, while once more glaring directly into George's still smiling eyes. "What's this I hear you've been selling blown up photos of our oldest son, so as to deter people from overeating?"

The humor that was already in motion only grew in volume as the comical remarks continued, while George answered Judy's question. "I don't know who's been feeding you such information, but I think they should at least get it correct. The photos weren't meant to discourage people from 'over-eating'. They were supposed to make them think twice about having 'kids'. The fat remark made was when your oldest son 'Wubbles' was a baby and we joked about having the fridge door handle lowed because of the way he used to go through his food so fast. But now, after looking at the size of him, and as to probably why I'm so broke, I said I think we would have been better off if we'd just out right removed the handle instead. And finally, since he's got a job, I haven't had to oil the hinges on the fridge door so much, not to mention that the food inside now finally has a chance to get 'cold'."

The instant it looked as if Hubby was going to pause long enough to catch his breath, after such a long babbling run, Judy quickly added a little rebuttal of her own. "Let's not overlook that we now also get to save on hydro and light-bulbs from burning out, for the fridge."

"The reason I didn't mention that" George smiled sarcastically, "is because we lose it all back by having to use the kitchen's regular lighting to illuminate the area instead now."

The low blows, as well as earning him an, 'I'll get even with you later.' glare from in Judy's direction, was also worthy of a friendly light slap in the back of his head from one of the women sitting close to him.

It was a tiny pleasure the woman often eagerly enjoyed delivering for each other, so Vicki smiled, "I got him this time for you Judy. I'm sure the way the 'boys' are acting, you'll be returning the favor before the night's over,"

Another apparent victim of 'mid-life', 'mid-rib bulge' crisis, and neighbor who knew from past gatherings that his size wasn't far away in either conversation or everyone's thoughts, was sufficiently suicidal enough to say, "Being pleasingly fat isn't the worst thing that can happen to you, you know. It's a proven fact that a lot more people die from booze and smoking than from being overweight."

"Don't you believe him." his wife just as eager as everyone else to keep the conversation in motion replied. "He's just bragging because he gave them both up last week. He's also been nibbling none-stop ever since. I swear that if he doesn't take one of those vices back real soon, he'll probably end up exploding! And with my luck, I'll not only be in the room when it happens, but I'll be the only one available to clean him up afterwards."

"Are you sure he didn't just fall asleep in the tub with his mouth open?" Fred half-whispered in George's direction, someone else also whispering, "It'll have to be an awful big room for both of them to be in it at the same time.'

"His nickname at work is 'O Crane' because whenever he wants to walk from one end of the shop to the other, the crane is always considered as a means of getting the job done."

Bill's answer of a Ralph Cramdon like 'Hardy-har-har-har!' was totally obliterated by the wave of reverberating laughter the remark had brought, as Ken did his imitation of something slowly expanding. And someone else quickly added, "I'd ask you why you don't just take up weight lifting, but by the looks of the size of ya, you're already lifting enough weight every time you stand up."

In an effort to save a little face, as well as keeping the happy mood flowing, Dave immediately replied, "I already thought about taking up lifting weights. But I gave it up as soon as I remembered that all of the young guys at work who 'pump iron' have no pecker."

"Well, if you're only using it for 'peein' out of any-ways," Kim added dryly, before taking a sip from the drink in her hand, no doubt to make sure she had everyone interested, "What does it matter how big it is?"

Before anyone could answer, "It's the 'magician' and not the 'wand' that does the trick, lady." someone else snidely butted in with their own answer to the blow against the male ego. "Isn't it funny how size never seems to matter whenever the women are in heat. But just let a group of you get together, and all of a sudden you sound as if Abraham Lincoln was a liar when he said 'All men are created equal'!"

"Well I'd be happy as Hell if my just hung below my knees, wouldn't you?" someone hiding behind his booze bragged in the background. But as always, not to be outdone, another of the inebriated instantly offered, "I sure would! At least I wouldn't be tripping over the bloody thing every time I was walking!"

As expected, most of the women gave out a long drawn out, "A-w-w." in response to the remark, something else that did nothing but further step on the already bruised men's integrity. But it did warrant another verbal response at boosting it back up where it belonged, when another of the men responded. "I may not be big enough to get into the movies, or even scare any women, but at least I did my part in getting three kids born, and that's what really counts."

"Well from what I've seen of you men wearing shorts," Betty Faylen giggled, "I don't think there's much fear of any movie 'talent scouts' scrambling to break down doors to get your signatures on the dotted line. And don't give me that old line about where you have to put a fold in hour pecker just to keep them from falling out, or strap them to your waist so that they don't hang down and throw you off balance by swinging back and forth as you walk"

"Really!" one of the men said his voice full of surprise. "All this time I've been cutting a hole into one of my side pockets just so I can tuck it into there And hold onto it in order to stop it from rubbing against my leg in order to keep it from staying hard!"

As one of the women chuckled, "Dreamer." another adding, "Don't you wish." Betty smiled, "Unless your so called 'it' catches a nasty cold and starts sneezing and dripping all over the place, I think it's safe to say the men are lucky to have women as compassionate and tolerant as us."

"Compassionate! What's so compassionate about a poor guy who accidently makes a mistake by saying about his wife's home made pie that it's almost as great as his mother used to make. And then she in reply comments that if he ever expects to get 'pie' of any kind around there ever again, he better soon learn how to appreciate all of her cooking."

"Ya, and if some of you ladies are going to wear really short shorts to our get togethers', then I think the most you can do is to start trimming your 'mustache' before you come out." Ken laughed, to which he was just as quickly punched in the arm by someone else's wife closest to him.

And as a bunch of the men there, in almost unison, moaned while reaching up and holding onto their own arms, it encouraged, "I don't know about some of you guys, but ya know you're in trouble when you catch the wife lying on the bed in order to get her slacks done up."

"I don't know about you bums." came out of the gathering. "But I'm still more interested in when my wife's taking he pants 'off', not putting them 'on'!"

"Don't judge the rest of the world by your marriage." George said in his neighbors' direction. "We've got a little group of 'man haters' at work passing as woman who could probably use a new recruit. Would you like me to mention your name?"

Seeing that her hubby's remarks were starting to bother Betty, Judy quickly jumped to her defense and answered the question that really didn't need answering.

"Don't bother, smart-ass. You've already managed to scare off her hubby. What do you want to do, intimidate her to?"

Throwing his hands in the air, finger tips upwards, after having given Judy a quick wink, George then stood erect in order to refill his once again empty glass, while saying, "Pardon me for living! I was only trying to make conversation!"

"Ya, well the type of conversations you make are either 'booby' trapped, or explosive." Judy shot back, as George grinned while bowing and backing away from the gathering, one of the women clipping at the back of his head again as it passed.

"How do you stand him?" Betty laughed, a little nervously.

"Generally in the corner, like any other bad little boy." Judy laughed. And before the atmosphere could get too hung up or deteriorate any further, she shifted the conversations onto another topic. "Speaking of the kids," she smiled in Helen's direction. "Got any pictures of the little darling yet?"

Even as his wife's fingers busied themselves in her purse for snapshots they had taken of their new son, Bob answered, "Ya, but I'll warn you now, you'll be sorry you asked."

"Why?" Ken snapped. "Does he look like you?"

"Let's hope "God' in his mercy let the little guy take after his mother's side of the family." Chris added.

" Can't be any worse than yours." One of the woman close by giggled, booze no doubt starting to do her thinking for her. "I was over at your place the other day and noticed that some of the pictures were turned to face the wall. When I asked why, I was told that those were all of the ones showing 'your' side of the family."

By this time Helen had found the pictures she had been after. And as she started to pass them around she smiled, "Well, at least I haven't had to give the little guy a shot of 'rye' in order to get him to get him to go sleep yet, unlike his father often does. And when I use the word 'little' this time, I am referring to the baby."

"Very funny!" 'Pop Bottles' jokingly sneered in his wife's direction, while taking the first picture and then passing it on without even glancing at it. "Did it ever dawn on you that I need a little 'shot' of false courage because our bedrooms not dark enough when we're in bed."

Helen wasn't fast enough with her remark about how that it was a lot of 'hogwash', because once he took his glasses 'off' he generally needed a 'seeing eye dog' to refined them. Especially since a comedian beside Bob, after accepting the first photo, jumped back so fast in fright that he spilled most of the drink in his hand back in Bob's face. The hand still holding onto the picture, after he had said 'Sorry!' in Bob's direction, as everyone else laughed, then went to cover his shocked heart, no doubt in effort to deliver the rest of his comical routine. He then pretended to peel the picture slowly from his chest, sneaking a gradual bit of the images on it, a little at a time.

"Very funny, wise-guy!" Bob remarked, wiping at his face with the towel that had come out of the crowd. "But don't try to kid us into thinking you haven't been that close to 'ugly' before. Or would you have us believe that there are no 'mirrors' in your house? Besides, we've all seen your kids up close too, remember? Or would you like me to call them over here for verification?

"How many times do I have to remind you," Eagle Beak laughed while passing on the photo he had been making so much fuss about, "When they're this young, we call them children. It's not until they turn into teenagers that we call them kids. And the only reason I can say that, its because I've already survived both age periods."

"Listen to the old 'pro'," George butted in, as he rejoined the group. "There was a time when he used to brag about how smart and cute his kids were. Why I can still remember how he used to brag about being so intelligent as a baby that he himself was walking by the time he was only six month's old. That is until I put a stone in his boot by saying that the only logical reason for it being true is - "

"Ya, we all know." Eagle Beak smiled. "It's because I was so dam ugly nobody wanted to carry me."

Still occasionally monitoring their parent's antics, wisely from a distance, George junior could almost word-for-word read his father's gestures, as he watched him comically spray bits of potato chips into the face of his best friend Fred. And just as Eagle Beaks son Ron caught him breaking out into laughter, he trailed his line of vision while asking him just what so funny.

"Have you ever laughed until you thought you'd cry?" Wubbles asked.

"Sure." Ron shot back, as other kids with them eagerly listened on. "I saw my dad trip over a garden rake once. He caught me laughing, and then 'I' cried. But what the Hell's that got to do with your old man."

"Everything!" Junior answered a hint of humor about him. "If I hadn't learned to laugh at everything my dad says or does, I'd either have ended up crying a lot, or committing suicide."

"Such as?" one of the other kids asked.

"Well," George junior continued to smile. "Being around Pop when I was growing up was often a real treat. If I wasn't lookin into his 'zipper' while he was scolding me, I was 'walkin' behind him at just the wrong height to be in the line of fire after his Thursday nights out. There was even a few times where I thought for sure the whole 'bloody' world was shrinkin all around me."

"Ya." Ron laughed. "There was times I could never understand my parents reasoning either. For years they sent me to bed while I was wide awake, and then made me get up when I was still sleepy."

"Parents 'are' weird!" one of the 'Hubba Bubba Club' added. "If I was bad when I was little, I used to get grounded for a week. Now my dad just throws me out of the house until 'he' feels better."

"Not mine." another offered. "I still get grounded. Only now it's called 'house arrest'."

"Hell. I wish it was that easy." another of the giggling group added. "If I was bad, I always got a spanking." And when my Pop asked me if I knew what it was for, I used to end confessing to about a half dozen dumb things before he finally cut me off with "No, that's for getting caught'!"

"Oh, you mean the 'ol do as I say, not as I did routine." Ron added.

"You guys should have lived in our house." another of the club smiled. "If I hadn't of had such a gullible younger brother, I never would have made it sanely this far. Sometimes I swear he was born to fit that comment. 'He was born stupid, and has been loosing ground ever since!"

"My Dad always used to say he was born broke, and has been walking backwards ever since."

"Naïve or Stupid?" Ron asked, hoping to encourage more laughter. But when one of the bolder young women there answered "If you want to talk about your family, wait your turn." He wisely did just that, especially since her remark got a bigger chuckle than his did. And not even the occasional spray of water being splashed from the pool by kids to young to be interested in anything not within their age range could distract them from trying to outshine each other.

"As I was saying, before someone changed feet, my little sister would believe any and everything I told her, especially when it came to 'show and tell' time at school. The first time I got her to take condoms to show as special party balloons, or the time I gave her a couple of mom's wigs and convinced her that whenever mom wanted a new style or color she could just grow a new head of hair instantly. But the best and one that almost got me killed was when I had her believe dad could blow cigarette smoke out of his rear end. And when I gave her a pair of his under-shorts with nicotine stains on them to prove it at 'show and tell time', well, I spent so much time in my room that I almost became turned into a mushroom addicted to 'soap operas'."

Laughter and its reasons for existence was just as necessary to the kids as it was to the adults, only the teenagers could be crueler if desired. But when one asked Darryll why his brother George was so much bigger than him, the answer he got border lined on maturity.

"Rumor has it that when we were growing up we didn't have enough beds to go around, so we hung him in the closet at night, if you can believe it. But personally I think it was just a case of dad leaving his doniker in a little bit longer then necessary."

"So beating you and Ian to the table at meal times had nothing to do with it?" someone chuckled.

"I think it was more like first 'come' first served." one of the older kids sneered, mostly to ears not old enough to catch his play on words.

As laughter flowed among even their limited grasp of the grownup world, another youth offered. "I can always tell when mom and dad have managed to sneak upstairs for a little 'sanity time' as he likes to call it. Mom's always humming some old tune, and he always seems to have one of his socks or tee shirt on inside out."

When another of the Bubba group said, "You mean your parents still do things like 'that'?" A much younger youth asking, "Like what!" young George chuckled. "My dad says it's the best way he knows of to settle an argument. He's even told me, after making sure mom's not around, that he deliberately on occasion will start a disagreement."

"Golly, and here I just thought my mom could see in the dark." one of the older girls said a little sarcastically in her younger sister's direction.

And when the child said, "How's that?" she continued to frown, "I've heard her say many a-night, 'Not tonight. You haven't shaved yet, hon.'

"Better they pick on themselves then us." Wubbles said.

"Or give us such confusing advice." Darryll quickly added in his brothers' direction. "Whenever he sees me with Pat lately", the young girl blushing at the sound of her name, "he always tells me 'No hanky panky' or not to play to much 'grabby, grabby' as if I knew what the 'Hell' they meant.

"You will." George laughed in his brothers' direction. "Believe me, you will, and not to far down the road I might add."

"Now there you go, sounding just like 'dad'. What in the 'Hell's 'going down the road' got to do with anything we're talking about!"

It was obvious by the way their heads were snapping back and forth between the strange conversation going on 'over their heads' that all of the younger children there were not only confused, but also missing out participating in the reasoning behind the laughter. And to make up for it they jumped into the strange verbal barrage in front of them.

"When I told my old man I got ninety-five out of a hundred on my history exam," Ken smiled, "He simply replied that I must have got a good seat close to someone smart."

"You didn't tell him your actual school marks." George laughed. "Let them ask you how close you got to an 'A', and then just tell them 'Oh, about three seats."

"My parents told me that when I'm old enough to start dating - to remember that kissing a girl who smokes, would be just like' licking' an ashtray." Brian frowned.

"Sounds more like they're not fussy on people who smoke." Ian offered.

"Sounds more like the ol 'Do as I say and not as I do!' routine again." one of the older boys offered.

"Unless they're on 'fire'!" junior quickly laughed.

"Well, personally I can think of worse things to 'lick'." the same youth grinned devilishly.

"Don't be 'rude' in front of the children." George continued to laugh. "We don't want to shatter their little protected worlds too soon for them. Like dad always says to us, you'll get 'too old too soon', and 'too smart too late', soon enough."

In a state of apparent frustration, one of the youngest children there blurted out, "Will somebody please talk about 'anything' I can understand! Is it just me," he then added, "Or don't any of you ever get spanked?"

"A spanking is what they give you when you're little like you Danny." George smiled. "At our age, when your parents want to 'thump ya' it's called a 'lesson'. so the answer to your question is, of course they do, but not necessarily in a physical manner anymore. But they do," as he spoke he smiled into both of his brothers smiling and affirmative nodding heads directions, "find other ways to punish us."

"Ya!" Ian added. "Our dad likes to classify it under the label of 'doing ones chores."

"Not to mention, "Darryll cut in. "when you want a little bit of extra spending money, he wants receipts!"

"And when they finally 'do' give out with the 'loot'," Brian scoffed, "they always make sure to give you a little bit of well deserved advice with it, such as "See if you can make this last for awhile. Or at least last a little bit longer than it took me to earn it!"

"Or go as far as you can!" George chuckled. "And my favorite answer to that one is, 'I'll make it go 'so far' you'll never see it again'!"

"Hell, if I ask my parents for any 'scratch', they always tell me I'm to old to be begging for money," one of George's friends said dryly.

Already laughing, just as his father would, George quickly added the words, "Tell them you're not 'begging' your 'praying'. And if they come across with a large chunk of cash, you might put a good word in for them."

"It won't work." the same youth frowned. "When I was little I used to think that dad was really Santa Clause in disguise. But now that I'm older, I know he's really Scrooge reincarnated."

"If he knew some of the pranks you've been in on," George continued to chuckle, "your old man might realize just how well he's doing his job!"

"Very funny." the boy answered. "I'm sure I could open your father's eyes a lot about what his namesakes been up to."

"Go ahead." George grinned, while gesturing in the direction of the grownups. "Around here I need all the recognition I can get! And while you're at it have him show you the vanishing dollar trick."

Even as the youth replied with a confused, "Huh?" George started to prepare for the demonstration needed to explain the very trick he had just mentioned. "Here, let me show you." he said while taking a dollar bill out of his wallet. Ian and a few of the Hubba Bubba group, already knowing what the stunt involved, slowly backed away from where George was standing. And as everyone else in the young gathering inquisitively drew in closer to the dollar bill he was placing under a glass of water, Wubbles then drew the rest of them in even closer. "I'll bet one of you this dollar that I can pick it up and you won't even see me do it."

"What?" the close by youth scoffed, glancing around the gathering, as if maybe one of them already knew how the stunt was done or might even accidentally give the secret away. But when most of them simply shrugged their shoulders, indicating that they were just as mystified as he was, he then took the bait. "Okay, it's a bet."

In one fluid motion, possibly so as not to allow for his friend to figure out what was about to happen, or maybe even change his mind, junior picked up the glass and tossed its cold contents smack into the center of the boys' face. And as the surprised youth instinctively put both hands up to wipe away the dripping water, George junior easily picked up the dollar with his other hand and stuffed it back into his pocket.

Needless to say, even though some of the bystanders had gotten sprayed accidentally by the cascading splash of fluid, the already busy night air was filled even more by the loud outburst of youthful laughter. And not even the boy who had been the but of the joke could keep from adding his humor to the group.

"Want me to show you the one about the fighting human hairs next?' George chuckled.

"No-o-o-o-o thank you!" the youth answered, instinctively backing away while still trying to shake away the water he had just accumulated onto his hands. "Just tell us about it. Don't show us."

"It's not as much fun if I just 'tell' you." junior smiled.

"We'll chance it!" another of the youths' close-by quickly offered. "Just say it, don't spray it!"

"Well." George continued to smile, his friends and Ian still holding their ground. "I'll try." Then without any warning he reached out and quickly yanked a hair out of the head from the unsuspecting youth closets to him. The small "Ouch!' that came with it was totally lost as he, while pulling a hair form his own skull, spoke, "What you would do is to place both of these hairs into a puddle of water laid out on a flat surface for everyone to see. But they have to be from two people with different personalities."

Wisely, as he did exactly as he was saying, now even everyone was reluctant to move in closer.

"Then you would tell everyone to watch the hairs from two different heads wiggle and fight in the puddle. And as soon as anyone was foolish enough to bend over closer to the hairs, you would smack the puddle of water, only hopefully drenching more people this time."

Once more, especially since it was the type of trick the kids could relate to and would 'love' to pull on each other, their laughter was in competition with that of the so-called adults. It was so loud in fact that it warranted an inquisitive glance from some of the parents within hearing range.

"And you dad teaches you those kind of tricks to play on other people?" one of the girls asked.

"It's worse than that," Ian grinned, while glancing briefly in his fathers direction. "He teaches us the hard way! He pulls them on us."

"Gee." someone else chuckled. "I find it hard to even imagine my parents doing anything like that."

"You're right!" Wubbles grinned, while twisting his negatively. "I can't picture your parents setting a booby trap by 'passing wind' into his 'beer fridge' - then closing its door real quick, to wait for a victim."

"Or-r-r putting it on tape so you can play it over the phone to someone you don't like!" Ron chuckled out.

"That stuff went out with kindergarten!" a younger brother to one of the Bubba club members giggled. "Grown ups got more class then that."

"Yeah, right!" Ron acknowledged a little sarcastically. But before they became 'grownups', they were 'us'. I've heard my dad telling your pop about how they used to play the 'ol lost wallet on a string' routine. Or exchange burnt out light bulbs from 'car lots', with good working ones in alleyways or above their neighbors garage doors."

"I heard from one of my uncles how my old man used to make a parachute by using a blanket and a garbage pail, and then throw it off an apartment buildings roof, with a cat for a passenger inside!" another of the Hubba Bubba club chuckled.

"Hell, the boldest thing my pop ever did was to spit on a car's windshield." another of the kids remarked.

"I think the boldest thing 'your' dad ever did, was to marry your mother!" George shot back.

Ignoring the remark, as those of the other kids who understood the slamming laughed, the same youth quickly tried to get even. "I'll bet your dad was one of those who used to shit in a paper bag, put it on someone's front porch, light it on fire. Then he'd knock on the door, and run like 'Hell'!"

"Better than that!" Darryll beat George. "He probably invented it! And another of his favorites was where he and a bunch of other kids his age used to go into an apartment building, find two occupied apartments where their doors were almost directly across from each others'. Then with a piece of rope they'd tie one end onto one door handle, and the other end onto the opposite door handle, leaving about a foot of hanging slack in the middle. Knocking on both doors at the same time, they'd all run like the devil was after them!"

As soon as each youth mentally visualized the humor in someone opening one of the apartment doors, one of them in pantomime going through the motions of the act described, and then inquisitively sticking their head out through the small opening to see what was going on. Only to have their own door whack into the back of their heads when the door opposite theirs is pulled open, their laughter acted as if it was contagious.

"The devil wasn't chasing them." one of the kids roared "He was running with them!"

"They were no better than us." Ron said in between chuckling. "And we still basically do the same thing."

"Ya!" Darryll replied slightly annoyed. "Only some kids nowadays 'smash' the light-bulbs, break into cars or snap their aerials off, and still throw cats off rooftops, only without a parachute!"

"Oh how 'cruel'!" Patty cringed, do doubt her imagination well into images of what had just been suggested.

"We don't do things like that!" Ron quickly replied. That's only a rare few bad kids!"

"Maybe we should just grow up and be like our parents." Someone added.

"Not me!" George laughed, deliberately trying to put the disturbed atmosphere back into a better mood. "When I get as old as my ol man, I'm going on a 'strict' diet. And I don't mean one of those comical 'sea food' diets, where you 'see food' you 'eat it'!"

When someone in the gathering said 'Any special color?' Ian cracked "Well if you start right now, I'm sure dad's going to be able to financially retire a lot earlier."

"Not really!" George said, while reaching out for his younger brother. "He'd only end up spending the extra cash on a funeral, yours. Especially if you keep coming up with 'wise cracks' like that."

Making a break for the safety of the house, Mark Faylen following him, Ian laughed back in his oldest brothers' direction. "Knock it off! Or I'll tell everyone how dad used to put you into a green garbage bag and then suck all the air out just to calm you down, so mom could feed you!"

"You keep eating all that candy mom finds hidden in your room and you'll be shittin zits."

Pretending that he was going to chase after him, George played up his part while laughing just as hard as everyone else, as Mark and Ian disappeared into the sanctuary of the house. It was a little skit that didn't go unnoticed by the grownups, as one of them commented, "It's good to see the kids getting along so well with each other. Little do they know how brief this stage of their life is going to be. Well at least they'll live long enough to out grow it. Just think of those heading into old age. From what I've seen, they not only don't get another chance at it, it also generally doesn't even last very long for some of them."

"Take it easy lady!" Sid chuckled. "It's to early in the evening to start sobbing into your beer. Besides, you'll dilute it!"

Fred, feeling a lot more at ease now since his and Nancy's arrival, was doing his best to make sure everyone there knew he and the once missing debatable 'better half' were getting along just fine right now. And he repeatedly made an effort to 'touch base' just long enough to make sure her refreshment was far from getting low, while still jumping in and out of the conversations.

"Ya - but that was before most of the younger whipper snappers started in the plant. It was a time when George and I really had to work for our money, not just show up like now and automatically get paid."

"A lot of things have changed." George smiled. "especially since we've had our kids, diapers being about the biggest! They'll never know the joy we had in using reusable cloth diapers. They may have been a lot more work, not to mention a little raunchy," he wrinkled up and pinched his nose to emphasize what he was getting at, but they did have an occasional humorous aspect to them from time to time."

"If you mean fun times," Judy over-exaggerated, "You obviously never got any 'shit' under your nails. Or do you mean like permanently staining the hardwood floors if I forgot and left a wet one sit in one spot to long. So don't give me any 'cra-a-a-p' about those being the good 'ol fun filled days'. You're talking about something you only 'think' you know something about, I was raised on them, remember?"

"Oh, you're still mad because I used to gripe about your mother being around the house so much when we first got married."

"Why didn't you just tell her to go home?" Pop Bottles said. "I find it hard to believe that 'you' could be afraid of her."

"I couldn't! George grinned broadly. "It was 'her' house we were living in at the time!"

Those who didn't laugh, booed George, as he kept on talking. "But getting back to the kids. If you think getting your fingertip pricked for a blood sample is bad , you should have been there when the kid was dirty and good ol mom wasn't around to change him. The safety pins we see today are nothing compared to the barracudas we used to end up stabbing into the bones of our fingertips back before throw away disposable diapers were invented. Not to mention occasionally pinning the poor kid to the mattress. Could you just imagine what would happen if there had been waterbeds back then? And if it hadn't have been for the occasional game such as seeing how many flips you could get out of a hard green turn when you snapped it into the toilet-bowl, well, we probably would have thought that having children was a 'pain' in the prostrate."

"You call that fun!" Ken and Kim said in almost unison.

Everyone there instinctively pivoted their heads in George's grinning direction, because they not only wisely realized that it didn't pay to but into the 'Axe-man's' pearls of wisdom, but also possibly because he still likely had more humorous tidbits still up his sleeve.

"Well at least we didn't have to worry back then about someone's cat or dog tearing open plastic bags in search for dinner, thereby ending up with raunchy dirty diapers spewed all over the neighborhood. I'm sure everyone's heard the pun about how nothing grows where 'Fido' goes.

Well the one about dirty strewn diapers is, only 'Nasa' could re-grow the 'grassa'."

Instantly, especially the people in the group who could relate to such a situation, broke out into almost knee slapping laughter. And George, basking, quickly added, "Why on a really hot summer's day I've seen the 'garbage men' shoot off a gun' in order to get all the flies off the bags of someone who still has a kid in diapers. Not to mention they then had to walk upwind backwards just to get close enough to handle the garbage pails."

Smiling in his wife's direction, Bob said, "They make it all sound so awfully 'encouraging' - don't they?"

"Sounds 'awful' something!" Helen laughed back. And as Pop Bottles' smile faded into a grimace at the images now 'popping' into his head, he looked in George's direction before speaking again.

"Maybe we should have done what George suggested last year. Maybe we should have just rented a baby off someone for awhile like he said, just to find out what we were letting ourselves in for again."

George, as almost everyone started to laugh, gestured as being a bit confused by shrugging his shoulders and holding his hands palms outward. When Judy pretended again to glare in his direction over the advice that sounded exactly like something he would say, he then smirked in her direction. "Honestly I don't remember saying that. Personally I feel every health young man should have the opportunity to take a little kid into a 'kiddy-pool' at the beach. You'd be surprised how many over-endowed young mothers 'hang out' there, bending over and dipping or walking their babies in the shallow water."

This time it was Kim who was close enough to slug George in the arm for his remark, as well as a smack at the back of his head by another of the woman presently scolding him. But before she could give him the verbal lashing she knew Judy would want to deliver, the sound of a high-pitched scream, preceded by a hollow sounding 'plop' and spray of water from the pool area, just naturally drew all of the grownups attention in its direction.

George, in his wisdom, once realizing that it was only the kids involved in watery horseplay immediately capitalized on the interruption by pulling off his tee shirt as he jumped erect, and yelling, "Last one in the pool buys the next round!"

Needless to say, the challenge was instantly answered by most of the men, in one loud flurry of half-toppled lawn chairs, flailing bodies tearing at their clothing as they moved in a human wall towards the pool. The wives wisely, in between trying to stop chairs and drinks from being spilled or knocked over, laughed out-loud, while making no effort to join in the childish looking antics of pushing and shoving presently going on around them.

It wasn't until most of the physical commotion had moved towards the pool area did they realize that two of the husbands, two men who obviously had not intention of being anywhere near the last into the pool, had jumped into the water with all of their clothing still on. And it was only because of this, that any of the ladies made any real effort to get out of their own seats.

Somehow even 'Woody' had even managed to end up in the water without being last, his artificial leg now comically bobbing up and down in the waves. And as the kids wisely quickly vacated the pool, his voice in between coughing and spitting up water joined the others - as they too sputtered out what kind of drink they would like, in Rustys' direction.

Sensibly, some of the kids, mostly the Hubba Bubba club - had ended up on the wooden deck surrounding the pool. And even though they could have supplied the name of the of the individual who had 'really' been the last body into the water, judging by the silly antics and noise now unfolding before them, they just as intelligently stood by and enjoyed the sights. It was not only all familiar recent antics, but also the kind of horseplay that if they had been guilty caught performing, would have been scolded for. Instead, they just silently lined the perimeter of the pool, content with the knowledge that in all probability after about five or ten minutes of such silly physical antics, they would have the water back all to themselves. But soon to their surprise and dismay the horseplay now started, such as 'belly-flops' and 'cannonballs' from the neighbors garage roof, soon had every indication of carrying on far past that estimated time.

Gradually age and conditioning, along with encouragement to do so from their wives, prompted some of the men to start slowly remove them-selves from the pool. One by one, with most giving the excuse that they were falling seriously behind on their drinking on their drinking schedule, the choppy water in the pool eventually settled into small pulsating rings of transparent mounds. And when no-one looked as if they were coming back, leaving just George, Fred, and Ken in deep conversation in the pool as some of the kids sat with their feet dangling into the water, George knew that it was time to rekindle the excitement back into the gathering.

Swimming under the water he grabbed a distracted Ken by the legs, and then easily toppled his unsuspecting already half submerged form. From there, especially with grinning Fred's prearranged help, it was fairly easy for the two of them to slip off Ken's almost skintight swim trunks.

Noisily resurfacing, with Ken's excited voice and grasping hands at arms' length, George threw the captured prize into the once again seated crowd of guests. Jeers and laughter instantly broke out as soon as they heard and saw the wet swimsuit, even before knowing exactly whom it belonged to. And since the pool area was very well illuminated thanks to the flood lighting system George had installed, Ken was smart enough to make sure to let only his head project out of the transparent excited waters surface, while using both hands to cover the often bragged about family jewels.

Before Kim could react to her husbands almost whining pleading words of, "Hey hon, toss me my swimsuit back in here, will ya?" one of the other men quickly scooped it up and proceeded to twirl it around out of her reach over his head. Walking back in the pools direction he comically started singing, "Come and get it yourself Mister Macho Man. Now's your chance to show the women what a real 'stu-u-u-d' you are."

This time the women came with the men, joking and chuckling, as they noisily converged on the pool. Bob was still swinging Ken's bathing trunks over his head, even though Kim had repeatedly unsuccessfully tried to snatch if from his grasp. And Ken, if possible, tried to submerge himself even deeper into the rippling water, as the gathering positioned them-selves all around the outer edge of the pool.

Fred and George still hadn't made any real effort to climb out of the water, even though each had since the attack repeatedly received a verbal barrage of comical insults from Ken for their treacherous actions. But both of them were also smart enough to relocate themselves at opposite ends of the pool, just in case an attack or reprisal or necessity was made on 'their' swimwear.

As the crowd around the pool grew, even the most of the kids were there also, so did the noise and antics. Some of the women, as others joined their husbands into trying to coax Ken out of the pool, gave out a series of long loud 'wolf whistle' calls. A few of the 'shit disturbing' ladies teasingly dipped a toe or foot into the water, in response to the awkward bobbing movement still being made by Ken, his hidden manhood obviously still his biggest concern.

But as usual, it was George's loud joking voice that drowned out everyone else's, as he shouted. "Hold it everybody! I guess it's time to give him back his swimsuit. If he keeps trying to get down any deeper in the water for protection, he's libel to drown himself!"

As expected, as he spoke, everyone's attention was focused solely onto George, himself, even though Fred was also still in the pool. And even though a few verbally objected to what he was suggesting, everybody except Ken obviously over enjoying what was happening, it was easy to see that what he had suggested was soon about to happen. But then, when George's attention seemed to suddenly wander in another direction, everyone's curiosity, even Ken's, naturally froze in what they were doing in order to find out just what the sudden interruption was all about.

For some unbeknownst reason, Ian and Mark were now moving among the group surrounding the pools' perimeter. But it wasn't so much their sudden presence, but rather what Ian was holding in his hands right then, that caused George's voice to excitedly accent what was now in his thoughts.

"Hey! What are you doing down here with that thing? I thought I told you to keep that aquarium and those 'damn' fish strictly in your room!"

Instinctively everyone's eyes automatically shifted first to Ian - and then solely to the murky water-filled tank he was cradling in his arms, as he answered, "I just wanted to show the other kids here the fish!"

"Well, you had no business bringing those dam ugly things down here!" George answered, more angrily than loud.

'Piranhas' are too 'bloody dangerous' to be just shown to anyone. Now be careful and get them back upstairs!"

Strangely enough, just hearing the name 'Piranhas' was almost like shouting out 'Fire!' Or even 'Free booze!' to this group. So some of them, especially the so-called mature ones, just naturally and curiously, while repeating the deadly fishes' name, crowded in around Ian's already adolescent clumsy movements. All commotion about Ken's still naked form squatting in the center of the pool, even Kim had stopped trying to retrieve his evasive trunks, was temporarily forgotten about. Forgotten that is, as curious human eyes pushed in nearer and nearer in an effort to get a closer view of the shadowy evasive deadly fish.

Poor Ian, Mark now totally pushed to the rear of the grown-ups, was just about to become a forth member in the watery pool, when someone fortunately grabbed the back of his 'beach bum' shirt just in time. Unfortunately though, all eyes there becoming hypnotized by young Ian's awkward balancing act, the aquarium he had been so carefully cradling broke totally free of his grip to become subject to the gravity filled air now surrounding it.

During the elongated frozen seconds it took for the fish tank to complete its downward journey into the pool, a few daredevil hands grasping at air now free of where it had been, its arced path magnetically held everyone's complete interest. Strangely one loud trailing 'scream' was heard above all other noise and activity Ian's apparent carelessness had brought forth from all those around him. Later speculation would have George senior as the owner of the high-pitched hysterical outburst. But for right now, as soon as the aquarium finally disappeared below the surface of the pools water in one long loud 'plop', it was only 'his' emotional filled voice that could be recognizable among all of the bewildered others.

Even as he shouted, "Holy shit! Everybody get out of the water! - The Piranhas are loose!" he was already in a state of excited motion trying to do exactly what he was shouting out.

Fred's almost comical looking movements were only a fraction of a second behind George's. They were both within a foot of the pool's perimeter and apparent safety, but poor bewildered Ken was still stuck squatting in its center. And his mind, as it mentally called back the images of the ugly little beasts eating in a frenzy earlier, it totally abandoned his present embarrassing condition, sending him scurrying for safety also.

And when poor George miscalculated his balance when pulling himself up out of the pool, only to end up falling spread-eagled backwards to land with a noisy 'smack' back into the water, Ken's little bit of remaining reasoning abandoned him totally.

Using both hands like giant shovels, digging the water in front of him into a frothy foam Ken dragged himself forward through the normally restrictive liquid almost as easily as if it were only air. Somewhere along the way, his mind must have envisioned the greedy razor-sharp teeth of the fish nibbling as his stately manhood, because he suddenly found himself pushing his naked body up and out of the pools liquid entrapment, even before Georges' now totally submerged body had a chance to even resurface.

The excitement that had started as soon as the aquarium had landed in the pool grew even louder now as all there suddenly realized that Ken was standing among them, naked as the day he was born in his 'birthday suit', except for the watch he was wearing that is. Only a few of them had bothered after that to let their attention shift briefly back to the pool in time to watch George finally emerge out of the water. But even they soon rejoined everyone's building humorous excitement when a series of short bright white flashes briefly illuminated the air around them.

There could be no doubt now that a camera was busy making its presence know. But things were still in such a confused state that no one yet realized the full potential of what was actually happening. No-one that is, except Ken, as his still excited racing thoughts told him that only 'he' and his present lack of attire seemed to be the new main topic of focus in the camera's eye.

As his hands once again instinctively repositioned themselves over his temporarily forgotten and exposed 'hammer', this was the first time in his life that he could ever remember wishing that it was indeed smaller than it actually looked. As someone in the crowd said, 'Poor Kim.' his slowly returning reasoning started to tell him that things were somehow not exactly what they seemed to be. It was also a soon to be proven sense of reality, even as all of those around him broke out into sidesplitting laughter. Laughter that was totally justified and confirmed when George's almost hysterical form positioned itself directly in front of him, while trying to hum the theme music from the ever famous shark movie 'jaws'.

Suddenly, instead of bewildered confusion filling Ken's head, it was just plain anger that started to make its presence known. The blush that leapt to his face was now through the realization that he had been used, used as a laughing figure for everyone else's pleasure. And as the words, "Why, why, you, you,!" stuck in his throat, George cut him off laughingly with, "Now you know how terrified all the fish you've bloody swallowed alive over the years must have felt!"

The swimsuit that had remained so evasive earlier suddenly appeared as if on cue in front of Ken's surrounded nude form. By now, even though his face was still noticeably flushed with anger, even his wife had joined in on all comical and verbal remarks still filling the air. But it took the sudden bright illumination from the camera in Fred's hands to cause Ken to spring into a responsive reaction.

Suddenly lunging forward while remarking, "Gimme that bloody thing!" his left hand exposed the territory it had sworn to cover while snapping out to grab his swimsuit. His right hand also was on a mission of its own as it tried to snatch the instrument that had been recording his embarrassing condition. It was an attack that failed to reward him with the camera, but did manage to have him comically end-up back in the pool after miscalculating his angry steps. And ironically, it had all been arranged when he had left a trail of water puddling after having climbed out of the pool only moments earlier.

The sight and sound of Ken, this time it was him screaming, while hitting the water just naturally drew everyone once more like the ever proverbial magnet back to around the pool's perimeter. And as their loud commotion again grew in hysterical antics, a sudden burst of shoving soon had almost half of them joining him in the pool, drinks, clothing and all. Then finally out of those who had managed to avoid being knocked into the water, only about six didn't voluntarily themselves join those in the churning wet liquid.

Such behavior soon gave two of the men, Chris and Terry, a chance to use the old comical routine of one laying on his back while the other primed one of his legs like an old water pump. The horizontal form in turn would then start spewing a stream of water out of his mouth, just like he was a fountain. As always it was much the way things went, all pain and no gain, one of the jokers along the way stealing Woody's wooden leg. And when Ken finally managed to get a few undisturbed moments alone with George, each smiling into each others face although being able to read one another's thoughts, he lets his words drip with intimidation. "Of course you know this isn't the end of your little prank. I'll get even with you, and then some, for as long as it takes."

George, even though his body was now dry, let the words roll off his back while chuckling, "I'm sure everyone hopes it's not the end of our little 'get even' prank. You know why?" he taunted him. "Cause I know we're going to have a lot more fun with it yet. And I sure as Hell hope you're willing to keep your threat for revenge!"

Anyone close bye to see their attitudes in motion would have just thought they were in all likelihood planning something else. But it wasn't just their antics that went on well past eleven o'clock.

By this time most of the younger kids had either disappeared into the warm sanctuary of the house in order to watch a movie, or a place of chosen privacy for their own benefit, such as Darryll and Patty had. The so-called adults on the other hand, were well inebriated and still going strong in antics and loud conversation about everything from what had happened so far, as well as finding Judy's and Betty Faylen's friend Lucy Carlson spread-eagled the proverbial 'tits up', passed out in one of the lawn chairs. It was all just more of what gave no indication of wearing down.

Randy, his wife only now noticing that he had accidentally put his running shoes on wrong, was also well into the making of an absolutely envious great hangover. And when Tracy said to him, "You're wearing your shoes on the wrong feet hon." he groggily looked down at them and hesitated only a few inebriated seconds before answering, "No I don't! These are the only feet I've got!"

Most had returned to their original seating arrangements, George junior and the rest of the 'Hubba Bubba Club' having positioned themselves close-by, just enough so that they could if necessary become a part of the silly happenings. And it was during one of these pauses, after someone had noticed that Pop Bottles was missing, but his glasses weren't, that Helen found him sitting at the bar in the basement, talking to a mirror image of himself. Plus there was Rusty saying to Kim, after his own latest journey to the 'little boys room' as some of the woman would attest, "I just love using a washroom after a woman."

Kim in turn, not normally slower than the average 'beaver', foolishly replied, "Why? A man doesn't have to sit down to 'squirt'."

"Hell no!" Rusty quickly shot back, total satisfaction grinning on his thanks for the opportunity to use one of his favorite standard answers, "But it sure is lovely to have a nice warm toilet seat to rest one's doniker on when taking that much needed tinkle."

But unfortunately with the good vibrations occasionally there also came along a little irritation. Someone along the way had made the foolish mistake of reviving Lucy with a pail of water from the pool. And she in turn was trying to persuade Fred into dancing with her, in the pretext that it would warm her up. And the amount of antifreeze being consumed by all, everyone realizing that it was damn close to 'last call for alcohol', was more than enough to let normally controlled logic and inhibitions go for a walk, with Nancy being no different than the others.

Not wanting to make a scene or endanger their renewed torrid relationship, even though it was obvious Fred was doing everything within his power to politely unwrap the octopus tugging as him, Nancy made sure that he alone caught the short wink of her eye.

"I'm afraid I'm starting to get a really bad headache hon."

She also, as everyone else smiled, wrapped one of her own arms around Fred's while saying, "It's been a long day. Why don't we turn in early tonight hon, tomorrow's going to be another busy one."

Most of the woman there, as someone in the background shouted, "Let me be the first to thank you for leaving!" gave an understanding wink of their own, while independently saying that they all understood and hoped her headache would soon go away. But Lucy, even after Judy and Betty had also tried to redirect her interest, persistently asked, "And do you get these headaches very often?"

In an almost sarcastic catty grin that only another woman on the prowl would fully understand, Nancy showed more 'teeth' then 'claw' this time, while answering and flaunting her grip still on hr. husband's arm.

"Not so much in the past, 'Dearie.' But I've got a funny feeling that they're going to pop up just often enough in the future."

Never in the past on similar such occasions had Fred and Nancy been the first to leave, for just regular or any special get together. In fact, it was generally the opposite, they often had to be reminded that they had a home of their own, 'anyplace' but where they presently were. But since there is always a first time for everything known, apparently tonight was to be 'their' time to call it quits first, and head for the exit. And as they did exactly that, both Judy and George almost protectively walked them to their parked vehicle, but not until George had made sure that at least one of them was sober enough to keep their car pointed safely in the right direction.

Things had gone a lot better then anticipated, especially after his earlier conversation with Judy after she had warned him that she had invited Lucy. And when she had then tried to get out of what she had done, after hubby had asked her why Lucy was alone, by saying that the only reason she had shown up without a companion is that it had been to late to find anyone available. To which he, as always, had instantly put his foot in his mouth by adding, 'Ya, I can see your point, especially since it's now against the law to tamper with a grave.'

Each of them inwardly wanted to talk about what was happening between the two of them, but the sudden familiar sounding loud rattle of a motor working overtime cut their time alone together short. Making sure to emphasize how happy he was that they were back together, George excused himself, but not before punching Fred's arm and promising to talk to him tomorrow. As he ran back into the yard, mischief on his face and mind, Judy explained with humor in her voice that the loud sound of an approaching snow-blower coming from their neighbor's yard was all about, and just what George in all probability would be doing about it.

Almost as soon as George had disappeared into the house, his guests already laughing about what was going on, the ear piercing sound of a speeding locomotive that gave every indication of passing within feet of the house made even Judy laughingly shout, "See what I mean! This is how they get even with each other lately. It also let's Betty know that it's time to come home."

Induced to quickly climb into the car, their hands over their ears to help block out as much of the strange mixture of noises now filling the midnight air as they could, Fred smiled for the both of them while saying in a forced loud voice." Somehow I think it's a very good idea to leave now!" He then, between smiling and shaking his head, started his car and slowly crept off into the night.

Judy, now alone after having returned Fred and Nancy's departing wave, silently mouthed the words 'Drive carefully and hurry back!', couldn't help but grin at the childish antics of 'hubby' and Jim next door. And as she wondered to herself how he kept his high revving snow blower from blowing up, her train of thought was broken by the approach of Betty briskly walking in her direction. And as she first apologized sternly for Jims immaturity by promising to give him a good smack across the back of his head, her temperament did a total about change and smiled "Thanks for the invite Judy. I'll call you tomorrow and check to see if and when the coast is clear before I come over." Smiling back, "I'll do worse then that to George. I'll accidently misplace or even burn that tape of his , just as soon as he has a chance to put his mind onto shit disturbing someone else." She then likewise returned Betty's goodnight wave, before walking back in to join the almost just as loud party.

Dropping her tired frame back into the seat it had vacated only moments earlier, her heart skipped a beat when she scolded herself for saying, "perfect timing." when her cheeks registered on the first drops of rainwater starting to fall from the black overhead void. Grudgingly getting right back out of her seat, the gathering now active for just the same reason, the laughter that had been at home in their throats for most of the night stayed there, as she watched and listened to the rest of her hustling departing company.

Rushing towards their own vehicle, kids darting everywhere to gather up their things, Chris and Vicki shouted in Judy's direction as they passed, "Don't bother George! We'll all throw ourselves out!"

Hobbling by, the ensuing rain no doubt probably making whoever had hidden his leg earlier return it, Jamie Weir smiled while putting one hand out palm upwards, and offering, "As always, thanks' for the wonderful night of entertainment, and tell George I'll catch him at work next week." And in keeping with the humor that had been a constant companion with them throughout the night, a few of the others offered comical suggestions about what was really going on, with the one that

George was probably on the other side of the house causing the rain with the garden hose, just to get rid of us?" being the best.

Now that they had mentioned it, Judy said to herself, it was exactly the type of stunt George would be capable of playing if really wanting to encourage company to leave, but it wasn't. And for some strange reason, for which she would later scold herself, she briefly glanced in the direction of the accused culprit still resting in its hanger at the side of the house. Besides, she smiled to herself, if hubby wanted to give them a hint to head home, he'd want to do it face to face, just so he could enjoy the mixed variety of expressions on their gates. Like the time nearing the end of another of their legendary parties he'd slipped away, only to reappear in a pair of gaudy pajamas, whose she never really found out. And then stood at the opened front door while winding an alarm clock, periodically putting up one of his hands to his yawning mouth.

At the sight of the next couple leaving Judy started to reach for an umbrella close-by, and had it ready to offer in their direction just as they were within feet of where she was standing. But as soon as Eagle Beaks wife detected the offering of shelter she waved it off, while saying, "No thanks! I'll just walk under Terry's nose!"

Finally walking back out of the once more quiet house, one hand holding a new refreshment as the other overflowed itself with potato ships, George raised the drink and shouted his own rendition of 'Thanks for leaving!' in everyone's quickly disappearing direction. And in that same instant, as if suddenly remembering something apparently very important, he shouted, "Wait! Hold it! Hold it! the hand filled with chips letting them fly in all directions as he waved it over his head in such a manner to enhance his excited voice. "I almost forgot, we still got one last thing to do before we can call this a great night!"

Judy, hoping that she was going to finally get to tell George about the strange incident with the colored women and child from earlier in the day, accepted that she was just going to have to wait a little bit longer. And as she watched George first whisper something into the small circle of men still there, something which seemed to have the capability of rejuvenating them, she couldn't help but smile along with the remaining women as they watched the childish gathering disappear around the far side of the house.

Once more finding and filling her chair, Judy sat back and briefly enjoyed just her own company for the moment. Maybe, she thought to herself, while also wondering what kind of hellish prank her screwball hubby and gang could possibly be up to at this time of the night, it could be a blessing in disguise. With any luck he would be to 'pooped, or pissed', to question her deeply about what had happened earlier. As of now, she merely wanted to get the nights activities out of the way. Ribbing him about what the woman had been trying to insinuate, no matter 'what' it was really all about, after swearing Betty to an oath of silence, was something she had no intention of sharing with anyone else, at least not just yet.

Chapter 10

'Bare Knuckles and Knees'
Or
'A show of affection'

Being a Monday and the start of another new workweek was normally in itself bad enough. But having more unpredicted damp drizzling rain added on top of it was definitely adding insult to injury for George and most of the regular carpool riders. Also for strange reasons, and the very cause why they were close to fifteen minutes ahead of their regular schedule, the least bit of water or snow always made most drivers cautiously over react. And as such it presently dictated the reason they were presently travelling as such an irritably allotted for slow speed.

But fortunately for George and his coworkers this time, Saturday nights' barbecue and Friday's close call with death was still fresh enough in their thoughts to give them more than enough subject matter to jokingly whittle away at the usually monotonous long moments. Nothing and no-one, again, was left ignored as they systematically relived each humorous moment they had experienced during those nights, with Ken and the fish-tank just naturally being the absolute highlight of their conversations.

"I never once said you were an alcoholic." George grinned. "All I remarked is that if you ever accidentally caught on fire you'd probably burn for five days. And just because you're wearin' your favorite 'scratch and sniff' tee shirt don't think anyone's going to be fooled because it's hiding your gut."

"Hardy har." Ken shot back. "Next time you walk past a mirror do a profile. Anymore calories and I'm sure Judy's going to have to take a piece of furniture out of the front room next time you want to go in there for a sit down."

Now even the spontaneous incident on Saturday where some of the men before leaving for home had picked up George's irritated next door neighbors small European car and deposited it on the next adjoining family's lawn came next to hilarity. But when George started to whistle in Pop Bottles direction, the old Gene Autry's 'I'm back in the saddle again.' an accepted tune they all from past similarly related experiences with resumed sex after childbirth, their happy mood continued to evade the 'Monday blahs', especially when a small blush of acknowledgement instantly broke out onto the Bottles face.

After their arrival, their funny mixed half run and quick walk from the parking lot into the plant was made even more humorous looking by the way they had each pulled the back of their spring jackets up over their heads in an effort to keep dry. In doing so it had forced their arms to stick out sideways just enough so that they resembled a group of galloping penguins at play. And when two of the plants tough and rougher looking women grinned while passing them, George mistakenly thought that it was no doubt because of their comical looking appearance, or just maybe they had already heard about Saturday's get-together. In fact, he was so pleased with their reaction that he totally kept to himself the thought, 'I wonder if they're somehow related. They both have the same moustache.'

The trip to the change-house was just long enough for George to comment, "How many stations can you get with that thing?" as they passed miserable Motor Mouth's umbrella totting figure. And when he was instantly rewarded with an expected, "Kiss my ass!" George felt totally justified to laughingly answer, "Okay! But get your nose out of the way first." before leaving him behind them, once more having to fight only the wind. Ken, talking to no-one in particular, mumbled, "I'd like to kiss his ass - with the flat end of a big shovel. He's the type of guy who'd turn Santa Clause in for pissin in the snow."

"Now, now." George grinned. "Let's not be catty. I like to think of him as being a throwback to before humor was invented."

"Well as far as I'm concerned," Ken grinned. "They didn't throw him back 'soon' or 'far' enough. I could have lived without his presence long ago."

"Look," George half laughed now, one of the other men commenting, 'Who's presence - his or Santa's'?', the conversation fuelling his day, "If you're going to get into being obnoxious, why don't you try being original for a change."

"Hey!" Ken reacted, pausing only briefly in his stride before continuing, "Besides, aren't you the one who always says the good ones are worth repeating? Or do you mean something like being really 'rude and crude'?"

"Ya, exactly." George answered devilishly. "Something really vulgar, or overly stupid."

"Sure I can." Ken beamed. "But why can't you do what you're already famous for? Why don't you help somebody like that too verbally 'crash and burn'?"

Widening the distance between them as they continued to walk, George almost apologetically said, "I can't. At least not while you're still alive!"

Fred, looking healthier and by far happier then he'd had a right to be for months,' was already seated at the lunch table awaiting George's arrival. For reasons known so far only to himself and his best friend, the depressing weather outside was obviously having no noticeable effect on his presently smiling attitude. And as he held up a small brown paper bag containing the three 'survival kits' he had picked up on the way in, he grinned out, "Morning buddy." George in return, after returning both words and gestures, seated himself, while extending the pleasant gestures to everyone else also there.

"Sex sure seems to agree with you, 'Stud'." he then added, in between glancing back in Fred's direction and playing with the bag in front of him. "It looks like 'mister Pop Bottles' isn't the 'only one' who should be humming 'I'm back in the saddle again.' or at least limping a little when you walk."

Their own immediate laughter, once the rest of the men at the table realized that the little skit in front of them was over for now, was instantly acknowledged with a round of mixed smiles and contagious 'Mornings!' as well as laughter from everyone else there. But it wasn't until the foreman decided to make an early visit to their gathering that things really verbally got going, especially since George was noticeably wearing one of his best tee shirts that read 'Some people are like a baby's diaper when they're on someone's ass. It's usually because they're full of 's - - t!'

Feebly making his presence known by faking a small cough, while also frowning his disapproval after having read the lettering on the shirt, the Evil Dwarf waited until he had everyone's attention before finally speaking. "I don't know if any of you have heard or were involved, but we've had a few lockers broken into sometime during the weekend again. We haven't at this time been able to find out who the culprit or culprits are as of yet, but the standard forms for compensation of stolen articles are available in the office if any of you need to make a legitimate claim."

Without even a second's hesitation George, in one of his best shows of seriousness, snapped out, "Good! I lost a Ford Escort and a 36" front projection color television set!"

Only the Dwarf filed to laugh at the silly remark. But when someone else half-heartedly added, "I finally lost that old measuring tape you gave me."

"Ya, I'll bet you did." the foreman smiled, No doubt trying to be a part of the gathering. And when he added, " You probably lost it in your garage, like half of the other stuff that goes missing around here, no doubt for company." His attempt at humor only fell half flat on its face. And when a loud round of elongated 'He-e-e-e-re's' from a few of the men filled the air around the table, George content to remain quiet and let the Dwarf enjoy the moment, someone else remarked, "Did you check all the foremen's lockers first?"

The Dwarfs 'nature', as it did now, often worked against him as he snapped out, "I'm not accusing or saying anyone here is guilty of anything, just as I'm not eliminating anyone either."

Rusty, while winking at the other men, lost no time in retaliating with, "Boy! Somebody's sure wearing the touchy skin off their ass on their forehead this morning. I'll bet there's something else you're not telling us. What's really wrong?"

What was left of the happy mood, dropped to a lower level, as the Dwarf's face, now void of any pleasant looking emotion, snapped out, "What are you, the 'shop cop'?" And then, as if an almost second thought, those of the men not in shock snickering, he quickly added, "Or do you know more than what everybody else does around here?"

"I'm afraid you're giving him to much credit." George butted in, in an effort to relieve the noticeable tension now in the air. "He not only doesn't know any more than everyone else around here, I'm pretty sure it's safe to say he knows a 'Hell' of a lot less then everyone else around here, even 'Joe' the janitor!"

The Dwarf, even though a slight blush had leapt to his face, as one of the workers yelled out at George 'What the 'shit' you picking on 'Joe' for?" was just smart enough to realize that the tension that had been in the air a moment ago, was gone. And as he cursed at himself for once more failing to keep the promise he had made to avoid such similar situations, everyone's attention was diverted by the verbal arrival of Bill Langley. "Morning everyone! what's on the menu for today?"

In a short abbreviated sentence, between his arrival being verbally recognized and the Dwarf pretending to busy himself with the papers in his hands, Fred quickly brought him up to date. And the big grin that instantly appeared on his face totally confused the other men, until he said, "You mean nobody here knows that our mister Farkas' locker was broken into also? Only instead of taking something 'out', some 'sick, sick, sick person' put something rather disgusting 'in'!"

There was no doubt in anybody's mind that Bill had been strictly overly polite when talking about their foreman, undoubtedly because he was standing right their within eavesdropping range. And the looks of confusion that had blossomed on most of the men's faces grew even broader, as one of them willing to play the part of a shit disturber asked, "Huh? What are you 'barkin about?" while glancing in Farkas' still noticeably irritated direction.

Looking into the glare that was now diverted at him alone, Bill nodded slightly in the Dwarfs position, while adding, "I think it would be more polite if I let him tell you. What I heard was only second hand 'poop' and I might get the 'messy' details all out of proportion." an even bigger grin now growing on his face.

Of all the now suddenly slightly grinning faces that were turning in the foreman's direction, George's was no doubt the sadistically happiest. The Evil Dwarf in turn, the red on the whole of his face now an almost purple blush, stared mostly straight ahead while forcing the answer he was choking on out of his mouth.

"Someone! Somebody, with an apparent 'sickness' - 'excreted' into a paper bag." The words still obviously having trouble being born, "And then, then they were sick, mentally degraded enough to -."

Before he could finish tripping over the rest of what could only be the remainder of what was left to say, someone, one of the other men apparently now emotionally tickled by what his mind had figured out what was yet to come, blurted out, 'Holy shit!'

It was an exclamation that only George could instantly pick up on, and quickly add to. "Say - - isn't that what you get from 'sacred cows in India'?"

As the men instantly reacted to the silly remark, in their expected usual manner, the Dwarf had to raise his unimpressed voice above theirs to be heard. "And as soon as I find out who is responsible, 'he' or 'they' will be 'fired' immediately, 'on the spot'!"

Sometimes to quick for his own good, like now, George had to bite his tongue in order not to deliver the overly rather obvious reply of 'You mean in like in 'Johnny on the spot?' So instead he delivered the next, and what he thought might be an even funnier and closer to the truth remark, "Hold it! You can't 'fire' us! Unless the rules have changed. You have to 'sell' a 'slave'."

With what looked like foamy acid forming around the rim of his mouth, the Dwarf didn't care who was listening as he snarled, "Always the wise-ass! You think you know the answer to just about everything, don't you?"

"Let's just conservatively say," George smirked. "I've probably gone and forgotten more than you'll ever know."

"Don't say that!" Fred quickly cut in with, much to everyone else's surprise. But when he next said, "That would still classify you as legally brain dead."

No-one lost any time in understanding the unexpected putdown, contagiously laughing out-loud almost instantly, which only fanned the flame under the foreman's still building irritation.

Suddenly, as if deliberately rigged to break up the brewing verbal battle between George and the Dwarf, the company's shift starting horn let out one singular long irritating ear piercing blast. The foreman, his raised blood pressure induced face just as flustered as when he had started, froze the comment on the tip of his tongue "As far as I'm concerned, you all got 'shit' for brains!" instead said, "Alright everybody ,same jobs, and I'll visit you later. Now let's get to work. And try to stay away from the shops motto, "If it isn't broke, break it!"

George again wanted to reply, "You shouldn't use words you don't know the meaning of." but instead simply smiled before turning in Fred's direction to give him a short know-it-all wink, while standing erect. He then smiled at no-one in particular, while saying, "Well gentlemen, so far it looks like it's got the makings of a great week."

As the rest of the men at the table slowly climbed out of their seats and started for their jobs, a smile also on their faces, Farkas repositioned himself in front of Fred and George's forms, just as Bob in a half run joined them.

"Sorry I'm a bit late boss!" he more panted then said. "But I'm afraid I'm not used to your local traffic yet, and this bit of rain threw me."

Only George and Fred's grins were for real as they each smiled in his direction. And after George commented, "If you think it's bad now, wait till payday." Farkas lost no time in continuing with what he was there for. "Is there even the remotest chance of the three of you getting that mill job finished sometime this week?"

"What, are you grumbling about now?" George almost snarled back, in an attitude almost identical to the one apparently still looking for an excuse to argue.

"You've been farting around with that job for almost a month now!" the Dwarf shot back. "We've got other breakdowns waiting for repairs ya' know!"

"Look!" George smiled, Bob and Fred wise enough to remain spectators, as he drew out the words, "Stop, treating, us, like, prostitutes. We, are, not, on, 'piecework'!"

If there was any good in the animosity between the Dwarf and George, it was that either could say to each other exactly was on their minds at any given time, now being a prime example as the foreman snapped back. "You could be. Especially the way you're 'effin' the bloody job to death!"

"Whoa!" George retaliated. "It's not our fault that when we go to the overloaded storage area to pick up ordered pieces for the job it takes so long to find them. What are we supposed to work from, 'blueprints' or 'treasure maps'? We backtrack to the missing parts to the company stores, wait in line for two hours to be served by someone who just short of suggesting that you should sacrifice your 'first born' before he can serve you. Then, after another half-hour wait, he comes back from who knows where they've gone to hide to say that he can't find the parts either, but will put them on backorder. We in turn, 'knowing' that you are thinking we're milking the 'proverbial cow dry', hunt down what we can from one of the storage areas through-out the company containing any extra parts not used from past repairs. Now, is this a legitimate excuse to argue over, or are you just trying to get even with whoever you can for what someone did to your locker? Get your thinking off 'search and destroy' before you 'self destruct'! You already know none of us are 'Jewish', therefore that can't be why you're on our asses. So if it is the locker incident, and you want to give 'shit' 'back' to the person responsible for why it happened, then you're going to have to find a mirror. Then you're going to have to stand in front of it and take a good look at the person looking back at you, for awhile."

Glancing briefly at Fred and Bob, both men smiling and looking as if they had just taken a big breath of air to regain the wind spent on George's long speech, Farkas pretended not to understand the good advice that was just indirectly given to him.

"And just 'what' is that supposed to mean?"

By this time all of the other workers had disappeared into the buildings interior. But for what George had on his mind, he wasn't really looking for an audience.

"What it means," standing almost toe to toe with each other, "is that you are your own worst enemy around here. Your attitude 'sucks' and your personality is the 'shits', to which is no secret plant wide. Whither you can accept it or not the truth of the matter is that the men like us working under your 'thumb' are the real ones responsible for making this place perform. The sooner you get the fact into your head that the more you aggravate or try to screw any one of us, the more you're committing suicide. And with the way you treat everybody lately, the only one I think of who would be glad to see you, is someone visually impaired."

"I don't need 'you' or 'anybody's' help!" Farkas said stiff faced.

"Yes I know." George acknowledged. "And if I was on 'fire' and you were the only one close to me with a pail of water in your hands, I wouldn't let you 'throw' it on me either! But that's what everybody around here expects the two of us to feel about each other. I know it's a form of entertainment for most of the men, but for me I just look at it as a sort of game. And believe it or not, I always kind-uv thought you took most of it the same way. So take, or leave. And if you plan on leaving it, just make sure you're willing to step right into the shit as deep as we are. "

George's last words', as almost always, had an immediate effect on those within hearing range. So justifiably Bob and Fred were having trouble suppressing the laughter now building within their bodies. And as much as it was on the tip of Bob's tongue to say, "Boy' I'm sure glad I haven't got your nerve in my bad tooth." he instead wisely bit his lip. In itself, Fred still silently just smiling, it was a very wise decision, as he tried to look as neutral a bystander as his limited acting ability would allow him to be.

But old Farkas continued to be almost expressionless as he asked, "Are you really speaking for everyone? Or is it just your own opinion you're expressing?"

With a soft smile that he normally only shared with those very close to him, George did something that even he wouldn't have believed himself capable of at any other time, he was genuinely sincere when he next spoke.

"Look. Believe it or not, I actually do enjoy out little occasional verbal spats. But that's the way I am. Now if I was really the only one who felt about you the way I had just 'said', then I would tell you right off to your 'puss' that if you stay out of my face, I will stay out of your stomach. But then again, if it's a 'coronary' you're really lookin for, then I can be the right guy to keep 'buttin heads' with."

Strangely, Farkas made no effort to interrupt or even question any of the information being offered, which didn't slow George down one bit.

"Now then, since I am trying to give you a little bit of 'free advice', if you'll notice I didn't use the word 'friendly', I said 'free'. I'm sure that if you start treating everybody around here just a teensy bit more human, then I'm also sure they'll start acting it. 'Plus', if you even mention to any of the other men our little conversation, the three of us here will totally deny any part of it ever having taken place. 'And', to make it even easier on your ego and more appealing, 'I' don't have to be in that group."

The humor that had been showing on Bob's and Fred's grinning pusses had slowly drained away with each passing word out of George's mouth. It was as if they both had found it hard to accept what their ears had been a party to, even if what their buddy had just said was already common knowledge to everyone else, everybody accept the Dwarf that is. And when Farkas recognized their confused reactions for what they were, he also did something almost totally against his expected nature. For the first time since any of them could remember, even if it was being forced, he smiled just as softly as his voice sounded, "I thank you, for being so honest." before turning and walking away.

In stunned belief, more Fred than Bobs, their chins as if joined at the lip, slowly sagged with each step of the Dwarfs departing figure. And just when it looked as if he was about to go into noticeable epileptic shock, which instantly changed Bob's reactions back into laughter, Fred stammered in George's direction. "I don't 'believe' what I just heard and saw. Am I hallucinating! Or is this some kind of sick conspiracy you and the other men have concocted and are playing on us? - Aren't you at least going to harpoon him with one of your old 'ego slamming' favorites, 'Hurry back! Or, 'Thanks for leaving!'?"

"No, not this time." George half smiled, while also watching their foreman disappear. "Although, I will admit there were times I'd have given a million dollars or more, just to get the sound of his voice out of my memory."

Then, as if suddenly realizing just how nauseatingly friendly he had just been with a man he had jokingly said on more than one occasion that he wouldn't walk across the street to look at him in his coffin. Only to quickly add, 'On second thought, oh yes I would, just to make sure he was really in it! 'Hell'! I must be getting old!"

Fred, still shaking his head in disbelief, instantly added. "Or going 'senile'! If that man's got any 'friends', I've never met 'him'!"

"As I said earlier," everyone else by now had long disappeared,

to which was easily quickly confirmed by a series of short related glances split among the three of them. "I think I must be getting old enough to start showing signs of degenerating to the funny farm."

For some strange reason it seemed to be effecting Fred the most, as he continued to slowly twist his head back and forth sideways, while muttering to himself. Bob meanwhile, not having enough history between his foreman and George, remained just a grinning bystander as Fred finally offered. "Or all that alcohol you've been pouring down your gullet over the years is finally starting to pickle your grey matter." And as George instantly started to node his grinning head in confirmation to his friends' suggestion, Fred kept right on slamming him. "And if we can believe that theory, then it sure justifies why you're also starting to look as rough as you do!"

Maybe it was just because they were presently so involved with the Dwarf or even due to the fact Fred presently had enough emotional problems on his plate, but George totally let the barbs slide, while saying, "If nothing else, it'll drive ol' Farkas crazy for the next hour or two wondering if I was really being honest with him, or just setting him up for something else."

"Boy! I'm sure glad none of the other guys were around to hear any of that sickening dribble." Fred then frowned "Along with ruining our tarnished reputation, they'd also think you've lost your toe hold on reality."

"From what I've seen so far," Bob grinned, " I doubt it!" And as both Fred and George glanced curiously in his direction between their walking forms, he carried on with the rest of what was in his thoughts. "From what you told me about your barbecue by the time it gets around the rest of plant about what you said you did to Ken, Nobody will ever believe you were capable of treating their foreman the way you did back there. It's just not your nature. By the way, how the Hell 'did' he get to be foreman?"

"Probably by being someone's 'love toy'" Fred chuckled. Then, just realizing what Bob had said about Ken, he quickly added, "Say, how'd you get to know about the barbecue?"

Before Bob could answer, George cut him off with the real truth. "Do you think you were the only guy I phoned yesterday?"

Letting out a soft chuckle of his own in acceptance of the answer, George caught him off guard by throwing his hip sideways just enough to knock his unsuspecting form off balance, sending it into Bob's just as surprised and unprepared body. But it wasn't enough of a distraction, as Bob's reflex's returned the 'pinball' like ricochet maneuver, to keep him from continuing with, "Ya, I guess you're right. I'd say there's still no fear of anyone accusing the ol 'Axe-Man', or should I say, 'Mister Acid Tongue" of ever getting close enough to the 'Evil Dwarf' to be referred to a touchy hemorrhoid. Ah, pardon me, or should I have said 'asteroid'!"

Fred's attempt at humor worked simultaneously on all of them, which they kept going by taking turns telling Bob in detail more about of what had happened at the party he had missed, as well as in detail what had happened at the 'Meat Market.

If there is any 'real truth' to the 'old wives tale' about when if someone was talking about you your ears would be burning. Or that if a chill ran down your spine it was because they had just trampled across your grave site. Then George's neck should presently be like an equator with his ears burning to a crisp, with his back cold enough to make ice cubes on. Far across the plant, in one of the women's washrooms, he was presently being raked back and forth across the proverbial 'hot coals' by a group of ladies with only one thing on their revenge filled mind's, Georges demise.

"That's too damn simple!" Carla snapped, her face distorted to match the thoughts of painful vengeance she was presently experiencing inside her minds eye. "He'll not only see that immature prank comin a block away, he'll also know it was pulled by us. If we're going to get revenge," she continued, while slamming the fist of her right hand into the palm of her left for effect, "we're going to have to make sure it's something simple enough to trick his male 'ego' into letting itself be embarrassingly trapped!"

"Well, after Friday's retched attempt, he isn't exactly really going to believe just anything that come along now." Mary added.

"Our biggest mistake was in thinking that we could get at him through his wife." Carla frowned. "She's obviously been conditioned not to believe anything out of the ordinary that her husband might be mixed up with."

"Guarantied it was a 'great' idea, but did it ever dawn on any one of us to try and find out in advance if he'd had a 'vasectomy'. And if so, 'when'?" one of the women asked.

"I'd sure like a chance to 'fix' him!" Carla continued to carry on. She was in one of her moods where if she presently came across any of the men within the plant, they had better be prepared to defend themselves, or at least one of them should be carrying a tranquillizer gun. "Only I'd have used a dull rusty knife!" she quickly added.

"Ya right!" someone else laughed. "Why don't you just tell it like it is. You'd really like to use your teeth, wouldn't you?"

"Or maybe even 'bloodless' castration. You know, like they do with cattle." Kit snickered. "With bolt cutters!" she added, an invisible pair now being held out in front of her, busy squeezing the mentioned appendage of just an also invisible animal.

"Knock it off!" Carla growled, in between glaring at those in their gathering who were now still smirking or now grimacing at Kit's remark, while pacing the floor. "We're here to get at 'George Stone', not each other!"

"Well, I thought for sure he had his sidekick's 'chestnuts' in the proverbial 'ringer' after we'd accidentally found out about 'hooker' and poker night. Especially when we tipped his separated wife off." Kit added more seriously now.

"Hooker, and, poker!" one of the women started to giggle, and then laugh uncontrollably. And when the so called lady beside her asked he just what the Hell was so funny, she answered, "Don't you get the connection between the two words? Think of it. What do you do with a prostitute, a 'hooker'? You, 'poke', her! Get it? 'Poker'!"

It took almost a whole minute for Carla to be able to glare away the instantaneous laughter that had broke out. But as always, she soon had full control of the gathering once more.

Of the five women there, and mainly because it was her name and embarrassing situation a week earlier that they were presently using as a crowbar to want revenge on the men in the plant, Louie was definitely more emotionally worked up. But it was strictly for an altogether different set of reasons. At first, she had meekly tried to talk the gathering out of their idea for seeking vengeance on any of the men, especially since Mister Stone had been singled out as the one to be the victim. But when the older and definitely more aggressive women in the gathering had loudly protested her strange behavior, she wisely decided to follow in with their ideas, solely with intent of keeping the attack as non-violent as possible. And the comment about most men being lower than snake shit in a wagon rut, would have to run its own course into oblivion.

"I wish I had never been born with these things!" Louie frowned, her eyes pointing down at the well-formed mounds she was referring to. "They're all some immature men ever think about."

"Damn!" Mary said a little wistfully. "If you can think of any way to transfer them over here honey, I'll be glad to take their burden off you chest!"

Once more most of the women started to chuckle, even a now blushing Louie, at the pun just made. But it all quickly faded when Carla added, "It just goes with what I've been telling you people all along. All men are 'pigs'! And I wouldn't trust any of them, even if they were related to the Pope."

"Well when it comes to endowments, they're a problem if you've got them dearie, and a bigger problem if you don't." a voice of apparent experience sighed.

"Okay. So, as easy as it would have been with a grease-gun, filling George Stone's locker full of axle grease is out of the question." Kit now said, getting the subject back on track, her favorite tee shirt 'Beware of dog!' getting full exposure as she joined Carla pacing back and forth in front of them. Some of the crueler men, never George, when taking their turn at expressing their displeasure about not just Kit. But also the other rougher looking man-haters, had even gone so far as the old, 'Did you get the name of the truck that hit ya?' "But we have to think of something real soon, or the men will get the silly idea they can pull pranks on us and get away with it anytime the want to."

"They already think that." Carla frowned. "But not all of the 'rats' out there are happily serving their 'life sentences'. We'll just have to a bit more careful and dig a little deeper into their marriages."

"Too bad 'black balling' is strictly a man's prank." Mary chuckled, as a women's crude rendition of raunchy 'wolf whistles and calls' instantly broke out. Carla straight-faced mistaken in her beliefs added, "black-balling' someone is merely a figure of speech, although I'll admit I do love the implications of the deed. Now let's get serious!"

Slight embarrassment let itself show on Mary's face, but she quickly flushed it away behind a half-disgusted mask of frustrated anger, while continuing with, "Well 'excuse' me, for thinking out-loud. I didn't nickname them "horseshoe' and 'hand grenade' just because George and his best friend Fred always seem to be someplace close-by whenever something happens to one of us. You said you wanted something sexually embarrassing. Well, as far as I'm concerned, there's nothing more painful to the male ego than playing havoc with his 'ego-testicular' pride and joyous sex organs."

Once more the women proved that they could be as 'rude and crude' as those they wished to torment, indicating that most of them eagerly agreed with Mary's statement. Then all of a sudden, as if she had just mentally discovered the true meaning of life, Carla excitedly blurted out, "Wait! Wait, that's it! By God I think I know how we can fix George Stone's and every other 'male chauvinist pig's' wagon in this plant."

Carla's' sudden enthusiasm, as well as the tone of her voice, instantly drew the gathering in tighter around her. And as she started off with the words, "Now here's our 'new plan'." each woman inquisitively leaned even closer in eager anticipation of the no doubt devious idea - eager all that is except a worrying Louie.

Meanwhile on the other side of the plant, their job site now in view, it was George's voice that again dominated the conversation. That is, still in motion, having changed only direction, not purpose.

"Hell, I'll be damned if I can figure out how he can stand up so straight. Everyone knows he's got no 'real' backbone."

"I'll say." Fred quickly offered. "Normally he wouldn't have enough courage to sneak up on a glass of water, without warning it first."

While chuckling at the description they were both giving him on one of the men they had passed along the way, Bob made no effort to verbally interrupt the humorous description still coming in his direction.

"Normally," George continued." if you told him he did a good job on something, he'd thank you for having such a high opinion of himself.

"And if Ron wasn't the type of guy that you just couldn't help but like, George would've slammed him by saying that with his ability there was really no place for him to go but up." Fred laughed.

As habitual instinct unlocked their first the tool boxes and then set the job up for working on, Bob still fresh enough to follow and acknowledge their routine, both George and Fred kept at their humorous catty remarks of recognition, with a winking George taking his turn once more.

"Why I can still remember when Ron used to complain about the muscle on the back of his neck being so tight from looking over his shoulder wondering where the foreman was, that it kept him from laying his head flat on the pillow at night."

"Not to mention that it was also responsible for him slowly drifting to that same muscle's side when he walked." Fred added, still half-laughing. "But lately, everything he puts his hand on, even if it ends up screwed, he comes out smellin like the proverbial 'bucket of roses'. I even heard some of the other guys saying they think he must have the 'almighty' on his side."

"I doubt it." George butted in, a huge smile on his face. "After some of the 'booboos' Ron's made in the past, I don't think even 'God' has that much pull!"

The instant humor that came to each of them, which was also becoming much more frequent, had them laughing in almost unison when Bob finally added something to the conversation.

'I don't know how things are arrange around here, but from where I came such treatment as he's been getting generally can only mean one thing, the company's 'groomin' the guy for a foreman's position."

"Of course. That's got to be it!" Fred chuckled. "Well it won't require much of a change in position as far as he's concerned. Instead of 'kneeling down' he'll be just 'bending down!'

"Easy does it." George said. "He's still one of us remember."

"What else could it be?" Fred continued. "The way he's been darting around here from job to job lately, he picks up any more speed and he'll probably be able to get the wife pregnant even before she realizes that she's been 'diddled'."

"Or at least enter a new 'time zone." Bob chuckled, until he realized that he was working alone.

"Could be. But I sure hope not." George said dryly this time. "Personally I liked ol' Ron a lot better when he was so pessimistic about always coming in last on everything, especially the 'human race'."

"Kept him kind of humble, didn't it?" Fred smiled softly.

"Ya." George grinned back. "And he's so used to lookin' at nothin' but 'assholes and elbows' I doubt if he'd recognize just anybody face to face. I just can't envision him having enough intestinal fortitude to go through the ol' 'bare knuckles and knees' routine under the foreman's desk. But, what the Hell, let's not commit him until we're sure he's certifiable. Besides, ya know my standard theory on rumors, 'they're all born pregnant, and have the tendency to have multiple births by the time they've traveled the full distance of the shop."

Work, as was universal throughout the plant, was having a tendency to get in the way of their spermatic conversations. But as inconvenient as it presently was, they dug in and did just enough of it to financially ensure that the company's stocks didn't presently go 'tits up' on the stock, market. And even when Dick Dryden, alias "Sominex', showed up briefly in search of something he needed for his job site, they surprisingly kept right on working as they talked. In fact, their strange behavior was instantly rewarded by Dick with the comment, "Look, I don't mind if you guys want to do imitations of what 'real' workers do, and work your assholes off while I'm around, but do me a favor while I'm still here will ya, don't get to close. With my luck lately your phobia for imitating physical activity just might be dangerously contagious. and I'm in no mood for visiting 'detox central'.

Even as they chuckled as the remarks, Fred couldn't help but feel justified to use one of George's favorite old put downs.

"There you go again 'Sominex', usin' words you don't even know the true meaning of, 'physical activity! - Work!'

"Very funny." Dick said sarcastically in answer to Bob and George's laughter. "But that old line's already been overworked. Can't you come up with anything at least a little more original?"

"Sure I can!" Fred beamed in his direction, while George and Bob looked on as if referees. "But the best 'slamming's' are always worth repeating whenever possible, just ask anyone."

Unfortunately for him, Ol' 'Sominex' wasn't long on standing 'toe-to-toe' with anyone to match their verbal assault for equal abuse, as was becoming evident by the slow burn now showing in his cheeks. But just as fortunately for him George knew exactly when and how to handle such situations. So he wisely waited until the two men in front of him looked like they were about to go into another of the company's many fake knock em down, Indians circling the wagons, fake fist fights, before he as 'Acid Tongue' could make an effort to take the building tension onto his own shoulders for awhile.

"Don't mind him Dick. Since the little head's been 'back in the saddle' he's been on an ego trip ever since someone told him they thought he was younger than me."

For a fraction of a second, as the realization that what he had just heard was meant to be a pun, Dick looked as if was actually about to say "But he 'is' younger than you!" he quickly caught himself and instead remarked, "Ya, but what they should have said was that unfortunately he's just ugly enough to be someone's 'father'." Little did he realize just how close he had come to the truth, especially since that information was still strictly only know in the workforce between Fred and George.

And once again only Bob was new enough to Dick's personality to be confused by his strange remark. But fortunately he was also smart enough to know that if Fred and George thought it comical enough to chuckle at, then so should he. It was also a maneuver that made Dick pause long enough to regroup his composure, after having glanced in his direction, while picking up the giant adjustable wrench he was there to borrow, before saying, " So far - the only thing I can see that you might have in common with those two out of work comedians," his head acting like a pointer, "is that you're not 'black' either."

Bob then, while biting his tongue so he wouldn't reply, "Maybe if I let you come home and kick my dog you'll feel better." Only gave one of his best forced grins, while joining George and Fred's stares in 'Sominex' departing direction. And as he walked there could be no doubt that the occasional comical looking and verbally cursed partial trip was not only for their benefit, but also to let them know that he knew very well that they were watching his departure. And not until he was totally out of sight did Bob finally say, "Boy!, is he always just short of 'exploding'?"

"Aw, he's really harmless." George answered, while letting his eyes slowly drift back onto the job in front of them. "He's like an old barking dog. His bark at times is a lot more threatening them his bite. It's not until he asks you how many wrinkles there on a big prick, and then starts to count the lines on your forehead while you're thinking about the answer, that you're in trouble."

"That, I can believe." Bob grinned. "But why the nickname 'Sominex'?"

"Oh that's just because he's generally always looking for a place to lie down and imitate the dead." Fred offered. "I'm the one who came up with that handle."

"He's one of the few men in this place that's actually got another nickname." George offered. "Sometimes they also call him 'Blister', because he has the tendency of generally showing up once the work's all done."

"And if he can't find a place to go horizontal, " Fred smiled, "he's actually perfected the ability to go to sleep vertically erect -- anytime -- anywhere -- with his eyes wide open."

"Which goes for half of the lumbering people in this place." George added, his eyes passing briefly and suggestively over Fred, no doubt hinting he just might be one of those individuals he had just slammed.

Even as he laughed, Bob offered what they used to call such workers. "You mean, 'the walking dead!'

As they all started to enjoy the remarks, Fred quickly added what the men in the plant had in similarity.

"We also have a saying something along those same lines. If you don't believe the 'dead' are capable of coming back to life, then you ought to be around here at quitting time."

Mother nature's beckoning beat the ten o'clock coffee into calling them off their job. Fred, volunteering to show Bob where a new "pit stop' was located, already knowing that he was to deliberately drag his 'bony buns' while doing it, just in case George ran into a little bit of difficulty with his part in what they had planned. George in turn, "When you guy's get back we'll have our break. Until then, I'll get a bit more done around here." turned his full attention towards doing just that.

But little did he suspect that he was far from being alone, even though he had watched his two colleges leave. A pair of eyes that had been watching him even before Bob and Fred had disappeared, checked the surrounding area one more time just to make sure that 'they' were finally alone.

Humming to himself he used a small dolly not unlike the one a mechanic would use when crawling under a car, to slide his frame beneath the supported massive hydraulic ram they were there to repair. And if his pranksters mind had been more on the task in front of him rather then what he had planned for later, he just might have been aware of the work boots now standing as the end of where his own 'shit-kickers' were protruding out from.

If their sudden presence alone were not enough to startle him once detected, then the sound of the familiar soft female whispering voice calling out his name, was. "Ah - Mister Stone. Ah, may I talk to you, please."

Between being both startled and confused George pushed the dolly his form is laying on so hard that he accidentally caught Louie off guard just enough to kick her feet out from under her. And as fate would have it, although most of the other men in the plant would have called it 'luck', her shapely body falling across his as it came out from under the machinery that a brief second earlier had been directly over him. Instantly, George wasn't the only one surprised by her wriggling presence suddenly so close to him now.

Both being shocked by the entanglement they were now in, each awkwardly, and just as comically, tried to unlock their bodies from the presently close predicament. Louie, as George finally wisely kept both of his hands tight against the sides of his body, excitedly said "I'm getting up! I'm up! I'm up!" while finally pushing herself away and erect. George, working his damndest to keep his also blushing face from smiling, inside of his head fought the words," So am I Louie! So am, I!" before realizing that he also was just short scant seconds shy of screaming wordlessly at himself, "Do-o-o-wn boy! Do-o-wn!"

Slowly standing up himself, his mind fighting his bodies instinctive emotions as Louie was nervously busy using both hands to brush away that might have stuck to her during their little close encounter, while obviously keeping her head tilted just enough to keep from making eye contact with him, George pretended to cough as he imitated her movements. All that is, except from being able to keep his eyes totally away from her shapely jiggling form, which was magnified even more by her rising and falling chest with each breath she took. And when he started to apologize for what had just happened, "I'm terribly sorry Louie, it was all my fault!" she did her best by claiming that everything was really all of her doings. "No, no, Mister Stone!" her timid eyes finally looking up at his, while continuing to apologize. "I should not have startled you that way. Please, please forgive me!"

"Think nothing of it. No real damage done." he continued to smile, an act that did manage to ease the tension that had sprung up, or anything else for that matter. And when her eyes darted away briefly to check the surrounding area, he used the brief distraction to imitate her gesture, before saying, "Now then, there must be something terribly wrong for you to chance a face to face meeting with big 'ol' bad me, what is it?"

"It's, it's Carla, Carla and her gathering." Louie stammered.

" I wanted, to return that favor you did for Corey and me last week, - and I needed to talk to you alone. There's something I have to warn you about!"

"Favor?" he butted in. "You don't owe me any favor. The fact that you and Corey are still together is more than enough reward for our private conversation earlier. And by the way, we agreed it would be only 'George', remember? Guaranteed I'm almost old enough to be your 'much' older brother," he winked, "but 'Mister Stone' only makes me feel ancient." he smiled again.

Whatever the problem was - his grin seemed to take a bit of the edge off it, as she smiled back. "Sorry! But there's something I feel I 'must' warn you about!"

"Warn me?" he continued to smile. But even though his thoughts were at present justifiably confused by both her strange sudden appearance and jittery behavior, his face showed that it was controlled by his pleasant nature. "Warn me about what?"

"It's, it's Carla, Carla and her gathering" she stammered. "they, they're planning something terrible, just terrible. And I think it's going to be aimed at just you!"

"What do you mean?" he chuckled again, obviously not yet phased by what he had heard so far. "Why should those bunch of 'whale harpooning' 'barracudas' be after me?"

"Because unfortunately your reputation is known plant-wide and they totally blame you for that stunt last week! And even if you're 'not' involved in just about everything that goes on around here, they reason that any successful lingering blemish on your reputation would serve as a slap on the face against all males within the plant."

This time he chuckled out loud, even if Louie obviously still didn't share his lax attitude. But his reaction was due to his devious mind at work once more. He even briefly thought about mentioning the 'boob' of a prank someone had tried to pull on Judy last Friday, as well as the strange phone calls with no-one answering from the opposite end she had also been getting lately. But now that he thought about it, it was obvious that they in all likelihood were probably the very same women. But then again, why offer up something she may not even know anything about. Why emotionally upset her even more than she seemed to be. So he let the idea pass.

Still noticeably bothered by his apparent lax attitude Louie half-scoffed, "Laugh if you want to, but I wouldn't underestimate that darn Carla Daniels. She and some of the older women who've worked here as long as you have, want to carry out whatever it is they're planning. Even though they let me be a part of their group, they also don't let me in on everything their planning, it's as if they don't trust me totally yet"

George tried once more to smile away the growing alarm in Louie's behavior, even if her vision was now less interested in the area around them, as she added, "They honestly believe that you're the one who masterminds all the pranks that go on around here, and then puts the men up to them. I tried to tell them that what happened wasn't only your fault, but they wouldn't listen. I even tried to steer them away in another direction, but they won't settle for just anyone. They insist that it must be 'you'!"

George didn't have to work very hard to get the grin on his face to fade, as his mind raced ahead of Louie's words. And in the brief silence that followed her warning, his face slipped right into one of deep thought before saying, "And you say you don't have even the slightest inkling of what it is the women are planning?"

Clamping her mouth tightly shut, no doubt in an effort to emphasize her answer, while letting her head tilt slightly forward just as obviously ashamed, Louie slowly shook her head sideways in a negative reply to his remark.

This wasn't the first time someone in the plant, and not just the females, had felt the necessity for some sort of revenge. It had been tried before and no doubt as now it would be attempted again some time in the future, if not for reasons other than those Louie was now concerned about. And even though it had been on a very rare occasion when someone had managed to successfully get revenge, it was mainly because George and others had done their best to work it out that way. He also mentally told himself that if the woman in the 'man-haters' club did manage to get the best of only him this time, then he would somehow make sure that both sex's could walk away from whatever it was without feeling the desire to keep the feud escalating.

"Well," he finally continued in exasperation, Louie trying to read every ever changing expression on his face, "I guess I'll just have to play whatever it is they come up with by ear, hopefully making the best of it as I go."

"I, I guess," Louie faltered, noticeable regret written all over her emotions, "It's all my fault! I should have tried harder to stop Carla!"

"No-o-o-o! - Hell no-o!" George quickly beamed back, using a soft genuine smile to sooth her mood. "We have to let this thing, whatever it may be, happen, no matter what now. If we're all to go on living and working here together for years to come, then we have to let these 'old dragons' have their chance of immortality. Now that I know they're up to something, it gives me a chance as it plays itself out to hopefully somehow turn it into a humorous situation."

"I think you know my feelings about good times and personal emotions being more important than bad vibes between any of the workers in the plant. As for me, if necessary, which I doubt, I'm expendable. Just as long as both sides can laugh it off, before either gender has a chance to get nasty about it."

Having risked another quick scan of their surroundings as he had been speaking, Louie once more gave him her total attention while saying, "But how are you going to do that if you don't know what it is that they're planning? again sounding a little frustrated. "Carla wants your 'ass' in a sling!" A slight blush leapt to her face once realizing she had just used one of the words she considered as very unladylike - especially around a man. But she was feeling mad now, which was only encouraged when he let out a brief chuckle at its mention also, and she didn't let it stop her from expressing how she presently felt. "Damn you! Can't you ever take anything seriously?"

"Whoa, slow down lady." George snapped out, his tone now all serious. "Take it easy, please! What you've been seeing is just a 'suit' I wear most of the time in this place, which doesn't mean I'm not also a little wiser. So far the only thing we're in agreement with about is the fact that nothing noticeable has happened yet, am I right?"

Slowly nodding her head once more, her anger apparently having drained with each of his words, she offered a simple and weak "Yes." to George's logic.

George, fighting to regain lost ground grinned openly again, only now a little bit devilish once more. "I have a reputation to live 'down to' you know."

"But what, what if whatever they try on you isn't funny?" Louie let her composure slip just a bit again, there was little doubt it could be due to the emotional attachment she had developed for 'one Mister Stone'. And when a following scary thought entered her head in answer to her own remark, her voice started to quiver at the horrible idea.

"What if, if they start a rumor, a terribly horrible rumor that you've got a lover, a 'male' lover!"

Without even hesitating, as usual, "Well the 'high side' of that prank," he half laughed, " is that at least we won't have to worry about him or me getting pregnant!"

For the first time since he had known or talked to Louie, he heard her do something that was the closest thing to a laugh he could imagine coming from her lips, she giggled. Enjoying it briefly, he felt his fatherly instincts kick in again, while saying, "Sex, believe it or not, isn't the only thing that is connected one way or another to everything that goes on in this often wacky place. Humor, a very wild varied form of humor also lives within these walls. And people, especially most of those I work with, believe me can find something to laugh about on even the most morbid of topics. As for the male lover theory, well, the way this crazy world is going I don't doubt that some day it won't matter one way or the other."

Leaning just a little bit closer to her perfumed form, genuinely pleased when she did noticeably likewise in his direction, his voice was just above that of a whisper as he continued with, "Just between you and me, I guess I'm definitely one of those mentally unbalanced people. No matter what any of those 'sharks' can come up with, I'm pretty sure I'll be able to turn it around into something comical. That's what I often do 'best' around this place, remember?"

As the tension that had been playing 'hop scotch' with her emotions once more started to fade, George chased the rest of their noticeable presence away by smiling, "Trust me! I know it's a corny phrase usually at home on the lips of someone often dubious, but I really do mean it. 'Trust me!'"

Fighting the impulse to reach out and rest a hand on her shoulder, he instead let a smile return, while saying, "Let them try their best. It's better if they concentrate on just me - that way there's less chance of anyone else getting hurt. Those ladies have failed on more than one occasion in the past, and I'm sure they'll be just as successful in the future."

Seeing that she possibly was judging his reasoning, while his senses unwillingly filled themselves even more with everything pleasant about her, he glanced at his watch before panning the area one last time. And as his brain first told the animalistic maleness in him to get back where it belonged, it then reminded him that he probably only had about five or ten minutes to play with, before saying what had to be done to get her on her way.

"I really appreciate what you're trying to do, but I think it's best if we separate ourselves from each other as quickly as possible, and then stay that way. If the ladies get wind that you've been anywhere near me, I'm sure they'll be tougher on 'you' than they plan to be on 'me'. Besides, I've been around long enough to realize that not everyone in 'Hooterville' is out to get me."

Instantly realizing that he, and not just for the most obvious reasons, was referring to 'her' as being the one on his side, Louie blushed slightly, while mouthing the words, 'Thank you.'

"And here's something you might want to think about." he added. "Nothing around this place goes further to release tensions among the workers than a good joke, even if it's only a verbal one. No sarcasm or animosity intended, but you're a blond. And I'm sure you must have heard your share of blond jokes over the years. I'm also pretty sure that if you can come up with a good one, backed by the nerve to tell it, I'll guarantee you'll not only help break down some of the wall of animosity between the sexes, not to mention that you'll own the heart and soul ever male in here, forever."

"Now then, " using both hands hanging at his side like giant scoops, he pushed at the air between them to help suggest that she should get moving. "You get back to where you are supposed to be, and I promise you , I'll be extra careful. Now scoot!"

Hesitantly at first, no doubt evaluating his every word, Louie turned to retrace her steps, but not before giving him the type of smile that any beautiful woman with her endowments would have been rewarded with anything in the world her little heart desired. And as she started to hurry away, soft words saying "Thank you again Mister Stone - ah I mean, George." In turn he swallowed hard while saying to himself, "Who-ow! You can bet your 'sweat bippy' this meetings going to leave memories I'll take to my grave."

In allowing himself one last pleasant view of her departure, George missed a piece of what was also a part of their surroundings. He and Louie had not been the only ones very well acquainted with the plants internal structures. The still undetected female, who had not only taken polaroid snapshots of their contact with each other, as well as overhearing most of what they had talked about, now made no effort to go unnoticed with her rapid jogging own departure. In fact, she herself became a victim to a pair of eyes whose owner made sure to give her and her kind as wide a berth as possible whenever passing.

Inwardly George 'thanked God' that everyone else in the area seemed apparently busy. No doubt, he told himself, with their coffee breaks - which in turn had left the area they had met in so isolated and destitute of human activity. And when glancing back again after having only traveled about ten feet, Louie was now magically gone, which strangely triggered the sort of soft smile he usually kept for only those closest to him.

It took him just a little bit less time to briskly walk the distance to the lunch area where the mill's regular personnel ate then it did to talk to the individual he was after. The 'crane-man' was a friend from a long ways back, and his similar taste for humor had brought them together on more than one occasion in the past. In fact, just their presence together was usually enough to let others around them know that something memorable was in the making, even though no one else was generally let in on what it was that they were up to. And after George had delivered a few grinning whispers into his friend's ear, his still smiling departing form, was just naturally and inquisitively watched by the rest of those also seated at the table.

A quick glance at his watch told him that no matter what he did - he was going to be later then anticipated by the time he got back to the job site. And the brief consideration to 'jog' in order to save some time while retracing his steps, was startled out of his thoughts when Louie's voice once more called out to him from a location so tiny that he would have missed it if he had blinked.

"Mister Stone! It's me again, Louie!"

Instinctively turning his head in the direction of the sound of her voice, he was just about to do the same with his body when she called out to him, "Don't look at me! Just listen, and pretend your busy checking something in your wallet or something, while I tell you what I think has happened."

Doing exactly as suggested, a quick rub at the back of his neck first telling him that if anyone else was in the area, then they must be invisible, cause he sure as 'Hell' couldn't detect them. He then let his fingers noticeably take a small searching walk through the contents of his wallet, as his ears picked up on every whispering word from Louie's lips.

"I got a brief glimpse of the back of Kit Fishers form hurrying away from where we were talking. I don't know if she saw or heard anything, but I'll figure out some way to check on it. Personally I don't think she's as bad as the rest of Carla's' group, but she still is loyal to the gathering. It just might be my imagination working overtime, but I think it's better we should be safer than sorry. If I find out anything, I'll pass it on to you through Corey. If you don't hear from him within the next twenty-four hours, you can go back to just worrying about what I first warned you about. Sorry."

While still glancing down at the contents of his wallet, he kept his voice as low as hers had been while smiling, "Don't worry about it young lady. Remember what I said, we'll handle whatever comes along. Now - say 'hi' to Corey for me when you see him, but first get back to work!"

Stuffing his wallet back into his rear pocket, only silence coming back in response to what he had just said, he continued to grin while starting to whistle before starting on his way once more.

After re-evaluating his thinking George was just short of running when he arrived back to the job site. Fred and Bob were busy locked in conversation until they detected his presence, to which Bob jokingly said, "Where in the name of 'h-e-double upside down sevens' have you been? Your caffeine's cold and what's left of the break is just short of being over!"

"Give it a rest." George winked so that only his best friend could see. "You know that when we're working in the mills we go by their time, which is generally whenever they feel like it. And right about now I'm so hungry I could eat the asshole out of a skunk, providing someone else held up the tail."

Starting to seat his still grinning form across from theirs, a short blast from the factory whistle confirming Bob's remark, George flipped open his lunch's container while chuckling, "I may miss a lot of things around here, but never a coffee break. But then, the company's loss is our gain!"

"You mean 'weight gain'." Fred mumbled, under Bob's words, "Well of all the things I've lost, the thing I miss the most is my sanity!"

"You better be careful around whoever you make remarks like that in front of." George chuckled between large bites of his sand-which. "You don't throw out comments like that, unless you've the right ammunition at hand to fight off any sarcastic rebuttal it might bring you."

Fred, after doing the exact opposite to his lunch bucket, bent a little forward while asking, "What did happen to you buddy? You're not out laying landmines for ol' Farkas are you?"

"Only time will answer that question." George answered, with one of his best shit-disturbing smiles. "But let's just say I ran into a little extra business, and leave it at that for now." before cramming the remainder of his lunch into his mouth.

Fred knew that if his 'bud' wanted him to know why he was so late getting back from an errand that should have taken less than half of the time they had allotted for, then he would have freely offered the information. So rather than pursue the mystery and jeopardize what was yet to come, he wisely changed the subject by saying, "You should 'a been with us. Someone's been pulling pranks on poor ol' Joe the janitor again."

George, his thoughts already ahead of his ears, smiled a half mumbled, 'Not again!' as Fred lost no time in offering evidence to his remark.

"When we walked into the 'john' Joe was just gettin' ready to rinse down the floor with that special rubber garden hose he keeps in there for just that reason, you know the one I'm talkin' about. Well - I was just about to get him and Bob more aquatinted when Joe, while holding onto the end of the hose with one hand, used the other one to turn open the tap it was connected to."

So far Bob had been content to sit there quietly smiling. But suddenly, no doubt because he already knew what had happened, broke out into a snickering chuckle, which instantly made Fred pause enough to glare in his direction, saying, "If the 'peanut gallery' will contain itself, I'll continue!"

Bob, feeling more and more at home each day with the two men across from him, forced himself to hold back on the laughter fighting to get out, while saying, "I'm sorry, so solly! Go ahead."

A still smiling George, as a small snicker did manage to get past Bob's lips, between bites said, "Sounds like this is going to be a knee slapper." before Fred continued. "Well, as I was saying," his own body straining and failing to hold back the humor already in his thoughts, giggled while getting the rest of the story out. "Before I was so, how should I put it, so 'childishly' interrupted. Well, poor poor unsuspecting Joe was standing there with the hose in one hand and the tap handle in the other, when all of a sudden he was totally engulfed in a barrage of thin spraying water. It would seem that someone had drilled the hose with holes so tiny that they couldn't really be seen until the rubber was under pressure. Fortunately for us we were at the other end of the room, and didn't get wet. But poor Joe, even as fast as he could react and shut the water back off, got totally soaked. After that we were laughing too hard and he was so mad and cursing that I didn't dare stop and talk with him."

"Ya." Bob added, his voice reverberating with laughter. "You should have seen the poor little guy. In the spray there for a minute he looked like a statue on someone's lawn."

Since the three of them were all starting to not only look at things in the same way but also along the same lines pertaining to humor, George did his part in making it grow by pretending to choke on some of the food still in his mouth. Quickly taking a sip from the still lukewarm coffee supplied by Fred, he used it to wash down the blockage. With tears now in his eyes he looked at Bob while picked up where Fred had left off.

"Someone's always playing tricks on that poor little Italian. Sometimes I swear that if you shaved all the hair off his head, you'd find God's 'thumb-print' on the top of his head. But he's not the only one. Every once in a while even one of us gets slammed when we're in the 'library' too."

Hearing the washroom referred to as a 'library' brought a puzzled look to Bob's face, which once noting the reaction made freed say, "ya - library. That's just one of the many nicknames we have for the 'john'. Sometimes we call it the 'lou', 'pisser', 'KY bow', the 'head', the 'water-trough', the 'crapper', or even 'voting booth' when election times roll around. But whenever someone goes in there with a book or magazine to just 'pass' only time, we refer to it as the 'library'.

As George Pretended to clear his throat once more, Fred instantly realized that he had committed the proverbial 'no, no'. He'd cut into his buddy's explanation of even 'them occasionally getting slammed. But just as quickly he wisely turned Bob's distracted attention back in George's direction with the words, while letting one hand gesture towards where his words were intended, "Anyhow, as our 'fearless leader' was about to offer before being so rudely interrupted."

In the brief fraction of silence that followed after Fred's eyes had turned towards George's, Bob's vision quickly imitated the maneuver, but was still a fraction of a second behind the words. "What I was about to warn you about 'Robert!', is that the 'library' the 'shithouse', is a favorite location, if you'll pardon the pun, to be caught with you pants down."

Forgetting himself Fred instantly let out with an elongated 'E-e-e-e-w-w, while pinching his nose to emphasize that something really stunk, mainly George's last words. Bob, briefly imitating the gesture, then grinned just as widely back at George as he continued. "By that I mean dear friend, is that you are less apt to be able to retaliate if attacked. Instead of that old saying, 'Is nothing sacred?' we always answer 'No!' and everyone's fair game."

"Such as?" Bob continued to grin.

"Well, the gentle attacks, especially if they don't recognize your feet, you may get bombarded with from the centers out of old toilet paper rolls, to wet paper towels someone leaving has just wiped their hands on. But if they do know who you are, they might simply wedge the door shut so you're locked in, or they'll reach under and grab your pants with the intention of pulling them off your legs and leaving you really --- em-bare-assed!"

The noticeable punctuation of the last word made the grin already on George's face grow even broader, as Bob's voice joined Fred's to quickly 'Bo-o-o-o' the pun. And just as everything was purposely meant to be, George used both friends' spontaneous reaction as fuel to encourage him on.

"But of all the stunts that might be pulled on you, there is only one that you really have to be alert for"

It was apparent, as Fred started to chuckle that he already knew what was coming next. But Bob, his curiosity only raised higher by Fred's' actions, gave George a grin that begged to hear the rest of George's wise words.

"The big one!" George's voice now rose and accented each word for effect. "The prank that'll clean you out for a whole week, and have you answering telephones for about as long, not to mention getting' your hemorrhoids sucked into your throat, is everyone's favorite 'Enema in a can'!"

By this time Fred was just short of hysteria, as his mind's eye visualized a scene from just such an incident he'd been part of in the past. But when Bob made no effort to coax the definition out of what the hell 'enema in a can' could be, even though George was now pausing long enough to give him time to attempt to, he eagerly smiled out the answer anyways.

"Why is it I sometimes feel that I'm playing lip service to a dead audience? And when Bob still gave no indication of what he was talking about, except that he had apparently just been picked on, George shrugged his shoulders in Fred's' grinning direction before continuing for the benefit of Bob alone.

"'Enema in a can' is where a prankster takes an empty pop tin, fills it with a mixture of oxygen and acetylene, then puts a long paper wick into the open hole. They then wait, most times with an audience, until someone with a paper or book has occupied one of the stalls. But it has to be someone who is definitely not there on regular company business. They then stick the pop can just inside the washroom door and ignite the paper wick. What happens next, thanks to testimony from those who have survived such a cleansing experience, is a magnified explosion. It is so loud and has such pressure that not only does it accomplish all of what I've already told you, but also gets all the loose dust off the walls ceiling, and almost totally unwraps what ever is left on the toilet roll dispenser. It also leaves you for at least the next week ending every question you're asked with the singular word of, 'What!'

By now Bob, as George had expected, was involved in humor almost equivalent to Fred's. He was also eager to add his own bit of strange humor to their gathering, just as soon as the laughter gave any indication it was about to subside.

"How do you, do you know," he said while shaking with laughter, "When you've really had a good dump?"

"I'll bite." Fred quickly answered, just as broken up. "I don't know! how do you tell when you've had a really good crap?"

"That," Bob chuckled, "That's when the guy in the stall beside you either lets out with a moan mostly associated with childbirth, or he has tears in his eyes when he stops to wash his hands besides you before leaving."

As they each broke down again, Fred had to force his next remark out. "I often wondered if anyone ever tried to find out just why 'Shit' smells so bad." George always at the ready, lost no time in replying,

"Well, if it didn't have such a repugnant look or odor to go along with it, some idiots might be foolish enough to start saving up, possibly as a hobby or something. Then where would we be?"

"Sooner or later obviously up to our necks in the disgusting stuff." Fred grimaced, his face matching the look Bob's imagination had also conjured up.

Bob, glad to keep things going, quickly added, "And once it got up over our waists, that's waist spelled 'w-a-i-s-t' not 'w-a-s-t-e', all the companies who make 'bum wipe' paper might just as well go out of business. And I'm sure nobody here wants to do anything that might put any red blooded individual with an overworked sore ass out of work."

It was easy for George to see that the present level of their 'crap' dominated conversation had every indication of going down the toilet. Making no attempt to hold back the chuckle the thought had tickled out of his sense of humor, he deliberately worked at altering their avenue of thoughts by interrupting it. "Ya, but anyways, if the time comes that you're ever in an emergency and the booths are all full, don't be afraid to peek over the top of the stall. In the past smark-asse's have been known to use old work boots and pants hanging on strings to make it look as if that trap's occupied. That way they know there's always a seat available, if they should need one."

'Well, believe it or not," Bob grinned, "some people have been known to smell a Hell of a lot worse than what comes out of their insides, especially after a very memorable weekend."

Wrinkling his nose in reaction to the very odor normally associated to the kind of repugnant smell he was talking about, Fred asked him in between chuckles, even though he and George already roughly knew what he was leading up to. "Normally I'd jump on the last part of statement by giving you the obvious, 'Sounds like the voice of experience.' But I'll just go with, 'How's that?'"

Pausing for effect, his body still pulsating with bits of broken laughter, Bob smiled. "Back, back on the old job, we used to have our own, little K'K'K' committee."

"You had members of the 'Klue Klux Klan' workin' in your plant?" Fred blinked exasperatedly, the humor on his face totally replaced with one of surprise.

"Kind of," Bob grinned, only wider than normal thanks to Fred's almost comical looking reaction. "Only ours stood for the 'Kama Kasie Krew'."

"Oh-h." Fred responded. "I see. he quickly added, even though he really didn't, with his face telling the same story.

"Their mission was to track down fellow workers with known allergies to 'soap and water'. Once they cornered one, which you didn't need a 'bloodhound' to do on a hot summer's day, it was up to them to convert a 'pig pen' into a 'mister clean', if possible. Verbal diplomacy was always tried first so as not to invoke any hard feelings, but if all else failed, they, as a last resort, the Kama Kassie Krew, cloths and all would pick up the selected individual and carry him into the running showers. In there, they give him a cleaning that would 'gag a maggot'."

Needless to say, laughter paid them another brief visit. Then George, while standing erect as an indication that they could walk and talk at the same time, spoke as he led the way back to work.

"I think we'll have to consider such a committee for around here in the future. In case your nose has been on the 'bummer' and you haven't noticed it in the change-house yet, we have a few such individuals with a similar form of hygienic impediment. And I'm not talking about those you hear doing 'duck calls' to clean out their clogged noses, and then saying to the recently vacated, something like, 'Okay, it's time you got out and walked. You've been hitching a ride along enough.' There are a few who haven't seen the backs of their lockers in probably five years, not to mention they no doubt ever take their work clothes home for a baptismal dipping in soapy water. Then there's the guys, for those of us who still have the capability of detecting odors from other than this place, who take their work socks at the end of each shift and throw them at their locker door. It's their way of judging that if they don't stick by the end of the week - they're good enough to wear for another five days. And if you're unlucky enough to be close-by to witness this ritual, it'll have you looking forward to any shifts opposite theirs."

As Bob instantly went 'E-e-w-w-w!' through a scrunched up nose, the words, "It's true buddy." were the first out of Fred's mouth. "There was a case just last year of just such a guy where everyone thought the old bachelor had taken an early retirement, especially since no-one had seen him for almost a month. But when security and the janitor went to finally hygienically clean out his locker, they found the old boy still wearing his socks, stuck to the inside wall of the locker."

Not until now, as both George and Fred broke out into a series of short snickers in one another's direction, did Bob have any reason to suspect Fred's remarks were anything short of the gospel truth. And as his face quickly imitated their, it was more through common sense then the sight of his two chuckling friends that made him realize they had been pulling his leg.

The three of them were still busy laughing away each other's company when 'Sugarlips' Larry Gilbert, lunch pail in hand, shuffled up to join them, the words, "Hi guys!" warning them of his approach. Having a happy go lucky attitude not unlike theirs always made his presence welcome. And because of his continuous affair with sweets, he was also sometimes referred to as the 'Candyman'. His friends often joked that he in all probability walked around with a constant erection every Easter. His arrival, like the majority of the plant's personnel, was welcomed with a smile and comment in unison from Fred and George.

"Well, hello, Sugar Lips!" But only Fred kept it going. "Long time no see. Welcome back! How was Cuba and the sugarcane crop this year?"

Even at the worst of times Larry like George was never at a loss for words. And since it usually was the Axeman himself who always got the last word in or was slamming him each time they joked around together, he looked straight in his direction only, while giving the answer he had worked on all through this years vacation, for just this occasion.

"To tell the truth my friend, it was a whole lot like my sex life." he verbally exaggerated. "It was 'far' to short, and 'over', long before I could 'really' start to enjoy it!"

As the remarks all around got the humorous results they had been designed for George asked, "And the weather this year?"

"It didn't 'monsoon', if that's what you're hinting at?" Larry jokingly snarled.

"Too bad." George smiled. "I've been thinking about sending your name in to the national farmers drought association."

"I know I shouldn't be helping you," Sugarlips continued to smile sarcastically. "But, for what?"

"Well." George grinned, first at Bob and then Fred. "the way it usually downpours whenever you take off on your vacation, I figured that if the farmers ever needed rain real bad any place special, they could give you a call. You in turn would just have to set up a tent in the middle of a chosen field, and before you know it, 'zap, crackle, boom!' everything they owned not tied down would soon be floating away."

Chuckling himself, Larry grinned, "It's still that way. I lied about Cuba. I went out West this year to visit my brother for a week. Not only did it rain 'cats and dogs' for the whole time I was there, but his house sprung a major leak."

As they were laughing George introduced Larry to Bob. Bob in turn then felt justifiable in offering him own little witticism.

"You better not let the Arabs find out about you. At least not until they find out how to irrigate all that sand some other way!"

Figuring it was his turn, Fred offered his bit of continuing humor. "I guess the only one who'd be really glad to hear about your misfortune Sugar lips, is 'Smokey The Bear', especially with all those forest fires now raging away out of control."

"Say!" George half-laughed, "That's a great idea. I can see it now Larry. You're up in a plane with a group of professional firefighters. All attempts to extinguish a raging inferno have failed and they're about to try their secret weapon. The other men in the plane are all lined up ready to jump, their knapsacks loaded down with all sorts of fire fighting equipment. They jump, and then it's your turn. You step up to the door just in time to watch the other men's huge white mushrooms float gently towards the ground. After sticking one of your fingers into your mouth to wet it, you then stick it out through the open doorway in order to check which way the wind is blowing. Finally, you use the same hand to pinch the end of your nose, no doubt so you don't get caught in an updraft, and float, up instead of down, you jump while shouting "Cannonball!' Almost instantly, 'poof', a huge colorful kitchen tent instead of a parachute unfolds all around you during your decent, both of you getting to the ground just before a record-breaking cloudburst lets go overhead!"

Sugarlips wasn't the only one to go "Whew!" But he was the only one to add, "Boy! Give the man an audience, and he'll go on forever!"

The job needless to say was abandoned early, sort of in honor of their guest. But before they could all sit down at the portable table provided at that particular work site, George asked Bob if he would mind doing him a favor first.

"Sure." Bob smiled, glad to be trusted enough to ensure that he was definitely an essential part of the group. "No problem."

"Good." George beamed back. "Do me a favor. Nip over to the next building and tell - "

"Nip!" Bob indignantly cut him off, just loud enough to drown out George's voice. And when he repeated it, he said it even louder. "Nip!" the friendly smile that had been on his face only seconds ago now totally gone.

Almost instantly, as Fred and Sugerlips looked confused by Bob's harsh reaction to the obvious word "nip', George alone realized that he had unintentionally used a slang word meant to describe the Japanese people during the second world war. And just as quickly he tried to justify his usage of the word.

"Sorry!, Sorry Bob! no disrespectful pun intended. For most of us the word means a small bite or quick trip to someplace. I only meant that I wanted you to jog over and tell the guy in the crane next door I need to see him for a couple of minutes. It's about the shop's yearly stag! honestly!"

"We-e-e-ee-ll," Bob squinted, a hint of humor now around the corners of his eyes, "No offense taken. I just wanted to see how fast you could 'back-paddle' while squirming."

Even if he hadn't already anticipated George's immediate reaction - he still would have had more than enough time to expertly avoid his weak effort at punching him in the arm - while cursing. "Why, you!" And as Fred and Larry laughingly enjoyed the little demonstration unfolding in front of them, Bob started to back away while grinning out his best Charlie Chan imitation. "Now then , where was it you wished your humble servant to go"

Half-laughing, his steps matching Bob's, George once more swung at nothing but air, while answering, "Normally I'd say 'to Hell', but you'd probably only answer, 'Why, you lonely or something?"

"It'll have to be a bit closer than that!" Bob laughed. "I've only got a half hour for lunch, remember?"

"I remember." George shot back. "But can you remember that lunch area we showed you in the building beside this one last week, It was located next to the spare parts storage area."

Widening the space between them, Bob continued to grin. "If not, I'll ask somebody."

After glancing at his watch, George picked up from where he had been distracted. "Well 'nip' over and tell the crane-man I need to see him. We're still a little bit early for lunch yet, and I want to talk to Larry about his vacation and secret sex life. I'd send Fred with you but I think this would be a good time to see if you can find your way around here all by yourself. But now, I guess it wouldn't be such a bad idea if you did 'get lost!' he leered. "But if you do, just ask the first guy you see if "Noah' is around."

Instantly realizing that he had just mentioned a nickname they had not used around Bob yet, George didn't even pause slightly with his word. "Noah's the nickname of the shops welder, because he gets all the jobs that have to be watertight. He and Steve always keep track of each others snooze spots, just in case their foreman is trying to track one of them down, or catch them horizontal when they're supposed to be vertical."

"You won't need the bloodhounds for me." Bob continued to grin, especially at George. He then started to move in the direction he was about to visit, but quickly stopped in his tracks long enough to ask, "It's not that I'm nosey, but maybe it would help if I knew who I was looking for."

Instantly, smiling back through two rows of shinning ivories, George pretended that it had been purely accidental when failing to tell him to ask for a Steve Laslo.

As soon as Bob was no longer in sight, Fred had followed him just far enough to make sure he was headed in the right direction. George in a half run gestured for Sugarlips to follow them, while explaining where they were going, as well as why. Using another of their short cut they were only seconds ahead of Bob's whistling form, which fortunately was just enough time for them to comically get out of sight.

Unsuspecting Bob, still murdering a tune only a deaf man would be glad to hear, did exactly as George had recommended. Flashing a smile he asked the first man he caught site of, where he might find someone by the name of Steve Laslo, crane driver.

Lifting one hand to point at the overhead crane parked about fifty feet from where they were standing, the worker answered, "Rip Van Winkle doesn't come down for his breaks. Right about now he's probably watchin' the inside of his eyelids. Just call up to him, he should hear ya.

"Thanks." Bob continued to smile. And as he headed towards the crane, his expression and movements gave every indication that he had no idea a dozen pair of eyes were glued onto his every move. Stopping almost directly under the crane's cab, his eyes easily picked out the protruding elevated crossed bottoms of a pair of work boots. They were stuck out through one of the cubicle's open windows, clearly indicating that their owner was resting lower out of sight. Raising one cupped hand to the side of his mouth, as if to keep the words he was about to shout from straying in every which way direction, he then shouted upward. "Hey, Steve! Steve Laslo!"

Almost instantly, the protruding pair of boots that had been as stationary as the crane itself disappeared inside. Then slowly, indeed as if it had been inconveniently disturbed, a human head gradually peered out from the same window opening the shoes had been occupying only seconds earlier. And once its eyes had finally located the source of the disturbance calling its name, a rough voice called down in Bob's direction. "Ya, I'm Laslo. What do ya want?"

"I'm a friend of George Stone's." Bob shouted back, while walking to an area where the crane man could view him better. "He sent me to get you. He wants to talk to you about the retirement stag that's comin' up."

There was no doubting that there was a hint of irritation in the voice from the head still peering down in Bob's direction, as it reluctantly said, "Oh. All right!" and as it disappeared briefly from view once more, it could be clearly heard to say, "Stay there! I'll be right down."

With patient hands thrust into his back pockets, Bob's head was just naturally still tilted upward in the crane cabs direction, when something happened that took him totally by surprise. For the first split second even his trained body couldn't react to the sight now unfolding before his eyes. But in the remaining end of that same instant, as his brain acknowledged the fact that human beings don't really fly through the air without any form of assistance, his body's automatic reactions finally kicked in. And when they did, his eyes growing wider at the sight of the airborne human body rapidly descending towards him, his arms and feet functioned in total conflict with each other. Even though his arms formed into a cradle to catch the form cascading towards him, his feet instinctively and defensively backed his body safely away.

The exploding words out of his mouth of "Holy - Shit!" that had accompanied his reactions, seemed to hang in the air around him - long after the human form had landed with a dull flat "Thud!' on the ground in front of his feet.

Other automatic body reactions caused Bob's eyes to snap shut at the same instant the awkward looking form made sickening contact with the concrete floor beneath his feet. In reality everything had happened so fast it was all over in a nightmarish flash. But the next following seconds, as the sound of his own pounding heart blocked out all other existence around him, seemed like an eternity, before he finally felt able to reopen his windows to the world.

Less than five feet in front of him, face down and in a position anatomically impossible for any normal human being, was the motionless twisted form Bob had just seen viciously sucked downward by the earth's gravity. Justifiably, as he tried to squeak out the ridiculous words, "Hey! Are you okay?" his eyes and attention remained glued to the still dormant heap only feet away.

Slowly, even though his brain had already told him that no human could have possibly survived such a fall onto the concrete, he forced his own body to start moving forward towards the still unresponding heap. And not until he was close enough to be able to reach down to touch the figure, did his still shocked senses finally pick up on what was also happening around him.

Loud sounding 'woof whistles' mixed in with hand clapping and cheers were now filling the air. Snapping his head from first one unknown face now approaching him to the next, Bob was still totally confused. Confused, that is, until his vision finally rested on someone he couldn't help but recognize, George."

Now, and only now, did the reality of what had truly happened finally start to seep through into his confused brain's racing reasoning, as his vision now fell on another strange sight. One of the apparent secret admires, or maybe just someone else who was a part of whatever had just happened, was having so much trouble controlling his laughter that he apparently felt it necessary to hide his face in one of the shop's garbage pails. Any ridicule or laughter he had hoped to achieve, was justified when his head reappeared splotched with black grease. And what happened next as an apparent worker late for the prank while running in slipped on a small puddle somehow left on the floor only to end up with one of his feet elevating just enough to be stopped be another unfortunate coworkers unprotected groin area - just somehow seemed appropriate. Especially after the recipient buckled over into a little hobbling dance that just naturally involved a prayer that his family jewels were not about to become worthless.

Letting his eyes drop back to the form at his feet, Bob used the tip of one workboat to roll the body over onto its back. Instantly, as his vision locked onto the brightly hand painted face on the rubber mannequin dressed up in work clothing, Bob's body was totally consumed remembering how funny his actions must have looked to the workers now gathering around him. And it took the sound of Fred's familiar voice grinning, "Now! Now you're truly one of us my friend!" to get his attention back to where it belonged.

By now, George's chuckling form was almost at his side, as Sugar lips laughed out "Welcome to the family buddy." And with his arrival Bob used his expert training to snap out and gently deliver a series of short jabs to George's and Fred's unsuspecting midsections, while saying, "I sure hope I made everybody's day!"

"I don't know about anybody else." George replied, while failing to block any of the attack licking at his body. "But you sure sugar coated mine so much that if I was a kid, and depending on what age, I'd probably be sprouting a big 'zit' or an even 'bigger' erection."

Reaching down and picking the dummy up backwards by the shoulders, as the grinning crane river joined them, Bob then held it at arm's length, as all the men around him continued to laugh. He then kicked the mannequin's lower rear anatomy, which only served to fuel the humorous antics around him, still out of control.

Finally George, laughter still rocking his body, reached out and rescued the poor dummy, while saying, "You keep that up much longer and Herb'll be eligible for disability leave."

"You even named the 'dummy'!" Bob shot back.

"You ever meet a 'dummy' who didn't have a name? George smiled, while passing the poor creature into more caring hands. He then quickly added "Think about that for a minute."

No doubt doing exactly that, Bob's face went lax for a few seconds, before once more filling itself with a grin that ran from the proverbial ear to ear. He then stared directly into George's eyes, just so there would be no doubt as to who he was talking about, while answering, "Ya! When you're right, you're right! I can see now where I was kickin' the wrong 'dummy'. And as soon as I get back from the washroom after taking a 'valium' to slow down my racing heart, and scrappin' the 'crap' off my legs, I just might do exactly that!"

Instinctively backing up in order to avoid an attack that never materialized this time, George continued to smile, even as he spoke. "Let's not do anything we'll definitely live to regret later. If you'll think back a bit, you should remember how when you started working here, I warned you to watch out for everyone, even me. Well you just saw the proof of that statement. Besides, if we don't get movin', we'll miss what's left of our lunch break. And only a real 'dummy' would do that!"

The rain that had led them to work earlier that morning, was still there at quitting time to hound them all of the way home. For some, especially those involved in fender benders, it had been the type of day that would die a long memorable hated death. But for George and most his path had crossed so far that day, later reflections would bring a smile to their owners' faces, each time they recalled the prank played on Bob. And even though it truly and definitely rated what had been what some liked to call a 'red letter' day, for George it was what living was really all about, good memory material. It was definitely what he in his books rated as one of his real 'Wow!' days.

Supper, as well as the remainder of the day, passed as rapidly and effortlessly as hundreds of days just like it had become history before. Not even the brief inquisitive comment from Judy that a woman who refused to give her name or remark as to why she was calling for George again, could alter the family atmosphere. Fortunately George's answer that it was probably only someone playing games again, after mentally telling himself that the woman from work were no doubt behind it. But it was enough to temporarily satisfy Judy's curiosity, even though she hadn't totally believed it, especially after last week's illegitimate child visit.

But age and patience had not only brought wisdom, it had taught Judy - especially after another phone call that she had answered was rewarded with only a loud 'click' from whoever was calling, she would eventually figure things out. If George himself didn't want to tell her anything about what was going on, that is if even he knew about whatever the mystery was, then the passing of time eventually would. But all of the strangeness running around tripping over itself inside of her head, could have been put to rest if she had ever had the opportunity to meet Louie, especially since it had been her on the phone each time.

Chapter 11

'Did ya.'
Or
'The humor mill.'

On 'Fat Tuesday' appropriately named by the men because of their ongoing ritual for picking that days shifts to use overweight jokes or comments as put downs against each other. As for the damp 'crappy' weather - the majority of it had apparently decided to move on and annoy some other part of the state. The day had started off with only a very slight drizzle, but by ten o'clock even it was alien to the surrounding area. And George, his body also rocking with laughter like the rest of those around him, was presently involved with a retaliating reply to an attack that had been made about his growing middle age spread, proving once more that not all of the kids were 'not' in school.

"I don't think the 'pot' should be calling the 'kettle' black 'porko'. I'm not the guy who has pictures of mouth watering juicy hamburger and greasy fries topped off with a big swetting milk shake hanging around his work area, instead of the usual explicit girlie pinups. And one look at you, even a visually impaired person could see that you obviously didn't have to sing for your supper! Not to mention, in your case, it's rather noticeable that when you did hoorf down any groceries, you must have destroyed an awful lot of contagious 'ugly' food in there too.

Ernie's instant rebuttal of "Very funny!" was almost lost in the barrage of elongated 'He-e-e-er's!' that followed George's words. The more so, because it was expected than necessity, he continued with his defense.

"If you're referring to this little bit of extra skin here," while speaking he grabbed and he pulled away from his body the two very noticeable fat deposits all the commotion seemed to be about, one in each hand. "My wife likes to refer to them as her 'love handles'.

The term 'love handles', or 'energy packs' as a few liked to call them, was not new to anybody there in the gathering. But most of the men just thought of them as to much stomach, with not enough back. All of them on one occasion or another, George possibly more than the others, had used the words to excuse away the storage bins of excess cellulite accumulating around their midsections. But it was also just a friendly term that wasn't always accepted, especially now, especially by 'shit disturbing' George.

"Love handles!" George exclaimed. "I think your wife's just being conservatively kind. Everybody here knows that when a woman's sittin' in the saddle, she shouldn't need anything extra to hang onto, especially if the horn is long enough. Know what I mean, 'jelly bean'?"

"Indeed I do!" Ernie chuckled, the rest of the gathering eating up every verbal morsel dropping all around them. "But I doubt if you do. As much as it hurt my eyes, you have to remember that I've seen you in the shower too."

"Oh! One of 'those' guys, eh?" George shot back. "And all this time I thought you were honestly just 'accidentally' dropping your bar of soap on the shower room floor!"

"Say what you want." Ernie answered, feigning a little bit of sarcasm. "Besides, everyone knows it's not the 'size of the boat' but 'the motion of the ocean' that gets the job done. So eat your heart out."

"No thank you." George smiled, even as a few of the men gave him his own rendition of the 'Get that into ya' slamming. "You're the one who looks like he's already done just that, as well as anything else you might be able to sink your greedy little ivories into. In fact, and I'm sure I'm not the only one here who's noticed, but you're startin' to look more an more like the 'Good Year Blimp than it does."

All of them being guilty as ones never to linger to long on any one individual, one of the other workers followed right in behind George's words with, "Here's something you might be interested in Ernie. I've heard that one of the big name pizza joints in town is having a blitz to draw customers away from the chicken burger troughs. Seems they're giving out cards to be stamped with each pizza sold. Twenty cards, and they give you a bigger belt."

"Well I knew it was time to lose weight," someone laughed, "When I rolled out of bed the other day, and the pillow came with me. Seems it was caught in one of the folds in my neck!"

"If you think that's embarrassing," George shouted into the hysterics now in control of the gathering. "Just before the barbecue last week Judy sent me to the mall for some last minute pickups. When I got home she gave me Holy Hell for cheatin' on the diet she had put me on. At first I thought she must be psychic. How the shit did she know I'd stopped off at the doughnut joint and downed a half dozen sinkers in the car on the way home. And when I just as sarcastically snapped back in response to her accusation as to how the 'shit' could she accuse me of such an atrocity, she shot me out of the water by pointing out that I had a piece of napkin stuck in my teeth!"

If the men hadn't already been busy laughing their way into the day, then George's remark would have been enough to encourage it. And when someone added, "Hell, the quickest way I know of that when it's time to go on a diet, is when I put my hands in my pants pockets and my 'fly' pops open. In fact it was so bad, and I was so hungry there for a while, I thought my asshole was re chewing my food one more time, before letting it go."

"Well, I try to watch my weight whenever I can." Ernie smiled. And George just as quickly put a pin in his balloon by chuckling, "You keep making food disappear the way you have been, and you won't have to turn your head very far in any direction to keep an eye on any part of it."

The slamming as usual got the appropriate recognition from the other workers. So George just naturally kept the mood going, by adding, "Normally I'd give ya the old line about there's no such thing as being 'fat'! But then there's 'fat fat'! And last but not least after there's 'really really' 'fat', there's 'you'!"

"Well you're no 'Nick Charles' yourself, you know." Ernie smiling barked in George's direction. And the broad grin he was now enjoying was more from having used one of George's favorite detective heroes from the famous 'Thin Man' movie era, to slap him back with.

"Personally" George answered, while doing his best to look as if he actually had been slapped across the face, "I've decided that there's actually a thin guy living inside of me, trying to get out. But I've found that after about two bags of potato chips. a chocolate bar, and a big tug at a glass of cola, he's actually content to stay exactly where he is."

As the other workers kept right on doing what they now seemed to be best at, Ernie used one of George's own remarks to zing him once more. "Sounds quit possible to me. Only in your case I think there's enough room inside you for him and a double dating twin brother!"

"Well, if I've got twins," George expectedly shot back, the rest of his body now arching itself into a position that looked as if he was ready to draw a pair of invisible guns from just as imaginary holsters, he sneered out his best 'Whipply Snidelash' imitations, before finishing with, "you can make any area qualify for standing room only!"

As Ernie quickly copied his antics, everyone else totally engulfed in their little two man play, he pretended, facial expressions and all, to be stepping over some just as imaginary animal droppings, while snarling,

"Well next time I need a work belt for my pants for 'here', I'll just let you give me one of your old 'ones'. I can always cut it down to make 'two' my size! Whatever's left I'll just throw away."

"Ha!" George answered, himself moving sideways as if to better his position in their imaginary gun fight. "Well next time you're barkin' at the wife as to where all the food money has gone, just tell her to get a big mirror, and then hold it up in front of you!"

Ernie yanked the first of his invisible weapons from their present resting spots, verbally adding the sound effects necessary to make it appear that outward stretched guns pointed at George's heart had just gone off. And as George in turn slowly melted to the ground from his fatal imaginary wounds, some of the other men indulged in a brief barrage of just as invisible crossfire, before bad acting had them falling to the ground. A few even managed to end 'tits up' across the lunch tables.

As always, because there was never any real intentional animosity of a hateful nature in the present group of men, not one of them hesitated to then add fuel to the 'cutups' and slamming's now going on all around them. Some of them, just as now, even accidentally set themselves up when trying to fan the flames during someone else's turn in the 'barrel'.

"The 'Axeman' is right you know." Bob chuckled, while leaning on the handcart he had been using earlier. "Yesterday on the way into work I saw six guys pick up and use Ernie for an umbrella so they wouldn't get wet on the way in.

Frowning in Bob's direction, Ernie put a hint of sarcasm in his voice while replying, "Someone here order a 'rickshaw'?"

"Not really." Bob continued to grin, especially after George blew him an undetected kiss. "The buggy is here just in case you need help in getting back to your car later. From what I've heard about those six men yesterday being off with hernias today, I just thought I should be prepared."

"That's a lie" Fred quickly jumped in, much to everyone's surprise. 'I don't believe ten men could pick Ernie up!"

In the background, in an almost whisper, someone offered "Well just as long as he can't be picked up by just 'one' man either."

Instantly, just as quickly as the innuendo had been delivered, a contagious and growing 'E-e-e-e-w-w' from those not participating briefly filled the air.

"Well!" Ernie snapped in Fred's direction. "Shall we duel again? I hear the three of you jokers are becoming almost inseparable!"

"Not me." Fred smiled back. "Personally I don't think either one of them needs any help to handle anyone like you. But thanks for the recognition anyways!"

"Well I don't care if the toilet bowl does let out a little moan every time I sit down lately." George smiled at Ernie. "As long as the wife doesn't complain. that's all that really matters. And unlike some people I know," his eyes now passing over a few of the bigger boys there, "I don't have to worry about listening to the sound of cracking cement under my feet as I walk"

"Or any other floor 'mumble an obscenity' whenever you trod over it." Fred added with a grin.

"Ya, I know what you mean." someone else noticeably a bit over weight offered. "Every time I go into a fast food restaurant lately, they all want me to pay in advance. And last night after noticing I had a little gas, my wife asked, "What's the matter Hon? the baby kicking?"

"I guess I should lose a couple of pounds too." another of the men chuckled, obviously begging for his share of the attention going around. "my shorts were so tight last week that when I sat down on the couch they split the crotch open just enough for my passing daughter to notice and asked me if I had two noses. Apparently she thought she saw a piece of my moustache and a part of my right nostril sticking out."

As everyone kicked in with their laughter Fred lost no time in adding his silly remarks to the gathering. "You guys ain't kiddin'. Whenever there's a gathering like this lately I feel like I'm in the middle of a 'baby boom'!"

"Baby! Boom! You isn't kiddin'!" George half laughed sarcastically. "Back to back puns. Boy, being 'back in the saddle' sure has loosened up your clogged brain cells hasn't it?"

Fred made no verbal attempt to retaliate against his buddy's close to home slamming. But instead satisfied himself with the childish gesture of simply putting the tip of his thumb on the end of his nose. The rest of his hand was spread wide open, while sticking his tongue out in grinning George's direction. An as yet unheard from voice, raising his hands to help avoid the spray now coming from Fred's lips which was the expected follow up to the rest of his gesture, picked up from where he had left off.

"Well I don't know about you bums, but really fat people scare me. I'm afraid that one day one of them is going to blow a button, and with my luck I'll be close enough to lose an eye before I even had a chance to hear it whistling in my direction."

"Imagine how they must feel." George chuckled. "Every time they climb out of a small car it must feel like they're being reborn. They go into a restaurant with a special on for all you can eat for one flat price, and the manager comes out and commits 'Harri Karri' tits up across their table."

"Or if one of us goes on vacation for awhile, some wise guy," Ernie looking directly at George while speaking, "someone always nails you when you come back with, 'Been in hiding because the price of meat went up again, eh?"

"That's not my favorite." George quickly joked back in Ernie's direction. "The way I like to put it is, 'If the price of meat keeps going up the way it is, you're liable to wake up one morning hanging by your ankles from the showerhead, with you know what cut."

Only those who hadn't heard George's crude remark before, made a disgusted gesture with their face. And as usual, it only served to encourage someone else to try to get an even bigger chuckle from the men with his own remark.

"That's almost like saying fat people always look great in something white - like say, a big freezer!"

Ernie instantly rewarded the owner of the wisecrack with a quick jab of fingers into his ribcage, which only provoked more such verbal abuse from another source.

"Well at least now I know why I always see chunky people walking in the park with a little animal of some sort close-by. All this time I had thought they were like everyone else - just taking their pets there to get rid of little excess food. But now I realize that's not the real reason. They're probably just keeping a portable 'survival kit' close-by, you know, just in case they get hit with a snack attack, and can't maker it to the fridge in time."

The remark, for those with a wicked imagination, was instantly acknowledged with a similar reward from Ernie, before he said, "Well, since I'm gettin' a little tired of trying to sleep on my stomach, only to end up rolling out of bed, right after the stag I'm on a strict diet. Well, I've found that if anyone's 'really' 'really' serious about loosing weight, and fast, just make sure everything you put in your mouth is Ex-Lax based."

"That doesn't always work!" someone smiled. "I tried it once and almost shit myself blind!"

"Well then I think some of us should make sure the last thing we push down our throats when eating, is our biggest finger." George laughed. "That's got to be better than the kind of diet I know most of you're going on."

George's reputation betrayed his face, and as he opened his mouth to deliver more of his expected customary comments. Ernie instantly cut him off with, "Ya, we know, a 'sea food' diet. Every time one of us sees food, we eat it!"

"I wasn't going to use that corny old saying again!" George replied, as the rest of the men laughed. "Personally I don't care if some of you bums do look like the cause of a famine. I like you all just the way you are. If your idea of reading material at break time is to browse through a cookbook full of over enhanced colored photographs, that's your business. Personally I just love standing beside any of you with your face all lathered up in the shower room. Strangely it not only makes me feel good, it also makes me feel like I'm standing next to the big 'ho, ho, ho, man himself, Santa Clause!"

The sudden loud interruption from the shop's horn informing them that their break period was supposed to be over went totally unrecognized at first. But when Fred accidentally happened to catch a glimpse of the Evil Dwarf's figure approaching in the distance, it only took the words of 'Oh, oh. Headhunter approaching at seven o'clock!' to break up the gathering. As the men seemingly started to disappear into thin air, more through the desire of avoiding the boss's aggravated presence than fear of his authority, George led Bob and Fred directly into the enemy's territory.

Bob, having almost totally blended his brand of humor in to match that of George's and most of the men in the plants by now, tilted his head slightly in George's direction, while whispering. "I think Farkas is starting to lose some of his homosexual tendencies towards you since your little talk with him.

"How's that?" George grinned back, Fred's eyes and ears locked on them.

"He doesn't seem to be trying to 'screw you' as much lately as he used to."

"Bob's right, you know." Fred quickly added." Shop rumor has it he's now on your side."

"Right idea, wrong location." George answered through the side of his mouth as the distance between them continued to dwindle. "It's not my 'side' 'ol Farkas is on, it's on my 'back'!"

The snickers his remark brought didn't go unnoticed, as they stopped only feet away from the still advancing foreman. Farkas in turn, his face almost expressionless as his personality usually was, sounded like his old self and was strictly business when he spoke.

'One of you were supposed to call the office and let me know how bad that pump is I sent you to work on."

"We did phone." Fred quickly offered. "But your line was busy both times I called."

The happy atmosphere that had been with the three of them was noticeably showing signs of fading, but not quite enough to start to match the Evil Dwarf's cold voice. It was an unpleasant and unnecessary sensation that George had no intention of letting linger around them too long.

"It needs new seals and has to be repacked." he offered. "We're on the way to stores right now to pick up everything needed to fix it."

"And it's going to take the three of you to carry everything?" Farkas asked with just enough hint of sarcasm in his voice to add truth to the look in his eyes as they passed first from Bob and Fred and then back to George.

"Bob's coming with us so we can show him where the storage and supply location for this end of the plant is located, just in case we need anything else while we're in this area in the future."

"And I have to get something out of my locker along the way," Fred quickly offered as the foreman's eyes flickered briefly in his direction. But instead of speaking to him as expected, Farkas' stare moved back to George alone, while remarking.

"I just heard a little rumor from one of the woman, and I was hoping' you couldn't convince me it isn't true."

"Couldn't!" George exploded, noticeably perturbed. "You mean you're going back to your old ways and convicting me of the crime before I've even had a trial? Why is it I hear my brain yelling, 'Is anybody out there!' whenever we have these altercations?

"Anybody else but you, and I normally wouldn't have been so easily convinced." the Dwarf answered. His sudden change in reaction very noticeable, telling those smart enough to recognize his gestures that he was probably now doubting what he had just suggested. But as quickly as the doubt had shown on his face, it just as quickly disappeared, as if admitting to himself that he was correct to believe what he had heard.

"You've got to admit, you are the logical choice, especially as 'your' name always seems to be the first and last one most people always come up with when in doubt about who is responsible for whatever it is that's going on."

"Boy, you must wake up in the middle of the night wonderin' if there isn't something else you could do to take more advantage or make those around you more uncomfortable."

"Not anymore." the Dwarf answered, surprisingly. "The way damn things keep popping up around this place, I don't have to go out of my way to work at making anything up against the workers around here."

"Well then what is it that's biting you on the ass this time?"

George frowned, even more frustrated. "Maybe I 'will' be able to make your day."

For one brief second it actually looked as if ol' Farkas was actually about to smile, but he didn't. Instead he let Bob and Fred once more know that he was their boss, and therefore, above them.

"I don't know if it's the type of thing you want said in front of just anybody,"

"Don't worry about them!" George snapped out, his voice and gestures now indicating that he was capable of showing a little bit of authority himself if necessary. "I have no secrets to hide. A secret's too much like a lie. You not only have to remember exactly what it was - but also whom you have and whom you haven't told it to. And if you keep going the way you are, you're going to end up in one of them famous little padded rooms. You know, the one's where they give you a 'Nerf' airplane to throw. It has a pressure gauge taped to its nose that tells them how hard it hits whatever you throw it at. Only in your case - instead of throwing it thirty feet, you could probably toss it right through the closest wall!"

"Very well." friendly emotion still a stranger to his actions, the Dwarf answered, "If you insist!, It's been brought to just 'my' attention, that you've been spying on the women's end of the change-house. I believe that some of the men in the plant like to refer to it as 'Hooterville'."

"I don't believe it!" Fred said exasperatedly before George had a chance to speak. "I'll be damned if he doesn't believe you've been taking part of 'the great cross country' 'beaver hunt'!"

The smile that had vacated George's face since their meeting was instantly back almost in full force, as he almost laughed directly into Farkas' face.

"A couple of years back someone told me something so stupid I told him that if I ever lived to be a hundred I would probably never hear anything so ridiculous ever again. Well guess what? You just took his place!"

Under normal circumstances the remark might have received a grunt or two of appreciation, but since this wasn't to be that time, he continued with. "Sorry to disappoint you. But firstly, I don't believe in torture, good 'o-o-o-r' bad. And secondly, if I may put it so kindly. I believe that after looking at some of the older ladies around here, that they no doubt not only definitely look better fully clothed, but also are the main reason God in his almighty wisdom invented the 'dark'. Otherwise, I might add, a lot of poor ugly kid's wouldn't be getting a chance at being born."

Fred and Bob, as always, instantly saw the humor in the remarks. The Dwarf, in turn, was still successfully managing to keep himself from letting a smile express itself on his face. But the words that rolled off the end of his tongue next caught the three of them totally one and ten hundred percent off guard, not to mention surprised as Hell.

"I, I believe that you are telling the truth. I heard you use something once, and even though I've been saving for a long time for just a time like this, I'm not going to use it."

"And which little gem was it?" George asked, apprehension in his voice.

Keeping his own face almost totally free of emotion, the Dwarf answered dryly, "You shot the man down by saying, 'The next time you open your mouth, take your foot out!"

For almost the first time, especially since Fred and especially Bob had known him, George was noticeably hesitant with a reply, which more than hinted he was possibly at a loss for words. But then just as quickly, even though his face had temporarily betrayed him, he finally came up with the response, even if it was kinduv flat for a man of his capabilities. "Well, as much as I never thought in my life time that I would ever be saying any such words in your direction, I thank you!"

And before the situation could get any stranger than it had just become, Farkas started to walk away, while adding.

"Please remember what I said earlier, only 'I' have been made aware of this accusation. So unless someone informs those in higher management, the allocation dies here. Now let's get back to work. Our standing here isn't making the company any money."

For another brief moment, as they watched until his departing form was far in the distance, they each now seemed to be at a loss for words, as George's brain instead told him that no doubt one of the vengeful women was undoubtedly responsible for the silly rumor maybe even what Louie had been trying to warn him about.

Finally when one of them did speak, Bob was still leery enough to say out loud what he thought might be going on. Fred instead said, "I'll be damned! Is it me, or do you think he's smart enough to be trying 'head games' on us? One minute he makes you want to see the back of his head, and now he makes you wonder if maybe you aren't being a little bit too hasty!"

"I think I know what his problem is." George smiled. "He's probably trying to change his attitude and is finding himself in uncharted waters. And he just doesn't know how to go about finding his way our, let alone doing it yet."

"Maybe, maybe he's just havin' a bad day." Bob grinned.

"He usually doesn't have bad days." George answered, a doubtful look on his face. "He's know more for having bad weeks!"

"Or even bad months." Fred laughed.

Once more starting to move towards their next destination, a figure that had managed to hide undetected nearby joined them by matching his steps to theirs. It was one of the same men who had magically disappeared upon the boss's detected arrival earlier. Returning his smile-George simply said two very descriptive words. "Chicken shit!"

"Boy!" Ernie chuckled in reply. "You and the Dwarf sure seem to be getting alone pretty good lately."

"Ya, I know." George grinned in his two friend's direction. "I call him 'P.F.', and he calls me 'Son'."

"Keep it up." Ernie laughed, as Bob and Fred let only the expressions on their faces indicate the pleasure the present conversation was giving them. "And you'll be eligible for a very 'responsible' position around here."

George's sense of humor wanted to reply, "Hell! If I could 'keep it up', I'd be in Vegas right now sellin' it to the 'blue tinge'." But instead he continued to smile, "I already have one of those." knowing perfectly well Ernie was hinting at him being eligible for a foreman's position. "I'm already in a position that if anything goes wrong around this place lately, everybody here automatically thinks 'I'm responsible'."

"You mean that 'whoosh' I heard earlier as you and Farkas were talkin wasn't you passin you-know-who on the way up for a foreman's job?"

"The only 'whoosh' sound you could have heard," George winked in his two partners direction, "was the air in here passin' in through one of your ear holes, moving right on through to the other side and then back out again."

The low 'He-e-e-e-r!' that simultaneously slipped out of both Fred and Bob's lips were more habitual than necessary. But it was only Fred who then quickly added the extra slamming of, "Get that into you 'Gout Ball'!"

"Never mind the old 'You're so stupid,' jokes." Ernie snapped, while throwin' George off balance with a bump from his hips. "This is 'Fat Tuesday' not 'Simple Saturday', remember?"

"Oh, he remembers!" Fred quickly offered before George could. That's the trouble with George, he remembers 'everything'. And that's one prime reason why he'd never make a good foreman."

"I know, I know." Ernie answered a little frustrated. "He gives elephants memory lessons. We've all heard that line one more than once before, remember? But that doesn't mean he can't be debriefed enough to make him pull a 'Bogey" on us, and think about 'goin' over to the other side."

"Bogey?" Bob said, just barely enough to be heard. "What's the hell's a 'bogey'?" As spontaneous as he was, he couldn't figure this one out. Plus, he didn't want to miss out on what the referral stood for.

Fred's right hand, with his index finger extended, started up slowly towards his own nose. George's hand shot out to smack at it, while laughingly saying, "Don't bother being disgusting." His eyes then shifted back to Bob before answering his inquisitive remark of 'Bogey'?

"In the movie 'The Maltese Falcon' Humphrey Bogart played the part of a detective by the name of 'Sam Spade' who spends most of the picture trying to find out who bumped off his not so honest partner. Ya know, 'code of honor' and all that stuff."

"Now that you mention it, I do vaguely remember a bit about that old movie." Bob offered.

"Well then you should know what the Hell a 'Bogey' is!" Fred shot in his direction.

Seeing the confused expression still on Bob's face, George quickly offered, "At the end of the movie, Sam Spade, Humphrey Bogart that is, finally figures out just who was really responsible for the death of his partner."

"That, I think I can remember too." Bob offered. "Wasn't it Bogey's, ah, Spade's potential girlfriend in the movie, Mary, Mary, Mary Astor?"

"Very good!" George smiled. And as soon as he added the singular word of "And?" in an inquisitive manner, recognition lit up Bob's face.

"O-o-o-oh." he said, as soon as his brain finally grasped the information necessary to figure out what a 'Bogey' was. "When Bogart told her he wouldn't be anybody's 'fall guy' and was sendin' her over to the other side to pay for her crime of murder. And Ernie suggested you might be 'goin' over to the other side, he meant that you might be becoming a part of the enforcement agency, meaning the company management."

"Give the man a big fat cigar, for scoring one hundred percent!" Fred laughed.

"I would, if he smoked 'em'." George offered. And Ernie, while fishing a so-called 'coffin nail' out of his own package, added.

"Well I do smoke. And I think I'll 'cremate' a little something in his honor, right now."

Failing to get the 'Zippo' lighter that he had pulled from the same pocket to ignite, Ernie quickly gave it a few forceful shakes, while complaining, "This damn thing's getting' to be a real pain in the ass. I don't know what's wrong with it. Half the time it'll light, and half the time it won't. It's as if it's always running out of fuel."

"Here, let me have a go at it." George offered, while extending an open hand in his direction. "I know just how to fix that problem."

"Really!" Ernie replied, while sounding surprised and doing exactly as he had requested. "I thought you didn't smoke?"

"I don't." George answered, before dropping the lighter to the floor in front of them, and then smashing it with the heel of his safety boot.

And as Ernie excitedly shouted, "Hey! What the Hell did you do that for?" George calmly answered. "Well, now you'll no longer have to worry about if the 'damn' thing is going to work or not. Now you know for 'sure', 'it doesn't'!"

As Ernie continued to stare down in hypnotic astonishment at what used to resemble his lighter, the unlit cigarette now sagging from between his lips, Fred and Bob made no attempt to suppress any of the humor his present predicament had brought to them.

By this time they were within feet of splitting to go their own different ways. And because of what had just happened, it prompted Ernie to jokingly snarl in their direction.

"Well, I guess it's plain to see that the rumors about the three of you becoming a close knit 'rat pack' are true." He then, after glancing back one last time to the messy spot where his lighter had ceased to exist, altered his direction from theirs, while shaking his head silently. And just as quickly as the distance between them started to grow, George called out after him.

"The biggest trouble with 'rumors', Ernie, is that they don't always pay their 'rent' on time!"

The glow that instantly came with George's remark, as they continued to watch Ernie's shrinking form, uncontrollably suddenly became magnified as their vision took in the sudden comical antics of his body excitedly jumping what looked like about ten feet sideways. His hands weren't far behind as they instinctively leapt up to totally cover his ears. And as the obvious reason reached them only a fraction of a second later, someone was using a pneumatic air hammer on the opposite side of the tin wall Ernie was passing, each of their senses of oddball humor was 'gang raped' even more.

"You okay?" George, as the noise disappeared as quickly as it had arrived, more laughed then called in their departing friends direction.

James G. Davies Sr.

"I don't know, you tell me!" he shouted back, while probing a baby finger into the ear that had been closest to the wall. "I know I usually have a 'dump' about this time every day, but I'm normally one 'Hell' of a lot closer than this to a toilet bowl at the time!"

"Sounds like a possible 'lost time'!" a meaning associated with time off work, Fred shot back, his voice just as tickled with humor as George's had been.

"I'll let you know if I need witnesses after I hit the first aid office!" Ernie called back, one of his hands now cupping the location of where his heart would normally be under his work shirt. And just before turning a corner to disappear out of their view, knowing perfectly well that all of their eyes would still be on him, he paused long enough to left his left leg just high enough off the ground to be able to wiggle it. It was an act that was more for their benefit than to really check if their was something damp or loose unseen between his leg and pants.

In a half chuckle, George said to Bob, "Well, if 'Porko' wasn't already a candidate for menial work today, he is now!"

"Menial work?" Bob asked, once more noticeably confused.

"Ya!" Fred continued to laugh. "High criteria jobs!"

Bob only had a chance to acknowledge Fred's words with a singular "Huh?" before George offered n explanation as to what they were referring to.

"Special jobs! You know! The kind of work where you don't need a blueprint or any special instructions to work from."

"Ya!" Fred offered again. "Such as what you had mentioned earlier, cleaning out the old used staples from the bulletin boards throughout the plant, to see if they can be reused for thumb tacks."

"Or the inspection of burnt out light bulbs, so as to see if they can be recharged." George laughed.

"Oh!" Bob smiled back. "You mean such as shaving broom bottoms so as to ensure that all of its bristles will touch the floor equally at the same time when in use."

"Now, you've got it!" George grinned.

A small detour that George had genuinely forgotten to mention to the foreman was required into the service shop's welding area. It was necessary in order to pick up an ordered mounting bracket necessary for the job they were going to be working on. And since it was another location that Bob would sooner or later have to be familiarized with, George mentally passed off the oversight with Farkas as totally immaterial just now.

Most of the men in the enclosed small shop were familiar with both Fred and George, music from the odd cubicle they approached and passed easily detectable, so they both automatically returned the grins and friendly gestures aimed in their direction. But even before they reached the area George was leading them towards, Bob's silent inquisitive glances at what was going on around them as they walked, was more than enough to tell him that this little area apparently also had its own humorous gathering. And it wasn't just the guy alone who had mounted a small telescopic radio aerial out of the top of one side of his hearing protection cups that started him thinking that way. But rather the fellow using the flint lighter held up beside his head and snapping it like a flash bulb while pretending to take their pictures was another story.

Even from where they were walking, after watching another grinning worker purposely step on the dragging loose end of an air hose a fellow bud was carrying, Bob could see the makings of another prank underway. And even before the one carrying the airline had it yanked off of his arm as soon as the dragging slack had been taken up, Bob was already chuckling. But where one prank seemed to end, another was also there to follow it up. On one side of a thin metal painted flat black wall two men, one of them resting by leaning against the wall with the palm of one hand, were busy in conversation. On the opposite side of the wall another man, a lit heating torch in his hands, was just in the process of applying the soft flame from the torch onto the same area almost exactly opposite to where the leaning man's hand was touching the steel protective barrier. It didn't take any Einstein to figure out what was about to happen next. And as Bob altered his attention just long enough to inform George and Fred about what he anticipated, both men instantly acknowledged his still unspoken words with a silent mischievous all-knowing smile of their own, as George whispered,

"Watch the Oscar performance about to come from the comedian holding up the wall."

Almost instantly, no doubt due to the heat from the torch now penetrating the metal wall, their eyes were rewarded by a comical scene of the man in question as he yelped while jerking himself erect before doing a little dance any Indian would have been proud to know. They were actually close enough by now to hear the quick short puffs of wind being expelled from the still dancing man' lips. And their laughter was topped only by the worker who had been standing talking to the one now bouncing and shaking his whole arm, all enhanced with sporadic spitting at his apparent wound.

Anyone with common sense knew that a possible burn was anything but funny, regardless of man's nature to instantly laugh at any such humorous looking antics. But so far no one had ever credited any of the onlookers as being owners of any such sense, which was no doubt why they each continued to snicker out loud.

"Looks like Harry's going to have to do without sex tonight!" Fred laughed.

"Not really." George added. "Why did ya think God in his wisdom gave you 'two' hands?"

"No doubt just in case 'one' has a headache." Bob quickly chuckled.

"Right on!" George smiled. "But ol' Harry loves to over react just as much as the rest of us. His paw will probably only be sore just as long as it takes for quittin' time to get here,"

"Or right up until after he's home, when he picks up his first bottle of ice cold 'brown pop' Fred added.

"Either way," George said to Bob. "He's only getting back a little bit of his own medicine. Two weeks ago he gave the guy holdin' the heating torch a hotfoot much the same way. And if you thought Harry looked funny, then you should've seen Ted hopping around here like an inebriated one-legged stork, trying' to keep all of his weight on the cold foot, while fighting to get a hot work boot off the other."

"Now 'that', was funny!" Fred laughed, while doing a poor imitation of what they were talking about. "Especially when he ended up stickin' his leg, boot and all, into one of the tanks of cold water they keep around for coolin' hot jobs down."

"But you gotta realize most of these guys have been inflicted with one or more forms of welder's disease during their years here." George smiled.

"You know," Fred butted in. "they're the one's whose attire is all pock marked like someone has burned a million small holes into their clothing, the kind caused by hot sparks from when they were welding."

"Exactly," George butted in. "But the real veterans are the guys you see in the shower room with 'two' holes in the end of their 'donikers'. One porthole they were born with - the other they got when a red-hot molten gob of metal had landed in their lap when welding. It then burnt right on through onto the end of their 'knob'! Now when they take a 'leak' they have to put a finger over the end of one hole - or they end up with one jet stream going into the urinal, with the other water spout pissin' out onto the floor. And if you think that's not bad enough, just envision the poor bugger who ends up doing the splits when slipping on the wet spot!"

"Don't forget the joy of having the potential poison from the hot metal burn having to be 'sucked out'. And then applying hand cream to the infection." Fred smiled.

"At our old place," Bob laughed, "We used to identify most of our welders by the areas of arc burn under their chins."

"Ahhh! the 'big hickey'" George smiled, while nodding his head in recognition of his best buddy's remark. "And let's not forget the classic way we identify those of them who are smokers."

"How's that?" bob asked.

"By the way that one of their shirt pockets are generally missing, gone, burned off, just a hole surrounded by browned singed material."

"How come?" Bob continued, still looking confused.

"Think about it." Fred smiled, before George started to answer. "If you were a smoker, you'd probably keep your smokes and matches close-by in your shirt pocket. And if you were a welder, where do the hot sparks generally end up while you are welding, why in any convenient close-by opening. Thus, for those of us who know, a book of match's once one match is ignited, the rest generally follow right in behind. And by the time the individual realizes what is happening - he tries to slap out the ensuing bon fire, only to end up loosing his pocket and contents along the way."

His face cringing at the mental images George's little horror story had conjured up, Bob said. "That's scary!"

James G. Davies Sr.

"It sure is." George grinned. "Especially if the fire takes the hair in your nose with it. Just think of all those opportunities you'll miss out on, if you can't smell the wife when she's in 'heat'!"

With Fred laughing, while Bob was shaking his head in 'sick joke' response, George picked up the bracket once more, and started to lead the way. And after glancing over his shoulder, he commented, "We don't want to hang around here any longer than we have to. These guy's don't always just pick on each other."

"You can believe that!" Fred frowned. "Stupid me, while passing through here once paused long enough to wait for what I thought would be the humorous results of what would happen after I saw one of the men filling up another guy's air hose with water." And as he paused long enough to roll his eyes upwards in an effort to enhance what he was saying, grinning Bob quickly asked, "And what happened?"

"Nothin'! At least not to the guy I was naive enough to think was being 'set up'! Me! I almost drowned standin' up!" Fred carried on, now noticeably frustrated. "While I was lollygagging to see someone's area get sprayed with water - - the real joker in the overhead crane rolled up behind me and drove me to my knees with a pail of water he had hidden up there. Seems I was the real target and the other guy was just a 'red herring'.

As always when they were together now, once started laughter was again extremely contagious. And Bob, his backbone growing larger with each passing day, wasn't about to let either of his two best friends supply all of the laughs.

"We used to have water hose fights, but the best drowning you could catch someone with was when they were the most vulnerable. You'd wait till the target was busy in the crapper next to you. Then you'd pour a pail of water over the stalls wall while he was caught not only with his guard, but pardon the pun, but also with his 'pants' down."

"Different prank, same results." George laughed, just as their next destination grew in front of them. "The boys in this place are famous for everything from hot teabags under your bum just as you're ready to sit down, to welding each other's lunch buckets to their lunch table."

"At my old place," bob chuckled, "they used to put a solid block of steel in each other's lunch pail. That way anyone in a hurry foolish enough to forget to check his bucket first usually ends up either just ripping the container's handle clean off, or being rewarded with one arm ending up longer than the other."

"Same here." Fred laughed. "Only with us it was usually just through nailing the poor soles pail to the table."

"Hell, we even used to bet who'd get the furthest." Bob laughed.

The change houses were only a quick short cut away from the company's supply stores, and as Fred turned to briefly break up their trio - George's departing words of, "We'll meet you at 'Did-Ya's'." went along with him. Bob in turn, his face already showing the question forming in his mind, didn't get the chance to ask it, as George once more beat him to the punch.

"Did-Ya's just another one of the nicknames we have for one of the older guys around here you haven't met yet. This guy's real moniker is Ron Chalmers, but no one ever calls him that anymore. 'Did-Ya's' his nickname, and 'Did-Ya's' all he ever goes by now."

As they walked, Bob shifted the weight of the pump packing they had also acquired, which George had given him as his share of the load, from one hip to the other. It was in his thoughts, even though he was still smiling inside at the sign they had seen on the company's outer door, 'Back in 15 minutes. Gone 10 already!' to comment about the weird name George was presently giving a going over, but he didn't. Instead, as he had come to learn, he just waited patiently for George in his own way and time to tell him, and he had also learned since their times together that it was inevitable.

"His nickname's such a natural, although no one really knows for sure who originally gave it to him, even though there are those who will swear it was them. It all started when Ron used to be the plant's all-time best joke teller. People, more so now, used to come from all over with the intent of trying to stump him with the punch line of a joke. And just naturally the first words out of all those people's mouths were -."

By this time Bob had no trouble in figuring out in advance what the last words would be next in coming out of George's mouth - and he proudly beat him to it. "Did-ya hear the one about?"

There was an equal smile on both of their faces now, and George asked if maybe he thought he might have an old or new joke 'Did-Ya' might never have heard yet.

"Could be." Bob, the confirmation written all over his face, that he had figured out the origin of 'Did-ya' before George was able to tell him - smiled "Let me think about it for second."

More than once in the past when doing his best to tell what he believed was an all out 'knee slapper', he had felt that those in the presence of his greatness must have surely been sitting on their hands when he delivered the hilarious punch line. But, for whatever reasons, he had no intention of letting George know that.

"Well if you're going into the 'gray matter vault', you'd better dig real deep." George grinned devilishly. "It could either make or cost you some serious money."

"Huh?" Bob said, confused.

"Well," George chuckled out loud as they walked. "like I said earlier, "Did-Ya's' reputation for almost knowing the punch line to every joke going around got to be a challenge to a lot of the guys working here. And when one of them bet him that there was no way he could possible know the punch line to a joke this guy had heard on his vacation in Europe only a week earlier, money just naturally became a part of every joke test after that. In fact, I know personally that there have been some months where he's almost made over a hundred bucks off guys willing to gamble that they could stump him."

"A 'hundred' greenbacks!" Bob said, before letting out a long slow whistle. "Wow! That's a lot of bread! - Just what kind of coin does it take to find out if he already knows the joke you're testing him with?"

"He always leaves that up to the person with the joke. But to make sure no one individual gets burned to bad in either direction, he keeps the maximum bet at two bucks." George answered. "But the real money to be made is in 'side bets'. The guy with the joke can gamble anywhere from two bits to two bucks. And if anyone else there thinks that 'Did-Ya' isn't going to know the punch line, and believe me, they've generally already discussed or done research on the joke, they can each bet the same amount."

"Sounds a little lopsided against old 'Did-Ya' doesn't it?" Bob said, once more repositioning the load he was carrying. "What's the odds against him knowing the punch line on a joke from halfway around the world, as well as having already been dissected by a bunch of seasoned co workers?"

"Exactly!" George grinned again. "And that's why he gets two to one odds on all jokes tried on him."

"Ah - - that sounds a little better." Bob smiled. "And does he ever get really abused?"

"Occasionally he gets stumped." George answered. "But not very often. speculation has it that he's almost made enough to retire on." he chuckled. "The men may seemingly have the odds in their favor by first trying the joke on each other and asking around to see if anybody's already heard its punch line, but ol' 'Did-Ya' does his homework too. I've heard that he has friends and relatives picking him up joke books from all over, wherever they travel. It may sound like a lot of work for a chance at some money, but personally I think he does it more for the fun of the men's company and reactions, not to slam them."

Bob was just about to tell George that he might just have a 'stumper' or two that 'did-ya' could never have heard of, when George spoke first with the simple words of, "We're here!"

The only immediate noticeable difference Bob could see between the little work area they had just entered and a dozen more just like it scattered throughout the plant, was that this one was seemingly overpopulated with human activity. And as George's presence was noticed along with the stranger he had brought with him, his arrival was both acknowledged and welcomed by most of the men they walked past.

Easily blending in with the crowd, there was someone already presently trying to stump the very one they had come to see, George quietly introduced Bob to a few of the men they paused alongside of. While Bob, looking at the man wearing the tee-shirt labeled 'Did-ya' bring your money?' George asked one of them what was the first part of the joke 'Did-ya' was now trying to answer.

With a big grin on his face, possibly because he already knew the punch line of the joke just asked, one of the men whispered in George's direction. "Dandy just asked 'Did-Ya' if he knew what the blind man answered to the department store clerk who had rushed up and excitedly asked, 'Sir! Can I help you?' as the blind guy was swirling his seeing-eye dog as the end of its leash, out over the top of his head."

As humorously exaggerated mental images of the poor air born dog at leashed end formed inside their heads, even though each didn't really know the punch line, both Bob and George couldn't help but let their faces imitate the ones already smiling around theirs. And while moving in a little closer in anticipation of 'Did-Ya's answer, not even a remark of, "Hey! I don't mind you two guy's standin' still, just don't do it in front of me!" could wipe the anticipation of laughter from their eyes.

'Did-Ya', obviously enjoying the sea of grinning faces before him, deliberately fuelled the building emotional fires of anticipation by pretending to be a little doubtful about the jokes potentially hilarious punch line. And in order to prolong, as well as escalate his co-workers hopes, he slowly, as always, repeated the joke out loud.

"Now let me think. What did the blind man swinging his seeing eye dog at the end of its leash over his head in the middle of a department store answer to the clerk who rushed up and asked, "Sir, can I help you?"

Pausing briefly, one hand stroking his chin while saying, "Hu-u-u-m." every man there hanging on his every word and gesture, 'Did-Ya' then let his now excited face indicate that he had finally figured out the blind man's humorous probably reply, before answering. "Why he must have answered something like, 'No thank you! I'm just taking a look around!" to the clerk.

His words, even though everyone except George and grinning Bob already knew the answer was almost word for painful word one hundred percent correct. It also instantly caused the whole surrounding area to be filled with a wave of loud moaning broken laughter. And even the men now busy passing a small amount of change and paper currency in smiling 'Did-Ya's' direction couldn't help but smile themselves.

Everyone was apparently happy, 'even' the guy who suddenly let out with a loud verbal barrage of obscenities, verbal remarks that somehow never seemed out of place in some work places. But it was enough to make George instantly place the bracket he was now holding down onto the floor in front of him, before quickly reaching out and cupping his hands over Bob's ears, while saying, "Pul-e-ase! - Not in front of the new man!"

'Did-Ya', obviously there for his benefit as well as theirs, grinned a singular word of "Next!' into the crowd, without waiting for the snickering humor around him to subside.

Shifts

When no one spoke or stepped forward, George dropped his hands back to his side after nudging Bob, before whispering into his ear, "Go ahead! Try to stump him."

And just as quickly as George had poked him, Bob shyly declined. But when George persisted a little more loudly now so that the other men there would obviously notice, "Go ahead! I'll back ya!" Bob reluctantly and gradually weakened while his brain started to search the corridors of his memory for just such a joke.

Finally, as others there who still didn't know him from 'Adam' coaxed him on, Bob hesitantly let the words of, "Oh, okay. I, I think I've got one." slowly escape from his lips.

As should be expected, all of the men's eyes instantly shifted in his direction, with their interest likewise riveted to his every following word.

"Did ya hear, the one about these two young guys who used to go to the same beach all the time. One used to constantly have beautiful shapely young females falling 'all' over him, while the other poor fellow could never get a single girl to come anyone near him - not even for a very short time?"

A small ripple of whispers immediately flowed through the crowd, as the workers tried to find out if anyone there had even remotely heard of the joke. And when they had failed to finally get even one person's acknowledgment to the gag, everyone's eyes just naturally shifted in 'Did-Ya's' silently smiling direction.

Panning the crowd first, he stared directly into Bob's nervous face, before answering, "Around here 'sonny', it usually costs a little something to get the answer to a question like that."

"Oh, oh, ya." Bob quickly fumbled. And as he answered, "Would a dollar be too much?' 'Did-Ya' lost no time in replying with, "Sounds about right for a starter."

He then let his age-wise eyes once more pass among the crowd, while continuing with, "Anybody else here feel lucky enough to gamble on whether or not I know the punch line, that is after he gives me the rest of it? And if it'll help some of you fence sitters grow a backbone, I'll swear on a stack of bibles that I've never set eyes on this man before today and up until right now." Altering his attention just long enough

James G. Davies Sr.

to smile in Bob's direction, he then added, "Is what I just said not true young man?"

Even before Bob's head started to nod in affirmation to the question, a small ripple of conversation had started to pass among the expectedly 'gun-shy' workers, with the final result being that only George seemed willing to match his as yet untested friend's finical wager. And when Bob, his attention distracted just long enough to notice that Fred still hadn't shown yet mentioned it to George, George joked it away by saying that Fred had been known to get lost in a one door shithouse, so not to worry about him.

Now, as earlier, 'Did-Ya' expertly played the gathering by slowly mouthing Bob's last words, before finally saying towards the crowd. "Okay, go ahead. Let's hear the rest of it, right up to the punch line."

"Well," Bob started, noticeably nervous, especially since the sound of any other human voice was noticeably missing, everyone's interest now locked onto solely him. 'Well,' he swallowed hard before continuing, "Finally at the end of one day when the two guys just happen to be in the change house at the same time, the fellow not getting any girls asks the other guy what the secret of his success is. The other fellow tells him that to get the young stuff all excited he puts an elongated hard thin potato about six inches long on the inside of his swimsuit before going out on the beach.

The first poor fellow thanks him and it's just about a week later that they run into each other once again in the same change house. The lucky stiff usually getting all of the woman's attention asks the first fellow how it's been going, to which the poor chump frowns, "It's worse than ever!"

Letting a few seconds of silence pass before continuing, indicating that he was finished with his end of the joke, Bob sheepishly nodded 'That's it.' in 'Did-Ya's direction. And as the silence that had been 'golden' only brief seconds earlier was broken by the gathering 'Did-Ya' once more noticeably enjoyed his part of the action. Exaggeratedly scratching his chin, while mumbling to himself in words just loud enough for those closest to him to hear, 'Gee. That's not much to work with.' He then let his eyes squint upwards while the rest of his face indicated that he was now searching deep inside the 'storage chambers' of his head, 'Did-Ya' stalled for as long as he dared, before finally handing his loss in Bob and

George's direction. It was a gesture that instantly had the air around them filled with cheers, almost drowning out his voice.

"I give up! I guess you got me with the ol' beginner's luck! and to top it off, being a new and first timer, you get 'face value' on your wager. So, what 'is' the punch line?"

Happily and eagerly accepting his share of the wager, Bob almost giddily answered, "Well, the guy who always 'gets' the girls takes a step backwards, a look of puzzlement on his face. He then proceeds to walk around the first guy still in his swimsuit, before finally stopping in front of him again. Then in one quick movement, he leans forward just far enough to whisper into the poor other fellow's ear 'The 'potato' goes in the front!'

The cheers that had subsided just long enough to hear the punch line - exploded into a roar of similar sounding happy laughter. It was also punctuated with a few elongated 'He-e-e-rs', both in recognition to the hilarious punch line - as well as the fact that just maybe a new someone had finally brought fresh material 'competition' to their gathering. Noticeably also enjoying the moment, 'Did-Ya' shrugged his shoulders in apparent dismay, before once more simply saying, "Next!"

As had happened before, it was a gesture that briefly went unnoticed, as a few of the men quickly tried a few lesser and obviously universally more recently well-know small jokes on each other. and when someone started it off with one of their crowd pleasing old favorites, 'What has six wheels and flies?' a handful of them instantly shouted out in almost perfect unison, 'A garbage truck!' the humor was instantly contagious - especially when someone else kept it going.

"I've heard that the definition of a 'born loser', is a guy who goes to a hooker and she says, "Not tonight honey, I have a headache!"

From there it carried on with a rapid burst of short one-liners that were answered in almost the same manner.

"Why did 'God' invent wheelbarrows?"

"So Italians could learn to walk!" the group cheered.

"Why don't cannibals eat clowns?"

"Because they taste funny!"

"How do you know if your nose is to big?"

"It blocks out most of the floor space in front of you!"

"What do you say if all your kids are ugly?"

"They're adopted!"

And when it looked as if the 'one liner' jokes were about to become scarce, someone always seemed to have 'two' and 'three liners' ready to take over.

"What's the definition of a true friend?"

"That's a guy who goes to town, gets 'two' blow jobs, comes back home and gives 'you one'."

"What's the difference between an optimist and a pessimist?"

"The 'pessimist' is a guy who thinks that when the end of the world comes, he'll be in the 'john' with his pants down around his ankles. The 'optimist' is a guy who hopes that when the end of the world comes, he'll 'be' the 'john' in the bathroom with his pants down around his ankles!" As a few of the gathering made sour faces at the suggestions behind some of the jokes, someone in the excitement of the moment answered his own riddle when saying,

"Why are electric trains like a woman's 'boobs'? Because even though they're intended for children, it's the fathers who always want to play with them!"

"I think I can relate to what that born losers been going through." someone close to George said. "My wife's always using four letter words whenever we're having sex lately. And all of them are like - 'Stop!' 'Don't' 'Can't!' And 'Won't!'"

"Ya, well, you could be worse off." another co-worker snickered. "You could have married my wife! Ice wouldn't melt on her forehead when we're having a little 'nookie'."

"That's nothin'!" someone else frowned. "Mine has a cool 'mist' comin' out of her mouth whenever I'm tryin to lay a little 'pipe'!"

"I don't see what you bums have got to grumble about." a new voice in the crowd complained. "As soon as my wife takes off her underpants - the 'furnace' comes on!"

It was apparent that the jokes were starting to drift towards what was considered as 'risqué', material generally left for the lunch table or change house conversations. So George, especially after noticing that not everyone there was not enjoying the quality of the material now being spoken, did one of the many things he was well know for, he tried to salvage it.

"Am I missing something? Are you guys forgetting what 'day' this is?"

A voice yelling out 'It's 'Friday'! The day before two days of parole and freedom!' led the way into a series of just as noisy whistling and cheers from the crowd. And George, as Bob enjoyed the comradery, gave a long high-pitched whistle of his own, before adding. "It's also double up 'Fat Friday' time. All the jokes you never had a chance to use or hear on 'Fat Tuesday', now get a chance to come into play again. Or have you bums forgotten that?"

The words were like a spark to dry straw, which instantly set the men on fire with comments like, "He must be referring you Pete. The word must have gotten out that you've got the 'skinniest' pets in town - no doubt because there's never any leftovers at your place after mealtimes"

Instantly the 'insulted' became the 'insulator' with, "Don't start a fire you can't put out. I'm not the guy walking around with a portable radio strapped to my hip and listening to all the commercial jingles being played, just so I can keep track of which fast food franchise has the best 'junk food' deals on for the week."

"Hey, and I'm not the one who after the company picnic with all its 'free food' who couldn't fit into his car and ended up staying to the very end!"

"That's only because I temporarily lost my car keys, and didn't find them until the next day, smart-ass!"

"Where'd you find them," one of the other workers quickly asked, "In your 'poop'?"

"Easy does it Dougy." Pete smiled. "I'm not the one who looks like that when I was little my mother not only beat me with an 'drum' stick - but also with an 'ugly' stick, Not to mention looking as if she also fed you with a 'shovel' instead of a 'spoon'!"

Once started, which was often, those sitting by and enjoying the little battle of witticisms, sometimes felt the need to throw in a tidbit of spiked information they believed would not only keep the intended war of words entertaining, but also ongoing. And as the words, "Don't forget to mention his big lunch-pail!" came out of the crowd - they were just as quickly used as retaliating ammunition.

"Lunch-pail! I wouldn't call anything with three handles, one on each end and one on top, a lunch-pail. A mid sized garbage pail maybe, but never, ever a lunch-pail!"

"If he put wheels on it, he could use it for a wheel barrel! came out of the gathering.

"I think we should be calling it a 'waste basket'?" someone else in the gathering offered. "By the time he's finished sacrificing to the 'God of poop' everything that wasn't absorbed, whatever was digested generally always ends up showing around his 'waist'!"

"If you want to elaborate on it being referred to as a 'waste basket', why not go the whole 'nine yards' and call it what it will eventually be, especially if he keeps 'chowing down' at the rate he's going. Call it a 'casket' and get it over with. After they cremate him, it's just the right size."

"The amount of food he can consume is one thing, but the way he can inhale and make it disappear is another. I swear he must have taken a course in magic!"

"A-a-h. The 'big gulp!" someone added.

As those sitting close to the one who had just spoken grinned, Doug also smiled in his direction, before adding, "The 'big gulp'. I haven't heard that one for a long time. I can still picture how it got its name. A man would scoop all of the food on his plate into a pointed mound, hang himself upside down overtop of it with his mouth wide open, and then 'cut' the rope."

As those with vivid imaginations chuckled when envisioning the scene just described, some apparently feeling neglected, started to pick on themselves. It was a strange and contagious phenomena that always seemed too sooner or later pop up at the gatherings.

"I've put on so much weight lately that instead of telling me to go to my room when we're arguing, the wife tells me to go to my stall."

"I know what you mean. Instead of going for a jog after supper like I used to, I now feel like I'm going for a waddle."

"If I don't find something to do after supper, I always end up guarding the couch until it's time for bed."

"I can't remember when I last saw my dick." Someone then foolishly offered.

"I sure hope everybody else here can say the same thing about your pecker." 'Randy' chuckled.

"I would've been happy if he'd just said he could see his shoes or toes." Doug frowned. "Now I don't know if I'll be able to get to that image out of my head and sleep tonight!"

"Lately all it seems I have to do to gain weight is to just think about food. I swear the only sure way to loose some weight is to either stop eating completely, or die!"

"Which strange enough, is true." someone chuckled.

"Well at least you're not starting to look like a bag of garbage tied in the middle."

"Apparently we've all got problems of one kind or another. I'm starting to feel that I just gotta get me a bigger car. Every time I try to get out of mine lately, it fits so tight that I swear it almost reminds me of what it was like being born!"

"And here I was going to compliment you on not having any wrinkles for your age."

"All I know is that I've got to do something. When I tried to sneak up behind the wife and surprise her from behind by puttin my hands over her eyes, she said my stomach arrived first gave me away."

"Are you sure it wasn't the sound of the floor moanin or crackin?" another heckler quipped, only to be slapped with, "Listen 'Slim'. I'm not the one who resembles the 'Pillsbury Dough Boy' - hooked on steroids.'

And then there were those among the gathering who tried to be just short of invisible to the heckling and barbs. Such was the individual trying to silently 'suck back' a fresh pink 'Twinkie', only to have its ripping wrapper give his presence away. And when the man beside him started to sing, "Twinkie a Twinkie, fun for girls and boys. A Twinkie a Twinkie," the worker next in line quickly laughed, "That's a 'slinky', 'pea-brain'."

"Boy! Someone's showin' their age."

"That's not all he's showin'." came from somewhere within the gathering, " He's showin' about eight months pregnant!"

"Who'd have thought having a wife who makes sandwiches that need the 'jaws of life' to bite into would ever come in handy?"

"Well if some of you guys want to really loose some calories - just try pretending the refrigerator is locked next time you plan sneaking downstairs in the middle of the night to 'hump' the poor bugger."

"I've heard it said that some people's eyes are bigger than their stomachs. If you think you're one of them, try closing one of them next time you sit down to eat."

"Or if exercise isn't for you, and you can't do the odd 'push up'. try doing the odd 'push away'. Try pushing your chair away from the 'trough' next time you think you're so hungry you could eat a 'horse'."

"Now that you mention horses," Doug smiled, after noticing 'Did-Ya' glancing at his watch. "That reminds me that I've heard there are actually people out there who don't eat 'meat', you know 'vegetarians. I think they go by the name of 'vegans' now."

Even as the thought, 'Well if they don't eat 'meat', how do they ever expect to finally win an argument?' popped into George's head, one of the men close to him started to offer his own commentary. And as soon as he started with, "Only 'whusups' are afraid to eat 'meat'! A 'real' man would not only," he quickly reached out and used one a hand to cover the mans mouth. And when others close by, as well as the one he had cut off in mid remark gave him a confused look - he smiled and waved his finger in front of his own nose, before offering, 'Now then, think before you speak. Remember that saying about 'It's better for one to be thought an idiot, than to open ones mouth and remove all doubt'. Well it also goes for being 'rude and crude'.

Fortunately for George his reputation 'did' precede him. A lesser man would possibly have remained silent, and then snickered at what the rest of the crude remark was leading up to. But his little gesture didn't go unacknowledged, as the worker remarked, "I sure hope that's not the hand you wipe your 'ass' with." To which George grinned, "Na-a-aw. That's the one I pick my 'nose' with. Your nose should have told you that."

And as those close enough to be a part of the little verbal skit laughed, another high pitched whistle brought everyone's divided attention back to where it had all started.

'Did-Ya' than smiled devilishly in their direction while saying, "Anybody else here to bet the wife and kids. Or is that it for today?"

As earlier, it was soon obvious that the men were still a little gun-shy about testing him just yet. But Bob, apparently a bit overly confident and cocky about winning money on his very first try, stepped a little closer while saying, "I think i might have another joke for you, that is if you still want my money?"

"That's what even the cowards are here for son." 'Did-Ya smiled in his direction, noticing that he also had most of the men's attention. "Go ahead, spit it out. Or do you just want to open your mouth and I'll read what's on the tip of your tongue?"

Also noticing the he had everyone's interest, Bob chuckled, as some of them edged him on. Turning his head in George's direction just long enough to ask him if he wanted to split on this joke also, George grinned back, "Sure, why not? It's only money." The reply was not only as Bob had hoped it would be, but it also gave him back some of what he felt like he was starting to loose - courage. Moving on to give the crowd a bit of a cocky grin, a gesture which prompted a 'Wise man once say, even fool know not to prod the panda.' from his partner, he quickly lost it before looking into 'Did-Ya's' 'spider to the fly's' face, before starting.

"Did ya hear, the one about the little old fragile lady who was affected by the weather. It seems that whenever she had to go out on a damp rainy day she always used to end up with a terrible hot burning rash between her legs by the time she got back home?"

Exactly like earlier the men, after trying to read 'Did-Ya's' face for any hint of a clue that he might know the answer, quickly took turns putting their heads together while mumbling among themselves'. Reading them as they had read him - 'Did-Ya' did what he always did, encouraged them to enter his den.

"Anybody here with enough intestinal fortitude wanting to make a side bet?"

Suddenly, possibly because Bob was betting the limit on the success of his first joke, more than half of the men exploded into a barrage of one and two dollar bets. In fact, some of them were so overconfident at Bob's as of yet unheard rib tickler, they were willing to make more than one wager.

George now, for some strange reason know only to himself, suddenly spoke up and said that he was willing to cover some of the men's extra bets. It was a maneuver that instantly made Bob sarcastically smile,

"Thanks for the vote of confidence, friend. Trying to cut your losses, huh?" before continuing with the rest of his joke.

"Well, one rainy day she couldn't take the pain any longer, and went to see her doctor. She told him her condition and after he had checked her out on the examination table, he understood what her problem was. Without giving her a chance to object or using any anesthetic, he dug right in. After a few bewildering minutes he told her to hop back down onto the floor. Gingerly doing as requested the poor thing slowly took a few timid steps as also suggested. And when to her astonishment the burning sensation was totally gone, in utter amazement she asked him what he had done.

Pausing now, a big grin on his face, Bob then said in 'Did-Ya's' grinning direction. "That's it. Now then, what did the doctor answer?"

"Oh, that's easy." 'Did-Ya' shot back, while moving closer to the wagers each gambler was holding in his hand, "The only logical response the doctor could have made was, 'I just cut two inches off the top of your rubber boots'!"

Even before Bob could start to offer his and George's money in 'Did-Ya's' already opened-handed direction, most of the men there somehow just knew that the answer they had just heard was about to cost them their money also. And as soon as Bob's hand, his face already telling the whole story, started to return the loot and more he had won only moments earlier, a low series of 'Oh no's! Not again!' flowed through the crowd as other losers reluctantly prepared to do the same.

"Look fellas," 'Did-Ya' smiled, while gathering in his winnings. "I'll give everybody here a chance to win their money back. All any one of you has to do is give me the answer to this riddle. Why is a good haircut like sex?"

Instantly the workers exploded into half whispered conversations, with strictly the hopes once again of improving themselves financially. But when almost a whole minute passed with no suitable answers being offered, 'Did-Ya' smiled while saying,

"Sorry guys. But why is a good hair cut like sex? Well - because if either experience is a really good one, it doesn't bother you anymore. But if it's a botched job - it irritates you right up until you do it again."

Shifts

Between the mixed reactions of moans and groans that instantly flowed from the men, 'Did-Ya' still noticeably content with him-self smiled, "And then there's always the one about the Southern Gentleman who had the word 'South' tattooed onto his pecker. And when his wife asked him why, he had replied 'Because I'm positive that the 'South will soon rise again, good woman'!" and as soon as most of the moans turned to chuckles he quickly went right into "Next!" while counting his winnings. George's similar actions were only feet away from his, but totally unnoticed by everyone else there, all except Bob. But even stranger to him was the sudden reaction the singular word was now having on each of the other men. It was if it had actually been a challenge to serve as a command to encourage everyone's immediate departure. And the slight humorous grumbling that followed the men's sudden evaporation was just as customary as it was unbiased.

When finally only a grinning George and a confused Bob were left in 'Did-Ya's presence, once someone had yelled out 'Who cut the mustard!' George made sure to walk his and Bobs nostrils a safe distance away from the now contaminated area and all of the other likewise instantly departing men before acknowledging his old friend's contagious smile with a simple quick seemingly all-knowing wink. And once 'Did-Ya had wordlessly answered Georges eye twitch in much the same manner, George then lead Bob into new territory.

Once alone again, Bob curiously asked his friend if he and the apparent 'king of punch lines' weren't taking advantage and teaming up on their apparently slower witted co-workers.

The undetected wink he had given 'Did-Ya' moments earlier repeated itself, only this time with more of the 'devilish prankster' in it for Bob's benefit.

"No! I thought by now you would know me better than that. It's just that I personally don't think there are jokes 'Did-Ya' doesn't know the correct or possible answer to. I also think he deliberately lets the odd gag get by him, just so he can not only suppress some of his winnings, but also so as to keep the men happy and coming back for more. And to give you a better understanding of the man for next time your paths cross, believe it or not there are times when he'll actually disqualify himself if the joke has already been tried on him.

Don't go underestimating the other men either. They know what he can do, and what they think he can't do. And believe me, they all also know that he's not the type of guy to take advantage of his buds.

"Well, thanks for warning me." Bob said with just a hint of sarcasm still detectable in his voice, as his face slipped into a Confucius like mask. "I can see where it's true when they say 'A smart man learns by another man's mistakes, and a fool repeats them'."

"Why should I warn you?" George half-laughed while shifting the weight of the item he was once more carrying, his hand then digging into his right pant pocket. "You didn't loose anything. I just got to carry our money for us for a little while."

Waving the small pile of folded paper bills he had won under Bob's nose like a fan, he added, "The next 'feed bag' stops on me."

The fact that Fred was still nowhere in sight now had George a little concerned, But not by the type of worry that yet warranted a search party. And when Bob once more mentioned Fred's absence, only after catching George's curious searching stare around the building they were now passing through, George again shrugged it off with a comical response.

"Oh, I'm sure he'll show up sooner or later. It's for guys like him that elevators only go up and down, not sideways."

Jumping out from behind a steel supporting girder he had been hiding behind, as if materializing on George's command, Fred loudly shouted out, "I heard that!"

Instinctive reflex's made both George and Bob comically jerk away sideways in surprise. But the grin that almost instantly came to George's face when his eyes settled onto Fred's familiar form was a full second behind Bob's other instinctive defensive reactions. And as Bob's trained body leapt with one foot menacingly parallel forward in Fred's direction, while letting out a yell loud enough to make a deaf man flinch, it was Fred who became noticeably startled. Up until now Bob had never had a chance or reason to experience Bob's expert reflex actions. And he was genuinely startled enough to let out a 'Yikes!' of his own, especially when Bob's work boot whooshed less than in inch past the side of his head.

George, once more startled even though he knew what was coming, naturally couldn't contain his laughter. And when Fred finally realized that Bob wasn't about to kick him into the middle of next week, he gradually imitated the two friendly faces now smiling in front of him.

"Where the 'Hell' have you been?" George asked.

"Ya!" Bob quickly added. "We could have used your money and support at 'Did-Ya's'

"Oh don't give me that." Fred grinned back into Bob's face. "If you were with mister sarcasm here, you must have made money!"

While waving the winnings in front of Fred's face, George grinned, "Only one person here didn't know that you would already know that we won some 'scratch', and he thinks the jokes might have been fixed. But two of us here have absolutely no inkling as to why the 'shit' it's taken 'you' so long just to take a 'crap'!"

The humor that had faded from his best friends face came back in full force as his minds eye previewed the information he was about to give out, in order to answer George's aggressive question.

"When I was in the change-house," he chuckled. "there was a couple of guys who had been working overtime getting' ready to wash-up and go home. I was just reaching my locker when all 'Hell' broke loose. Sometime during this morning and the first coffee break, someone, speculation already has it as being the women, somehow managed to sneak food-coloring dye into the liquid soap dispensers mounted over the washbasins and in the shower rooms. Apparently it was that granular clear stuff that only activates and changes color once mixed with water."

"Two guys usin' the washbasins only got their hands stained. But the poor buggers in the showers got the stuff all over their faces, as well as not to mention the family jewels. And if human emotions are truly associated with colors, then these guys are rightly shaded for deep anger."

Needless to say, as he continued to over-emphasize his closing words of, "And 'that', gentlemen, regardless of the prank already having been played on us more than once, is why I am so late!" Bob and George, once more telling himself that this is another of the things Louie had warned him about, were in deep laughter.

Once again, as Fred quickly joined in, it was apparent that each of their warped sense of humor was closely matched. And each and every time they came across a familiar fellow worker willing to listen that day, it wasn't Bob's initiation with 'Did-Ya that received all of their attention, but rather the comical change-house incident. Also fortunately for all encountered, as most other happenings within the plant, it was over-exaggerated over blown and greatly out of proportion each and every time it was told, told, and then re-told.

Chapter 12

'Blood suckers.'
Or
'Pecking order.'

Fortunately for those in the world whose stomach instantly flip flops at the sight of blood, there are others who can take its life giving crimson red color in their every day stride. Bob, his past in such matters still a secret but with a slight queasiness in his stomach confirming his previous thoughts, was starting to regret that he had let George talk him into volunteering to join him at the company's quarterly 'Blood Donor Clinic'.

But it was far too late to back out now, especially after having 'wowed' most of the men there with his masculine Karate demonstration back at the Meat Market. He just knew he was going to have trouble going along with the contagious conversation now taking place around him. And, as he moved one step forward along with the rest of the human chain he was now standing in, not even the caption from a world famous Jim Unger cartoon hanging only feet away, could perk up his spirits. The sketch was of an apparent idiot with a bandage wrapped around the bicep of one arm. And as the other held up a bottle half full of the rather obvious liquid to a nurse dressed in a red cross outfit, the caption below it read 'Who said you could take it out yourself?'

"Remember," George grinned into his face, while nudging him with a shoulder, "try to get a nurse with 'no blood' on her uniform!"

"Ya." Fred quickly added, his face just as lit up as his best friends.

But if Bob thought his little charade of bravery was fooling George or Fred, then he was in for more of a surprise than he had even started to imagine so far.

"Once we're in there and you should get one who nervously asks you if you feel alright," George went on, "or suddenly says something like 'Oh shit!', then you know it's time to worry, cause you're in trouble."

"In trouble!" Bob more said than asked, with a noticeably weak grin on his face. "What kind of trouble?"

"Oh, nothing serious." George grinned devilishly now. "Nothing that is, unless she suddenly grabs you by the ankles and starts to pump your legs sideways like a giant set of 'bellows' that is! That's their way of letting you know that you're not bleeding fast enough. - But then again - to me there's nothing encouraging about being a 'fast bleeder'."

Bob faked another short laugh while inwardly praying that he didn't copy the reactions of another first time blood donor who had just short of fainted in line when they had first arrived. Even though it had looked totally hilarious, especially after someone in the crowd noticing the poor mans condition had yelled 'Timb-e-e-er!' he prayed he had no lack of intestinal fortitude to keep from repeating the mans performance. Inwardly he knew he would just die of embarrassment - especially after seeing the other workers comical reactions when the same poor individual had ended up on his hands and knees, pushing his lunch pail in front of him while heading for the clinic's rest area. And as comical as the scene first looked, most of the men instantly stopped laughing, when a few rushed forward to help a hurting fallen comrade.

Waiting until he was sure no one was paying him any real attention, George and Fred apparently content to giving him a bit of a break by briefly joking with someone else in line. He swallowed hard before hoping to find some perverted relief in the variety of funny tee shirts and hats being worn around him. With such a large number of personal to draw from, many an apparent jokester also, he had no trouble finding ones he thought were surely only meant to be seen around the worksite.

Deliberately seeking out the shoulders of a worker only two people away in front, it was easy to work up a grin over the saying 'I'm a sucker for big boobs'. And on the back or someone even further up the line, 'If you don't think you can afford a body like this - I'll loan you the money.' made him smile even broader, especially since he also was wearing a hat with an old regular 'I'm so broke, I can't even pay attention!'

The standard mall bought shirts such as, 'To all you virgins out-there - thanks for nothing!' or 'P.O.W.' which as all workers knew as standing for 'Prisoner of war'. Then an old regular 'Some day my ship will come in, and with my luck I'll be at the airport!' or 'You can't scare me, I've got kids!' on to 'If I want your opinion, I'll beat it out of you!'" were always good for a smile. But the personnel or homemade story telling sayings were the ones that usually got the most respected laughs. Such as 'If it's true that to much wild sex can cause blindness, I'm willing to risk one eye!' or 'It's only an infected pimple.' to 'Where's the nearest washroom!' for those men sporting big guts. or 'My wife says General George Custer started it all, when he yelled 'Charge!' were also just as good. And the occasional front and back shirts were also often just as funny once put together as a commentary. 'Po-o-o-or me -!' on the front, And on the back the rest of the strange comment, 'another drink!' Or, on the front 'I'm a sex toy!' with on the back, 'Wind me up, and I'll follow you anywhere!' on to 'The wife just left me!' in bold lettering on the front, and then onto the back 'Thank goodness!', Then, a more aggressive, 'People are often like a toilet seat!' on the front, 'Sometimes they get pissed off!' on the rear.

But the one that broke his sanity bubble to make him chuckle out loud, was in total on the back of 'Beautiful Brad', 'I'm against all women having sex, every chance I get!' But where the snicker had brought him humor, it also had lost him his brief brush of neglect, as George smiled, "Something tickling you where I can't see?"

"Oh, just reading some of the 'billboards'." he grinned back.

Glancing around as if to confirm what Bob was talking about, George chuckled himself, before adding a few of his favorites to the group.

"One of the old standards I like best is the one that reads, "I'm with stupid', and then shows an arrow pointing towards the individual they are walking along side of."

"I've seen that one." Fred but in. "But it's even funnier when you see a husband and wife team, both wearing the same tee shirt, only with the arrows pointing towards each other."

"Or the one on the noticeably overweight guy we passed on the way here, "Baby under construction." Bob laughed.

"Fred's favorite," George added, "is the ol' 'I'm a member of the 'E.I.C.I.O.' Club. 'Everybody I see I owe.' "Sounds more like the lead into the 'Old MacDonald had a farm' song to me Bob laughed.

"Not anymore." Fred cut in. "My newest one is from a tee shirt I saw in the mall last week. It was so good I'm thinking about using it every chance I get."

"Well spit it out. Maybe we all can use it too." George said.

'It read." Fred started to chuckle even before he could start speaking, and Bob reached and to gave him a punch in the arm to help get him back on track. "Sorry guys. It read, 'Since I've used up all of my 'sick leave', I'm phoning in dead!'"

As Bob instantly started to chuckle at the comment, George frowned in his buddies direction, "It sounds like something you'd think up - just to get out of work."

Suddenly, as if in another answer to Bob's earlier silent unspoken prayer for something to take his mind off what he was about to become involved in, a brief diversion exited from the rest area they were now passing. And as soon as his vision passed over where they were standing, he gave every indication he was about to stop alongside of George to talk.

"Hey, Georgie! You old snake!"

George, using body language to emphasize his true feelings about the older co-worker now smiling in front of him, lost no time in grinning his standard acknowledgment to such a remark.

"Hay! Isn't that the stuff farmers sometimes get subsidized not to grow, as well as it growing up to about this high?" one of his hands held out palm downward and waist high. "And as for being a 'snake' if it wasn't for people like me, you'd have no one to look up to, everybody else is obviously already too far up out of your reach."

Without even hinting that George's little slamming had been heard or registered, especially since he and George knew too much gossip about one another to dare to really antagonize each other, the in reality truly old friend continued with that he had really stopped to talk about. And as he said, "How'd you like to buy a ticket on a raffle?" the tickets in question magically appeared in his hand.

"What's it for this time Harry? George answered. His face, a grinning Fred and Bob leaning a little bit closer, was also a mixture of whimsical smile and half-dubious frown, as one hand started for his wallet.

"It's for widow Brown." Harry smiled back, his anticipating hands separating one ticket from the small packet he was holding. "It's been a year now since Jack's passing, and we've heard through the grapevine that she's still carrying a few small bills."

"What in the Hell would he do with 'widow Brown'?" Fred whispered in Bob's direction, a big grin on his face. "George can't afford the one he's got at home now. And if he tries to bring the 'widow Brown' home, I'll be selling raffle tickets on George's 'demise'. Meaning his 'death' for the uneducated." he grinned into Bob's face, "And within a week I'd say."

Being multi crafted George ears and mind didn't miss any of Fred's little speech. And with a smile matched only by Bob's, he deliberately chose to remain silent. Silent that is until after he had finished with his friend, while handing a five dollar bill in his direction.

Harry, his face and voice obviously still unaffected by the attempts for humor at his expense, silently gave George the single ticket in return for his money, before turning his attention in Fred's direction.

"I'm sorry Freddie. I don't think I heard you right. Did you say you wanted a ticket also, or were you just blowin' wind?"

Not being the Don Quixs that his best friend was, a slight blush starting to make its arrival present on his face, Fred made a weak attempt to redirect the laughter now going on around him back in its perpetrator's direction.

"That's not 'gas' you detect Har Har Harry. It's just your breath blowin back in your face. Besides, I hear you've been workin' so much overtime lately- why don't you buy all the tickets, or do you like hearin' your kids call you Uncle Charlie whenever you go home?"

Rewarding Bob's wisely offered five spot with a ticket and a smile, "I like your new friend already." Harry smiled at George. He then helped Fred with his decision, as if he really really had one, on whether to buy a ticket or not by holding one out in his direction and grinning.

"Can you think of a better place to hide than here when you're arguing with the wife? Even the foreman nags less than she does. Besides, I'd rather come here and get paid - than to go home and work my 'ass' into the ground for free."

"I believe ya," Fred laughed, while exchanging the money in his hand for the ticket. "Millions wouldn't, but I believe ya." and after glancing briefly at his change, no doubt as a humorous insult on possibly being short changed, he carried it even further by frowning, "Boy - you sure know how to punch a hole in a twenty, don't ya?"

As Harry occupied himself with stuffing the newest addition of cash into the already crowded envelope now in his hands, George turned his head so that only Bob could hear what he was about to half whisper.

"He's been workin' so much overtime lately, that when he goes shopping now, he doesn't have to worry about being picked up by the plazas security cameras for shoplifting!"

"Ya don't mean he's one of those guy's," Bob smiled back, "that now gets his mail delivered to this place."

"Sounds possible." George chuckled, Fred's own ears now tilted close enough to catch most of the humor. "But just to be sure, I think I'll look up his home address and phone number in the book, first chance I get."

While stuffing the wade of cash back inside of his baggy shirt Harry's face suddenly lit up, as if just suddenly remembering something, something at times best left unsaid, such as now. "Say! Didn't I hear big rumors about you also having a big argument with your wife, and something about how you were going to straighten her out with a forty-four, and I don't mean your I.Q. size."

The blush that had started and then subsided in Fred's face grew back in an even deeper shade of noticeable red. But George quickly saved the day by answering before his best buddy could.

"Not really." he half laughed. "He just forgot to allow for crosswind. But then for someone who's not actually sure as to which end of a gun to point away from him, I wouldn't go around putting ideas in someone else's head. That is, unless you've already decided where you want your body found! Do ya know what I mean, jellybean!"

As always, and expected, the diversion he had hoped for, worked. Somewhere in the past one of them had apparently pissed in the others cereal, and as to where and why he decided to leave alone. Neither man had dropped so much as a hint in his direction as to what was driving a wedge between them, and he had learned long ago never to pick sides in disagreements. So he made sure to keep the close to home innuendoes away from both men he liked to think of as friends, even if one was years removed from the other.

"Speakin' of tickets, Harry," George quickly added, his right hand retrieving one of the yearly stag tickets he always carried from its hiding place, inside his wallet.

"Did you get yours for the company's stag yet?"

The question and gesture, as he and a few others around him remembered, had an instant noticeable effect on Harry. And just as anticipated, Harry started to make a hasty departure, using the words, "Uh, uh, I'll get mine at the door George. Excuse me will ya. I promised to meet someone in the canteen. It's my turn to buy, and I don't want to be late!"

The snickers, peppered with a series of squeaks and duck calls that followed Harry's hasty departure from some of the other men close enough to over hear what was going on, were explained away to those who hadn't understood.

"He'll get his all right some day, but not from anybody on this planet. I wouldn't say ol' Harry is cheap, but that's only because the word 'cheap' doesn't do him justice. That 'squeak' you heard as he left, wasn't from his shoes, or the fact that old age is setting in."

"You can say that again!" someone further back in the line offered, and obviously another pupil aware of Harry's tight grip on a buck. "His mother must have been part cash register and when he was born she thought he as a 'wooden nickel', and spit him out!"

"Ya!" Fred quickly added, especially since he and Harry were constant sparring partners, whenever the opportunity arose. "I'm surprised he hasn't had his nostrils enlarged, considering air's free?"

"Okay, that's enough." George butt in. "Guaranteed Harry's no doubt got the first dollar he and half the guys in this place ever made, but he isn't stingy when it's time to help those having a run of bad luck. We all know he'll give you anything but money, and even 'his time' is worth something, considering ya can't put it in the bank."

The laughter that had been filling the air, 'Isn't that what you're always saying about 'sex'!' someone mumbled, died only a little with George's sobering words of reality. But it wasn't enough to stop the put downs, now that they had been started.

"I still say he's tight enough to have embarrassed the king of cheap 'Jack Benny'!" someone in line offered.

"I'll bet ya his favorite toy at Christmas time when he was a kid," Fred smiled, "was a printing press."

"Are you hinting he did time for counterfeiting?" Bob asked, much to George's surprise.

"Could be." another worker answered. "I've never seen him spend any 'real money'."

"Ya know, now that you mention it, you're right. George said straight-faced. "Boy, you talk about the ol' proverbial 'getting blood out of a stone'. Why I remember once - - -."

Before he could continue, even if he did have everyone's attention and the realization of what he had really just said still an apparent stranger to even his quick form of warped humor, Bob cut him off. "Well, isn't that what you're here for?"

George's face as everyone else there listening was also just as confused, proving that they had trouble thinking in anything but an unbroken straight line, was one of genuine confusion when he acknowledged Bob's strange remark with a singular confused word of "Huh?"

"To, get, blood, out, of, a, 'Stone'!" Bob answered, his big grinning face already far ahead of his long drawn out words. And as the significance of the word 'Stone!" sank in, a large barrage of chuckling 'Bo-o-o's! and 'He-e-e-er's! filled the air. George himself simply smiled into Bob's face, while sticking one finger into his mouth in order to wet it and then mark an invisible number one into the air in front of him for everyone to see. He then continued to grin out, "Can I pick a nickname, or can I pick a nickname."

Bob pretended to blush, as Fred slapped him on the back and added, "Nice going 'Slingshot'. You not only got out one of the greatest and most perfectly timed puns I've ever heard , but you also briefly stumped one of the company's most recognized, as well as greatest 'shit disturbing' 'slam artists'. And if I know my buddy here mister 'Stone', uh pardon me, Mister 'Acid Tongue', you're probably going to have to look over your shoulder for the rest of our life. You give him an opening at any wound or soft spot you've been protecting so far, and he'll be all over you like ketchup on French fries. If you think the only sex you've been getting is at home, then you just quadrupled your time. I can personally guarantee that 'the Axe-Man' here will 'bone' you mercilessly."

All the while Fred had been speaking, Bobs eyes darting back and forth between him and Fred, George had simple kept quiet - while giving Bob one of his best puritan smiles every time his vision had fallen on him. But now, while overreacting and hamming it up, he let his gestures speak what he really meant, instead of what he was saying.

"Don't listen to him, old buddy. You must know by now that I'm not really like that."

Instantly, and in almost unison, a loud pulsating moan flowed through the small crowd still involved with what was going on, while someone offered the words, "That'll be the 'Frosty Friday'. But George totally ignored the slanderous attack on his character, while saying with an angelic face. "In my younger days I may have said about Harry that the only difference between him and a canoe, was that a canoe would tip. But since I've matured." another wave of exaggerated laughter flowed through the gathering, causing George to pause long enough to appreciate its delivery, "But since I've gracefully matured, I always try to look at the bright side of things. Why, we could've been related."

Instantly the air was once again filled briefly with a mixture of jeers and laughter, which George comically bowed to, before continuing. But this time he deliberately chose and emphasized every intimidating word he delivered in only Bob's direction.

"Now then, if I was really out for 'blood'!"

Noisily slapping his forehead with the palm of his own hand, Fred comically fell backwards into George's already anticipating waiting hands, before saying, "I don't believe it. He snuck in the big 'B' word again!"

Someone further back in line, probably a wise coward since he let only his altered voice indicate his location, added his two cents worth to the flowing laughter. "George don't need to blow his own horn, at least not while Fred's around."

"If you could 'blow your own horn'," George shot back, his head turned searchingly in his attackers direction, "I bet you'd still be single."

But when his gaze or slamming failed to pick out any grinning face familiar enough to dare such a comment, he tried to prod the individual out into the open by smiling, "What's the matter - nothing else to say? Come on. It's safe to speak up., My mother always taught me to be kind to dumb animals!"

Raising his body up higher by standing on tiptoes, as Fred and Bob imitated his gesture, George's eyes fell on a small group of woman further back in the line. One quick glance was more than enough to see that it was Carla with a few of her regular man haters, and it made Fred comment, "You'd think once a month would be more than enough for some people wouldn't ya."

Before the atmosphere had a chance to deteriorate any lower, a loud shot-like bang reverberated down through the thin corridor they were occupying. And as George quickly remarked, "That oughta get the slow bleeders off the beds a little bit quicker!" everyone's attention automatically stared into the grinning face responsible for the loud noise. The worker then half laughed, "Just checkin' to see if we have any faint hearted donors in the crowd." before bending down to pick up the paper cup he had squashed beneath one foot. Someone, apparently politely waiting their turn to speak, finally added, "Well thanks to you 'smart-ass', I think I'm going to have to go to the 'first aid' after I'm done here, and get my leg scraped!"

From there, as another worker said, "Aw, did you hurt yourself?" while someone else added, "Could be. It's startin' to smell like a possible lost time accident to me." "Speakin of 'smell," the first guy added, "With his breath, I'm sure nobody will notice the difference." The grade of humor once started, as always, started its decline to lower levels once more, all of which made their day more enjoyable.

It was only the fact that it was now George's Bob's and Fred's turn to enter the room where they would answer standard universal questions before being able to donate blood, that saved each of them from joining their co-workers now splashing around in the grade of crude mud-slinging humor.

After giving his name, shop's location and badge number to the woman checking it with the computer terminal just inside the room's entrance, George moved on to the next stage in the whole blood donating process. Being a regular, he made sure to smile back into the familiar

Shifts

faces he passed. And when a new young nurse asked him, "Sir, have you read and understand all of the questions on the questionnaire in front of you?" he couldn't help but smile back an answer he'd heard used many times in the past. "Yes, I have. And I can honestly say, regardless of what the company does to us at times, that I'm not pregnant."

The young woman, apparently new to both the men and the clinic, blushed noticeably, while continuing. "Other than that sir, are you feeling normal?"

As Bob's eyes were busy eating up everything new going on around him, eavesdropping Fred leaned closer to his best friends form and said over his shoulder, "Lady, he's never been what I'd call 'normal' since I've known him." And as the blush on the young woman's face deepened, Bob started to laugh as soon as he saw George reach back and goose where Fred's testicles should be just enough to cause him to jump backwards and shrieking slightly in unexpected surprise.

The high pitched sound of Fred's voice more than his quirky movement brought an instant reaction from the staff trained to watch for just such reactions. And as a few of the nurse's started to rush fore-ward in his direction, Fred's face now the same shade of red as the stunned receptionists, he quickly blurted out, "I'm okay, I'm okay! honestly. I just accidentally bumped my knee on the edge of the desk."

This time, between laughing and jesting, they stuck together when it was time to move into the next both. And when a nurse pricked the side of George's finger in order to get a blood sample, he was almost positive he saw Bob out of the corner of his eye, jump more than he had. In fact, he was so curious about what he thought he had detected, that he decided to try a little experiment, when it was 'Slingshots' turn to get stabbed.

Pretending to have his attention focused on something else going on in the room, as the nurse was using one of her hands to grab and steady Bob's middle finger before pricking it, George lowered his as yet undetected right hand down behind Bob's rear end. And, his face already starting to give away what he was up to, he gently pinched his newest buddies bum at exactly the same time the nurse let the pin in her hand do the job it was there for.

Instantly as a small 'Yelp' escaped from his lips, Slingshot Bob involuntarily jumped. And in the same instant that followed his comical little reaction, as the nurse apologetically said, "I'm sorry." George also spoke, only under his breath. "So-o-o. We're a little goosey about givin' a pint, are we?"

When Bob's eyes finally had time to search out the culprit really responsible for his present embarrassment, George's eyes were once again busy someplace else. Unfortunately this left Fred's present silly grinning puss open for retribution.

But Bob was smart enough by now to realize that here or the present wasn't the time for revenge, so he satisfied his burning humiliation by silently mouthing the singular word of 'Asshole!' in Fred's still smiling, but now confused face. Also George, his best acting ability at work once more, looked genuinely puzzled when he glanced at Fred in the same instant, and asked, "Why, what was that all about?"

"Search me?" Fred laughingly and puzzled shrugged.

Bob, suddenly and somehow realizing that he had singled out the wrong person, turned his attention now to grinning George, while continuing to silently mouth the new thoughts now in his mind. "Not Fred ol' buddy. - You! You're the 'horse's patoot'."

"Why thank you." George softy grinned back, the woman in front of them still occupied testing Bob's blood sample. "A little bit of recognition every once and a while never hurt anybody."

Leading their little trio, George led the way to a row of chairs provided as a last resting spot before the final act of actually giving blood itself. But before any of them even had a chance to kiss any of the chairs with their posteriors, a young nurse's soft voice said, "I have a bed available for anyone wishing to use their left arm.

George's quick thinking and reflexes instantly answered for all of them. "My friend Bob here's left handed. He'll take that bed." He then turned and grinned devilishly directly at Bob, just so there could be no doubt as to who he had been volunteering for, while saying, "Remember ol' pal. Look to make sure you've got a nurse with no blood on her uniform.'

While hesitantly heading in the available bed's direction, the smiling nurse leading him by the arm, a frown a yard wide suddenly found its way to his face. But it wasn't enough to stop him from saying in his two grinning friends seated location, "You bum's haven't heard the last of this yet."

"Right!" Fred chuckled, obviously having a punch line ready. "It isn't over till 'the fat lady 'Stings!'. Right!"

"Only in our case, in other words," George added. "if you'll pardon the familiarities, it isn't over until the bleeding stops!"

Even though he couldn't be sure, George once again thought he detected Bob nervously reacting by swallowing hard. But before anything more could be added by any of them, the same young nurse's voice asked, "Either of you gentlemen have an arm you prefer to use, or that you bleed out of faster?"

"As for an arm my friend here prefers to use," George smiled. "well - it's gettin' a little personal when you start askin' about his sex life. But if it's getting blood out faster that you're after, then there's a couple of guys farther back in line to chose from that you can probably take the whole pint just out of their nose."

"Ya," Fred said, before leaning close enough to George so that only he could hear, the nurse close-by letting the children she had grown accustomed to dealing with have their fun. "And if 'Harry the Horse' does comes in here, they better hope he doesn't he gets sexually excited, or there won't be enough blood left in the rest of his body for them to even get their sample."

George, already comically envisioning what Fred's words were suggesting, lost his control and couldn't help but laugh at the very true suggestive remark. Starting for the cot now ready for him, the humor still more than evident on his face, when he happened to pass the bed Bob was occupying. Glancing only briefly at him, his minds eye still occupied, it was a gesture which only encouraged poor misunderstanding Bob to remark, "A real friend wouldn't get that much pleasure out of watching his buddy in agony."

The reality of the words made George freeze in his tracks just long enough to caringly look down at Bob's horizontal form to say, "Sorry ol' pal. But it's not you I'm laughin' at." And as a gesture to add affirmation to his words he rested a hand gently on Bob's left leg, while quickly adding, "Do your share for humanity and I'll explain it all to you later in the recuperation area. And before moving on to the cot still awaiting his arrival, he also gave Bob a short emotional grin.

Within what only seemed like minutes Fred and George found themselves lying in separated beds alongside of each other. And after verbally finding out that neither had seen anything of Bob since passing him, a volunteer leading a noticeably pale face individual resembling him exactly approached them. Not only was she steering Bob's movements, but she was also helping as he pressed three fingers of his own hand over the inside elbow area where they had tried to take blood from. Stopping almost opposite their cots, after Bob had mumbled something into her ear, the nurse helped him into a position only horizontally matching theirs, before saying, "Now you take it easy - and I'll send someone out with a bit of ice for your forehead."

"A little rough huh buddy." George in a definitely caring manner asked. But before Bob could answer, the nurse did it for him, by saying, "I'm afraid not all people are destined to become blood donors first time out sir." As Bob silently nodded his head in agreement, she smiled down at first him, and then in George's and Fred's inquiring direction, while adding. "The spirit was strong, but unfortunately the flesh was a little weak at this time." Turning her full attention back solely to Bob, she rested a hand on his shoulder, before saying. "You take it easy and we'll try again in three months, at the next clinic.'

As the volunteer headed back into the room she and Bob had just left, all three of them trailing her pleasant looking departing form, George waited until she was totally out of sight, before saying in Bob's direction, "Don't sweat about it ol' buddy. At least you tried - and that's a 'Hell' of a lot more than most of the workers in this plant ever do."

"And let's not forget the 'Angels of mercy' who get to put up with the variety of characters that come through this place." Fred added. "If we were at war - they'd all get a medal for acts of bravery for up and beyond the call of duty."

"Don't ask him why." George smiled, noticing that Bob was looking a little confused. "You'll only be encourage him."

But smiling Fred wasn't about to be deterred, and his buddy's interruption only encouraged him to add more body English to match what he was saying. "Not everybody comes from the shower room to here, like we did. Some of the guys come from straight from the mills and their jobs, so you can imagine what they might smell like on a hot sweaty day. And their 'breath'!" he used one of his hand like a giant waving fan in front of his face to emphasize what he was saying. "Some

Shifts

like to compare it to as that of a lions. But whatever you want to liken it to, I swear some of them have breath so strong, it could stop a bullet!"

"And let's not forget the men who use language so 'blue' it's enough to curl the wallpaper off the wall." George chuckled.

"It's not always just the men." Fred quickly added defensively.

"You're right." George apologized. "Although it's not very nice to admit, but I've heard some of the ladies put words together that could make even the hardest of grown men around here blush."

To further help chase away any bad feelings of thoughts he might be having about himself Fred with George sat up on the edge of their cots, eager to tell him just what it had been that they had been laughing about when passing earlier. Bob, slow at first to return their smiles, was a lot quicker in realizing that his failure to donate was no longer a secret, and also knew that it would never be mentioned by the two friends now working overtime to take his mind off of that fact. And as he waited along with them for bandages to be applied over their sometimes referred to as 'a victory bite' area he had no trouble copying the laughter now being brought on by topics totally unrelated to where they now were.

Leading the way to their next brief stopover, a free coffee and doughnut station provided by the company exclusively for those having donated blood, as usual it was George's joking voice that dominated the trio's conversation, once more back on the 'Dwarf'.

"I know there are times he acts like he couldn't fall over without directions first. but instinct tells me he just might get a case of the smarts some day and try to work with the men instead of against them. But then again, don't go by what I say. Remember I'm one of those guys who thought that 'Pac man' was just a silly game for kids."

"Boy." Fred smiled. "It sure sounds as if you you're getting a little 'senile' to me."

Without almost any noticeable hesitation, Bob instantly raising his good arm stiff as a board out in front of him, proving he was fitting right in with them, its fingertips eventually pointing just above eye level. He then, once sure that all eyes were on him, deliberately did the goose step while they walked. And as the hint of a confused look leapt to Fred's face, George couldn't help but start to chuckle, while saying, "Fred said 'Senile'! You bloody idiot! Not 'Zig-hile'!"

Fred lost no time in letting his humor match his buddy's. But it was still his voice that filled the terrazzo-floored hallway they were walking along, as Bob gradually faded back into temporary obscurity. "Do me a favor will ya. Let us know when it's going to be your last day working for this place. We'll throw a party in your honor, about a week after you've gone!"

"Speakin' of parties." George smiled. "You both better make sure you get to the stag tomorrow night bright and early. My instincts tell me that the woman just might have a little something special planned, and I want you guys to help me check the place out before anyone else arrives.

"Oh?" Bob more asked than said. "And just what could the women possibly do to intimidate any of us?"

The smile already on George's face, grew even broader in response to what he had just heard. "I don't believe you said that!" But it was Fred who chose to answer the silly remark with first only a singular over emphasized "Ha!" before finally continuing with, "Once you've been here for one of the yearly stags you won't dare ask such a stupid question. Given the opportunity, half the 'man haters' working here would just love to bite someone as naïve as you right on the round hump of your 'ass', in public if need be. And I don't mean as a gesture of sexual pleasure."

As their destination came into view, Bob and George expressed their pleasure at Fred's emotional little display by simply grinning from ear to ear, as he kept talking.

"If some guy ever tells you that the older you get, there's no such thing as an ugly woman, don't believe him. Anybody who's been married will tell you that every year there's getting to more and more leaders instead of followers. Personally I think God in his wisdom,"

Just as they were about to finally enter the room they were after, a new voice calling out George's name made them stop in their tracks to look back in its direction, with Bob completely loosing track of what he was about to finish saying.

As George smiled the words "It's Ketchup." the dream of the shop." Bob's once more confused face made Fred this time lean a little closer to him, and half whispered in his ear. "He's not nicknamed "Ketchup' because that's what he likes on everything he eats. He's really the kind of guy that's going to be late for his own funeral. Everywhere he goes, he's either totally late or hurrying to 'catch-up' to everyone else, as well as often as not presently being someone's nightmare."

A grin still on his face - George's words were also whispered, as he said out of the side of his mouth, "Ya better hurry up and tell him the rest of it. The 'red mud's' almost here.'

"Well," Fred frowned at George, no doubt for interfering. "other than often being so dirty he tends to draw flies in the summer - and make everyone else around him look sterile clean," Only George caught Bob's stiffening arm start to rise straight out in front of him, to which he quickly slapped down. "it's rumored that the only way he can get the built up grease out of his clothing at the end of the week is to wash them in gasoline, and then dry them with a match."

"You mean he's like one of the people you were referring to earlier?" Bob said.

"Exactly." Fred answered, while pinching his nose quickly to infer exactly that.

By now 'Ketchup' was almost within hearing distance. So in one last half laughed low voice, Fred shot out the words, "And next to 'Mister Acid-tongue' here, especially if he thinks you can't take it, he just loves to cut you up verbally. Oh, and by the way, he's ugly to."

As the man in question, puffing slightly, said, "Thanks for waitin' guys." he was instantly rewarded with a reply of "Afternoon Terry. Long time no here.", which instantly brought both a smile and a reply of "Ya. It has been about three months hasn't it."

Bob could see now that his face did indeed look as if it had undergone cosmetic surgery, with the doctor apparently having used a shotgun for a scalpel. And as the rest of his dirty greasy looking apparel also came under the scrutiny of Bob's inquisitive eyes, while George was busy introducing him, Bob's senses instantly told him that the man indeed had the potential for making anything come out smelling like a bed of roses. It was a fair and not malicious evaluation, Bob told himself, considering the man did smell like very aged old fertilizer.

Continuing on into the room, 'Ketchup's words now filling the air almost as much as the strange odor he had brought with him, they quickly occupied a table just far enough away from the men already there to ensure privacy. "I'm not the only one in the plant who's noticed how strangely sociable the woman around here have suddenly become. Now I don't know about you characters, but when my wife starts actin' that way, I know that sooner or later somethin' costly or abusive is comin', and I better be careful where I step!"

The sudden arrival of a round of coffee and doughnuts appearing at their table brought a pause in their so far one-sided conversation. But as soon as the smiling older volunteer had departed - George quickly said, "I've had the same uneasy feelin' a lot lately. But until we get some positive proof they're up to something all we can do is to be on the alert. And if we do pick up on whatever it is, let's not overreact. I know some of the older woman's bite is a Hell of a lot worse than their bark. But if they realize that they can successfully upset or intimidate us, then they're going to continue to concentrate on makin' our lives miserable around here."

"Do think it's related to that prank you guys pulled on Louie Zupanic?" 'Ketchup' smiled.

"Probably." Fred replied, a little sarcastically. "Probably just that, or as well as a dozen other good reasons I could give you."

"Don't bother." George laughed. "Just give him one."

"Go ahead and laugh!" Fred retaliated. "Maybe they're still mad about the time, but I won't mention any names," his eyes staring directly into George's, "Maybe the women are still a little pissed off because someone slipped weight reducing water pills into their coffee maker. Most of them then spent half the day squattin' in the washroom dabbin' their derrieres dry, after having relocated excessive amounts of consumed hot tea or coffee."

Especially for the two at the table who had been present at the mentioned prank last month, laughter instantly flowed over and out of them like a small wave. But it was Louie's prank that apparently was still in 'Ketchup's' thoughts, and he let it show by holding his hands cupped over his nipples and saying, "Louie Zupanic! Now there's a real woman. If my wife was built like her, I'd be at home right now trying to save my marriage."

As both Fred and George, in an almost word for word reply to the comment, thought, 'That one's already been used. Get some new material.' It was their newest team member that did justice to the remark, also within his thoughts. 'Not without a shower first!' But as always it was George's mind that worked overtime, and quickly added, "Only if her eyesight's failing." And then, again, his mouth kicked in and spit out what was now crossing his brain.

'I like 'big bo-o-o-obs' too." he smiled. "Why else would I enjoy workin' with guys like you so much."

As closely eavesdropping ears comically let out a low long disgruntled "O-o-oh." Ketchup retaliated with "From what I can remember of seeing' you in the shower, you're no prize catch for any woman either."

"That's okay." George shot back. "Lucky for me that wife of mine doesn't mind more ammunition than weapon."

"Never mind that!" Bob offered, apparently already felling at home in "Ketchup's presence. And he leaned noticeably closer in his direction, a maneuver his sense of smell instantly and dearly paid for, while peering directly into his face before saying, "Just what the 'Hell' you doin' in the shower room checking' out someone else's family jewels, or does everybody here do it?"

"Ya!" Fred quickly piped in. "It's startin' to look as if the ol' rumor about your wife stayin' with you only because your ears are great for holdin' onto, is true."

"Go ahead, indulge yourselves." 'Ketchup' pretended to smile, as the men did exactly that. "I can handle a little jealousy."

"Well if you'd learned to handle yourself in the first place," George said suggestively, "you'd probably still be single, and probably rich!"

Ketchup lost no time in providing more fuel for their verbal feuding as the laughter grew slightly in volume, by directing his words solely in George's direction. "Well thank God it's only women I'm havin' trouble with."

"You thank him." George retaliated. "I'm sure he'll be glad to hear from someone like you."

"Whatever." Ketchup grinned. "From what I've been hearing around the plant lately, a lot of guys feel as it they owe you a favor. As long as the foreman is busy trying to figure out a way to 'shaft' you, he's too busy to be out botherin' anyone else."

"George can take it." Fred quickly offered. "He's got broad shoulders, and you've got no broads!"

"What's this, gang up on me day?" 'Ketchup' frowned.

"Relax." George smiled. "You know the rules. If we didn't love ya', we wouldn't talk to ya. Besides, just think of it as your day in the barrel."

"But that doesn't mean we wouldn't not talk about ya!" Fred smiled.

"Well you know what they also say," Ketchup shrugged his shoulders while grinning. "As long as you're talkin' about me, you're leaving someone else alone."

Enjoying the comradery, George flexed his arms and chest, before adding to his own defense. "Ol' Farkas bites me, and I'll just bite him back. After I get a tetanus shot, that is."

'I'd be doin' a Hell of a lot more than just barkin' back." Ketchup said, his voice and face showing that he seemingly had no love for the man either. "Id be foldin' the ol' fibers inside his ears over on their sides if he ever tried to shove his authority on me."

"He does it to everybody." Fred offered in his best friend's defense. And George was just about to offer his two cents worth, when Bob surprisingly also came to his defense.

"Next time you see our boss, take a seriously close gander at his neck. The blemishes you'll see there aren't hickeys from his wife. They're bruises from where the 'axe-mans' fingertips have been wrapped around his throat from the last time they met."

Realizing he was way outnumbered, 'Ketchup' wisely joined in the laughter surrounding him, while changing the topic.

"Personally, if it wasn't for an affliction for food, I wouldn't work in this dump."

"Stop complaining." George mercilessly and quickly half laughed. "I wouldn't exactly call what you do around this place as 'work'!"

"Nice guy." Ketchup answered, his head slowly twisting in a negatively disappointed manner. "I stick up for you, and you in return stick it 'up' me!"

"Sounds about right to me." Fed laughed. "They usually say that the best defense is a strong offense. And you're about as 'offensive' as they get around here."

"You been coaching this guy?" Ketchup half laughed, a grinning Fred waiting for the next volley of words between them. And to prove that their sparring was nothing more than music to each other's ears, he let him have it with, "Don't jerk me around right now, or I'll hit you so hard you'll have to jog for three days just to get back here!"

"Well the nicest thing about that," Bob quickly butted in, "is that as least you won't be here when he does get back." "Wait your turn." Fred smiled at Bob. "My reply comes first. And it would have been. "At least that's three days I wouldn't have to look at your stubby puss."

Shaking his head negatively again, his eyes passing over the grinning trio he was still foolish enough to be sitting with, Ketchup couldn't keep the humor he was feeling out of his voice, as he fought back. "Talkin' to you guys is like passin' wind. I get temporary relief, but the results stink. I can see where the rumor about you bums being the new Three Stooges isn't too far fetched."

It would have been easy at this point in time for George or Fred to take a low blow and suggest that the reason Ketchup usually ended up eating alone was because of his breath, but that was never intentionally their desire or way. And as always in the past, and now, whenever slamming's' were on the verge of getting painfully personal, it was always accepted procedure to take your lumps and move on down the road to another topic, rather than add an enemy to the ones you already didn't need. So instead of being acid-tongued, George simply smiled in Ketchup's direction, as he was finishing the remnants of his coffee and sinker left in front of him.

"I'm sure if you ask politely, they'll probably let you put a couple of doughnuts in your wallet for later."

It was easy to read the signs that Ketchup was about to make his departure. And even as he started to stand up, his face now contorting itself to best imitate what he thought someone being simple minded might look like, he comically answered, "Gee. Do you really think so?"

"When I was a kid my mom always said that if I kept making stupid faces like that, it would probably freeze that way?" Fred half laughed.

Keeping his features humorously distorted, Ketchup' slammed Fred just as easily and effortlessly as George would have done, if Fred had not been his closest friend. "Well in your case ol buddy, I'm sure it would have been nothing short of a great improvement."

Bob, as George laughed, couldn't help but give Fred a slamming he had grown to like since arriving within the plant, an elongated "He-e-e-re!" as 'Ketchup' started to move away from the table. And right after saying, "See you comedians at the stag tomorrow night." George quickly added, "Sure thing. Oh, And thanks for leavin'!"

Now that they were alone again, milking the break for everything it was worth, George smiled in the man's defense. "Ketchup's basically good people. Even with his hygiene problems I'd rather be around him than some of the 'jerks' we've got in the plant."

Fred, even though he knew he was probably the reason for Bob's silly smirks each time he looked as him, softly added, "You can spray that again. He can sure slam people when he wants to. But more importantly, he can at least take it in return too."

After pushing what was left of his own free refreshment to the center of the table, he then stood erect while saying, "That's enough for me." Fred and Bob were only seconds behind him, as he started to move away from the table, while adding, "It's time we showed this place what our backsides look like."

Leading the way towards where they had entered, George would have made it safely out of the room, if his head and attention hadn't been twisted back to answer a remark made by Bob. So when his body collided head on with that of another unsuspecting human being, he was genuinely apologetic, 'Oh! Excuse me!' even before realizing just who he was talking to. And after everyone there, first reeling back in shock got over seeing just what two people were involved, only Bob and Fred broke into instant laughter, especially since the person

George was apologizing to now had their reputed very big butt kissing the terrazzo floor.

Even though it was instinctive politeness that made him finish saying, "Gees, I'm awful sorry! Please excuse me!" the same instincts told him to brace himself for a barrage of unrepeatable or even unladylike ear stinging verbal abuse. Especially since it was a well know fact that most animals are most dangerous once injured. But instead of using his hands to cover his far from virgin ears, he stepped forward and offered an outstretched hand in assistance to the surprised female figure still seemingly stuck to the floor, both of her hands braced behind her sitting position.

There seemed to be little doubt, Bob and Fred still failing to suppress the humor they were presently experiencing, that the woman, her face only now briefly flashing the anger expected from her, was now at a temporary loss as to either slap away or accept the gesture of help. And when the more surprised than George, especially when a female shaped hand far rougher and abused than his, reached up and grabbed his offer.

Pulling her erect with more physical strength than just the smile on his face, the anticipated harsh remark of 'Why the Hell don't you watch where I'm going you idiot!' failing to materialize, no one was more surprised then George. Fred's own reflex's for self preservation causing him to comically take two steps backwards, George once more apologized for knocking her down. And when the woman simply smiled a grin that was definitely and noticeably forced, her own still silent friends in apparent shock, she then wordlessly walked around them and on her way into the room they were just leaving. But of everyone there, it was only Bob's untarnished thoughts that accepted the normally hostile woman's strange behavior.

Still locked in bewilderment, it was Fred's confused voice that finally broke the silence now surrounding them, while George comically pretended to check and see if any fingers were missing from the hand he had just used. "If I hadn't seen it with my own eyes," his two hands tight fisted and rubbing at them as he spoke, "I wouldn't have believed it!"

"Ya, well, I saw it to." George continued to grin. "And for those of us who chose to stay and face the enemy, I don't know if it means that all the strange rumors we've been hearing are true. And we're in trouble, or that we're really really up the creek, in for some deep shit!"

"What was so special about her?" Bob finally asked, his tone indicating only now that he was confused about the little comical looking incident he had been a silent witness to.

"A Hell of a lot!" Fred shot back excitedly. "That was Rita Elston, commonly know as 'No-man's land'! Why else would a woman that looks like she could kick all of or asses into the middle of next week, with both hands tied behind her back, act so contrary to her reputation?"

"Is she really that bad?" Bob grinned, while watching George first yank and then repeatedly count his fingers once more. George, once more proving that he had the potential to walk, talk, and chew gum at the same time if necessary, answered before Fred could. "You wouldn't need to ask, if you ever saw her wearing one of her true to life tee shirts around the plant."

"I know you're setting' me up, but I'll ask it anyways'." Bob smiled. "What kind of tee shirt are we talkin' about?"

"Oh nothin' the women working with her have to worry about." George half laughed, only because he had already seen the image of a large black gorilla pounding one hand into the palm of the other and wording in question. "But if I was you, and you even 'thought' about giving her advice on anything, jut make sure she isn't wearing the one that reads, 'If I want your opinion, I'll 'beat' it out of ya!, because believe me, she can!"

Pretending that he could almost still see the rough looking woman and her trailing entourage in tow, Fred shook his body in a manner indicating that someone had just poured ice cold water down the center of his back, before adding. "Somewhere in this world, out there there's an awful lucky man who didn't marry her!"

"He's right." George chuckled. "Blood donor or not, she's got a neck on her even Dracula wouldn't touch."

"Meaning?" Bob smiled, as they continued to walk.

"Meaning, she generally has to plaster on some makeup before she can even start to begin being called 'rough'.

"Now is that spelled 'r-o-u-g-h' as in appearance, or 'r-o-o-o-f' as in a dog barking?"

"Now that you mention it," Fred chuckled, "I guess you can say they both apply. Normally the only thing nastier than her is her disposition."

"I thought only the women were supposed to be 'catty? Bob snickered, before adding, "I'm sure glad we're all on the same side, especially with the way I look."

Stopping dead in his tracks, Fred so close he bumped into him, George looked at his two friends and straight faced commented. "You're right!, We are starting to act worse then a bunch of old hens, pickin' on those no worse then us. Just because someone who in our eyes has chosen to live a lifestyle not preferable to our, we have no right to judge them. And a women who was working here years before I started in the plant, and if my memory stands correct about her being jilted at the alter, then I'm absolutely positive, I'm going to make sure 'I' apologize to them and the ground they're walkin' on, for having bad manners."

"We!" Bob gasped. since when did I become one of the 'hens' 'pecking' on the misfortunate?"

"Since you became part of the trio." Fred smiled. "And that makes you guilty by association. And speakin' of guilty." he said directly at George. "Since when did you develop a guilt complex?"

Giving out with a short, 'humph' before starting to move again, George replied, "It's not guilt. It's humility. Every once in a while I feel a little shot of humility helps take us back down to where we really belong, in the dirt with the rest of the working class."

"If you keep this up," Fred frowned. "I'm going to get out my fiddle, and play a soppy tune to go along with it."

"Fiddle!" Bob laughed. "Why even where I come from it warrants at least a bow cello!"

"If you tone deaf musicians care to get down off the stage," George chuckled, "maybe we can lay off slamming the poor woman, even if she believes all men should end up circumcised eunuchs just so they can sing the high pitched notes in a choir. Or, being sterilized by being castrated with a dull razor dipped in iodine and using no anesthetic."

"Whoa!" Bob chuckled. "I thought you said you wanted to go easy on her?" "I do." George laughed. "But I felt like I had to get in a few last good 'zingers' of my chest before I go on the wagon."

"And if she had been in her car when you bumped into her," Fred added. "Right about now we'd be lookin' at two rows of Good-Year radials running horizontally across your chest."

"Speakin' of woman drivers," George continued to chuckle, "do either of you know what the difference is between a clown or a woman driving a car?"

"I know! I know!" Bob answered, like an excited little boy. "One's not funny!"

Smiling out "Someone's heard that joke before." George gave him one of his best 'Tisk' 'Tisk' looks while adding, "Who gave you the answer, Charlie Chan or Mister Motto?"

Instantly slipping into character, Bob answered, "Confucius say man who let woman drive transportation, have long ears and belong in front, in harness."

As George was busy laughing, Fred tried to copy Bobs accent while saying, "My Confucius say 'Foolish man who trust woman to do anything correctly, belong 'just' in harness - straightjacket."

Joining in on the laughter, while pinching his nose at Fred's rendition, Bob moved on to ask, "Which of you guys do I believe? Heckle or Jeckle?"

"Neither!" George quickly answered. "Do you not remember what I told you when we first met? Never ever get involved or pick sides. You form your own opinions about everyone and everything around here. That way - "

"Ya, ya. I know." Bob cut in. "That way, if something goes wrong and you end up getting burned, you've got nobody but yourself to blame."

"Let alone help you put yourself out." Fred quickly grinned."

"By jove!" George smiled, while using a strong English accent "I think he's got it!"

"He's right." Fred grinned at Bob. "I was only trying to give you a little history on Rita, not trying to turn you against her. Heavens knows you'll eventually make enough enemies of your own around here, without us picking some out for you."

"Well 'exc-u-u-u-se' me!" Bob laughed, while doing what he believed to be a true to life comical rendition of one of the day's better-known comedians. "I was only trying to find out if she was future prime material worth picking on, not dating stock."

"You try mixing it up with her or her group, and the only memorable date you'll end up with, is the one on your tome-stone." George frowned. "And if she was still within hearing distance," he added in a whisper, "Only someone with suicidal tendencies would even consider using their own tongue as a rope, to hang themselves."

"What about you?" Bob grinned in Fred's direction. "You got any suggestions?"

"Well, my first act would be is to make sure I've got lots of accident insurance, you know, just in case I accidentally trip over my own tongue. Then, I'd pick out a location where I'd like my body found, again just in case I accidentally disappeared from public view for a period of time. But then, on the other hand -,"

"Ya, we know, four fingers and a thumb." George butted in. "That's enough. You're starting to scare him!" he then laughed.

"And you think I wouldn't stand a chance?" Bob asked, now with a tone of indignation in his voice.

"Only if you grow 'bigger balls'!" George laughed.

"How big is big?" Bob asked, his words now sounding more like a challenge.

"Well," George frowned as one hand stroked his chin, a squinting eye giving every indication it was searching for just the right answer. "Remember that rickshaw you were pulling back at the 'meat market'?"

"You mean the wheel barrel." Bob chuckled, while jogging on the spot, Fred's grinning silence saying just enough to tell anyone who cared that he staying out of the battle of 'quips' going on in front of him. "You think that would be big enough to carry my giant 'balls' around in?"

"No." George chuckled. "I think it would be big enough to carry just 'one' of your big 'balls' around in. The other testicle you'd have to string over your shoulder and hope you don't have to reach for it if it gets itchy. You loose your balance and the extra lopsided balance just might end up spinning you around so hard it could end up screwing you right into the ground. And yes, I know I said every dirty old mans favorite word, 'screwing'!"

Even though he had anticipated their eventual arrival, George still wasn't nearly fast enough to successfully avoid the series of lightning short jabs Bob expertly delivered to his midsection, in retaliation to whimsical sarcasm he was dishing out. And Fred, apparently foolish enough to feel left out, tried to punch one of Bob's preoccupied arms. But like his best friend, after ending up fanning at free air when his target had easily danced away sideways from the attack, he then found himself a victim of the same type of physical abuse, a grimacing George was presently still flinching from.

Chapter 13

'Countdown & winning'
Or
'Working on Louie's revenge'

Saturday's yearly stag prevented the shop's usual verbal bantering from receiving the normal amount of recognition they were justifiably entitled to for a Friday. But that didn't mean those men in the shower looking eight months pregnant, and recipients of the 'Dickey Doo' award, that was where your stomach now sticks out further than your 'dickey do'. And let's not fail to mention that those caught in any other silly predicament weren't going to get verbally slammed at every opportune moment also.

Instead it just meant that after such types of incidents were acknowledged, the remaining part of any conversation immediately went right back to the stag and its potential of related information. Almost everyone involved, mainly by past association or experiences knew and expected pranks were either already in motion, or being deviously planned for that very night. And as for the 'Dickey Doo' award, it not only existed, it actually gave out professional looking certificates to be 'hung' on a wall. It showed large gold trimmed white alphabetical letters highlighted at the bottom reading, 'You might as well 'mount' this, since with the shape you're in now it's probably about the only thing you'll be 'mounting' in the future.

It was just such conniving that was also presently going on in the woman's location of the change house, only with humiliating revenge in mind for some at the small gathering. The woman were in a sense, something more than just one of them enjoyed seemingly more then life itself, re-chewing someone's butt more than once, before spitting the bigger chunks out.

"And again, I say he is!" Carla said harshly, her rough fisted right hand slamming at the metal locker opened in front of her. "George Stone may not be directly involved with every demeaning prank ever pulled on us during the last year, but I'll bet you dollars to doughnuts he knew about them. And I'll give ten to one odds he laughed just as hard as everybody else did!" her hand slamming at the door one more time.

"That's the point!" one of the other older women quickly offered. "And I'm not sticking up for him, heaven knows he's more than capable of doing that for himself. I'm just saying that our revenge for what happened to Louie or any of us has to be directed at or inflicted on all of the men in the plant, and not become a vendetta to single out just one lone individual."

"She's right." Louie offered, a little sheepishly. "Even though I'm the one that was embarrassed, I think that they all should be made to pay, and not just Mister Stone."

"Humph." Carla muttered, her hand once more playing the same tune on her locker door, only at a lower octave. "You cowards don't realize that to kill a snake you have to first cut off just its head. The body will wiggle for a little bit after that, but then it will stop thrashing about real soon too. We stop George Stone with an embarrassing stunt that'll stick with him for years, and we'll never have any more trouble from the rest of the weak-kneed wimps in this plant."

Carla, pausing long enough to let the sneer on her face show contempt as to how she presently felt about someone she considered to have no backbone, quickly added what she hoped would be one more piece of damning evidence against a gender she had grown to hate so much. "Doesn't it bother you Louie," one of her hands pointing at the items in question, "when the men refer to your 'tits!' as Hewie and Dewie!" She then growled more as an explanation then a question. "They're really the ones who are the 'boobs'! And if I had my way I'd smack each one of them so hard across their face that it would make their heads spin. Hell, they'd be able to see out one of their 'ears' by the time I was finished with them! They're the 'Stooges' lady, not us!"

As an uncontrollable blush leapt to Louie's face, an instant wave of mumbling flowed through the gathering, making it evident that the group was sharing mixed emotions as to what they had heard so far. Realizing that if a vote were taken to decide on what to do right now, it would in all probability be close enough to go in favor for or against a personal revenge. Carla's right hand Rita, always ready to stand beside or back up her mentor when necessary voiced her strong one-sided opinion. "There's one thing all you weak-kneed wishy-washy jellyfish better remember. If you decide to let all the dirty rotten pranks the men have pulled on us in the past or any embarrassment in the future slide into obscurity, then you better also be prepared to live with it for as long as you plan to work here."

"And don't forget that it'll be almost another full year of such 'crap' before we're in a position to get even like this again." Carla quickly added with no doubt in hope of fueling the already mixed emotions some of the women were still mumbling among themselves. She deliberately hadn't mentioned that certain steps had already been taken by now for Mister Stone strictly because she and a few like her had every intention of following through with their scheme whither the rest of the woman there agreed with it or not. And there was sure as Hell no sense in letting these women make a decision on something they just might let out of the bag, especially if not agreeing with her idea of revenge.

Another of the older, matured with exposure woman offered, "I say the smoke screen we've just set up, as well as what we have planned for the stag is more than a justifiable rebuttal towards what we've gone through!" Her eyes, slowly taking in most of those there as she spoke, fed her the results on their faces "I personally don't like the word 'revenge', as well as what it invokes back in retaliation. The pranks we've pulled on the men may not have equaled theirs in some of you others eyes, or obviously satisfied you, but they have been enough to let the men in this plant realize that we can and will retaliate when necessary."

"Why is it sometime I get the feeling we're just a bunch of pussycats on a hot summer day hanging around the drippy watermelon, just so we can chase the flies." one of the woman chuckled. It was an attempt to keep the mood mellow, which also instantly brought a reply of, 'I've seen a couple of 'flies' I wouldn't mind attacking. 'Zippers' for those of you who can't figure out what the Hell we just said."

"Guaranteed we've never drawn blood," the older woman, now chuckling, picked up from where she had been interrupted, "but then in actuality neither have they. The only reason it seems they are getting the best of us in each prank they pull, is because the numbers are in their favor. There's a Hell of lot more of them then there are of us, but we still make our presence felt when we do stick it to them, no matter how weak or trivial the rebuttal from our side may have been. Don't ever forget they we are' the gender who used to wipe their runny noses and cuddle them when they were hurt. Anything we do to them now, has to hit closer to home with them, whether they show it or not."

As most of the women started to nod their heads in approval to the common sense they had just heard, Rita while standing next to Carla, once again made her presence and feelings known "Oh sure! Graphite on their toilet seats and stink bombs in their showers are really going to leave them mentally frightened, just like they've done to some of us during the last year. I can be a forgiving type of person when you come right down to it. But when it comes to some of the ethical jerks around here, the only forgiving I'm interested in, is for giving them a big slap up one side of their fat heads!"

"After that stunt they played on us with the water pills, I'm proud to say we delivered a pretty good blow for our side when we retaliated with the ex-lax chocolate chip cookies strategically placed in a few shit disturber's lunch pails."

One of the two older women who had spoken earlier remarked "Ya! And once they got down to dabbing instead of wiping their bums at the end of the day, you can bet they sure knew what their assholes were created for after that."

The dirty girlie magazines with circled ads in their lunch pails just before they went home was pretty good too." someone giggled.

"If I'd been in on that one," Carla snarled, "it wouldn't have been girlie sex books I'da sent home with them. It would have been 'gay' magazines with circled adds that I would have planted."

"I think we get even with most of them." Louie offered, while checking for herself just how the crowd was reacting.

"Of course we do deary." another of the older woman answered with a smile. "And once you're married to one of them long enough, you'll really understand just how easy it is to upset and manipulate them."

"Exactly!" Jane, the most seasoned older worker standing beside Louie grinned devilishly. "Only the young naïve ones foolishly think they're superior or masters over their mates. It's the men who have been seasoned, after even a very short time away from their freedom, that know who the 'real' bosses are. Just ask my Stan."

As one of the woman joked, "If you can find him." another of the more experienced and just as obviously wise of the woman offered her tidbit of wisdom.

"Jane's right. Some of the men might kid themselves and their friends into thinking they wear the pants in the family, but it's not the pants they are wearing that decides what goes on in their marriage. It's when ours are off that the rules are made. As for the stink bombs and graphite, just remember that most men's stomachs aren't the rock of Gibraltar they would lead us to believe they are. And speaking of the graphite, well let's just say that we found another opening to apply it to today"

"Just wait until some of the perverts next door press their little peepers up to one of those peepholes they think we don't know about. That graphite with a little bit of layout ink added in doesn't all wash off as easy as everyone might think it does. After today we'll get to know who some of the Peeping Toms are by just looking at their pusses. They'll have marks so red around one eye from rubbin' that stuff off, that'll it'll stick out like a great big giant hickey. It'll look just as if someone suffering from a strong affliction of being in 'heat' had tried to suck one of their eyes right out of its socket!" another of the woman giggled girlishly.

By now some of the women were laughing out loud, with a few 'Here'! 'Here!' and 'It'll look good on them!' comments thrown in. It was mostly a contagiously happy mood, unfortunately and noticeably not shared by all that was kept alive by those who could relate to the remarks.

"And let's not forget that those same peepholes work in both directions. I'm sure some of those Polaroid snaps we took earlier in the week are now hanging on strategic bulletin boards throughout the plant, no doubt startin' to draw results. As well as a few crowd's." Jane laughed.

"You didn't shoot the right part of their anatomies!" Carla added harshly. "Not to mention, it's rather obvious that some women out there are still marrying for money!"

"Oh yes we do!" someone quickly laughed.

"Well with what I've seen from the photographs," Jane smiled. "compared to the rest of their anatomy, I'd say we got them showing their best features."

As the present laughter pulsated briefly in volume, Rita said a little sarcastically, "Oh, wow! those are real knee slappers'. a couple shots of the 'Pecking Order Club' showing full moons and I'm sure a few of them after viewing the snapshots would be too em-'barr-assed' to look us in the face, let alone become involved in any future pranks."

With a bit of a frown on her face, Jane let it be known that she had never really been overly fond of Rita or Carla, let alone with what Rita had just suggested. All were good points for which was possibly one of the main reasons why she retaliated with her own feelings about what had also in the past been referred to as the 'Short Order Club'.

"The 'Pecking Order Club' Rita was not formed by us to single out any one particular male worker in this plant. It was created to be used exclusively as an aid, biologically, financially, psychologically, and physically, in helping 'us' choose any available bachelors that might become fair game within the plant. Then match them up with any unmarried relations we might have, or even know of. It is hoped that we might be able to save any of those people from going through any mistakes or nightmares we may have been through ourselves."

"And another thing those holes in the wall could be used for," someone piped in, "A few well placed cream pies at peep time should get as a little more humorous revenge."

"Or we could just seal them up permanently from our side." Louie offered, her voice low and still noticeably a bit sheepishly.

"And that's it!" Carla said, her words dripping with disgust and clearly from the opposite end of the emotional scale to Louie's. Her poor locker door was then once more made to become being the sole receiver of her physical pounding anger. "That's all the 'revenge' you wimps want!"

"No-o-o!" Jane answered, her own voice and demeanor very calm and collected. "That's all the 'retaliation' we require. 'revenge' is something inflicted upon your enemies. Retaliation is a 'tit for tat', for people you expect to be around for the next couple of years."

"Shoot yourselves!" Rita shrugged, as Carla noisily delivered the final deathblow by slamming her locker door finally shut, and locking it. Then, with irritation still abundantly present, she cut into Rita's reply. "Just don't come crying to us after they pull some of their corny jokes on you at the stag tomorrow night. And you can bet your big fat asses they've got some real beauts planned."

"Maybe so." Jane smiled. "But God's been known to take care of his own."

"Ya! And God also said that vengeance is his too."

Rita half laughed sarcastically. "But personally I'm the impatient type. When the time comes, I'll do the job for him 'now', and then he can thank me later when we meet."

"I doubt if your type will ever get to Heaven." another new voice giggled.

Rita opened her mouth, after turning her head in the voice's direction, and snarled, "How'd ya like a chance to meet him right now!" But Carla quickly cut her off by saying, "This is great! Instead of gettin' even with the men, we're standing here fightin' with each other!"

"Don't we always." Rita finally said. And as Carla started for the room's closet set of doors, he head shaking in disgust, Rita and a few followers who obviously agreed with her way of thinking, quickly followed in behind.

Jane, a tiny wicked smile on her lips as she fought to keep from saying in Carla's direction, "Don't go away mad Carla. Just go away!" instead turned her attention to those who had stayed behind.

"Let's not let them wreck our plans. So far it looks like we just might have the jump on the men today, maybe we'll get the last laugh on them at the stag, too."

And when one on the women snickered, "There's a couple hunks out there I wouldn't mind jumping on. Or even letting them jump on me!" To which her best friend quickly slammed her with, "Well at least now I know why you're buying a new mattress every couple of years."

Shifts

"Well if they're built for 'bounce to the ounce'," the woman beside her chuckled, "I'm surprised you get that much time out of them at all."

"Let's not start all over on the 'fat' slamming's. You've had all morning to get them out of the way. Right now we've got other more important issues on our plates, so let's not bite off more than we can chew at this time" Jane laughed. Only a few of the swifter women joined her, as soon as they put the word association of food and plate together. From there it went onto one of the grinning women holding her open hand in front of her face, palm inward, to totally mask her facial expression. And once she was pretty sure that the rest of the group was watching her, she slowly pulled it down to show that the smile was total gone, leaving only a blank looking stare on it.

The rest of the gathering, as someone commented, 'I thought she looked better with her face covered.' another adding 'I think I heard her husband say the same thing once.' broke into almost hysterical laughter.

If there was ever only one thing the women could say they were thankful for learning from the men, then it would have to be that right from the word 'go' they had liked the idea of having sessions where they could relentlessly with no animosity intended jokingly pick on each other. It not only kept them from breaking up into small independent groups - but also allowed for everyone willing to do so, to get a chance at 'zinging' in jest anyone they feel might deserve it.

Carla's presence may been out of the room, but an extension of her ears and eyes weren't. In the past Ruth Peddler had only been suspected of being a two faced double secret agent for Carla, something one of the other women had joking said that it was very well possible, considering that she was big enough to build two people, if necessary. But today she was about to prove most of it was true. Laughing right along with everyone else. She made sure her ears picked up as much as her limited intelligence could hold onto, before heading out for her job when the others did likewise, only with the intention of getting the news of what she had heard to Carla. And even though she, unknowing to her, wasn't considered to be trustworthy enough to be considered as part of the inner circle, she was taken as reliable when reporting any rumors she might have picked up on. Strangely, almost like a puppy's loyalty, she probably wouldn't have cared that Carla had refrained from telling her about the two prostitutes hired to make trouble at the upcoming stag. But what was presently going on just south east of where she was heading, also one of the many pranks unknown to her, was all tied into the women's everlasting tit for tat for equality.

Normally a half hour at the end of the sift on Friday would have been considered as more than enough time for a shit shower shampoo and a shave, or as some of the men liked to call them, five dollar 'shits' and twenty dollar 'showers'. But not today. Because of his large involvement in the stag and a long list of things still needing to be taken care of, George was presently way behind his intended schedule. If nothing else it gave him an excuse to more jog than walk towards the change house. A short glance at his wristwatch also told him that if was just minutes since he had left Bob and Fred, once reminding them that they had promised to give him a hand with a few of the items on his last-minute list.

Entering the change house, George was surprised slightly when human traffic appeared to be a lot lighter than he had anticipated. The regulars' who always found it habitually hard to work a full forty-hour workweek, especially on any special occasion or long weekend, appeared to be long gone as he hurried into the main corridor leading to his change isle. But even though he was rushing, his senses, especially his nose, told him that something strange was in the air. And as he rounded the first corner leading to his locker, his eyes first picking up the abused naked human form of 'Sugarlips' his vision also then found the apparent reason for what his 'Beak' had already tried to warn him about.

On more than one occasion in the past he had made humorous remarks about how it looked as if it had snowed around the lockers of men sprinkling themselves with white talcum baby powder. But now, its sudden surprising overabundance caused him to stop dead in his tracks as his eyes took in the vacant aisles in all visible directions being totally covered in the mysterious white stuff. Instantly, as his warped sense of humor would have it, a big grin was born to his face, when his vision next picked out the occasional faint trail of human footprints in the powdery floor.

"What the Hell happened in here!" he half laughed in 'Sugerlips' direction. "We get a surprise visit from Frosty The Snowman or something?"

"Naw!" Larry smiled back, soap and towel in hand, while pausing briefly to answer George's remarks. "Rumor has it the company's sprinkling out some new kind of poison in order to get rid of all the ants and silverfish we've been getting' in here lately."

Never being the one to pass over an obvious opening for a pun, no matter how much he was pressed for time, George quickly said, 'Ants!, What about the uncles? Aren't they going to get awfully lonely?"

Pretending to ignore the words at first, Larry Gilbert let his actions lead his next remark by sniffing at the air around them. "If it was anybody else but you, I'd say it's time to stop showing the limits of your intelligence."

"Smart move." George grinned softly as Larry kept talking. "Boy, that powdered poison smells so sweet that maybe it doesn't kill the little buggers outright. Maybe they'll smell so good to each other that they'll just 'screw' themselves to death."

"It can't be done." George laughed. Starting to move towards his locker once more he now deliberately used his work boots to stomp on the floor and make loud plopping noises in the powder, just as he did in the snow when he was a kid. But part of his mind was also still on Larry's last remark. And he used it to finish the rest of his own reply to fuel his departure. "I know for a fact it can't be done! I've tried it at least a hundred times with my wife!"

The, 'Don't you wish!' comment and laughter that trailed him was as always pleasant to both his ears and ego. But what he next saw, while turning the last corner into the aisle containing his locker, just about made him double up with laughter. 'Scratch', also wearing an abused birthday-suit and ready for the showers, was in the process of closing the doors to his lockers, when his head had instinctively turned in the direction of George's noisy approach. And as he stared directly into George's humorously distorted face, he was at first confused, and then irritated, before finally and just naturally expecting something sarcastic from the "Axe-Man.

"And just what the 'Hell' are you laughing at, 'smart-ass'!"

"Oh, nothin' nothin'." George answered, while working very hard to control the half chuckle now in his voice. "I just left 'Sugar Lips', and he had told me a 'very, very' funny story."

Passing behind 'Scratch', the mans head twisting just enough to keep 'Mister Acid Tongue' in full view at all times, George tried not to stare at the very noticeable big almost circular gray smudge surrounding most of his right cheek and eye. But before he could make it the rest of the way to his locker, his deranged sense of humor won out and he failed to hold in any longer a barrage of short chuckles.

Now apparently more irritated than baffled by George's strange behavior, Scratch glanced curiously down briefly at his own body, before turning his attention back in George's direction to say, "I've seen you in the raw, and you're no prize catch either ya know! Hell, I don't even think you're a keeper!"

Now back to only a half chuckle, George just smiled, 'I know. I know." while still failing to totally force himself to concentrate fully on the lockers now in front of him. And even though it was in his thoughts to ask 'Scratch' if he had been peekin' through one of the peepholes into the women's end of the change house again, he deliberately didn't. It didn't take an Einstein to read the obvious evidence arousing his curiosity.

Systematically stripping off his dirty work clothes after watching 'Scratch's' mumbling departure, George couldn't keep either his mind or body from occasionally reacting to the humorous images still within his thoughts. Stuffing his dirty cloths into his duffel bag, he then slipped his feet into a pair of well-aged flip-flops before closing his locker doors. Then, in an attempt to force his warped mind back onto the reason why he was there so early, he started to hum to himself, while forming a mental list of what he wanted to do as well as to what order to do them in.

Soap on a rope, towel, and other cosmetics in hand, he retraced some of his original steps in order to get to the shower room. He thought he had just about managed to control his wandering thoughts when his eyes fell on another sight that instantly told him he was never going to be able to keep a straight face as long as he was still within the plant.

Directly in front of him balancing on one foot and looking like a pear-shaped ballerina, was 'Sugarlips'. Leaning against one of the corridor's walls for support, he had one arm straight out sideways, as the fingers of his other hand were vigorously scratching at the bottom area and toes of one foot pivoted upwards. His face, and voice, 'If I ever get my hands on the dirty rotten son on a bitch' were also feverishly protesting his present apparent discomfort.

"What's the matter now?" George grinned, the answer to his question already vaguely in the back of his mind.

"If I didn't know better," Larry cringed, his fingers still viscously attacking the area between his toes and along the bottom of his right foot now, "I'd swear I was havin' an attack of 'athlete's foot'!"

"Can't be!" George laughed. "You don't exercise enough at anything to warrant 'athlete's foot'. But on the other hand, besides four fingers and a thumb, I'd say it looks like a bad case of 'itchin' powder blues to me."

The next word that came out of 'Sugar Lips' mouth, was both aggressive and explosive. "What!" And as quick as his brain would accept the information, his body reacted by jumping into the small clear areas provided by George's flip-flops. As giggling George started to move once more, Larry lost no time in matching his stride, while mumbling under his breath, "'God' damn women! Wait'll I get a chance at one of them!'

Leading the way into the shower-room, 'Sugarlips' still following close enough to start the wrong kind rumors if detected, George broke up once more when detecting "Scratch and another familiar face both at work scrubbing various parts of their bodies. And as soon as 'Scratch picked up on George's presence, he lost no time in shifting some of the aggravation he was presently going through into George's direction, sarcastically.

"Thanks for telling me about my face, 'Pecker-Head'!"

"Don't mention it!" George smiled back, while reaching out and flipping the shampoo cap in 'Scratch's hand end for end on the bottle he was irritatingly trying to screw it back onto.

As frustrated as he actually was, 'Scratch' totally succumbed to the humor of what he had been trying to do. Straight faced as possible, he grinned back at George "That was my next try!"

Behind him, after having paused long enough to give his own feet one last verbal scratching, the second worker added. 'It's bad enough you guys occasionally get in my mouth, now you want to be manhandled?" George then continued to chuckle while giving them what he surmised was happening.

"I think we've been attacked by the opposite sex. Which to me," he leered, "is all that any healthy man could really wish for."

It took only seconds for everybody else there to figure out what his words meant. And as each man scrubbed ruthlessly at their body, with only George's laughter filling the damp raining cubicle, they all took turns expressing how they felt about tricks they had been victims to, swearing to deliver personal revenge later at the stag.

By the time George walked squeaky clean back out of the shower, it was apparent that someone else must have also figured out what the white talcum on the floor had really been there for. Nice in the sense that whoever the individual had been, they'd had the incentive to wipe clean all of the visible itching powder. And after allowing himself the pleasure of one last laughter-filled moment in honor of remembering what had just happened to his work mates, George felt that now was as good a time as any to make a much needed rumbling pit stop.

Positioning himself directly in front of the first of a short row of four snow white porcelain urinals along one wall outside the shower stall, his head still occupied with the now clean floor behind him, he didn't hold back one iota when releasing the pressure built up in his bladder.

Almost as instantly as his lower naked body registered the warm liquid spraying back in his direction, George's automatic reaction couldn't help but let out one quick surprised loud shriek, before instinctively jumping backwards away from the golden showers that had been coming in his direction. Looking down at his now once again wet and now smelly body, his dripping fingertips now released and held as far away as possible from the weapon responsible for his present predicament, he let out a short burst of obscenities that he would have washed his kid's moths out for using. And when enough reasoning had returned to make him glance back at the real culprit, the open face of the urinal had been covered over totally with a piece of practically undetectable transparent food wrap, George couldn't help but let his warped sense of humor run free and loudly enjoy the prank, like the others who had come to investigate what the commotion was all about had. But the part that made him laugh the hardest was the fact of realizing that he too was now a victim of one of the women's pranks.

Back at his lockers, after a quick and total rescrubbing, George was just slipping on the last of his shoes, when the noticeable echoing sounds of some new, as yet unknown, commotion beckoned him back to the area of showers and washrooms. Letting his ears lead him, along with others now there and a pleasant smile already at home on his face, he followed the route laid out by the noisy commotions growing volume. As he walked back into the area he had left only brief moments earlier, a wall of variously dressed human flesh separated him from the source of the loud air singed complaints.

Squeezing his way through the semi-confused and half laughing gathering, the words 'What's all the excitement about this time?' on his lips, he didn't eve glance in the direction of the answer that came back at him.

"I think someone's got 'shit' all over their Jell-O, or something like that."

Although George thought the voice responsible for most of the disturbance did sound a little familiar. He was genuinely surprised when he found himself standing almost face to face with "Scratch' once again. Beaming out a "What the Hell you squawking about now?" look on his face, he as always once more let the humor still within him fail to keep from expressing itself.

"It's those bloody women again!" Scratch exploded, while raising his hands up for everyone to see.

"Don't tell me they've slammed ya twice in one day!" George laughed, with most of the other men also there instantly imitating him.

"Well what the Hell would you call it!" Scratch irritably answered.

Raising his hands over his head and shaking them in a frustrated manner, it was easy to see now that from about his wrists down to the tips of his fingers on both hands, 'Scratch's' skin was a bright reddish-orange in color. The laughter that had started with only those close enough at first to see, was now enjoyed by all. And as such, just as always, instantly encouraged a barrage of loud spontaneous long jeers and elongated 'He-e-e-res!'

James G. Davies Sr.

Even though he was enjoying the display just as much as everyone else George finally managed to ask. "I just know you're looking for someone to 'bark' at - but you've tickled my curiosity just enough that I've got to ask you, 'what did you do this time?'

In between still vigorously shaking and rubbing at his hands, obviously hoping that the color would somehow just fly away through the aid of centrifugal force or gravity, 'Scratch' growled out "I made the mistake of using the 'john'! And like any normal human with an impediment for personal hygiene, I washed my hands afterwards! One of those poor excuses for a woman, one of those 'Bitches!', must have somehow managed to slip some red vegetable food dye into the colored hand soap dispenser mounted over just this basin!"

Only noticing now that some of the apparent grinning idiots that had been so far content to silently just stand and listening to his sob story, were letting their limited intelligence show by deliberately starting to imitate his flailing arms and hands, 'Scratch', in return, gave them one of his best and meanest 'Piss Off!' expressions, before calling them 'Assholes!'

"You idiots got nothing better to do?" he then added, the small betraying grin now growing on his face saying that he was enjoying just as much of this bad situation as they were. "Remember, I know where most of you bums live. So if you don't knock it off, I'll drive by your place on the way home and ask your wife why you haven't been here at work all week!"

Almost instantly, just as if someone in the crowd had released a gagging 'room divider' into the crowd, most of the still smiling bystanders started to evaporate. And as a few hung back to find out what was going to happen next, George being one of them, he picked up from where he had left off.

'Boy, this just isn't you day, is it 'Scratch'. But then it's just as much our fault as it is for some of the shit disturbers next door. The stags only a day away, and it's not their fault we forgot about them pulling the same prank on us at about this time two years ago."

Still grinning while turning, since his hands were already stained, Scratch scooped the remainder of the powdered soap out of its dispenser and into the washbasin, one of his feet on the lever that let water flow into the basin. As he, along with everyone else watched the soap start to disappear, he pretended to be still upset while commenting to George.

"You wouldn't think this was so funny if the women ever got you with one of their pranks."

"Oh, but they did!" George grinned. "Only ten minutes ago they got me with the ol' transparent 'saran wrap' across the urinal trap."

"Really!" Scratch chuckled. "Well now I don't feel so bad."

"You shouldn't" George chuckled, his ever working 'quick-wit' kicking into gear. "No one outside of this place is ever going to see the results of what was pulled on me. But you - look at the bright side of it. If that bright dye doesn't wash off - you can always get a job down at the airport, waving in planes as they're taxing in for parking spots."

"Ve-e-ery funny!" Scratch said, straight faced and in between the small barrage of slamming's not unlike those heard earlier. "Now why don't you pretend you're one of those planes, and take off outa' here!"

When the last of the gathering wise enough not to trip or fall into the little verbal bantering going on in front of them instantly broke into a repertoire similar to what they had bestowed upon scratch only seconds earlier, George half bowed to them as an appreciated actor on stage would do to a delighted audience, before walking away, head held high.

Once back at the sanctuary of his locker again, George reached inside and pulled out a small note pad, the very reason he had sneaked away and taken the early shower for. But before giving it his fullest attention he let something that had also been on his mind lately bother him briefly. It wasn't that the women seemed to be pulling so many pranks on the men lately, as to how they were managing to do it and go undetected. And his devious logic being what it was, even if a few of the women in the right light could almost pass for a man, was that one of their own was working for the enemy. After all, most women under the right circumstances can get the proper man to do anything she wanted, especially since he believed that sex sells and controls almost everything else in the world. And as terrible as the thought also might be, there were a couple of men in the plant, married or not, that he considered as unsavory enough to be willing to trade their co-operation for a 'rattle' or two.

But instead of this being a negative he believed it was going to work out as a positive in everyone's favor, especially since he thought he knew just who the collaborator might be.

Sitting himself down as comfortably as possible on his duffel bag of dirty clothing, willing his ears to turn off all contact to the world around him, he leaned back against the cool stone wall opposite his lockers, and then flipped the small pad open. Inside, on a page numbered one, was a rough outline and list of things he was involved with at the yearly stag. And even though he already knew most of the pages' contents by heart from past experiences, he mentally in his mind's eye went through his duties once more.

Sitting motionless with eyes shut so as to enjoy the past images now floating through his mind, it took the sudden and loud mention of his name to snap him back to his world of often abused reality.

It was Fred, and as he grinningly fumbled with the lock on his cupboards, he continued with the words, 'Ya better wake up buddy. The dwarf was on the job site chasing' your ass! But Bob and I covered for ya. We said we hadn't seen you all day either."

"I'll bet ya did." George smiled. "Have I still got a job?"

"Not really." Fred grinned, still occupied with getting undressed. "We told him how far we were along on repacking those valves. I said that if he didn't manage to track you down, or you failed to find him before quitting time, then you would fill him in on Monday morning."

"With my luck, he'll probably bring it up at the stag." George frowned. "Or did you forget old' Farkas will in all probability be there?"

"I didn't forget." Fred frowned. "I was kind of hoping that if I didn't mention tomorrow night, maybe he'd forget about it and not show up."

"Boy - you are dreaming." George continued to frown, his eyes rolling 'Eddie Cantorish' skyward. And even if it looked like he was trying to be funny, it was really only in an effort to let his attitude match Fred's. "He hasn't missed one since he's started here!"

"We can always hope can't we? Or maybe we should be wishing with all our might for his absence." Fred smiled sadistically, while stuffing his work cloths into a duffel bag not unlike George's.

"When it comes to wishing, you better do it all." George grinned, his humorous wit apparently returning. "I must have used all of mine up when I was little, cause' they sure don't seem to work for me anymore."

"Serve's ya bloody right for being so greedy!" Fred chuckled. Fortunately, as almost always when they were together, his emotional behavior patterns were very susceptible to best friends. And it proved so now, as he twisted his head from side to side while adding, "If you were smart, you would have saved at least a few of them for when you got older."

"If I was smart," George shot back, while shifting his weight into a little more comfortable position, "I'd have been rich enough to retire by now. But if I was really, really smart, I wouldn't, "

"Ya, Ya, I know." Fred quickly cut him off. "If you were really, really smart, you wouldn't be hangin' around with guys like me."

Faking emotional pain even before Fred had a chance to totally finish the very phrase that he had himself was about to make, George made no effort to convince him of the phony pride he was presently experiencing because of what he had said. "Would I 'ever' say something as 'crude' as that?"

"Every chance you get buddy." Fred chuckled. "In fact now that I think of it, every chance you 'got'!"

"Well, if you think so." George replied, with phony emotions once more on display and exaggerating pain Fred really knew he wasn't experiencing. Also wearing a smile turned upside down George then added, "That hurts." Then suddenly, in less than a split second, he snapped right back to what everyone close to expected him to really act like. "Well, so much for the mellow dramatics. But getting back to hanging around, how is it, hangin'?"

By now Fred was as naked as the day he was born. Except for the odd extra wrinkle, not to mention some areas being noticeably bigger than when he had first started out, he calmly reached inside of his locker to grab his towel. He then looked directly at best friend's silly still grinning face, and answered nonchalantly, "We're expectin' the scab and swelling to be gone in a few more days"

"You mean that thing's going to get smaller!" George chuckled in disbelief.

"We are what we are." Fred answered with his expression and tone unchanged. Then using his towel as a whip, he snapped it just short of George's already anticipating cringing position, while adding, "Some of us just have to make the most of what we can, with what we've got. You included."

Turning with the showers as his next objective only in mind, Georges laughing words, "If you'll pardon the pun." following in behind.

"Ya, I guess you're right buddy. But in your case, I think it's best if you don't set your sites to high."

Watching Fred's unperturbed body until it rounded the last corner at the entrance to the isle they were in, his ears picking up the faint mumbled words 'My sites, what about Judy's?' With a smile on his face George turned his attention back onto the pad still opened in the palm of his hands. The thought to warn his best friend about all the traps presently planted by 'boobies' had crossed his mind, a trip others had often stated as requiring only a very short journey. But he thought that now was as good a time as any to have him pay for his departing mumbled slamming. But just as quickly as the thought had entered, even though he was willing to gamble that there were probably still as unyet detected tricks around someplace, he put it out again. Fred's a big boy he told himself. There's nothing out there that will hurt him or anybody else slow enough to get caught in any of the pranks, after all, he had.

Forcing himself to purge his head of everything except the whimsical speech for the stag he was trying to memorize, the occasional urge to chuckle at issues he would be talking about showing up as images inside his thoughts slipping out. The minutes and background noise flashed by again, in what seemed like only seconds. And again it was the sound of Fred's familiar voice that once more broke into his repeatedly tickled concentration.

Glancing up from the note pad just in time to catch his friends laughing form walking back around the same locker he had seemingly just stepped behind, George habitually started to grin even before asking him what was so funny.

"Someone, Someone just, found," whatever it was that was still tickling his funny bone so vigorously, Fred found that he had to sit down if he was going to develop the ability to try and spit out a full unbroken sentence. "One of the men, found a, a polaroid snapshot in one of the shit house cubicles, of 'Beautiful Brad.' Apparently mo-oo-onin' for the camera!"

George's immediate reaction was no different than Fred's, as soon as a mental picture of Brad in the raw, an 'ass' and best face foreword he'd seen naked before, jumped into his thoughts. And with that image, came the instant memory of when one of the other men had doctored a similarly viewed phony identification pass for entry into the plant, a few years back when the company was on a security binge. The guards at the gates, no doubt through frustration, had been stopping everyone entering or leaving the plant for seemingly any old reason. Possibly in the hope that if they irritated enough people, word just might get back to the higher-ups to knock off their silly time consuming inspections. And when Ron Richards had handed one of the security men a pass that showed him 'mooning' the camera, the guard, without even the faintest hint of faltering or hesitation held the card up alongside of Ron's face briefly, before saying, 'Okay. You can go. But I gotta' say, you sure do look different after just a shave and a haircut!'

With that memory had also come the realization that again there was no way he was going to be able to concentrate on the pad he had been staring at. So he closed and slipped it into a shirt pocket, before offering, "There's not only a photographer out there who has a dedicated sense of humor, but also he's an individual who apparently has an awfully strong stomach, too."

Slipping into his clothes as he spoke, Fred answered a little sarcastically, "You're not kidding! There's a couple of other guys in here with bodies so abused that with pictures like that of them it would undoubtedly scare the Hell out of a lot of kids, and back into puberty."

"If you're even close to the same two guy's I'm thinkin' about," George cringed. And they looked even a little bit like they do now before getting married, I doubt if any horny old women would have gotten close enough to contemplate the possibility of offspring, even if they were giving away free television sets after each wrestling match."

Breaking out into almost equal and unison body shaking appreciation of each other's humor, George and Fred were totally involved with their own company when a new and also familiar sounding voice broke into their antics.

"What the poop's takin' you two so long?" It was Bob's voice. And when both men looked in the direction his words had come from, they found only his head and fingertips from both hands sticking out sideways from the last locker at the end of their isle. At first glance, it almost looked as if he was actually somehow standing in a horizontal position halfway up the locker's height, giving the impression that he was being subjected to a different plane of gravity.

"We're comin'!" George shouted back, as they watched the rest of Bob's body seemingly melt slowly out through the locker door's face, finally into full properly vertical view.

"I thought we were supposed to be getting' out of this place a little bit ahead of the rush?" Bob smiled as his lunch pail and dirty laundry hung at his side.

"We are." George grinned. "We're just waitin' for old slow poke here. You ought'a know by now that he can't walk talk and chew gum all at the same time. Just look as his tee shirt! It ought'a give you a good idea of what kind of brain tissue he's workin' with."

Always eager to please, Fred stood erect so that Bob could read what was on his sweat shirt. "And no, it's not Halloween!" he then blurted out. Bob in turn, once getting a full view of the colorful image of a dim witted looking little man, finger protruding from a singular hand pointing straight upward, with the lettering 'I'm with stupid' in brackets underneath, couldn't help but snicker.

Slamming his locker doors closed and locked before picking up his work bag in one fluid motion, while saying, "I don't know who you bums are supposed to be waiting for - but it isn't me." Fred started in Bob's still smiling direction. George, jumping erect and scooping up his own clothing while mumbling, 'Why you asshole!' half ran until he had caught up to his two grinning buddies. And as they passed a mixture of men also on their way home, especially those with noticeable red eye and cheek bones, not to forget those unfortunate enough to be just starting their shift, the camaraderie that passed between them occasionally spilled over each time they came close to anyone commenting about what the women had been up to.

Bumping noisily through the doors leading towards the time clocks the humor that had been fed by the females pranks, continued to dominate their conversation. And as their feet eagerly ate up the distance still separating them from their next destinations, fate led them directly into the paths of some of the ladies who were in all probability involved in some of the very stunts they were still laughing about.

George was the first to notice the small group of women approaching in the distance. Without even missing a breath, he shifted their 'catty' like conversation smoothly onto them alone. "Here comes some of the 'rat pack' now. Whatever you do, don't let on that anything out of the ordinary's been happening in the change house. These barracudas get even a hint that they've gotten under our skin, or we've been intimidated in any way, they'll laugh us the rest of the way to our cars."

Giving the approaching group a quick once-over himself, Fred instantly lowered his voice while leaning in closer and whispering, "I don't see any of the 'sugly isters' in the pack. Maybe we'll get by them without any need for a course in self defense."

Bob was still fairly virgin enough to most of the plant's female workforce that in all likelihood they still didn't even know that he existed yet, or at least so he thought. And he in turn, even though he had heard a lot of scuttlebutt about which women to watch out for and avoid whenever possible, wisely once more offered only a Charlie Chan- ish smile to the ongoing remarks between his two friends.

"I doubt it." George remarked out of the side of his mouth, even though the women were still to far away to possibly hear their conversation, or they the one apparently the ladies also appeared to be having. "It looks like Kit Fisher's leading' the pack. The fact that she looks more like a man than you do Bud, doesn't please her any more than it does any of us - or her poor husband I've heard. And she'll jump down your throat if she even thinks you're contemplating thinking about her appearance."

A Dolly Parton she wasn't, and now that you think about it most of the other women in the plant weren't also. But in her case it could truly be said that if she ever tripped and fell face down, the first thing in all probability to touch the floor first, would be her nose. And as the group rearranged itself as it moved, a new and familiar face showed itself from the rear of the pack.

"I see Louie's with them!" Fred chuckled. "I heard that when she was little she played all kinds of sports. I guess she always wanted to be just one of the boy's."

"It's hard to believe she was ever 'little'!" Bob snickered.

"Well, and I'm sure I'm speakin' for the rest of the other animalistic 'oink oink's' in the plant, I'm sure as Hell glad she never made it!" George groaned.

His delivery copying George, Fred added, "Ya! Those pants she's wearin' are so tight they gotta be hurtin' her when she walks."

"I'm only watchin," George leered in a sigh of a whisper, "and they're killin' me."

Whacking George in the arm as his own body shaking humor matched both of his friends, Fred's next words were barely detectable. "Judy catches you talkin' like that, and the first thing she'll do is too order the flowers. Then she'll 'kill' ya!"

George hadn't anticipated the 'sucker' punch in the arm Fred had given him , but his reflexes were still fast enough that he had no trouble returning the horseplay as Fred had been finishing what he was saying. The women by this time were walking almost parallel to them and since they had no trouble seeing their silly antics, it prompted one of them to comment, "You learn that from your kids, or vice versa?"

Delivering a wink that only Bob and George were in a position to see, Fred immediately did his best to put his foot in his mouth. "We were just practicing our answers for when you ladies ask us to dance at the stag tomorrow night."

Most of the women instantly laughed sarcastically at the remark. But Kit, obviously taking his words to heart lost no time in expressing her personal bitter feelings about what he had suggested.

"It'll take a Hell of a lot more than a new pair of glasses or a face full of booze before any of us will ask you snakes to slither across the dance floor!"

With every intention of making the confrontation come out on a friendly basis, George smiled pleasantly while saying, "When the time comes, can we hold you lovely ladies to that offer." Quickly then, after using his arms to reach out and wrap themselves into an embrace around an invisible dance partner in front of him, George waltzed to music that was just as imaginary.

Shifts

Only Louie in the group of women anticipated what he was up to. So she instantly reacted to his gestures by pretending that his arms had ticklishly encompassed he body. And as even the slowest to catch on of the women recognized what she was insinuating, she kept squirming while giggling, "Please Mister Stone! Not so tight!"

But Kit was having nothing to do with fraternizing with the enemy on any kind of basis, regardless of what she knew. Glaring into Fred's eyes, if looks could indeed kill then he would surely by now just be ashes in an urn, she coldly remarked, "No doubt your dirty imaginations will leave you animals endin' up grabbin' more than just air!"

While Bob let out a long elongated moan at the blow rightly belonging to George, who was busy already laughing, those of the women smart enough to stay out of the remarks giggling amongst themselves, Fred pretended to dramatically take an invisible arrow dead center in the middle of his chest. And as he continued with the humorous-looking charade by staggering backwards from the pressure of the invisible shaft, all of the women except Kit threw caution to the wind and laughed out loud as Fred directed his rebuttal exclusively in her direction.

"I guess we'll just have to try fishin' in another location at the stag."

"Oh ya!" Kit instantly snapped in his direction. "Well there may be other fish in the sea, but from what I've heard some of you boy's are going to need a Hell of a lot more tantalizing 'bait' than any of you heroes have got, before you'll ever stand a chance of enticing them onto the hook!"

Mean to or not, Kit had accomplished exactly what George had hoped to do, especially after Fred took the second imaginary arrow noisily in the heart. Staggering even more wildly after letting his pail and work bag drop to the ground so as his hands could clasp his chest, other passing workers pausing only long enough to verbally rate his hammy performance from one to ten, Fred finally laid his act to rest - so to speak. Falling to the ground, tits up, he finished it all off by letting one of his legs give out with one last reverberating death kick, eyes closed and his tongue exposed hanging out the side of his mouth.

There was no animosity in the second round of cheers and laughter that instantly filled the air around Fred's now motionless form. Even poor Kit, realizing that there was no way she could be the winner in this battle of 'twits', stepped close enough to Fred's horizontal dormant form to pretend to give it a nasty kick, while saying, "Oh, 'pa-lease' let this be true!" She then, while still over reacting herself, pretended to limp away in a huff, satisfied that although she may not have been a winner in the battle she had willingly tried to fight, she could be content that she was at least not a loser either.

As the other still giggling women automatically started to follow in behind her departure, the odd one pausing long enough to send an invisible arrow back in the men's direction, the wink that went also undetected this time was between George and Louie.

Offering Fred a hand in order to help his still horizontal form up from the ground, something just short of tears rolling down his cheeks, Bob was still laughing quite noticeably when he offered the words. "I think you've got at least an 'Oscar nomination' coming for that performance." George in turn, while scooping up his best friends discarded pail and work bag, offered his own humorous view as to Fred's possible future potential. "Personally, I thought you were puttin' yourself into a position of someday wakin' up in a pit full of lye, especially after 'you-know-who' hears about this."

Brushing the knees of his pants clean, his own face now lost in laughter also, Fred acknowledged George's remark with a simple, "Well, they say into each 'lye', a little 'pain' must fall."

Giving the terrible little pun exactly what it deserved, a quick low 'E-e-e-ew! Bob finally offered his own comments on what he had been a witness to. "That woman sure provided a legitimate reason to any man for sneaking into a monastery to become a monk.

"Could be!" George grinned, while starting to move once more towards the cars. "I wouldn't be surprised if her old' man got freezer burn on his shorts whenever it's time to relieve a little bit of the old eyeball pressure."

"Isn't that why we're born with two hands?" Fred grinned, while glancing at his own. "You know, just in case one gets injured, or has a headache."

"Regardless." George smiled while still leading the way. "Just keep it in mind that in all probability you just earned a spot for your name closer to the number one notch on their 'hit list'."

"Did you say 'hit or 'hate' list?" Bob asked with his face still lit up in a broad smile.

"They're one in the same." Fred frowned. "But what George was really saying is that although it's important to remember your friends, it's a Hell of a lot 'more' important to never forget your enemies!"

"Well maybe it's the wrong time of the month for old' what's her name Bob grinned.

"If you mean Carla" George smiled, "It could be. Especially since her curse seems to linger for about four weeks out of a month."

Suddenly for some strange reason known only to himself Bob asked, "Don't you guys ever think you owe Carla even a little bit of sympathy?"

As George instantly answered with "No-o-o-o!" Fred remarked, "Aw 'sympathy'. How well I remember you, ah, your, ah, smiling features."

As a questionable look of confusion instantly leapt to Bob's face, George answered the question that was no doubt now forming in his mind, just one more of the hundreds still yet to pop up.

"Sympathy's a nickname for one of the women you haven't had the, ah, pleasure of meeting yet. And the reason the boys call her 'Sympathy' is because at one time or another, she's been felt by most of the available men in the plant."

With a devilish look in his eyes, Bob squinted at George, 'Even you?' and George in a half laugh, lost no time in blurting out, "Hell no! I have hopes of living long enough to see my pension ya know, with both of my testicals in tact!"

"Don't forget to tell him that your wife rapes you regularly once a month too." whither you need it not " Fred chuckled as they started to split for their cars.

"You mean you still 'do it' at your age!" Bob exaggerated at George.

Letting his fisted right arm snap out, and fail, to make contact on Bob's already evasive shoulder, George chuckled, "It's the fastest and best way I know of to settle any and all arguments. It's our little way of, lets say, clearing up any old business and having a clean slate to start the next month with."

"Not to mention that under those circumstances it's truly better to 'Give!' 'Give!' 'Give!' Till it 'Hurts!' 'Hurts!' Hurts!' Than it is to 'receive'!" Fred laughed out loud, after having finished with the little lewd bit of body English body langue he had used to emphasize his words.

With the cars now in sight George had one last thing he wanted to cover. "Before we split, did either of you happen to notice anything strange about one of the women in the group back there?"

As Bob, his face suggesting that he was searching his memory, while shaking his head in a negative manner, Fred answered, "No, not really. I was having too much fun being the entertainment then watching the audience. Why?"

While glancing back to where their confrontation had taken place, the females all now long out of view, George offered, "Oh, nothing important. I thought I detected something on one of the women's faces."

"You look at their faces?" Bob chuckled, cynically.

"He likes to get the 'whole' picture." Fred grinned back rudely, before commenting in George's direction "Right buddy?"

"Well." George smiled. "Sometimes you don't have to actually see a lump of 'shit', just to know you're standing in it."

"Did we miss something?" Bob asked.

"No, not really." George lied, the image of one of the ladies sporting a slight red tinge to one eye and cheekbone, something he'd already seen more then once day. "But the ladies have been getting the best of us all day, and it would be nice to think that maybe they got some of their own back."

The image, as he couldn't help but start to smile again, was enough to tell him that 'yes' the men did have an ally in the woman's area.

"If they did or didn't," Fred smiled "tomorrow's another day. And we've still got a few tricks up our own sleeves for the stag, right?"

"Right!" George said forcefully, Bob still smiling. "By Monday we'll know who wears the 'trousers and makeup' in this place."

"Do we really want to know who or if some of the men wear 'makeup'! Bob chuckled.

"Not really." Fred with a look of disgust on his face.

"But if we do!" George smiled. "Then we forget who they are, just as fast as we can."

Their farewells, even though it would be hard to match the comradely they had already experienced, was just as sweet as George again briefly reminded them of what they had already agreed upon in order to help make his involvement in the stag flow easier. And it wouldn't be until they were long gone and home in almost opposite directions that the stage would be set for one last potentially humiliating laugh on each of them.

The overly large brazier that Bob's wife wouldn't find in among his dirty work cloths until Sunday, when the kids were off to bed, would easily and laughingly be explained away when he would tell her that it must have fallen in from someone changing beside him, especially since it was 'way' to small to be his size. And as if to give credence to his explanation he held the piece of apparel up to his chest as he had been speaking, before adding, "Besides, does this look like something I would wear?"

For Fred, especially since he and his wife Nancy were only just back together, it would take her strong desire for them to remain that way, even though he repeatedly apologized that he had nothing in connection to the pair of torn pantyhose hidden inside of his workbag. Not until he had reassured her repeatedly that it must be something left over from the barrage of pranks the women at work were playing on the men, did he realize a now grinning Nancy was just adding her humor to the gag.

And last but not least, our boy George, even though he already knew that the over exaggerated look of skepticism in Judy's eyes when finding the bright red silk panties in among his bag of filthy laundry within minutes of his arrival home - didn't have to be explained away. He simply and placidly smiled off his own surprise by saying, "Well don't look at me! You know I won't wear anything red! - It clashes with my personality!"

Frowning, Judy added, "They may not be yours, but I did get a woman phoning here last week asking for you. And now this. Maybe, if she calls back I should tell her it's okay with me if she wants to drop by and pick you up!"

"And you forgot to tell me!" he pretended to explode, Totally ignoring her attempt at humor. "It could have been about something related to the stag."

"Well if it was, she's had all week to contact you. And if it was that important, she would have called you back. "

Letting a smile float to his face, a sure sign that he was yanking her chain just as much as she was pulling his leg, he added, "I think you're right. I think whoever called, already has made contact."

Quickly filling her in on what he believed to be going on, George added a little bit of body English when coming to the part about just before leaving the parking lot. And after finishing it all off by asking 'How long before supper hon?' he fished a beer out of the fridge and headed for the kitchen's table, the notebook once more in hand.

So far everything was wishful speculation, as he used his Perry Mason powers of deductive reasoning. But with the hope that he did have someone or even maybe someone's' on his side you might say, it also brought with it that the same individuals just might be the ones who had pulled the nasty prank on Farkas, and that he didn't like to theorize about. But then again, like he had suggested to Fred earlier, Monday just might be the beginning of a new era within the plant. And sometimes change, as any optimist or pessimist is willing to tell you, isn't always for the better.

Chapter 14

'Fantasizing Fathead.'
Or
'All together now - 1 - 2 - 3.'

As a stranger to the mature concept of death, even though he was in a sense taking his life into his hands, or even as others would like to describe it as putting his 'butt' on the line - Ian crept on hands and knees towards the window now only inches away in front of him. What he presently lacked in maturing years was overly and abundantly made up for by being protected with a sense of humor that had him giggling to himself, solely for what he was about to do. And once he was secure in the sanctuary he had been after, he lifted his head just high enough to be able to peek out and down onto the yard across from him, with its two unsuspecting occupants. With only the sound of his own giggle to keep him company he slowly lifted the Polaroid he had purposely brought along and tilted it towards the provocative images he hoped to capture. Like most things in his protected world he foolishly believed that what he was about to do was strictly for his own beneficial use and survival.

His brother Darryll, more in the past then now and no more than his older brother had done to him, had seemingly taken very great pleasure in occasionally irritating him in his little existence. But now, especially since Darryll was strangely spending most of his time with the girl next door, something he explained to himself as probably being due to the fact that she had something of value that he must be after, he knew that if need be a few snapshots could be a very valuable bargaining tool in the future. Little could he even begin to suspect at this stage of his life just how close he was to the actual truth, for 'both' wild summations.

Still a little strangely confused by the pleasant warm sensations he felt each time he was now with someone he could remember teasing and avoiding whenever possible only scant years earlier, Darryll wondered to himself if there wasn't something terribly wrong with himself. He had no trouble remembering the explicit, yet weird at the time sex education class he had been exposed to during his last year in school. But the bewildering things that were starting to happen to his mind and body, more intimidated than scared him. He didn't mind the new growth of hair sprouting out at the strangest yet predicted parts of his body, but the sudden way it behaved whenever noticing the body transformations of young girls he had grown up around him, did. Having to stay on a vibrating bus ride for almost four stops past where he had wanted to get off, or regularly now having to carry his books in front of him as he walked from classroom to classroom was sometimes proving to be embarrassing. And as he sat there, occasionally taking a sip from the can of soda pop resting beside him and his lawn-chair, he more than once asked himself 'What the Hell's happening to me!'

It was a good question, especially since he swore that he could actually see the tiny chest mounds on the napping form sunning itself in front of him grow to almost five times their actual size, only to then shrink again, each and every time she took a breath. Cursing wordlessly at himself, especially when remembering that it also hadn't been that long ago when she had fit the nickname of 'Fatty Patty', he repeated the small simple slamming he had just given to himself when realizing just watching her also made a tiny bit of his body uncontrollably grow. And if he'd been called upon to explain what it felt like, he would have replied, 'It was like having a magnificently total body pleasing itch, that simply just scratching at it briefly wouldn't make it go right away. In fact he found that it often did quite the opposite. '

With a big seemingly all knowing smile on his face, his head twisting itself from side to side while glancing at the view visible through their neighbors open fence gate, George junior mumbled to himself, 'Poor little brother. Someone's got him on a short string through the ring now in his nose, and he hasn't got the foggiest idea what to do about it. I thought Pop would have given him the same 'father son' fantasy 'pollinating the flowers' by now that he gave me, but I guess I'll just have to sneak a couple Playboy magazines under his pillow later. Maybe then he'll get a small inkling as to why I joined all the sports activities, basketball, baseball, and football at school. Where else can you go and get a free front row seat of the schools hottest chicks physically showing off while flashing their pink panties and shapely bodies, not to mention the side benefit of them hanging around and clamoring all over anybody on any of the teams.

But as junior's attention was locked on Darryll, Ian grinning from overhead, was now going over the snapshots he had just taken did not notice another pair of eyes watching only him. And it took a repeated rap on the kitchens rear door, blended in with the sound of his paging name, 'Georgy!' to snap his attention back to where he was.

"Come on in Uncle Fred, the door's not locked."

Fred wasn't really related, but George had more than once requested as a sign of respect for his kids to please refer to him in that manner. And Fred, already knowing himself that he really didn't need permission to enter his best friends abode, always returned the honor by making sure his presence was known before doing just that. Saving his normal 'How's it hanging?' comment for work, he instead gave a younger rendition of the same phrase in junior's direction. "How's it going Georgie, still keepin the fridge company I see.'

"If it's Pop you're here to see," Junior smiled, "I'm afraid ya just missed him. He was updating his manuals when he got a phone call from someone from work and said they had to meet at the mall over something that has to do with your yearly stag. At least that what I heard him tell mom.

"That's okay." Fred smiled, his head tilting itself just enough forward to check the adjoin rooms for any other human activity. "I'm really here to talk to your mom. Is she home?"

"Last time I saw here she was loaded down with dirty cloths, no doubt heading for the laundry room in the basement. - Want me to call down and let he know you're here?"

"No, that's okay." Fred smiled. "I'll go talk to her down there. Besides, what I have to say will probably have to be cleaned up before it's worth talking about any-ways."

Even as occupied as she was, her ears already tuning into the fact that Fred was now overhead in the house. Judy was only briefly attempted to hide in behind the laundry room door, in order to jump out shouting 'Surprise!" when he arrived. Even though the brief thought had brought her temporary humor, she was even happier to know that he and Nancy were genuinely making progress at repairing their bruised marriage, especially since there was now soon to be a baby to help with the healing process. Besides, if their impending family was hopefully about to grow, she didn't want her sudden loud shock of 'Surprise!' to scare him 'sterile' like hubby, who she often reminded sounded more like to what she actually at times thought he was, 'senile!'

Letting his ears lead the way, not that he didn't already know where Judy was, it was solely with the intent of making sure that no one else would be within hearing range for what he presently had on his mind. But just in case she wasn't aware of his presence in the house, after getting no reply after calling out 'Judy!' from the top of the stairwell, he made sure that the sound of his size nines on the cellar stairs might help announce his approach. And just when he was about to question if Georgie had made a mistake about the whereabouts of his mother, Judy's soft voice finally came back in his direction, "I'm in here Fred."

Entering the small area housing the homes washer and dryer, the dryer still busily announcing that it was quickly approaching the need for a new belt and bearings, Judy repeated the almost exact same information about Hubbys' whereabouts as her son had, even before he asked for it.

"It wasn't George I was after." Fred answered, this time his eyes assisting his ears as he let his vision pan the area around them. "I actually came to see you."

For the first time since Fred had become a regular part of the family, Judy thought, this would be the first time she had actually been both alone in the house with him, let alone be the reason for his visit. And it only took a brief glance at the look of nervousness now on his face to get her to drop the bed sheet she was presently folding, while answering.

"Let's take this to where we can hear ourselves think if we have to." she smiled. And as she led the way to the rec room, after making sure to close the door to the small laundry room behind Fred, she then added "The boys are occupied with themselves and in there we can talk in peace and quiet.

Even before he had a chance to seat himself, Judy asked, "Can I get you a drink, pop or coffee?" already knowing that Fred was an occasional ale drinker alright, but 'Ginger ale' was the one she had been referring to.

As appealing as the thought of a cold beer might sound at this time, Fred had no intention of not only indulging without the presence his best friend, but also because he needed to keep a clear head for what he was about to ask. And even though the words were on the edge of his lips, it took Judy's voice to get them started on their mission.

"Now then," she smiled, "if you're not here to see George, and I already know that he has the ability to make anyone nervous, so what's Nancy up to?

"She's home packing." Fred tried to smile. "Her fathers not doing to well, so we thought we'd drive out and break the good news to them face to face with the hopes that it will perk him up."

"I'm sure they'll be more than pleased, all the way around." Judy quickly offered, hoping to encourage more out of him. "But you could have passed that information on through George. So why are you really here?"

Shaking his head briefly in disbelief before saying, "I guess I should have known you would have suspected why I'm here. George always says he sometimes feels as if you already know what he is about to say, even before he does."

"Save the flattery." Judy smiled. "Most men are like an open book, and what you and Nancy are about to go through, especially for the first time, is enough to scare any man."

"Regardless of how you do it," Fred started, now a bit more at ease, "you're right, about everything. Best friend or not, I can't talk to George. With his since of humor he's more likely to laugh himself silly if I ask him what to expect or should be doing to help Nancy. I can already hear him chuckling, 'You've already done your part in helping Nancy.

You've' done what men done with woman since the dawn of time, to get their first born here."

"Don't worry about him laughing himself 'silly'," Judy smiled. "Believe me, most of the time he's already 'silly'."

"Ya, right." Fred chuckled, as his brain did an instant trip down memory lane over some of the crazy things they had done together over the years. And then in almost that same instant his face seemingly sobered up, while adding, "Like I said earlier. George is my best friend, and because of that, I guess 'that' by proxy also makes you my best friend also."

With only a smile, Judy confirmed what he had been saying so far, before wisely letting him carry on uninterrupted.

"If you don't mind, I'd like to be able to occasionally ask you for a few pointers along the way. You know," he almost blushed, while seemingly fighting for the appropriate words to continue. And again, no doubt from having been around George so long, his manner quickly turned to humor. "You know, having had the repeated benefits of being a three time winner, of the 'Meddle of Honor'.

Even as she laughed, 'You got that from George, didn't you?' Judy kept right on giggling, while adding, "Of course I'll do what ever I can do to help the both of you get through this blessing. And I'll warn you right now - it's a lot more then it's cracked up to be! There's going to be times when you think you can't take anymore, but the 'makeup times' will inspire you to want to do it all over again, especially when you get to hold those little extensions of yourselves. Besides, what kind of friends would we be if we didn't help each other out occasionally. Right off the bat I'd suggest, if you plan on having more than one kid, now might be the right time to consider a big house, especially if you can afford it. And take into consideration that as the years go on your present wage should go up. Thereby letting you grow into a mortgage you might think you can't afford just now. That was one of the deciding factors when we bought this place. You might say we not only grew into the house, we also grew up to and even passed the range where we could eventually afford it."

"And that's how you decided on this place, you planned on having three children?"

"Not really." Judy smiled. "Neither of us really planned on having three kids. But when the children stopped showing up - we stopped moving."

"Kinduv makes thing about that old question I've often heard the men ask each other at work, you know the one where if they could go back and start all over, would they ever have kids again."

"That's an easy one to answer." Judy smiled. "And the answer would be, of course!"

"Why?" Fred answered genuinely straight faced.

While letting her head slowly pan the area, maybe she was evaluating the house and its contents, or even just checking on where the kids presently were, Fred couldn't begin to understand. Having 'been there' and now living in the latter part of 'done that' she smiled, "Because when I was little I can still remember my parents and friends often asking each other the same question. And even though some of them had jokingly shouted at each other 'No way!', it was all just an act, especially if there parents had not only thought the same way, but had in actuality decided not to have children. So consequently, logic suggests that if your parents had acted the same way, none of us would be here right now having this conversation. And the bottom line is, if we're not 'here' to get others like ourselves 'here', then what the hell are we really 'here' for?"

Instantly laughing to just himself, especially since the old 'If you're not 'here-after' what I'm 'here-after', then you're going to be here-after I'm gone!' joke just naturally jumped into his head, he let it just as quickly depart. Especially since he already knew the answer to her comment and had heard George more than once jokingly say that she had been no doubt put on the face of the earth just o make his life miserable. And to mention it, would no doubt open a can of worms he had no desire to be a party to.

So instead he forced the grin off of his face, and got back on track.

"Well, " he stammered once again. "There's a bit more to it, Hell! There's a lot more to it! We were hoping, that when the time comes, you two would consider becoming Godparents."

The smile that had already been on her face grew in volume, as she answered, 'You can count on it!"

"But what about George, shouldn't you talk it over with him first?" Fred asked seriously.

"This isn't one of those situations where you need a second opinion." she continued to grin. "Hasn't he told you by now that whenever we have a disagreement or when I want his opinion - I generally just beat it out of him."

"If you do," Fred chuckled. "you'll be the first person I've ever met who ever 'really' got the best of him."

"It's not as hard as everyone thinks - especially if you know how to get back at him. And believe me, I've had over forty years to learn where and which buttons to push." Judy half laughed.

"And letting him do anything he wants to ," Fred asked, "is how you control him?"

"Exactly. That way he thinks he's the Captain of his domain, without even suspecting that it's the one who rows or steers the ship who is really the one in control.

"Well what's his ship doing at the mall? Fred Smiled.

"He said he had last minute business there with someone involved with the company stag." Judy smiled back. "But then you probably already know that, you're his best friend."

"He said he has a sort of secret agent working for him in the woman's camp, but he couldn't risk telling me who. It is. Maybe that's the person he's meeting." Fred offered.

"Do you think," with a hint on concern in her voice now, "she's the one whose been calling all week, and then hanging up whenever I pick up the phone?

Hesitating for a few seconds before answering, no doubt evaluating the information, Fred's' voice was just as concerned when answering. "Let's hope so. I don't know if he's told you, but it's his head painted on the bull's-eye of the shit-list of the companies so called 'man haters.'"

"He can generally take care of himself." Judy chuckled. "Now here's a bit of that free helpful information you haven't asked for yet. Make sure you and Nancy have some time to just yourselves after work each day. We do. It's during those times we've occasionally laughed about such things away. We have no real secrets from each other."

"I envy your commitment to one another." Fred smiled.

"But aren't you even a little bit concerned, especially after that potentially wicked mother and son visit George says you got?"

"Even if he didn't already have a 'bullet proof' way out of that one," Judy chuckled, "I'd still have given him the benefit of the doubt. He may not be overly bright sometimes, but he's more loyal then a Saint Bernard."

Sharing the instant thought that entered his head, "But that could have only been the prelude, or maybe even a distractor. The ladies have already been up to their old pranks and more at work. And we're almost as close as we're going to get to the stag. If they can pull something off between now and tonight, there won't be enough time to prove or disclaim whatever it is, let alone have any time for retaliation."

Judy once more tried to laugh it away with, "Oh he's probably just trying to sneak in another face full of junk food, figuring if he's that far away all traces will be gone before he has a chance to get home again."

"I don't know." Fred started to twist his head side to side in a negative fashion in order to give credence to what he was saying, "I'm getting a really bad feeling about this. I think I better go to the mall and check this out, just to be safe."

"Stop it!" Judy smiled. "You're starting to scare me."

"Laugh if you want," Fred said straight faced, while turning to head for the door. "but he 'is' my best friend, And friends back friends, in good as well as bad weather. Now, did he happen to tell you which mall or plaza he was going to?"

"Oh, somewhere on the other side of town." Judy answered. "He said they wanted to meet someplace where there would be less chance of running into anyone from work."

"That in itself sounds a little bit suspicious." Fred answered. "But there is an out of the way place where we've occasionally gone for coffee and doughnuts. George likes to call it his 'safe-house' away from home, because we very rarely run into anyone from work. Are you sure that's what he said?"

"Okay, you got me." Judy continued to smile. "We may not tell each other everything, but we never lie to one another. And you should know Georges philosophy on telling lies."

"Ya." Fred said straight faced. "But that's only if he thinks someone's telling him the truth."

Pausing for a second, no doubt pondering the facts up to now, Judy continued to smile while saying, "Hold it! If you think it's worth checking on, give me a second to grab my purse and tell the boys they're on their own for a little while. I'll meet you at the car. And you're driving!"

He was about to say, as she started to move also, that she didn't have to leave the boys alone, bust just as quickly realized that by now they were all old enough to watch each And even though he could check on Georges' situation all by himself, he also quickly remembered that when Judy said anything, it was generally good enough to be etched in 'stone', especially where 'George Allen Stone' was concerned. Instead he just offered, "We better hurry. If he's where I think he is, he'll already be there, and probably into his second piece of cake."

While licking from his finger tips the last remnants of two glazed sinkers he had just managed to inhale, smiling like the cat that had just swallowed the unguarded canary, George wordlessly smiled, "Lets see if she can smell that on my breath later." A brief glance at his wristwatch told him that he was still long minutes ahead of the time he had agreed to meet Louie. And as it privileged him enough time to glance around it only took a second to see that something other than his rendezvous was apparently in the wind. There in plain view through the window of one of the malls better woman's orientated cosmetic stores was the image of Dick Dryden, alias 'Sominex'.

George rationalized that this was a need to know situation and he had just enough time to satisfy his curiosity. Disposing of the last of the drink in his other hand, another quick chuckle in memory of Judy's warnings, he then made his way into the scented store.

Wordlessly walking up behind his co worker, his surprise, as Sominex jumped at the sound of his voice, was just as genuine when getting a view of the startled face now looking in his direction. And as his inner voice commented, 'I don't believe it!' his voice matched the surprise he was presently feeling while looking at the red area around Dick's right eye.

Sominex, 'You scared the shit out of me George!', was still obviously unaware as to why his friend was acting so strange. But as soon as

George remarked, 'There are those in the plant I would expect of being a 'Peeping Tom', but not you Dick.' he knew he was now in more trouble then had been in when entering the store.

"Stop right where you are George. I promise you, it's 'not' what it looks like!"

"I'm glad you can read what's in my thoughts!" George said, his voice still dripping with a hint of disbelief. "Then you'll also know that with my devious mind, you better have a really good believable excuse as to why your presently sporting such an obvious red blemished area on your face.

"Believe me, I have." Sominex blushed, the rest of his face now shifting to match the area around his cheek and eye. "I'm in here for a very good reason. But before I tell you, you've got to swear you'll never tell anyone as long as we're both alive."

Risking a quick glance at his wristwatch, George forced a smile onto his face, both because he hoped that his first assumption was wrong, and in the hopes of relaxing his friend. "I think we know each other well enough that if I give you my word, it's good. But before I give it to you, you'll have to earn it."

Swallowing hard, 'his' eyes now scanning the area, Dicks voice was both hesitant and just as shaky as the hand coming up to point at the area in question, as he started. "Well, firstly, I'm here to purchase some skin colored makeup. Something that will hide this approaching shiner."

The obvious question of, 'Who, as well as how in the Hell did you get a shiner? was replaced with "You're already starting to tickle me inquisitive funny-bone, that alone making it hard for me to promise you my word." George offered.

"Bare with me!" Dick quickly cut in. "It's just, just that - what I have to tell you is more embarrassing then believable.

"Try me." George smiled.

"Well, I guess you might say it all goes back to how I got my nickname 'Sominex'. It's no secret sometimes I snore so loud that anyone I'm around has trouble getting any sleep. Just ask the men on my crew each time we work twelve to eight, like last night."

As the saleslady returned long enough to hand Sominex his purchase and change, George used the brief interruption to check the time. And as Dick led them towards a small bench just outside the store, he kept talking.

"It's gotten so bad over the years that the wife and I finally decided to do something about it. Hearing that a friend had beat the smoking habit through the help of hypnosis we decided to give it a try, just last week in fact. Well, and I swear I'll get even if it takes be the rest of my life if you ever tell anyone, especially anyone form work."

"Calm down." George smiled as they sat down. "You're going to hyperventilate if you don't take a few deep breaths. And besides, I'm not so heartless that I can't see that this is really bothering you. So once again I, give, you, my word of honor!"

While smiling slightly, "Sorry buddy. My eye is really starting to hurt, and no doubt effecting my since of reasoning."

"That's okay." George continued to smile, while once more glancing at his wristwatch. "But I'm afraid you're going to have to pick up speed. I've got an important meeting to get to soon. And no, you can't ask what it is until you're totally done."

"Agreed." Sominex grinned. "Well - like I was saying, we decided to go the Hypnosis route. And believe it or not it actually seemed to work, as far as the snoring went. But without me knowing it, the wife had the doctor throw in a little something extra with the subliminal message. In her little evil, or should I say 'horny' mind, she had him put in that if she was to touch any part of my inner ear cannel, I'd instantly get sexually aroused."

Even though still not knowing exactly what had happened, Georges mind was miles ahead, as he remained silent and forcibly straight faced once more.

"Well, you know as well as I do what the showers are like at work. Here I am standing in the raw beside someone I didn't know from the mills also drying himself, only arms length away. And almost instantly as I crammed and twisted one tip of my towel into my ear, I started to get a 'Bonner' that you could have tripped a charging elephant with."

Even though the corners of Georges mouth were starting to curve up, Dick kept right on with his story, possibly with the intention of getting it over with and out of his stomach as fast as possible, no doubt hoping that whoever he told it to might just be able to take away some of the pressure he was presently experiencing.

"Needless to say, the fellow drying himself beside me didn't accept my just as instantly embarrassing surprise in the same manner I did. And when I just as instinctively tried to smile my present situation away with a nervous big smile, he no doubt took it to mean anything else but."

Using a finger to delicately touch the enflamed area on his face for proof, he took another big breath before continuing, George remaining a true friend by successfully refraining from laughing. "Once again I was instantly surprised, with this, which just as strangely chased the reason for the entire incident instantly away. As soon as I had enough sense to call home, and just as soon as I could get the wife to stop laughing, she told me what she had done. Needless to say until we can get this predicament rectified, I can't go to work, let alone the stag. With a red area around one of my eyes, especially since most of the men know this kind of thing's been associated with those peeking into the woman's change house, I'd be a nonstop target for every innuendo anyone is willing to throw in my direction. So, you can understand why I'm so far off the beatin path buying cover-up cream for my face.

Once more proving that he was still a friend, while commenting inside his head, 'And a belt to strap your doniker down to the side of your leg!' George smiled, before glancing at his watch and saying "I promise I'll take it with me to my grave buddy."

Even though his smile was fueled as much as Georges' Dick quickly thanked his friend for understanding his present predicament, and then added, "Now what about you? What brings you here?"

"Well, " George grinned Devilishly, "as we used to say when we were kids, only in reverse. 'You showed me 'yours', now it's time to show you 'mine'. And 'mine' has to do with work."

Deliberately and visually panning the area briefly before continuing, George could almost feel his dicey words magnetically draw Dicks body in closure.

"I've got a sort of 'secret agent' working for me inside the plant, in the woman's camp. Someone who is going to let me know what the Barracudas might have in plan for later on at the stag."

Scanning the area around them again, George, while this time using a finger to indicate Sominex should lean in closer so that he might whisper 'his' secret for him alone to hear - he waited until his friend had done exactly that. Then in one swift motion, as Dicks vision briefly strayed to follow where his had gone, George dipped a still sugar flavored finger tip into his mouth just long enough to wet it, before then sticking it briefly into the unsuspecting orifice now only inches away from him. And as Sominex instantly pulled away in surprise, George was already on his way out of his seat and heading in the direction he had originally been moving in.

Even as startled as Dick was he instantly in more ways then one realized what his co worker had just done. And even before he had a chance to offer the obscenity that had also arrived with that information, 'Why you son of a bitch!' the sound of Georges own laughing voice was already starting to over shadow his thoughts.

Having stopped about ten feet away, George laughed, "I only gave my word not to tell anyone else buddy. I didn't promise I wouldn't take advantage of it myself!" And after watching Sominex quickly sit back down after starting to stand 'erect', apparently something else beating him to it, he quickly added, "Take it easy 'Dickie'. If I don't see you at work by Tuesday, at least I'll know where to 'come' and find you!"

Starting off again, another quick glance telling him he is within seconds of being late, George spotted Louie's familiar figure through one of the stores he was rushing past, and it is not their agreed meeting spot. Hurrying in to stop along side of her, his sudden presence seemingly undetected, Georges' voice was almost as soft and low as the stores background music, as he smiled, 'How's it going young lady?' And even before the young woman moves, as she starts to turn in his direction, he suddenly realizes that he has not only made a mistake, but an apparent real blunder. He was about to realize, as the woman indignantly blurted out, "Are you talking to me!" that not all things are as we perceive them to be. The woman, even though she was of the same stature, and familiar features, as she instantly followed his, 'I'm terribly sorry mam, I thought you were someone else.' with 'That's what they all say mister!' It is also instantly obvious that she totally lacks Louie's' demeanor. And yet, apparently also lacking personality as she continued to frown at him, she did resemble Louie's beautiful scented features enough to almost be a definite sister.

Starting to back paddle as fast as his tongue would let him, 'My apologies again miss. Please, please excuse me! It's just that I mistook your beauty for someone else I know.' He suddenly had a terrible feeling that he was only digging the hole he already seemed to be now standing in, deeper.

"Ya, I've heard that one before to." the total stranger continued to frown. And then as if to deliberately make him feel worse, she used words he honestly believed never would have come out of Louie's mouth, let alone temporarily leave him at a loss for words. "You wouldn't have been my first experience with a 'rubber'!"

"A what!" he stammered, his usually sharp wit tripping over itself.

"Oh don't play coy with me!" she quickly added, other customers closely stopping long enough to watch the little incident unfold in front of them. "You know perfectly well if I hadn't stopped you, you would have brushed your body into mine, pretending to have accidently bumped into me!"

Feeling a hot flush growing on his face, George offered one last quick, 'I'm afraid you've got me confused with someone else lady!' before excusing himself and heading back out of the store as fast as his feet could keep from looking as if they were running, her voice trailing him, "You better run! I'll remember your face and will be keeping an eye open for you from now on every time I'm in this mall!'

George didn't care if any of the other customers in the store were still paying him any attention, he just wanted to get away from there as fast as he could. And when his eyes next fell upon Louie in the distance sitting in the food court directly in front of him, the panic that he was normally a stranger to him started to subside. But it was to be a short departure when his vision briefly passed over another form he again instantly mistook for Louie's, when he had looked briefly into another store window he was passing. Stopping cold on his tracks, his mind already confessing that it must be playing tricks on him, he backed up just far enough to glance through the window once more. And just as he thought, it was, for the familiar form wasn't there or anyplace else to be seen.

Telling himself to 'Smarten up!', something he realized that he should have done wordlessly when a couple he was passing gave him a look that suggested that just maybe he shouldn't be allowed to be out unattended, he once more concentrated on Louie's form alone. And as the distance separating them disappeared he was just as glad to see the huge smile on her face once detecting his arrival as he was to see that she obviously recognized him.

Dropping his frame into the seat opposite hers, as she asked, 'Wouldn't you like a coffee or something before we start?' he answered 'No.' with just a shake of his head. And just when he thought his sanity had totally returned, while pointing in the direction he had just come from and saying, "You won't believe what just happened to me!" the potential nightmare returned.

Now stepping out of the store he had just hurried away from was the very woman that had in all probability had made his blood pressure temporarily shoot up a couple hundred points. But as bad as it looked, it got even worse when she started to head straight in their direction. If possible he was once more seemingly at a loss for words, not even aware that Louie was also staring at the approaching female figure. And if that wasn't bad enough, things got worse, when the second female form he had thought only existed inside of his imagination, also stepped out of the store he had just hurried past.

Time must have sudden started to stand still, especially since George was locked frozen, his eyes blinking jaw drooping and one hand pointing at the two females now close enough to seemingly be smiling at him. And if it hadn't been for the close sound of Louie's soft scented voice saying, 'Mister Stone, George.' he would have in all probability have stayed that way, looking ready to be carved in granite.

His composure slowly returning, while his eyes involuntarily blinked with each step the in almost perfect unison two jiggling beautiful forms took, it was as if his throat had just gone magically bone dry, before he could slowly force out the words to nobody in particular. 'H - How - how is this, possible?"

And not until Louie giggled out the words, 'They're my sisters, silly.' did any form of real reasoning start to reappear for George.

Of course. That had to be it, even though his mind had temporarily screamed to itself, 'Holy shit! I'm dreaming again!' But logic was now instead scolding him by accepting, the logic of 'You idiot! What else could it be? Moron!'

Manners had him out of his seat even before the two hypnotic creatures were at the table. And as his ears filled with the words being spoken to Louie upon their arrive, from the first one he had encountered, she then chuckled, 'You're right Honey, he's precious. But don't let him fool you Sis, he's just as gullible as the rest of the men are in this world.'

The warm blush that had started earlier was back again, but now for a totally different set of reasons. Inwardly, and he kept it to himself, he knew that any man in the plant would gladly give a months pay just to be in standing in the middle of his present predicament. And as the realization of how much beauty there presently really was around him grew, even as the sister he had not personally met yet had added to the end of her sisters statement, "Oh-h-h-h, I want one!" he just knew the 'blush' was going to hang around, quite possibly for awhile.

Fighting to hold ones own in a group of men was one thing. But being in the middle of three extraordinary beautiful looking women, was even for George, intimidating, especially after Louie told him that one of them was actually her twin.

With a smile that would undoubtedly win over any mans heart, Louie said, "I see you've already met my sister Eileen. I hope you don't mind - but I showed them a picture of you. It was one that one of the woman at work had snapped when they thought they had caught you doing something they might use against you at the right time. But when the gathering couldn't find anything to pin on you, they threw it away. Fortunately for me I just happened to be there when they did, and of course I also couldn't help but tell my family about the wonderful fatherly like man that was presently watching over me at work."

Accepting Georges big grin for what it was, even though the words 'fatherly like' had unknowingly 'wounded' his ego slightly, she didn't even pause before carrying on with, "And this is my twin sister 'Maureen'."

Even as his mind instantly started to play games with the name 'Maureen, more, moe.' he more than once rolled it over in his thoughts. And as soon as the last three letters had entered his brain 'Moe!', his eyebrows arched in automatic reflex as he instantly put it all together with, "Oh my God! We not only have 'Hewie' 'Dewie' and 'Louie', now we're going to end up with 'Curly' 'Larry' and 'Moe'!"

Depending on whatever is presently taking a short trip through ones thoughts sometimes thinking out loud isn't always considered as being a good thing. Just like now being a prime example, as Maureen asked, "What's he talking about?"

"You don't need to know. You'd love it. But believe me, you don't need to know." Louie smiled in Georges direction, before then adding, "And fortunately for us he's not into 'dumb blonde' jokes. So if you tried to tell him that you once read information stating that 'blondes' aren't really dumb, they're just full of 'us less' information, he'll laugh, but he won't try to add to it."

As the word 'Useless!' the words are not 'Us less!' it's 'Useless'! jumped into his thoughts, George had to almost bite his lip to keep from blurting it out. And it wasn't something that went unnoticed, by Louie, as she continued to grin after sneaking in an undetected mixed wink of appreciation and realization that he was indeed biting his tongue on a reply, before turning her full attention back onto him.

"I know we have come to trust each other in the last month Mister Stone, and there generally isn't much that goes on in the plant you don't know about. But -"

Instantly, just as soon as Louies voice faltered, George knew that something important was about to take control of whatever it was that he had been called there for. And even though her tone had dropped to match her line of vision, her voice was also even softer as she continued. "Cory asked me to marry him a week ago. And I wanted you to be the first to know before it gets out or around the plant"

Instantly, as he strangely felt that he should now be putting his arms around her as a sign of congratulations, his inner voice screamed 'Oh my God!' and then quickly followed up with 'Why that lucky dog!' 'Finally the little head making the right decision for the big head!' and then onto 'Have I got a spiel for you.' while genuinely smiling and kicking into overdrive. Want to or not he couldn't stop a lot of the old comical putdowns and remarks from starting to fill the vast void between his ears. Why should he - it had done whatever it wanted before. And even though, especially with his sense of humor wanting to ask 'Shotgun?' he threw it away, taking the advise that if given the choice 'a man should always marry an ugly woman, because if she ran away, who cares!' with it. And anyone with any kind of taste, and I don't mean the kind you find in your mouth, could see that in no way could Louie come any where within a million miles of that kind of reasoning. Even the brief image of Cory kneeling at the alter with the words 'Help Me! printed across the bottoms of his shoes wasn't given a seconds thought. He instead silently just hoped that the biggest obstacle in most marriages when first starting out, money, didn't come between their attachment with each other.

He also knew that just as soon as this juicy bit of information hit the plants gossip hotline, they were going to be in for some ribbing not for the faint at heart. He'd already heard from the men's side a few of the milder snide remarks that had been commented on separately about Louie, her getting more than her fair share of the available oxygen around us, and Cory, him being about as exciting as watching grass grow. As for the female side of the workforce, he knew he couldn't do justice to what they might have come up with. But as soon as either side of the gender tied them in together, well, Cory was rumored to be needing an extra size nine shoe when seen walking naked around the shower room. Whereas if Louie had any desire to gallivant around in her birthday suit, all that extra oxygen she had been suspected of stealing would be needed to revive half the men in the plant if they had caught even a glance of her bobbing around in that same manner. And he, as always, would do whatever he could to make sure neither of them was permanently scared by any of it.

His immediate genuine reaction to their sisters good news didn't go unnoticed, as the words 'You're right! I want one just like him too.' as well as 'Oh! He's such a dear!' brought forth two more attacks on his wandering male ego.

But it wasn't enough to not have him carry on with, "You know I'm all for it. And I'm sure most everyone else in the plant will also feel the same, when 'You or Cory' decide to tell them." he then added, his mind reminding him that without their secret help keeping him abreast of information from both battle fronts he would never have been privileged too.

"We knew you would be." Louie returned, one of her hands just short of touching the one George presently had resting on the table. "I phoned my sisters right away and they insisted on immediately coming here to meet him. But that's not why I asked you here. I wish it was, but it's not. There are those at work who still want to single you out tonight for what they think is wrong within the plant."

"Like I've said earlier" George grinned reassuringly, "when that time comes, I'm sure it's not something we won't be able to handle. Unfortunately, and I don't think I'll ever know why, but a few of them if you'll pardon the expression 'hard nosed ladies', have 'tunnel vision' whenever my name comes up. And if that's the way things have to be, then I'll just have to make sure I'm leading the rest of the convoy in an 'armored truck!"

"But I think this is something really serious. Something you should know about! She quickly added. "Something I felt I just had to tell you face to face!"

Ego or no ego, George had no intention of letting the happy mood acquired through or at the expense of his male ego deteriorate. Smiling even more, he offered, 'If you're going to make me feel older than I already do, then at least let my 'fatherly image' work its wisdom to whatever it is that is bothering you."

As Louie's twin smiled, 'You can be my 'Sugar Daddy' anytime.' Maureen fluttered her eyes to, "I'd never say 'No!', to any gentleman that asked if he could buy me a fur coat, and then ran his fingers over if for long hours at a time." Louie quickly grinned, 'Easy girls, easy. I can guarantee you that this tigers still got all of his teeth. And when he gets to know you better, he'll be more than glad to,' pausing long enough to wink undetected in Georges direction, she then finished with, 'bite either or both of you on the ass!'

It was, by Louie's standards, a crude suggestion that was instantly rewarded from an over emphasizing emotional Maureen with, "Oh, kinky sex, again! How exciting!"

"Me too, me too!" Eileen quickly squealed.

Feeling as if he was back in charge, after returning Louie's wink while her sisters were giggling into each others face, George continued with, "Now then. What's got you so upset that we needed to meet way out here in the boon docks, in secrecy?"

"Well," Louie started, after having taken in a deep breath, "I knew Carla and her inner-circle were up to something by the way they would stop talking or start to whisper whenever I showed up around them lately. But whatever it was at that time they wouldn't let me in on it, no doubt because they didn't trust me a hundred percent. But from what tid-bits I have managed to pickup on, I think she has hired a couple of, ah, 'ladies of the evening' to infiltrate the stag, no doubt to cause some serious trouble."

"Prostitutes?" George smiled, as if indicating that just maybe this wouldn't be an all bad thing. Right off the top of his head he could think of a few comical ways to turn their presence around to work in the men's favor, especially if the Dwarf was there at the stag.

"Yes. Hookers, Prostitutes, Ladies of the night, Home wreckers, whatever you men might call them." Louie blushed. "At quitting time I saw Carla, wearing one of her 'Don't piss me off!' faces, pass an envelope to two such ladies in a car in the parking lot."

"Did you happen to catch a name, or get enough of a good description to describe them?" George asked.

"Let's just say they definitely looked and dressed like they were not the type to be working in the plant. One I would guess as being midd thirtyish, tall, lean, and while wearing enough makeup to paint a small car, had the facial features to be a model. The other, was definitely about ten years younger, and dressed in the same manner. If I was to guess at their height, the older was I'd say five ten, with the other was about a half head shorter, broader at the shoulders, and well, you know."

As she had gotten to 'and well, you know.' Louie had brought both of her hands up and held them palm inward within inches of her own breasts, which not only made George grin, but also told him exactly what she was referring to. Watching a woman describe another of the same sex in such a manner was strange enough, but seeing Louie do it, was actually a surprise, considering how timid she normally seemed to be. But, no doubt her sisters presence had given her a little extra courage, it had also sounded slightly familiar, as he asked, "She didn't have long blonde wavy hair and a build that well over emphasized her own rather large pronounced lung capacity, or better yet, two rows of ivory like perfectly white teeth, did she?"

"Why, now that you mention it, I think she did." Louie answered puzzled, letting the remark relating to 'big boobs', 'hooters', 'mammary glands', 'knees caps pushed up through the top of your sweater' 'breeding stock' slide. She'd heard them and one Hell of a lot more while growing up. But because of her fondness for the true friend in front of her now, obviously enjoying the moment, she let it all slide. In fact she was even briefly astonished that he would have gotten past the woman's oversized chest and taken the time to notice the rest of her features. She had know lots of men who wouldn't, especially at work. "But, then again, how would you know that?" she then asked.

"Oh," he continued to smile, while thinking, if 'lady luck' was on the job, she was probably having a good laugh right about now. "Just a lucky guess. You might say it's a male thing. I guess at one time or another all boys as they are growing up fantasize about what certain women might look like when first hearing about their professions."

"But if they are, uh, professionals?" Louie started to ask.

"Oh don't worry about that." George with a big smile cut in, also already telling himself that if indeed his suspicions were right, then he definitely had the upper 'gland' you might say. "I'm still sure we can get through whatever the ladies might have planned."

"Well, if it'll help any," Louie quickly offered, the sudden slight blush in her voice matching her actions, "I'm sure you can talk both of my sisters and myself into crashing your stag while wearing white dresses, white wigs and pushup bras'. And if we did it, we could call it our tribute to Marilyn Monroe! And if we did that, maybe it would distract everyone from anything else that might happen."

'Pushup bras'! he thought. 'W-o-o-w!' He had to admit that this was not only an unexpected or unprepared for side of Louie, but also a positively pleasant unanticipated side of a woman he had never even suspected as having existed inside of her. And as his overactive debatably mature imagination instantly ran blindly into images of the three of them looking like what had just been offered, the fact that he was still a healthy male also causing a slight stir deep in his loins, he blushed once more while answering, "Please ladies ,please! Remember, I love my wife! Besides, a few of the men still have 'Norma Jeanne' ah 'Marilyn's' Playboy pinup in their locker. You ladies dress up like her, and they'll think they've died and gone to "Playboy' heaven. And as far as the heaven part is concerned I can't be sure if any of them will make it that far. But if their wives catch them drooling over any of you in those scanty outfits, not that I would blame them, you can bet they'll soon qualify for the 'dead' part of the statement!"

'Hell', he thought to himself, if you ladies dressed up like 'Charlie Chaplin' the men would at least have a good excuse for walking with the toes of their shoes pointing almost sideways. Ya know what I mean, jellybean?

Maureen, one of her hands scratching at the top of her head, apparently giving adage to the saying 'picking ones brain', and definitely about to prove that she had a mind just as twisted and warped as some of the men in the plant, smiled as she offered, 'Well, what about entertainment? You must have speeches or presentations of some sort. And I'm sure the men would be okay with the three of us jumping up and down on 'pogo sticks' in rhythm with some kind of music in the background.'

As the new images of the three of them in unison bobbing up and down on pogo sticks jumped into his head, his face wearing a big smile betrayed the wonderfully evil thoughts jiggling there with them. And as he started to say, 'As much as I like the suggestions, personally', Eileen quickly cut in with, 'While wearing matching polka dot bikinis' of course. The images 'pogo sticks' had invoked were bad enough in themselves, but when you add 'wearing matching polka dot bikinis' the new scantily clad gyrations that they brought when put together were instantly too much for even someone as devoted to a happy home as George was. And as he sputtered, "Whoa! Ladies! Please! Please not that! You're giving me one 'Devil' of a headache!" He also had to fight off the words of, 'Kind of gives a warm pleasant purpose to the old phrase 'Keep your eyes on the bouncing ball!'

As if almost being able to guess as to which 'head' George was actually talking about, the three women each giggled, especially while watching him twisting his head from side to side, apparently trying to shake those very wicked images out through his ears. It was a comical reaction that only encouraged them to lean their scented for trapping bodies in even closer, as Maureen, as you might say, 'kept the balls in play'.

"Well, what if we just coached our sister on how to tell the joke about the 'milkman and the blonde', at the stag. She told us that you had mentioned that if she could only loosen up a bit and find a joke that would endear her to the men, then everyone in your plant just might get along a lot better."

'I know I shouldn't be asking this, especially from a lady," George smiled, hoping a new train of thought might help him regain most of his composure, especially after the way they had been toying with him, at least he sure as hell hoped they were only playing with his since of humor, "but what milkman and what blonde joke would that be?"

"Well -" Maureen started. But then smiled first at George and then onto Louie, while adding, "Why don't you give it a go Sis. You know, a sort of test run."

Already guessing what her sister might be up to, Louie had a noticeable blush to her face as she first tried you might say 'dodge the bullet' but finally gave in when realizing her audience now would be a lot easier than the one she might be facing later, especially after George smiled, 'Go ahead. Believe me - there's no way any of the men are going to give you a rough time about anything you say or do. They'll be to hypnotized just looking at 'you'!'

Encouragement or not, especially after the slight blush had temporality grown to a full bloom once realizing the meaning behind her smiling friends words, Louie took a deep breath before saying, "Well, I hope the men will realize that this must be a very old joke, considering that there was a time when people used to get certain items delivered straight to their homes' door. – But, well, here goes!"

As far as George was concerned, if she did the same thing before starting the joke in front of the men, taking in a deep breath that is, she would have brought them all more instant pleasure than the joke ever could.

As if being able to read Georges present thoughts, when in fact they just realized that he was in all probability just like any other hot blooded male, Maureen quickly puffed up her own chest, an obviously contagious act as Eileen instantly imitated her, she smiled at Louie, "He's right! I know for a fact most horny men can only concentrate one, ah, two, things at a time. Louie, only a fraction of a second behind realizing what her sisters were up to, lost no time in copying their present gesture, before starting.

"One day this blonde lady meets her Milkman at the door and says, 'I've heard that bathing in milk is great for your whole body and complexion. If it's even remotely true, I'm willing to give it a try. How much do you think I'll need?' And when the grinning milkman asks her 'Pasteurized?', she replies, 'No silly. Just up to my 'tits'! From there I can splash it up onto my face.'

Biting his lip, physically as well as literally, George tried to keep as straight a face as possible as Louie asked, "Well? What do ya think? I know I'm not going to get a standing ovation, but do ya think with a bit more practice I'll have a chance at making a standup comic?"

Not until he had glanced at her sisters, more or less seeking permission if it was okay to tell the truth, he took their heads nodding to the unasked question as a yes. Swallowing hard, a big smile leading the way , he finally answered, "Uh, she tells that one, and I can guarantee you she'll get a 'standing ovation'!"

George, always the 'In for a penny in for a pound' type, as all three devishly grinning so called ladies in almost perfect unison slowly let out the deep breath they had been holding onto, Louie then blushed while her sisters laughed out loud, then added, "And after that, if Cory or the wives don't step in, she'll be in a position to make every available man at the stags life a finally realized fantasy ."

Louie, quickly realizing that this was one of those times when you let the innuendo's' slide, giggled herself, as George added, But more importantly, she'll instantly own within hearing distance every true red blooded man's heart, forever and a day!"

If beauty was indeed in the eye of the beholder then George obviously needed sunglasses, as he happily basked in the sweet smelling beauty now surrounding him. And as they continued to giggle among themselves, mostly over him, he wisely kept most of whatever jumped into his thoughts to just himself each time they sexually spared with him again and again, and again. It wasn't hard to do, especially when Eileen and Maureen had placed themselves along side, with each holding and hugging one of his arms. But wisely one of the lewd remarks he thought, while risking a quick peek, 'And all this time I thought those things were 'mammary' not 'memory' glands!' he kept just to himself.

But like the old saying that goes, 'Just when you think things can't get any worse in ones world, although he honestly believed his were getting better, fate proved the second half of the proverb true, and stuck a big sharp pin into his presently inflated 'egos' bubble, just to prove that it could 'indeed' get much worse.

Far off, and once more in his present line of vision, the distant images of Fred and Judy could be seen hurrying through the spinning doorway leading into the mall. It was an unexpected sight that instantly activated his subdued emotions back into hyper drive. And just as sure as he could easily see them, especially after they had paused long enough to read the schematic view explaining the malls layout, he was just as positive they could see him, as they once more hurriedly headed straight in his direction.

Mans hereditary instinct for survival instantly kicked into full force, pushing his body straight up out of the chair - the ladies there protesting immediately at his sudden and just as strange behavior. And just like the deer trapped in a cars approaching deadly headlights, especially since he had been already caught in a very compromising situation, he quickly jerked his hands free of those still holding onto his. Forcing the smile that should have come naturally to his face when seeing his wife, his present emotions also betrayed him with an over pronounced smile that anyone could see just didn't look right there. And the look of surprise on both Judy's' and Fred's faces, their arms also waving just enough to confuse him about the words now shouted in his direction, 'Look out! It's a trap!' only drew his attention away to allow what they were trying to warn him about, to happen undetected.

But the attack they were there to originally warn him about, had nothing to do with the one now rushing up from behind in his direction. And as the extended wet finger of the attacker easily completed its deliberate mission into Georges unsuspecting right ear, reactions that were born into each of us instantly had him jumping sideways, away from the crude damp sensation that had also come with it.

The instant reflexes of youth are without a doubt, a wonderful thing. But as we get older they sometimes will help some out of one predicament, only to throw us right into the path of another, especially if not working together. Where his reflex's had easily taken him away from the surprised attack from behind, they also threw him right into an area already occupied with a group of vacant plastic chairs belonging to another table closely. Once again called upon to help him keep from loosing his balance, they failed as they tripped first over the seating arrangement, and then over his own already confused feet. And as his ears filled with the close sounds of woman's almost hysterical voices shouting over concern for his safety, another rose above them shouting out the singular word of 'Go-o-otcha!'

As the floor rushed up, his automatically extended arms grasping at mostly air as he went down, it was only a leg of one of the plastic chairs that stopped his head from coming into contact with the tiles now beneath everyone else's feet. It was to be one of those instant strange unplanned for accidents you got to share with someone, instead of just suffering alone. But with the surprised 'thump' had also come a temporary dizziness that left him looking up at a circle of fluctuating faces now looking downward in his direction. The view, far from unpleasant as most of the area within his range filled with almost perfect matching paired mounds of supported hanging flesh, was also yet strangely intimidating.

Normally it would have been just another of most men's fantasies fulfilled. And even though there was a barrage of pulsating mixed emotions also peering down on him, it was the sound of the harsh sounding words, 'George Stone!' that shocked him the most, as his brain fought feverishly to put everything into it's proper perspective. But it wasn't the way he was being harshly paged that added to his confusion, it was the way that the words now coming out of Louie's mouth sounded syllable for syllable exactly like his Judy's'. And it was as also confusing that the way she was repeatedly shouting them, didn't quiet feel like they belonged there, let alone to just him. In fact, as well as his middle name not being 'Andrew', something she might or might not have known, why did her voice have such a noticeable feeling of intimidation and anger to it?

Chapter 15

'That was then. - This is now.'
Or
'Vengeance is mind.'
Or
'Home Again.'
Or
'The round up.'
Or
'Rules of engagement!'
Or
Oh - what the 'Hell' - you pick one!

Each of the above potential titles 'all' fit within the chapter below leading us out and back unfortunately into the real world. So enjoy yourself. It might be awhile before we get the chance to meet again, and believe me there are still volumes to talk about!

"George! George Andrew Stone Junior! I am not going to call you again! You and your brothers get up here now! Some of our guests are going to start hinting that they have to get home soon, and you three have been hiding down there for over an hour. So all of you get your buns up here and show some respect! , I said now!"

Picking up the page marker from beside where he was sitting, while yelling in response, 'Okay Mom! Sorry! We'll be right up!' he then tucked it into the fold between the open pages of the book now resting in his lap. Looking back down at the diary he was still holding, a soft smile still on his once youthful face, he 'flopped' it closed, while adding, 'Sorry Pop! Mom says we have to go. But don't go away! We'll be back as soon as we can.'

With a grin on his face he turned Darryll's direction, Ian once again doing one of his best 'imitating the dead' impersonations on the rec rooms' Davenport, George Junior broadened his smile even more, before saying, "Just remember it's your turn to read out loud next time. We can't let 'Mister sleeping sickness' over there do it, or he'll have all of us snoring inside of the first two pages, or should I have said he'll have us all comatose within minutes?"

Placing the diary back inside the padded box he had watched his father build long ago, Junior tucked it back along side of the other two he had also been reading from that day, while commenting "Did you know there are still another six more diaries and about three films in here? Who knows how up to date they are. If we'd known about these things when we were kids we probably could have used some of the information we've come across just today alone, like, like say a, 'Get out of jail free.' Card'!"

"You must be talking about when we were in our teens." Darryll continued to grin. "Any earlier than that and we would have been to busy standing with our pants down around our ankles, waiting for him to realize that he had sent us up stairs for a spanking, never mind remembering what the ass tanning session was for!"

"Ya." Ian butted in. "And by the time I was in my teens, for years I was way to scared to touch anything that belonged to Dad, especially after that 'fart jar' fiscal we had."

"Don't be such a 'wussap'." Darryll laughed, in Ian's direction. "After spanking us till his hand hurt, Dad was so tired he generally just forgot all about you!"

"Tell im bro." Junior laughed, his eyes also on his little brothers still horizontal form. "I'll bet we could count on one hand, the number of times you got spanked, and we'd still have enough fingers left over to count up to three. And if he ever found out it was you who was responsible for the sudden presence of a foul odor in his favorite chair every time he sat down - he'd probably give you a good spanking right now!"

"Ya!" Darryll laughed, instantly relating to the incident just mentioned. "I still can't believe he never figured out it was just you passing wind in it every chance you got when he was at work."

Picking up a film labeled 'Company Stag - 1977' George then commented to no one in particular, 'Shit! Since we found out during our last visit Dad hid these things, I've been looking foreword to viewing this baby all week. On second thought, I hope the old spool to spool projector is still working. Otherwise it's going to be tricky sneaking these things out of here and then brought up to date on discs without anyone else finding out about it.'

Lifting up the similarly dated photo album that had been resting in his lap, Darryll had been scanning through its pictures to use as a visual aid when imagining the comical situations they had just been reading about, he held it open and pictures facing outward while saying, "Get a load of this snapshot showing Louie and her sisters when they showed up for the company stag that year! Dad always said you could never see enough of a pretty woman, 'see' obviously being the key word in this case!"

As a soft 'wolf whistle' first escaped from Juniors lips, Ian lifting just his head to get a full view of the photo, he then added his interpretation of the three scantily clad figures in the center of the photo, with just a small animalistic like growl. Darryll, after first offering, I'll second that, which he did with an 'E-r-r-r-r!', then moved on to add, 'Any or all of these ladies could have easily been Playboy 'Bunny girls'."

"I'm sure if Dad was here he would have added his two cents worth, and changed 'Bunny girls.' to 'Money girls!'. Ian laughed, while allowing his head to fall back onto the cushion it had originally been resting on.

"Which he probably already did at the time the photo was taken." Junior quickly added. "Especially if Mom wasn't within hearing distance."

Darryll turning the photo to face himself, took another long look at the picture before adding, "Mother of two teenage girls or not, Missus Allen still has all of her looks, as far as I'm concerned. And if I was more her age and had to quote one of dads more cruder and appropriate comments here, I'd have to say, 'I sure wouldn't kick her out of bed for just eating crackers!"

"I don't think she's looking for a 'boy toy'!" George chuckled. "But if she was, I'm pretty sure Louie would chew you up and spit you out on your first outing."

"Who cares." Darryll quickly laughed. "As long as I get a first 'inning'!"

Ian's 'E-e-e-w' was only a fraction of second behind his oldest brothers. And it also prompted an additional response of, "Pat hears you talking like that, and I don't think they'll ever find your body!"

"We keep this up and the wives find out, I don't think they'll find any of our bodies!" Ian smiled.

Turning the photo album back in his brothers direction, Darryll continued to smile, while saying, "Well if we can't talk about beauty, let's pick on a couple of beasts. Take a gander at the group shot of these so called ladies. Each one looks like she could take any of us nine out of ten times in an arm wrestling contest."

"Oh, you mean Carla and her 'mean machine'. Junior grimaced, his upper body shivering as if someone had just poured a glass of ice cold water down between his shoulder blades. "I remember Dad telling me that if I ever encountered anyone like them once I'm old enough to join the workforce, I believe his words of wisdom at that time were 'don't stroke or poke the kitty cats'! They have nine live each, whereas I only have one. And if I happen to be married by that time, even that 'one' life is no longer mine to throw away."

"If you think that group shot was hard to look at," Darryll cut in, while flipping to almost the last page in the still out held album, 'take a gander at the size of this gathering."

Fortunately someone on the yearly stags committee had enough foresight to suggest that as well as the regular photos taken through out the nights festivities a collage of those willing to be involved that one large photo taken midway through the night would be a good idea. Unfortunately they had failed to take into consideration that not only would some of its participants be unwilling to be seen within arms length of each other, but also pockets of the rest being a combination of leftover class clowns onto a those wanting to stand out in every crowd they would be a part of. And within the first second of glancing into the photo any sane person would realize that there were very few people with their amount of rationality staring back at them. For every couple or individual standing prim and proper for the picture there were just as many doing everything from posing rubber faced to holding up two fingers directly behind the heads of the unsuspecting persons posing in front of them. But the most noticeable couple, especially for the boys, was Mom and Dad in the back row, embraced and kissing."

Once more turning the album in just his direction, Darryll said, more to himself than his brothers. "Even after the three of us, they still had the hot's for each other. Kind uv makes you wonder why they never had any more kids after us."

But George, like his namesake, couldn't resist adding, "Either of you bother to take a good look at yourselves in the mirror when your shaving in the morning. I have. And I think it's safe to say there's no fear of any of us being scooped up by a talent scout looking for the likes of Paul Newman or Robert Redford stand ins on a movie set."

"Or the wives filling in for 'hot!' Elizabeth Taylor." Ian quickly added.

Closing the album with a loud 'plop', a sour look on his face, Darryll grumbled, "I guess it's lucky for us it's not like one of Dad's other favorite old sayings. 'It's the magician that does the trick, not the wand.'"

Ian, still apparently pleased with himself for his last comment, added his favorite. "Don't forget - 'It's the motion of the ocean.' he also used to say."

"Well, my favorite still is, 'If it wasn't for the dark, a lot of ugly kids wouldn't get born'." Junior smiled.

As something new, for who knew what reason, popped into his thought, Darryll continued to keep the sour look on his face when adding, "Can you imagine what it would have been like if they would have had any more kids, and one of them was a girl that resembled any of us?"

Shifts

"Ya!" George laughed. "And I'm willing to bet that she'd probably still be single! But if you think about it, they were still willing to have you after me. "

"Well I guess that would explain why there were no more kids after Ian." Darryll chuckled, in George's direction.

Ian, unable to control his own since of humor, simply smiled while adding, "Sticks and stones, boys. And I'm not the only 'Stone'! So I'm not the only reason there are no girls in the family."

Once more picking up the album that had made its way back to his lap as they had been talking, each of them letting out their own versions of 'E-e-e-w!' in response to whatever image their imagination had come up with for a sister, Darryll got up and placed it back onto the bookshelf along with others of its kind. It had not only helped give truer youthful faces to most of what they had just been listening to, but passing of time had actually been kind. It had also in a sense, helped them understand better what direction they should expect their futures could be headed in.

Then, his still over active mind no doubt still enjoying the time period of his Dads' life just read about, a sudden realization that came with it made him respond, "Hey! I just realized that all those boxes of old joke books Dad sold at a garage sale about five years ago must have been tied in with the segment at work where the men often tried to stump someone referred to as 'DidYa'. It would seem that he and Pop were working in cahoots to take advantage of their fellow man, or should I say 'fleece' the other sheep!"

'Kind of makes ya proud, doesn't it." Ian chuckled. "Our Dad. He wasn't only King of the wisecracks, but also had a little bit of larceny in him also. I think it safe to say our old man, at one time or another, had his 'mind' in every conceivable kind of 'pie' out there at the time."

George, meanwhile making a mental note to himself along the lines of, 'Maybe I can come up with some excuse to encourage Mom to have one of her Sunday suppers again real soon.' was to occupied at first to hear Darryll comment about the other photo albums on the shelf.

"Ya know, with any luck we'll find some information to go along with all those weird party pictures Dad had taken over the years."

"That would be neat!" Ian piped in. "I liked the ones taken from the album marked "Come as you were in '1957'. Boy, seeing Mom wearing snow white socks and a green polka dot dress with a big bowed ribbon to match in her hair was bad enough. But getting a gander at Dad in a pair of big cuffed jeans, penny loafers, a jet black tee shirt with the sleeves rolled up and a cigarette package tucked in on one side, and hair swept up from both sides of his head and rolled into a large pointed wave on top, all topped off with a pair of dark sunglasses, 'boy', that did take nerve!"

"And the music at that time!" Junior smiled. "I can still remember Pop mentioning titles like 'Jailhouse Rock!' 'Wake up Little Susie' 'Whole lot of shakin' going on' and 'Long Tall Sally'. But one of his favorites to jump all over the dance floor was, 'Great Balls of Fire'!"

"Makes sense to me!" Ian laughed, while shaking his arms and legs in wild gyrations. "I know that if 'my balls' were on fire, I'd be doing a lot more then just a 'little dance' all over the place! In fact if there was even a little bit of Indian heritage in our bloodline, by the time I was finished flailing my arms and bouncing all over the place, you'd probably have the biggest cloudburst in recorded history!"

"Speaking of crazy music." Darryll laughed, in first Ian's' and then Georges direction. "My favorite party was one of the ones where everyone was allowed to come dressed as a record title, and then the other guests had to guess what the name of the record was. I remember the one where Mom was dressed in Dads old work cloths. She was also wearing a tool pouch filled with tools, and carrying his Craftsman's' toolbox. It hear it took a few guesses, but almost everyone finally came up with 'Handy Man', which I personally think was just her way of getting in a little 'zinger' at Dads 'all thumbs and no fingers' fixer upper abilities."

"But Pop's costume, as expected, got the most laughs. He wore a pair of held up by suspenders, cut off at the knees shorts. Knee high socks and running shoes. A mosquito netted cap with a peek that stood out about twelve inches, sneakers, four cameras in cases and about three pairs of binoculars. He had everyone stumped until Mom had quipped, 'What's 'his' and half the other bums he works with favorite pastime?' In less then ten seconds most of the women there had blurted out 'I'm a girl watcher'!

"Can you imagine what it would have been like if they had some of the expressions of freedom back then like they have now-a-days.

Braziers, or 'over the shoulder boulder holders' as we liked to call them, are to be referred to simply as 'bras', something to be conveniently dropped down in public by some whenever it's feeding time."

"Not to mention what they're expected to carry after Silicon enhancement. It's not like it was when Mrs. Allen was naturally born well endowed. Today it seems to be whatever the backbone or budget can carry, as well as any other part of the body that can be 'nipped' tucked' sliced' or 'injected'. Darryll frowned. "If there's one thing I don't think any of needs at this stage of our lives, is a reason for a third pant leg."

'You wouldn't have thought like that if you were still single" Ian laughed. "Hell, I know I would have been willing to risk it, or at least just enough to need an extra pocket to put it in."

"You're a 'Stone'!" Darryll, while puffing up his chest, said forcefully. "We already got more than our share. And I've got the 'zipper mark scars' to prove it."

"Dream on." Junior chuckled. "But can you imagine what it's going to be like once the new millennium gets her in almost ten years. I don't know about you guys but I'm already having trouble adapting to the new technological toys on the market. Right now my own kids are so far advanced with the changes going on, I have to ask them for their help if I want to assemble or install anything new to the stereo and television set."

"What about 'thongs'? Junior cringed. "Once they were just shoes. Now it's barely an eye patch riding up the crack of your ass! That reminds me," he continued to frown, "does anybody here know if they wash and re use them, or just throw them away after one use?"

"Lets change the subject." Ian cut in. "I'm all for anything that will enhance the males sexual arousement, especially it it'll keep the old dreaded 'I've got a headache. ' at bay. But now, first you talk about something to get the ol juices up and flowing, and then you go into the kind of images I don't need. Especially, I might add, after seeing some of the older women at the beach wearing thongs buried so deep I actually felt sorry for someone I'd never met yet, their husbands!"

"Well at least you didn't say that it was the men wearing the same type of thong that threw you off your lunch." Darryll chuckled. "Besides, if memory serves me correctly, I can remember your boss telling mine how you used to get the 'dry heaves' just watching the babies green diapers being changed."

"Let's not go there either." Ian frowned with a wrinkled up nose, with one hand caressing his tummy. And as both brothers chuckled at his reactions, there was no doubt in their minds that little brothers memory was apparently presently bringing back both the image as well as the smell that had come with that fond period in his life.

Things get any worse," Junior then continued to smile, wishing no doubt to get in his evaluation as to what was wrong with the world today. "and the way technology is advancing they'll be expecting us to being able to breast feed! Besides, we haven't got time to due justice to everything that's changed since Mom and Dads quieter era. According to the pictures showing the variety of parties and shenanigans going on, they were always nice, especially since we're in the 'middle' of one right now."

"Those photos," Ian, while chuckling no doubt to his own set of memories from those times, cut in, "also helped explain not only why we had to go to bed so early on those weekends, but also why there was always so much noise coming out of the basement or backyard."

Darryll, first kicking at his younger brothers protruding feet, then snickered at him. "Ya, well that was then and this is now. If you don't stop working all the bloody overtime you can 'suck up' to, your kid's are going to start calling you 'Uncle Ian'!"

Replying, 'If you worried about your kids as much as you do about mine,' while trying to rub some of the tiredness from his eyes, Ian shot back, "then our wives wouldn't be all hush hush while whispering about a potential wedding in the near future." He then quickly, before Darryll had a chance to retaliate, turned to give his attention in his oldest brothers direction. "Did I miss much when I dozed off?"

"No more than usual." George smiled, while bending down just enough to slide the box past the curtain Darryll was holding aside. And as soon as it was back into its former resting place, behind a small piece of loose wall paneling, he stood up beside his closest brother and took a second to also enjoy what he was now looking at. Etched into the door frame was a series of pen pencil and even crayon lines, dates with names beside each one, to signify that it was the height of each brother on the dates listed beside them.

"It's hard to believe we've now got kids taller then most of those markings." Darryll sighed.

"Maybe a couple of 'old timers' like you two have," Ian laughed "but my boy's still two inches short of where I was at his age. I sure hope the next one takes after 'our' side of the family."

"Well since we already know you can't be talking about his sexual attributes, especially since being any shorter and he would have been a girl, I guess we'll never know about the next one just as long as the 'bun is still in the oven' Darryll chuckled

"Don't you mean 'rice cake'? 'Rice cake' is still in the oven'!" George laughed.

"Hey, hey! No 'ethnic' put downs, remember? If Dad had been here and heard you say that, he'd remind you that you're still not so big you can't have your ass kicked around the block a few times" Ian retaliated.

"And if he couldn't do it," Darryll, with a snicker, came to his younger brothers defense, "then your wife's father sure could, especially after he saved Dad and a bunch of their inebriated co workers once from getting their faces re arranged outside of a bar one night. And besides, it's not our fault you were a late bloomer. I can still remember the big silly smile on Dads face when you brought home your very first real girlfriend."

"That wasn't a smile of happiness." Junior chuckled. "That was a bloody sigh of relief."

Coming to the defense again of what was and always would be their 'little brother' Darryle grinned, "Hey. Not all of us got to go to college and meet our future wife."

"Just because Carol and I were fortunate enough to end up with a few extra letters behind our names has never made us flaunt it, let alone ever talk down to anyone."

"Relax brother." Ian started to chuckle. "You know as well as we all do that the only way you or your wife would ever talk down to any of us is if you two were standing on the roof and we were all down below looking up shouting 'Jump!'. Besides, he's just trying to get under your skin."

"Under my skin! Boy, does that comment take me back. Talk about quoting Dad."

"Well at least Pop had a chance to fix things up between himself and your father in law, before he passed." Ian offered sadly, in Darrylls' direction.

As their mothers words, "Are you boys coming, or do I have send your bosses down there to chase you up!" broke the deteriorating atmosphere, each of them chuckling back in her direction. "We heard you the first time Mom!"

"We better get moving before she carries out her threat." Junior chuckled. "If you remember, Dad may have worn the pants in the family when we were kids, but when it came down to the real 'nitty gritty' it was Mom who wielded the belt the hardest!"

"Kind'uv makes that promise we all made to Dad that when he ends up in that big party in the sky we are to take the next man Mom decides to spend the rest of her life with off to the side and give him a good whipping. Then we're to tell him it was from the last guy who lived here. And if he doesn't treat Mom right, there'll be one Hell of a lot more where that came from."

"Ya right." Darryll chuckled. "There was a time when we may have had to honor Dads' last wish - but not now. When we were kids it may have seemed that Mom was just a pussycat most of the time, but now that we know she's just a tiger with a wicked left hook laying in wait to pounce on anything or one who stirs her up, she can more than take care of herself."

The memory, true or not, actually did get them out of the rec room. Laughing among themselves as they jokingly took turns pushing each other up the stairwell and towards the backyard, each added their own comment about what might lay in wait for them.

"You go first, I'm to young to die."

"No, you go first. Being firstborn you always were her favorite."

"Na, na, na. Let him go first! She would never hit her baby!"

Little did they suspect that the afore mentioned ladies were waiting in the kitchen for them, their ears apparently already having told them of their impending eventual arrival.

Age having its privileges, as well as wisdom, Ian was the first one through the cellar door and instantly found himself being burdened down with, 'Take the buns and spread them around the tables we've set up Hon." And as soon as he instantly started to roll his eyes for not

Shifts

only in response, but also as a sign that he wasn't exactly happy about what he had been told to do, something he had come to expect between him and his wife over the years, flowed right in behind his noticed by all antics. "And remember, 'Chose your words wisely if wishing to pick on someone. Many a man has been hung by his own tongue - usually after it has first been used to dig his grave'."

Quickly shooting back, 'As you can all hear, my wife more than just looks like her father, Ian was quickly reminded that he was only a Stone in name, with the words, 'Oh, and don't be afraid to spend some time with our son. That family photo on the mantle is almost over five years old, and I don't want him to forget what his father looks like now.'

Blowing his wife a kiss before once more retaliating with, 'I see you've still got most of your father's wit. But just remember what happened last time you thought you had the final word. I told Bobby you wanted a nice little baby sister for him, and he wouldn't talk to you for almost a week."

Family photos apparently being the present method for attack, with the college over the fireplace also now in clear view through the living room door, Darryll couldn't help but do a mental count of the family members almost filling the pictures frame. And it wasn't so much the norm for the day number of five grownups and six children that suddenly seemed so important - but rather the years that had passed to make them all possible. But the photo for some strange reason, probably because subconsciously it and the father-in-law were each so close together in his thoughts, made him silently wish he could come up with one to cover the comical incident he and everyone else in the family had been repeatedly subjected to, which in this case involved Dad and Ian's father-in-law within their first years together.

The way he had heard it happened was that on one more than normally hot summer day, no doubt a lot like todays, when the temperature had everyone working in the plant dropping a few sweaty pounds. Uncle Fred Dad and Ian's father-in-law were all working on the same repair job. Big floor fans had been brought in order to help displace some of the hanging warm air away from the job-site, hopefully to give relief to those working there. While helping clean up the area Dad had accidently knocked a welders firebox containing white baking soda, used to smother out any possible fires, off the top of the repair mans welding machine. And not only had the box spilled its entire contents right out in front of one of the large fans, the one as luck would have it directly in front of Uncle Bob, its vacuum like drawing power instantly sucked in the big white cloud that had resulted from the spill, totally and temporarily obliterating Ian's father-in-laws unsuspecting form from view.

It was reportedly to be one of those 'not needed to be reported accidents' that had left the men far to stressed out and over tired to work after having laughed themselves silly. Especially once seeing the father-in-laws totally white, all except for his blinking eyes, kneeling form with hands clasped in prayer in front of him, singing 'Suwanee, how I love y, how I love ya, my dear ol Suwanee!' And forever from then on, there was never any doubt that he had fit right in with Fred and Georges' strange sense of humor.

It would have been one of those legendary conversation piece Kodak photos worth a lot more than its weight in gold, especially when needing to get the occasionally knit picking old fart off his younger brothers back.

Patty, loading Darrylls arms up in the same manner, only with three stacked platters of cut vegetables and mixed meats, smiled, "Try not to drop them this time. Mom says the poor dog had the shits for a week and almost scrapped all the skin off his bum dragging it across the grass after helping us clean up the hot chilly peppers. And then you can call the kids out of the pool and tell them to get dried off, quick."

Junior, his arms and hands still his to use as he pleased, used one to point at his brothers, the other cupped his groin area, while silently mouthing the words, "Boys, boys, boys. Where's your Gahanna's?" It was a gesture that although meant for just brothers didn't go totally unnoticed by all of the women in the kitchen, as his wife mouthed in his direction, 'Same place as yours smartass.' And it was more than enough recognition to magically have his arms rise outstretched ready for his part of the chores. But it wasn't enough to keep him from smiling while laughing, "And you both can paint the house if you have a little time left over."

But this, possibly because it had been spoken out loud, was a wisecrack that was instantly rewarded with a small quick smack across the back of his head, as Carol showed the rest of the woman who was boss in their house also. 'You can put these trays of treats, one at each end of the tables, and then keep out of them until after everyone else has had a chance to eat. And make sure Jr. Jr. doesn't get into them either. He keeps going the way he is and next time he tries out for the football team, he'll 'be' the team!" Turning her head in the other woman close by enough to add, "And I know what you two are thinking - but don't say it. It's okay if I comment that he's more like a 'chunk' then a 'chip' off the old block!"

"Oh, he's still hasn't gotten rid of all of his baby fat." Junior joked. "Just give him some time."

"Oh, he'll get plenty of time!" Carol shot back. "Especially if he tries to burn the fat off trying to make a 'baby' before he's married!

"Is it just me, or does all this sound a lot familiar?", Darryll said, no doubt trying to regain a little bit of dignity. "Aren't all you ladies stealing Pops' putdowns?"

"Well he always did say the good ones were worth repeating." Carol chuckled, while placing both of her hands onto her hubby's back and steering him in along behind with his brothers out through the back door.

Walking into a barrage of clapping hands, amidst mixed shouts of, 'We were beginning to think you'd gone home!' 'It's about frickin fracken fruzzle time!' 'Never mind them, drop the goodies off over he-e-e-re!' 'I don't see the ketchup!' a few of the younger kids started running for seats at the lined up lawn furniture. And as the grown ups, drinks in hand, started dragging their chairs towards the spaces allotted for their eventual arrival, the food was starting to be deposited exactly where suggested earlier. But it wasn't the only activity going on. Down at the mouth of the driveway Judy was just walking back around the edge of the fence that separated their yard form the Faylens, Betty in tow. Each had their arms full carrying mixed bags of picnic necessities and junk food.

Yelling, "Give your Grandmother a hand." his own still occupied, Darryll smiled at Pat, "You know it's your fault I have to remind the kids to help without being asked. You should have let me beat them more when they were growing up." he then smiled.

"Ya. Just like your Dad beat you and your brothers." Pat smiled, while spreading the food he was holding out onto the table.

"Well, like Dad used to brag, I wouldn't be beating them for their benefit - I'd be beating them for mine! But then he had three of us to spread his frustrations out on. I've only got two."

Frowning in her hubby's direction, even though he hadn't started to smile and grin yet, she didn't really believe him, "I don't ever remember your Dad being anywhere near that mean. If he had a real temper - he's sure kept it well under wraps, and nobody's that good with a secret. So admit it."

"He wasn't, ever." Darryll finally chuckled. "Every man likes to think he has control over his children. And if he didn't he sure as hell never let any of his friends know it, let alone the kids"

"Well it hasn't slowed him down any over the years." Pat smiled. "During almost every special occasion he's been feeding his grandchildren tales involving either all those practical pranks he was involved in at work or you shady characters!"

Coming to his fathers defense, Darryll smiled, "Ya - but he generally cleans them up first." And he then wordlessly thanked the Almighty that Dad had never brought up another of his favorite topics, about being so poor when he was a boy that they used to have the bottoms of their pant pockets cut out - just so they would have something to play with."

With a look of skepticism in her eye, Pat gave a short 'Humph' before continuing with, "What with the present collection of pirate movies flooding the screens during the last few years I can't wait to hear how he's going to clean up one of his old favorite Halloween comments whenever a kid dressed as a pirate come to the door yelling 'Trick or treat!' Not everyone, regardless of their age, gets your fathers innuendoes."

"Well I thought it was funny when I first heard it - and I still think it's funny now." Darryll chuckled. Shocking vulgarity is never going to go away, and anytime it can be cleaned up so as to be presentable for where the actual words they insinuate are replaced, well, I'm all for it."

Telling the joke how when he was giving out candy one year and came across a youngster dressed as a swashbuckling pirate, big hat and all, he smiled 'Where's your Buccaneers?' to which the kid in return replied, 'Under my buckin hat!' isn't offensive?"

'Only if you're old enough to have lost your since of humor." Darryll chuckled "Would you rather have him tell the kids about the reputed time in his youth when he went, except for wearing a full body sock and a pair of roller skates to a Halloween party as a 'pull toy'. Besides, he not only hasn't told that pirate joke to any of our kids, he hadn't even mentioned it for years before they arrived. Maybe in his old age he's having a lot of 'senior' moments - and has forgotten most of his, crude as you call them, wiseacres."

"You're forgetting, I've seen you many times in almost similar attire, just next to being totally nude. And I'd be more willing to call your looks actually more a curse, then a compliment."

"What part are you talking about? The part about being well hung - or just our overall good looks?" Darryll laughed.

"Don't you wish!" Pat frowned. "Besides, any man who constantly remarks that he gives elephants memory lessons, isn't going to forget a joke or 'any' comment that receives as much of a humorous response as you're having right now. And I can't believe we're picking on your Dad when he isn't even here. Boy, you talk about beating the proverbial dead horse."

"If 'my' memory still serves me correctly. there was a time not that long ago when you thought most of what my father did spontaneously was quit funny. You liked the fact that he had talked us all out trying a tattoo, at least until they became washable. By that time we'd all matured enough to realize they just not be as appealing as the older we got. And you didn't seem to mind it when he bought us all those comical undershorts, especially mine that read 'Home of the whopper'. And how about when he bought a bunch of those 'Clapper units'. You know - the ones where you used them to either turn on or off a rooms table lamp with a simple clap of your hands. And when you asked him why, he had replied that he wanted to use them to keep track of everything from his car keys, to where we or mom were located, just to make sure that he needed to be someplace else at the time, at least as far as where Mom was concerned."

"I didn't have the heart to tell you at the time, but I guess some of your fathers wit had already rubbed off on me, especially when first seeing you in your shorts I couldn't help but keep thinking of the other sales promotion that went 'Where's the beef!' and let's not forget the time he was going to become the 'French Fry King of the neighborhood' with one of those 'Handy Dandy slice and dice' units where you could run out hundreds of fries in a matter of seconds." Patty smiled. And don't think I didn't hear you and your brothers jokingly referring to them as contenders for instead of 'The Punch and Judy Show' as 'The Paunch and Judy Show!' for a couple of weeks. "That is until he got the slicer going so fast at one time it took a mixture of sharp pain and red blood to get his attention onto the fact that he had run out of potato, and was now working on slicing just 'ham!"

"Maybe so," Darryll chuckled, while proving that he could still work and talk at the same time by re arranging the food on the tables in front of them, apparently unlike her. "but if you also remember he had quickly pointed out that it is our country that 'one' is supposed to bleed for, not 'ones' French fries."

"But you gotta admit his heart's always been in the right place. Let's not forget those winter time 'pocket warmers' he was going to buy for everyone, but wisely decided to try them out on himself first." Patty smiled, while reaching out and smacking free the handful of potato chips presently heading for a new home. "I'll admit at first I thought your Dad had finally come up with something everyone could benefit from, until he almost set his own pants on fire!"

Those close enough to see the air born potato chips, looking strangely from a distance just like a small flock of butterflies attempting a small burst of energy towards freedom, had already started to laugh before Darryll could outdo them, when adding, "Maybe so. But I'm too much of a gentleman to tell you the instant side effect the sudden rise in extreme heat had brought to another part of his body located in the same area. Besides, if it wasn't for Pop we wouldn't have understood what 'rug burn' was caused by. And as for good ol 'Vaseline- it kind of gave a whole 'new' meaning to 'chapped lips', not counting that we now understand why when we were little we occasionally found it on the door handle leading into their bedroom."

As the light bulb suddenly went off inside of her thoughts as to the why she had occasionally also found it on the door handle leading into their 'love shack', as hubby liked to call it sometimes, Pat let out a slight 'Oh.' when realizing that it had helped keep their own kids out whenever they had wanted a little bit of privacy. And this time the smack delivered in his direction landed on his rear end, along with the words, "The first one was for snacking before supper. And that one was for what I 'think' you just meant." All of which was topped off with a short wink and smile before continuing.

"I still can't believe he actually bought one of those new portable cellular phones that 'vibrates' almost enough to register on a 'Richter Scale' whenever anyone is calling. And then really had the nerve to go on and tell anyone he strapped it to his own leg, before putting it on redial and dialing his own number."

While rubbing at his backside, Darryll himself grinned, while getting even. "If that was for just what you 'thought' I was insinuating, then you're no better than my Dad when it comes to thinking dirty. And if you're so worried about just some legendary words out of the past, how come you're not bothered by the way George's and our boys are leering at and following the Allen's twin teenage daughters around right now?"

Snapping her head in the playful kids direction just in time to catch them throwing water filled balloons onto each other, one of her hands instinctively grasping at her chest as the memory of how she had done something along the same lines to unintentionally help trap Hubby, popped into her thoughts. Especially when the water bombs exploded over the protruding chests of Louie's just as well developing young daughters, instantly turning the tee shirts they were wearing almost totally transparent. And instead of letting out the excitable words of 'Oh my babies! My babies!' that were also now exploding inside of her head, she instead quickly turned her full emotional filled attention back onto Darryll, and gave him another even harder whack while growling, "Get over there and break that up, n-o-o-o-w! And get that silly smirk off your face, or I'll smack you into the middle of next week!"

The silly grin and whack were only a prelude to what he was going to get next, as he followed Pats present staring direction just in time to catch the boys sticking last years water toys, small plastic darts with suction cups on their ends, to their chest areas. And even though he wasn't looking at her he could still hear the big gasp escape from Pats lips, leading both the word 'N-o-o-o-w I said! and a slap still much harder then before, especially when he made the mistake of chuckling out loud at the sight of all of the kids themselves laughing at the prank.

And as soon as she added, "And if your Dad starts throwing around the same kind of innuendo comments like he did when we got engaged, then you better get used to having the back of your head smacked on a regular bases."

"Oh," Darryll smirked. "you mean like why buy a cow if you're getting your milk free! Or, never buy a pair of shoes without trying them on first. Or, if it wasn't for the dark, a -" but quickly stopped when he detected Pats hand starting to rise up from her side. And after making sure he was out of arms reach, he quickly added, "Ya, I know what you mean, jellybean!" while starting to jog in the playful kids direction.

More than happy to presently be back as just a stationary pedestrian instead of a participant if necessary, each sporting a new comical age related Tee shirt that had been supplied by their hosts, Cory used the end of his fresh ice cold beer bottle to tap at the side of Bob's just as replenished drink. And after once more reading, 'I'm retired! Fix it yourself!' he continued to grin, "Come on now. We've had our nap. We're not only more than half inebriated, as well as all alone, but we're also well out of earshot of the nosey wives. Truthfully now, was there ever a day when you regretted letting George and Judy into your family circle."

For some strange reason the thought popped into his head. "Let them into 'our' family! I was lucky to get into 'theirs' after making the mistake of setting Judy up for a zinger by George when thinking that I was giving her a compliment as I had said to him, 'I hear your wife is very outspoken.' Which he instantly turned into 'Not by anyone I've ever met!' and her only feet away at the time. And as soon as he could get it out of his head, he quickly got back to what he had just been asked. Smiling back, while also once more reading from the Tee shirt in front of him, 'I'm not really in my 50's. I'm actually only in my twenties - with over 30 years of experience!' Bob then chuckled, after having wisely checked for just his own wife's present location. She, along with Betty and Louie, all wearing the woman's' standard shirt reading 'I'm with what's his name.' were all presently busy at the barbecue, no doubt with some form of gossip presently on the coals also. And as to why Darryll was presently laughing while being plummeted by his boss, he was sure he had seen the familiar looking antics before, only the blows being delivered were with the aid of a rolled up umbrella. But, for whatever reason, he didn't really care, just as long as it didn't give his own wife any such abusive ideas.

'Not a day! A year or two, maybe!" Bob grinned devilishly. "But never just a day!" which led into a hearty laugh. And then, as if only now questioning the strange remark, he quickly added, "But why are you asking me that? You got any plans on infiltrating the enemies camp?"

"Naw, not really. Especially if ever returned to his old wild 'yahoo' days." Cory smiled. Then, as if the gulp from the drink in his hand had flushed a thought loose, he suddenly realized that Mister Stone had really and noticeably mellowed from long ago in the plant. He also realized that he couldn't exactly remember when the big transition had taken place.

"Now that I think about it, when did George decide to slow down. He hasn't exactly burned himself out, but his 'anything for a laugh days' sure seem to have dwindled."

"Probably around the same time I decided it was time to grow up and take my position in life more seriously." Bob answered, straight faced.

"You!" Cory chuckled, already expecting he was about to get some more oriental 'words of wisdom' advice.

"Ya, me!" Bob smiled. "And your time's comin. Maybe not for another five years, but it's comin."

"And whatever it is that's on its way, when it gets here it's going to force me to change my ways, and even mellow out?"

"Believe me," Bob answered. "It happened to George and he changed almost over night. It happened to me and I changed, without even knowing it at first. And when your time comes, your first grandchild gets here and calls you 'Papa' your heart will melt like butter on a hot stove. And all those things in life you still thought important, will evaporate, leaving you and Louie beaming with joy each and every time you see or hear them. All special occasions in your life will seem to take on more meaning and be more enjoyable just seeing smaller versions of your own kids running around and calling you Nana and Papa or even Oma and Grampa." In a split second, he slipped into one of his better oriental philosophers, 'Grandparent so simple, even child may operate. And the seed once planted to bloom, once having done so, never ever dies."

As strange as some of Bob's words of wisdom may sound at times, Cory found that as he got older, strangely enough a lot of them did start to make sense. Smiling while glancing in his own kids direction, Cory tipped the top end of his beer in the group of playful kids direction, strayed from the topic at hand long enough to say, "Looks like a little bit of 'puppy love' going on over there."

Bob, taking in a quick view of what Cory was referring to, himself smiled, while using one of his 'words of wisdom' deliveries again, "Any married man tell you, 'puppy love' only start of 'dogs life'!"

Cory, realizing that he had started something, after saying 'Ouch.' with a smirk, then carried on with, "Give us a break 'Charlie'! They still haven't got all of their looks yet!"

Apparently his own age was starting to wear Bob down, as he slipped out of character just long enough to chuckle, before continuing with, "Two things make person look good, dark or distance."

Glancing briefly in Bob's wife's direction, Cory shuffled himself and his chair out of arms reach before grinning at Bob. "And did you have one eye or both eyes open when you decided to get married?"

Pretending to accidently drop the drink in his hand, his instant reflex's still fast enough to make Cory flinch, Bob then said deadpanned, "Wise man always remember, most mans wife ventriloquist. And best way to remember wife's birthday, is to just forget it once."

"Bin there done that!" Cory chuckled. "Louie's' always telling me we're going to live to be a hundred? And whenever I reply 'Who the hell wants to owe money that long!' she always lays one across the back of my neck before saying, "Well since I was always told when I was little by my father that there is no sense in two people worrying about money, so why don't you just keep on earning it, and I'll worry about how I'm going to get rid of it."

"If you have done wrong," Bob added. "one should not be ashamed to make amends."

"That's it!" Cory deliberately played into Bob's words of wisdom. "Take the wife's side."

"A great man is always calm and at ease. But a petty man is always worried and filled with stress." Bob chuckled, seeing that Cory was about ready to give him something just short of a smack, verbal of even physical, if he dared. And he was right.

"Why is it every time we get into these type of conversations, you slip into one of your philosophical characters, and "I always end up getting a strong craving for Chinese food?"

"Okay, okay." Bob laughed. "Just one more. And I promise you, you'll always remember this one. "A great man never travels in solitude. He always brings friends."

"Finally! One I get." Bob smiled. "You're talking about George, and us, aren't you."

"That, any wise married man may relate to." Bob continued to grin. And we are supposed to be talking about the Stone family, are we not?"

"But we are talking are we not? Are you worried about something in particular?"

"Not really." Cory smiled. "We're hoping the girls have still got the rest of high school and a few years of collage in front of them yet. But then, when the time came, you didn't get to choose for your kid either, did you? Or to quote one of your favorites, 'Man marry once and have good life, once enough. Man marry once and have bad life, once to many!'

Continuing to laugh while glancing in his daughter and husbands seemingly playful direction, they were presently busy trying to stuff an ice cube down the back of one another's neck, Bob slowed down to just a chuckle, before giving what he figured would be some father to son like advice. "I've heard in some cultures where someone has believed it necessary to sacrifice their firstborn, and if twins were involved, they would forever be in the Gods favor. But in all these years I never once figured your wife still felt as if you or she owed George such an endowment, just over one little incident. But, if the fates 'are' working against you -."

Chuckling first, then pausing long enough to let his vision float over to where all of the kids were still busy enjoying themselves, George Jr. Jr. and present squeeze now in with them, he took a deep breath and sighed, before letting the truth out. "If it's my personal opinion you're after, well - you could search forever and a day, and you won't find a more caring or loving family on the face of this earth to become a part of."

Seeing on Cory's face that his answer was having only an apparent partial satisfactory answer effect, he carried on with, "I'm sure we've both had our share of visits here over the years." to which Bob nodded affirmatively. "And no doubt you've also had the opportunity to see the inside of our couples home, if only to relieve your bladder." while holding up the bottle of beer in his hand as evidence of what he was referring to. "Well, have you ever taken the time to stop and look at some of the photo colleges George has put together over the years?'

"I sure have." Cory smiled. "And that picture of George and Judy on a motorcycle before the kids started showing up sure gave me a chuckle."

Grinning himself, especially since he could remember the picture, Bob got on with what he was really after. "Never mind just that one. What about the rest of the pictures they have all over the house. Did you notice them also?"

"Sure I saw them." Cory continued to smile. "It's kinduv hard not to notice them. They're plastered everywhere."

"Well if you've just 'seen' them, then you've missed the total picture. They represent the lives of a 'family'. And an obviously proud 'family man' took most of them. So I think it's safe to say, if you have chance to join them, as I have, you better be prepared to prove that you've worked for and earned that honor."

"Oh, I think I've earned it!" Cory frowned, while pausing long enough to take a big gulp of the drink in his hand. "On more than one occasion! I still haven't forgiven him for the time he talked me into shaving my head. He convinced me that the look was reputed to drive woman into a sexual frenzy when laying a little 'pipe'. He said that he had seen magazine reports that stated that just the appearance and touch of such a large smooth round object in a wife's hands at the right time was much better than an aphrodisiac!"

Even though he was laughing, Bob offered, "That's nothing! Didn't you ever hear about the time last year when he wanted to find out if one of those new sex enhancers on the market really worked, so he gave some to my big black lab. I had to feed the poor dog by hand for almost a week, after it had tried humping one of my plastic garbage pails nonstop for two days. I swear I don't know who shed more tears, the dog from crying, or George from laughing! Not counting how long it took before we dared letting anybody's kids see of go near the dog!"

"Well how about the time he talked Judy and Louie into letting us try one batch of that home made beer. And once they had agreed he bought enough supplies to fill our bloody swimming pool!" Cory half chuckled.

"Well can you imagine how I felt when I was ready to retire and he had dated posters with my name on them made up to hang on the outside of telephone booths all over town, reading, 'Come one! Come all! Bring a friend, and enough quarters to make a long distance call!'"

"Well you know what he's always said for years. If he didn't like ya, he wouldn't pick on ya!"

"Well ya gotta admit." Bob smiled. "He sure must have an awful lot of friends, cause he's sure not afraid to take a verbal shot at anybody I've ever seen him with over the last thirty years!"

Then, perfect timing once again taking a hand, and just as quickly as he had allowed himself to become mellow, Bob instantly returned to his former self as the sound of a short horn blast in the driveways direction instantly chased the mood away. "Oh shit! Speak of the Devil!"

Almost as if by reflex, Cory's' mouth started to open, but Bob quickly reached in a pulled out the words he had already heard George more than once over the years reply, whenever the 'Devil' was brought into the conversation. "I know, I know." he chuckled, "The Devil couldn't make it, so he sent me to fill in for him until he was available!"

Knowing the routine by heart Cory beat Bob out of their lawn chairs, but it was Bobs' voice yelling at the kids to gather around the pool for the 'happy birthday' sing-along that was now customarily also only minutes away. Cory in turn, doing a quick visual on where as well as what Louie and the girls were up to, turned his head in the driveways direction just in time to catch 'Stanley and Livingston' enter the yard.

Using the only part of his body not presently busy manipulating the packages he and George were fumbling with, Fred used his rear end to hold open the gate leading out of the yard into the driveway. And as Judy magically appeared alongside the struggling duo, picking away enough of their load to make everyone's journey bearable, she also lit into him. "Where have you two been? Apparently I sent two 'simpletons' out almost two hours ago to pick up a few 'simple' items, and I've had to consider calling the armed forces and reporting both of you missing in action! So you might want to choose your next words wisely! And I don't want to hear that ol routine of yours where you had to plan your trip by going from fire hydrant to fire hydrant along the way there and back"

Fred may have been smart enough to use his best friend as a shield, especially after being refereed to as a 'simpleton', but in his desire for self preservation he put himself in harms way just enough to likewise be scolded when Betty in the distance lowered her eyebrows before frowning in his direction. But it was George who was presently in the line of fire, and friends helped friends if they were in danger, but not this time, not that his buddy ever needed any. So before he excused himself to head off in his better half's direction he paused just long enough to say in Judy's direction.

"Ya better be kind to him. We also picked up the winning Lottery tickets for tomorrow night. You give hubby any static and I don't think he'll even send you a postcard after he's picked up his share of the winnings."

Lifting one of her arms high enough to catch Betty's already interested attention, Judy used one of her fingers to point downward at Fred's' departing form, while mouthing the words 'He's all yours.' She then turned with every intention of giving smirking hubby the second barrel.

"Well since you're retired and can't go in and 'shit in your work boots' like you always said you would if you ever won the big one, where 'are' you planning to 'dump' now, or should I have said 'who'? And don't think I've forgotten that add for the newspaper you used to joke about with the kids at work. 'Wanted! Woman with no headache. We can work the rest out later'. Or how you were going into work wearing a brand new suit everyday, until they couldn't stand the sight of you. Heaven knows you've always had the 'sight of you' effect on most people you've come into contact with."

Forcing himself to stop laughing long enough to answer, "Firstly, who? Whom do I plan on 'dumping'? Do I really still look that stupid?" And as Judy knotted her head in affirmation to his question, he kept on with, "I'm not going anywhere! It's taken me this long to train you so that I know your every thought and move. So if you behave yourself, I just might let you help me count our share, especially after I get it all in small bills and loose change."

Trying to keep a straight face, Judy just short of chuckled, "Your math was never that good."

Finally deciding that it was time to give up with one of his best 'always attack when you're being attacked' defenses, especially once noticing that most of the guests were watching, he got back on track.

"Listen Lady, why don't we arm wrestle over this more aggressively after our guests have gone home. As for my 'math' it was good enough to 'add' three kids into our household! And who said anything about my bladder holding us back. Finding selective games or items for the pool wasn't easy. And you know that whenever I'm going to entertain the grandkids afterwards I like to use as many visual aids as I can get my hands on. It's not easy finding birthday gifts or props that can function almost totally without the aid of batteries or some form of plug in adapter. Each year they're getting harder and harder to find, let alone replace.

"They don't have it as good as we did when we were growing up. Our toys generally required personal hands on involvement inside outside night or day - and nine times out of ten it was something we either assembled or even created ourselves. There were no portable phones, no computers, no D.V.D. players or films. We had friends, but we generally walked or rode our bikes to their house. We played sweaty sports, ate the same dirt, shared our drink and food, and nobody broke out into a contagious rash. If we were bad at school or anywhere else, we got the strap or were grounded to our room with nothing more than a bed and dresser for company. Mom ran the home and after letting Dad work hard and pay for everything, he occasionally got to state his opinion, which Mom sometimes agreed with."

"Why I can remember -."

"Remember!" Judy butted in, hoping to cut short a spiel she already knew by heart, just as well as his reputed trips to school on raining or snowy days being 'up hill' both ways. "If I want to send you to the store to pick up anything - I have to give you a note, which half the time you forget to take with you. Why your memory's startin' to get so bad lately - you'll - you'll - soon be able to hide your own Easter eggs!"

And everybody knows we can't put an empty shopping cart in front of you, you'd only fill it. So consequently it just happens that it took me a little bit longer then anticipated. Now then," leaning his head slightly forward in Judy's' direction, his cheek protruding out the most, he then continued with, "unless you're going to give me another black eye like you did last year, which I'll have to lie away to the kids again, let's say we get on with the show."

"You know as well as I do, even if you have already used the same excuse long ago, that it really was an accident." Judy scoffed as they walked, Fred wisely shuffling on ahead. "And if you hadn't blown it all out of proportion by telling everyone that it was the result of my leotards snapping out and whacking you in the puss while helping me undress, it would have all been over and forgotten in a few days."

With a sometimes seemingly thousand years of such verbal setups already behind her Judy was ready for hubby's remark. "Are we talking about our sex life or my black eye?" But George, while adding in a mumble, 'I guess there's no sense on fantasizing about any of that for later.', still managed to get out of the way of the shoulder 'whack' now being delivered in his direction, while asking "Where's Ian? He already knows I was going to need his help in getting something else from the rear of the car."

"What have you got back there that one of us couldn't carry?" Judy asked, a hint of 'I know you're up to something 'Mister Stone' in her voice.

Wearing a grin even before starting to reply, the results of an age old childlike answer he normally would have instantly replied with, 'What are you, a 'cop'? and then "Why do you want to know, you writing a book'? Instead he did something totally out of the norm, he told her the truth.

"Well, you know one of my favorite flashbacks is that summer when he brought those ugly fish home to babysit." He didn't get a chance to finish the obvious, before Judy cut him off. "Don't you dare, tell me you brought home two piranhas, just so you can go through that story one more time! They're so damn ugly you'll scare the shit out of the kids."

"Okay! I wont' tell you I brought two ugly fish home, especially since I only got one, and it's only rented." George beamed, ready to take a protective step sideways, just as soon as it looked as if he was going to need it. "Besides, out of all the grownups here, you and I are the only ones from the original gathering mature enough at that time to understand what was really going on. All of our present guests only know the story by word of mouth. And the boys were still young enough to only think they understood the full reasoning behind the prank. After the kind of horror movies that are playing on television and in movie theaters now-a-days, I don't think the sight of an ugly fish in a little tank is going to traumatize any of our grandkids too much. 'Hell', I wouldn't be surprised if they scared the poor bloody fish!"

Judy just knew, by the way he was grinning, that there had to be more up Georges sleeve than just his arm, especially since now she had to agree with him about its real shock value on any of todays kids. And as she watched him finally zero in on Ian's whereabouts just long enough to give their son a nod towards the car, she made her objection know with, "You're going to trust 'Mister Fumble Fingers' himself, with a tank of water and a live fish? I swear, if you're up to something, just remember that little bit of naked land in the garden beside 'Snowball'. And you can be sure her marker will still be a lot larger, nicer and definitely more cared for than yours by the time I'm finished with you."

"Look!" George grinned. "If it'll make you feel any better, I'll just get him to give you a hand with this stuff. Then only I'll be the one handling the fish tank."

Opening her mouth to reluctantly protest, George cut her off by stopping Ian in his tracks and instruction him to instead, "Put this stuff on the deck, you know where, and then give your mother a hand in passing the pool gifts around Son."

Giving her a 'Are you happy now?' grin, he raised one of his now free arms and shouted 'Hello everybody! Georgies here! it's time to let the real drinking begin!" Pausing long enough to say at her, 'Okay?' he didn't even wait for an answer.

Deliberately not even waiting for George to be totally out of hearing range, Judy gave him a little slamming, another dig at proving she was still capable of getting in the last word. "Well, now that we've got him out of the way again, lets really get this party rollin'!"

It was plain to see, even after almost fifty years of marriage, they still had an ever ongoing 'love, hate' relation ship. They each still just loved to antagonize or pull a prank on one another, just as they both hated to see the other get in the last dig or word from any such situation. Their antics, as George disappeared back in the cars direction, was noticed by all of the grownups, but appreciated by only a few, as the kids in between grumbled and made faces at each other.

But it was soon to be proven that such a considered juvenile antic, while claiming a spot along the edge of the pool and using their feet like giant egg beaters to whip the water into a froth foam, knew no specific age limit. And as if to prove it, as their parents with drinks in plastic cups slowly joined them, the kids energetic antics weren't to be the only form of entertainment. As the larger and much older delinquents passed, each took turns pushing their own unsuspecting child into the pool. It was a stunt that was just as quickly retaliated with protesting palm thrusts of water back in their passing direction.

Yelling for the kids to split up and gather alongside the rim of the pool, a soon to be boys against the girls formation instantly taking place, Ian took the far side of the pool as Judy started along her half. And as she was in the middle of handing Cory's' daughters a matching set of pump up water floatation wings, something to help them float, noticeably not really necessary in their case, Ian gave the boys a choice over varying size of brightly colored squirting water guns or blow up plastic floating mattresses.

Glancing up just in time to see the top of Hubby's thinning crown as he was himself occupied bending down to display the contents of the very container she had not wanted presented, Judy was horrified as the déjà-vu memory from out of the past started in almost slow motion to repeat itself. She had honestly believed that as long as Ian was occupied on the opposite side of the pool, especially if he and his father were in cahoots, at least she would be able to control whatever it was that they might have planned. But the thought of their relative through marriage, as Bobs' bare foot came out and touched Georges protruding rear end just enough to send him and the contents of what he was holding forward into the pool, had never entered her head. And just as those close started to shout in glee and laugh, panic took ahold of Judy's reasoning as she jumped up, letting everything still within her grasp fly skyward, screaming for everyone to 'Get out of the pool!'

At first her crazy panic like antics only invoked more wild screaming laughter, uncontrollable laughter that reigned only until Georges submerged form shot straight up almost totally out of the water, his own high pitched voice yelling, 'Get out of the water! Everyone out of the water! Now!' And as his body then totally submerged below the waters disturbed surface once more, those who instantly stopped laughing to scramble for the safety of the pools deck were instantly joined by the remainder of the kids when George noisily once again popped up holding onto one of his ankles and screaming for them to run for their lives.

Not until now, as he once more slipped beneath the water, did Judy have a chance to fully see the tee shirt he was wearing, confirming her earlier suspicions. And even though she was speaking out loud, her words were meant solely for her and her benefit alone. "Dam it! I knew you were up to something, you sneaky old fart!"

Watching where he had just disappeared once more, the panic in her turning to one of wanting revenge, she thought to herself, 'So you want to play dirty by wearing that old tee shirt dedicated to my mother do you? Well shit disturber, it won't save you this time!'

It wasn't the necessity for air that finally had George once more shoot up wiggling like a fish hooked on a invisible fishing line almost totally out of the water, Judy's eyes instinctively going to the wording she already knew by heart, 'Irean Goodnight Irean, Irean goodnight. Goodnight Irean, goodnight Irean, I'll see you in my dreams!' on his tee shift. But it was more for his own benefit and all for show, hands and arms tight against his side, as he boldly brandished the tail wagging piranha in his teeth.

Already heading for the pools leaf skimmer, the rest of the gathering in physical turmoil with Ian now by her side whispering into her ear, 'Relax Mom. You know Pop when he gets into one of his pranks. Besides, it's only a harmless kids windup toy!'

Not even breaking her stride, she excitedly commented 'That's not the only thing that kid's 'wound up' today!' while jerking the basket and pole from its resting place."

All of the kids, grownups alike, were each seemingly to still be over emphasizing everything they were presently involved in. Like out of the past, as a few of the jokesters fell arms flailing wide open noisily backwards 'whack' into the pool - each of their parents was hysterically yelling at one another while frantically trying to pull them back out.

In all of the wild turmoil, Ian hoping to catch either of his brothers attention, everyone else seemed to be too involved with their own present problems, could see that he was going to be all alone with the task of trying to calm down his fuming mothers escalating emotions.

"You're not going to try and catch Dad with the little net on the end of that pole are you! You might hurt him!" he protested, reaching for the metal shaft while positioning his body between her and his once again submerged fathers.

"Net him!" Judy mumbled just loud enough to hear, while first yanking the pole out of her sons protesting hands and then easily side stepping him before yanking the hooped net off the end of the shaft.

Only now, in the background, did some of the other grownups finally take notice as to what was strangely taking place at the far end of the pool. And as Darryll and Junior jumped into the water, no doubt to offer their father assistance, Bob and Cory started to ran with out stretched arms in their direction, reasoning of what was about to happen apparently having entered their heads, they in almost perfect unison each shouted out, 'No!'

Judy, now this side of mumbling, but definitely loud enough for all of those within hearing distance, carried on with her one sided conversation. 'So he wants to 'arm wrestle' does he, eh! Ha! It's more like the old days of 'Indian leg wrestling' he's interested in! Again I say 'Ha!' As if that's going to ever going to happen, tonight or any other night!"

She then spread her legs in a bracing manner, while holding the pole in one hand high over her head and facing the pools still rippling surface, as if ready to toss it like a long distance javelin thrower. Turning her still hinted at frustrated looking face in Ian's direction, her loud shout words etched the look of confusion already there, even deeper into his features.

"What in the name of this side of 'Hell!' ever made you think I was just going to try and 'net' him! Even I know that your grand standing ego manic fathers 'inflated fat head' is much to big for that skimpy little nets tiny opening!

Besides! They 'harp-o-o-ned' 'Moby Dick'! Didn't they!"

"Look! - - - Thar he blo-o-o-o-ws!"

Epilogue

Well, what do ya think? I tried to warn you right up front that our boy was one of those rare individuals who often found humor in not just anything, but in almost everything. But most important, and here is what life is really all about, I hope you enjoyed visiting our boys fictitious often crazy little world as much as I did, especially while going there to write about it.

Even at the end of where we last parted, although he hadn't really abandoned everyone most important to his world, he was busy affirming that age knows no boundaries when it comes to having a good time. Once more our boy George had left them not only laughing uncontrollably, but also once again departed leaving them wanting 'more', and 'more', and as always, even 'more'!

The End

CPSIA information can be obtained at www.ICGtesting.com
234164LV00001B/6/P